Tom Holt was born in London in 1961. At Oxford he studied bar billiards, ancient Greek agriculture and the care and feeding of small, temperamental Japanese motorcycle engines; interests which led him, perhaps inevitably, to qualify as a solicitor and emigrate to Somerset, where he specialised in death and taxes for seven years before going straight in 1995. Now a full-time writer, he lives in Chard, Somerset, with his wife, one daughter and the unmistakable scent of blood, wafting in on the breeze from the local meat-packing plant.

Find out more about Tom Holt and other Orbit authors by registering for the free monthly newsletter at www.orbitbooks.co.uk

The Divine Comedies

TOM HOLT

Here Comes The Sun

Odds and Gods

www.orbitbooks.co.uk

An *Orbit* Book

First published in Great Britain by Orbit 2002

This omnibus edition © Tom Holt 2002

Here Comes the Sun
First published in Great Britain by Orbit 1993
Copyright © Kim Holt 1993

Odds and Gods
First published in Great Britain by Orbit 1995
Copyright © Kim Holt 1995

A CIP catalogue record for this book is available
from the British Library.

ISBN 1 84149 145 4

Typeset by Palimpsest Book Production Limited,
Polmont, Stirlingshire
Printed in Great Britain by
Clays Ltd, St Ives plc

Orbit
An imprint of
Time Warner Books UK
Brettenham House
Lancaster Place
London, WC2E 7EN

CONTENTS

HERE COMES THE SUN

For
MY MOTHER
But for whose tireless encouragement
And selfless dedication to the furtherance
of my writing career
(To the neglect and detriment of her own
prodigious talent as a crime writer)
I would now be the son and heir
of a bestselling authoress
Instead of just another
Penniless
Author

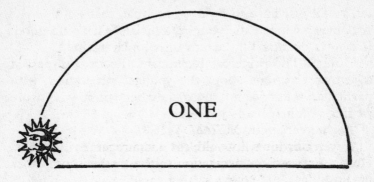

ONE

The sun rose.

It was dirty. It was late. It was thirty billion miles overdue on its next service. There was a thin film of oil on its surface, the result of a sprung gasket. But it was up and running, and that in itself was something of a miracle, all things considered.

'Over to you, son,' said the Principal Technical Officer, wiping his forehead with the back of his hand. 'Just don't drop it, all right?'

The Assistant Technical Officer scowled. 'You always say that,' he replied. 'And have I ever . . . ?'

'Not yet.'

The older official looked down at the great fiery disc and smiled in spite of himself. True, he could hear the distinct grinding noise and smell the burning oil, but it was still an impressive sight. They'd built things to last in those days, which was just as well. Of course, they had the funding, then.

'Here,' said the younger official. 'The gyro's packed up again.'

'Gyro,' replied his colleague scornfully. 'Bloody modern

tat. You'll just have to fly it on manual, that's all.'

'Oh *no*,' whined the younger official. 'That's no good. If I gotta do that I'll have to miss lunch again.'

'Tough.' The Principal Technical Officer's soul passed a few observations about the younger generation, with particular reference to those members of it who wore earrings. 'When I was your age . . .'

'Yeah, yeah, you told me.'

'Given anything, I would, for a chance to fly her solo.' He paused, remembering. 'We took a pride in our work in those days,' he added.

'Yeah. Well.'

The younger official had a point. Things were different now, the Principal Technical Officer admitted to himself as he packed up his knapsack and put on his bicycle clips. Not quite so run down for one thing. The Great Bear wasn't held in its place in the firmament by three hundred thousand miles of insulating tape and a bent nail.

'You should think yourself lucky,' he said without conviction, 'that you've got a job at all.'

His junior colleague didn't even bother to reply; he was leaning on the dead man's handle, eyes vacant, Walkman headphones on, staring down towards Betelgeuse. Something told the Principal Technical Officer that if humanity made it through to nightfall with nothing worse than a few hours of inexplicable darkness it should count itself lucky.

Still, he said to himself, as he hoisted himself on to his ancient bicycle and pedalled stiffly away across the sparkling freeway of the stars, if you're going to take a pride in your work, your work's got to be something you can take a pride in. And if the whole shooting-match is virtually derelict, what can you expect? No wonder the boy's demoralised. Where's the point in bothering when nobody else seems to give a damn?

His way home took him past the moon-sheds and, following this train of thought, he slowed to a halt, leaned on his handlebars and looked in through the great double doors. Inside, the moon was being winched back into dry dock for the day. From a distance, it never failed to take his breath away. Seen up close, it wasn't a pretty sight.

'Strewth,' the old official muttered under his breath.

Admittedly, it was quite some time – centuries, probably – since he'd taken the time to stop and look at it this closely, but there was no denying the fact that the old girl was in pretty poor shape.

'What have they been *doing* to her?' he said aloud.

One of the maintenance engineers, an alarming-looking youth with a Mohican haircut and a ring through one nostril, looked round and stared at him. He didn't seem to notice.

'What's up with you, grandad?' the youth demanded.

'You're not going to use sandpaper on her, are you?' the old official said, horrified.

'You what?'

No wonder, the old official reflected. No wonder the poor old bus has got all those great big pits and craters all over her once-smooth surfaces. He sighed; he knew there was no point uttering the words that were trying to squeeze their way through the gap in his teeth, but he said them anyway.

'You shouldn't use that stuff on the outer skin,' he said. 'First thing you know, you'll get pitting.'

'So what?'

So what indeed? Nobody cared, obviously; and as he cycled away, the old official couldn't find it in his heart to blame them. Where was the point in trying to keep it going when it was patently clapped out? They were going to scrap it soon in any case, they said, commission a brand new one. They'd been saying it for a long time now.

As usual, he stopped off at the Social Club for a tea and a bacon sandwich before going home. He parked his bicycle, chained it to a lamppost, and walked into the room, which looked like one of the more run-down East German railway stations. Another example, he couldn't help reflecting, of the way this whole operation is going downhill.

'What's happened to the pool table, Nev?' he asked.

'Jammed,' replied the steward, washing glasses. 'They're sending someone later on.'

'Right.'

'Or at least,' the steward added, 'so they told me.'

'Right.'

The steward made an indeterminate noise and put the bacon sandwich in the microwave. Another bloody innovation.

'Looking forward to the darts match tomorrow, Nev?'

The steward sighed. 'Cancelled, George old son,' he said. 'Due to lack of interest. Hadn't you heard?'

Jane stopped what she was doing and looked out of the window at the sun.

This, she reflected, is what they call too much of a good thing. All very well looking fondly back on the long, hot summers of one's childhood, but when you're stuck in an office with a glass roof, windows that don't open and a heating system mysteriously jammed on, even in summer, you start thinking nostalgically about good, solid rain.

'I can remember rain,' she said aloud. 'Gosh, that dates me.'

Three weeks, give or take a day, and already the newsreaders were smugly saying gloomy things about standpipes and hosepipe bans. What's wrong with a country where three weeks of sun turns the reservoirs into dustbowls?

She turned away from the window and tried to concentrate on the VDU in front of her. It was staring back at her with a sort of blank look, as if it had been sniffing glue. She picked up the phone.

'Trish,' she said. 'What's wrong with the screens?'

'System's down at Reading,' Trish replied. 'Back on after lunch.'

'Great,' said Jane. 'Tell them we'd be better off with a card index and a notched stick.'

Never mind, there's plenty I can be getting on with till then, said Jane to herself. Staring out of the window, for instance.

Instead, she looked through her handbag, found her address book and dialled a number.

'Apollo Staff Bureau,' said a voice like a lady Dalek at the other end of the line. 'Can I help you?'

'Yes,' Jane said brightly, 'I want a new job, please.'

'We could advertise it,' said the Chief of Staff.

The rest of the committee looked at him.

'Well,' said Personnel eventually, 'it's an idea, certainly. Where would you suggest?'

'Um.'

'Tricky one to place, don't you think?' Personnel continued, with the air of someone getting ready to ram a point into the ground. 'I mean, it's not one for the *Exchange and Mart*, is it?'

'Let's try being positive for once,' Staff replied testily. 'That's the problem, really, we're all too keen to look at the disadvantages and not the . . .'

'Absolutely,' Branch interrupted. 'With you all the way there. But I think Personnel's got a point too, you know.'

All God's children gotta point, said Staff to himself, it's just that some of them are bloody silly ones. He drew a spaceship on the agenda and tried to calm himself down.

'I still think,' he said, putting the tips of his fingers together as a means of stopping his hands clenching, 'that we should advertise it. I mean, why not? It's what they do in the private sector. They don't keep staff vacancies a deadly secret, like they were something to be ashamed of. They go out and they ask people to apply.'

'Right on,' said Personnel, with all the enthusiasm of a corpse. 'So where do we look?'

There was a silence.

'All right,' said Staff, 'what do you suggest? We need someone and we need someone quickly. You're the Personnel Officer. What's your considered opinion?'

'I think it needs thinking about.'

Another silence; during which Staff noticed that the burning thrones they sat on, as a mark of their superior executive status, didn't burn any more. They just glowed intermittently and hummed.

'Have you thought yet?' he enquired.

'Not yet, no.'

'Fine,' Staff replied. 'You take your time.' He crossed his legs and started to doodle ostentatiously.

'Why don't we use the usual procedure?' asked a voice from the other end of the table.

'Because . . .' Staff started to say, but checked himself. There were times when his paranoia slipped the lead and got mixed up with his angst, when he sincerely believed that Finance and General Purposes was a management plant, deliberately seeded on to this committee to make sure that nothing ever got done. Since it was very probably true he invariably dismissed the idea from his mind; it is not just mankind who cannot bear too much reality. 'Because,' he went on, 'there's three feet of moss growing in the usual channels and something's got to be done.'

'Oh, we're all agreed on *that*,' Branch said. 'No question about it, *something*'s got to be done. On the other hand, we don't want to rush into something without having worked it carefully through. I mean. . .' He made a slight but expressive gesture and went back to impersonating a doorstop. Staff took a grip on himself, straining something in his integrity, and tried to sound conciliatory.

'All right, then,' he said, 'what about an agency? I gather they're very good at this sort of thing. You know, head-hunting.'

'Which agency had you in mind?' said Personnel.

'Look,' said Staff, 'this is supposed to be an ideas session, right? We're supposed to be a think tank, bouncing ideas off each other. Has anybody got any ideas at all?'

There was a slightly embarrassed pause; and then Personnel, judging his timing to perfection, smiled and cleared his throat.

'I've got an idea,' he said. 'I've got an idea that this needs thinking through carefully.'

'Me too,' said Branch. 'Looking at it in the round, I mean.'

'I think,' said Finance and General Purposes, 'that we should go through the established procedure.'

Staff closed his eyes. 'Good God, Norman,' he said to the ceiling, 'what an absolute stroke of genius. Yes, let's all do that, shall we? Well, thank you very much for your time, gentlemen. I honestly believe we've all made very real progress today. Same time next week then?'

Instead of going back to the main building, Staff turned left down the corridor, walked briskly on past the post room, turned right by the file store and pressed the button for the lift. Two minutes later, he swore at the lift-shaft and started to climb the seventeen flights of stairs that led to the DA's office.

'I'll show the bastards,' he muttered, rather breathlessly. 'Just for once, I'll damn well *show* the . . .'

The further up he went the dustier it got. There was something about the decor, something very subtle which you couldn't put your finger on, that suggested that nobody had been this way in a very long time, and that there was probably a very good reason for that. Perhaps, Staff said to himself, it's the fact that all the treads on this staircase are rotted half through.

At last, breathless and sweating, he found himself at the top of the building. It was dark here (no light bulb), and cold, and ever so slightly spooky. It was *years* since he'd been up this far. It was a fair bet that there was nobody here any more.

In front of him there was a glass door so grimy that he had to wipe it with his sleeve before he could read the lettering on it. But there was a light behind it, implying the presence of sentient life. That, as far as Staff was concerned, would make a pleasant change. He screwed up his eyes and read the inscription on the window.

D. GANGER

it said, and in smaller letters underneath:

DEVIL'S ADVOCATE

'Oh well,' said Staff to himself, repressing a shudder, 'I'm here now.'

He knocked smartly on the door and turned the handle.

'Try a bit of silver paper and some gunk,' said the Technical Adviser into the receiver.

The voice at the other end crackled at him. 'Will that work?' it enquired.

'Dunno.' The Technical Adviser leaned back in his chair and put a peppermint in his mouth. 'Might do.'

'Look,' said the crackle. 'I've got a bloody great disc of helium broken down over East Africa. Things are starting to get burnt. Suggest something.'

'Not my fault,' replied the Technical Adviser automatically. 'I told 'em at Depot it needed a whole new gearbox, but would they listen? Nah.' He crunched the peppermint into the mouthpiece, sending a noise like the end of the world down the wire. 'Look,' he said, after he had cleared the shrapnel off the roof of his mouth, 'tell you what I'll do for you. I'll send out Maintenance with the van. They'll have you back on the road again, no worries.'

The crackle reminded him by way of reply that the Maintenance Unit had been disbanded two years ago as part of the cutbacks programme, and its staff reassigned to Oceans. 'What about the backup team?' it suggested.

'Nice idea,' replied the Technical Adviser, thumbing through a roster. 'Trouble is, they're down at the Social Club at Depot fixing a jammed pool table. You want them, you got to fill in a Yellow at least forty-eight hours in advance.'

'Then what do you suggest?'

'You could get out and push.'

The crackle considered this, gave the Technical Officer some advice of an intimate nature, and disconnected itself.

The fish in Lake Victoria were finding that the ceiling was rather nearer than usual.

'Come in.'

Rather to Staff's surprise, the door opened easily. He blinked.

It wasn't quite the way he'd expected it to be. For one thing, it was clean. Cleaner, in fact, than the rest of the building. It was newly decorated. In one corner there was a highly advanced fax machine, flickering quietly, bringing up its lunch, while in the other stood a computer terminal which looked like the sort of thing George Lucas would have dreamed up if possessed by devils. There was also, Staff noticed, a substantial potted plant. Real, not plastic.

'It's because we're separately funded,' said a voice behind him. 'The benefits of decentralisation and all that. You're Chief of Staff, aren't you?'

The figure standing behind him was almost as disconcerting as the environment. It looked young, vibrant, full of energy. More amazing still, it looked like it was capable of enjoying itself.

'You're . . .' Staff said. The figure grinned.

'My name's Ganger. We haven't actually met, but it's my job to know things.'

By way of a disorienting remark, said Staff's soul to any part of his brain that happened to be listening, that's got to be in the running with *Are you sure you're feeling all right?* and *Excuse me, there's a bomb inside this banana.* Throwing people off balance was probably part of the job, too. Staff forced himself to relax.

'Sorry to barge in like this,' he said, 'but have you got a moment?'

Ganger nodded. 'Sure,' he said. 'Carol, I'll be engaged in the back office. Anyone calls, take a message.'

Staff's head swivelled like a windmill and he caught sight of a blonde head between two earphones. Laid-back nonchalance is all very well but there are limits.

'You don't mean to say,' he whispered, 'you've actually got a *secretary*?'

'Two,' Ganger replied, and Staff gave up the struggle. This was the sort of man who had a My-other-car's-a-Porsche sticker in the back window of his Maserati. 'Come with me. Coffee?'

Staff made a little noise without opening his lips. 'I suppose your secretary will bring it through to us?'

Ganger raised an eyebrow. 'Well, yes,' he said.

'One of your two secretaries?'

'That's it. If that's all right with you, that is.'

'That's fine,' said Staff. 'I think I've come to the right place.'

It seemed like a very long walk through to the back office, until Staff realised that it was the effort of walking through the carpet. You could easily lose a Mayan city in the pile and never know it.

'So what can we do for you?' Ganger said, waving his arm at a chair. Staff looked at him carefully. Perhaps it was an invitation to sit on it, but it seemed unlikely. It had the appearance of the sort of thing you pay money just to look at.

'Sit down,' said Ganger, 'please. We don't stand on ceremony here.'

Maybe not, but you sure as hell sit on luxury. Staff sat back, panicked for a moment until he got his bearings again, and cleared his mind.

'Actually,' he began to say, 'all it was . . .'

His lips froze. Ganger followed his line of sight and raised an eyebrow.

'It's a photocopier,' he said. 'You know, you put pieces of paper in one end . . .'

'I'm sorry,' Staff muttered. 'Like I was saying, I'm in a bit of a quandary, and I thought, you know, a fresh angle on the problem . . .'

Ganger nodded. 'I know,' he said. 'Do you advertise or do you go to an agency? Good question.'

'Look . . .' Staff tried to sit up, but the chair wouldn't let him. He struggled. Self-esteem wasn't the most significant part of his personality, but he was damned if he was going to end his career by slipping down the back of a chair.

'How do I know all this?' Ganger said. 'Simple. It's my

job.' He paused, then smiled gently. 'Try straightening your back,' he said. 'It'll push you forward out of the cushion.'

Staff did so, then he scowled. 'You're a . . .'

'No, I'm not, actually,' Ganger replied. 'It's possible to read mortal minds, of course, but not ours. Jamming devices, you know. Really, it's just intuition and psychology.'

'Oh.'

'And microphones too, of course.'

'Ah.'

The door opened, and a female person brought in a tray with two cups of coffee. With saucers. Saucers that matched. I'd honestly believe I'd died and gone to heaven, thought Staff . . .

'Only that's not possible in the circumstances,' Ganger said, and laughed politely. 'Thank you, I'm flattered. All it takes really is good taste and careful management.'

'And separate funding.'

'That helps, certainly.' Ganger looked at him over his cup. 'My money's on an agency.'

'Really?'

Ganger nodded. 'Every time,' he said. 'Saves time, and in the long run money. Neither of which, if I'm right, you've got a great deal of.'

Staff tried unsuccessfully to balance his saucer on his knee, but the chair seemed to be breathing. 'All right,' he said. 'And what do I tell the rest of the committee?'

Ganger looked surprised: probably a whole new experience . . .

'Not at all,' he said abruptly. 'Things surprise me all the time. Who gives a toss what the committee thinks? Anyway,' he added, 'if you're at all bothered about it, don't tell them.'

'But I've got to tell . . .'

'Why?'

Staff was shocked; it was like being asked to justify breathing. Then the penny dropped. Different rules . . .

'You tell me,' he said.

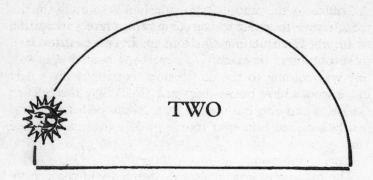

TWO

Jane was not a naturally discontented person; or at least, that was what she'd always led herself to believe. It was just that there were certain things that she found hard to put up with. These things tended to change their shape depending on circumstances, just as clouds can sometimes be great fluffy dragons and sometimes wisps of low-quality cotton wool; sometimes it would be the plight of famine victims, sometimes it was the incredibly feckless way the stationery supplies were managed at work, and sometimes – quite often, and in point of fact, right now – it was the punctuality of the 42A bus that really managed to get to her. If there was a common factor, it was probably sloppiness.

The weather could do with sorting, too.

The British Nation, she said to herself, and its unique relationship with water: we either sail over it or stand under it. It took the Chinese, though, to invent the umbrella.

Since the 42A had patently been ambushed by the Hole in the Wall Gang, set on fire and abandoned somewhere further up the line, she decided to walk the mile from the office to the station. She splashed resolutely up the road, trying to avoid the larger puddles and speculating as to whether ditching fins and growing legs had been the evolutionary breakthrough everyone reckoned it was. She was coming to the conclusion that the really smart move would have been wings and floats, like the Spruce Goose, when she bumped into a fellow-pedestrian and nearly knocked him over into a puddle the size of Lake Van.

'Sorry,' she said.

The man, who was so sharply dressed you could have used him for open-heart surgery and, despite the lack of hat or umbrella, as dry as a bone, smiled at her.

'Not at all,' he replied. 'But you're wrong about the wings, you know.'

Jane's jaw flopped down like undercarriage. 'What?' she said.

'Wings,' the man replied, still smiling. 'If the ancestors of mankind had grown wings, they wouldn't have needed to develop manual dexterity and the use of tools. That way, their brains wouldn't have adapted and become what they eventually did become. Result, you wouldn't be a human, just a big pink bird, and the chimpanzees would be feeding you breadcrumbs in Trafalgar Square. Think about it.'

He nodded, side-stepped into the puddle (which divided on either side of his foot) and walked on, leaving Jane standing in exactly the right spot to receive the full force of the spray when a 42A bus went neatly through the puddle a few moments later.

Staff was reading a letter.

It wasn't easy going, because the script – and, indeed, the language – it was written in had died out centuries before; but he could understand that. The writer of the

letter probably hadn't found the need to put pen to paper
for a very long time.

Dear Sir, it said, translated:
*I have to inform you that I resign. You probably don't remember
me though I saw you once at one of those receptions over the
top of someone's head, you were shaking hands a lot and
opening something. I've been raising the Sun for 777 years, 7
months and a week Thursday, but this is too much and I've
had enough. It's a scandal, that's what it is, and they ought
to do something about it. I have the honour to remain, etc.*

Staff sighed, and put the letter face down on his desk.
   They ought to do something about it.
   Too right, he said to himself, and they will, just as soon
as they find out who they are. And normal service will
be resumed as soon as possible. And, naturally, we apologise for any inconvenience in the meantime.
   'Hell,' he said aloud.
   'Sorry, wrong floor,' said a voice from the other side
of the desk. He looked up and saw Ganger, DA, sitting
in the visitor's chair, smiling and looking far more
comfortable than he would have imagined possible.
   'It's a knack,' Ganger replied. 'You just have to wriggle
about until you find a part of the seat that fits.'
   That's what he does, Staff realised; he replies before
you speak. Bloody irritating, of course, but certainly
conducive to efficiency. Like a fax machine or something.
   'And?' he said.
   'Yes,' Ganger replied, and pulled a sad face. It looked
hopelessly incongruous. Ganger's face was pretty exclusively smile-shaped. 'The problem is, how?'
   'Exactly.'
   'Well,' Ganger said, leaning back and folding his arms
behind his head, 'there you have it. In a nutshell.'

Staff capitulated. 'All right,' he said. 'Can we go back over that and fill in the blanks, please?'

The sad face melted into the usual grin, like grilled cheese. 'You were thinking, Shit, there's another irreplaceable employee gone and handed in his notice, and what the hell are we going to do now? I replied, "Yes", because I'm buggered if I can think of anything either. But the fact remains that he's got to be replaced, because otherwise it's going to be all jam for the electric torch manufacturers but no fun for everybody else, plus you'll have to pay the man in the moon double time and a half. The problem is, how do you fill a vacancy like that from the load of rubbish you've got available?'

'Exactly.'

'And there you have it,' Ganger said, smirking, 'in a nutshell.'

'It's very impressive, the way you do that.'

'Flashy,' Ganger replied. 'Telepathy is like television or tele-anything. Looks good, but doesn't actually help very much in the final analysis. Not,' he added quickly, 'that it really is telepathy; more a sort of partial insight. It comes in useful in our work.'

'Ah yes,' said Staff, leaning forward slightly. 'I meant to ask you about that.'

Ganger hitched up one corner of his mouth into yet another isotope of his perpetual smile. 'You're quite right,' he said. 'Up to a point.'

Staff growled at him. He laughed.

'It's all right,' he said, 'I'm on secondment. That means I have to play fair. That means you can trust me. Okay?'

'Perhaps.'

Ganger stood up and walked to the window. 'Good view you get from here,' he said.

'All the kingdoms of the earth,' replied Staff absently. 'Look, who exactly are your lot?'

Ganger continued to look out of the window. 'Simple,' he replied. 'We're them rather than us, but we're on your side really. Is that enough?'

'No.'

'Okay. We're a department, same as all the other departments, but we're pretty well autonomous within the quite strict confines of our brief. And the head of our department gets abjured a lot at christenings.'

Staff nodded. 'And all his works?'

'Right on,' Ganger replied. 'Also his pomps, not that he's got any really. Not in the last five years, at any rate.'

'Five years?' Staff raised an eyebrow. 'What's so special about . . . ?'

'We got put out to tender,' Ganger replied. 'We were the guinea-pig, you see. Five years ago, we were the most hopelessly inefficient department in the whole set up . . .'

'Surely not?'

The back of Ganger's head nodded. 'Straight up. Hopelessly overstaffed, but undermanned at the same time. Work backing up, souls not getting processed, furnaces still powered by expensive, ozone-unfriendly sulphur, and worst of all, costing an absolute fortune. Really, the whole system was on the point of collapse. In fact, there were those who reckoned it had collapsed years before, only in the nature of things nobody had noticed.'

Staff picked up a pencil and started to fidget with it nervously. 'Nobody told me,' he said.

'Didn't they?' Ganger leaned on the window-sill and swayed slightly. 'I'm not in the least surprised. Not something they'd want you to find out about, really. Anyway, they reckoned that since nothing they could do could possibly make things worse, they'd try an experiment and put the whole operation in the hands of outside contractors. My lot got the contract, and since then . . . Well, you can judge for yourself.'

There was a silence, during which you could have counted up to seven comfortably, and ten if you gabbled a bit. 'Then you're not . . . ?'

'Qualified?' Ganger laughed. 'Oh yes, we're all qualified. I'm not a mortal, if that's what you're thinking.'

'But if you're not a mortal, then you must be . . .' Staff's voice trickled away, like the last drops of water from a turned-off hose. The back of Ganger's head shook.

'Not necessarily,' he replied. 'Common misconception, that. Most of us are left over from the previous systems, but . . .'

'Previous systems?'

'Ancestor worship,' Ganger explained. 'Classical mythology. Odin and Thor. There's one chap works in Accounts who used to be Osiris, or is it Anubis? Odd sort of bloke, but in his line of work it's actually an advantage to have the head of a jackal. Me, though, I'm from Philosophy.'

'Philosophy?'

'Absolutely,' replied Ganger, with a hint of pride in his voice. 'Personification of an abstract concept. I'm a child of late nineteenth-century German neo-nihilism. One of Nietzsche's gentlemen, you might almost say.' He laughed briefly at his own joke. 'Sorry, I'm drifting away from the point rather, aren't I? What I was going to say is that in our department, we do have a few members of staff who were originally mortals.'

Staff tried to find an appropriate word, or at least a noise, but there wasn't one. Instead, the room was filled with the noise of a jaw dropping.

'I have that effect on people sometimes,' Ganger agreed. 'I startled the wits out of a girl in the street earlier on. I want to talk to you about her later, actually.'

'You use *mortals*? On *official business*?'

'Ex-mortals,' Ganger replied gently. 'There are limits, naturally. But within those limits . . .'

'You can't,' said Staff, controlling his anger with difficulty. 'It's unheard of. It's against the rules. It's . . . it's . . .'

'Evil?' Ganger chuckled. 'Well, it would be, wouldn't it?'

'Will you kindly stop reading my mind?' Staff shouted. 'It's bad enough my having to live in it without strangers poking their dirty great snouts in there as well.' He pulled himself together. 'I'm sorry,' he said. 'But please, just for the time being, could you possibly?'

There was a pause. 'Could I possibly what?' Ganger said.

'Thank you,' said Staff. 'Could you possibly just wait for me to say what I'm thinking, rather than going and looking for yourself? For one thing, it's bad form. You know, like reading the end of a book before you get to it. And it puts me at a disadvantage.'

'Not really,' Ganger replied. 'I can only read what's there, can't I? And anyway, it's not telepathy, it's just . . .'

'Insight, I know, you said.'

'Now you're at it.'

'Oh shut up.' Staff reached for the pencil again and started to chew it. 'These mortals,' he said tentatively.

'Ex-mortals.'

'Ex-mortals, then.' Staff felt his teeth meet around the graphite core. 'I suppose they're all, you know, in menial capacities. Hewers of wood, drawers of water, that sort of thing.'

Ganger shook his head. 'Not really,' he said. 'Upper executive, lower administrative grade, mostly. None in the upper grades of admin, but that's because they're relatively new and it all takes time. Dead men's shoes, you know, that sort of thing.'

For some reason, the phrase made Staff shudder a little,

in context. 'But that's really . . .' He diluted the thought rapidly, just in case someone was peeking. 'Not really on, you know. I mean, mortals . . .'

'It's never been tried here, you mean.' Ganger turned away from the window, and Staff noticed, in the brief fraction of a second it took him before he could cauterise that part of his brain temporarily, that he looked a bit different. 'I know, it's hard to accept. But we're doing it, and it seems to be working. That's the joy of effectively running our own ship. If we do something outrageous, then who cares? It's just us, going to the devil in our own way. So to speak,' he added deliberately. 'And if it works . . .'

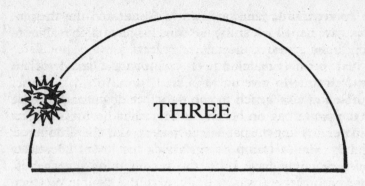

THREE

Between the acting of a dreadful thing and its first motion, all the interim is like a phantasma or a hideous dream. The genius and the mortal instruments are then in council, and the state of man suffers the nature of an insurrection.

'Oh hell, why not?' said Jane suddenly, aloud, and crossed the road into the shop.

'Two cream doughnuts, please,' she said to the girl. 'No, make that three. The fresh cream, not the artificial.'

Eyes like molybdenum steel augers bored into her soul as she fumbled in her purse for a pound coin, trying her inadequate best to look like someone who is buying cakes for three people, not just one.

'And a penny change,' said the girl. 'Thank you.'

Well, Jane thought, as she walked on down the street, it seemed like a good idea at the time. Eat a doughnut, girl, said the Father of Lies, you won't know yourself afterwards. Whereas in fact, her better part of reason told her, the only perceptible change will be round the back of her buttocks. Girls who eat three cream doughnuts have only themselves to blame if they end up looking like hovercraft.

'Never mind,' Jane said firmly. A man in a fawn over-coat gave her a look and quickened his pace slightly. Never mind, she repeated *sotto voce*, at least it isn't chocolate. When you start mainlining chocolate in the middle of the day, it's time to give up and die.

She found a bench in the park, sat down and looked at the paper bag on her knee. Cream had saturated it in patches, making the paper transparent, and she shuddered slightly. Had a tramp been passing just then, he would most certainly have been the recipient of unexpected charity; but there was nobody, except a couple of glue-sniffers under a plane tree on the other side of the Oriental pond, and the distant prospect of a jogger. She was going to have to eat them herself.

The first one wasn't too bad, although she was painfully aware that the cream had got out and was roaming around her face like a Dark Age horde. The second one wasn't too bad until about halfway through; and she abhorred waste, and you look such a fool walking around with one and a half cream doughnuts in a paper bag. So she finished it, sent her tongue snowploughing through the sweet slush on her upper lip, and closed the bag firmly. She felt slightly sick.

'It's a symptom, you know,' said a voice beside her.

She jumped. It was bad enough being addressed by a strange man in a park; the fact that it was the same strange man who frightened her half to death the previous day by reading her mind and then walking away dry-foot through a huge puddle only served to add inches to her take-off.

'Eating,' the man went on, smiling. 'Atavism, pure and simple. The hunter-gatherer inside us all reckons that if you've got something to eat, then that's all that matters, and so at the first sign of trouble we reach for food. It's all stress related, of course; and the things we eat make the stress worse. For a purely instinctive reaction, it's pretty counter-productive, wouldn't you say?'

'Go away,' Jane replied.

'You've got cream on your nose.'

'I'll call a policeman.'

The man smiled. 'For all you know,' he said, 'I am a policeman.'

'Then I'll call another policeman. Go on, get lost.'

The man crossed his legs and folded his hands round the junction of his knees. 'Another slice of atavism,' he said, 'though marginally more sensible. What a mess humanity is.'

He vanished.

In the ensuing cloud of mental static, Jane became aware that she had somehow managed to sit on the third cream doughnut. It's odd, the way you notice things like that.

'Where have you gone?' she said.

'I haven't gone anywhere,' replied the voice. 'Did you realise you're sitting on . . .'

'Yes.'

'There you go,' said the voice. 'Telepathy. We can really get a move on now, don't you think?'

Jane stood up to walk away, turned and brushed ineffectually at the adherent doughnut. 'Don't you dare,' she said.

'I wasn't going to,' replied the voice. 'Being a spirit, I am not susceptible to mortal desires; and even if I was, I'm not sure removing flattened cream cakes from the back ends of people would be quite my thing. If you sit down again, nobody will see you've got a doughnut sticking to your . . .'

Jane sat down. She didn't like this one little bit; but of all the things she was, she wasn't afraid.

'Well?' she said.

The air hung around her, empty and quite blatantly transparent. She began to wonder whether . . .

'Sorry,' said the voice, 'I was forgetting. I'm still here.'

Jane stared straight in front of her. 'Are you a ghost?' she said.

'No,' said the air. 'The term ghost implies someone who is dead. Never having been alive, I cannot be dead. Next question.'

Jane turned her head and looked slowly around. There wasn't a tree or a bush for ten yards around, so it wasn't some silly fool ventriloquising. The voice was quite soft, but distinctly external. She didn't know what voices inside your head sound like, but this was definitely an outside broadcast. She turned her head back and continued to stare forwards.

'Well?' she repeated.

'If you continue sitting on that doughnut,' the voice replied, 'it'll ruin your skirt. Compacted fresh dairy cream and gaberdine don't go, or so they tell me.'

'If you go away,' she said, 'I will remove the doughnut. While you stay here, visible or not, I have no intention of indulging your warped sense of humour.'

There was a long silence, and then the voice spoke again. This time, though, it was definitely *inside*.

'Happy now?' it said.

'Certainly not,' Jane replied. 'Go away.'

'I just did,' replied the voice. 'I went back to the office and I'm making myself a cup of tea. What the hell more do you want?'

'Don't you dare make a cup of tea inside my head,' Jane replied. 'I won't have it, understand?'

'What'll you do, then, blow your nose?'

Jane wriggled violently in her seat, trying to dislodge the doughnut. Inside her head, she could feel laughter.

'Stop that,' she said, 'you'll give me a headache.' The

walls of her skull stopped vibrating. As far as she could tell, the doughnut was still there.

'Who are you?' she asked.

Her brain hummed, and the message, when it came through, was wordless and vague; repellent, but attractive too. What remained of her defence mechanisms prompted her not to understand it.

'Very well,' said the voice, audible inside her head once more. 'Here's three clues for you. Talk of me and I appear; the proverbial alternative to me is a lot of sea water; and, like your average cream bun, I have a tendency to take the hindmost. Or at least,' the voice corrected itself, 'those should help you identify our head of department. Actually, though, we're more of a team. The cult of personality, though . . .'

'I see,' said Jane, primly. 'I'm afraid I'm going to have to insist that you leave.'

'You can't insist unless you've got an or-else,' replied the voice. 'What'll you do to me if you don't?'

'I shall make the sign of the cross,' Jane replied awkwardly. 'So there.'

The voice smiled – it was that sort of voice. It would have had a radio producer standing on his hands with pure joy.

'Can if you like,' it replied. 'Won't do you the slightest bit of good, and I shall be bitterly offended. We have feelings, you know. All these spiritual stereotypes would be history in a truly enlightened society. But we're used to it. We make allowances.'

'Can I get rid of you?'

'Not really,' the voice replied. 'I suppose you could get one of those portable stereo things with earphones and try and blast me out, but I'm not sure that that wouldn't be counterproductive. I mean, I'm not vain, but which would you rather have banging about inside your head, me or Def Leppard?'

Jane considered this. 'Are you planning on staying long?' she asked. 'Because if you are, it might just be worth it. And there's other things beside heavy metal that you can play loud, you know. I was on a train the other day with a man who was listening to *Götterdämmerung* on his Walkman. You could hear it buzzing away from the buffet car.'

'Threats,' said the voice coldly, 'are the last resort of the inadequate negotiator. Were you thinking of the Solti recording, by the way, because I prefer it, on balance, to the Karajan.'

'Why can't I get rid of you?' Jane demanded. 'You'll make me late for work.'

'You let me in,' the voice replied. 'You listened to temptation.'

'Did I?'

'What you're sitting on proves it,' replied the voice, smugly. 'Go on, I said, be a devil. I didn't actually mean it like that, of course, but you seem to have got the message.'

'That makes sense,' Jane replied thoughtfully. 'As a rule, I don't even like cream cakes. What are you doing here, anyway? Do you want me to sell you my soul or something?'

The voice laughed, making her hair shake slightly. 'My dear girl,' said the voice, with genuine amusement, 'why on earth should I want to do that? I can get souls any time I want, trade. The public,' it continued, 'have this peculiar idea that all we care about is souls. Me, I can take them or leave them.'

'So what do you want?' Jane demanded.

'I want,' said the voice, 'to offer you a job.'

Jane caught her breath in amazement. Unfortunately, in doing so she inhaled the last of the cream, huffed for about a tenth of a second, and then sneezed mightily. When she'd recovered from the shock, the voice had gone.

★   ★   ★

Staff looked at his watch.

'Well?' he said.

There was a squelching noise, and Ganger materialised on the other side of the desk. Staff was amused and pleased that, for once, Ganger wasn't looking like a designer-shirt advertisement. He was wet and shaking slightly, and his stiffed-up haircut had been blasted down over his forehead.

'Sorry I'm late,' Ganger said. 'I got sneezed.'

'That's all right,' Staff replied equably. 'How did you get on?'

'I'd say,' Ganger replied, mopping himself with a handkerchief, 'that she's thinking about it. Either that, or she's booking in at one of those places where they don't mind if you think you're a tree just so long as you don't drop leaves on the stairs.'

Staff tapped his teeth with his pencil. 'But she didn't give you a decision?'

'Lord, no,' Ganger replied. 'Wouldn't have expected her to. In fact,' he admitted, 'I'd only just introduced the subject when I had to split. It's typical of the problems I have with women,' he added. 'I just get right up their noses, you know?'

Fine, said Staff to himself, I'd always wondered who writes the script for *Spitting Image*, and now I know. 'But you did tell her about the job?' he said. 'I mean . . .'

'Well, I mentioned it.' Ganger shrugged. 'You can't rush these things. It's one of the lessons we've learned in our own mortal recruitment programme. Anyone who wants the job really isn't going to be suitable.'

Staff nodded. 'So?' he said.

'So,' Ganger replied, reaching in his pocket for a comb. 'The next stage is, we scare the poor kid absolutely shit-less. You can leave that bit to me if you like.'

Staff pursed his lips. 'Is that going to be, you know,

absolutely essential?' he asked. 'I know you lot are allowed a certain latitude in the way you do things, but over here we've got to watch ourselves.'

Ganger nodded briskly. 'Absolutely essential,' he said. 'You've got to do that to induce the right ambience of mild paranoia. Like they say, nobody in their right mind would do this job anyway.'

'Well.' Staff opened the top left-hand drawer of his desk and found a peppermint. 'Let me know how you get on.'

'Will do.' The chair emptied itself. Staff sat for maybe thirty seconds, looking at it. Then, with one smooth easy movement, he reached into the open drawer, grabbed an inhaler and sniffed ferociously. There was a sort of peculiar popping noise, and Ganger was lying on his face on the floor beside him. Staff put the inhaler back in the drawer and closed it.

'Serves you right,' he said. 'I thought I'd made it quite clear that I didn't want any of this mind-hacking stuff, but I suppose you didn't listen. In one ear and out the other, that sort of thing.'

Ganger grinned ruefully and rubbed his knee. 'Force of habit,' he said. 'Won't happen again.' He got to his feet, dusted himself off and walked to the door.

'By the way,' he said, as he turned the handle and half-inserted himself into the gap. 'While I was in there, I couldn't help noticing. That stuff with the blue stockings and the polar bear. Very original.'

He closed the door just before the stapler hit it.

In the Blue Mountains, high above the encircling plain, a woodcutter paused from his work and leaned on his axe. The sun, chugging along on two cylinders and with a pair of tights doing service for a fan belt, glinted on his curly red hair and fearless blue eyes. Far away, a bird sang.

'Greetings, Cousin Bjorn,' said a voice behind him. 'Yet another really beautiful day, is it not? Pleasantly mild, yet neither too hot for work nor too cold for a moment merely standing and listening to the voice of the stream as it laughs its way down the hillside to our tranquil village.'

'Drop dead, Olaf,' Bjorn replied.

Olaf shrugged. 'It is a pity that one so young and so blessed by Nature should be as sour at heart as a green apple,' he observed tolerantly. 'Nevertheless, I am sure that sooner or later you will overcome your internal anguish and find true peace. In the meantime, there is wood to be cut.' He shouldered his axe and walked away down the hill, whistling a folk-tune.

Bjorn could take a hint. He lifted the axe, whirled it round his head, and brought it down on the base of the tree. The head flew off and landed in the crystal waters of the stream.

'How unfortunate,' observed a white-haired, rosy-cheeked woodcutter, who had been tying his shoe behind a venerable elm.

'Yes,' Bjorn agreed. 'Another eighteen inches to the left and it'd have taken your leg off.'

The elder, whose name was Karl, sighed, seated himself on a tree trunk, and motioned the young man to join him.

'Hostility,' he said, offering Bjorn an apple, 'is like a rough-handled axe. It wounds those you use it against, and it blisters the hands of the user. Try and be a little more peaceful within yourself, Cousin Bjorn. Life is a wonderful thing.'

'Apples give me gut ache,' Bjorn replied. 'Specially bloody Cox's.' He threw the apple away over his shoulder. 'Now would you mind shifting yourself, because if you don't you're going to be right under this tree when I chop the bugger down.'

Karl shook his head and smiled. 'You'll have to find your axe head first, Cousin. Always remember that,' he added, as he got up and walked away. 'Always find your axe head before you start to cut down your tree.'

Bjorn made a rude noise and stumped across to the stream. It took him quite some time to find the axe head, during which his shoes got absolutely soaked.

'Good-morning, Uncle Bjorn,' said a voice above his head. He looked up to see a little girl, about ten years old, in a pretty blue dress. 'Mother thought you might be hungry, so she sent you some food. If you would like a refreshing draught of beer, I can run back to the house and get some for you.'

Bjorn lifted the napkin and made a face. 'Leave it over there,' he said. 'And tell the dozy cow I can't stand waffles, right? Waffles give me wind.'

The girl nodded. 'Uncle Bjorn,' she said, 'I was running blithely through the woods just now and I saw a beautiful flower, as blue as the heavens themselves. Look, I picked it to show you. It's such a lovely flower, I'm sure there must be a wonderful story about it and how it got its name.'

'It's called dungwort,' Bjorn replied. 'Use your imagination.'

'Oh.' The girl curtseyed prettily. 'Well,' she said, 'I'd better be getting back to the house, before Mother wonders where I've got to. Do be careful with that great sharp axe.'

'Scram.'

The girl curtseyed again and danced off down the hill, leaving Bjorn alone at last with the trees, the birds, the squirrels and his ingrowing toenail. For a while he stood and looked aimlessly about him, until his eye lit on one tree that he recognised. It was a tall, ancient oak and he remembered it well; he had climbed it as a boy, and his grandfather had often lifted him up into its branches, pointing out to him all the marvellous things he could see. How wonderful it is, his grandfather used to say, to sit in a high tree and look out over all the kingdoms of the world, as if one were God's own eyes!

Bjorn braced his feet, grinned, and set about cutting it down.

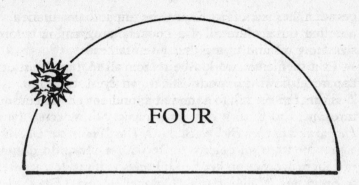

FOUR

It's a strange feeling, knowing that someone else has been inside your head; halfway between having a beetle down the back of your neck and being burgled.

Jane's first instinct, on getting home after an afternoon at work when she had got precisely nothing done, was to wash her hair; but it didn't really do the trick, somehow. She still felt that sensation – irritating more than anything else – of being bunged up with something, the way you feel after you've been underwater and got water trapped inside your ear. Holding her nose and trying to blow through it didn't really achieve anything either, however.

Silence made it worse, and so she switched on the television. At first the mixture of irritation and fascination inspired in her by the discovery of a brand new Australian soap opera distracted her, and she spent at least six minutes sitting in front of the screen trying to work out whether Terry was Gloria's sister or Tracy's boyfriend's son; and then she started to get the unpleasant feeling that all the voices were inside her head, and several generations of brown-skinned, bright-eyed Aussies were conducting their tangled personal relationships right between her ears. Hurriedly she flipped channels and watched three minutes of a cookery programme before switching off and trying the stereo instead.

That seemed to work. She remembered that, for all its apparent show of bravado, she'd got the distinct impression that the voice had sounded apprehensive when she'd threatened to flush it out with music. She selected *Fifty Favourite Marches By The Band Of The Coldstream Guards*, a present from an elderly uncle with a very odd notion of generosity, put on her headphones and sat down. After ten minutes ('Lilliburlero', 'Colonel Bogey', 'The Girl I Left Behind Me' and, incredibly, 'When I'm Sixty-Four') she came to the conclusion that demonaical possession was a damn sight better than premature deafness, and turned that off, too.

She made a cup of tea.

'All right,' she said, 'I know you're in there. Come out.'

Absolute silence, both internal and external. Perhaps, she said to herself, I'm going mad.

This possibility (oh hell, the milk's gone off, I'll have to use powdered) hadn't occurred to her before, but her innate sense of logic recommended it to her most strongly as an explanation consistent with the known facts. If it was the right explanation, it would require serious thought and quite possibly a major adjustment to her lifestyle. Girls who hear voices inside their heads have only two options: they can raise armies and drive the English out of Aquitaine, or they can seek professional help.

'I wouldn't do that,' said the voice. 'You're not like her at all.'

Jane relaxed. She wasn't going mad after all.

'Out,' she said firmly. 'Where I can see you.'

'Very well.'

The man materialised against the worktop, picked up

her cup of tea, and sipped it. She switched the kettle back on and took another mug down from the rack.

'Not like who?' she said.

'Joan of Arc,' the man replied. 'Funny girl, our Joan. Not mad, not by any stretch of the imagination, but definitely the sort that gives sanity a bad name.'

'That's my tea you're drinking. The milk's off, by the way.'

'In addition to which,' the man went on, 'because she spent so much time in a helmet she had *the* most appalling build-up of wax in her ears. It really puts you off, that sort of thing.'

'You've just made that up,' Jane said. The man grinned.

'Ten out of ten for intuition,' he replied. 'You're quite right. When Joan of Arc was around I wasn't more than a niggling little theory at the back of the European subconscious. I got all that stuff from one of the blokes in our department. Claims he invented the wax cotton jacket back in the fifteenth century just through having to crawl in and out of her ears all the time.'

'Fascinating,' Jane replied. 'Look, is there any point to this persecution, or is it just my bad luck? I must add at this point that I'm not the slightest bit frightened of you.'

'You're not?'

'No.'

'Oh shit. That's a nuisance. I have this theory about fear as an organic component of any fully integrated recruitment programme.' The man sipped his tea thoughtfully and Jane observed that the level in the cup hadn't changed at all. The little white flecks that signified needled milk, however, had vanished.

'Now that's odd,' she said. 'I thought your lot were supposed to turn fresh milk sour, not the other way round.'

'Static electricity,' the man replied, sipping again and

pulling a face. 'Personally, I hate fresh milk. It sets my teeth off edge. Nine out of ten for observation, by the way.'

'Only nine?' Jane enquired, as the kettle boiled. 'Why's that?'

'Because,' the man replied, 'you should have recalled that the milk was fresh on the doorstep this morning, and it's been in the fridge all day. It's my presence that turned it bad, and now I'm doing the decent thing and turning it good again, by reversing the flow of ions temporarily.'

'You can do that, can you?'

'Oh yes,' the man replied, widening his grin as an archer draws his bow. 'I'm very versatile. You might say that I've got a lot of ions in the fire.'

'You might say that, yes.'

Jane dropped a teabag into her cup and poured water on to it from the kettle. It was stone cold.

'Childish,' she said.

The man lifted his left foot like a horse being shod and inspected the sole of his shoe. 'Not really,' he replied. 'Empty it out and have a look.'

Jane scowled at him and tipped the cup out into the sink. There was a clatter, and she saw four or five little lumps of what looked like glass.

'Diamonds,' the man remarked casually. 'Produced by electrolysis. They're not stable, mind,' he added, as Jane scrabbled frantically for them. 'They'll turn back into quick-dissolving sugar in a moment, just you see.'

So they did. Jane drew her breath in sharply.

'You haven't answered my question,' she said.

'Nor have I,' the man replied. He sat down on the kitchen stool, picked up a slice of Battenberg that Jane had been saving for a rainy day and bit into it. Its surface area remained undiminished, despite the crunching noises the man was making. 'Another proverb bites the dust,' he observed with his mouth full. 'You want to know why I'm haunting you?'

'I thought you said you weren't a ghost.'

'I'm not. I'm a . . .' He hesitated.

'You're a devil,' Jane said, calmly. 'I'd gathered that.'

But the man was frowning disapprovingly. '*Not* a devil,' he said. 'We don't use that word, it's got overtones. We consider that word pejorative and demeaning. We are a distinct metaphysical group with our own unique cultural and spiritual identity, and I'd be grateful if you'd respect that.'

Jane nodded. 'Okay,' she said, 'I can understand that, just about. What are you, then?'

The man's frown deepened slightly and he put the cake back, apparently untouched, on the plate he had taken it from. 'On the whole,' he said, 'we don't hold with generalising descriptive nouns. We firmly believe that each and every being in the cosmos is an individual, and . . .'

'Yes,' Jane said, folding her arms, 'that's fine. You're an individual. An individual what?'

'We don't like to . . .'

'Come on.'

'Well.' The man seemed distinctly embarrassed now. He picked up the salt cellar, shook a little out into the palm of his hand, and threw it over his right shoulder. 'If pressed, we prefer to describe ourselves as dæmons.'

'Demons.'

'Dæmons,' the man corrected her, hamming up the diphthong. 'From the Greek *daimon*, meaning a spirit, supernumerary god or præternatural entity. We feel . . .'

'But your leader is Satan, right?'

The man now looked distinctly offended. 'Wrong,' he said. 'Look, when you go out and buy takeaway chicken, you don't honestly believe that the business is still run by a seventy-year-old Texan colonel with a little white beard, do you? It's the same with us. We've kept the name, I suppose, or at least parts of the corporate identity, but we've moved on a long way from those days, I can tell you. We've diversified our interests into completely new areas.'

'Like the Mafia.'

'*Not* like the Mafia. Like Rupert Murdoch or Howard Hughes, even. We really aren't in the same business that we used to be in at all, even say two hundred years ago.'

'Don't tell me,' Jane said. 'You're moving into the area of communications and information technology. Or financial services, maybe. I could believe that,' she added thoughtfully.

'Let me make you a cup of tea.'

Jane shuddered involuntarily. 'No, thank you,' she said. 'I like my tea made with wet water and organic tea-leaves. I don't imagine there's much of either of those in any cup of tea you'd make.'

'You're being very hostile,' the man said.

'And you still haven't answered my question,' Jane replied sweetly. 'Why me?'

'Like I said,' the man replied. 'We want to offer you a job.'

'As a devil? No thanks.'

'Will you please not use that word.'

'You look rather silly when you're upset,' Jane observed, 'and not at all the way I'd expect a demon – sorry, dæmon, I hope I pronounced it right . . .'

'Perfectly. And how should I look?'

'Don't change the subject. I know the one about Jesus wanting me for a sunbeam, but I reckon your idea's a bit over the top, don't you?'

The man sighed, and Jane suddenly felt a pang of sympathy for someone else who'd had a long day. 'I'm sorry,' she said. 'Tell me about the job.'

The man looked suitably grateful. 'Thank you,' he said.

'And I'm sorry I sneezed you earlier,' Jane added. 'That was an accident, actually, honest. I get hay fever sometimes, in the summer.'

'How unpleasant for you. Basically, the job . . .'

'Yes?'

The man thought for a moment. 'Actually,' he said, 'it's a bit tricky to put into words, really. If I could just pop into your head for a moment . . .'

'I'd rather you didn't,' Jane said quickly, and then added, 'But thank you for asking, anyway.'

'Okay then,' the man said. 'I'll see what I can do just explaining it verbally, and we'll take it from there. Basically . . . Oh, *nuts*!'

Jane looked startled. 'What is it?'

The man looked sheepish. 'It's my bleeper,' he admitted. 'I'm on call, you see. Can I possibly borrow your phone a minute?'

Jane suppressed a giggle. 'You're the duty devil tonight, are you?'

'Will you *please* . . . ?'

'Be my guest,' she said. 'It's in the other room. Not long distance, is it?'

The man made a sort of simpering noise. 'Not at all,' he said. 'It's about a mile and a half to my office, as the lift-shaft plummets.' He walked through, shutting the door behind him. Somehow, Jane managed to keep herself from listening at the keyhole.

The door opened, and the man's face appeared round it. 'Sorry about this,' he said. 'Something's cropped up, I've got to dash back to the office. Look, can you forget all about this for the time being and we'll talk later?'

Jane nodded. 'Though I can't promise to forget *all* about it.'

'Don't you worry about that,' the man said. 'And I'll take care of the phone bill, too. Thanks for the tea.'

He vanished.

Jane stood stock still for about twenty seconds. Then she blinked twice, shook herself, and realised that she was in the flat.

'Funny,' she said aloud. 'I can't remember taking my coat off.'

She considered the matter for a while, until something at the back of her subconscious assured her that it really wasn't worth worrying about. Instead, she decided, she'd have a nice cup of tea and a slice of cake, wash her hair and then watch the telly for an hour or so before going to bed.

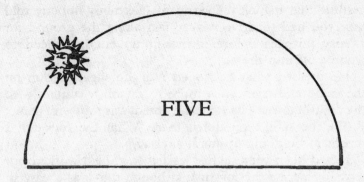

FIVE

Wayne, trainee technical assistant (second grade), looked down over the dashboard of the sun and wondered if something was wrong.

If it was, he told himself, then it wasn't his fault. He hadn't asked to be transferred at a moment's notice from Tides, where he had just mastered sweeping up the staff canteen floor, and to be given this bloody great big thing to fly. Nobody had told him how to fly it, probably because nobody seemed to know. The sum total of hands-on vocational training he had received comprised the words 'I think the ignition is that one there'.

Why was everyone down there looking at him?

He'd heard somewhere that mortals aren't supposed to look directly at the sun, because it damages their eyes or something equally feeble. Pretty well everything damaged mortals, as far as he could gather. If half of what he'd heard was true, it was a miracle there were any of them left.

It hadn't been easy getting the stupid thing off the ground in the first place, and the damage wasn't his fault either. After all, anybody with any sense would naturally assume that it took off vertically. Certainly nobody told him you had to drive it very fast along the ground for twenty minutes before it picked up enough speed to wobble off into the air.

He pressed what he hoped was the speak button on the radio and tried once more to establish contact with the control tower. His voice, he noted, was thin with panic.

'Oi,' he said, 'you down there. What the fuck am I meant to be doing up here, anyway?'

It had been very slightly easier once he'd worked out how to operate the joystick; although that was a case in point. You'd think that if you pushed it back it would make the thing go upwards. It didn't, though. Remarkable how quickly an ice-cap will melt if you do low swoops over it.

'Is there anybody down there, for shit's sake?'

He gave up. On the left-hand side of the console there were some buttons he hadn't pressed yet. He pressed them. They didn't seem to make any difference.

There had to be some way to make this thing fly steady. If he could get down lower, perhaps somebody on the ground would know what to do, and they could shout up at him and tell him. He noticed a lever with a red knob on it, and pulled. That certainly made a difference.

'Help!' he screamed.

About five minutes later, once he'd got used to flying along upside down, he managed to grab hold of the lever again and tried to pull it back. It wouldn't budge. It was stuck.

At least, he said to himself, I can't see what's going on on the ground. I don't think I'd want to know, somehow.

Instinct told him that since he couldn't see where he was going, the sensible thing would be to try and go higher, because the higher up you went, the fewer things there were that you could possibly bump into. The odd star, perhaps; maybe a comet or two. Not the ground. He wrestled with the joystick, but now that was jammed too. He had a notion that he was going into a spin, zooming downwards. If the great burning disc he was attempting to manipulate hit the ground, the chances were that it would probably perform a massive leg-break and whizz out into the back end of the universe for six byes.

Not my fault, he muttered, as he strained against the stick. Not my fault, not *my* fault, not my *fault* . . .

Jane woke up and sat bolt upright in bed. Something was wrong.

It was, she realised, the dawn. It was doing something it shouldn't be doing. It was flashing on and off.

With her head still full of damp, heavy sleep, she stumbled out of bed, clumped to the window and hauled on the curtains. Dear God, she thought, I'm right.

The sun, riding high – very high – in the morning heavens was flicking on and off like a huge, blazing indicator. Blinding flashes of light, then sudden darkness, twenty times a second. All the signs were that planet Earth was approaching a junction and preparing to turn left.

Perhaps, Jane said to herself as she struggled into a pullover, it's an eclipse. Lots of eclipses. Perhaps they're using up an enormous backlog of eclipses before they pass their best-before date.

She stopped and thought for a moment. There was, she realised, something else.

Very slowly, she turned round and looked for her watch. It was difficult going, because the stroboscopic effect of the flashing sun made it impossible to focus or judge distances. Eventually, though, she found it and peered at the dial. It was half-past eleven. At night. She'd only gone to bed an hour ago. What the hell were they doing having dawn?

Perhaps, she thought, there'll be an announcement in a moment. There is no cause for alarm, it's only a drill. We're having a dawn-practice and we forgot to tell you. Sorry about that.

Then she twigged. The sun was going the wrong way. Instead of East-West, it was going West-East. She could tell this because, in addition to flickering away like very old film footage, it was going at one hell of a lick.

Jane stood there, one small mortal trying to make sense of the Universe. All things considered, it was a pretty ambitious undertaking, and nobody could have blamed her if she'd not even tried. Aristotle had tried, after all, and Thomas Aquinas, and Descartes, and Einstein, and a lot of others too, all of them better qualified and probably far better paid than she was. The combined results of their researches, one had to admit, had not been impressive. Nobody could possibly have reproached Jane if she had failed. But she didn't; in fact, although she wasn't really conscious of it, she hit the nail on the head dead centre and with considerable force.

'Oh dear,' she said. 'Somebody's made a banjax.'

As if to congratulate her on the accuracy of her summary, the moon rose from behind a clump of very frightened-looking clouds, zoomed across the sky, stopped just underneath the sun and hovered there. On the perfectly blank silver sphere of its face, Jane was sure she could make out an expression, and it reminded her of her geography teacher at school. Jane frowned.

'Honestly!' she said.

Then she drew the curtains tightly and went back to bed.

Wayne, trainee technical assistant (second grade), opened his eyes and looked up.

Not that it was up, strictly speaking, because he was

still flying along in a dead spin, upside down, straight towards the centre of the earth. As far as he was concerned, however, it was up. They call it relativity, and up to a point it works.

'Ger,' he said.

Directly above, or perhaps below, his head, he could see the moon. What was more, he could see the man in the moon. And the man in the moon wasn't pleased, apparently.

To be precise, he was standing up in his cockpit waving his fists in the air and shouting. He was too far away for Wayne to be able to hear him, let alone read his lips, but he had a pretty shrewd idea of the general gist of what was being said.

'Not my fault,' he yelled. 'Not my *fault*!'

What the hell, the man couldn't hear him anyway. Wayne shrugged, relaxed his shoulders, and leaned back in the seat. Any minute now, he reckoned, he'd collide with the earth and none of it would matter very much anyway.

As he slid back in the seat, it so happened that his elbow banged against the control panel, and something got switched on.

'. . . THE BUGGERY DO YOU THINK YOU'RE DOING, YOU DOZY YOUNG BUGGER, PULL THE BLOODY STICK BACK AND OPEN YOUR SODDING FLAPS!'

Ah, said Wayne to himself, that must have been the radio. Now perhaps we're getting somewhere.

'Here,' he shouted. 'Can you hear me?'

The voice from the radio, which he assumed was that of the man in the moon, didn't answer his question in so many words, but the impression he got was that yes, they had established radio contact. He took a deep breath.

'Here,' he said. 'How do you fly this poxy thing?'

There was a moment of stunned silence.

'You mean you don't *know*?'

Wayne scowled. 'Course I don't bloody know. You think if I knew I'd be flying it upside down straight at the bloody ground?'

The moon wobbled on its course. 'Didn't anyone, like, *tell* you before they let you take her up?'

'No,' Wayne replied. 'Look . . .'

'All right,' said the man in the moon, quickly, 'keep your head, there's nothing to it really. You see that stick thing in front of you?'

Wayne looked down. 'Yup,' he said. 'I tried that.'

'Shut up and listen. That's your joystick, right? Now to the left of the joystick there's some levers. That's your flaps. Now, ease the stick back with your right hand, lift the flaps with your left. Easy does it. I said easy! Gently!'

Amazingly, Wayne could feel the sun responding; levelling out, slowing down. He gripped the stick hard. The voice over the radio sounded quiet and reassuring with just a soupçon of blind terror.

'Now then,' said the voice, 'just by your left foot there's a pedal. That's the brake. You got that?'

'Yeah.'

'Gently mind, that's it. Not too hard, mind, or you'll stall her. Now then, ease forward on the stick, that's it, lovely job, and open the throttle just a crack . . .'

'Which one's the throttle?'

'Right foot. No, no, that's the clutch, *that*'s it. Just a crack, mind, or first thing you know you'll be up the back of the Crab Nebula. Come on now, son, just a little bit more, you've got it. Now hold it like that.'

'Like this?'

'NO!'

There was radio silence for a moment as sun and moon took evasive action. By rights, the violent jinking of the moon should have whipped up a tsunami that would have gone over North America like a carpet-sweeper and given Japan a spring-clean it would never have forgotten. As it happened, however, they were hopelessly under-manned at Tides, owing to the secondment of key personnel to other departments, and everything stayed exactly as it was.

'USE YOUR BLOODY STICK!'

'Like that?'

'Yes. More so. Put your back into it.'

'Like this?'

'Yes.'

The sun seemed to hover for a moment; then it seemed to drop like a stone, just for a fraction of a second; then it caught itself, wobbled heart-stoppingly, and pulled away, flying straight and level. The moon closed in and followed it cautiously.

'Nice work,' said the man in the moon, with a trace of admiration cutting the fear and the relief. 'Just one more thing.'

'Yes?'

'Switch the bloody flasher off, will you? You're giving me a headache.'

Wayne crunched his eyebrows together. 'Flasher?' he said. 'What's that?'

'The flasher. The emergency warning lights. You've been flashing on and off, didn't you . . . ? By your left hand, it's a little blue button with an arrow on it . . . That's it. You're doing just fine.'

In the cockpit of the moon, George let out a long sigh and wiped half a pint of sweat off the bald dome of his head with the back of his hand. Bloody short retirement it had turned out to be, after all. Still, he said to himself, the lad looks like he's got the hang of it, amazingly quickly as well; a natural, obviously. Just as well, too.

'Right,' he said. 'All we've got to do now is to turn it round.'

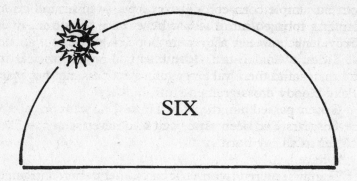

SIX

High above the peaks of the Blue Mountains, the sun, under escort, completed its banking manoeuvre, straightened out, and began to head East. On the ground, all the villagers except one threw their hats in the air and cheered.

'Well, well,' said old Ari, the blacksmith. 'It's not every day you see something like that.'

The other villagers were silent for a while. Even by their standards of simple-hearted straightforwardness, old Ari did come out with some pretty asinine comments from time to time. Still, he made a cracking good horseshoe, so nobody really minded.

'There's something to tell the grandchildren about, eh, Bjorn?' remarked Gustav, lowering the shard of smoked glass through which he had prudently watched the whole thing. 'Remarkable.'

Bjorn said nothing. He was fitting a new handle to his axe, having broken the old one when he lost his temper earlier on. Bjorn got through more axe handles than the rest of the community put together.

'I never cease to wonder,' Gustav went on, knocking

out his simple corn-cob pipe on the sole of his boot and stuffing tobacco into the bowl, 'at the infinite variety of Providence and her astounding . . .'

'I don't,' said Bjorn. 'If you've got nothing better to do than stand there yakking, you could pass me that rasp. Poxy bloody cross-grained stuff, hickory.'

Gustav passed him the rasp. 'I mean,' he went on, 'sixty-seven years I've been alive, and I've never seen the like. Never in all my born . . .'

'I have.'

Gustav's merry, weather-beaten old face contracted into an unaccustomed frown. 'You have?' he asked.

'Oh yes. More times than you've had hot dinners. Give me the wedge. No, not that one, the small one.'

'That's very remarkable, neighbour Bjorn,' said Gustav, with a voice entirely devoid of disbelief. 'I haven't, and I'm much older than you.'

Bjorn stood up and banged the axe head three times on the ground to seat it in the handle. At the third blow, a long crack appeared in the handle. He swore, broke the handle over his knee, and reached for the auger.

'You should be more careful,' Gustav said. 'You could hurt your knee, doing something like that.' Bjorn laughed unpleasantly.

'Fat chance.'

This was, Gustav couldn't help feeling, a typical sort of conversation with young Bjorn. Strange, he looked a pleasant enough sort of fellow. Perhaps he had had an unhappy life before he came to the village.

'Are you sure you've seen things like . . . ?' Gustav pointed at the sun. Bjorn nodded.

'Yeah,' he said. 'I used to work for them, didn't I?'

Jane looked suddenly round, the toothbrush still in her mouth.

'Look . . .' she started to say. The man made an apologetic gesture.

'Sorry,' he said. 'I didn't realise. I can come back later if . . .'

Jane looked at him. Yes, there was something about him that told her that he was another one of Them. What was it, now?

'You're a different one, aren't you?' she said. 'I mean, you're not the same one who came before, are you? Or are you him with a different body on?'

'No,' the man replied, 'I'm a different one. My name is Staff.'

'Staff?'

The man shrugged slightly. 'It's not my actual name,' he said, 'but it's what everybody's called me for longer than I can remember. It's short for Chief of Staff.'

'Ah.' Jane extracted the toothbrush and laid it down on the soap-dish. 'I wish you lot wouldn't keep creeping up on me like this.'

'I didn't mean to creep,' Staff said. 'I just . . .'

But Jane wasn't going to be conciliated that easily. 'I mean,' she said, 'there I am, brushing my teeth, and suddenly there's this face over my shoulder. Did you ever work for a man called Hitchcock by any chance? Fat bloke, big nose.'

The man looked puzzled. 'Not that I can remember,' he said.

Jane smiled apologetically. 'Sorry,' she said. 'Human joke. I don't suppose you devils know much about the movies.'

The man looked hurt. 'Actually,' he said, 'I'm not a devil. Not at all.'

'Sorry,' Jane said, 'I meant to say dæmon, it just slipped out.'

'I'm not a dæmon, either,' the man replied. 'I'm a . . .'

He paused, and blushed. 'Well, I'm not a dæmon. Different department.'

Jane thought for a moment, and then a slow grin spread over her toothpaste-flecked face. 'I've got it,' she said. 'You're an angel.'

'Please,' said the man, 'I really would prefer it if we didn't use that word. It's so . . .' He waved his arms helplessly.

'Well,' said Jane. 'What word should I use?'

'Public servant,' said the man, firmly. 'I think it's a much better word, really, don't you?'

Jane nodded, and looked at the man carefully. Tall, grey-haired, thinning a little on top and thickening out a bit round the middle, with a lot of hair on the backs of his hands and wearing a suit with rather shiny cuffs. Public servant did seem to fit the bill rather better than angel. 'Quite right,' she said. 'Look, can we get out of the bathroom, please?'

'Yes, of course.' The man moved awkwardly and opened the door for her. Jane tried not to mind.

'Coffee?' she said.

'Yes, er, thank you.' The man sat down on a straight-backed chair and folded his arms. He looked embarrassed.

'I've put the kettle on,' Jane said. 'Now, is all this connected with what happened to the sun just now?'

The man nodded. 'You're very observant,' he said.

'Not very,' Jane replied, wrinkling her nose. 'I mean, look at it sequentially. The sun goes haywire, supernatural beings start following me about, you don't have to be Aleister Crowley to get the idea that there may be a common factor . . . Sorry, did I say something wrong?'

'No,' said the man, 'or at least, you weren't to know. It's just that we don't mention that person in the Department.'

'Person? Oh!'

'Exactly,' said the man. 'You may remember Peter Wright; you know, *Spycatcher*? Well, think on, as we used to say when I was a boy.'

'Oh.' Jane bit her lip. 'Look, can we get to the point? What do you lot want with me? The other one – the, er, dæmon – said something about a *job*, but I . . .'

She tailed off. The man was nodding his head.

'A *job*?' she repeated. 'You can't be serious, surely.'

The man stood up and walked to the window. 'Well,' he said, drawing the curtains slightly, 'you saw all that today, I take it? The sun and everything?'

'Yes indeed.'

The man cringed slightly. 'Wasn't very impressive, was it?'

Jane shrugged. 'I don't know,' she said. 'Was it supposed to be? I mean, I'm not really up on portents and things like that. I thought that sort of thing only happened when people like Julius Caesar got stabbed, and there isn't anybody like Julius Caesar about much these days. I mean, you've got to be realistic, haven't you? The whole lot of them aren't worth a light shower between them.'

'It wasn't a portent,' said the man quietly. 'You'd guessed, hadn't you?'

Jane nodded. 'Have you got my mind bugged, or something? Because if you have . . .'

The man shook his head firmly. 'Nothing of the sort, please believe me,' he said. 'But we at the Department . . . well, you had guessed, hadn't you?'

'Yes,' Jane said. 'If you mean that business with the sun was a cock-up, then yes.'

'It was,' said the man, and shuddered. 'Staff shortages.'

Jane raised an eyebrow. 'Staff shortages?'

The man nodded. 'It's a nightmare,' he said. 'An absolute bloody nightmare. Honestly, I haven't the faintest idea where it's all going to end.'

From the kitchen, Jane heard the click of the kettle switching itself off. She decided to ignore it.

'But how can you have staff shortages?' she asked, bewildered. 'I mean, I thought the whole point of you . . . you public servants was, you go on for ever. Immortal, you know.'

'Immortal,' said the man quietly, 'doesn't mean you go on working for ever, it just means that you have a very long retirement. Which means,' he added, 'that with each year that passes, paying the pensions takes up more and more of the available budget. At the moment, pensions account for ninety-nine-point-nine-seven-two of our available revenue. Think about it.'

Jane thought about it. 'I see,' she said.

'Exactly,' said the man. 'And that's only part of it. Put bluntly, we're running out of manpower. You see, every time a public servant retires, there's a vacancy, right?'

'I suppose so,' Jane said. 'I hadn't thought.'

'Take it from me,' said the man. 'There is. Now, the number of . . . I don't know how to put this.'

'You don't?'

'No,' said the man, shaking his head. 'It's delicate. Um. Where do you suppose angels – public servants – come from?'

Jane felt her tongue go dry with embarrassment. 'Er, mummy public servants and daddy public servants?'

The man scowled. 'Certainly not,' he said. 'It's a metaphysical impossibility. No, the stork brings them, of course. And do you know what's happened to the natural habitat of storks in the last fifty years?'

'Um.'

'Well,' said the man, 'I think you can see what I'm getting at. The storks are dying out, so we're . . . well, it makes recruitment a problem. A bloody great big problem. And that's where you come in,' he added.

Jane felt herself going red all over. 'Now look,' she said.

'No, no,' said the man quickly, 'not like that. I mean, we've decided, or at least Mr Ganger and I have decided . . .'

'Mr Ganger?'

'You've met him,' said the man.

'Oh.'

'We've decided,' the man continued, 'that the only way out is to start recruiting mortals – suitable mortals, obviously – and, well . . .'

'Well, what?' said Jane. Her voice, incidentally, would have frozen oxygen. The man swallowed hard, and then made a show of noticing his watch.

'Good lord,' he said, 'is that the time? Anyway, you'll think about it, won't you? I mean, you'll be, like, the guinea . . . I mean, a pioneer. That's right, a pioneer. The whole success of the programme . . .'

'No.'

'And if it works,' the man said quickly, standing up and knocking over a small pile of tapes on the floor, 'it'll mean that we can start replacing key staff, reorganising the whole running of the department, and . . .'

'No.'

'So you'll think about it. Good. Well, I'll be saying . . .'

'No.'

'We'll be in . . .' The man suddenly became translucent, 'touch. Please give it very serious . . .' Then transparent, 'thought.' Then invisible. 'Thank you.'

'No,' Jane said. 'Absolutely not. No way.'

She stopped. She suddenly had the feeling that she was talking to herself.

'Honestly!' she said.

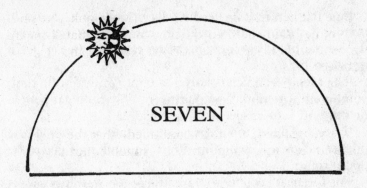

SEVEN

Look in Sir Isaac Newton's *Principia Mathematica* and you will learn all about gravity.

Gravity, according to Sir Isaac, is a natural phenomenon, as immutable as it is impersonal. Because of gravity, objects stay attached to the surface of the planet instead of flying off into the void. There's nothing mystical or even intentional about it; it just happens, because that's how the great machine works.

In all fundamentally important respects, Sir Isaac was right. Gravity is, as he observed, a physical force resulting from the interaction of bodies possessing mass upon each other. It is not dependent upon the whim of any deity or supernatural entity. It can, in other words, be relied on; provided, of course, that somebody remembers to grease the main drive-shaft once in a while.

'It's not my job,' complained the Head Technician loudly, above the ear-splitting scream of grinding diamonds. 'By rights, it's down to Maintenance to . . .'

The Technical Supervisor snarled at him. 'Well,' he observed superfluously, 'whoever was supposed to look after the sodding thing, it's seized. The gearbox's completely stuffed. Look out!' he added, as a chunk of diamond shrapnel flew past his ear. 'Bugger me, Fred, the whole bloody thing's breaking up. We'd better get it switched off quick.'

The Head Technician stared at him. 'You can't do that, you lunatic,' he said. 'Switch this lot off, you'll get people drifting off into space, we'll be lynched.'

'Look,' replied the supervisor, 'either we switch the bugger off or it'll switch itself off. Something's got to be done, right?'

For the next second and a half, speech was impossible, as the bearing manifold suddenly shattered, spraying egg-sized diamonds about like birdshot. The Head Technician dived behind a flywheel and put his head between his knees.

'Come out of there, you coward!' yelled the supervisor.

'Not my problem,' the Head Technician shrieked back. 'You look in the files, chum, you'll see. I wrote a memo about it five years back. I warned you lot that if the whole gearbox wasn't renewed . . .'

'Shut up,' the supervisor observed, 'and bring me a spanner. All we've got to do is slip the clutch and let it freewheel while we bodge up the transmission. Its own momentum'll keep it turning for hours.'

The Head Technician considered this for a moment. 'Bollocks,' he opined. 'It'll just grind to a halt, and then you'll have all the mortals floating upwards yelling at us. You may not give a toss about your pension, chum, but . . .'

The ball race chose that moment to fuse, filling the air with a sparkling cloud of diamond dust. Planet Earth wobbled sharply on its axis.

'All right,' hissed the Head Technician, 'only if this goes wrong, you just remember it was your idea, right? Like, you gave me a direct order and . . .'

'Shut up,' the supervisor reiterated, 'and find me that spanner.'

A few moments later, Planet Earth stopped shuddering and began to spin noiselessly, easily round its axis. It began to slow down . . .

'Ouch!' said Jane, aloud.

It hadn't been her first choice as a flat; it wasn't really her kind of neighbourhood: it was a fair old hike to the station every morning, the bedroom wall needed papering badly, the doors stuck in winter and there was something of a condensation problem in the kitchen; but hitherto at least, she'd never had any problems with the ceiling being too low. Until now, apparently.

She looked down. Yes, there was the floor, just where she'd left it. There was her furniture. Same old furniture, mostly the unsuitable and heterogeneous offerings of relatives and friends, except that previously it hadn't shown any signs of wanting to jump off the ground and float about the place like a shoal of dazed tuna. And there was her breakfast – mug of coffee, slice of toast – swimming obligingly towards her through thin air.

She grabbed at the coffee-cup as it floated past, missed the cup but not the handle, and split the coffee. It fell upwards and splashed against the ceiling.

Gingerly, and conscious that there were rather more cobwebs up here than Mrs Beeton would have approved of, Jane raised her left hand above her head and pushed the ceiling away from her. She felt herself bob downwards for a few feet, and then the current, or whatever the hell it was, caught her up again and lifted her slowly upwards. She kicked violently with her feet, but it didn't help. She hit her head gently on the lampshade, pushed off again, and walked on her hands across to the door frame.

'Somebody,' she said to a passing telephone directory, 'is going to have some explaining to do.'

The directory fluttered its pages and continued to drift

upwards, until it was splayed open against the plaster-work. Jane gripped the wooden frame of the door with both hands and tried to haul herself downwards.

'That's better,' she said, as her feet connected with the carpet. She looked down. The fibres were trying their best to stand on end, giving the impression of one very fright-ened Axminster. Worse still, all the dust she hadn't got around to hoovering out of it was slowly rising. It got up her nose and she sneezed.

A flower vase drifted past her, upside-down and bobbing about erratically as air escaped out of its inside. This wouldn't do at all. She managed to propel herself on to the back of the kitchen table, which was passing by slowly and ponderously, a mere foot or so above the ground. As she had hoped, her weight helped to push it down, and she found herself a mere six inches above floor-level. What she needed now, she reckoned, was some sort of punt-pole.

A passing golf umbrella solved that problem, and soon she was punting cautiously across the floor, steering clear of drifting armchairs and trying not to hit the walls too hard, towards the window. She had an idea that things were going to be a bit surreal out there, and it was a pity that her camera was presently nuzzling against the ceiling-rose like a small black remora.

'Good lord,' she said.

In a way it was really rather beautiful. Peaceful, certainly. The drivers of the cars had mostly had the sense to switch off their engines and they were now simply drifting aimlessly, a few inches off the ground, while airborne pedestrians hung on to their door handles. A school of red buses sailed gently past the request stop opposite the corner shop, while the newsagent's stock in trade sailed gracefully, almost majestically, into the air, flapping their leaves like enormous, slow-motion herons.

An open umbrella fluttered away past her window on its way to the stars.

'You see what I mean?' said a voice above her.

She looked upwards to see Staff flat on his back against the ceiling. She tried not to laugh, but there are limits.

'I'm sorry,' she said. 'But you look so . . .'

'I know,' he replied sadly. 'You think you're having problems. Just count yourself lucky you've got a corporeal body. You have no idea how difficult it was getting here.'

Jane pushed hard on her umbrella, and the table rose upwards. She was just able to grab hold of Staff's left foot before it fell floorwards again, and she towed her visitor down with her. As she had expected, he weighed nothing.

A little undignified scrambling enabled Staff to get on the table, and he secured himself to it by wrapping his arms round one of the legs. Even so, the lower half of his body pointed resolutely upwards, with the result that he looked like nothing so much as a large, respectable tadpole.

'Anyway,' he said. 'Surely now you can't deny that there's a problem.'

'Oh, there's a problem all right,' Jane agreed. 'Like how I'm going to get coffee stains off the ceiling. It's Artex, you know.'

'I gathered,' Staff replied. 'It's like sandpaper, that stuff. Oughtn't to be allowed.'

'Sorry.'

'Not your fault. Look,' he went on, 'unless we find some way of getting things sorted out, it's going to get worse. You must see that.'

'But,' Jane started to say; then she corrected herself. 'Are you sure I'd be able to help?' she said.

'Yes,' Staff replied, 'you and others like you, but you

first. You see, if you make a go of it, we can recruit others. Management won't be able to stop us. We'll be able to fill all the vacant posts, get the plant and machinery properly serviced; that way, we won't have all our staff and resources tied down coping with emergencies.' He paused to fence away a teapot that seemed to want to get inside his jacket. 'Come on,' he said, 'what do you say? Anything's got to be better than this.'

Suddenly, the world started to move again. For a split second, Jane felt it distinctly; the violent shock of an incredibly rapid acceleration, rather like the awful feeling you get the first time you're in an aeroplane taking off. Then she was rather too preoccupied with the spectacle of all her possessions falling to the ground and smashing into tiny pieces to bother with detailed observations of that kind.

'Right,' she said and, using her thumb and forefinger, picked a razor-sharp shard of casserole out of her hair. Outside, the air was suddenly full of the sound of many motorists restored to normality and lamenting their lost no-claims bonuses with the help of their horns. The last glossy magazine twirled a few times in the air and flopped to earth like an exhausted pigeon.

'You're on,' she said.

'Tell me,' said Gustav tremulously, 'all about it.'

The fire burnt low, so that the interior of Gustav's small but cosy cottage became full of deep shadows, each one a curtained doorway into hostile infinity. Using his teeth only, Bjorn removed the crown cap off a bottle of Carlsberg and spat it accurately into the grate.

'Not a lot to tell, really,' he said. 'I applied for the job, got it, tried it, didn't like it, told them to stuff it, moved on. Simple as that.'

'Um,' said Gustav, 'yes, I suppose it is, really. But tell

me,' he went on, overcoming his feelings of acute apprehension. 'What was it really like? Being an angel, I mean.'

There was a silence: a huge, heavy, abrasive silence you could have ground corn with. The firelight glinted red on Bjorn's eyes, making Gustav shrink back into the chimney corner.

'You ever call me that again,' Bjorn growled, 'I'll pull your lungs out through your nose and make you eat them, okay?'

'I'm very sorry,' Gustav squeaked. 'I'd got the impression . . .'

'Because,' Bjorn went on, 'we don't like that name, right? It's a poncey name. Makes you sound like a right fairy, being called that.' He paused to glower savagely into the fire. 'Makes you think of little lacy dolls with wings and Christmas trees shoved up their jacksies. Anybody tries that with me, they'll get what's coming to them, understood?'

'Understood.'

'Fine.' Bjorn took a long pull of beer and burped assertively. 'The lads and me, we used to call ourselves "the Boys from the Blue Stuff". Sounds better, you know, meaner. More macho. And we didn't fart around playing harps, either.'

'Absolutely not,' Gustav agreed, nodding furiously. 'Right on,' he added.

'Right on what?'

'Sorry.'

Bjorn drank some more beer and scratched his ear thoughtfully. 'I'm not saying we didn't have a few laughs, mind. I mean, it wasn't all answering prayers and polishing the sun. Bloody awful job, that was,' he parenthesised, 'took all the skin off your knuckles if you weren't careful. Bloke I worked with, he got his fingers caught in the works when he was trying to clean them out and nobody noticed. They launched the damn thing same as usual and he was left there, trapped, dangling by his fingers, yelling his head off, but nobody heard. You just imagine that,' he went on, after a deep shudder that started just below his neck and finally earthed itself out through the soles of his feet. 'Just imagine it, hanging by your fingers from that bloody great hot thing, miles above the ground, for a whole day. And when he tried to get compensation, what did they say? Should have observed the safety proce- dure, they said, all his own silly fault, served him right. He went a bit funny in the head after that so they put him on Earthquakes. Nobody notices if you're a bit funny in the head on Earthquakes.'

'I see,' said Gustav. 'Well . . .'

'We were always having them,' Bjorn ground on, staring straight in front of him into the fire. 'Industrial accidents they called them, only some of them weren't accidents if you ask me. You can't tell me a grown man suddenly falling off a perfectly wide, fenced-off catwalk into the works of the grass-growing plant was an accident, or a coincidence. Just so happened he'd found out about the foreman and the cocoa money, that's all. Of course, they hushed it up. Blamed it all on the frosts, they did.'

Gustav smiled and tried to seep away into the cracks between the stones, but there was too much of him for that. 'Gosh,' he said.

'Right bastards, some of those foremen were, mind,' Bjorn went on. 'There was one when I was on Miracles – some years ago, this is, because they've closed that department down now. Evil Neville, they used to call him. Short, round bloke, face like a road map. Whenever we were told to turn water into wine, he'd be in there with his mates and a couple of hundred jerrycans, and the poor bloody punters would have to make do with water turned into lager. Couldn't tell the difference half the

time. No wonder the whole department got such a bad
name with the high-ups. Talking of which, you got any
more?'

He waved the empty bottle, and Gustav, simpering,
fetched another. It had cobwebs on it.

'Cheers,' Bjorn said. He decapitated it, absent-
mindedly swallowed the top, and slurped deeply.

'It sounds very unpleasant,' Gustav said.

'Unpleasant!' Bjorn sniggered noisily. 'You're telling
me, sunshine. I could tell you some stories, no worries.
What about that time we were working Nights and Norm
the Headbanger got completely rat-arsed and left his
brother's old van parked right in the middle of the Great
Bear? Or there was that time Mad Trev and me were
working on Rivers, and Trev got taken short just before
the flooding of the Nile. Those Egyptians sure got a shock
that year, I'm telling you.' He laughed brutally. Gustav
closed his eyes and felt sick. He had a little picture of an
angel over his bed: his mother had put it there years ago,
telling him that it would watch over him while he was
asleep. As soon as he was alone in the house again, he
told himself, he'd get a shovel and bury it under the oak
tree.

'Not that it was all bad, mind,' Bjorn was saying.
'There was guard duty, f'rinstance. I liked that. They
gave you this flaming sword and you stood about in
front of the gates of Eden, and anybody who was daft
enough to try and get in there – shunk!' He made a
sharp, graphically illustrative movement with the bottle,
spilling the few remaining suds it contained over the
back of his hand. 'Don't get up,' he said. 'In that
cupboard, right?'

He lurched to his feet and went to the cupboard. Gustav
shut his eyes.

'Here,' he heard Bjorn call out. 'There's no more beer

left, that's a bummer. Hold on, though, this'll do. Cheers.'
Oh wonderful, Gustav thought, he's found the paint
thinners.

'Help yourself,' he said, in a small, tinny voice he barely
recognised as his own.

'Anyway,' Bjorn said, sitting by the fire again and wiping
the neck of the bottle. 'I stuck it as long as I could, but
in the end I couldn't stick it any more.'

'Really?'

'Yeah.' Bjorn drew heavily on the bottle, winced and
licked his lips. 'I reckoned it was, well, brutalising me,
you know? Like, when I was young they said I was sort
of sensitive, you know, feelings and all that. So I reckoned, if I stick this job any longer, what's going to happen
to me? I could end up turning into a really nasty person
if I wasn't careful. So I quit. Probably I was just imagining it,' he added, 'but you can't be too careful, right? I
mean, there's integrity, for one thing.'

'Er, right.'

'So,' Bjorn said. Then he sat silently for a very long
eight seconds, glaring viciously into the fire. Just as Gustav
was beginning to feel a scream welling up inside the pit
of his stomach, Bjorn got up, drained the bottle, and put
it down on the table with a bang. 'You know what,'
he said, 'it's done me good, you know, talking about it. I
feel –' he burped savagely '– much better now. In fact,
we must do this again sometime, right?'

Gustav closed his eyes. On the one hand, his mother
had told him never to tell deliberate lies. On the other
hand, his mother had told him a lot of stuff about angels
that had turned out to be rather wide of the mark.

'Right,' he said. 'I'd like that.'

'Yeah.' Bjorn rose to his feet, groped for his axe, and
staggered clumsily to the door.

'Strewth,' he said, poking his head out into the cool,

sweet, night air and sniffing distastefully. 'Smells like armpits out here. Cheers, then.'

'Cheers.'

Gustav closed the door after his guest, bolted it, put the shutters up, and collapsed into his chair, trembling. From the distant village street he could hear the distinctive sound of a man with an axe playing Try-Your-Strength games with the village pump. He winced.

The picture of the angel disappeared from above Gustav's bed shortly afterwards, and was replaced by a Pirelli calendar.

'Oh,' said the charge-hand.

Far below, an enormous brown snake of muddy, foulsmelling water thrust its snout into the gaps between the skyscrapers. Apart from the occasional crash of falling masonry, the great city was quite astoundingly quiet.

'I thought you meant Memphis, *Tennessee*,' the charge-hand went on, slightly apprehensively. 'So there's another Memphis, is there? That's confusing.'

'Isn't it?' his superior replied, through tight lips. 'Sorry, perhaps I should have explained a bit better. I thought it'd be clear, even to a complete idiot, that when I said flood the Nile as far as Memphis, I meant Memphis, Egypt. Obviously, though, I was wrong.' He pushed his cap on to the back of his head and scratched his bald patch thoughtfully. 'You know what,' he added, after a moment. 'This is going to take a bit of sorting out, this is.'

'Ah.'

'I mean,' he went on, 'just to take the small details first, there's your crocodiles, right?'

'Crocodiles?'

'Crocodiles.' He pointed. 'Must've got swept along with the current or something. Look, there's one now, just crawling up the steps of the Fire Department building.'

'Oh yes, I can just make it out. Gosh, that's . . .'

'And in ten minutes,' his superior went on, 'when we whack all the pumps back into reverse and start draining the water away . . . Well, there's going to be a lot of them left behind, right?'

'Um.'

'But,' his superior went on, 'that's really a minor point, and probably nobody's going to notice, what with rebuilding the whole goddamn city, and flying in emergency aid, and what not. Still, I just thought I'd mention it. Let you have the fully-rounded picture, so to speak.'

'Right.' The charge-hand nodded. 'Got that.'

'There's also,' his superior went on, his face gradually tightening like an overstretched guitar-string, 'the fact that the Egyptians are now one river short. They're not going to be pleased, you know. I get the feeling they're, you know, attached to it.'

'Yes?'

His superior nodded. 'You been working in this department long?' he asked. The charge-hand did some mental arithmetic.

'Not *very* long,' he said.

'How long exactly?'

'Um, eight hours,' the charge-hand replied. 'Before that, I was on Truth.'

'Truth. I see.' His superior nodded a couple of times, and then a few times more simply out of momentum. 'Doing what, exactly?'

'Mumblemumblemumblemumble.'

'Sorry?'

'I made the tea,' the charge-hand replied. 'And sometimes I went out to the shop to get doughnuts and things. We used to do a lot of just sitting about in Truth, see.'

'That follows.'

'It's the Daughter of Time, you know, Truth,' the chargehand added, nervously. 'Not many people know that, but it's . . .'

'Right.' His superior jammed his cap squarely on his head, lifted his sagging shoulders, and scribbled on his clipboard so hard that the point of his pencil snapped. The fragment of graphite flew wide, tumbled down through the firmament, hit the Earth just outside Petrograd, and ended up in the State Geological Museum marked *Fragile*. 'I guess we'd better make a start on getting it sorted, then. First, we'll need a Form KRB1, supported by a blue chit and a Requisition in Form 4.'

The charge-hand made a note in his pocketbook. 'Got that,' he said. 'Right.'

'After that,' his superior went on, 'we'll need a couple of buckets and some mops.'

'Two – buckets,' the charge-hand said slowly as he wrote, 'assorted – mops. Yes?'

'That'll do to be going on with,' said his superior. 'So I'll leave you to it, all right?'

'But . . .'

'After all,' said his superior, a rainbow plainly visible through his torso, 'you're the charge-hand. It says so on your badge. Good luck.'

He retreated rapidly, and soon was nothing more than a tiny speck, indistinguishable among the flock of ibises circling the helipad on the roof of the First Consolidated Bank.

The charge-hand stood for a while, looking in the direction he had taken, and then frowned and said something under his breath. It might have been 'bucket', or at least something quite similar.

'Excuse me.'

The charge-hand turned to find a smallish female mortal standing behind him. She was wearing, he noticed with mingled amazement and disgust, a bright blue lapel-badge with 'Inspector' written on it.

'Where did you get that from?' he demanded.

'The badge, you mean?' Jane said. 'Oh, a man gave it to me. A man by the name of Staff, if that means anything to you.'

The charge-hand blinked four times, said, 'Oh,' and then took off his cap. 'How can I help you, miss?' he added warily.

Jane looked down at the city below her. Out of irre-sistible force of habit, the mighty river was depositing its massive cargo of alluvial silt in through the windows of third-floor offices. She wasn't quite sure what the people in those offices did for a living, but she was prepared to bet money that it wasn't growing rice.

'It's more a case of how I can help you,' she said. 'You see, I've been assigned.'

'Assigned?'

'To help,' Jane explained. 'I'm new, you see. It's a . . .' She searched the back end of her mind for the right phrase. 'It's a management training programme. I'm here to learn the work of various departments, before I'm finally placed where they think I'll be most suitable.'

'I see,' said the charge-hand. 'You, er, know something about tidal rivers, then?'

'Not a great deal,' Jane replied. 'I had a sort of idea that they aren't supposed to flow slap bang through the middle of major urban thoroughfares, but maybe I'm a bit behind on the latest developments.'

The charge-hand sat down on a lump of scrap cloud, put his index finger in his ear and wiggled it about. 'If that's irony,' he said, 'then it's not allowed. There's strict rules about irony.'

'Really,' Jane said, looking at the city. 'You know, I think we ought to do something, don't you?'

The charge-hand sighed. 'Yeah,' he said. 'All right. I'll fetch the buckets.'

Jane looked at him for a moment and considered reminding him about the irony statutes. Then it occurred to her that he might be serious.

'No,' she said, as calmly as she could. 'Don't do that. I've got an idea.'

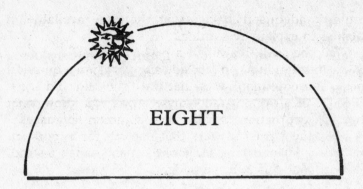

EIGHT

It was lucky that the Mayor's office was on the top floor of the City Hall building. Had it been anywhere else, it would have been flooded out, with grave consequences for the smooth and efficient administration of the City. As it was, the nerve-centre of the governmental system was intact and functioning, which made up to a certain extent for the fact that the rest of the system was under three feet of muddy water. The Mayor, a pragmatist whose electoral image was 'early laid-back pastoral', had decided to face the challenge posed by the inundation, borrowing a hat with some hooks stuck into it and hanging a sign on his door-handle which read *Gone Fishin'*.

'Come in,' he said, in answer to the knock on the door. Then he frowned.

'How did you get here?' he asked.

Jane came in, shooed out an inquisitive crocodile with her handbag, closed the door behind her, smiled, and sat down. 'Easy,' she said. 'I walked.'

The Mayor was about to argue when he caught sight of the bright blue badge. For some reason which his mind couldn't adequately process in the time available, it seemed to explain everything.

'Well,' he said. 'We've got a problem, right?'

Jane put her head on one side and gave him a quizzical look. 'You could look at it that way,' she said. 'I'd see it as more of an opportunity myself, but you know what they say, two nations divided by a common language.'

The Mayor tried to work that one out for a moment, but it was beyond him. He looked at the badge instead. He had confidence in the badge.

'Opportunity,' he repeated.

'Don't you think so?' Jane smiled. 'Millions of cubic tonnes of mineral-rich alluvial silt deposited right on your doorstep,' she said, 'not to mention your window-sill,' she added, 'at a time when the situation in the Middle East means that the price of phosphates on the world commodities exchange is pretty near an all-time high.' She winked. 'I think somebody up there loves you, don't you?'

'Um,' said the Mayor. He could feel a sort of prickly itch in the small of his back. 'Mineral-rich, you said?'

'Very much so,' Jane replied confidently. 'Pump out the water and carry it away and sell it, simple as that. I suggest you put it out to commercial tender.' She stood up and straightened her skirt. 'Then you use the proceeds to rebuild the city, you see. And, well, I don't have to tell a man of your obvious intelligence and sensitivity what a wonderful opportunity this'll be to get on with all those wonderful slum clearance and highway improvement projects you've been talking about all these years. You know, show the voters that you really are a man of your word, that sort of thing. But I expect,' she added sweetly, 'I can leave all the details to you.'

On her way out, her high heels pecking at the surface of the water as she went, she met the charge-hand. He had a full bucket of water in each hand, and was trudging slowly east.

'You needn't bother with all that now,' she said brightly. 'I've sorted it. We'd better be going.'

'How d'you mean, sorted it?' demanded the charge-hand. 'I mean, who's going to clear up the mess?'

A crocodile the size of a middling to large park bench waddled towards them, jaws agape. Jane tossed it a peppermint and it retreated, coughing. 'The mortals,' she replied. 'Coming?'

The charge-hand frowned. 'Will they want paying?' he said. 'Because there's not much left in petty cash after we bought a new handle for the mop, and you can't go using the cocoa money, the lads won't stand for it.'

'They'll do it for free,' Jane replied. 'Now hurry up and get rid of those buckets, and then we'd better nip over to Egypt.'

The charge-hand rubbed his chin. He didn't want to be caught out a second time.

'That's Egypt in Africa, right?' he said.

'More or less,' Jane replied. 'They don't know it yet, but they're just about to discover that this is a heaven-sent opportunity to build hydro-electric plants without the water getting in the way. All right?'

The charge-hand furrowed his eyebrows, and then he caught sight of the badge on Jane's lapel. It was very bright and singularly blue.

'Yeah,' he said, relieved, 'right. That's a pretty good idea, that is.'

'Ingenious,' Ganger said, leaning forward and switching off the monitor. 'Don't you think?'

'Novel, certainly,' Staff replied. He put the tips of his fingers together and frowned.

'Not all that novel,' Ganger replied. 'It's been done

before. Basically, it's just persuading the mortals to turn our mistakes to their advantage. And you've got to admit, it's worked all right in the past. Think,' he added with an involuntary grin, 'of manna.'

In spite of himself, Staff grinned too. The manna story was an old chestnut in Departmental circles; the story of how a containerised shipment of manna had got spilt all over the Sinai desert once upon a time, just as a party of mortals came wandering along and walked right into it. The fortunate part of it was that, although the Public Servants knew precisely what manna was (hence the Departmental expressions 'dropping someone right in the manna' and 'up manna creek without a paddle'), the mortals had never come across the stuff before and were quite remarkably taken with it.

'Maybe you're right,' Staff said. 'I'm not denying the girl has –' He paused while the librarians of his mind shuffled their card-indices furiously, '– talent, but that's not what I'm mainly concerned about. There's a lot of people out there with talent, some of them,' he admitted, 'mortals . . .'

'Most of them,' Ganger interrupted softly. Staff didn't contradict him.

'On the other hand,' he went on, 'talent's no use if using it is counterproductive. If it, well, rocks the boat.'

Ganger frowned. 'It strikes me,' he said, 'that nobody notices very much if you rock the boat when it's sinking rapidly anyway.'

'Don't you believe it,' Staff replied sharply. 'I read a book once,' he added, and Ganger noticed with surprise that his voice had dropped rather low, until it was scraping its hubcaps on furtiveness. '*Social Interaction In The Workplace*, it was called. There was a rule in it.'

'Get away.'

Staff scowled. 'Don't be so bloody funny,' he hissed.

'It's a prohibited book, I'll have you know.'

Ganger nodded. 'I'm sorry,' he said, 'I was forgetting where I was. Where I used to work, remember, all we're allowed is prohibited books. I remember the scandal once when someone smuggled in a copy of *The Swiss Family Robinson*. They were fighting like maniacs to get hold of it . . .'

Staff blinked and paused until he could remember where he had got to. 'Anyway,' he said, 'this rule said that in order to preserve the natural equilibrium within an enclosed workplace, the pressure of internal paranoia rises to counter-balance the level of external pressure from without. It's a well-known phenomenon, apparently.'

'I think I get you,' Ganger replied, stroking his chin. 'Sort of, if you can't stand the heat, knife the chef.'

Staff raised an eyebrow. 'You could say that,' he replied. 'What I'm getting at is, the worse things get, the more touchy and difficult the high-ups are going to be about anybody trying anything that isn't, well – you know, done.'

'Not a lot *is* done around here these days,' Ganger couldn't help replying. 'Specially maintenance. But I think I can see what you're getting at. This is one sinking ship where the rats are staying put and everyone else is leaving, yes?'

Staff fiddled with his propelling pencil, breaking the lead. 'Indeed,' he said.

'So we've got to be careful, in other words?'

'Yes.'

'Right.' Ganger stood up and put his hands in the side pockets of his jacket, his thumbs remaining outside. 'So we'll be careful. No problem. What'll we try her out on next?'

Rocco Consanguinetti was one of those people who do one thing at a time, and do it well. At the moment, he was making a pizza, and he was concentrating. The result was obvious; it was the sort of pizza that would get hung in the Metropolitan Museum of Art one of these days if some thoughtless idiot didn't eat it first.

'Rocco, for Christ's sake.' His sister Rosa's head snaked round the swing door and scowled at him. 'There's people chewing the tablecloths out there. How long does it take to make a pizza?'

'It takes as long as it takes,' Rocco replied without looking up. He had a feeling that he had used one olive too many, and Rocco felt about waste the way Nature feels about vacuums. 'Give them some more bread or something.'

Rosa scowled at him. 'Bread costs money, Rocco,' she replied. 'Also, if hungry people stuff themselves full of bread, they make do with *antipasti*, they don't want the main course as well. They certainly don't order ice-cream to follow. We owe the bank money, Rocco. Work faster.'

But her brother merely set his jaw and studied the pizza from another angle. He had been wrong. The tenth olive was indispensable.

'Finished?'

'No.'

'Oh, for . . .' Rosa retracted her head, and Rocco started to lay the pepperoni; slowly, one slice at a time. A Double Roman isn't built in a day.

The jaw he had set was rather a remarkable one. It projected. It had magnitude. You would feel comfortable about mooring a new and expensive yacht to it if you wanted to be sure it would still be there when you came back from the Casino. It was, in fact, the Hapsburg jaw, as worn by Charles V, in full and exuberant flower; and Rocco, completely unknown to himself or anyone else, was, and had been for some years now, the Holy Roman Emperor. His election had been perfectly valid, and he had even been properly and correctly crowned and anointed – under anaesthetic, admittedly, while he was under the impression that he was having his teeth capped.

As the saying goes: just because a river goes underground doesn't mean it stops flowing.

It is, after all, essential that there be an Emperor: without him, absolutely nothing at all could be done. As the very title suggests, the post represents the fusion of temporal and celestial authority, and the Emperor himself is the spark-plug who transmits the divine fire to the profane cylinder of humanity. His assent (albeit given in his name by his agents under the authority of an eleven-hundred-year-old power of attorney, mistakenly signed by Charlemagne, who thought he was giving someone his autograph) is a prerequisite for the ratification of any statute, human or superhuman. But centuries of experience have taught the College of Electors that if the Emperor ever gets to realise what he actually is, he tends to interfere, usually with tedious results. On a need-to-know basis, therefore, it is generally held that His Majesty doesn't.

Apart from his virtually undiluted Hapsburg blood, Rocco VI was chosen because of his wisdom, his tolerance, his broad grasp of current affairs and because the present College of Electors (who are also the Emperor's trusted advisers and agents) like to do business over working lunches. A really great Emperor, they argue, ought to know how to handle anchovies.

The agenda for today's cabinet was short, even shorter than usual.

'To start,' said the Lord High Cardinal, 'I'll have the minestrone. Phil, you're having the *insalata di mare Adriatica*, Tony's plumped for the fish soup, and Mario's going to try the artichokes. They are fresh today, aren't they, Rosa?'

'They're always fresh,' replied the Emperor's sister. 'How many years have you guys been coming in here, anyway? You ever know the artichokes not to be fresh?'

The Lord High Cardinal assured her that he was only kidding. 'To follow,' he went on, 'I'm having the Sardinian veal, plus two sole. Mario, do you want the Messina chicken or the veal?'.

'I'll have the veal,' confirmed the County Palatine. 'Chicken I can get at home.'

When they had all finished eating and drunk their coffee and picked their teeth with the proper wooden toothpicks you got at Rocco's instead of those damned plastic ones they have everywhere these days, the cabinet turned to the last item on the agenda. It was Mario's turn.

'Any other business?' he asked.

The Lord High Cardinal looked at his watch. 'If there is,' he said, 'it'll have to be adjourned till next time, because the game starts in half an hour and I need to go to the drugstore first. Next Tuesday?'

The other Electors confirmed that Tuesday would be fine. Then, in accordance with ancestral tradition, the Imperial Treasurer took four toothpicks from the glass and broke one, and they drew lots to see which of them was going to sign the bill.

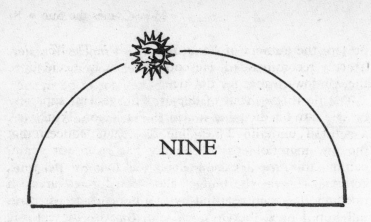

NINE

'Thank you,' said Staff, cautiously. 'That's very, um . . .'

Clerical gave him a slightly distant smile and returned to her desk, leaving him with rather mixed emotions. On the one hand, it was touching to think that she had remembered his birthday; on the other hand, it was profoundly tiresome that she had chosen a present more than usually unidentifiable. If he assumed it was an executive paperweight and left it lying on his desk, it would most probably turn out to be a labour-saving kitchen device and its continued presence in the office would cause immortal offence. If, however, he took it home and put it in the big box in the cupboard under the stairs, it would undoubtedly turn out to be an executive paperweight, and he'd end up having to make his own coffee every morning for the next two thousand years. Difficult.

'Many happy returns, Skip.' It was Denzil, from the post room, with a palpably bottle-like shape suffused in brown paper. Staff smiled warmly. He didn't drink, but at least he knew what the present was and could guess approximately how much it had cost. It was the sort of present the authors of *Social Interaction In The Workplace* heartily recommended. He could give it, he decided, to the window-cleaner for Solstice.

'Memo to the head of department, general supplies,' he said into his dictating-machine. 'Re, colon, Truth with a capital T, underlined, new line. I note with concern that the raw material cost of Beauty has risen yet again, comma, this time in excess of six point four two per cent, comma, whereas the budget allocation for resources in this area has been reduced by two point eight per cent, full stop. I must therefore ask you to revise the existing Beauty oblique Truth ratio as from the first of next month full stop. I would propose that until future notice, comma, Beauty shall be sixty-six point six per cent Truth, comma, with a proportionate adjustment in the inverse ratio for Truth oblique Beauty, full stop. New paragraph, row of dots. Chief of Staff etcetera. Thank you. Tape ends.'

He put the tape in the tray for Clerical to collect and sighed. Everyone was going to blame him, and it really wasn't his fault. Never mind, it couldn't be helped. Nothing can be helped, ever. He shuffled about in his in-tray, looking vainly for something he felt he could manage to cope with.

'Hi.'

He looked up, and saw Ganger, in his usual stance, half-in and half-out of the doorway.

'Happy birthday,' Ganger said. 'I got you something. Quite fun.'

He threw a small parcel through the air. Staff caught it and, feeling rather self-conscious, unwrapped it.

'Thank you,' he said, after a long pause for inspection. 'It's really, er.'

Ganger smiled. 'There's a leaflet inside the box,' he said, 'which explains what it is.'

'Ah.'

He found the little piece of paper and unfolded it. BLANK PAPAL BULL, it read. FOR YOU TO EXCOMMUNICATE THE PERSON OF YOUR CHOICE. There followed two columns of instructions in small print.

'The receipt's in there too,' Ganger said. 'If you don't like it, you can change it. What's the plan?'

'Ah yes,' said Staff, putting the box carefully away in his top desk drawer. 'I've been thinking about that.'

'Me too,' Ganger said.

'What I'd decided,' Staff went on, raising his voice slightly, 'is something a little bit less risky this time, something more straightforwardly administrative. I mean, we don't want to put her off by just giving her crises to sort out, do we?'

'All right,' Ganger said, sitting on the corner of the desk and picking up the Executive Present. 'What had you in mind? Hey, a mate of mine's got one of these. They're very good if you can get them properly tuned in.'

'Yes,' Staff replied firmly. 'I was thinking of Records.'

Ganger gave him a look. 'Oh come on,' was all he said. The rest could easily be implied from context.

'Yes, I know,' said Staff. 'But we don't want to give her the wrong impression, do we? I mean, seventy per cent of what we do is just plain, unexciting clerical work; sorting papers, answering queries, filing, ordering, that sort of thing . . .'

He stopped. There was something extremely inscrutable about Ganger's usually mobile face. 'Maybe you're right, though,' said Staff quickly. 'We can put her on that later. How about a tour of duty on Earthquakes?'

Ganger shook his head. 'No,' he said, '*you're* right. Absolutely. No, don't bother to get up, I'll deal with it. I'll let her know straight away.'

He stood up, pressed a switch on the side of the present that Staff had completely overlooked, and left the office.

As he closed the door, a few wafer-thin rose-petals formed spontaneously in mid-air and drifted floorwards. When they touched the carpet, they melted like snowflakes.

'Records,' said Staff aloud. 'Records.'

A small red light suddenly appeared on the side of the present, then it went out again. Staff spent the next quarter of an hour staring at it and then covered it up with an office circular.

'Records,' he said a third time. '*Records*. Beats me.'

'It's very simple when you get used to it,' said Norman, the supervisor. 'Once you've been here a few months, you'll find the work is pretty straightforward.'

Jane nodded. First impressions, she knew, can be deceptive, but it looked to her as if straightforward was putting it mildly. As far as she could judge, it consisted of picking the envelopes out of the trolley, reading the number stamped on the side, taking the envelope to the appropriate shelf and leaving it there. She could, she decided, do it in her sleep; in fact, that would probably be the best way to approach it.

'If you need any help,' Norman was saying, 'just ask.'

Thanks, said Jane to herself under her breath; the sort of help I'm going to need here is not the sort you're likely to be able to supply. She smiled, and headed for the trolley.

On her seventeenth visit to the shelves, she collided gently with a bespectacled male person, who fell against a shelf, dislodging its contents.

'Sorry,' she said.

'Don't worry about it,' said the person. 'These things tend to happen in an infinite universe. By the way, you're standing on my foot.'

'Oh. Sorry.'

'Not at all. Thank you, that's *much* better. Do please

continue with what you were doing while I laboriously put all this lot back.' He scowled at her, and stooped wearily down.

'Please,' said Jane through stiff lips. 'Let me help you.'

The person gave her a prickly smile. 'How excessively kind of you,' he said. 'Gosh, how original of you! For years now, I've been putting them in numerical order, but you're quite right. Think what an exciting challenge it'll be for the researchers if they're all jumbled up together like that.'

Jane drew in a half-lungful of breath and started again, while the person looked at her.

'You're mortal, aren't you?' he observed.

'Yes,' Jane replied. She stood on tiptoe to replace 26576768/766543765/2308J/3C.

'Do pardon my saying this,' the person said, 'but wouldn't you perhaps find it rather more – conducive, let's say – back on Earth with all the other, er, people? I understand,' he added, 'that there's plenty of room for everyone down there. Up here, on the other hand, it's a touch on the cramped side, if you're not used to looking where you're going.'

For a moment Jane stood with her mouth open; then it occurred to her that she should have prepared herself for this sort of thing. Since she hadn't, she determined to ignore it.

'Not really,' she replied, therefore. 'In fact, it's pretty much the same up here as down there I find. Would you be very sweet and put this one back up on the top shelf for me? I can't quite reach.'

The person glowered at her, and then complied. 'It's been a funny old day so far,' he observed, groaning as he stretched. 'I overslept, arrived here late, found that someone had moved my trolley, forgot my sandwiches, slipped on the polished floor and bruised my knee, and

now I've been knocked to the ground and trampled underfoot by a mortal, and it's still only ten-thirty.'

Jane allowed herself a smile. 'That's unusual here, is
it? Sounds like an ordinary day where I come from.'

The person raised a corner of his mouth. If hyaenas
are dogs, it was a smile. 'So I'd gathered,' he replied. 'In
fact, I understand you people have a special word for it.
Life, or something like that.'

'Fancy you knowing,' Jane replied. 'Thank you so much
for your help.'

At a quarter past eleven there was a coffee break. To her
disgust, Jane found that Departmental coffee tasted very
much like the coffee she was used to at home, except that
it had even more chicory in it. Her back hurt and her mind
had got pins and needles in it for want of activity. For the
first time ever she began to wonder whether data inputting
at Burridge's had been quite as horrible as she'd thought.

'My word,' said the person, suddenly appearing behind
her shoulder as she drained her coffee down to the silt.
'What a lot you've managed to get done.'

In spite of herself, Jane felt pleased. She wanted to say,
'Of course I have; I'm a mortal, after all,' or something
equally inflammatory, but she very sensibly didn't. Instead
she made vague and quiet thanking noises.

'Beats me how you can do it so fast,' the person went
on, 'ordering them, stacking them, *and* writing the
numbers up in the Register.'

Inside Jane's heart, something small but not entirely
trivial broke. 'What Register?' she asked.

The person smiled, properly this time. 'The Master
File Register,' he replied. 'Didn't they tell you about it?
You write down the number of the file, and what shelf
it's on, and under which section of the shelf, and other
things like that. Otherwise, you see, the researchers won't
have the faintest idea . . .'

'Thank you,' said Jane. 'I see. Nobody did mention it, actually, but I suppose I should have worked it out for myself.' She put her cup down on its saucer. 'I suppose I'd better go back and do that, hadn't I?'

'That would be a splendid idea,' the person agreed. 'Oh, by the way. Aren't we forgetting something?'

Jane stopped still and turned her head slowly. 'Are we?' she said. 'Sorry, we didn't mean to.'

'Thirty zlotys for the coffee,' said the person sweetly. 'We always put the money in that tin on the shelf there. It helps,' he added, 'to avoid bad feeling and disruptive outbursts of temper.'

Jane sighed. 'That's a nuisance,' she said. 'You see, I've only got terrestrial money. I don't suppose they accept that here, do they?'

The person shook his head. 'Not really,' he said. 'I mean, yes, it's the thought that counts, but it doesn't actually buy a new catering-size tin when the present one runs out. Let me,' he added unpleasantly, 'lend you thirty zlotys until you get paid.'

'Thank you.'

'Don't mention it.'

The person, having watched carefully while she put the money in the tin, walked away, leaving her to scream silently in peace and quiet. Then she found Norman and asked him to explain properly about the Register.

There was a crash. The four intruders stopped dead in their tracks, or at least they tried to. Alcohol, however, tends to enhance momentum. They fell over each other. In the far distance a dog barked, then fell silent.

'Mind where you're putting your bloody feet next time,' Darren hissed. 'There's guard dogs about. I heard one.'

'Bollocks,' Jason hissed back. 'Haven't had dogs here for years. Cutbacks. Didn't you know?'

Darren shrugged and fumbled in his pocket for the key to the hangar which he'd lifted off the hook four hours earlier. He was still worrying about the possibility of dogs, but he wasn't going to let his mates see he was worried. He had his cloud credibility to think about.

The lock clicked and he pushed hard on the door. As it rolled back a single piercing ray of light speared out into the blackness. Jason hurriedly threw himself against the crack.

'You prat,' he snarled. 'All that bullshit about dogs and then you nearly let the light show. What a *wally*!'

The four adventurers squeezed through the crack and then drew the door to behind them.

Inside the hangar it was, of course, as bright as day; in fact, very considerably brighter. For a moment they all stood dumbfounded by the sight; even Darren, who worked in the shed during the day, had never been this close to the thing before. It was enough to fry your brains.

Dave was the first to break the silence, and he did it with a nervous giggle.

'Oh come off it,' he said. 'We're *never* going to be able to fly this thing.'

It was intended merely as an observation, but somehow it got badly mutated on its way out past the gate of Dave's teeth, and by the time it reached Jason's ears it was a challenge with a strong superficial likeness to a taunt.

'You reckon,' Jason said. 'Watch this, then.'

'I didn't mean . . .' Dave started to say, but his friend was already halfway up the ladder towards the cockpit. There was nothing for it but to follow.

'I'm beginning not to like this,' observed a voice from the foot of the ladder. 'Why don't we just forget about it and do something else? We could go and smash up a few phone boxes or something instead.'

'You've lost your bottle,' Jason sneered. 'You haven't got the nuts, have you?'

'No,' replied Adrian, with a remarkable note of sobriety in his voice. 'Not for this I haven't, anyway.'

Dave and Darren paused on the ladder because this was somewhat disturbing. It was commonplace in their social circle that Adrian played the complete head-case, afraid of nothing. His favourite way of letting off steam, it was widely rumoured, was spray-painting graffiti on the sides of moving asteroids. If Adrian didn't fancy it, the chances were that there was an element of risk.

'Stuff you, then.' Jason's voice drifted down from the top of the ladder, but it sounded far away and hollow. He had clearly found out how to get into the cockpit. 'Hey, those morons left it unlocked. What a load of pillocks, huh?'

'Nobody gives a toss,' Dave agreed, but his thoughts were elsewhere. Maybe this wasn't such a good idea, after all. It really was very big, very big indeed.

'Gotcha!' There was triumph in Jason's voice, and the other three exchanged glances. 'You coming, Ade, or not?'

Adrian paused for a moment; then he shrugged and shinned quickly up the ladder. He wasn't afraid any more – it had gone past that stage – and he was very curious to find out what was going to happen. 'Coming,' he said.

'Only if you're not going to bottle out,' Jason shouted back. ''Cos if you suddenly get scared, I'm not stopping, right?'

'Get stuffed,' Adrian replied, and from his tone of voice the others could tell that he was himself again: the same Adrian who thought nothing of playing Chicken on the edge of Time. 'We'll see who shits himself first, my son.'

Jason grinned. He was sitting in the pilot's seat, trying to guess which controls did which. He hadn't, he realised, the faintest idea.

'Here,' he said. 'How do you make this thing go?'

Adrian shrugged. 'I dunno,' he said, and leaned forward. 'Let's try this.' He sprawled his hand out into a pink fan and pressed as many buttons as he could.

'Don't do that, you luna . . .' Dave started to scream, then his mouth went dry and his tongue became inextricably welded to his palate. The hangar had suddenly become filled with the most agonising light, and all around them they could feel the pulsing of a planet-sized engine.

'Switch it off, for fuck's sake!' Dave yelled, but nobody moved. They were all paralysed with terror, and besides, it was painfully apparent that it was too late now. The thing was beginning to move.

Slowly at first; then, as it built up momentum slipping down the ramp, very fast, then faster and faster still. As if in a dream, Dave noticed that the hangar doors were firmly shut. But the chances were, he felt, that that wasn't going to make much difference. In fact, it was extremely doubtful whether anything was ever going to make any difference ever again.

The four joy-riders had just enough self-possession left to hurl themselves to the floor of the cockpit as the giant machine ploughed through the diamond-and-titanium doors of the hangar like a bullet through a bubble, left the ramp, hung for an everlasting fraction of a second in mid-air, and then began to drop like a very large stone. Then the engines fired.

It is at such moments that essential character, distilled and compressed, is most easily observed. Dave and Darren both howled 'Shiiiiiiiiiiiiiit!' and tried to squash themselves into the same small space under the computer console. Jason sat flattened against the back of the pilot's chair, his face apparently splattered across the front of his head in an expression of sheer horror that would be worth millions to an ambitious film producer. Adrian grabbed wildly for the joystick, and pulled.

The sun checked itself, seemed to hesitate, and then lifted.

The sun rose.

'Where is it now?' Staff demanded.

There was silence at the other end of the wire.

'Well?'

'Well,' said the voice, and Staff could feel the effort of self-control running up through the wire. 'You know that sort of lacy constellation just under the armpit of Sagittarius? Like an ammonite with woodworm, I always think. It's out there.' A pause. 'Somewhere.'

Staff let the hand with the phone in it wilt. Disasters he could cope with – anyone whose days are spent in any form of high-level administration gets withdrawal symptoms without at least one disaster before breakfast – but there are limits. His lips went through the motions of repeating the word Somewhere, but his larynx wanted no part of it.

'You still there, Chief?' said the voice.

He put the phone back by his ear. 'Yes,' he said. 'Look, I know this is a damn silly question, but I owe it to myself to ask. Is there any chance whatsoever of getting it back?'

'None, Chief. Sorry.'

Staff winced like a salted slug. 'Right. Fine. Thanks for letting me know.'

The line crackled a bit. 'So what do we do now, Chief?' said the voice nervously.

Staff sighed. 'Heaven only knows,' he said, and put the phone down.

He was, of course, lying.

*   *   *

Jason was worried.

He had good reason to be. He was a long way from home, his companions had blacked out – for good, by the looks of it – the fuel gauge was deep into the red bit on the far left-hand side of the dial, and there was a funny rattling noise coming from under the bonnet. The only good thing about running out of fuel, as far as he could see, was that when it happened, then the bloody thing would slow down and perhaps even stop. He had been trying to make it do that for some time.

The monotony of the view from the cockpit window didn't improve matters. It had been as black as two feet up a chimney for the last forty million light years, and that sort of thing can get to you once the effects of the beer start to wear off. To put the tin lid on it, he found that he'd run out of cigarettes.

And then he saw the light; just a tiny little pinprick, far away in the distance, but definitely light. For a few seconds he was elated, until he remembered that (a) light didn't necessarily connote safety or help, and (b) even if it did, he couldn't steer the damned thing towards it anyway.

He needn't have been concerned. The engine chose that moment to drain the last drop of fuel in the back-up reserve emergency tank, and the sun decelerated and started to drift. A few minutes later, the gravitational field of whatever that bright thing over there was started to have effect, and the whole contraption slowly turned and started to travel towards the light. Jammy.

The light was a star. The star had a planet; you could see it from light years away. It was big and bright, and blue with the most incredible oceans Jason had ever seen. It was, he realised with a leap of the heart, inhabited. And he was headed straight for it, at a nice slow drift. He'd have called it Destiny if it wasn't for the fact that he'd worked there for six months and knew how it really worked; so he called it bloody good luck instead.

Soon, much sooner than he had imagined, he was close enough to see the two wide belts of golden asteroids that encircled the planet, and a few miniscule sparkles of flashing metal which could only be space stations. He was nearly there.

'Help!' he screamed. It was, he knew in his heart, a bit early to expect anyone to hear, but there was no harm in just warming up, so to speak. He also stood up in his seat and waved both his arms.

And then . . .

It was one of those moments when the soul dies: when all the lights go out and all that remains is the horrible feeling of having got it wrong. He shaded his eyes with his hand, hoping against all the probabilities that he was mistaken, but he wasn't.

They weren't space stations; they were parking meters, and he had no change of any sort whatsoever. Likewise, the things he had taken for a twofold belt of golden asteroids were something rather more prosaic but utterly unambiguous. They were double yellow lines. To ram the point home to the point of complete and utter superfluity, the planetary authorities had picked out the words

NO PARKING

in glowing red dwarves right across the azimuth.

'Fuck,' he said.

If it had been a smaller planet, of course, it would have had to orbit him rather than the other way round. As it was, there was nothing he could do except scream a lot and wave his fists about and, after a while, once the lack of food and the helium-rich atmosphere began to tell on him, he couldn't even do that.

When he had been there for a very long time, so long that he could no longer quantify the time with any degree of accuracy whatsoever, he became aware of strange, immaterial figures wandering about the cockpit. They spoke in strange, distorted voices and had a disturbing tendency to walk right through him and out through the cockpit into the blackness outside. They ignored him completely, being apparently entirely engrossed in inexplicable conversations of their own which he was quite incapable of following beyond a few tantalising phrases.

There is no reason to believe that he isn't there to this day. Certainly, the inhabitants of the planet would have had no reason to disturb him, given that his timely arrival saved them the expense and trouble of launching a purpose-built satellite to bounce their afternoon soap-operas off. The fact that, by some strange quirk of optical distortion, Jason occasionally features in some of the episodes, probably adds to their overall enjoyment.

'Now then,' Staff said. 'Let's just pause there a moment, shall we, and recap for a minute. We have the following suggestions.'

It was an hour and seven minutes later, and the pale, taut faces round the boardroom table were uniformly blank. Nobody was in any hurry to say anything.

'First,' Staff continued, 'we have the proposal that we get the moon back down, spray it all over with luminous paint, bang it up there at sunrise, and hope nobody notices. Now, it strikes me that there are a number of potential difficulties with that idea.'

He proceeded to enumerate them. When he had finished, nobody spoke, and he took the silence as his cue to move on to the next suggestion.

'Next, we've got the proposal that we shove a big illuminated sign up in the sky saying *Normal Service Will Be*

Resumed As Soon As Possible.' He breathed in, and then out again, with the air of someone making the most of it while he still could. 'Now I've got nothing against that, nothing at all, as far as it goes, but in the longer term . . .'

There was no need to go on. The heads nodded. Ways and Means, Staff noticed with a flicker of amusement, was already fast asleep; which, given the circumstances, must be a Pavlovian reaction to being in Committee.

'As for the idea,' he went on, 'that we run out an extension cable from the heart of the Great Cloud of Unknowing and try and rig up a set of floodlights as a temporary measure: I've got to admit that as far as I'm concerned it's the best one we've come across yet, but I still think we've got some way to go before we're actually there. I mean, logistically . . .'

There was a cough from the side of the table, and everyone looked round at a small but extremely – well, *normal*-looking figure standing there holding a large tray.

'Excuse me,' said Jane. 'You ordered coffee.'

She had been working late, trying to sort out the mess she'd made earlier on in the day, and when the Committee came stumbling in to use the boardroom, she had been told, as the only female life-form in sight, to get coffee for twelve. Being female, she had managed it.

Staff smiled bleakly. 'Thanks,' he said. 'Just put it down there, we'll help ourselves. Now then . . .'

'Excuse me,' said Jane again. Everyone looked at her.

'Sorry to butt in,' she went on, 'but I couldn't help overhearing, and I was just wondering if you'd considered . . . ?'

Finance and General Purposes sat upright, looking like a stick of anthropormorphic dynamite, but Staff caught his eye and he subsided.

'Well?' he said.

'Only,' Jane said, in a small but clear voice, which

reminded Staff of something vaguely familiar, something he seemed to remember from a very long time ago. What was it? Ah yes, he suddenly remembered: it was the sound of somebody being sensible. 'Maybe you're approaching this from the wrong direction, if you see what I mean. I know it's really nothing to do with me,' she went on, 'but perhaps . . .'

There were signs of unrest from around the table. Either this person – this *mortal* – was going to offend their ears with a stream of idiotic and untimely nonsense, which would be bad enough; or else she was going to make an intelligent suggestion. For her part, Jane was aware of a squashed feeling, as if she was an over-boiled potato under a steam-roller. As was her habit when she felt nervous, she smiled.

'It just occurred to me,' she said, 'and I hope you don't mind me saying this, but if you're trying to find some way of bodging up some sort of substitute thing so that nobody'll notice, I don't really think you're going to have much luck. No,' she said, shaking her head. 'What I reckon you need is a diversion: you know, something to take people's attention off the sun so that they wouldn't notice even if there was nothing there at all.'

There was quiet in the boardroom, compared to which the inside of the average tomb would sound like Rome in the rush hour. Just as the silence was about to solidify and start dripping down the walls, Finance and General Purposes shook off his air of stunned torpor, fitted a less than pleasant expression to his face and cleared his throat.

'Very good,' he said. 'And what would you suggest?'

'Well . . .' Jane said.

In the grey desolation of the small hours of the inter-stellar morning, the big abandoned lot, out round the back of the Great Cloud of Unknowing, hummed to the roar of an infinity of different kinds of power tools, variations on the scream of metal cutting into metal, instructions and swear words. The activity was indescribable; usually movement is perceptible because it is seen against a background of rest, but here there was no background.

Everyone – the whole supernatural host, everyone – was on overtime.

There were two main groups. The smaller group, comprising about a sixth of the whole, was cutting an enormous disc out of a galaxy-sized sheet of the first quality sixteen-gauge celestium carbonate, while an army of gantries stood by to install a million miles of electric flex and twelve billion light-bulbs. A sub-section of the group was fitting a huge black velvet bag over the moon and rigging it up with a tow-hook. In the distance, a fleet of astro-freighters were bringing home a hastily gathered harvest of small and relatively unimportant stars which were going to be used for fuel to run the generators.

The other group was five times larger and infinitely busier. They were loading the boots of 10^{23} cars with 10^{74} cardboard boxes.

Staff, watching the proceedings from a point of vantage on the roof of the Fate Office, glanced down at his watch and bit his lip. Three hours to go. Either this was going to work, or else he was going to look the biggest prawn in the entire universe of time and space.

'All right,' he muttered into his walkie-talkie. 'Tell Phase One to move out.'

The empty vacuum of the back lot was suddenly stiff with the tortured vibration of sound-waves as the buzz-saws jarred through the last few miles of celestium carbonate. The disc leaned horribly and fell free on to the supporting cat's cradle of titanium cable. There was a dazzling flash of welding gear as the electricians set to.

The engines of the moon began to hum as her crew warmed her up for her unscheduled flight.

'Phase One,' said the walkie-talkie. 'Ready, and rolling.'

On a signal from the control tower all the 10^{23} cars started their engines at once. Trying to encapsulate the effect of so much noise in mere adjectives would be like trying to squidge the sea down into an egg-cup; suffice to say, it was *loud*. The column began to roll.

'This had better work,' Staff growled, as the structure of the cosmos braced itself to withstand the vibration of so many humming engines. 'Because otherwise . . .'

'Oh, I expect it'll be all right,' Jane replied, pouring boiling water from her thermos on to a teabag. 'I mean, everyone was always saying how the old one was clapped out and on its last rays anyway, and wouldn't it be a simply splendid idea to get a new one, except it would cost too much and take too long to build. I expect the idea was to save up Esso tokens for the next sixty thousand years and finance the refitting programme that way.' She sighed. 'It really only goes to prove that you can get things done around here, just so long as it's an absolute emergency, and they think you're doing whatever it is you're doing for a totally different reason. Funny, don't you think, the lengths you have to go to?'

The new model sun, its lights blazing, was lowered from its scaffolding on to an enormous trailer, while the two-rope was lowered into position and made fast to the back bumper of the moon. Painfully slowly, complaining every step of the way at the unaccustomed weight, the moon began to taxi down the strip.

'Here goes,' said Jane. 'Fingers crossed.'

The details of the Great Diversion are so well known and form the basis of so many religions that it would be superfluous to recount them here. All that needs to be mentioned for our purposes is that when humanity awoke in the dim light of a weak, flickering 60-watt dawn, it didn't notice anything funny about the lighting. Everybody's attention was riveted to the towering letters of fire, pinned to the back of a rainbow that arched across the firmament and announced

BIGGEST EVER CAR BOOT SALE NOW ON!!

to all mortals, creatures of a day, buyers on impulse, across the face of the globe. No sooner had their brains digested the message than the encircling horizon glared yellow in the indeterminate grey light with the glow of innumerable courtesy lights as 10^{23} car boots opened as one car boot, and mankind, lifting its eyes heavenwards, saw that it was true. As one leading theologian is reported to have remarked, as a way of proclaiming a New Covenant, it beat rainbows into a cocked hat.

Those who comment on such things in the calm seclusion of history point out that, as diversionary tactics go, the Great Diversion was a pretty neat piece of thinking. Not only was mankind's attention distracted long enough for the workshops of heaven to cast, found, finish and launch a brand new, all-alloy sun with teflon bumpers and an ABS braking system; the proceeds of the sale were enough to pay for the thing with enough left over to repaint the outside of the hangar and fit a proper padlock on the door, and the warehouses of General Supply were purged of twenty thousand years' worth of accumulated junk; which in turn provided Norman and his staff in Records with the storage space they needed to put in place a new and vastly more efficient data storage and retrieval system. In fact, some commentators say, bearing in mind the circumstances of the event, and the person whose idea the whole thing was, there's a good case for saying that that was in fact the underlying point of the whole exercise.

'Well?' Bjorn repeated. Old Gustavus looked sheepish and evaded his eye. He muttered something about a once in a lifetime bargain.

Bjorn grinned. 'Yeah,' he said. 'Only you don't know what it is.'

'Um.'

'And it doesn't work.'

'Um.'

'And bits keep coming off in your hand every time you pick it up.'

'It was a *bargain*,' Gustav retorted, stung. 'Twenty-four ninety-nine. And I beat him down from thirty-five.'

'I know what it is.'

'And it was the last one he had left,' Gustav continued. 'In fact, he said he was saving it for someone, but . . . You do?'

'Yes,' Bjorn replied, and yawned. 'You've been done,' he added.

Gustav scowled. Then he noticed a mark on the back of the casing, took out his handkerchief, spat neatly on a corner and rubbed the spot until it was clean again. 'Nonsense,' he said. 'It was reduced. Slight exterior damage, he told me, doesn't affect the working in the least . . .'

'Right,' Bjorn said, and bit the top off another bottle. 'And I can see how, you being a woodcutter, it's really essential for you to have a temporal distortion refractor that you know is going to work. Yup,' he added, with a positive nod of his head, 'I guess you're right, at that.'

Gustav blinked. 'I'm sorry?' he said.

'Temporal distortion refractor,' Bjorn repeated carelessly. 'Used to use them a lot when I was on the Time gangs. They're really good for flattening out time warps. Of course,' he added as an afterthought, 'that's not a whole one, that's just the mainframe stabiliser unit. Still, if you can get it to work, maybe the next car boot sale you go to, you'll find the rest of the gear – you know, the rocker box, the induction manifold, all that stuff – and then you'll be in business. And you'll need the batteries too, of course.'

He grinned again and drank some beer while his neighbour sat and stared at his purchase for a while. In the distance could be heard the soothing coo of a woodpigeon, sleepy in the warmth of a late summer evening.

'I think,' said Gustav firmly, 'I'll put a tablecloth over it and stand it in the corner by the log-basket. It'd look nice there, and I could use it to display my bowls trophies.'

'Yeah,' Bjorn said. 'Or it'd make a great footstool.' He parked his boots on it, folded his arms behind his head and lay back.

'Did you go to the sale, neighbour?' Gustav enquired. Bjorn shook his head.

'Listen,' he said. 'Any old Departmental stuff I wanted, I nicked before I packed the job in. It's all a load of crap anyway, most of it. All clapped out, and it was junk when it was new, as often as not. Buy it cheap and flog it to death, that's their motto. You take leap year, for instance.'

Gustav raised an eyebrow. 'Leap year?' he said.

'Yeah,' Bjorn replied. 'Leap year. Bloody typical, that is. I mean,' he went on, warming to his theme, 'suppose you were building a Seasons plant, you wouldn't cut corners and go around buying in second-hand tat from the breakers' yards, would you? No way. Stands to reason, you buy the real thing and then it's not going to break down and you don't have to go fixing it every five minutes when it gets out of sync. That's not the way they see it, of course, oh no. And that's why we've got leap year. You didn't think it was, like, deliberate, did you?'

'Um.'

Bjorn sniggered unkindly. 'No way,' he said. 'Main bearings completely shot, so a bloke I used to know on Maintenance told me once. Miracle the whole thing doesn't pack up on them. Serve them right if it did.'

He fell silent and lay on his back, scowling at his toes. A family of chipmunks scampered up and down the branch above his head, chirruping wildly. A dragonfly droned past, the sun flashing on its kaleidoscope wings.

'What a beautiful day,' Gustav remarked involuntarily. 'Really, neighbour Bjorn, it does my old heart good to see it. Can't you just –' He paused. He knew he was wasting his breath, but he couldn't help it. The infinite wonders of nature never failed to move him, even at his age. 'Can't you just *feel* the thirsty earth drinking in the life-giving warmth and the seeds bursting into life under the soil. Can't you just . . .'

'Yeah.' Bjorn was looking puzzled. 'Yeah,' he repeated, 'you've got a point there.' He frowned, sat up, absent-mindedly swatted the dragonfly with the back of his hand, and stared thoughtfully at the sun for a very long time.

'Funny, that,' he said.

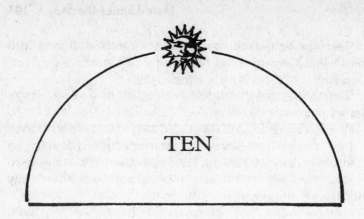

TEN

'Ah,' said Jane briskly, 'I was hoping I'd get a chance to have a word with you.'

Ganger's hand had been on the door handle. He froze; then he turned round and smiled.

'Sure,' he said. 'Look, just got to make a few quick calls, then . . .'

'It won't take a moment, I promise,' Jane replied grimly – you could have sharpened chisels on her tone of voice – so that Ganger subsided and seemed to lose about an inch in height.

'Fine,' he said. 'Come on in.'

Although she'd spent the last two hours waiting for Ganger outside his office, this was the first time she'd actually been inside it. She wasn't impressed. An office, her expression clearly said, so what? The fact that it has recording angels instead of dictaphones makes it different, not necessarily better. Ganger wilted a little more; if he'd had petals, some of them would have fallen off by now.

He perched, nevertheless, on the edge of the desk, and waved her to a chair. 'What's all this about then?' he asked.

'Just one or two things,' Jane replied. She dipped into her bag and brought out two copies of a neatly typed list. Ganger's smile became a windscreen.

'First,' she said, 'I thought that perhaps we ought to get straight exactly what it is I'm doing here.'

'You're doing fine,' Ganger said quickly. 'Next question.'

Jane glazed her expression of respectful contempt to the consistency of ceramic armour plate. 'Thank you so much,' she said, 'but I asked *what*, not *how*. What's my job description, precisely?'

Ganger sucked his cheeks in slightly. 'We-ell,' he said, 'I don't know about you, but I'm all for flexibility in these things. You know, the broad outlook, the adaptable definition, the overall view . . .'

'Yes,' Jane said, 'I'm sure you are. It wouldn't do if we were all alike, would it?'

For a moment, Ganger's perennial smile had a lot of big sharp teeth in it which hadn't been there a moment ago; then he recovered himself. 'Fair enough,' he said. 'Well, I suppose we could say . . .'

'I thought Management Trainee,' Jane interrupted. 'Oh, by the way, you don't mind if I take a few notes, do you? It does so help when you're trying to remember what you said later on.'

Ganger's throat moved slightly, as if he were swallowing a small plum-stone. 'No,' he said, 'you go ahead, that's fine. Well, yes, I suppose Management Trainee covers it more or less, you know, in general terms, bearing in mind that . . .'

'Next,' Jane continued, 'I think it's time we had a little chat about salary, don't you?'

The upturned corners of Ganger's lips flickered briefly. 'Salary,' he repeated.

'That's right,' Jane said. 'I've been asking around, and . . .'

'I beg your pardon?'

'I've been asking around,' Jane said, with very slightly exaggerated clarity, 'and the general opinion seems to be . . .'

'You've been *asking* people what they *earn*?'

'That's right, and . . .'

'Just walking up to them and *asking*?'

'Exactly. Now . . .'

'And they've actually *told* you?'

'Yes,' said Jane. 'And the impression I get, and of course you'll correct me if I'm wrong, is that the going rate for junior management in this setup is twenty-five thousand kreuzers per annum. That seems reasonable enough, doesn't it?'

Ganger sat monolithically on the desk-top with his mouth open.

'Subject,' Jane went on quickly, 'to upwards review every six months, naturally. Now, the next thing I wanted to talk about . . .'

There was a noise from the back of Ganger's throat. 'Twen—' he croaked.

'I'm sorry?'

'Twenty-five thousand kreuzers,' Ganger said. 'My dear girl . . .'

It was unequivocally the wrong thing to say. To do him credit, Ganger realised this before the fatal words were more than a few inches out of his mouth, but by then it was too late. Before he could speak again, Jane's eyes filmed over with permafrost, and her lips set in an invisible line.

'Right,' Ganger said, in a very small voice. 'Yes, that's fine. I'll see to that straight away. Yes, absolutely. Now then, was there something else?'

'Yes,' Jane said. 'Please don't think I'm complaining, but it does seem a bit of a waste of my time to have to commute here from Wimbledon every morning. I have to change trains twice just to get to the stellaport, and then there's all that hanging about getting through Customs . . .'

'I'm sure we can do something about that,' Ganger said quickly. 'I could have a word with the guards, you know . . .'

'I was thinking,' Jane said, ignoring him completely, 'about a relocation allowance. Plus superterrestrial weighting, of course, because . . .'

She stopped speaking. Ganger had gone a very funny colour.

'Um,' he said. 'Look, I'm going to have to talk to some of my colleagues about that, because . . .'

'Alternatively,' Jane said, 'I gather there's going to be a staff flat falling vacant soon in the basement of the Weather building. I could have that, couldn't I?'

Ganger had agreed, enthusiastically, before he suddenly realised that he'd been outgambited. He opened his mouth to speak, and then subsided.

'Just a few more things,' Jane went on. 'Holidays, normal working hours, pension scheme, that sort of thing. We might as well clear them up now, while we're on the subject, don't you think?'

There was a long silence, and Jane could feel Ganger trying to prise a way into her mind, for all the world like a psychological double-glazing salesman. She put the chain firmly on the door of her subconscious and gave him a look.

'Yes,' he said quickly. 'Why not? I suppose,' he added, 'you had something in mind?'

'As it happens,' Jane replied pleasantly, 'yes. Now, then . . .'

'The work we do here,' said the director, 'is specialised. Very specialised.'

He pressed a button on the console, and the far wall of the enormous room flickered and became one huge screen. At first sight, while Jane's eyes were getting used to the brightness, it looked blank; then she realised that it was cross-hatched with millions of tiny fine lines, connecting hundreds of thousands of minute points of pink and blue light.

'Each little light,' the director went on, 'represents one of our clients – we like to call them clients, you know, because we feel that above all we strive to offer a person-alised service.'

Jane thought of the name of the department – Office of the Director of Star-Crossed Lovers – and felt the urge to protest, but she didn't.

'Ah,' she said.

'The pink dots,' the director went on, 'are our lady clients, and the blue ones are of course the gentlemen. The lines connecting them are what we call the fate-lines. You'll see,' he went on, pointing at the screen witha lectuer's stick, 'that one tends to get a few patterns emerging on a fairly regular basis. Here,' he said, pointing, 'we've got a classic eternal triangle – lovely example, this; you'll notice that all three sides are precisely the same length. Quite rare, nowadays.'

'Really,' Jane said. 'Gosh.'

'Yes.' The director stood speechless for a moment, transported by the geometrical perfection of the thing. 'Remarkable specimen, all things considered. When they're that precise, you know, the links are quite extra-ordinarily strong. I'm writing a paper on them, as it happens,' he added diffidently. 'Just a little monograph, of course; but, I flatter myself, not without a certain intrinsic interest.'

'Absolutely,' Jane said.

The pointer moved to another sector of the screen.

'And this,' the director said, with a glow of pride, 'is a quite lovely example of an H/A Syndrome Major. Bless my soul, yes,' he added, leaning forward and squinting. 'Exquisite. Just look at those reciprocities!'

Jane coughed slightly. 'H/A?' she asked.

'It's short for Heloise/Abelard,' the director explained, 'although there's a tendency in some circles nowadays to call them R/J's.'

'Romeo/Juliets?' Jane hazarded.

'That's right,' said the director, with slight distaste. 'But really, that's a misnomer, because properly speaking the R/J Minor Syndrome is an entirely separate and self-contained sub-group, with its own characteristic matrix of tension. They're quite rare, unlike H/A's, which are quite common, in their natural state. Ah, now here's something I want you to see. Look.'

He directed Jane's attention to what looked to her like a small, perfectly symmetrical spider's web, with four or five separate points of pink and blue light flickering desolately in the meshes. Jane swallowed hard.

'Classic trifoliate misunderstanding,' the director said, 'with an impacted rebound just here, look. They're completely self-explanatory once you get the hang of them, of course.'

For a moment, Jane couldn't quite grasp what he meant; then, as she concentrated on the spider's web, it all became lucidly clear. The two brightest points of light were palpably the original lovers (sorry, *clients*), but the thread that had originally joined them was hanging loose, broken in two equilateral parts. Around each original client there was a separate web, into which another client had been drawn (the rebound, presumably), thereby creating another little separate vortex of misery for the jilted partner who should have been linked up to the reboundee. From a distance, the overall pattern was immediately apparent and infinitely depressing.

'The wonderful thing about this particular formation,' the director was saying, 'is that, where conditions are right, potentially the pattern is infinitely self-repeating. It just goes on and on and on, duplicating itself over and over again.' He uttered a small, weak academic laugh. 'We sometimes say it has a life of its own, but of course, that's not strictly true. Eventually, something happens to break the sequence and then the whole thing grinds to a halt.'

'Um.'

'Yes, it's a pity, in a way,' the director sighed. 'It's such an intellectually satisfying configuration, in my opinion. Not like this,' he added, pointing at another section of the screen. Jane looked across, and saw something which immediately put her in mind of what usually happened to expensive pairs of tights.

'This,' said the director, with a perceptible curl of the lip, 'is what we call an HBH Convergence.'

'Right,' Jane said. 'HBH standing for?'

'Heartbreak Hotel,' the director replied. 'It's not a very common phenomenon, although they're on the increase, I believe.'

Jane peered; and again, the thing became obvious. There was one big blue dot, she observed, and lots of little pink dots, which had torn away from their ordained pairings and followed the blue dot, like iron filings with a magnet. She frowned involuntarily; she knew the feeling. In fact, she had a shrewd notion she knew the blue dot concerned. Nigel something, used to work in Accounts . . .

'And over here,' the director said, 'we've got the main-frame computer, which we use to plot out the various conjunctions and configurations before we put them up on the screen. In the old days, of course, we used to have to do it all by hand. It made life terribly simple.'

'You mean,' Jane said, 'complicated, surely.'

'For the clients, I mean,' the director replied austerely. 'We just didn't have the capacity, you see; with the result that far and away the most common basic configuration, right up to about fifty years ago, was the absolutely basic BMG/BMG/HEA Simplex.'

'I'm sorry?'

'Boy Meets Girl/Boy Marries Girl/Happy Ever After,' the director translated. 'Millions of them, all dull and boring like that, simply because we didn't have the facilities. Now, of course, it's completely different, thanks to this little box of tricks here.' He patted the computer affectionately. 'This is only the third generation, of course. By the time we've got the sixth generation installed and operational, we're hoping to be able to extend our service to the entire mortal population.'

'Um.'

'And of course,' the director said, 'the marvellous thing is that the computer never sleeps. Which means that even now, when the Department has closed down for the night and everyone's gone home, the little black box is still awake, twitching a wire here, nudging a client into adultery there, on a twenty-four-hour, round-the-clock basis. Anyway,' he said, switching off the screen and putting the lid back on the console, 'that should give you an idea of the sort of work we do here. We're only a small department, but I think I can say we're a happy one.' He gazed self-containedly over Jane's head at a spot on the darkened wall. 'I always say,' he continued, 'that it's one of the few departments in the whole of the Service where you can point to an end result and lay your hand on your heart and say to yourself with pride, "I did that." Yes,' he added, 'I confidently expect that you're going to enjoy working here.'

'Yes,' said Jane grimly, 'I rather think I am.'

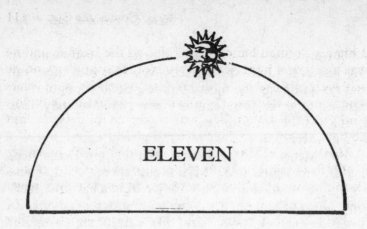

ELEVEN

The village cockerel woke up, glanced instinctively at the sky and did a double-take. Funny, said its genetic memory to its motor centres.

Little Helga (who was rapidly becoming Big Helga, but the inhabitants of the village affected not to notice) yawned, rubbed her eyes and set off to the dairy to do the early milking. She was just crossing the yard, pail on arm, when she stopped and stared. Then she dropped the pail and ran back to the house.

'Listen, everyone!' she called out. 'Neighbour Bjorn is leaving the village!'

There was, for the first time in the history of the family, complete silence in the kitchen. Well, not complete silence: Minoushka stepped back on the cat's tail, with highly vocal consequences, and there was a noisy clatter when Grandmama dropped the porridge spoon; but at least nobody spoke.

Little Helga, being young, misinterpreted the reaction as signifying disbelief.

'Honest,' she said. 'I saw him going up the path to the top of the hill, and he had his axe over his shoulder with a big red spotted handkerchief tied to the handle, and he was carrying a huge sack over the other shoulder, and he was wearing his Hell's Angels vest, which he only wears when he goes down to the town to buy intoxicating liquor. And the little brown dog was trying to follow him, but he kept stopping and throwing apples at it.'

More silence. Then Great-grandfather shook his head.

'It's impossible,' he said. 'Nobody ever *leaves* the village. People come here from the outside, yes, but they never leave.'

'Because of it being idyllic here,' Great-grandmother explained, with a microscopic quantity of residual wistfulness in her voice. She had fallen in love with the village the moment she set eyes on it sixty-two years ago, but before that she had lived in Chicago, and she couldn't help remembering, sometimes, that in Chicago they were admittedly short on idylls but hot as mustard on sanitation and running water. 'The whole point of idyllic is, you stay.'

'Oh dear,' said Grandmother. 'If he's leaving, it can only mean he's been unhappy here. Oh, the poor man!'

'We must counsel him,' said Grandfather firmly, rising from the table and removing his bib. 'We would never forgive ourselves if he left and we didn't try to stop him.'

'We would have failed him,' Grandmother added, 'in his hour of need. It would mean we are bad neighbours.'

Helga lowered her head and peered out of the window. It wasn't easy to see through, because the unutterably picturesque leaded panes were so distorted with genuine age that light only squeezed through them after a severe struggle.

'Do hurry,' she said, anxiously. 'He's stopped to try and find more apples to throw at the little brown dog. If you hurry, you might just catch him.'

So Grandmother and Grandfather and Great-grandmother and Minoushka and Little Helga and Lazy Olaf and Little Torsten dashed out of the house and up the hill, to where Bjorn was taking careful aim with a suitably aerodynamic Granny Smith.

'Surely,' panted Grandfather, catching his breath. 'Surely, neighbour Bjorn, you don't propose to leave us without even saying goodbye.'

'Goodbye,' Bjorn replied. 'Satisfied?' He let fly, and the little brown dog finally took the hint and retired, hobbling, to the woodshed. Bjorn picked up his luggage.

'But why?' Little Torsten demanded. 'Have you not been happy here, dear neighbour Bjorn?'

'No.'

'Where will you go?' wailed Grandmother. 'What will you do?'

Bjorn considered for a while. 'First,' he said, 'I'm going to find the nearest town that's got a halfway decent bar and a cinema that shows dirty movies, and I'm going to . . .'

'Why does he want to see dirty movies, Grandmama?'

'Hush, Torsten.'

'Yes, but Grandmama, if the film's got all dirty, doesn't that mean the pictures will come out all blurry and . . .'

'*Hush!*'

'And after that,' Bjorn went on, 'I'm going to find out what's happened to the sun. All right?'

The villagers stared at him as if he was mad.

'What do you mean, neighbour Bjorn?' asked Lazy Olaf slowly. 'It's the sun, that's all. There's nothing wrong with it. Look.'

He turned and pointed at the sky. The sun, as it happened, was obscured by a blanket of cloud.

'See?' Bjorn said. 'It's what we call a cover-up where I come from. Somebody's made one hell of a cock-up, and they're keeping it under wraps.'

'Maybe,' replied Grandfather. 'Or maybe it just means it's going to rain soon. Rain is good, neighbour Bjorn. It makes the crops grow and nourishes the little seedlings and . . .'

'Yes, yes, I know,' Bjorn interrupted impatiently. 'I used to make the stuff, okay? And I could tell you things about how we used to do it that'd make your hair stand on end,' he added. 'Look, just take it from me, all right? That is not the real sun. Something has happened to the real sun, and whatever it is they've got up there is a substitute, okay? Okay.'

He turned definitively and started to walk away. Little Torsten wiped away a tear.

'Don't go,' he whimpered.

Bjorn hesitated slightly, and then quickened his stride. Little Torsten started to cry.

'*Please* don't go,' he wailed through his tears. 'Even though you're grumpy and bad-tempered sometimes, and you never have a kind word for anyone and never help anyone out and never say thank you when Aunt Gretchen gives you griddle-cakes and you get drunk on Wednesday nights and go around being sick in people's hanging baskets and you're cruel to animals and you tread on the flowers round the village pump and you never go church and you haven't paid your contribution to the poor relief fund for three years and you park your cart in Uncle Gustav's parking space and you steal the food we leave out for the poor blind boy and you cheat at dominoes and you cut down Grandmama's cherry tree for no reason at all and when she complained you called her a rude word and you leave empty crisp-packets all over everyone's front gardens and you trod on my toy horse once and when I cried you laughed at me and Hilda says you've got the manners of a warthog and the weeds from your garden blow out all over Uncle Carl's potato patch and you put vodka in Big Peter's orange juice at his wedding and Uncle Christian swears blind you've moved your back fence three feet over into his garden and you drew a moustache on the picture of the Blessed Virgin in the little white chapel, we still love you.'

There was a thoughtful silence.

'Do we, though?' said a voice at the back.

'And he took my bicycle once without asking,' said Grandmama. 'And when I found it again, the forks were all bent.'

'And there's my lawnmower,' added Lazy Olaf. 'When am I going to get that back, I ask myself.'

'He still hasn't paid for that broken window.'

'Loud music all hours of the day and night.'

'Revving up his chainsaw when people are trying to sleep.'

Grandfather stooped to pick up an apple lying on the ground in front of him. 'Go on,' he shouted, 'get on out of it. We can do without your sort around here.' He threw the apple.

'And if he comes back again,' said Grandmama, savagely, 'we'll set the dogs on him.'

The little brown dog, which had come bounding out with its tail wagging, bared its teeth and snarled.

Halfway up the hill, Bjorn broke into a run.

'She's keen, certainly,' said the director. 'I have high hopes, you know. We need that sort of dedication and commitment in this department.'

The director's secretary sniffed. 'Look,' she said. 'Someone's left the lights on all weekend.'

'Oh dear,' the director replied, fumbling in his pocket for the key. 'Wait a moment, though. It's not locked. What on earth . . . ?'

He pushed open the door carefully and walked in to the main office.

'Good-morning,' Jane called out from behind the console. 'I worked over the weekend, hope you don't mind. You're right, it's easy once you get the hang of it. Of course, the computer helps marvellously. It's just like the one we used to have where I worked before, except that the memory's bigger, of course. Do you like it?'

The director was staring at the screen. From time to time, he made little choking noises.

The screen was different. Instead of the intricate cobwebs of inextricably tangled patterns, it looked like nothing so much as a very finely woven net.

'What have you done?' the director croaked.

'I've sorted it,' Jane replied cheerfully. 'Looks so much better like that, don't you think? Everybody living happily ever after, you see.'

'But . . .' The director struggled for words. 'But, you stupid girl, they're meant to be star-crossed lovers.'

'So,' Jane replied. 'I uncrossed them. Simple as that,' she added, and put the cover back over the console. 'It'll make life so much easier in the long run if people aren't having to cope with shattering emotional crises all over the place. Do you realise how many working days were lost in the Soviet Union last year because of emotional trauma? I looked it up. Four million. And as for Scandinavia . . .'

The director collapsed against a filing cabinet, breathing heavily. 'You – uncrossed them,' he gasped. 'My life's work, and you . . .' He made a noise like a horse whinnying and grabbed at the side of the cabinet for support. His secretary moved across to the desk and sharpened some pencils.

'And,' Jane went on, 'I've programmed the computer to make sure they stay like that. It's much easier that way, you know, and ever so much more efficient. In fact, all it'll take from now on is one full-time member of staff to make sure it's running smoothly, and a couple of part-timers to do the filing. I'm sure,' she went on relentlessly, 'they'll be ever so pleased to hear that in the Treasurer's Office.'

On the screen behind her, a galaxy of perfectly regulated blue and pink dots flashed in harmonious concord. All over the world, boy was meeting girl and falling in love, and they were immediately going out and choosing bathroom curtains together. The director's secretary shrugged.

'Well,' she observed, 'I'll say this much, it's a darned sight tidier than it used to be. I never could be doing with all those messy loops and squiggles.'

The director propped himself up against the filing cabinet and took off his spectacles. 'Miss Frobisher,' he roared in a voice like thunder. 'Be so kind as to get me the Chief of Staff on the telephone immediately.'

But Miss Frobisher wasn't listening. She was gazing, with an expression on her face like Stout Cortez finding a parking space in Piccadilly, at the electrician, who had come in to replace a light-bulb in the washroom. And he was gazing back.

'Bingo,' Jane commented. 'You see what I mean about efficient.'

With a cry of enraged anguish the director dragged himself to his feet, shook a fist in Jane's direction and staggered out of the door in the direction of the Main Office. For the record, he got no further than Accounts; where he happened to share a lift with a rather nice, motherly lady from Pensions. When, three months later, they got back from their honeymoon, he resigned from his old job and applied for the assistant librarianship in the reference section.

* * *

'This protégé of yours,' Ganger said. 'I'm beginning to get bad feelings about the whole idea.'

Staff checked himself between the second and third syllables of '*My* protégé?' and considered. He had, after all, been in the service for a very long time now, and one learned to expect this sort of thing. As the old Catalan proverb says: he who chooses to live among rats should not get aerated at the sight of paw marks in the butter.

'Why?' he said.

'Well.' Ganger took up his usual position on the edge of the desk. Obviously chairs were completely *passé* where he came from. 'Admittedly she's got talent. Talent, yes; also initiative, drive, authority, intelligence, all that stuff. But, you know, I can't help thinking she's getting above herself. I mean, first that thing with the sun, and now all this stuff with Star-Crossed Lovers. Like, wiping out a whole department overnight. You've got to draw the line somewhere, haven't you? She's making too many enemies too soon.'

Staff stroked his chin with the rubber on the end of his propelling pencil. 'And that means she's making enemies for us, you mean?'

'Naturally.' Ganger picked up a handful of paperclips and started to weave them into a chain. 'Major aggravation, at this rate. You don't need me to tell you that.'

They considered the matter in silence for a while.

'Finance and General Purposes smiled at me in the corridor the day before yesterday,' Staff said at last. 'I spent the rest of the morning searching this office for hidden microphones.'

'Find any?'

'No,' Staff replied. Then he put his finger to his lips, picked up his empty coffee-cup, inverted it and put it over the buzzer on the edge of the desk. 'Yes,' he went on. 'Six. I left that one where it was to make them think they'd won.'

'I wouldn't worry about it,' Ganger said, smiling. 'Sure, they've got every office in the building bugged – oh, and by the way, if you only found six, there's three more about here somewhere, I was talking with that kid Vince from Supplies. But it's nothing to worry about.'

'Nothing to . . .' Staff lowered his voice to a whisper. 'Nothing to worry about,' he hissed. 'Have you the faintest idea . . .'

Ganger shrugged. 'It all comes back to staffing levels,' he said. 'Think about it. So they've got the room bugged. In order for that to mean anything, think of all the backup you'd need. You'd have to have a guy listening in on each office, and another two guys to transcribe it all, and another guy to sort through the transcripts and put yellow highlighter on all the treasonable bits. With an organisation this size, you're talking maybe a staff of twenty thousand people. You know how many people work in Internal Security? Four, and one of them's a trainee. All they do is go around putting the bugs in, maybe fixing them when they go wrong, putting in new ones when they get found, and even doing that, there's a waiting list of maybe six years. Nobody actually *listens*.'

'Um.' Staff thought for a moment, then rather shame-facedly removed his coffee-cup. 'Even so,' he said.

'Exactly,' Ganger replied, leaning forward. 'Even so. We just can't afford to give those guys any more ammunition than we can help, and this crazy young kid of . . .'

'Not mine,' Staff couldn't help saying. 'You found her, remember.'

'Maybe, yes, but . . .'

'And you nagged her into joining.'

'Okay, yes, we're talking details here. It was your idea too. You didn't stop me.' There was a frown on Ganger's face; a very incongruous sight, like Genghis Khan in a dinner jacket. 'That doesn't alter the fact that we've got to be careful, both of us. It's a good idea, don't let's screw it up.'

'It was my idea to put her in Records,' Staff pointed out. 'And it was you who made sure she was on hand when the sun got stolen. In fact, I'm not so sure . . .' He stopped abruptly, aware that he'd been thinking aloud.

'Sure,' Ganger replied. 'I put those kids up to it. We needed a new sun. The old one was a goddamn liability.' He leaned closer forward still. 'Now you see what you're implicated in, huh?'

Staff half-rose; then he sat down again. 'You lunatic,' he said. 'What did you want to go and do something like that for?'

'Never you mind,' Ganger answered, infuriatingly. 'My department has a cross-departmental brief. I have to keep several things going at the same time.'

'Is that an explanation?'

'Yeah. Trust me.'

'Oh.' Staff bit the rubber on the end of his pencil in half and spat out the result. He was nervous when people from that particular department said 'Trust me'; he couldn't help but visualise the scene, many years ago now, when one of them had said, 'Go on, eat the bloody apple; trust me.' Of course, that sort of thing couldn't happen now, not with the New Covenant and mortals being so depressingly litigious, but old habits die hard. 'I think,' he said decisively, 'we ought to call the whole thing off. You're right,' he added quickly. 'You've convinced me.'

Ganger was taken beautifully by surprise. 'Hold on, now,' he said. 'I didn't say we should call it off. All I said was . . .'

Staff smeared a bewildered look on his face. 'You said she was becoming a liability,' he replied. 'I agree with you. By the way, what on earth possessed you to agree to all those demands of hers – pay and so forth? You realise that she's only down on the books as a trainee.'

'Wait a minute, now.' Ganger was distinctly flustered, and his smile was melting and dripping down the side of his mouth, like jam on the run from a doughnut. 'I couldn't help it,' he said. 'The kid's got personality, I guess. She just sort of came at me.'

'Right,' Staff replied, nodding. 'And now I think it's about time she came at somebody else around here.'

Another silence. In the corner of the room, unnoticed by anybody at all, one of the hidden microphones went wrong and began broadcasting the BBC World Service to its receiving station.

'Like who?' Ganger said cautiously. 'I think you're up to something.'

'Me?' Staff did a very creditable impression of startled innocence. 'I've never been up to anything in my entire life. I was just thinking that, if she's been attracting hostile criticism from certain quarters, then it's about time we turned her loose on her critics. What do you reckon?'

'I don't know.' Ganger stood up and walked across to the window, inadvertently treading on another hidden microphone and squashing it flat. The device in question had been installed by the trainee, and nobody had told him about putting them where they won't get trodden on. 'That could make things worse, you know? The last thing we want to do is precipitate a confrontation.'

'Don't we?'

'Well, not that sort of confrontation.' Ganger was starting to exhibit signs of great tension; that is to say, he appeared perfectly normal but his shoelaces were untying themselves and then weaving themselves back into fantastically intricate knots. 'What did you have in mind, anyway?'

Staff smiled; at least, he drew his lips across his face like the curtain of an old-fashioned proscenium-arch theatre. 'Nothing too dramatic,' he replied. 'I just think that the girl's proved herself perfectly capable in the field, so why not try her out in administration? After all,' he added carelessly, 'she can't get up to much mischief sat behind a desk all day, can she?'

'I don't know,' Ganger replied, and his face was a blank. 'Can she?'

Staff leaned back in his chair and put the tips of his fingers together. He was enjoying himself.

'Let's find out,' he said. 'Oh, and by the way.'

When one has worked in an office where mind-reading is the norm rather than the exception, one can't help noticing nuances of expression, just as a telephone can't get away from the fact that there are always people wanting to talk through it, regardless of whether it's in the mood. Ganger's face remained blank, but one of his shoelaces broke spontaneously. 'Yes?' he said.

'While we're on the subject of bugging.'

'Mm?'

'I saw a psychiatrist yesterday,' Staff said. He waited for some pleasantry or other from his interlocutor, and then went on: 'I told him – quite untruthfully, as it happens – that for the last few weeks I've had this extraordinary idea that someone's been listening to my thoughts. Inside my head, I told him. I didn't expect him to take me seriously, of course, but he did.'

'So I should think,' Ganger muttered.

'Well, he wasn't your run-of-the-mill shrink,' Staff admitted. 'In fact, he's the head departmental analyst, so he's used to that sort of thing, I should imagine. And do you know what he suggested I should do?'

Ganger beamed. 'Go on,' he said, 'you tell me.'

'He said,' Staff went on, 'that it's not a particularly uncommon condition in our line of work. He said – and this is just what he told me, mind – that the only odd thing about it was that I'd noticed. Funny he should say that, since I was making the whole thing up, wouldn't you say?'

'Hilarious.'

'Anyway,' Staff went on, 'the point he was making was that apparently, one of our own departments, or at least a department of what you might call an associated agency, has perfected a technique of mental bugging, just so's they can keep tabs on what the rest of us are thinking. A bit spooky, that, if it's true.'

'You've got my hair standing on end,' Ganger said. 'Do go on, please.'

'Oh, there's nothing to worry about,' Staff said reassuringly. 'Apparently, there's a very simple solution to the problem. The boys in the research lab tumbled to it almost immediately. All you've got to do is *this* and . . . I say, are you all right?'

Ganger, who was sitting bolt upright with a face as white as the proverbial sheet, nodded his head stiffly. His hair really was standing on end, Staff noticed.

'Sorry?' he said. 'I didn't catch what you said.'

'IIII sssaiiiid yyyyyessssss, IIIIyummm ffffiynnn, thannnnnx,' Ganger hissed. His eyes were bloodshot and he was starting to vibrate. 'WWWWwouldddddd yyyy kkkkkindlllleeeee sssstopppp ddddoinggg thattttt nnnow, ppppppl?'

'According to my friend the shrink,' Staff continued, looking away and affecting not to notice anything unusual, 'it's just a question of earthing the interloper into one's brainwaves. It's easy once you've got the knack, he says, though how you'd ever know you were doing it right beats me. Still, he says there's enough electricity inside the average person's head to fry an intruder like a sausage. I'm sure he's exaggerating. What do you think?'

'Gggggggggggggg.'

'Anyway,' Staff said, making a very slight movement, after which Ganger stopped looking like a cross between a straight-backed chair and a pneumatic drill and slumped on to the floor in a heap, 'it's just as well nobody's been trying to monkey about with the inside of *my* head, because he'd know he'd been in a fight if he did. My dear chap, what are you doing on the floor?'

'Resting,' Ganger croaked. 'I've had, you know, sort of a hard day.' He reached out a trembling hand and picked up the lenses of his glasses, which were all that was left, apart from a few droplets of melted plastic in the worn pile of the carpet. 'I think I'll get back to my office and do something.'

'Capital idea,' Staff replied. 'Mind how you go.'

'I will.' Ganger lifted himself on to his knees with an effort and crawled to the side of the desk.

'Want to borrow a comb?'

'Thanks,' Ganger mumbled. 'Don't think I'd have the strength to lift one right now, but maybe I'll take you up on it later.'

'Please yourself,' Staff said, picking up a file and opening it. 'You know what? The one thing that really cheers me up about this whole business is knowing that, come what may, you and I are on the same side. You know, implicit mutual trust, that sort of thing. It's a great comfort to me, it really is.'

'Um.'

'Cheerio, then.'

'Ciao.'

'Profiteroles,' said the Lord High Cardinal. 'I should live so long.'

The Count of the Stables winked at him. 'Go on,' he said, 'be a devi . . .' He checked himself. 'Go on,' he said. 'Tomorrow you can have a salad.'

The Lord High Cardinal shrugged. 'You convinced me,' he said. 'Or there's the *zuppa inglesi*.'

'Nah. That's for thin people. C'mon, go for it.'

'Okay.'

'Right,' said the Count of the Stables. 'That's six profiteroles. Hey, Rosa, six profiteroles over here.'

'I got it,' replied the Emperor's sister. 'Just give me a moment, will you? We got no help again today.'

The County Palatine clicked his teeth. 'You want to get shot of that kid,' he said, 'she's no good to you.'

Rosa gave him a withering look, the sort of look that scours roses of greenfly and lifts impacted grease off the inside of neglected ovens. 'You know how hard it is to get help – even crummy help – this time of the year? You don't. You let me run my business, okay?'

She scuttled off under a ziggurat of dirty plates. The Electors sighed.

'She works too hard,' opined the Lord Treasurer.

'It's a shame,' agreed the Count of the Stables. 'We should find her a reliable waitress.'

The Count of the Saxon Shore grunted. 'Anything that'd improve the service round here would be fine by me. You can get peptic ulcers waiting too long between courses.'

A match flared at the end of an eight-inch cigar. 'You've gotta look after your health in this life,' commented the Lord High Cardinal, 'because if you don't, nobody else will.' He burped smoke, like a dragon with carburettor trouble, while the other Electors exchanged surreptitious glances. They had an uneasy feeling that the Lord High Cardinal had just made a pronouncement *ex cathedra*; in which case, somebody really ought to write it down. 'Anyway,' he continued briskly, 'to business.'

The Electors stifled a selection of sighs and yawns. A working lunch, in their view, was a truly wonderful idea, but not nearly as truly wonderful as a plain ordinary lunch, hold the work. Still, they had a Duty.

'Well,' said the Lord Treasurer, 'I did the books last night, and they're looking pretty healthy. We got,' he reached in his coat pocket for his spectacles and yesterday night's wine list, 'we got income, seventeen point four four six four four million kreuzers, expenditure seventeen point four four six three nine million kreuzers, capital reserves nil, income transferred to capital account nil, fixed assets nil, short term liabilities nil, written down balance fifty kreuzers, transferred to cash account fifty kreuzers. Okay?'

The County Palatine frowned. 'What does that mean, Tony?' he asked.

'It means,' replied the Treasurer with a grin, 'today we can afford to leave a tip.'

The Electors nodded their approval, and the Lord High Cardinal cleared his throat.

'Policy review time next, folks,' he said. 'Anybody got anything to say about our policy?'

'I think our policy is just great, Rocky. What do you say, Tony?'

'Yeah, it's a great policy, Rocky. Where's that damn broad with the goddamn sweet?'

'Okay.' The Lord High Cardinal pencilled a little tick on the back of the menu. 'Now then, what's next? Oh, nuts, I forgot the minutes of the last meeting. Anybody take any minutes last meeting?'

'Nah.'

'Okay then, approved as drawn.' The Lord High Cardinal raised his eyebrows and scratched them with the end of his pencil. 'That just leaves Any Other Business, guys,' he said. 'Hold on, though,' he added, as Rosa approached with a tray, 'here it comes now.'

When they had finished Any Other Business, and the

Count of the Saxon Shore had had Extra Any Other Business with a side order of whipped cream, they sat for a while thinking and breathing heavily, until the arrival of the coffee recalled them to the next item on the agenda.

'Date of next meeting,' said the Lord High Cardinal. 'Thursday all right with you guys?' The Electors nodded. 'Okay, Thursday at twelve fifteen. Meeting closed. Hey, Rosa, where's the toothpicks? I got a big fat lump of veal gristle lodged behind my bridgework. You want me to choke to death here?'

Coffee was traditionally taken in silence, or at least without articulate speech, to give the Electors an opportunity to ruminate on the decisions they had just taken and if necessary review them or supplement them with a brandy or a small shot of grappa. It was, above all, a moment of tranquillity, essential in the headlong life of a monumentally important officer of state. Sometimes, however, something happened to spoil it; for example, the proprietor's sister tripping over her feet and depositing a plateful of tagliatelli verdi in the lap of the Count of the Saxon Shore.

'Yow,' howled the Count. 'You damn crazy bitch, that's hot!'

'Sorry,' said Rosa, perfunctorily. She leaned over and scooped the tagliatelli back out of the Count's lap on to the plate with a fork. 'You should count yourself lucky it was only a melted butter and cheese sauce. Bechamel sauce on a nice light suit like that, you'd be in real trouble.'

The Lord High Cardinal raised a caterpillar-like eyebrow. 'That's not like you, Rosa,' he said. 'You got something worrying you?'

Rosa sighed. 'That waitress,' she said. 'That so-called waitress. She only calls and says she's handing in her notice. On account of she's getting married and moving to Seattle. Some people just don't care.'

She bustled away to get a hot cloth. The Electors looked at each other.

'I move,' said the County Palatine, 'we find Rosa a new waitress. Seconded?'

'Seconded,' replied the Count of the Saxon Shore, grimly. 'As soon as possible. Wearing food isn't me, you know?'

'Right.' The County Palatine frowned. 'Anybody know of anybody?' he enquired. 'Gotta be somebody good, mind. You know, reliable, honest, intelligent, hard-working, efficient. Sure-footed,' he added. 'Good sense of balance, all that kind of thing.'

There was silence, during which the sun broke through the thick mantle of cloud that had masked it for a week or so now, flashed momentarily and then ducked away out of sight once again. A brief flare of dazzle on the outside of the window seemed to inspire the Lord High Cardinal, for he suddenly clapped his hands together and rubbed them warmly.

'Boys,' he said, 'I know just the person.'

George sat down at the controls, fastened the safety harness and switched on the intercom. There was the usual crackle.

'Helios One to Control Centre, come in please, over,' he said, but without conviction. Old dog, screamed every fibre of his being, new tricks.

'*Control Centre to Helios One, you are cleared, repeat cleared for commencement of preliminary take-off procedure in fifteen, one-five, minutes, over.*'

George growled. He didn't like talking to a computer; it made you feel odd, it was like talking to yourself. Makes you go blind, talking to yourself, so his mother had told him. He blinked.

Not, he had to admit, that a lot of it was not an

improvement. It worked, for a start. When you wanted it to turn left, you just wiggled the stick; you didn't have to lean right over and lean your back against the side of the cockpit. In fact, you didn't even have to wiggle the stick; something called an autopilot would do it for you. I wonder, George muttered resentfully to himself, how much he's getting a week. Probably non-union, too.

'Helios One to Control Centre,' he intoned. 'Commencing pre-take-off checklist programme, over.' He said it with roughly the same degree of expression and involvement as a forcibly converted Aztec saying the Mass in Latin, and without very much more idea what it was supposed to mean. It was all very well, sure; instead of having some brainless erk of a trainee standing out on the tarmac hauling on the propellor to get the thing fired up, all you needed to do was press a button. Provided, of course, you could remember which button. There were rather a lot of them, and they were all exactly the same shade of red.

Ah well. If things got tricky he could always ask the autopilot.

Instinctively he felt behind his seat for his thermos, and then remembered that in the shiny new design there were no convenient little ledges and nooks for secreting personal belongings in. Instead, there was a beverage control monitoring system, which unerringly threw a cup of warm, brown water all over him as he was coming into the bumpy stretch above 10.45 a.m. Time I retired, he said to himself. If only they'd let me, he added.

'Control Centre to Helios One, scheduled take-off time minus fourteen, one-four, minutes, over.'

If only, George continued to muse, the Boy hadn't gone off like that. He had talent for this job, the Boy had. Wonder where he was now? There'd been a rumour going about the Social Club that he'd packed in the Service altogether and gone off doing some job or other among the mortals. Still, they tended to say that about anybody who went missing for more than a week these days. Perhaps the Boy was going to be seconded back, now that they'd gone and bought this new model. A natural, that lad; fly anything, given time and provided nobody minded what he collided with while he was practising.

As take-off approached (what was wrong with calling it Dawn, by the way? Dawn had class; but you'd feel a bit of a Charlie talking about rosy-fingered take-off or the take-off coming up like thunder) something small but hard, like the ball in a pinball machine, started to roll about inside George's head; and maybe it was the faint jolt as the giant machine lifted smoothly into the air that finally gave it the impetus to roll into place. Anyway, roll it did. Clunk.

There was something very wrong with this machine, and nobody had realised. What the hell was it?

George flipped the intercom back to transmit.

'Helios One to Control Centre. Am cruising at five hundred thousand, five-oh-oh-thousand metres and climbing, all systems functional, over.'

He replaced the microphone thing, looked around to make sure nobody could see him, and switched off the autopilot.

'No hard feelings, chum,' he explained. 'You're doing a lovely job, but you know how it is. Always was a rotten passenger, me.'

He took hold of the stick and instinctively moved it to the right position. At once he became aware of a minute difference in the feel of the thing. The pinball rolled round in its hole and settled again, and in the back of George's mind, some coloured lights lit up and shouted 'Replay!'

Slower. Ever since he'd switched it on to manual, it'd slowed down.

George glanced out of the side of the cockpit at the ground. Centuries of practice flying the old sun on manual had enabled him to gauge the airspeed simply by watching the ground, while his brain made a series of subconscious, lightning-quick calculations. He *knew* he was flying at the right speed, just by the way the shadows of the trees below him shortened and lengthened again as he passed over. And yet just now he'd slowed down. It's impossible to confuse deceleration with any other experience in the world; like mashed swede, there's absolutely nothing you can mistake it for. Which meant . . .

'Bugger me,' George said; and, in spite of himself, he chuckled. It only went to show, you do no good by fiddling with things just for the sake of it.

It explained everything; the wilting crops, the freakish behaviour of the tides, the fact that the Pole Star was halfway up the back of Cassiopeia's Chair, the friction burns down the left-hand side of the Kalahari Desert, the way his wife always seemed surprised when he got in from work these days.

The daft sods had made the damn thing go too fast.

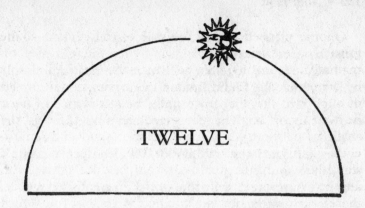

TWELVE

The alarm-clock buzzed. Jane made a squeaking noise, rubbed her eyes and extended an arm with the general idea of getting hold of whatever was making that horrible noise and throttling it. Then her memory fired up, and she groaned.

It was morning, and she had to get up and go to work. Oh *damn* . . .

She brushed her teeth like a well-brought-up robot, combed her hair and looked at herself in the mirror.

'Hi,' she said. 'I'm Jane. I help run the Universe.'

It didn't sound any better this morning than it had yesterday. She shrugged, blew her nose and went to see whether the ironing-fairy had broken in during the night and made a start on the blouse dump.

It hadn't. Bother.

Hanging at the back of the wardrobe and looking as if it had been dead for some considerable time, she found the old blue blouse with the Princess Diana collar that her mother had given her for Christmas, back in the days when you could buy a whole roast ox, watch the bear-baiting and still have change out of a half-groat.

On the other hand, she said to herself, it's the only clean blouse I've got.

She put it on, together with a few other jumble-sale rejects which she found hidden in corners, and stumped through into the kitchen to make herself a slice of toast and a cup of tea. The floor crackled underfoot as she walked.

'Yes, all right,' she said aloud, 'I'll clean you tonight if you'll just shut up.'

Don't suppose I will, though, she said to herself, as she stood waiting for the kettle. I'll be too tired. And anyway, people who run universes should have their housework done for them, surely. I mean, it doesn't say *and on the eighth day, He changed the bed, cleaned the oven and did the hoovering*, does it?

That's probably because He was a He.

Smoke curled out from under the grill and she sighed. Speciality of the house, she muttered to herself, Toast à la Pucelle. She grabbed a knife and started to scrape, until she was left with a large pile of black dust and about four square inches of toast.

Job satisfaction, she said to herself, that's what I've got. You know, the lovely feeling that I'm making the world a better place. *Really* making the world a better place. Or will be.

Staff had explained all that to her. Yes, she'd ironed out all the problems of human personal relationships at a stroke, but of course it wasn't as simple as that. A built-in fail-safe in the programme slowed the process down so that the customers wouldn't notice anything different. Wouldn't do for the customers to notice anything, they'd get restive, start believing in things, bad for morale. This way, she reflected bitterly, they'll be happy ever after without realising it, and so they'll go on being miserable, the same as before.

'Yes,' she said to the kettle, 'but I did manage to get them to replace the sun, remember. I mean . . .'

The kettle looked at her without saying anything. It didn't need to. She looked away and tried to crush rock-hard butter on to the porcelain-fragile toast without smashing it in the process.

There was nothing to show for it. The less there was to show for it the better, and so far she had a hundred per cent success rate.

'The hell with this,' she snarled at the kitchen clock. 'If I had any brains, I'd go back to working at Burridge's. At least I was sure of getting away at five-thirty.'

The clock ticked. A fat lot of help you are, she thought. Still, I have to talk to you, because if I start talking to myself, it'll mean I'm going mad.

She dumped the last few shards of toast in the bin and made a mental note to try and buy a sandwich at the station. The station . . . Well, it was a different sort of commuting; bus to Waterloo, train to Salisbury, change for Amesbury, bus to Stonehenge, bodily translation from there direct to the office. Unless there was a go-slow or track repairs, of course, in which case she'd be diverted to the Cloud of Unknowing and have to try and find a taxi.

'And you can shut up as well,' she snapped at the eggtimer.

At the back of her mind, in among the almost-forgotten birthdays and rotting scraps of Maths O-level, a small and badly underpaid member of staff coughed nervously and suggested that something was probably fundamentally wrong with the whole set-up. Either you work on earth, it said, and you get all this hassle, but at least you stay a human being doing sort of human things, plus the ironing; or you work in the Empyrean and don't have to be bothered with matters corporeal. And while we're on the subject, it added, looking nervously over its shoulder, I don't know about you but I think there's something extremely fishy about this whole work thing, and it really doesn't add up at all, because . . .

It would have enlarged on this theme if something large, panther-shaped and blatantly alien hadn't jumped out of the shadows on the edge of the subconscious and bitten its head off. The small knot of thoughts which had gathered to listen to it quickly melted away. A few fractions of a second later, strange shapes in black overalls came and cleared away the mess.

Leave the washing-up till I get home, said Jane to herself. Gosh, must rush. Don't want to be late for work.

'You'll like the work here,' Staff had said. 'Relaxing. No pressure or hassle or anything like that, just straightforward clerical and administration. You probably need a rest after all that, um, recently.'

The phone rang again. Jane stuck her tongue out at it, and then picked up the receiver.

'This is Phil from Audit,' it said nastily. 'Look, aren't those 1998 projections down yet? You promised we'd have them a fortnight ago and we're completely stuffed without them.'

Jane sighed and went into Ansafone mode. 'My name's Jane,' she said, 'I've only been in this office a week and I haven't the faintest idea what I'm supposed to be doing or what's going on. If you would care to explain exactly what it is that you want me to do, I'll get on to it as soon as I possibly can. Thank you.' Then, out of what could be described as sheer devilment were it not for the risk of causing confusion in the present context, she made a *beep* noise, and waited.

There was, as usual, a disconcerted pause of about three-quarters of a second. 'Look,' said the voice, 'it's just not good enough. Unless I get those breakdowns on my desk by half past four this afternoon, there's going to be ructions, okay?'

The line went dead. Jane shrugged, replaced the receiver and turned her attention back to the bulging tray of papers in front of her. They were all sorts of different colours, and they were covered in print, typewriting and office-person's handwriting (which is cursive, semi-legible and entirely uniform in every office in the whole of Creation) in a wide assortment of scripts and alphabets; all of which, curiously enough, Jane found that she could read without difficulty. The only problem was that none of them carried any sort of clue on the face of them as to what they were or what had to be done with them; apart, of course, from the ones with URGENT (or even occasionally *URGENT!!!*) stamped on them in red. Clearly, she was meant to worry like hell about those.

The phone rang.

'This is Sylvia from Mainframe Base, as if you didn't know,' it said. 'We're still waiting. However much longer is it going to take you?'

'My name's Jane. I've only been in this . . .'

'And another thing,' the voice continued. 'You promised faithfully you'd let me have the Directory back when you'd finished with it, and that was three weeks ago. Now I suppose you've gone and lost it. Again.'

'. . . In this office a week and I haven't the faintest . . .'

'Don't give me that, dear. Unless it's here, *on* my desk, *with* the reports filed to date, in the next forty-five minutes, I'm going to have to file a Blue. I'm sorry if that seems aggressive of me, but you don't really leave me any choice.'

Line dead. Shrug. Now then, what on earth is this big green thing meant to be? Which way up, for a start?

'Excuse me.'

Jane looked round, startled. Apart from the lost, violent souls on the other end of the telephone line, nobody except the tea lady had spoken to her since she'd started there. Most of the time the other people in the long, echoing hall yelled into their telephones and slammed them down again. For all she knew, they were the people who kept phoning her up.

'Sorry to bother you, but do you think you could possibly explain something? You see, I'm new here.'

The person, once located, turned out to be a small, wispy female who looked as if she'd last eaten back when mammoth steak meant just that. Odds on there was a face somewhere behind those spectacles, but probably not a face of particular relevance to anything. Jane felt a brief pang of sympathy.

'I'll try,' she said, 'but I doubt it, really. You see, I'm new here myself, and nobody's told me . . .'

'Oh, but you must know more than me,' replied the girl. 'You see, I've only been here two years, so . . .'

She tailed off. Obviously she didn't like the look of the way Jane was goggling at her, like an amateur sword-swallower faced with a chainsaw.

'Two *years*?' Jane said. 'And you still . . . ?'

'Haven't got the foggiest idea about anything, I'm afraid,' the girl replied, clearly deeply ashamed of herself. You could tell that from the fact that her fingernails were the least pink bit of her. 'Not a clue, honestly,' she added.

'But . . .' Jane pulled herself together. 'But what do you do all day, for pity's sake? I mean, you must do something.'

The girl nodded. 'Mostly,' she said, 'I answer the phone. I'm not terribly good at it, though, because I never know the answer to anything anybody ever asks me. I'm a bit worried about that. There's someone called Darren in something called Forward Budgeting who's been calling me every day for the last eighteen months, and . . .'

'I know him,' Jane interrupted. 'Wants it on his desk by two-fifteen or there'll be trouble.'

The girl smiled apprehensively. 'Yes,' she said, 'that's him.'

'And then he rings off without telling you what.'

'Yes, um.'

'Fine.' Jane breathed in slowly and deeply. 'And nobody else you've asked can help you?'

The girl frowned. 'Oh, I haven't asked anyone *else*,' she replied. 'I mean, they all look so busy, I was afraid to bother them. I only asked you because you look, well . . .' The girl trailed off; her fingernails now looked positively anaemic.

Jane looked around the room. It was true that, apart from herself and the girl, everyone else did look extremely busy. Mostly they were shouting into telephones and then banging them down; and when they weren't doing that, they were frantically rummaging through the coloured bits of paper on their desks, looking for something.

'Just out of curiosity,' Jane asked, 'what did they take you on as?'

'Computer operator,' replied the girl. 'Only the computer doesn't seem to work, does it?'

She nodded her head at the VDU on the top of Jane's desk. After the third day, when she still hadn't been able to get the bloody-minded thing to do anything more constructive than flash its lights at her and display the words *Hi! All rights protected!*, she'd followed what appeared to be the general practice of the office and converted the thing into a plastic cup stand. Some VDU's, she had observed, had several months' deposit of cups on top of them, which made the office look like a stalagmite farm.

'What is this office, anyway?' Jane asked. 'Someone told

me when I first came here, but I've forgotten what they called it. It didn't seem to mean anything much.'

'Oh, we're Processing,' the girl replied, with a hint of crazy pride in her voice. 'I think we're terribly important, or else why do people from other offices keep ringing us up all the time? Oh, do excuse me.' She looked away and answered the telephone on her desk. Jane didn't need a vast amount of imagination to reconstruct the conversation from the side of it she could hear.

'Let me guess,' she said, as the girl lowered the receiver. 'That was Dave from Throughput, and unless it's in his tray by three o'clock, the world's going to end.'

The girl stared at her. 'So you *do* know what's going on,' she gasped.

Jane shook her head. 'I'm just a good guesser,' she replied. 'Look, instead of just sitting here like a couple of decoy pigeons, why don't we go and find someone and ask them? Someone who *does* know, I mean.'

The girl looked at her as if she'd just suggested tarring and feathering the Pope. 'What, leave our desks?' she said. 'I don't think we're allowed.'

'Oh, I think we are,' said Jane firmly.

'But . . .' The girl shot her a look of pure terror; the sort of look one unborn twin might give to the other if it suggested going *up* the passageway instead of down. 'What if the phone were to ring while we're away?' she quavered. 'I mean, there'd be nobody to answer it.'

Jane shook her head. 'Highly unlikely,' she said. 'And even if it did ring, how would anyone ever know? You see, there'd be nobody to hear it.'

'The person at the other end would know,' replied the girl, her lower lip quivering. 'Wouldn't they?'

'Their word against ours,' Jane said fiercely – indeed, Henry V couldn't have said it better. In this mood, not only would Jane have had them into the breach once more, she'd have made them wipe their feet first. 'Come on.'

Without looking at her colleague, she grabbed her handbag, stood up, and began to walk in the direction she believed was most likely to be north.

'Wait for me!' the girl gasped behind her. 'If you leave me behind I might get lost.'

'Keep up, then,' Jane said. 'And follow me.'

Although she was only dimly aware of it herself, one of Jane's greatest strengths was her ear for the right choice of words to suit any given situation. Thus, when at last they came upon a man sitting at a desk who wasn't talking on the phone, some internal word selection system put the magic phrase into her mouth without her having to think at all.

'All right,' she said, 'where is he? I want to talk to him *now*.'

The man looked up at her, terrified. 'You can't,' he replied. 'He's in with Them.'

Jane tightened the focus of her ferocious expression. 'How long's he been in there?'

'Twenty minutes,' the man replied. 'Half an hour. Forty minutes. At least.'

Jane breathed out; and if her breath didn't consist of bluehot flame, it was only because of the No Smoking sign. 'Which room's he in? Come on, I haven't got all night.'

'Number Five.' The man pointed. As Jane turned her head to follow the line he was indicating, his phone rang, and he dived for it like a drowning man after a lifebelt. Two-thirds of a second later, he was shouting at someone.

'Right,' Jane said, and she beckoned to her acolyte. 'Now we're getting somewhere. Come on.'

The girl stood rooted to the spot. 'But we *can't*,' she said. 'He's in with Them, the man just said.'

Jane turned her head and smiled. 'Do you have any idea who he is?'

The girl shook her head.

'Me neither,' said Jane smugly. 'And what about Them? You know who They are?'

'No.'

'Well then,' Jane replied briskly. 'What you don't know about can't hurt you. Well-known fact. Coming?'

She marched up to the door, which had a big, slightly grubby '5' on it, knocked twice, and pushed open the door.

Then she stopped.

She was standing in a restaurant.

Furthermore, she was wearing a black skirt, shiny with age and the condensation of greasy food and sweat, topped by a white blouse and a pinny whose origins at least were decorative. She was holding a tray with three heaped plates of pasta on it. The door behind her closed.

'C'mon, for Chrissakes,' shouted a fat man, one of six fat men sitting round a table with a red and white checked tablecloth on it. 'There's people starving to death.'

'I know,' said a voice which Jane recognised as her own. 'Half the population of the Sudan, for a start. This lot'd keep most of them fed for a week, though it wouldn't do their arteries any good.'

Twelve round piggy eyes stared at her. 'Right,' she said. 'Who's having what?'

For six weeks, a long time ago now, Jane had been a waitress, in a Little Chef on a ring-road south of Nottingham. Six weeks was all she'd been able to take, because she'd come to the conclusion that feeding fattening food to fat people is basically immoral; but while she'd been there, she'd learned. How to balance seven plates at once while clearing up after a small child who's been sick after three consecutive knicker-bocker glories; how to serve a fried breakfast to three lorry-drivers who were trying to look down the front of her blouse, without hitting them with the ketchup bottle; how to watch thirty-seven eggs being fried simultaneously in dirty fat without becoming a vegan. She knew the ropes.

'Um,' said the fattest fat man, and pointed vaguely. Jane deposited the plates, turned on her heel and walked away as quickly as she could. Before she could make it to the door she'd come through, however, she nearly collided with a four-foot-high black-haired woman with her hands on her hips, who stood blocking her way.

'Listen,' the woman hissed, ''cos I'm only saying this once. Don't sass the customers, right? Now, there's two lasagnes over by the window.'

As if in a dream, Jane allowed herself to be diverted into what had to be the kitchen, where she found two plates of lasagne waiting for her. She picked them up and carried them to their recipients, who thanked her.

'Next,' the fattest man was saying, 'policy. Anybody got anything to say about policy, guys?'

'It's a great policy we got there, Rocky.'

'Yeah, don't let's fool around with it, it's working just fine.'

Jane's feet, meanwhile, had walked her back into the kitchen, where she took delivery of three portions of veal. There was a lot of cream on the veal, she noticed; in fact, if the proprietor of this restaurant took to buying his dairy products from Europe in future, there was a fair chance that the Common Agricultural Policy might make it after all. Jane frowned.

'Table for six,' hissed the short woman in her ear, 'and don't get fresh.'

'I thought you were only going to tell me once,' Jane replied, and darted through the door before a reply could be mustered.

'Stocktake,' the fattest man was saying. 'Anybody know if we got any stock, fellas?'

'Sure, Rocky, we got all the stock we can handle.'

'Don't you worry about a thing, Rocky. It'll be just fine.'

As Jane approached, the six men fell silent and she could feel their eyes on her again, like overfed leeches. She put the plates down and turned to withdraw.

'Did I hear you right, lady?' said a fat voice.

Slowly, Jane turned round. She was smiling.

'I beg your pardon?' she said.

'I said,' repeated the fat voice, 'did I hear you right just now?'

Jane identified the man speaking and looked him in the eye. It was rather like falling into something sticky, but she persevered. 'That depends,' she said, 'on what you thought you heard me say.'

The man jutted some chins at her. 'I thought you said,' he replied, 'something about my food.'

Jane looked down, to confirm that he'd had the pasta. 'I did indeed,' she said. Gosh, observed a part of her consciousness cheerfully, this is just like old times, isn't it? The rest of her consciousness pretended it hadn't heard.

'You *criticising* my food?' the man said.

'No,' Jane answered, as sweetly as she could. 'I'm sure it's lovely food. It's the company it keeps that I have my doubts about.'

There was a silence round the table, as the twelve eyes grew round with amazement. Finally, one of the fat men turned to another.

'Hey, Rocky,' it said, 'I thought you said this broad was okay.'

Rocky shrugged. 'So did I,' he replied. 'Hey, you,' he said, addressing Jane. She raised an enquiring eyebrow.

'Me?'

'You.'

'Well?'

The man seemed to be having difficulty with his powers of belief. 'Who do you think you are, lady?' he said quietly. Something struck Jane as odd about the way he said it, until she realised that, whether the man knew it or not, he actually did intend it as a question.

'My name is Jane,' Jane replied. 'I've only been in this office a week and I haven't the faintest idea what I'm supposed to be doing or what's going on. If you would care to explain exactly what it is that you want me to do, I'll get on to it as soon as I possibly can. Thank you.'

Ten little piggy eyes stared at her in complete bewilderment. The other two narrowed slightly.

'You're new to this work, aren't you?' said their owner quietly.

'No,' Jane said, 'I've done something similar before.'

'Is that so?' The man maintained his expression, giving Jane the feeling of being under a powerful X-ray that could see what she'd eaten for the last six days. Then one of the ends of his mouth flicked up a little. 'You like this sort of work?'

'No,' Jane replied.

'Not good enough for you, huh?' Again, Jane felt she was in the presence of a genuine enquiry.

'Let's say it doesn't tax me to the limits of my capacity,' she said. 'In fact,' she added carefully, 'it wasn't my idea in the first place.'

'No,' the man said. 'I guess not.' He widened the smile a micron or so. 'I'll say this for you, kid, you've got guts.'

'So have you,' Jane replied involuntarily. 'Lots and lots of them.'

The man didn't seem to mind; and Jane slowly became aware of a feeling she didn't like. Either the man was getting bigger, or she was getting smaller, or both. She broke off eye contact, and looked at the one piece of bread remaining in the basket.

'So what kind of work are you looking for?' the man said. 'Not office work, I guess.'

'I've done that,' Jane said quietly. 'Not really me, somehow.'

'I guess not.' Suddenly he chuckled. It was rather an attractive sound. 'Maybe you should try your hand at a few things, you know, look around a bit till you find something that suits you.'

'Thanks,' Jane said. 'I'll remember that.'

'Like I said,' the man repeated, 'you've got guts. Just don't make a pain of yourself in anybody else's if you can help it, okay?'

Jane mumbled something. Just now, she was thinking how nice it would be to get back to her desk and talk to somebody on the telephone. More her sort of level, somehow.

'Now,' the man said, 'let me tell you something.'

He half stood up, and began whispering in Jane's ear. It was rather like having your ears syringed by a blind octopus, but the words that she was hearing took her mind off that aspect of it.

'Thank you,' she said. 'You've been most helpful.'

The man smiled, widely this time. 'You're welcome,' he said. 'Oh, and kid—'

'Yes?'

'Before you go, tell Rosa this veal needs warming through,' the man said. 'Now get outa here.'

Jane pushed the door of Number Six. This time, she didn't bother to knock first.

The occupant of Number Six was not a human being, nor even vaguely anthropomorphous. What Jane found sitting in the expensive-looking leather swivel chair was a chipmunk.

'Excuse me,' Jane said.

The chipmunk looked up from the pile of papers in front of it and wiggled its nose. 'Well?' it said.

For a split second, something shorted in Jane's mind, and she couldn't think of anything to say. Anything, that is, apart from 'You're a chipmunk', which probably didn't need saying right now.

'Correct,' said the chipmunk. 'Did you come in here to tell me that?'

The short cleared. 'Not you as well,' Jane replied testily. 'Can everybody in this place read minds?'

The chipmunk's whiskers quivered slightly. 'I can't,' he said. 'It's just a ninety-nine per cent certainty I know what you're thinking. And before you waste your effort wondering, I can take any shape I like. I use this one for people who come barging in here without an appointment,' he added, 'because it disconcerts them.'

'Fine,' Jane replied. 'I want to talk to you about how this department is run.'

'I know you do,' replied the chipmunk. 'Now get out.'

By way of a reply, Jane sat down and folded her arms. The chipmunk sighed and nibbled a small area of veneer off the edge of its desk.

'I can give you five minutes,' it said.

'Thank you.' Jane smiled, opened her handbag and produced a notebook. 'I'll come straight to the point, then, shall I? This entire department is superfluous.'

The chipmunk stood up in its chair and waggled its forepaws briskly; then it sat down again, turned round three times, and crouched with its ears back. 'Rubbish,' it said.

'Fact,' Jane replied. 'The alleged purpose of this department is general administration for the whole operation.

It's superfluous because it doesn't administer anything. And the reason for that is that the system broke down 107 years ago.'

The chipmunk disappeared. In its place, there appeared a long, green snake with diamond markings. 'Really,' it observed.

'Really,' Jane replied. 'Take it from me. Ever since then, the input's been continuing to flow in, but the output's ground to a complete halt. Such administration as actually takes place is entirely spontaneous and *ad hoc*. I think that's the expression I want,' Jane added.

'It'll do,' the snake said. 'Where does your information come from, by the way?'

'A man in a restaurant told me,' Jane replied. 'For instance, this department is supposed to channel funds from the Treasurer's office to the Destiny department, via a system of requisitions and pink chits. In practice, Destiny keeps its money in a cocoa tin behind the clock in the machine shed. When there's nothing left in the tin, the duty supervisor sneaks into the social club while the barman's having his lunch, using the duplicate key belonging to the captain of the bowling team, and takes the change from the till. The barman in turn writes it off against breakages. Correct?'

The snake darted a fine tongue at her and hissed. Jane nodded and went on.

'This department,' she said, 'is also nominally responsible for the allocation of staff to, among others, the Perjury department, the main job of which is to strike perjurers with lightning. Perjury has a staff of seventy operatives and six supervisors, all on full pay, but nobody gets hit by lightning because the post of departmental head has been vacant for over 300 years. The net result is that, although perjury among mortals is regularly detected and noted in the Records, perjurers aren't being zapped at because thunderbolts can't be drawn from the stores without a green chit signed by the departmental head. All that the operatives can do, therefore, is stick their tongues out at the perjurers and shout rude words at them; and since all Perjury staff are required by the rules to be invisible and imperceptible to mankind . . .'

There was a soft rustling noise as the snake wound itself round the arm of its chair. 'Go on,' it said.

'Need I?' Jane replied. 'If you want me to, I will. I can tell you about how the staff pension fund never reaches the pensioners, not because the money isn't there, but because Gary in Pensions is waiting for the 1897 returns and can't issue a mauve chit without them; so everybody puts five kreuzers a week into the Solstice Club at the newsagents' round the corner from the Earthquakes building, which does the job perfectly well. Or there's stationery; shall I tell you about how the unissued stock of paperclips recently broke away under the force of its own mass and is now the centre of a whole new planetary system out the other side of Orion's Belt?' Jane paused for breath, and because she had run out of examples. The snake looked at her.

'So,' it said at last. 'There are hiccups here and there. Big deal.'

Jane bit her lip; was it her imagination, or could she hear the faint clunk of a called bluff? 'Hiccups,' she repeated. 'The sort of hiccup they had in San Francisco in 1906.'

The snake lifted its head, wondered what to do with it, and threaded it through the handle of its briefcase. 'We'll give what you say very serious thought,' it replied. 'In the meantime, perhaps you feel you ought to be seconded to some other department.'

Anger is a curious thing, with a behaviour pattern rather like that of a Honda CX550 motorcycle. Sometimes you can give the throttle just the slightest of tweaks, and the next thing you're aware of is the ambulancemen picking bits of hedge out of your lower abdomen. Sometimes you stamp the gear lever down into fourth and twist the throttle right round, and the beast just looks up at you out of its cow-like instrument panel and slows down to a gentle stroll. The only thing you can rely on is its habit of running out of petrol exactly halfway between filling stations.

Jane's anger, to continue the simile, had just boiled dry; and, as she looked the snake in the eyes and tried to think what to say next, something told her that it was going to be a long, hard push home.

'Perhaps that'd be best,' she said softly. 'Thank you for your time.' She got up, collected her handbag, and left the office.

As she was clearing her desk, the phone rang.

'You shouldn't have done that,' said Ganger's voice. It sounded cheerful. 'Not at all wise.'

'I expect you're right,' Jane replied. 'Who was that man in the restaurant?'

The line seemed to go numb. 'That was Rocky,' said Ganger, and his voice sounded as if he was speaking through two pillow-cases and a sock. 'You weren't supposed to meet him, either.'

'He seemed to be expecting to meet me,' Jane said.

'I know. Anyway, there we are. Come and see me at half nine tomorrow, and we'll talk. Oh, and by the way.'

'Yes?'

'You're doing just fine. Trust me.' Ganger smiled into Jane's ear, and hung up.

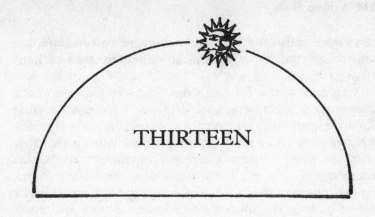

THIRTEEN

The sky is very high here.

In most places, the sky is just, well, high; a sort of blue tent that keeps the stars out and the air in. Here, it's different. Here, it's so high above sea-level that the existence of the ground is little more than an unsubstantiated rumour. There is also a castle.

A big, frilly, no-expense-spared, Ludwig of Bavaria special. And it's bobbing and floating about, like a balloon that's been at the sherry on an empty stomach, with nothing holding it up apart from the thought of the quite appalling effect it would have on the ground if it ever stopped floating.

When it comes to a bare-knuckle fight between gravity and social conscience, gravity loses.

As you approach, picking your way cautiously through the thermals and taking care not to tread on the heads of any high-flying birds, you can hear snatches of a strange and bewildering noise, wafted at you by the semi-feral winds that hide out in the major altitudes. From this distance, and bearing in mind the uncanny distortions of wind and the Doppler effect, you could almost believe that you were listening to several thousand people whistling – flat, off-key – the disjointed scraps of a half-familiar tune.

Welcome to the Castle in the Air, headquarters of the Department of Omens and Auspices. The men standing in inch-perfect rows in the courtyard are trainee Messengers. Once they graduate, they will spend their working lives delivering dreams, uncanny flashbacks, moments of déjà vu, and other similar communications. At the moment, they are being taught the extremely tricky art of making the unique noise known as the postman's whistle.

Now, supposing you look very carefully, you'll notice one small figure in the Departmental blue-and-gold uniform, whose hair is rather longer than the rest. If you can somehow force your ears to blot out the general cacophony, you'll notice that this one individual is defiantly whistling, in tune and without sudden disconcerting pauses, a tune which is unmistakably 'Sergeant Pepper's Lonely Hearts Club Band'.

Guess who.

'You mustn't think of it in those terms,' Ganger had said, as they trudged up the Castle's drive. 'That's negative.'

'Really,' Jane replied. She would have expressed herself more fully, but the gradient was steep, and her knees were beginning to feel as if some joker had whipped the sinews out of them while she wasn't looking.

'Believe me,' Ganger said. 'Even if we were trying to keep you out of the way for a while, which we aren't, we wouldn't do it by putting you in the Messenger service. It's far too high profile for that.'

'High,' said Jane, breathlessly sardonic (try it for yourself), 'profile. Running errands. Delivering messages.'

'Yeah.' Ganger stopped for a moment, ran his finger

round the inside of the button-down collar of his Abercrombie and Fitch pink shirt, and breathed in. 'Hardly hidden away in some out-of-the-way back office, is it?'

Jane wiped sweat out of her eyes with her thumb and forefinger. 'Not exactly challenging, though. Not precisely demanding the highest levels of executive performance. I thought you said I was a high-flyer.'

Ganger started to look down, then checked himself quickly. 'You want to go any higher than this, you can find your own way.'

Jane kept her face straight, just. 'You're not afraid of heights, are you?' she said.

'I'm bloody terrified of heights,' Ganger replied. 'Think about it, will you? My natural environment isn't high up on top of things; in fact, it's the exact opposite. I get vertigo standing on thick pile carpet sometimes. And,' he added, 'if you think that's so terribly amusing, we'll pay a visit to my departmental HQ one of these days, and we'll see how you like that.'

Jane made a contrite sort of breathless gasping noise, and they continued their climb in silence, or at least without words, for a while. Eventually, Jane bit her lip.

'Sorry,' she said. 'And I do appreciate you coming along to introduce me. Thanks.'

Ganger smiled. 'Think nothing of it,' he said. 'That's fine.'

'I'm sorry?'

'I said that's fine.'

'I'm sorry,' Jane shouted back, 'I can't hear you for the blood pumping in my ears.'

'It's not important.'

'Sorry?'

'I said it's . . . Nothing.'

'Are we there yet?'

Ganger opened his mouth, thought better of it, and nodded. In front of them, its drawbridge lowered over nothing at all and resting on even less, was the gatehouse of the Castle in the Air.

Over the keystone of the arch there was a board of wood. Wind at barometric pressure had long since scoured it of varnish, but still faintly visible were the words:

The Laurels

painted in faded white. Jane raised an eyebrow.

'We tried calling it that for a while,' Ganger explained, 'but it never seemed to catch on somehow. You wait there while I knock.'

He advanced up to the massive gate and lifted the knocker, using both hands and putting his back into it. He managed to raise it a full inch before he had to let go.

'It's not a real knocker, you see,' he said, rubbing his arms gingerly. 'Or at least it's real, but it's an ideal knocker. You know, the way knockers should be in an ideal universe. And in an ideal universe, people take a lot more exercise than we do.'

'Um.'

'So,' Ganger went on, 'I guess we'll have to do the next best thing.'

He stooped slightly and walked down under the gate. Jane followed, her belief not so much suspended as dangling by a thread.

'Mind how you go from now on,' Ganger called out to her as they emerged into the outer yard. 'The whole of this place is an Excluded Liability Zone.'

Jane blinked. 'Excuse me?' she said.

'Excluded Liability Zone,' Ganger repeated. 'Absolutely necessary, in view of the sort of work they do here.

You see, if we could be held accountable for any of the information that we pass on from here – in perfectly good faith, you understand – we'd be in court so fast our feet wouldn't touch. Talking of which, look out for tripwires.'

'Tripwires.'

Ganger nodded. 'And dogs, of course. It's part of the training programme, you see.'

'Dogs I can understand,' Jane said, thinking of postmen again. 'But why tripwires?'

'We deliver supernatural promptings to some of the best-defended people in the cosmos,' Ganger replied with a hint of pride. 'You know the sort of thing. Merchant princes who won't clinch a deal unless they get an okay from their astrologer. Lunatic third-world dictators who take their policy guidelines from the spirits of their ancestors. Identical twin brothers of Latin American drug barons. When you're on a job like that, tripwires come as light relief. And the worst part of it is,' Ganger continued, grinning, 'you have to keep whistling. It's the Code, you see.'

'Um.'

'Whistling, scattering rubber bands everywhere and never turning up with a Recorded Delivery unless you're sure the recipient is out. It's a point of honour. They're very strict about it.'

Directly under their feet the sun chugged past, twenty minutes ahead of schedule. Was it Jane's imagination, or did the pilot wave? Ganger stopped and straightened his tie.

'Right,' he said, 'we're here. Now then, I have a strange feeling you're going to do all right here.'

'Funny you should mention that,' Jane replied. 'So have I.'

'Naturally,' Ganger said. 'Think about it.'

*   *   *

Bjorn hesitated.

Some hard things have been said about him recently, so the record should be set straight. He had his failings, true, but when it came to balls, he had more of them than Dunlop and Slazenger put together. Equipped with an axe, a home-made grappling hook and Great-grandmama's washing-line, he was getting ready to burgle the Portals of the Sunset.

He reminded himself to stay cool, but it wasn't really necessary. Slowly and methodically, he checked his equipment, pulled his mask (one of Old Gretchen's black legwarmers with two eye-holes cut in it) over his face and crept forwards.

About here, somewhere, there should be an invisible electric fence.

He knew all about the fence. A long time ago, when he was working on Security, he and Thick Mick and Kevin the Pisser had had the job of installing it, one wet Friday afternoon. As he had anticipated, it did not detain him long.

The searchlights mounted on Number Three and Number Four observation towers would have been a serious hazard, if it wasn't for the fact that keeping the bearings oiled and in good repair had been the respon-sibility of Old Nobby from Maintenance ever since the Fall of Man. Nobby had long since worked out what axle grease was for. He ate it.

So far, so good. There were three machine-gun nests in Number Five observation tower; but what with the cutbacks and everything, the gunners were never issued with more than five rounds of ammunition each per year, and they were under strict orders to save those for the twenty-one-gun salute for the Commandant's birthday. Given this limitation, the gunners (probably still Daft Terry and Gormless Dave, even after all these years) tended to spend their watch in the guardhouse playing endless games of dominoes, which somehow or other neither of them ever seemed to win.

Having penetrated as far as the outer perimeter fence, Bjorn stopped and assessed the task now facing him. This was where the fun started.

For reasons which need not concern us here, nobody in the village had ever seen the need to spend good money on a pair of wirecutters. Bjorn, who had spent his meagre savings playing the Speak Your Weight machines at the Wolfhound bus depot on his way out, was therefore going to have to improvise. Over it, or through it.

He decided against over it. If memory served him correctly, the posts holding it up were put in by some friends of his from the Department of Works, and so the chances of it bearing his weight were not high. Through it, however, meant cutting a hole through the wire mesh without waking the entire guard. He frowned, and checked through his rucksack for inspiration.

Having rejected the spare pair of underpants, the roll of extra strong mints, the broken watch and the July 1985 edition of *StreetBike*, he was left with a tin opener, a leaky felt-tip pen and a Zambian Army Knife. The latter item had one overwhelming advantage over its Swiss rival which outweighed its various drawbacks in Bjorn's estimation. It was given away free with litre cans of lawnmower gearbox oil. He took it out of the rucksack and fumbled for the sawblade attachment.

It says something about the quality of Departmental fencing wire that Bjorn was through and out the other side in three minutes flat. (For the record, when the Zambian Army wants a fence cut, they don't hang around breaking their fingernails trying to get the sawblade out; they get on the radio for a squadron of MiGs.)

According to the periphery defences' design specification, there are seventeen acres of minefield between the inner and outer perimeter fences. According to the latest Security Department stock audit, the Department possesses five mines, at least three of which were in working order when last inspected. Bjorn gritted his teeth and ran for it. There are times in a man's life when he just has to ride his luck.

Which brought him, breathless but unscathed, to the foot of the inner perimeter fence. This was rather more of a challenge, since it hadn't been installed by the Department but taken over without substantial modification from the chicken farm which had been on the site before the Department requisitioned it. Here Bjorn suffered his first major setback. He tore the right leg of his trousers, about an inch below the knee.

'The thing to remember in this job,' said the Dream-Master General, 'is never to turn your back on small dogs.'

Jane nodded. 'Right,' she said. 'I think I can remember that. And all the rest of it,' she added, 'such as finding the recipient, climbing in through locked and barred windows, all that sort of stuff; I suppose that just comes by light of nature.'

The Dream-Master gave her a disapproving look. 'All right, Miss Clever,' he said, 'we'll come on to the various procedures in due course. We can't run before we can walk, you know. I was just telling you, for your own good, you look out for small dogs.'

'I always have,' Jane replied, with feeling. 'Especially when sitting down in a strange house. Look, I didn't mean to sound cocky, it's just that I want to get on with it. The practical side, I mean.'

The Dream-Master nodded. 'All in good time,' he said. 'Now, first you'll do your basic training. That's effecting entry, recipient identification drill, and elementary brain infiltration. That's the easy part.'

'Um.'

'The tricky part,' the Dream-Master went on, 'is getting out again afterwards.'

Behind the rail of Number Nine observation tower, Trooper 2314 Starspear identified his target and took careful aim. He sighted along the broad barrel, checked that his feet were braced and his arm was high and rigid, breathed deeply in and smoothly out, and . . .

'Unlucky,' observed Trooper 8345 Moonblade. He walked over to the board, pulled out the darts, and placed his feet on the chalk line.

'Double six for game,' he remarked confidently.

At the bottom of the tower, Bjorn paused and unwound ten feet of washing-line from inside his anorak. It was a long time since he'd done anything like this – in fact, the most recent occasion he could remember was when it was his turn to raid the Canteen at Destiny for digestive biscuits – but there are some things you just don't forget. He flexed his fingers and deftly attached the grappling-hook to the line with three superimposed granny-knots.

Far above his head – and below his feet too, for that matter, but let's not confuse the issue – the stars twinkled. A stray photon or so glanced harmlessly off the tines of the hook as he whirled it three times round his head and let fly.

There are, of course, other things that you *do* forget, and the art of throwing grappling-hooks is one of them. After a few minutes of serious thought, Bjorn picked himself up, rubbed the back of his head vigorously, and set about rewinding the rope round his forearm in long, slack loops.

'Double two for game,' said Trooper 8345 Moonblade

grimly. He steadied himself, threw his weight forward on to the front foot in the approved manner, and . . .

. . . And watched incredulously as a big black hook appeared over the rail of the tower, buried one of its talons in the dartboard, and whisked it off the wall and away into the darkness.

Far below, he could just hear a soft thud, followed by a faint cry.

'I think we'll have to call that a draw, Dave,' said Trooper 2314 Starspear, just managing to force the words out of his mouth before the whoop of triumphant relief beat them to it. Seven kreuzers had been riding on the outcome, and he had been on double one for the last six throws.

'Some bastard nicked our dartboard,' replied Trooper 8345 Moonblade furiously. 'Did you see that, Nev? Some bastard just . . .'

There was a whooshing sound, and the hook reappeared, hovered in the air for, say, a two-fiftieth of a second, and fell on to the rail. As it retreated, one of the tines caught and held firm.

'I think there's something in the rules about it,' persevered Trooper 2314 Starspear. 'I think what it actually says is if the dartboard gets eaten by a passing column of soldier ants, but it's the same thing really . . .'

'Nev,' whispered his colleague urgently, 'there's someone climbing up the tower.'

They looked at each other.

'We're being invaded, Dave,' said Trooper 2314 Starspear. 'Look, don't we have to do something, or . . . ?'

Trooper 8345 Moonblade gave him a long stare. 'Yeah,' he said, 'sure we do. We report it.'

Below them they could hear grunts and soft oaths, such as might be made by (for example) a large man climbing painfully up a thin nylon rope without wearing gloves.

'Report it?' repeated Trooper 2314 Starspear. 'You sure? I mean, don't we just, like . . . ?' He pointed to his rifle, which was leaning against the corner of the far rail. His colleague shook his head vigorously, dislodging various items.

'Don't talk bloody soft, Nev, for crying out loud,' whispered Trooper 8345 Moonblade urgently. 'For all we know, if we . . . start anything, it could be a thing. You know, diplomatic implement. We could really be in trouble. Just hold your water, wait till they've gone and report it, right?'

'But.' Inside Trooper 2314 Starspear's head, everyday civilian logic battled with military logic. 'But what if they, like, attack us, Dave?'

Trooper 8345 Moonblade stared past him to the rail, where a large hand was reaching up and scrabbling for a hold. He swallowed hard.

'Use your brain, son,' he hissed. 'We hide, right?'

Breathing hard, Bjorn hauled himself up to chin level, swung a leg over the rail, and flopped on to the floor of the tower. He lay for a few moments where he had fallen, catching his breath and swearing. Then he raised himself on his elbows and looked about him.

Nobody here. Well, he'd guessed that from the fact that he'd got this far without being shot. The odd thing was, though, that the only thing that gave you the impression of the place being deserted was the actual absence of people. Everything else pointed to active occupation; the still-warm mugs of tea, the glowing single-bar electric fire, the two rifles leaning against the rail, the forage caps hung on the radio aerial, the two pairs of shoes visible under the blackout curtain . . .

Bjorn froze for a moment. Then he grinned.

With an easy movement, he removed the grappling hook, transferred it to the opposite rail, and cast the line over the side. Then, with a slight wince and a muffled cry of pain, he hoisted himself over the side, slid down the line, and disappeared. A few moments later, the grappling hook wobbled, came loose and disappeared after him. Then silence.

'Oh look,' said a voice behind the blackout curtain. 'Here's the spare dartboard.'

'Dave . . .'

'That's lucky, isn't it, Nev? You know, thinking about it, I believe you're right. Drawn game.'

'Dave . . .'

'Mugs away, right?' The curtain parted, and Trooper 8345 Moonblade emerged purposefully and hung the dartboard on the hook.

'Dave,' said Trooper 2314 Starspear, 'we'd better notify HQ like you said, before he has a chance to get too . . .'

'I said,' repeated Trooper 8345 Moonblade meaningfully, 'mugs away.' He thrust the darts into his colleague's hands.

'But Dave, there's only one of him and if they start looking now, they'll find him and . . .'

'He'll tell them that two of the Department's crack special forces hid behind a curtain while he legged it over the side and got away.' Trooper 8345 gathered an ample handful of the front of his comrade's battledress lapels and held it for a few significant seconds. 'Look,' he said, letting go. 'You don't want to go around sending off daft messages like that. For a start, nobody'd believe you.'

'They wouldn't?'

Trooper 8345 Moonblade shook his head. 'Nah,' he replied. 'They'd just think you were making things up. Or imagining things, as a result of the nasty blow to your head.'

'But I haven't had a nasty blow to my head, Dave.'

'These things can be arranged, Nev.'

The two men exchanged non-verbal communication for two, maybe three seconds. You can say a lot in three seconds if you don't have to bother with words.

'Right,' said Trooper 2314 Starspear, placing his left foot carefully alongside the chalk line and taking the first dart in his right hand. 'Doubles for in.'

There was, Jane decided, nothing to it.

She turned and frowned at the window, which obligingly slid down and closed itself noiselessly. A sign with her left hand filled the room with a soft green light, imperceptible except through a Messenger's specially treated contact lenses, but more than adequately bright to illuminate the simple operation of dream delivery.

Jane pulled on her rubber gloves; then, with the tip of her extended index finger, she gave the sleeper the very gentlest of prods, just on the point of his shoulder. He made a piggy noise and rolled on to his side, right ear uppermost.

Piece of cake, muttered Jane under her breath. Too easy, surely.

From the black canvas holster slung from her belt she took the long black syringe, broke it open and felt in her hip pocket for the sealed foil capsule which contained the dream. Using her teeth as she'd been taught, she tore the capsule open and tipped its contents into the chamber of the syringe. As they fell through the air into the chamber the green light flashed momentarily on them. Jane nearly dropped the syringe.

For training, naturally, they'd used blanks. This was the first time she'd seen a live dream, and she didn't like the look of it one bit. It lay in the chamber, flashing and squirming. She shuddered.

In the green glow it resembled a transparent sausage, crammed full of little wriggling people and things, coloured lights, explosions and lightning changes of scene. Since the sausage was a mere three inches long, and apparently contained a cast of thousands, the individual items were all rather too small to make out, but the impression they gave in the round, so to speak, wasn't pleasant at all. She wondered for a moment who the recipient was, and what precisely was going to happen to him.

None of her business, she decided firmly. With an easy motion she clicked the syringe shut, flicked off the safety and poised it carefully over the sleeper's ear. Now then, she could feel her lips miming, this isn't going to hurt . . .

Quickly and firmly she shot the plunger home and pulled the syringe smoothly away. The sleeper jerked slightly, moaned and turned over on to his other side. Mission accomplished. Goody.

The sleeper sat bolt upright.

He was, Jane noticed for the first time, wearing a pair of dark purple satin pyjamas with a monogram on the pocket. Any nascent sympathy she might have had for the sleeper soaked quietly away between the floorboards of her mind. A quick glance reassured her that he was still fast asleep, eyes tightly shut, breathing regular.

'*Hey!*' he said.

Jane blinked. She hadn't been told about anything like this.

'*What the hell do you mean, the ides of March? It's the middle of September, and what are ides, anyway?*'

'Um,' Jane replied. The sleeper slept on.

'*That's not an answer,*' he said. '*Look, are you sure you've delivered the right message to the right person here?*'

'I think so,' Jane said. 'I mean, this is 47 Newport Drive, Cardiff, isn't it?'

The sleeper nodded. '*Yes, it is, but this doesn't make sense. I'm expecting a highly important dream about Marshfield*'

Consolidated 9^{1}/$_{2}$% Convertible Unsecured Loan Stock, and you come shoving my ears full of something about bewaring the ides of March. Are you sure you haven't got your wires crossed somewhere?'

'Hold on,' Jane said. She was beginning to feel distinctly uncomfortable. 'Let me just check what it says on the wrapper. Here we are,' she went on, smoothing out the foil and peering at the script. 'Jeremy Lloyd-Perkins, 47 Newport Drive, Cardiff. That's you, isn't it?'

The sleeper nodded slowly, like a puppet with rusty hinges in its neck. *'Sure that's me,'* he said. *'But that's not my message. They must have got them muddled up at the depot.'*

Jane wrinkled her nose. 'You seem to know a lot about this,' she said. 'For a human being, I mean.'

'I've been a subscriber for five years,' the sleeper replied, and Jane noticed how little his lips moved when he spoke. *'I suppose I should be used to it by now. Still, it's a bit poor, if you ask me. Only last month I was expecting a hot tip on the Beaconsfield International rights issue, and all I got was some load of old tosh about concelling my passage on the Lusitania. I don't want to be difficult, but it does make it hard to plan your long-term investment strategy when you can't rely on your supernatural advisers.'*

'Um.'

'Look at it from the other guy's point of view,' continued the sleeper, swaying slightly backwards and forwards. *'I mean, there's some poor sod somewhere who's going to have to face these ides of March things armed with nothing more relevant than an insight into the FT 100 Share Index for 18th September. He might get into serious trouble, you know?'*

'I'm sorry,' Jane said dispiritedly. 'It's not my . . .'

Without moving a millimetre, the sleeper managed to give a remarkably good impression of an impatient gesture. *'That's all very well,'* he said, *'but it's not helping me any, and I don't suppose the unfortunate bastard who sailed on the* Lusitania's *going to be feeling much more cheerful about it either. Even though,*' he added, '*he has the satisfaction of knowing that if only he hadn't drowned he could have cleaned up something rotten in early trading.*'

Jane shrugged. 'I'll mention it to them back at headquarters,' she said. 'But that's all I can do, I'm afraid.'

'*Oh no you don't,*' the sleeper said, and his arm shot out and closed around Jane's wrist. '*You're not going anywhere until I get my dream. And don't try struggling, or I'll wake up.*'

Jane felt her jaw drop, but she couldn't see any point in doing anything about it. When you're stuffed, you're stuffed.

'You're hurting my wrist,' she pointed out.

The sleeper sneered. '*Tell me all about it when I'm awake,*' he replied.

'Be fair,' she pleaded. 'How am I supposed to get you your dream if you won't let me go?'

The sleeper laughed, through nis nose. '*Not my problem,*' he said. '*I'm asleep, remember, I'm not in a position to do your thinking for you. Just get it sorted, or there'll be trouble.*'

'I see,' Jane replied, and there was an edge to her voice you could have shaved with. 'In that case, I'll see what I can do.'

With her free hand, she fished out another foil packet, chosen at random, tore it open and held the capsule in her teeth while she drew the syringe. She loaded it, noting with a certain grim satisfaction the nature of the contents. 'You want another dream, Mr Lloyd-Perkins,' she said. 'Here you go.'

Quick as a flash running for a bus, she drove the plunger home, and the transparent sausage sparkled briefly as it travelled through three centimetres of air. The sleeper jerked violently and let go his grip, and Jane dived for the window, remembering just in time to scowl at it. It opened briskly, apologised as she sailed through it, and snapped shut after her. As she landed lightly on the balls of her feet, she could hear Mr Lloyd-Perkins screaming in his sleep. His own silly fault, she told herself as she switched on the ignition of her starcycle, for trying to take it out on an innocent messenger.

When she was safely clear of Newport Avenue, she pulled up under a street lamp and examined the empty foil packet.

Nostradamus, it read, *Concerning the End of the World*, and below that, in smaller type:

BEST BEFORE: 17th FEBRUARY, 2706

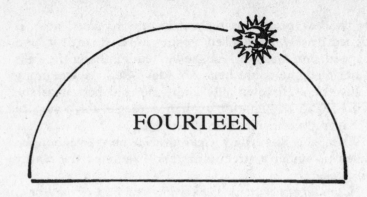

FOURTEEN

P art of Staff's duties was the inspection, on a more or less regular basis, of some of the outlying departments which had no internal review system of their own. He didn't enjoy doing it at the best of times, and Complaints was perhaps his least favourite.

Access to Complaints is, naturally, open to everybody and everything in the universe, regardless of species, metaphysical status or temporal orientation; however, for the sake of internal administrative efficiency, the Department reserves the right only to consider complaints which are submitted in the prescribed form.

The prescribed form is Form C301, a fifteen-page booklet printed on pages of beaten gold, twelve miles long by five miles wide. Once completed, the form must be submitted in triplicate, and the top copy must be countersigned by an apostle, saint (minor Celtic saints excepted), archangel, Bodhisattva, Taoist patriarch, dæmon of Grade 5 or higher, Elector of the Holy Roman Empire or other person of similar standing in the community.

'Hello,' Staff called, pushing against the door with all his weight and heaving. 'Anybody here?'

The door gave way, and Staff staggered, off balance, into the darkened office. He rummaged in his coat pocket for his flashlight and switched it on. This place always gave him the creeps.

'Over here,' said a voice, not very helpfully.

'Where's here?'

'What d'you mean, where's here? *Here.*'

Staff frowned, because the voice was coming from inside his head. 'Look,' he said, 'I've warned you about that already.'

There was a muted plop and Ganger was standing beside him. 'I know,' he said, 'and I'm sorry. It's just that I had to hitch a ride to get past Security.'

Staff nodded. 'Fair enough,' he said. 'So what was so important that it couldn't wait till . . .' The words evaporated on his lips like rain on a blast-furnace as the beam of his torch licked something huge and shiny in the far corner of the room. A part of his brain – the part where most of his thoughts refused to go, except in pairs in broad daylight – said I know what that is. The rest of his brain pretended it hadn't heard.

'I know,' Ganger said. 'A bit of a turn-up, really. Still, there's a first time for everything.'

Staff stopped dead, turned and looked at him.

'You don't mean to say,' he said slowly, 'that somebody has actually . . .'

'Complained, yes.' Ganger nodded. 'Fortunately,' he said, 'it isn't valid.'

The torch-beam flashed on what seemed to be an infinity of gold space, and the photons bounced, and bounced, and bounced. 'It isn't?'

'Nope.'

'Why not?'

'I don't know about you,' replied Ganger, 'but I don't think Colonel Gadaffi falls within the permitted class of counter-signatories. Apart from that, though, it's all in order and according to Hoyle.'

Staff scratched his chin. 'It's a moot point, actually,' he said. 'Anyway, we can leave that to the boys in Legal. Who's it from?'

'That's the puzzling thing,' Ganger replied, fiddling aimlessly with his key-ring. 'Nobody seems to have heard of him. Let's go see if the name rings any bells with you.'

With the help of a turbo-charged golf-buggy which they found in an outhouse, they made the journey across Form C301. Eventually, after taking a wrong turning just after paragraph 658(c)(iv) and running out of petrol on the slopes of the embossed seal, they came to the right place. Ganger put on the handbrake and replaced his sextant in the glove compartment.

'Here we are,' he said. 'Look.'

Staff moved his feet, and saw directly under them the words *Jeremy Lloyd-Perkins*, shallowly engraved in the soft metal.

'Who?'

'Search me,' Ganger replied. 'I tried looking him up on the computer, but of course the blasted thing was down again. I've got my secretary going through the card-index right now.'

Staff knelt down and ran a finger over the scored marks. 'So what's he complaining about?' he said.

'That's what I thought you ought to see,' Ganger replied. 'Come on.'

The draftsman who designed Form C301 had so many questions of an apparently irrelevant but of course strictly necessary nature to ask that the space left on the form for the actual complaint measured eighty millimetres by twenty. Mr Lloyd-Perkins, however, was gifted with small handwriting. Ganger produced a magnifying glass and held the torch while Staff examined the tiny words.

'Um,' he said.

'Exactly,' Ganger replied. 'It's not looking good, is it?'

Staff got up and brushed gold dust from his knees. 'I don't suppose it was her fault, though,' he said. 'You know as well as I do that the sorting office up there is a mess. That's one of the reasons why we sent her there.'

'Sure,' Ganger replied. 'That's not the point, really, is it?'

'It isn't?'

Ganger shook his head, produced a collapsible shooting-stick from his coat pocket, drove its point through the thin gold membrane, and sat down. 'Of course not,' he replied. 'Think about it, will you? Here's a mortal nobody's ever heard of, right? From what he says here, I gather that he's a subscriber to Oracle, for the financial news. In other words, he's got a soul equipped with Teletext, but otherwise he's probably just a small-timer. Okay so far?'

Staff nodded.

'So,' Ganger continued, offering his colleague a peppermint, 'you don't suppose for one minute that he's in a position to know about the complaints procedure. Even if he does, nobody's going to tell me that somebody who lives in a four-bedroom house in the suburbs of Cardiff can afford this much gold just to complain about a garbled message. No, somebody's put him up to it.'

Staff looked up. 'One of us, you mean?'

'Someone in the Service, certainly,' Ganger replied.

'With a view to implicating you and me, you reckon?'

Ganger nodded. 'Smart move,' he said. 'Whoever it was knew there'd have to be an inquiry, and even if she's cleared, it'll still bring the fact that she's a mortal, hired without the authority of a resolution, out into the open. Clever, no?'

Staff nodded, his jaws working slowly and methodically

on the peppermint. 'I'm not very happy about that,' he said.

'Me neither.'

'I think,' Staff continued, his brows lowering, 'that counts as playing silly-buggers, and I don't reckon we should put up with it.' He shook his head. 'No,' he went on, 'that won't do at all. Have you got any idea who . . . ?'

''Fraid not,' Ganger replied, standing up and folding the stick away. 'I'm making discreet enquiries, of course, but that's going to take time. I guess all we can do is be on our guard, and wait and see.'

Staff nodded. 'I suppose,' he said, 'sooner or later whoever it is will want to know why nothing's been done about the complaint. I don't suppose he knows it isn't valid.'

'Maybe not,' Ganger said. 'It could be that this is just intended as a warning, but I don't think so. It's a bit, well, monumental for that.'

'I've seen subtler hints,' Staff agreed, as the light from the torch played over the golden prairie all around them. 'Oh well, thanks for letting me know.'

'My pleasure,' Ganger said, and grinned. 'In the meantime,' he said, 'I suppose I'd better just get this cleared up. You know, put on microfiche.'

Staff nodded. 'Right,' he said. 'And, um, what happens to the original? The hard copy, so to speak?'

Ganger shrugged. 'Oh, I don't know,' he said with slightly exaggerated carelessness. 'Bin it, I suppose, or file it away somewhere. Mustn't let the place get cluttered up with piles of redundant old forms, must we?'

On their way out they were passed by a three-mile-long column of container lorries with an escort of soldiers equipped with axes, shovels and heavy-duty gear. As the lead jeep went by the driver raised his arm and gave Ganger a cheery wave.

'Friend of yours?' Staff asked.

'Never seen him before in my life,' Ganger replied. 'Keep in touch.'

'Hey!'

'What?'

'Over here.'

'Ouch!'

Bjorn stood up, stepped over the recumbent guard and ran swiftly across the short patch of open ground between the guardhouse and the hangar door.

It was a long time since he'd been here last, but he was still taken aback by all this security. The laws of departmental entropy dictated that there should be less security, not more, and that what security there still was shouldn't work. Even in his day, the hangar had been protected from the attentions of intruders by a wooden gate kept shut by a bit of wire looped round the gatepost, and a lifesize cardboard cut-out of an Airedale silhouetted against the sky. Actual guards with rifles and steel helmets (he rubbed the side of his hand vigorously until the circulation started to move again) would have been out of the question. It all went to confirm his earlier impression that something was going on around here. He leaned back into the shadow of the door-frame and, having checked to make sure the coast was clear, he fished in his pocket for his penknife.

Nailfile; no. Corkscrew; no. Tweezers; no. Thing for taking stones out of impalas' hooves; no. Ah, here it was; jemmy.

He extracted the blade, inserted it between the door and the hasp of the padlock, and jerked hard. The blade broke.

Astonished, Bjorn picked himself up off the ground and stared at the lock. Admittedly, you wouldn't normally rely on the metallurgical expertise of the Zambian State Arsenals for anything much more strenuous than opening a letter – an airmail letter, at that – but even so. This padlock was Departmental property. In his experience, a gnat sneezing a mile away should leave it hanging from its shank like a hung-over bat.

His train of thought was derailed by a sound like the Milan rush hour played at full volume on Dolby stereo, and he instinctively ducked. This is serious, he said to himself, covering his ears with his hands. A burglar alarm. A burglar alarm that works.

Something was *definitely* going on around here.

Bjorn burped disgustedly, unslung his axe from behind his back, took two steps backwards and let the padlock have it.

'Ugh,' said a voice behind him; followed by the sound of a man falling over. Bjorn looked over his shoulder, to see a heavily armed trooper lying at his feet, with a dent in his steel helmet you could store linen in, and the head of Bjorn's axe lying on the ground beside him. The padlock, however, was still there. Bjorn frowned, until his forehead resembled the knee of a pair of unfashionably wide cord trousers. This wasn't the usual sort of Department padlock, the sort that you get free at petrol stations if you stop off to ask the way to the M34 and don't buy anything; this was a *padlock*.

'Okay, chummy.' Bjorn could feel something cold and hard in the small of his back. 'Spread 'em, and no funny business.'

He sighed, turned round, picked the trooper up by his lapels, put him in a handily situated dustbin and rammed the lid down hard. Some things, he was relieved to see, didn't change. They may have snazzy new molybdenum steel padlocks; but the sort of men who end up working in Security are still the ones who get chucked out of

Earthquakes because they can't quite make the grade, intellectually speaking.

'Next time,' he said, not entirely unkindly, 'you could try holding the rifle with the bit with the hole in it pointing *away* from you.'

He gave the hangar door a final kick, yelped involuntarily, and trudged off into the darkness.

'Down there,' Jane shouted above the roar of the engine, and pointed. The pilot nodded uneasily.

'I still think . . .' he shouted back.

'Sorry?'

'I said, I still . . .'

'What?'

The pilot scowled. He knew she could hear him, and he was pretty sure she knew he knew. But for the life of him he couldn't think of a way of *proving* she knew he knew she knew. He gave up and decided he'd just fly the plane instead.

'There,' Jane was yelling in his ear, 'just by the big lake, can you see? That's it. Go down lower.'

It's not right, the pilot said to himself. We'll get into trouble. I'll get into trouble. I really shouldn't be doing this.

'Hold her steady,' Jane shouted. 'I'm going to release the rockets *now*.'

It's really down to what's allowed and what isn't, continued the pilot's train of thought – and as trains of thought go, this one's the Sundays-only 06.34 service from Llanelli, stopping at all stations to Neath; because if the pilot had enough brain to half-fill the cap of the average biro, he'd still be cruising at sixty thousand feet, with the intercom switched firmly off – and this has got to be something that isn't. He tried to communicate his anxiety to his passenger.

'Are you *sure* you want me to . . . ?'

'Sorry?'

The pilot swore under his breath and pushed the joystick down. He was going to regret this.

Crown Prince Konstantin of Anhalt-Bernberg-Schwerin, enjoying a pleasant drink beside the pool, saw something rather odd reflected in the plush blue water. He sat up and looked skywards over the rim of his Porsche sunglasses.

'Karl,' he said.

'Highness?' The footman, impeccable as always in the full dress uniform of an Equerry, Second Class, with crossed mulberry leaves and bar, materialised behind him. The prince noticed that he was trying, very hard but in vain, not to giggle.

'Karl,' he went on, running a finger lightly over the sabre scar on his left cheek, 'there is in the sky something not in the ordinary. Are you seeing it also?'

'*Jawohl*, Highness,' relied the footman. 'I am seeing it also.'

'*Sehr gut*,' the Prince replied. You can't be a Prince of the Blood and descended through fifty-nine unbroken generations from Charlemagne without having enough sang-froid to keep champagne chilled in a firestorm. 'For a moment I thought my eyes on me tricks were playing.' He pushed the sunglasses back to the bridge of his nose, said, 'That will be all,' and returned to his ski catalogue.

The footman clicked his heels, retreated soundlessly behind a row of mulberry bushes and collapsed into imperfectly muffled laughter, while overhead high-level winds started the long job of breaking up and dispersing an intricate pattern of vapour trails, which read:

KONSTANTIN VON ROSSFLEISCH YOU'VE HAD YOUR CHIPS

The heavens themselves blaze forth the death of princes; also their births and marriages, their official engagements, the dates of their more important garden parties, and all the rest of the mind-numbingly interesting information that one finds under such bylines as *Court Circular* in the newspapers with the awkwardly big pages.

Royalty are different from you and me. They don't panic. They don't run to and fro like headless chickens just because they get a warning from heaven telling them they're about to die. For example; the last thought that crossed the Prince's mind, about a seventy-fifth of a second before the bomb concealed in the four-foot-high inflatable rubber swan bobbing on the surface of the pool went off, was: How on earth did they manage to do the apostrophe in YOU'VE?

'In fact,' Jane continued, 'I don't see why we can't do the same thing right across the board.'

The Dream-Master General chewed a lump out of his moustache and swallowed it. 'You don't,' he said.

'No.' Jane sat down, uninvited, on the edge of the desk and reached in her bag for her notebook. 'I've been giving it some thought, doing a few outline costings, that sort of thing, and really . . .'

Very few people can say three dots and *really* mean them, but Jane could. The Dream-Master General picked up a heavy rubber stamp reading FRAGILE (for use on the dreams of idealists, naturally) and started to peel the rubber bit off the wooden backing.

'For a start,' Jane continued, 'this personal hand-delivering of everything. That's out. I mean, it's so inefficient it's positively prehistoric. I gather you've got one guy who has to dress up in a red bathrobe once every year and deliver presents to every child in the known world. Have you any idea what that costs you in overtime?'

'You don't feel,' said the Dream-Master, in the tone of voice you'd expect from a volcano with indigestion, 'that it's an essential part of a truly personal service?'

'No. Another thing that's got to be sorted is the sorting. You've got to face up to the fact that what we're dealing with here is messages, not premium bonds. Fair enough?'

'So what,' croaked the Dream-Master, 'do you have in mind?'

'Computerisation,' Jane replied promptly, 'and bar codes. It's very easy once you get the hang of it.'

'I see. In future, everybody's dreams are going to have little patterns of wiggly lines in the bottom right-hand corner, are they?'

'You can disguise them as railings,' Jane said. 'Or stationary zebras, or something like that. All you need is a little imagination.'

'You forgot to tell me,' the Dream-Master observed, 'how we're going to deliver the dreams without roundsmen.'

'Did I?' Jane smiled. 'By fax, of course. Direct instantaneous transmission, brainwave to brainwave. And all during off-peak hours, too. It'll be cheaper, as well as quicker and more confidential.'

'I see.' The Dream-Master leaned forward, with the air of someone playing an ace. 'And what about prodigies?' he demanded sharply.

'Sorry?'

'Prodigies,' the Dream-Master repeated. 'The skies raining blood. Spectral armies fighting in the clouds. Plagues of frogs.'

Jane shook her head. 'They'll just have to go,' she said. 'I mean, as information technology, frogs have had their day. So have plagues of anything.' She paused to examine a cracked fingernail, and then continued: 'You've got to meet the changing needs of the consumer. These days, if you get a plague of anything, people aren't going to go running to the nearest soothsayer. They'll be too busy organising emergency relief rock concerts.' She made an expressive gesture with her hands. 'It all comes down,' she said, 'to cost-effectiveness. Time and motion, if you like. Time, as in not wasting; motion, as in not just going through.'

'Really.'

'Anyway,' Jane said, standing up. 'It'll all be in my report. I expect you'll get your copy in due course.'

The Dream-Master stood up too, and suddenly banged the desk in front of him. 'And just who do you think you are?' he said.

'Easy.' Jane gave him a long, hard look. 'I'm a mortal. Or, if you like to look at it another way, I'm one of the poor bloody customers. The end users. The unfortunate souls who have to use the services all your blasted Departments actually provide. The punters, in other words.'

The Dream-Master grinned. 'Exactly,' he said.

Jane sat down again, put her head slightly on one side and raised an inquisitive eyebrow. 'Please go on,' she said.

'Think about it,' replied the Dream-Master. 'You've got mortals—' He picked up the stapler from his desk-top, moved it six inches to the left and put it down again firmly. 'And on the other hand, you've got us.' He lifted his coffee mug and placed it carefully on top of a pile of petty cash vouchers. 'Understand?'

'No.'

'Then I'll explain. Mortals have it easy. They're born, they lounge about for a few years, whingeing, they die. We have to work here. Mortals—' He pushed the stapler off the desk into the wastepaper basket. 'But we're different. We're for keeps.' He picked up the coffee mug, which a sheet of paper had fastened itself to the bottom of, and then put it down again. 'You want to grasp the fact if you're going to work here.'

'Another thing that's wrong with this Department,' Jane observed after a long pause, 'is the disgraceful waste of perfectly serviceable office equipment.' She picked the stapler out of the bin, dusted it off and put it back on the desk. 'I take it you're not really sympathetic to my proposals?'

'You could say that.'

Jane sighed. 'And you don't think that anybody else will be, either?'

The Dream-Master nodded. 'Let me give you a word of advice,' he said. 'Try and get it into your head that improvements are not necessarily good. In fact,' he added forcefully, 'usually quite the reverse. Remember that and you won't go far wrong.'

'Thank you.'

'I haven't finished yet,' the Dream-Master continued. 'Once upon a time, long ago, there was another bright spark, just like you. Originally worked in this Department, oddly enough. Thought everything around here needed a good shake-up, reckoned we were all far too set in our ways and a thorough pruning would do us all the world of good. Clear out the vested interests and the restrictive practices, start from scratch. That sort of thing.' He sighed. 'It all sounded so good that we tried it, just for a while. Biggest mistake we ever made.'

'Really.'

'Oh yes.' the Dream-Master lolled back in his chair and put his hands behind his head. 'The idea was to create a whole new level of staff to take over the running of the world, look after it, repair it, make sure everything was kept clean and tidy and in good running order. And that's what we did. We recruited them, trained them, and handed over the whole shooting-match. They were called,' the Dream-Master added, almost as an afterthought, 'the human race.'

'Um.'

'Yes,' snapped the Dream-Master, 'um. Bloody silly idea, wasn't it? And you know what happened to the bright spark who suggested it?'

Feeling like the poor fool who's lent her watch to the conjuror, Jane shook her head. 'No,' she said. 'Do tell me.'

A grin like a septic dawn spread over the Dream-Master's face. 'He got posted,' he said.

'Posted?'

The Dream-Master picked up the Fragile stamp, pressed it on an ink-pad and brought it down on the desk-top so hard that it snapped in two.

'Yeah,' he said. 'Posted.'

Jane considered this for a moment. 'Wasn't that rather difficult?' she enquired.

'Nah,' replied the Dream-Master. 'Once we'd got his head through the flap, the rest just sort of followed.'

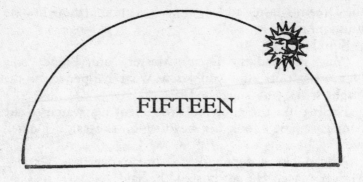

FIFTEEN

'Sod,' said Bjorn. He twisted uncomfortably round, and tried to see what had grabbed hold of his leg. The part of him that still occasionally harboured optimism hoped that it would turn out to be a smiling blonde air hostess.

It was, in fact, a man-trap. Close, but no cigar.

A fairly humane man-trap, it has to be said. The jaws weren't lined with inch-long steel spikes; in fact, they were padded with foam rubber and covered with chamois leather. There was also a notice, probably insisted upon by the Administration's hyper-paranoid legal advisers, engraved in tiny letters on the trap's upper mandible. It read:

CAUTION: THIS TRAP MAY BE DANGEROUS TO ELDERLY OR DISABLED PERSONS. MEMBERS OF THE PUBLIC ARE ADVISED THAT THEY GET CAUGHT IN IT ENTIRELY AT THEIR OWN RISK.

Bjorn grunted and tried prising the jaws apart with what was left of his axe. There was, of course, a man-trap-opening attachment on his Zambian Army Knife, but he'd broken that a day or so ago trying to cut into a pat of hot butter.

Overhead, the beams of many searchlights were producing a complex and geometrically satisfying display which, combined with the blaring of sirens and the thundering noise of many speakers playing back tapes of barking Rottweilers, added up to one of the most original *son et lumière* performances in cosmic history. You had to be there, of course.

Bjorn was, and wished he wasn't. The axe handle, seasoned hickory, groaned accusingly and splintered without shifting the jaws of the trap at all. The torches waving about in the distance wouldn't be in the distance for very much longer. What to do?

'Gotcha!'

A light shined straight into Bjorn's eyes, and he automatically shied away from it, raising his hands to shield his eyes. He had enough problems as it was, he felt, without having great big blobs of yellow custard cluttering up his retina for the next five minutes.

'All right, chummy,' said a voice from behind the light source. 'Throw down the gun. Easy, now.'

Bjorn sighed. It was going to be one of those nights, he could tell.

'How?' he said. 'I haven't got one.'

The torch-beam didn't blink exactly; but there was a sort of sympathetic modulation in the flow of photons as its owner registered surprise.

'But you're a dangerous intruder,' he said.

'Yeah,' Bjorn replied sourly. 'Looks like it, doesn't it?'

The torch came closer. 'So what are you armed with, then?' the trooper enquired curiously. 'Bombs? Gas grenades? Flamethrower?'

'No.'

The torch-beam wavered again. 'Don't believe you,' said the voice behind it. 'Come on, you've got to be armed with *something*. Nobody breaks into a high-security compound without something.'

Bjorn considered. 'I've got a bust penknife, a broken axe-handle and a pair of socks,' he said. 'Now, could you see your way to getting this fucking thing off my leg before it stops my circulation completely, please?'

The trooper hosed Bjorn down with the torch from head to foot, shrugged, and came closer. When he was within arm's length, Bjorn reached out, pulled his feet out from under him, and knocked him silly with the rim of his own steel helmet. Then he grabbed the man's rifle, and used its barrel to force apart the jaws of the trap. It wasn't easy even then; by the time he'd finished, he was holding the only rifle in the cosmos capable of shooting directly behind the person firing it. Essential equipment for self-defence in the corporate jungle.

Pausing only to stuff the socks in the recumbent trooper's mouth and steal his packed lunch, Bjorn jumped to his feet, winced, and ran off into the darkness. Behind him, very close now, he could hear the blood-curdling baying of quadrophonic Dolby hounds, with the occasional crackle.

Something materialised in front of his face and he ran straight into it. If the way he rebounded like a tennis ball and sat down with sparks coming out of his ears was anything to go by, it was quite possibly an electric fence. He forced himself to stop vibrating, picked a handful of spent volts out of his eyebrows and blinked four times. This was heavy stuff. Whatever it was they'd got in that shed, they didn't want anybody else to know about it. Which was odd, considering that it was hoisted up into the sky every morning where everybody on earth could see it.

'Psst.'

Bjorn lifted his head, spat out an amp and peered into the darkness.

'Over here.'

'Why?' Bjorn enquired.

The darkness hesitated. 'Look,' it hissed, 'do you want to be rescued or not?'

'Depends,' Bjorn replied. 'Who are you?'

'Dop sent me.'

'Oh.' Suddenly, a great light dawned in Bjorn's mind; figuratively speaking, of course. Otherwise, light would have seeped out through his ears and given the troopers something to shoot at. 'Oh, right. Coming.'

'This way,' hissed the voice. From the way it expressed itself exclusively in whispers and hisses, it was either the tutelary spirit of a cracked gas-main or a chatty snake. But if it was a friend of Dop's, that didn't really matter much.

Dop was the sort of bloke you could really trust.

From where Jane was sitting, wearing the great halo of noise and vibration like a hair-dryer, it looked like a giant millipede in dayglo socks. The more you looked at it, the less you actually made out. Everything just seemed to melt into a continuum of twinkling red and white light.

She switched on the intercom. 'It's very pretty,' she said. 'What is it?'

The pilot's laugh bounced around inside her headphones. 'It's the main stretch of the Renaissance bypass, between junctions 16 and 17,' he replied. 'Want to take a closer look?'

'Okay,' Jane replied, and the helicopter slowly lost height. As they closed in, the continuum became marginally less continuous. It looked less like a fibre-optic cable with indigestion and more like the pattern of millions of tiny dots of light, each close behind the other, each moving so slowly that you had to stare quite hard to perceive any motion at all.

'Fine,' Jane said. 'It's a traffic jam.'

'Almost,' the pilot replied, 'but not quite. Going in closer.'

Lower still, and the millions of tiny dots broke up into vague but distinct shapes, like a newspaper photograph under an extremely powerful magnifying glass. They reminded Jane of something – cars, to be precise, and lorries and motorcycles and vans – but it was only a similarity. They were palpably vehicles, but there the resemblance ended.

'What are those things?' Jane asked.

'Lives,' the pilot replied. 'No, that's not strictly true. If we're going to be all technical and correct, they're presents.'

'Presents?'

'That's right. And before you ask where's the wrapping paper and cards, I mean presents as opposed to pasts and futures. Okay?'

Jane frowned. 'I don't think I . . .'

'Well you wouldn't, would you?' the pilot replied. 'I mean, you're down there somewhere. Part of you is, anyway.'

'Um.'

So low now that each individual thing was plainly distinguishable from the mass, even if it didn't look at all like anything Jane had ever seen before. Try and imagine one of those old Heinkel bubble-cars that's suddenly come to life, and you may be able to creep into the corner of the same frame of reference.

'See the sign up ahead?' said the pilot. 'There's a clue for you.'

Jane peered forward. Despite the pitch darkness above

her, she could see reasonably well at ground level, thanks to the lights of the things. There was indeed a sign; very much like a road-sign.

'I can't quite . . .'

And then she could. It was an awkward moment. It read:

DEPARTMENT OF TIME
T49 CREATION-DOOMSDAY EXPRESSWAY;
RENAISSANCE BY-PASS NOW OPEN
ANOTHER CENTURY COMPLETED: AHEAD OF SCHEDULE
BY ELEY TIMESTONE PLC

At Jane's request, the helicopter climbed higher, until the continuum reappeared and the individual lights merged once more with the general flow.

'That's one of the good bits,' the pilot was saying. 'It's the bit they show in the reports. Further on, where the whole bloody thing's falling to pieces, it's not so pretty.'

'Um.'

'It's supposed,' the pilot continued, 'to be, like, continuous. Time, like an ever-rolling stream, and so forth. That's the theory.'

Jane swallowed hard, and tried to fool herself into believing that the heaving in her stomach was something to do with the way the helicopter was rocking about in the thermals. 'I see,' she lied.

'Doesn't work like that, of course,' the pilot went on remorselessly. 'I mean, it's becoming a joke. If it's not a whole carriageway coned off because they're repairing the membrane of the space-time continuum, then it's resurfacing; which means contraflows, of course.'

'Contraflows,' Jane repeated.

'Bloody horrible things,' the pilot said, nodding. 'Just up there, between junctions 19 and 20, they've rerouted

all five lanes of the Pastbound carriageway on to the hard
shoulder of the Futurebound, and they expect it to work.'
The pilot took one hand off the joystick, felt in his pocket,
and found a stick of chewing gum. 'No wonder you get
hold-ups,' he said.

'Hold-ups,' Jane said. 'In Time.'

'It can be a real bummer,' the pilot agreed. 'Not to
mention the confusion. I mean, there you are, quietly
edging your way through the first few decades of the
sixteenth century, and you look over your shoulder and
see all these blokes in bomber jackets and flared jeans
and Status Quo T-shirts zipping along past you on the
inside. I'm not at all surprised some of them freak out
and try and cut across the lanes.' A red light flicked on
just below the fuel gauge and started to flash alarmingly.
The pilot put his fingers in his mouth, and then reached
out and put a blob of chewing gum over it. 'I haven't the
foggiest what that light's for,' he commented. 'In the
manual it just says "Emergency".'

Jane opened her eyes – somehow or other they had
come to be shut – and nerved herself to look down. It
was like . . . Hell; there was no point her trying to fool
herself with similes. Now that she actually knew what it
was, there didn't really seem much to be gained from
trying to compare it with something it wasn't.

'But the hold-ups,' she repeated doggedly. 'In *Time*.'

The pilot chuckled. 'I bet you thought Time always
travelled at the same speed,' he said. 'Well, now you know.'

Jane felt her jaw sag, as if someone had cunningly
managed to whip all the bone out of it without her feeling
a thing. 'It doesn't?' she said.

'Course not,' the pilot replied. 'I mean, it's supposed
to, sure; that's what the speed limits are for. But does
anybody take any notice? Do they hell as like. And they
call that progress!'

Jane tried thinking about that one, but her brain wouldn't bite on it. 'Do you mean it used to be different before?' she hazarded.

'No,' the pilot said. 'They call it progress. That's the word they use for it. Or sometimes they call it innovation, or the relentless force of socio-political development. What they mean by that is, some flash bugger in a souped-up cafe racer doing a ton down the outside lane. It doesn't half screw things up when that happens, I can tell you.'

'Er.'

'That's if he's on the Pastbound carriageway,' the pilot added conversationally, 'because then he's going from the future into the past. If he's on the other side of the road, of course, he's a rabid reactionary trying to turn the clock back. Either way, if he gets done he loses his licence automatically, and a bloody good thing too.'

The calm, unflappable part of Jane's mind sorted out the words necessary for her to ask the pilot to confirm that it was possible for people to travel from the future into the past. The rest of her mind switched off the lights, locked up and went for a coffee. She closed her eyes, but it didn't seem to help.

'Can we get this straight?' Jane asked. 'There's people going from the past to the future, yes. I can handle that, I think. But people going from the future to the . . .'

The pilot turned his head and gave her a funny look. 'Yes?' he said.

'I'm sorry,' Jane replied, feeling rather as if she had a wet sock in her mouth. 'Is that possible?'

'It's more than possible,' the pilot said. 'It's absolutely essential. Can you imagine the mess you'd have up the top end if they didn't?'

Jane said nothing. The wet sock had become the last sock of all, the one you find wedged in a crevice in the back of the drum of the washing-machine three days after you did the actual wash. The pilot seemed to sense the difficulty she was having, for he changed his tone of voice down a gear and spoke a little more slowly.

'Look,' he said, 'you're a mortal, right, you've got all that blood stuff sloshing about inside you. Think what would happen if all the blood only went in one direction. You'd get a sodding great build-up in your feet, and the rest of you would . . . Well, anyway, think of it like that, if you can. Presents circulate in the same way. If they didn't, the past would go to sleep. You'd have pins and needles right up your racial collective subconscious. See what I mean?'

'You mean,' Jane replied, with extreme caution, 'that people keep going round and round in circles? For ever and ever?'

The pilot scratched his nose with the heel of his hand. 'Well,' he said, 'I suppose you could put it like that. It's more your classic river analogy, really, but I didn't want to explain it that way because it's such an awful cliche. You've got your river, right?'

'Which river?'

'Oh, any river. Rain falls in the mountains, it collects and runs across the plain in a river to the sea, the sea evaporates and falls as rain on the mountains. Now do you see?'

'No.'

'Fair enough.' The pilot's voice seemed very far away, somehow; or perhaps it was very long ago rather than very far away. 'Anyway,' he said, 'I gather that you're going to help us sort it all out. I bloody well hope so,' he added. 'It needs it.'

It's impossible to explain the operation of Time simply, especially if you're trying to fly a helicopter as well. Attempting to understand the way it works purely from a verbal description is like learning to play Mah Jong without a Mah Jong set. It can't be done.

Instead, look back down the carriageway to a point where the two streams of light eventually merge into one, then zoom in close and stare. This is Time, coming into operation . . .

. . . On a day when it's really slashing down, with the mud bubbling up around the ankles of the extremely self-conscious party of worthies in sodden grey suits and yellow plastic hard hats, standing around a length of damp pink ribbon stretched half-heartedly across the shining tarmac.

'. . . Gives me very great pleasure,' Staff is saying, as the rain drips off the peak of his hat on to his tie, 'to declare this astro-temporal expressway well and truly open.'

He reaches for the pair of scissors on the velvet cushion; and as his fingers make contact, he's making a very quick assessment of the whole idea, and thinking: Yes, but . . .

He's thinking: Okay, the old system worked, but that's not to say it's going to go on working, what with the vast increase in Time use expected in the next five million years. It's got to make sense to do it this way. Join it at the Big Bang, and then straight through to the other end without having to stop for anything. Absolutely no risk of anybody getting lost in the Industrial Revolution, or taking the wrong turning at the Fall of Constantinople.

And so he cuts the tape. And in that fraction of a second between the two blades of the scissors meeting, and the severed ends of the tape falling away, he thinks: Well, we all make mistakes.

Because, before they built the expressway, it worked. It shouldn't have, of course. It should have been absolute *chaos*.

Instead of a straight line joining the two ends of the universe, there was a maze of single carriageways and winding little lanes, creeping on its tortuous way from one crucial event to the next, completely haphazard, unco-ordinated and unplanned; rather like history itself. The traveller had to get off the ferry, thread his way through the back alleys of prehistory to get on to the Neolithic ring-road, pootle round that to the big roundabout on the outskirts of the Bronze Age, take the second turning on the left (otherwise he'd find himself evolving back into an ape) for the long drag across a thousand years of flat, boring timeways with no chance of overtaking until he got on to the downhill straight into the Roman Empire. Then he'd be faced with the sheer hell of cutting across the city traffic (you know what the traffic's like in Rome these days; well, it's actually improved out of all recog-nition) before taking the last exit for the gearbox-numbing journey through the Middle Ages – uphill all the way, stuck behind a succession of slow-moving ecclesiastical Long Vehicles – only to find himself confronted with the brain-twisting complexity of the sixteenth-century flyover network . . .

Anything's got to be better than that.

Wrong.

So wrong, in fact, that after the first of the disastrous multiple pile-ups on the Futurebound carriageway of the T7 there was a full inter-departmental inquiry. Needless to say, it never actually published any findings; but it leaked like a six-month-old torch battery, and the unauth-orised disclosures made alarming reading.

For a start, because the route was now so straight, everyone was travelling far too fast. Apart from the drast-ically increased risk of collisions, this meant that travellers were getting from one end of the universe to the other in at least half the time, often less; with the result that at the other end (where they have this really *amazing* set of traffic lights) the size and mass of the tailback was threatening to destabilise the equilibrium of eternity, quite apart from there only being three operational toilets in the cafe in the last lay-by. Unless something was done, there was going to be trouble.

So, very reluctantly, the Administration decided that there was nothing for it but to send the whole lot of them back the way they'd come . . .

The idea wasn't intrinsically bad. Instead of everyone trying to squash through the exit gates at once, there would be a filter system; any travellers who couldn't get through would be sent back round in a gigantic loop down the Pastbound carriageway to the start, and then they'd return back up the Futurebound side and have another shot at getting through the gates. It was a sort of holding-pattern, with presents circling in the system until they got clearance to leave.

What with the panic of getting the Pastbound carriageways built before the fabric of space and time got seriously bent, nobody had the leisure to think the project through; with the result that the awful consequences of having the same traveller driving along the same route two or three times *at the same time* – in two or three different instalments, if you like – weren't appreciated until it was too late. Reports of travellers on their second circuit driving too fast on the outside lane and running into the back of themselves still on their first circuit came as a complete and horribly unwelcome surprise. The difficulties over the insurance claims alone were enough to put a permanent kink in causality.

Each attempted solution led to further and worse problems. The idea of a speed limit was one of the least inspired; the sort of travellers who obeyed the speed limit were the sort who were already causing havoc by dawdling along on the inside – still faffing about in the Reformation when they should have been the other side of Napoleon, for example – while the tearaway element who were causing the problems simply ignored it. Putting sleeping policemen across the carriageway at notorious temporal blackspots did no good at all, particularly when the policemen started waking up.

Meanwhile, what with everyone driving round the system two, three or even four times more than originally intended, the carriageways themselves began to crack up. The tarmac simply couldn't stand it. Extensive frost damage along the entire length of the Ice Age didn't exactly help, and it wasn't long before, at any one time, up to a third of the entire system was coned off for repair, causing the worst problems yet. Discontented travellers began making their own unofficial exits off the expressway back on to the old, disused network of lanes and byways, with the result that they got to the Exit long before anybody else, themselves included. As a panic measure, the Administration introduced a number of diversions to get the traffic moving again, which meant that any number of crucial moments in history turned out not to have happened at all. The Trojan War, the reign of King Arthur, the golden age of English cricket all suddenly ceased ever to have existed, with side-effects that defied calculation.

One rather sad knock-on effect of all this was that Staff foresaw the whole ghastly mess just as he cut through the ceremonial ribbon. It would perhaps have been some consolation for him to know that the problem had already been solved, if it wasn't for the fact that the solution was destined to be held up in a contraflow on the T93 on the outskirts of Agincourt, finally arriving too late to be of any relevance, and being swept back into the stream of traffic.

The only person who derived any benefit at all from

the whole fiasco was the Flying Dutchman; who sold his ship, bought a set of spanners and a small yellow van, and is now doing a roaring trade as a breakdown service.

Staff closed the door and threw his raincoat over the back of a chair. It had been a long day.

Senior members of the Administration are expected to live close to the central office complex. Unless they're extremely lucky (like Ganger, for example, who was able to wangle a long lease of a houseboat moored on the left bank of the Styx) this means a tiny little flat in one of the five labyrinthine complexes that were built on the site of the old dockyards. For your premium of a billion kreuzers and your fifty thousand kreuzers a year ground rent and service charge, you get windows that don't open, lifts that don't work and condensation you could swim in. There are no roof-gardens or window-boxes, but if you have a horticultural streak there's always the mould on the curtains.

On the doormat there were three envelopes. Staff picked them up, poured himself a stiff shot of distilled water, and sat down in the one chair that space permitted in his living-room.

The first letter was junk mail from the United Perpetual Bank, offering him a discount on eternal life insurance and a credit card supposedly accepted by five million religions cosmos-wide. For an extra sixty thousand kreuzers a month, the United Perpetual people would be delighted to allow him to participate in their Special Select Reserve pension fund, which was guaranteed tax free owing to its registered office being situated in the Eye of the Beholder. If his application form was received within seven days, they'd even give him a free radio alarm clock.

The second letter was from the compilers of a publication called *Truly Important People of Yesterday*, and he was warmly invited to complete the enclosed personal biographical questionnaire in order that his biography could be included in the next edition, along with 190 million other truly important people who the publishers reckoned were good for the two thousand kreuzers they were charging per copy. He binned that one, too.

The third one he had saved until last, because it looked important. For a start, the address was hand-written, and his name was spelt right. He slipped his finger under the flap and pulled, and a moment later Ganger jumped out, landed heavily on all fours on the carpet and sat up, massaging his neck.

'Before you say anything,' he said, 'no, I don't think I'm getting paranoid about making sure we aren't seen together. Maybe I'm a touch overcautious, but there's no point in taking silly risks.'

Staff frowned. Entrusting oneself to the local postal system, which had the tendency to send all letters to a distant galaxy on principle, seemed to him to be the silliest risk going.

'Now you're here,' he said, 'can we get on with it? Only I've got a lot of ironing to catch up on, and . . .'

Ganger stared at him incredulously. 'Ironing?'

Staff flushed. 'Yes,' he snapped, 'ironing. And there's the kitchen floor to wash.'

From where he was sitting, Ganger could see the kitchen, and it struck him that it was so small that you could clean it very quickly just by spilling your drink. He confined himself to raising an eyebrow.

'Okay,' he said. 'I'll cut away to the main frame, shall I? It's vitally important to the entire future of the cosmos that we go for a pizza.'

Staff blinked. 'I see,' he said. 'Vitally important.'

'Vitally.'

'Who's paying?'

'I am.'

A smile like – well, in the circumstances, *not* like the sun emerging from behind a cloud; like something equally life-enhancing but without the overtones – flicked across Staff's face and earthed itself in his collar.

'Done with you,' he said.

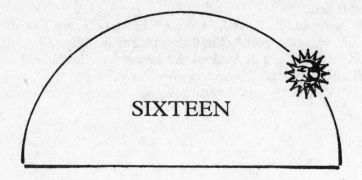

SIXTEEN

'Look,' said Bjorn, stopping suddenly and placing a shovelsized arm on his guide's sleeve, 'where is this?' There was a faint crackle and Bjorn hastily removed his hand. It was tingling painfully.

The guide pointed down the tunnel. 'Look,' he replied.

For the record, the guide was a small, hunched entity entirely wrapped up in what looked like an oversized monk's habit. In fact the costume was so voluminous that Bjorn had to take his own word for it that there was anyone in there at all.

'Where?' he said.

'There,' the guide replied. 'My name's Tzzx, by the way.'

'Sorry?'

'Tzzx.'

'I thought that's what you said.'

Bjorn's eye followed the line of the pointing sleeve and lit upon a sign nailed to the wall. By the dim ambient light – it gave Bjorn a really nasty shock when he realised that it was coming from inside Tzzx's cowl – he could just about read what it said.

It said:

PICCADILLY CIRCUS

It also said:

TIMES SQUARE

and

PLACE DE LA CONCORDE

and something else in cyrillic lettering, and something else in Chinese, neither of which Bjorn could read. To make matters worse, it said them all at the same time.

'Um,' Bjorn said. Tzzx chuckled, and a few blue sparks floated out from under his robe.

'I know,' he replied, and Bjorn noticed that he didn't so much speak as crackle. 'Confusing, isn't it? And now we'd better be getting on, or we won't miss the train.'

'Do we want to miss the train?' Bjorn enquired.

'Well,' Tzzx replied, 'since it'll be coming down this tunnel at approximately fifty-five miles an hour, I think it'd be sensible.'

Tzzx scuttled away up the tunnel, moving amazingly quickly, and Bjorn followed him. For someone who was completely swathed in ill-fitting brown sackcloth and had no perceptible legs, Tzzx had a fair turn of speed; and the way he managed to avoid treading on his own hem was little short of miraculous.

'We're in the subway,' Tzzx was saying. 'I thought it'd be quicker than walking.'

'We are walking,' Bjorn pointed out. 'Running, even.'

'Yes,' replied Tzzx, and Bjorn noticed that the gap between them was widening, even though he had broken into a jog, 'but we're walking in the subway. Makes a difference, you see.'

'Does it?'

'Naturally. Ah, here we are.'

The ceiling lifted and the walls became wider apart. On the left-hand side, Bjorn could see a platform, about two feet higher than the floor of the tunnel. It looked remarkably like a platform in a station on the Paris Metro.

'If you like,' Tzzx called out, 'we can take a train the rest of the way.'

Bjorn clambered up on to the platform and sat down beside the cowled figure on a bench. It took him several minutes to catch his breath.

'I bet you don't know how the subway works,' Tzzx said.

'You like betting on certainties, I can tell.'

Tzzx laughed again. Funny sound, Bjorn thought; like the noise you get when you accidentally put something metal in a microwave and switch on.

'The subway,' Tzzx said, 'is an urban short-haul passenger transport network, designed to take the load off congested surface routes in peak time.'

'Really,' Bjorn replied. 'You amaze me.'

A fat green spark floated out from under the cowl, drifted in the air for a few seconds, and vanished. 'All right,' said Tzzx, 'if you don't want to know . . .'

'Sorry,' Bjorn said. 'But I knew all that bit already. I've been on subways hundreds of times. But not this one.'

'There's only one,' Tzzx replied. 'Ah, here's the train.'

Sure enough, a tube train pulled into the station and opened its doors. Bjorn frowned. It was unmistakably a tube train. In fact, that was what was getting to him: it was the most quintessential tube train he'd ever seen.

'Come on,' Tzzx said. They climbed in and sat down. The compartment was empty, apart from a half-empty carton of pasteurised milk, which got up in a marked manner and moved right down to the other end.

'Milk doesn't like me,' sighed Tzzx. 'It thinks I turn it sour.'

'How do you mean, there's only one?' Bjorn said. As he spoke, he realised what his subconscious had been driving at. The compartment they were sitting in was every underground railway carriage he'd ever been in: in New York, Paris, Moscow, London, anywhere. All at the same time.

'Exactly that,' Tzzx replied. 'There is only one network. They just call it different things in different places.'

'Um.'

The train rattled away out of the station and into a dark tunnel. Bjorn surreptitiously fingered his penknife in his trouser pocket and tried to locate the two-handed claymore attachment by touch.

'It's a whole different dimension down here,' Tzzx went on. 'It really amazes me how few people notice. You'd have thought it'd have been obvious.'

'Should it?' No, that was the little plastic magnifying glass you couldn't actually see through. That's the scissors which will just about cut sellotape three times out of seven. And – ouch – that's the nail file.

'Think about it,' Tzzx replied. 'Name me a subway station.'

Bjorn considered. 'Oxford Circus.'

The cowl nodded. 'A classic example,' Tzzx said, shooing away a small steel bolt which had unscrewed itself from somewhere and was now buzzing round his head like a lovesick moth. 'Has it ever occurred to you that by the time you've gone down the escalator and trudged along all those miles of corridor to get on to the right platform for the Central Line, you've really walked a damn sight further than the actual distance between Oxford

Circus and Bond Street. And it still takes three minutes to get from Oxford Circus station to Bond Street station in the train once you get on it. True or false?'

Bjorn thought hard. 'Um,' he said.

'It's because of the dimensional shift, you see,' Tzzx explained. 'In this dimension, all the destinations are exactly the same distance from each other, and you travel—' He hesitated, crackled like a car radio under a power cable, and continued: 'Well, it's like at right angles to sideways, I guess. Or, more accurately, at an angle of 450 degrees to the vertical.'

Bjorn relaxed. When you are trapped in a strange dimension with a weird shapeless stranger in a cowl who gibbers to you about mathematics, there's nothing like finding a ten-inch length of copper piping filled with lead at the bottom of your knapsack. Bjorn wasn't a hundred per cent certain where it had come from, but he was very glad it was there. He wrapped a hand round it gratefully.

'Okay,' he said. 'Suppose you're right, how come you don't get on the train at Les Invalides and find the next stop's Tottenham Court Road?'

Under the cowl, a blue light glowed smugly. 'Easy,' said Tzzx. 'Nothing ever exists in just one dimension. When you get on the train, usually you're also in the dimension of Time, and a whole lot of other ones which we needn't bother with right now. They restrain you from getting outside the matrix. It's like a sort of seat-belt or something.'

In the sorting-office of his mind, Bjorn picked out the word in Tzzx's last statement that had triggered off the alarm system in his pineal gland. It was 'usually'.

'Right now, though,' Tzzx went on, 'we're sort of free-floating outside all the regular dimensions. If you're interested, the three we're in are Metro, Fear and

Bureaucracy. And if you hit me with that copper pipe, it'll be the worse for you.'

Bjorn tightened his knuckles around the pipe. There are times when it's appropriate to believe what you're told, and times when you hit people.

'You sure Dop sent you?' he asked.

'Ah.' Tzzx threw back his cowl and – this is a very approximate and inaccurate description of a profoundly complex operation – rolled up his sleeves. There was nothing to be seen but a fountain of blue and red sparks. 'I was having you on there, I'm afraid.'

Bjorn nodded, raised the pipe above his head and lashed out at the centre of the cloud of sparks with all his strength. There was a loud bang; then it started to rain molten copper.

'I was telling the truth about trying to hit me, though,' said a voice in the centre of Bjorn's brain. Then there was nothing except the rush of a few million particles being dragged apart and sucked away into an infinite vacuum.

Of the many results of this, the least significant was that an old lady living in a converted railway carriage somewhere in Nebraska received an electricity bill for eight million, three hundred thousand and thirty-six dollars, fifteen cents; which puzzled her. As she explained to her nephew, it wasn't the size of the bill so much as the fact that she'd only just paid the last one.

The forecourt of the offices of the Department of Time is about the only place in the entire Administration complex where you can ever have a hope of parking, and even then, you have to know the ropes.

What you do is this. Before you leave to go there, you phone Gerald, the doorman, and ask him to preserve a place for you. It's vitally important that you get the verb right. If in doubt, spell it for him; because if he just

202 • Tom Holt

*re*serves you a place, then by the time you get to park,
your vehicle will long since have fallen apart under the
normal pressures of entropy. *Pre*serving is different; it
involves using the Department's special relationship with
time to backdate your reservation a couple of centuries
or so. One final word of advice; it's well worth slipping
Gerald a minimum of fifteen kreuzers once you've parked,
unless you want to come back from your meeting to find
that your vehicle has been valet-parked a couple of
centuries away, probably in a stable and boxed in by ox-
carts.

'Thanks, Gerald,' Ganger therefore said, and there was
a clink of money changing hands. 'And do you think you
could get us a taxi?'

'No sweat, boss,' Gerald replied, and winked. 'When
were you wanting it for?'

(Please note Gerald's extremely careful choice of verb
tense; it doesn't do to be grammatically imprecise around
Gerald. The senior executive officer who once told him
'Call me any time you're ready' was forced to retire early
with critical tinnitus, because Gerald is ready pretty well
all of the time, and has been most of his life . . .)

'In about half an hour's time,' Ganger replied. 'In the
future,' he added quickly. 'Okay?'

In fact, there are a great many things about the
Department of Time which require extreme caution until
you're used to how they work. You need a postgraduate
degree in temporal theory just to walk through the
revolving door if you want to come out in the same
century you entered. This explains why Ganger and Staff
went in via the coal shute.

They found Jane sitting on her own in a large office,
behind a desk you could have played football on, hunched
over a thick pile of papers, a calculator and a six-handed
clock. She looked up as they walked in and frowned.

'Hello,' she said. 'You're late.'

Staff did a quick but violent double-take; Ganger merely smiled.

'I forgot,' he said. 'We should have known that you'd have seen today's rushes yesterday. Were we held up in traffic?'

Jane nodded. 'It's the one good thing about the old system,' she said. 'You can always take an advance look at what unforseen things are going to happen in the next few days. Gives you a chance to know what not to expect. Encourages sloppy planning, though.'

Ganger took his usual seat on the edge of the desk, noticing as he did so that the papers which covered the rest of it to a depth of six inches had been specially cleared away for him. Nice touch. 'Any progress so far?' he asked.

Jane shrugged. 'Depends,' she said. 'That's the tiresome thing about the whole set-up, really.' She sighed. 'For instance,' she went on, 'I finally managed to persuade the personnel people to try out some new staff rosters. Nobody liked the sound of them at first, but we negotiated a bit, and finally everyone agreed to give them a month's trial, starting on the twentieth.'

Staff nodded. 'Well done you,' he said. 'So where's the problem?'

'The problem,' Jane replied wryly, 'is that out there on the shop floor, it's been the nineteenth for the last three days. The same twenty-four hours, over and over again. I think it's called working to rule.'

Ganger clicked his tongue sympathetically. 'Never mind,' he said, 'it was a nice try. Come on, let's go and have some lunch. I thought we might try . . .'

'I know,' Jane interrupted. 'I booked us a table.'

'I recommend the veal,' Ganger said judicially, his finger traversing the menu. 'They do a very . . .'

'No thanks,' Jane replied. 'I didn't like it. There was too much tarragon, or something like that. I think I'll just have spaghetti.'

Staff looked up, with an artificially neutral expression on his face. 'What did I have?' he said.

'Scampi,' Jane replied, without looking up. 'It was cold, but you didn't want to make a fuss and send it back.'

'Thanks,' Staff said quietly. 'In that case, I'll try the osso bucco.'

'In fact.' Ganger leaned forward and pushed the menu aside from in front of Jane's face. 'In fact,' he said, 'there's not much point in us having this meeting, since you already know everything we said.'

Jane shrugged. 'Well,' she replied, 'I may, but you don't. I can tell you, though, it was a complete waste of . . . a complete wash-out,' she corrected herself. 'We didn't achieve anything.'

Ganger exchanged glances with Staff, and grinned. 'I know,' he said. 'Smart move, huh?'

Jane looked at him blankly. 'I beg your pardon?' she said.

'Think.' Ganger leaned back and snapped a breadstick. 'This meeting's already taken place, right? Nothing can change that, sure, but that doesn't mean to say you've still got to go through with having the veal. You can have something nice instead. True?'

'Well . . .'

'Likewise,' he continued, after he'd cleared his throat of bread shrapnel, 'we don't *have* to reach the same depressing conclusions I gather we're going to reach in what I would call the Authorised Version. Do you follow me?'

Jane bit her lip thoughtfully. 'Well,' she said, 'I certainly don't remember you saying that. You mean . . .'

'Exactly.' Ganger smiled. 'The first version is strictly

for the cameras. You realise that we were all under surveillance, of course.'

'Were we?' Jane asked. 'Or rather, are we?'

'Definitely.' Ganger unfolded his napkin and tucked a corner of it behind the knot of his tie. 'But the version the cameras will see is the Authorised Version. This one's one hundred per cent off the record.'

'It'll never have taken place, you see,' Staff broke in. 'So we can say what we like without fear of being overheard. It was his idea,' he added generously. 'This fellow here's got a brain like a pinball machine, but it does come in handy when the going gets devious.'

'I see,' Jane said, and in doing so told the truth. In exactly the same way, she could see a whole page of Chinese without understanding a word of it. 'So, what do we talk about?'

Staff poured himself a glass of mineral water, examined it carefully to make sure it was still there, and drank it. 'We felt it was time we sort of took stock,' he said gravely. 'See where we've reached, and so forth.'

'In other words,' Ganger went on, smoothly catching the narrative relay baton from his colleague, 'it's work-in-progress time. Mid-term report, if you like. Okay?'

Jane nodded. 'Fine,' she said. 'And before you start, if you want to call it a day, that's fine by me.'

The two senior officials looked at each other in surprise.

'Whatever makes you say that?' Staff demanded. 'Don't tell me you don't find the work challenging enough.'

Jane laughed sourly. 'Oh, it's challenging all right,' she said. After a moment's pause, she folded her arms and set her face in a grim, nobody-leaves-until-the-culprit-owns-up expression. 'I must say,' she said, 'I do think you two might have warned me before I started.'

'Didn't we?' Ganger said innocently. 'I thought we . . .'

'Did you hell as like,' Jane interrupted angrily. 'You

told me you wanted someone with a fresh perspective and no vested interests to sort out the way this Administration of yours works. That's fine. Maybe I might be able to help you with that, a little bit. What you didn't tell me was that you want me just as part of some horrible office-politics thing of your own. Well, I'm sorry, but no.'

Ganger, for once, looked confused. At least, he wasn't smiling, and without a smile to hold them together his features tended to sag like an unpropped clothes-line. 'Hold on,' he said. 'That's not . . .'

Jane ignored him. 'Let me just give you an example,' she said. 'Take this Time thing. You wanted me to sort it out. Everybody seems to acknowledge it needs sorting out. Fine. I thought about it, and I think I've come up with an answer that works.'

Staff's eyebrows shot up like the price of gold in an oil crisis. 'You have?' he said. 'How?'

Jane frowned. 'It's really very simple,' she said. 'Instead of having it all just lying about and slopping around, all like-an-ever-rolling-stream-bears-all-its-sons-away sort of thing, you should put the whole thing on rails. Then everyone'd know exactly where it was meant to be going and we wouldn't have any more of those dreadful flashbacks.'

'What flashbacks?'

'Then everyone'd know exactly where it was meant to be going and we wouldn't have any more of those dreadful flashbacks.'

'What flashbacks?'

'Then everyone'd know exactly where it was meant to be going and we wouldn't have any more of those dreadful flashbacks.'

'What flashbacks? All right,' Staff admitted, 'point taken. But just think of the . . .'

'And don't say it was because of the cost,' Jane interrupted. 'Again, it's as plain as the nose on your face that you finance it by bringing in private capital. The share-holders put up the cost of building the track, and in return they get a slice of the tolls and fares in perpetuity.' She thought for a moment, and smiled. 'And boy, do I mean perpetuity. But nobody's done it, have they? And nobody's going to do it either. I checked the files.'

'You did what?'

'I checked the files.'

'You did what?'

'Hang on,' Jane said, and she banged the side of the table with the flat of her hand. 'Loose connection some-where, probably. Sorry, yes, I checked the files. It's a funny feeling, you know, reading about what you're going to do in a dusty old file you find at the back of a pile of old boxes in the cleaning cupboard. Anyway, there it all was, and guess what? The idea was completely ignored, and I left the Department after fourteen days with absolutely nothing to show for it. Now then.' She leaned her elbows on the table and gave Staff the sort of look that would have made a mammoth in an ice-floe in Siberia start wondering where the sudden nip in the air was coming from. 'What's it all in aid of?' she asked. 'I mean . . .'

Before anyone could speak, they became aware of someone standing over them, radiating disapproval. Staff was the first one to remember how his voice worked.

'Right,' he said. 'To start with, I think we're all having the melon . . .'

'You maybe,' said the waitress, her notebook closing like a carnivorous plant. 'Her, no. She's barred, OK?'

Ganger and Staff looked at each other. 'I beg your pardon?'

The waitress tutted like a distant machine-gun. 'Your lady friend,' she replied. 'Calls herself a waitress. Insults my best customers, leaves without saying nothing, then thinks she can waltz in here ordering melon. No way.

Out. There's a Burger King two blocks down the street,' she added venomously. 'Say Rosa sent you.'

Idyllic. It was the only word to describe it.

In the far distance, a soft mist hung lightly over the blue hills. The long grass, still littered with pearly drops of dew, smelt fresh and clean. The slightest of breezes arched the long, stiff necks of the flowers that grew beside the gently murmuring stream. Here and there, a few sheep with pink bows tied round their necks lay under the shade of attractively gnarled oak trees, chewing slowly and counting humans. In the porch of the little loaf-shaped cottage, a young mother with a baby on her knee rocked slowly backwards and forwards crooning an ancient lullaby:

'*O abeth cynan sianon*
Cor-ara llana reanon
Y-tal ny rhian myanon . . .'*

Bjorn materialised, fell about five feet out of nothingness, landed heavily on all fours, recovered and looked about him. His senses took in all the available information and made a correct assessment.

'Oh *shit*,' he said. 'Not again.'

'Have a nice day, now.'

'Yes, thanks,' Staff replied absent-mindedly, and lifted the tray. He steered it back towards the corner table, hampered in doing so by the fact that he could only just see over the top of the chips.

'Oh,' said Jane. 'I thought I asked for the Double Chilli Nutburger with regular onions.'

'Did you?' Staff gave her a long look, combining threats with entreaties.

Lit: 'Listen, snotnose, go to sleep or I feed you to the dog, kapisch?'

'However,' Jane added quickly, 'this looks simply delicious, whatever it . . .'

'Right,' Ganger interrupted. 'Here we all are. To business.'

He twitched his handkerchief out of his top pocket and tucked it into his collar. The other two gave him hard, cold looks which he entirely failed to notice.

'Agenda time,' he went on. 'If we start off generally considering (a) our overall aim and objectives, (b) our achievements to date, (c) . . .'

'Your tie's just gone in the barbeque sauce,' said Jane.

'(c),' Ganger continued, moving his tie slightly, 'obstacles to be overcome, (d) . . .'

Staff coughed meaningfully. 'Yes,' he said, 'all right, we get the point. There's no need to be so damned ceremonious about it all.'

Ganger frowned at him; that is to say, he smiled at him with added eyebrows.

'(d) . . .' he said firmly.

Jane shook her head. 'Sorry to butt in,' she said, 'but can we start now? Only, I do have work I ought to be getting on with.' She stopped, and a sound like a laugh heard through a bacon-slicer came out of her mouth. 'Mind you,' she added, 'for the life of me I can't see the point. Can you?'

Ganger lowered his head and stirred his coffee with a pencil. Staff turned a chunk of crisp, golden something or other round in his fingers and stared into the saltcellar.

'Can you?' Jane repeated.

There was a moment of complete silence, except for the sound of 163 people eating and talking loudly in the background. Ganger removed his pencil from the coffee, wiped it carefully on the paper napkin and put it back in his inside pocket.

'Perhaps,' he said slowly, 'we ought to explain.'

Jane blinked, said 'Oh,' and instinctively reached for a chip. Ganger's elbow was in the way. Ah, but Man's reach must exceed Man's grasp, or what's a Heaven for?

'Go on,' she said, her mouth full.

Staff put down his crisp, golden whatever, which was moulting a sticky red and yellow sauce down the back of his hand, making him look like a wounded Martian. Then he looked Jane in the eye.

'It's like this,' he said. 'What we told you about the Administration being right up a tree and needing an outside view and a new broom and that sort of thing is absolutely kosher and on the level. You know that, you've seen for yourself. But there's more to it than that.'

'Yes?'

'Absolutely.' Ganger, leaning forward to emphasise the importance of his words, froze; then he slowly lifted his arm, inspected his elbow and shuddered. 'But really, it's all part of the same thing. I mean yes, the Administration is in a real mess. But how do you think it got that way?'

Jane thought for a moment. 'Things do,' she said.

'Of their own accord, you mean?' Staff said. 'Entropy theory and its application to practical office management. It's true enough, as far as it goes . . .'

'Too right,' Jane interrupted. 'Ask anyone who's ever been responsible for paperclip distribution. I never believed in black holes and time warps until they put me in charge of the stationery cupboard one week.'

'But,' Staff went on, 'it's not the whole story. You see, things in their natural state don't naturally gravitate into a mess. For instance, if you pour sand out of a bucket on to the ground, it forms a nice neat cone. If you spill water, you get a lovely pool with the sides all nicely level and a precisely flat top. It's only work that flops about all over the place if you drop it.'

'That's because work isn't natural, you see,' Ganger interjected through a jawful of bap. 'That's your basic thermodynamics.'

'Is it?'

Ganger nodded, and wiped his lips neatly with the corner of his napkin. 'Work,' he said, 'is defined as the result of applying energy to a stationary mass . . .'

'That's filing, surely,' Jane murmured. Ganger ignored her.

'. . . Which in turn results in the mass acquiring momentum,' he went on, 'which leads on to movement, which creates friction . . .'

'Depends what you move. I once moved someone else's pot plant because it gave me hay fever, and there was friction for weeks after that.'

'. . . Which dissipates energy, resulting in entropy.' He picked up a lemon-scented paper towel and began absentmindedly folding it in ever-diminishing squares. 'Because of entropy,' he continued, 'work sort of frays at the edges. Bits come loose and fall off. These in turn become random particles of disorientated matter, possessing momentum but not direction . . .'

'Ah,' Jane said. 'You mean auditors.'

'These particles wander about, collide with other bodies, and thereby create other little chips and splinters of disorientated matter. And eventually . . .'

'Eventually,' Jane interrupted, 'they end up in some poor devil's in-tray at a quarter past five on a Friday afternoon. I know, I've been there.'

Ganger looked down at his fingers. The paper towel had by now become so infinitesimally small that for all practical purposes it had ceased to exist. 'It's these little bits of stray work that cause all the hassle,' he said. 'But it's not in-trays they end up in. It's people.'

'So,' Staff said, 'in order to solve the problems, you

first have to solve the people. Agreed?'

Jane shrugged. As an original discovery, she felt the statement was on a par with trying to patent the wheel in 1986. 'Of course,' she said. 'But what's this got to do with . . . ?'

'Tell her,' Staff said. Ganger opened his mouth and left it open. If a medieval cook had been passing, he'd instinctively have stuck an apple in it.

'Well,' Ganger said at last, 'what do you do if you've got a blocked drain? Get a drain-rod and give it a good sharp poke. And that's what we're trying to do. Trouble is,' he said, looking away, 'it's not as straightforward as that, quite.'

'Oh?' Jane said. 'Why not?'

'Because,' Staff replied.

'Ah,' Jane said, nodding. 'Now I get you.' She frowned. 'But where do I come in?' she said.

'Simple,' Ganger answered. 'You're the drain-rod, as per the original brief. Except that we didn't tell you about the people, only about the problems.'

'Exactly,' said Jane. 'Why was that?'

Staff shifted uncomfortably in his seat. 'Well,' he said, 'the thing is, you coming to work for the Administration was strictly our idea, Ganger's and mine. We were supposed to clear it with all sorts of people: committees, departmental managers, sub-committees, all that sort of thing. But we didn't.'

'Why not?'

'Because they wouldn't have agreed,' Ganger said. 'Plus, they'd have guessed what we were up to.'

'They're the wet leaves we were talking about just now, I take it?'

'Some of them,' replied Staff, nodding. 'So what we were doing, being absolutely frank and open about the whole thing, was sending you in without any backup or support whatsoever, with the express purpose of getting up the noses of some of the most important people in the whole Administration. We knew they wouldn't let you do anything really useful; in fact, we're absolutely amazed how much you have managed to get done. No, the whole point of the exercise was to get them well and truly annoyed and angry; and then, with any luck, they'll make mistakes, and we'll have 'em.'

Jane sat for a moment. 'I see,' she said. 'But why didn't you tell me all that in the first place?'

'Because you'd have refused,' Ganger replied. 'Wouldn't you?'

'I suppose so,' said Jane thoughtfully. 'Probably not, actually. But I wouldn't have done it so well. I'd have been all furtive and apologetic about it, I expect, because I'd have known I was up to something sneaky.'

'Sneaky?'

Jane nodded her head. 'Sneaky in a good cause,' she said, 'but definitely sneaky. As it is, I've charged along thinking I had right on my side and it's them who're being difficult and obstructive. Yes, I get the idea now.'

'Good,' Ganger said, cheerfully. 'This coffee, by the way, tastes as if it's spent the last year in a gearbox.'

'It certainly explains,' Jane continued, 'why you two have been taking such a keen interest in everything I've been doing.'

'You noticed that, then?' Staff enquired.

'Yes,' Jane said. 'I thought it was odd at the time, two highranking officials personally supervising just one trainee. You said it was because I was a guinea-pig . . .'

'Not so much a guinea-pig,' Ganger said, half to himself, 'more one of those white rabbits you get in research . . .' Staff kicked him under the table.

'Anyway,' Staff said, 'we've come clean, so what about it? Are you still going to carry on?'

Jane scratched the tip of her nose with her plastic straw. 'Oh, I don't see why not,' she said. 'It's not as if I've got anything better to do.' Suddenly she stood up. 'Of course not,' she said. 'I think this whole thing is probably a bad dream I've been having, and unless I wake up pretty soon I'm going to miss my bus. What the hell do you two think you've been playing at, anyway?'

Staff was about to say something, but Ganger shushed him. Other diners turned their heads and looked at them.

'First of all,' Jane continued, gathering momentum but not appearing to dissipate any energy in the process. 'This weirdo here comes and tells me he's a . . .'

'Not that word, please,' Ganger said softly.

'. . . And that he wants me to come and work for him, and until I agree he's going to camp out permanently in my ear. Then,' she said, turning to Staff, who instinctively moved a little further behind his coffee-cup, 'you turn up and tell me that unless I pack in my job with Burridge's and come and work for you instead, the world's going to end. And somehow,' she added, with feeling, 'you convince me – probably because of a couple of conveniently timed natural disasters – and so that's what I do. And first I rescue a major city from a flood, and then I help you cover up the fact that you're so damned laid back that anybody can just walk in to your premises and help them-selves to the major star of their choice, and I somehow start believing, Yes, maybe this is for real after all. And then . . .' She paused, scrabbling around for words in the same way a motorist at a toll booth searches for an elusive coin. 'And then, just when I'm beginning to be able to look at myself in the mirror every morning without wanting to burst out laughing, you tell me that what I'm really doing is helping you two with some weird board-room coup or other. Well,' she said, 'you can take your job and you can stuff it, because . . .' She stopped dead.

'My God,' she whispered, 'I've been wanting to say that to somebody all my life, and now I actually have. Whee!' She pulled herself together, straightened her back and picked up her handbag. 'Sorry,' she said, 'but I'm through. I'd give you a month's notice, but after a week in the Department of Time I shudder to think what you'd do with it. Goodbye.'

She turned her head towards the door and started to walk towards it.

Bearing in mind the way the cosmos is run, and who runs it, credit has to be given for the fact that she got over halfway before the ground suddenly opened and swallowed her up.

SEVENTEEN

Bjorn carefully took the basin off the fire and tested the water with his finger. Then he took off his boots and put his feet in it.

He'd been a long way: up as far as the first range of picturesque blue hills to the east and halfway to the shadowy forest-clad slopes in the west, and still without finding so much as a kebab house, let alone the Kentucky Fried Chicken of his dreams. Shadowy forests and verdant meadows, yes; food, no. He poked his little fire with a stick and cast a furtive glance over his shoulder at a shyly grazing fawn.

This place, he said to himself, is the absolute *pits*.

Above him the sun shone, casting long, sharp-edged shadows on the bowling-green grass of the river valley. He lay on his back and stuck his tongue out at it.

Years ago, he remembered, I worked for those bastards. Best years of my eternal bloody life I gave them, lugging great heavy boxes about mostly. It wasn't fun, exactly, but at least a bloke could go down the Social Club with his mates, play a few frames of pool, have a couple of pints and a bag of chips afterwards, throw up over a parked car or two and trip over a dustbin before going home. At least there were pavements, and gutters, and the water came out of taps instead of lying around in river-beds where leaves and stuff can fall in it.

And then, he recalled, still years ago, I was working on the sun; nothing exciting, just cleaning it off at the end of the day, hosing it down, scraping the squashed flies off the windshield. And something went wrong or some daft bugger made a really big cock-up, and everybody reckoned I knew what it was, because I was in the sheds working when it happened, whatever it was. So they said, anyway. News to me, but still, they said that whatever it was had to be hushed up and I'd have to go, and I could either start a new life somewhere else, somewhere *idyllic*, or else . . . well, I can't remember what, I think it was just Or Else.

Bastards . . .

The fawn was looking up at him out of great round black eyes. He relaxed and smiled.

'Here, baby,' he chirruped. 'Whooza preddy liddle deer, den?' With some of those wild leeks from under the trees over there and maybe some watercress, he whispered to himself, you could do worse.

And then the fawn pricked up its ears, swivelled its head, and darted away. A forlorn attempt to hit it with a rock at twenty yards failed. Bjorn sat down again and started to massage the soles of his feet.

And then looked up. There was a girl standing over him: a tall girl, with long, straight hair, a sort of chestnut brown, and light blue eyes and a kind of mischievous-angel half-smile on her slightly parted lips. And, more to the point, knockers like footballs. Bjorn opened his eyes wide and let his jaw drop.

'Um,' he said, but it came out as a real thoroughbred mumble. 'Sorry, was that your, um, deer?'

The girl brushed a strand of hair out of her eyes and knelt down beside him on the grass. She was wearing a simple peasant blouse, the sort that they don't even bother putting the price on in Printemps, and in her right hand she held a basket of strawberries.

'*Na searan thu chulain-bach ma?*'† she said. Bjorn had a couple of goes at swallowing his Adam's apple and grinned stupidly.

'Er, yeah,' he said. 'Right. Um.'

The girl laughed; and her laughter was like the soft splashing of a mountain tarn; or alternatively, ice-cold lager hitting the bottom of the glass. Bjorn blinked and instinctively started to pull on his boots.

'*Be curailin suine pel-riath mo*,'‡ said the girl, and it occurred to Bjorn, apropos of nothing much, that her eyes were like . . . well, they were like . . . well, they were pretty neat eyes, you know?

'Hi,' he croaked. 'I'm Bjorn. Yup. Right.'

The girl laughed again, and this time, hell, you could almost taste the hops. Then she took a strawberry from the basket and popped it into his mouth before he could close it.

'Er, right,' he said. 'Thanks. Thanks a lot.'

The girl leaned forward and kissed the top of his head, and it seemed to Bjorn that the smell of her hair was like the first cigarette after a twelve-hour night shift in the explosives store. Then she giggled, stood up and walked away.

About five minutes later, Bjorn stopped staring at where she'd been, and spat out the strawberry. His left leg had gone to sleep and something small and hairy was running about inside his boot. In the shade of a thicket of wild

---

†*Lit:* 'Yeah. Your other brain cell burnt out or something?'
‡*Lit:* 'You could do your flies up too, while you're at it.'

laurels, two shy, velvet-antlered fawns were laughing themselves sick.

Jane opened her eyes.

And a fat lot of good it did, too. In order for your eyes to be of any use, it helps if you're not in a windowless cavern hundreds of feet below ground, with the lights off.

'Hello,' said a voice above her.

She tried to move, but that was a wash-out too. Somebody or something had done a pretty neat job of tying her to what her intuition told her was a railway sleeper. A long way over her head, more or less where her instincts suggested the voice was coming from, she became aware of a low crunching noise, like a steamroller creeping slowly up a gravel path.

'Hello?' she whispered.

'Oh good, you're awake,' replied the darkness. The voice was masculine, probably, but beyond that it was monu-mentally nondescript. It had no accent, gave no indication of age; and if it happened to be speaking in English, Jane felt, that was probably due to some fiendishly advanced simultaneous-translation system. 'My name is,' and it said something Jane didn't grasp, but which sounded very like Eyesee. Couldn't be that, of course. Stood to reason.

'What am I doing here?' Jane enquired.

'I don't know,' Eyesee replied, 'I can't see in this light. Don't you think it's terribly dark in here?'

'Yes,' Jane replied, trying to ignore the creeping sensa-tion she was experiencing, which felt rather the way she imagined it would feel if you had someone cleaning the marrow out of your bones with a pipe cleaner.

'Shall we have the lights on, then?'

'Yes, please.'

Well, we all say silly things sometimes, and she wasn't to know. So, when the lights suddenly came on and she started to scream uncontrollably, there was a small part of her brain that was able to say, 'Wasn't my fault,' and mean it.

'Gosh,' said Eyesee, 'is there anything the matter?'

By way of reply, Jane screamed some more; a lot more, in fact. Even when the lights went out again, she carried on whimpering and gibbering for nearly two minutes, which is a long time.

'Better now?'

'Nnnnnn.'

'Sorry?'

'Mmmmmmmmm.'

'I hope I didn't startle you,' said Eyesee. 'Perhaps I should have mentioned that some people find my appearance distressing. Me for one,' he added.

Jane subsided into a series of short, mucous gasps. The voice waited for a while, and then cleared its throat softly.

'It scares the living daylights out of me sometimes,' Eyesee said. 'Depending on what frame of mind I'm in. By the way,' he went on, 'my name. Actually my full name is Executive Officer i/c Reprogramming and Mental Aberration Adjustment. My friends call me Eyesee for short. Or rather, they would if I had any.' He paused. 'I don't, though,' he added. 'I think my appearance is against me, you see.'

'Mmmmmm.'

There was a sigh. 'Before that,' Eyesee went on, 'I was called Retribution, and I didn't mind that, because then I could be Rhett for short, like Rhett Butler. But the chaps Upstairs thought Retribution was a bit downbeat, so they changed it. These days they like to stress the *positive* aspects of the work we do here. Uphill job, mind.'

Jane sat frozen. She was aware of the inordinate length of time it was taking the big blob of sweat to reach the end of her nose, and it dawned on her, or at least upon a part of her mind that was playing roughly the same role in this episode that the orchestra played in the sinking of the *Titanic*, that Fear is another dimension.

'Anyway,' Eyesee went on, 'I don't mind what I'm called these days, now that I've had a chance to get used to it. It's pretty apt, really, because people see retribution the way they want to see it, so I look different to everyone. Horrible, of course, but different. So I think Eyesee is a pretty good name, don't you think?' The voice paused. 'Because it's up to your *eye* to *see* me the way you think I ought to be, okay? How did I come across to you, by the way?'

Jane swallowed hard, and discovered that someone had laid a thick concrete path right down her throat. 'You were very big,' she said. 'Huge. And slimy. And you had little strips of flesh still stuck to your bones. And there were these maggots . . .'

'Ah.' There was, far away in the darkness, a faint sniff. 'Seems like you didn't catch me at my best.'

'Um.'

'Maggots, did you say?'

'Mm.'

'What a perfectly horrid idea,' said the voice. 'I must say, you've got a rather nasty imagination there. Perhaps you ought to see somebody about it.'

There was a long silence.

'Well,' said Eyesee, 'this is all very well but it's not getting us very far. Look, would you mind awfully if I just had a little light? I promise to keep out of your field of vision. Only, well, the truth is I get sort of nervous in the dark. It's probably because I'm afraid that I'm out there somewhere. Maggots,' he repeated with distaste. 'Whatever next!'

'Go ahead,' Jane quavered. 'I'll shut my eyes.'

There was a click, and then a faint glow began to

permeate the darkness, like ink soaking into blotting-paper. 'People find that closing your eyes doesn't actually help,' Eyesee remarked. 'Tell you what, I'll hide behind the flywheel. You won't be able to see me then.'

Slowly and deliberately, Jane counted up to ten. 'Ready?' she called out.

'Ready.'

She opened her eyes. To her overwhelming relief all she could see was an enormous machine. It wasn't anything identifiable like a printing press or a hydraulic ram; imagine a top film designer had been told to design a machine for a horror-film set – that's what it was like. A really *top* designer.

'Where am I?' she whispered.

'Do you know,' said Eyesee's voice from behind the machine, 'it's amazing how many people say that. And before I started working here I thought it was only in books. You're in Justice.'

Jane's eyes widened, until her memory told her to pack it in. 'Department of Justice?' she said.

'Got it in one. This is the engine room, as you'll probably have gathered already. What you're looking at right now are the actual Mills of the Gods.'

'That grind slow but exceeding small, you mean?'

'That's them,' Eyesee replied. 'Actually,' he added, 'they don't, not just at the moment. Right now, they grind large and exceeding lumpy. In fact, ninety-five per cent of the time they don't grind at all.'

'Um,' Jane replied. 'What am I doing . . . ?'

'Partly,' Eyesee went on, 'because the nut on the drive shaft connecting the flywheel to the cams has stripped its thread, and would you believe, you can't get them in that size any more because these days they're all metric. Partly because even if they were in full working order they can't afford to run them for more than an hour a day because of the price of coal. Partly . . . well, mainly actually, because there's really no call for them these days.'

'Right,' said Jane. 'Look, why am I tied to this lump of wood, and what am I doing . . . ?'

'In theory,' Eyesee went on, and Jane began to wonder whether the maggots were really the least bearable thing about him, 'they don't need them any more because of me. De-automation, they call it. All the rage. Who needs machines when you can have people, they say. They don't give a damn for the effect it's going to have on the lives of hundreds of thousands of ordinary . . .'

Jane coughed sharply. 'Excuse me,' she said. The sound of her words faded away.

'What they say is,' Eyesee droned on, 'who needs Justice anyway? Outmoded concept, superhumanity has moved on since those dark and far-off days, that sort of thing. The idea is that they're phasing Justice out and replacing it with Retribution. Sorry, with Reprogramming and Mental Aberration Adjustment. That's me,' he added bitterly. 'And Rehabilitation, of course. He's about here somewhere.'

Jane swallowed. 'He is?'

'Unfortunately,' Eyesee sighed. 'Nasty piece of work. He makes me look like Tyrone Power, by the way.'

'Ah.'

'The idea being,' said Eyesee unpleasantly, 'that Retribution may be nasty but at least it's likely to be pretty exciting, whereas Rehabilitation is just incredibly point-less and boring. They're right about that, at any rate.'

Jane digested that statement for a moment. 'Are there any more of you?' she asked tentatively.

'Not full-time, no,' Eyesee replied. 'There's Govern-ment, of course, but she only comes in two mornings a week. Which is just as well if you ask me, because there's only two cups in the kitchen and if there's one thing I can't stand, it's having my morning coffee out of a mug.'

'Government?'

'It's got Snoopy on it, as well,' Eyesee went on. 'I'll swear it curdles the milk. Oh, yes, Government. You know, in a democracy people usually get the kind of government they deserve.'

'Oh. Right. Look, what *am* I doing here?'

There was a long, long silence, during which Embarrassment joined the host of other unpleasant things floating about in the stale air.

'Yes,' said Eyesee eventually. 'Look, it wasn't my idea. Not my idea at all.'

'Please . . .'

'I mean,' Eyesee said, gathering a bit of his customary momentum, 'it's bad enough being stuck down here in the dark and the damp with only Rehabilitation for company – the only card game he knows is snap, by the way, because of course he disapproves of gambling. He cheats.'

'Why . . . ?'

'Are you down here, yes, I was just coming to that.' There was another pause. 'And as for his charming habit of drying his socks over the radiator . . .'

'Please,' Jane said sharply. 'Why am I here?'

'You really want to know?'

'Yes.'

'You're sure? I mean, a moment ago you really wanted the light on, and . . .'

'I'm really sure, yes.'

'Well,' said Eyesee; and Jane would have sworn he was taking a deep breath if she didn't know for a fact that he'd have nowhere to put it, 'the truth is, you've been promoted.'

You could have heard a pin drop. It would have had to have been a largish pin, because of the background noise. A crowbar, say. But at least nobody spoke.

'Promoted.'

'I thought you didn't really want me to . . .'

'Promoted to being tied up in a dark cellar with a thing with eighteen-inch maggots crawling in and out of its . . .'

'Please!' Eyesee exclaimed. 'Oh God, you'll have to excuse me a minute.'

The light went out, and Jane heard the sound of footsteps, followed by retching noises. A few seconds later, the lights came back on.

'Sorry,' said Eyesee hoarsely. 'But I've got a weak stomach, actually, and the thought of . . .'

'That's perfectly all right,' said Jane, with feeling. 'It was thoughtless of me. But are you sure you mean promoted?'

'As opposed to what?'

'Well, found guilty, for starters. This really doesn't fit in with my definition of upwardly mobile, you know.'

There was a long sigh, and Jane tried not to visualise what the breath was coming out of. 'It's a bloody awful job,' said Eyesee at last. 'Still, someone's got to do it.'

'Oh,' Jane said. 'I think I see what you're getting at.'

'Do you?'

'Yes. I've been got rid of, haven't I?'

'That's right,' Eyesee replied, avoiding Jane's eye. 'I'm very sorry,' he added, 'truly I am.'

'Can they do that?' Jane asked, after a moment. 'I mean, is it, well, legal, just tying an inconvenient member of staff to a plank of wood and abandoning them in a cellar for ever and ever?'

'Oh, absolutely,' Eyesee confirmed, and a hideous squeaking sound suggested that he was nodding his head, or what had remained of it, vigorously. 'Their legal department's thought it all through very carefully. You see, the Code states quite clearly that the employer is obliged to pay the employee the correct salary – depending on grade and experience, of course – and contribute to the pension scheme and let the employee have the agreed number of days' holiday each year. There's nothing in there about what the employee shall or shall not be tied to.'

Jane giggled. There was a faint metallic ring to her voice which suggested that although she wasn't yet hysterical, this was only because she was saving hysteria for later. 'But I'm not really an employee,' she said. 'I mean, I'm mortal. If I stay here, then sooner or later I'm going to die. Doesn't that sort of put a different complexion on it?'

There was a long pause. 'Are we talking about statutory sick pay here?' Eyesee enquired cautiously. 'Because I don't know if death entitles you to that. Maybe it comes under the heading of early retirement. I think I'd have to look that one up.'

'Would you mind going away, please?'

'Sorry,' Eyesee said. 'I've offended you, I can tell.'

'It's not that,' Jane assured him, 'really. It's just that you might get embarrassed when I start screaming, and . . .'

'Got you,' said Eyesee, hurriedly. 'Yes, you've got a point there. Very considerate of you. I think I might . . .'

He stopped in mid-sentence, because a wall fell on him.

The way Bjorn had worked it out was like this.

There is no such thing as an idyll. Real life is nasty, sordid and boring, all about going to work and having to shave and the dustbin bags getting ripped open during the night by next door's cat. Even in an infinite universe, there is nowhere you can get a plastic fork that won't break.

Therefore, the idyll I've found myself in is artificial, and somebody's put me here to stop me wandering about.

Clever, really; if you want someone to stay locked up, put him in a prison he won't *want* to break out from. Or at least one where he only finds out it's a prison when it's too late.

He thought of Ilona's father, washing the ox-cart, not being allowed to walk on the floor, having to go out into the toolshed to smoke his pipe, and wondered what that poor bastard had done to offend the authorities. Something horrible, probably.

Having reached this conclusion, he set his mind to planning his escape. He reasoned:

This idyll is artificial, right?

That means somebody made it. It's a thing.

Things break when you hit them.

The trick was to find the right spot. Ten years of splitting logs in the other bloody idyll had taught him that it's no use going mad and slashing out wildly with the big axe, because all that happens if you do that is broken axe-handles. You have to find the seam, the flaw, the crack, the split, the lie of the grain, and you can be through it like ice cream through the bottom of the cone on a sunny day.

A hundred and seventy years in the Clerk of the Works' Department had taught him how to look at the sky and the horizon and find the join.

He waited till nightfall, hiding out in the hayloft behind the smithy. Just after midnight, he opened the skylight and looked up. It was a clear night, and the stars shone out of a black velvet sky like rhinestones. Good. That made it easy.

The sky, with its million twinkling points of light, is only wallpaper, after all, put there to cover over the cracks in the vault of heaven caused by the use of cheap, bulk-bought plaster. Like all patterned wallpaper, it's a real cow getting the edges lined up properly. If you look long enough, and know what you're looking for, sooner or later you'll find the point where the paper-hanger cocked it up; where the constellation whose real name is the Toothbrush of Adonis is duplicated on both sides of a millimetre-thick invisible line, and where the cosmos bulges out over an unsmoothed air-bubble. Follow the invisible line down to ground level, and you'll find a tree whose branches are a little bit higher on one side than the other. That's the join. Bjorn knew this because he too had served his time, up on a high stepladder with a bucket of paste and a long brush. He even knew what was underneath the stars . . .

(. . . A rather tasteless red textured flock, very frayed, with patches of mould in places and a few snags and nicotine stains here and there. Many people have wondered what was there before the Big Bang; well, where due north is now is where the dartboard used to be.)

If you're not in a hurry, it's possible just to peel the corner of the paper back, slip through and draw the paper back after you. If you couldn't give a toss, however, you simply pack dynamite round the roots of the tree, retire and light a cigarette, the butt of which you carelessly discard.

Eyesee brushed brick dust out of what for the sake of convenience we shall describe as his eyes and looked blearily upwards, to find himself staring at a distinctly unfriendly sight. It wasn't as bad as looking in a mirror, but it wasn't far behind.

'On your feet,' Bjorn said. 'Come on, I haven't got all sodding day.'

Eyesee blinked. 'Excuse me?' he said.

'On your feet,' Bjorn replied. 'Jump to it, or you'll get my boot up your . . .' He broke off, and frowned. 'Well, doesn't look like you've got one, but we can always improvise.'

Eyesee jumped up quickly. 'No,' he said quickly, 'I really wouldn't want you to go to any trouble on my account. What was it you wanted to know?'

'The way out.'

'Ah.' Eyesee cowered a little and backed away. He'd always wondered what it would feel like, being really frightened; well, he hadn't been missing much. 'That's going to be rather tricky, really, because there isn't one. At least, not in this dimension. I mean, not as such. Strictly speaking,' he added.

'Balls,' Bjorn replied. 'Talking of which . . .'

'This way.'

At this point, Jane woke up. She'd been hit, oddly enough, by a falling star, and a fraction of a second later by a hand-sized lump of plaster. She groaned.

Thirty seconds is plenty long enough for quite a complicated dream, and Jane had dreamed that she was lying, tied to a railway sleeper, in the vaults of some vague but sinister building, while a monster who somehow managed to look exactly like her worst nightmare hid behind a thing like a giant beam engine and explained that henceforth, everything in the world was now officially her fault. That's the trouble with the dreams you tend to get in the basement of the Department of Justice; no imagination.

'Oh,' she said. 'Oh *shit*!'

This is a complicated moment to describe, so we'll get Eyesee out of the way first. When Bjorn looked round, saw Jane and began staring, Eyesee ducked behind a lump of wall, tiptoed quickly away and found himself in the middle of a grassy meadow. Realising he'd come the wrong way, he turned to go back, only to find that the hole he'd just come out of had mysteriously vanished and been replaced by a slightly asymmetrical tree. He spent the rest of the night wandering about dejectedly, trying to avoid polished surfaces and pools of standing water, and at dawn came across a beautiful young shepherdess, who immediately took him home to meet her family. They were married three weeks later, and Eyesee now divides his time between washing up, exercising a small, vicious dog and painting the windows in the spare bedroom. Because he is simply Ilona's husband, nobody even notices what he looks like any more.

'Who're you?' Bjorn eventually asked.

'Queen Victoria,' Jane replied. 'Look, will you please get this log off me?'

Bjorn felt cheated. He'd wanted to make a good impression. He'd wanted to stroll over and say, 'Hey, lady, is that railway sleeper bothering you?' He'd wanted to cut through the ropes with one clean sweep of his Zambian Army Knife, but the big blade was stuck fast and the attachment for taking stones out of impala hooves was as blunt as an armchair. In the end he managed to saw through the rope with the tin-opener, but not before he'd trodden on Jane's foot and cut his fingers to the bone on the lanyard ring.

'There you go,' he said. 'No trouble.'

Jane sat up and massaged her foot. 'That's a matter of opinion,' she said. 'Look, you've broken my heel. Why don't you look where you're going?'

'Er.'

'Er, what?'

'Er. Sorry.' Bjorn stood on one foot and chewed his lower lip. Even thus might Perseus have looked, had he swooped down from the vaults of heaven on his winged sandals, decapitated the sea-dragon and then rounded it off by stepping backwards on to the tail of Andromeda's pet cat. 'Sorry,' he repeated helplessly.

'That's all right,' Jane sighed. 'Now, do you know the way out of here?'

'Um, no,' Bjorn replied, and blushed.

'You don't?'

'Sorry.'

'Never mind.' Jane stood up, took off her other shoe and neatly knocked the heel off against the side of the sleeper. 'They were new on,' she added ruefully. 'Oh well, can't be helped. Do you have such a thing as a torch on you, by any chance?'

Bjorn shook his head, unable to speak. To get a line on his state of mind, imagine you've just kissed the sleeping princess in the enchanted castle, and she stirs, and opens her eyes, and turns her head, and then you notice the book beside her bed is called *1001 Cures for Chronic Insomnia*.

'Well, well,' Jane tutted. 'We'll just have to try and find the light switch, won't we? Come on, try and make yourself useful.'

When eventually Bjorn did find it (by walking into it and switching it on forcefully with his nose) he was extremely grateful. 'Right,' he said. 'Hey . . .'

Jane gave him a look, and it wasn't friendly. Of course, it wasn't his fault that the switch that operated the huge machine was right next to the light switch, and that he had a fairly broad nose; but she really wasn't in the mood to make allowances.

'Don't just stand there,' she snapped. 'Switch the bloody thing off, quick.'

Bjorn reached out an arm, but too late. A force like a water cannon hit him in the chest and sent him bouncing off the walls like a squash ball, until he came to rest up in a corner of the ceiling. He had the unpleasant feeling that that was only temporary; basically, just so long as the ceiling could take the pressure.

'You *idiot*,' came Jane's voice from somewhere he couldn't see. 'What *have* you done?'

'Where are you?' he panted back. It wasn't easy; it was

as if someone was trying to fold his shirt without removing him from it first. 'I can't . . .'

'If you must know, I'm in the fireplace.'

Bjorn looked around, and noticed the tips of two shoes poking out of the chimney breast. Face facts, his soul whispered to his brain, even by your standards there have been more auspicious starts to a relationship.

'What's doing it?' he tried to shout; but his voice came out ironed and pressed.

'It's that stupid machine,' boomed the voice from the chimney. 'It's pumping air into this room faster than it can escape. Any minute now and I'll be off up this chimney like a bullet up a gun. Satisfied?'

'Hold.' Bjorn struggled, pitting his pectoral muscles against the force of the machine. 'On.' That's embarrassment for you; real, ear-tingling, bowel-churning embarrassment. Adrenaline is positively inert in comparison. 'I'm.' He kicked frantically against the wall, but all he achieved was a short rain of crumbling plaster. 'Coming.' His hand found the penknife in his trouser pocket.

'Great,' Jane replied. 'That's really cheered me up, you know?'

Until recently, Bjorn had always prided himself that he'd kept in pretty good shape – until very recently, in fact; right up until a few seconds ago, when Life had suddenly decided that he'd look better in just two dimensions – and there was the little matter of his self-esteem being at stake here as well. With an effort that a mere scientist would have dismissed as physically impossible, he pulled the knife out of his pocket, opened the big blade first go, and let the pressure do the rest. It drove the knife into the wall, which went pop.

Then there was a long, loud, extremely vulgar sound, followed by a thump as Bjorn fell off the wall on to his head.

'It's all right,' he gasped, a few moments later. 'I've switched it off now.'

'About time too,' came the reply from a long way off. 'Now will you please get me out of this chimney?'

That proved to be the hardest one yet; and Bjorn was on the point of cutting his losses and tiptoeing quietly away when he noticed that the machine had a gear lever. And the gear lever had two positions; one marked *Forward* and one marked *Reverse*.

'When you're *quite* finished,' said Jane, as she crawled out of the fireplace, 'maybe we can get back to looking for the door.'

Bjorn nodded. There were little bright dots and flashes in front of his eyes, and the rest of him felt roughly the way you'd expect a tree to feel after someone has just turned it into a newspaper. 'The door,' he whispered. 'Right. Um, I don't think there is one, you know?'

Jane breathed in deeply. 'We came in through the wall, you mean? Or did someone wash the Universe and it shrank?'

Bjorn nodded. 'I think I know this place,' he said doggedly. 'Used to work in this department once. This is one room where they don't need a door.'

The sardonic comment withered on Jane's lips. Instead: 'They don't?' she asked.

'No need,' Bjorn replied. 'The reason being, this place is basically, you know, inside your head. We're in Justice.'

'Justice?' Jane blinked twice. 'Look, where I come from, they have this thing called logic, and . . .'

'Yeah,' Bjorn replied. 'And Justice, like, it works by being what you think should actually happen to you. You know, conscience and all that stuff. So they don't have to bring you here, because you're already here to begin with. That's what they reckon, anyway,' he added. 'I never thought I had that much imagination, you know?'

Jane nodded. 'Nor me,' she said. 'I think they brought me here. If this was my conscience I reckon I'd have recognised it by now, it'd be full of unwashed cups and dirty kitchen floors.'

Bjorn raised an eyebrow. 'Since when did they need washing?' he asked.

'Later,' Jane replied. 'I think I've worked it out.'

. . . Very simple, though not very pleasant.

Where do you put inconvenient people so that nobody can ever find them? Inside your head, of course.

And suppose that you're not actually allowed to do it. You'd feel guilty, wouldn't you? Or at the very least, extremely worried about being found out. So, you put them in your conscience. Probably it just happens that way without you making a conscious decision, but it's a very suitable place, because, in the very nature of things, your conscience is the one part of your brain that's always kept sealed off from the rest.

'So where are we?' Bjorn asked.

Jane frowned. 'That's a good question,' she replied. 'First, I thought maybe I'd died and gone to Hell; but then I thought, Hang on, if this was Hell I'd be able to see the people who dreamed up the idea of putting fruit juice in little cardboard cartons with individual straws.' She sighed. 'So I guess it's option number two.'

Bjorn didn't actually click his tongue impatiently, because you don't do that sort of thing around visions of sublime loveliness. There was, however, a slight spasm in the muscles of his jaw. 'Go on,' he said.

'Which means,' Jane continued, 'we're inside somebody's head.'

There was a pause while Bjorn, for the want of a better word, thought about it.

'Nah,' he replied. 'We wouldn't fit, for one thing. You'd

have legs sticking out through ears and all sorts.'

Jane sat down on a lump of masonry and inspected the damage to her footwear. 'It's all a matter of dimensions,' she replied warily. 'I could be wrong, but I've got an idea that you lot are rather more flexible when it comes to that sort of thing than we are. I mean,' she added with a slight shudder, 'all that business with Time . . .'

Bjorn frowned. 'What's that got to do with it?' he asked.

'I don't know,' Jane confessed. 'During physics lessons at school, I was always the one at the back of the class drawing sea-serpents in the margins. I just feel that anyone capable of coning off two lanes of the later Roman Empire isn't going to have too much difficulty in tucking us two away between their ears.'

Bjorn digested this for a moment. 'Okay,' he said, 'so we're inside some guy's head. No problem.'

He stood up, grabbed hold of a large lump of rock and started banging it against a wall. Plaster fell from the ceiling in little clouds.

'What exactly are you doing?' Jane enquired.

'Well,' Bjorn replied, between gasps for breath, 'if you're right, pretty soon a big hole's going to appear and a couple of aspirin are going to come flying in here. That's when we make our . . .'

Jane sighed. 'Maybe I was over-simplifying,' she said. 'I mean, yes, we're inside this person's head, but we're also in a different dimension. These things are very complicated, you know.'

'Oh.' Bjorn sagged, and let the rock fall. 'So what've you got in mind, then?'

'Nothing, really,' Jane replied sadly. 'I think we're trapped, if you really want to know. I think we're stuck in here for ever and ever. Brilliant, isn't it?'

Bjorn shook his head. 'You're wrong,' he said. 'Look, everything that exists is a thing, right? And everything that's a thing can be broken, or smashed up, or knack-ered, right? All we've got to do is find where to kick it, and we're away.' He stood up straight, put his shoulders back and started to walk purposefully round the room, stopping occasionally to bang the walls hard with his head.

For her part, Jane put her arms round her knees and curled up. It was bad enough being stuck, she thought; she could really have done without the company. Her ideal companion for the rest of Eternity was . . . well, it wasn't a subject she'd given a great deal of thought to, what with one thing and another – A-levels first, and then briefly the rain forests and the threat of nuclear weapons, and latterly mostly the quantum mass of accrued back ironing – but it certainly wasn't a six-foot blond Nordic idiot whose reading probably stopped short at *Alcohol 4.5% by Volume. Please Dispose Of Can Tidily*. If someone was out to get her, so far they were doing a pretty neat job.

'Hey,' Bjorn called out. 'Sounds pretty hollow over here.'

'What does?'

'The wall.'

'Oh.' Probably an inter-dimensional partition of some kind. Gosh, thought Jane, I'm *hungry*.

'Definitely hollow,' Bjorn continued. 'Perhaps if I gave it a really good thumping with something hard and solid . . .'

'I thought you'd just tried that.'

'Well, it's better than just sitting there,' Bjorn replied coldly. He looked around, and then set about trying to lift a larger than average lump of masonry. He failed.

'Or there's the chimney,' he added. 'That looks like it goes somewhere.'

Jane sniffed. 'Quite probably,' she replied. 'Given that

the Universe is curved, it probably goes backwards. Up itself. Eventually, I mean.'

'Yeah,' said Bjorn uncertainly, 'right. You know, what I could really use right now is a bloody big hammer.'

'Look,' Jane snapped, 'you're just wasting your time. We aren't inside a room, we aren't inside anything. We're just inside.' She waved her arms irritably. 'So will you please stop banging around, because you're starting to get on my nerves.'

Reluctantly Bjorn put down the promising-looking slab of breeze block he'd been trying for weight and balance, and paced up and down a few steps, humming. Then he got down on his hands and knees and tried staring up the chimney.

'Maybe,' he said, 'if we're inside this guy's head like you said, this chimney is actually a nostril or something. Yeah,' he added brightly, 'and that pump thing, you know, the one we had on just now, maybe that's something to do with the breathing gear.'

'Please,' Jane mumbled, as she lay on her back with her eyes closed, 'would you mind terribly much just shutting up for a while, because I'd like to try and get some sleep.'

Bjorn glowered at her. 'All right,' he growled. 'Just let me have one more go, okay?'

'Please yourself,' Jane replied irritably, and turned over on her side.

Bjorn nodded purposefully. He was in love, he was trapped inside somebody's head, something he couldn't understand had tried to spread him all over the walls like butter, and what he wanted most of all in the whole wide world was fifty centilitres of ice-cold Budweiser. He spat on his hands, hefted the chunk of breeze block, and gave the corner of the mantelpiece a bone-jarring wallop.

Various things happened.

Several pieces of shrapnel broke off the mantelpiece; the lights flickered, Ganger materialised in mid-air, fell heavily and rolled on the ground, clutching his ankle and groaning; a hole appeared in one of the walls and the floor suddenly flooded with a sea of soluble aspirin.

The final event was Bjorn splashing across the floor, grabbing Ganger by the lapels and shaking him as if he contained a mixture of gin and vermouth.

'Dop, you bastard,' he snapped. 'What the hell kept you?'

Staff tightened his half-nelson on Finance and General Purposes' right arm and grinned like a maniac.

The trick was, apparently, to keep the bastard's mind occupied until Ganger could get out of it. This was getting increasingly harder.

'Another thing I bet you don't know about fifteenth-century Florentine religious painting . . .' he said.

'Dop?' said Jane. It wouldn't have taken much imagination to see wisps of smoke drifting out of her ears. '*Dop?*'

Ganger grinned sheepishly. 'D. Ganger,' he replied. 'What did you think the D stood for, anyway? Norman?'

There are times when you can feel the situation drifting away from you. 'But why?' she heard herself ask. 'Does that mean there's two of you, or what?'

Ganger shook his head. 'Coincidence,' he said. 'It just so happens that where I come from, Doppel is a very traditional Chri . . . very traditional name.' He paused. 'It's part,' he added, 'of our rich and ancient cultural heritage.'

'Where you come from,' Jane repeated. 'I thought you were a . . .'

'Yes,' Ganger interrupted, 'well, anyway. This isn't getting us anywhere, is it? Talking of which, I'll bet you don't know where you are. I mean, I could give you three guesses and you'd never . . .'

'Inside the head of the chairman of the Finance and General Purposes Committee,' Jane replied flatly. 'To be precise, locked inside his conscience.' She sniffed histrionically. 'Give me credit for a little common sense, please.'

Ganger sagged. 'Right,' he said. 'Now . . .'

'And I think I've seen everything I want to,' Jane went on brutally, 'so if you'll just see your way to getting me out of here, then I'll be very much obliged to you.'

'Right. Um.'

'And,' Jane added, 'you can accept my resignation. I've had enough of all this. I want to go back to being a terminally bored and frustrated human being stuck in the same old mindless rut, if that's all the same to you. In fact,' she added savagely, 'if ever I get out of this . . . this *head* in one piece, I'm going straight to the nearest poly to enrol for accountancy classes. Got that?'

Ganger nodded. And then vanished.

He re-materialised in complete darkness, but that was all right. Something soft broke his fall. Something soft and strangely comfortable. He reached in his top pocket for his slimline flashlight. Then he grinned.

He was completely surrounded by ironing.

Further inspection revealed that it was ironing strewn untidily across an unwashed kitchen floor, while on the edge of the penumbra cast by his small torch he could make out the silhouette of a sink piled high with saucepans and baking trays. He nodded. He'd come to the right place.

Look, said the walls and the floor, this is ridiculous.

'Maybe,' Ganger replied, lying back on a heap of creased and wrinkly cotton blouses and putting his hands behind his head. 'Quite possibly. But you can't blame me for trying.'

It's *absurd*, replied the walls and the floor. I'm inside his head, you're inside mine. It's going to end up like that trick where you have two mirrors facing each other, and the reflections go on and on for ever. For all I know, we could end up disappearing or something.

'Nah,' Ganger yawned. 'Trust me, I know about these things. I've been inside more heads than you've had hot dinners.' He paused and peered across at the sink. 'And that's saying something, apparently. Hey, Le Creuset. I've got a set of them.'

Leave my kitchenware out of this, replied the floor. And while you're in there, you can see for yourself. If you can find one scrap of remorse for me handing in my notice . . .

Ganger grinned. Then, slowly, he took a large, flat packet from under his coat and started to unwrap it.

Hey, shrieked the ceiling, that's not *fair*. You can't do that.

'Who's going to stop me?' Ganger said simply. Then he bit through a strand of sellotape.

But it's against the rules, howled the far wall. You can't bring things of your own into my head, it's brain-washing.

Ganger studied the floor pointedly. 'Looks like it could do with it,' he said. 'If your mother were to see this floor, she'd have a . . .'

You leave my mother out of this.

'I can do,' Ganger replied. He walked across to the sink, picked up a cheese-encrusted kitchen knife, and set to work with it on the wrappings of the parcel. 'Depends on how reasonable you can be.'

What've you got in there, anyway?

'Guilt,' Ganger chuckled. 'Highly refined, industrial-strength concentrated remorse. So don't sneeze or make any sudden movements, for both our sakes, or you'll spend the rest of your life with people hiding sharp objects whenever you come into a room.'

You bastard.

Ganger said nothing. He wasn't looking sheepish any more.

I think you're bluffing. You wouldn't dare.

'Bet?'

If you let go one drop of that stuff, as soon as you come out I'll kill you.

'Oh no you won't,' Ganger replied grimly. 'You'll be so sorry for everything else you've done, you'll positively beg me to let you carry on working for us. It's amazing stuff, this,' he added nonchalantly. 'In the plant where they process it, they have to stop every five minutes and confess.'

The walls seemed to shrink a little. The floor quivered.

'In fact,' Ganger went on, 'you wouldn't believe some of the things they confess to. We had an assistant production manager phone up the newspapers and claim responsibility for the San Andreas Fault the other day. Said San Andreas was framed. We had our work cut out hushing that one up, I can tell you . . .'

All right. You win. Put it away.

'I have a five-year contract in my left inside pocket,' Ganger said slowly. 'Also a pen. And something to rest on.'

All *right*. Just put it away before you drop it or something.

'Thank you,' Ganger said. 'You won't be sorry. Or at least, not half as sorry as you would have been if I'd . . .'

All *right*.

There was a blur.

It hardly lasted any time at all, which was just as well. Imagine a Cinemascope projection of the Rockies pulled through a two-inch hole, backwards.

'Here we are, then,' Ganger said cheerfully. 'All safe and . . .'

Staff looked up and let go of his prisoner. 'What the hell do you think you've been doing?' he demanded. The prisoner made a little moaning noise, sagged forwards and collapsed. Ganger looked at him.

'There wasn't any call to get heavy,' he said reproachfully. 'Besides, we need him.'

Staff growled. 'I didn't get heavy,' he said. 'Not unless you could call explaining the plot of *Tristan and Isolde* three times consecutively, *and* trying to make it sound interesting, getting heavy,' he added bitterly.

'Sounds pretty heavy to me,' Ganger replied. 'Never mind, though, here we all are.' He looked down and prodded the slumped body with his toe. 'Somebody throw a bucket of water over him or something.'

'Excuse me.'

Ganger and Staff looked round.

'Excuse me,' said Jane, 'but the deal's off. It was under duress, and absolutely unfair, and I'm not signing anything.'

She folded her arms, and Bjorn simultaneously took a step forward. There was an awful lot of him, and although it was undeniably true that mere physical violence wouldn't have any effect whatsoever on the likes of Ganger and Staff, they both shrank back a few inches. After all, there was no way of telling that *he* knew that.

'Who's this?' Staff asked.

'Ah yes,' Ganger replied, trying to smear a thin coat of self-confidence over his voice. 'Friend of mine I'd like you both to meet.'

Staff considered this for a moment. 'If he's a friend of yours,' he observed, 'then why's he holding you two feet off the ground by your lapels? Does that mean he's really glad to see you or something?'

'You bastard,' said Bjorn. 'You slimy, toffee-nosed little git. You went off and left me in that . . .' Bjorn paused and made a thorough search of his vocabulary for the right word; given the size of Bjorn's vocabulary, it was a bit like looking for a combine harvester in a haystack. 'In that *dump*,' he said decisively. Which only goes to show that you don't need to lug a dictionary round between your ears to be able to come up with the *mot juste*.

'Oh, come on,' Ganger replied. 'It wasn't that bad, surely.'

It was the wrong thing to say. Ganger suddenly found himself an inch away from the angriest pair of eyes he'd ever come across.

'Right, sunshine,' said Bjorn quietly. 'You can read minds, right?'

'Up to a point.'

'Maybe you'd fancy having a quick look round what I've got in mind for you.'

Ganger swallowed hard. 'I'd rather not,' he replied. 'You do realise, of course, that physical discomfort has no effect on me whatsoever.'

'Sure?'

Jane made a tutting noise. 'Put him down,' she said briskly. 'If you frighten him he'll probably go and hide in my subconscious, and I've had enough trouble with it over the years as it is. Who are you, anyway?'

Bjorn swung his head round, and blushed. 'Um,' he stammered. 'Like, well, my name's sort of Bjorn. That is . . .'

'Hello, Bjorn. Aren't you forgetting something, by the way?'

Bjorn's eyes filled with panic, as he struggled to identify the social error he'd just committed. Should he have shaken her hand, he wondered, or offered to give up his seat or carry her bag for her? Were you actually supposed to say your name on a first date? He looked around wildly for a door to open.

'I think she means about putting me down,' Ganger whispered.

Without moving his head, Bjorn relaxed his fingers slightly. There was a thump, and something down by his feet said 'Thank you so much.'

'How do you come into this anyway?' Jane was asking. 'You don't look like a . . .'

'He's not,' Ganger broke in. 'Or at least, he used to be. But he's not any more. Now he's a supergrass.'

Jane was just about to say 'A *what*?' and Staff was on the point of asking, 'Look, just what *is* going on here?' and Bjorn was poised to hit somebody, when the heap on the floor groaned and moved slightly.

And looked up. And saw Bjorn. And screamed.

Or at least one of him did.

One of the risks inherent in high managerial office, with all the accompanying stress and nervous tension of departmental politics, is that of developing a dual personality. Usually it's regarded as something to be avoided, but it can have its advantages.

To take a good example: it meant that whereas half of Finance and General Purposes' personality was making small squeaking noises and trying to hide itself in the pile of the carpet, the other half was striding angrily down the corridors of the Security barracks, yelling furiously and banging on doors with a riding crop. Where Finance and General Purposes had an advantage over the run-of-the-mill psychotic was being able to provide separate corporeal incarnations for each of his separate personas; or, to put it another way, two bodies to go with his two faces.

The one that went with his half-crazed-Dictator face was very big, dressed in the sort of black leather greatcoat the

SS would have gone in for if they'd had access to top-quality dragon hide, and draped liberally with interesting-looking weapons. You'd need an active, not to say warped, imagination to work out what they were designed to do to you, but any fool could see they were weapons. Fiendish ones, probably.

'Come on, you goddamn sons of bitches,' he was shouting. 'Move it!'

He moved the stub of a cigar round in his jaw as he shouted. Somewhere just north of his hip pocket, a particularly abstruse weapon shrugged and metamorphosed smoothly into a pearl-handled revolver.

As his footsteps echoed away down the corridor, two bleary-eyed spectral warriors opened their doors and looked out at each other.

'Now what?' yawned one of them.

'You know what?' replied the other. 'I have this feeling we aren't going to enjoy this.'

His comrade in arms suddenly became aware that he was still wearing his Snoopy T-shirt. He turned hurriedly away and reached for his regulation issue shapeless black cowl, and so failed to notice that his colleague had come to the door still holding the copy of *The Ballet-Goers' Companion* he'd been reading, under the blankets, with a torch.

'Better get ready,' said the closet balletomane. They both withdrew into their cells.

A few minutes later, they fell in for parade. Something about their leader's manner as he paced up and down inspecting them didn't do much to cheer them up. In this persona, Finance and General Purposes was sometimes known as the Grand Old Man, or Old Ironsides, or simply The General. And a lot of other things, too.

He stopped and pointed with his riding crop, his hand quivering with rage.

'Oh, shit,' whispered the Snoopy fan to his neighbour. They surreptitiously swivelled their eyes to the left, saw what the matter was, then quietly and sincerely thanked Providence that it wasn't them.

8765B had forgotten to take his face-mask off.

Accordingly, the row consisted of forty-nine billowing black cowls, empty except for a pair of indescribably horrible points of red light, and one pale pink face with spectacles and razor-rash. Forty-nine pairs of indescribably horrible points of red light closed, and the cowls surrounding them winced. A spectral warrior who turns out on parade improperly dressed doesn't get away with just whitewashing stones or cutting the grass with nail-scissors.

'You,' hissed the General. 'Fall out.'

The pink face sagged like a deflating balloon and fell down inside the cowl. 'But . . .' said a tiny voice, from a long way down.

'I said fall out, soldier. You deaf?'

'Sir.' There was a sigh of pity and terror – the proportions were approximately those of an extremely dry Martini – as first the cowl and then the rest of the habit slowly crumpled to the ground and lay there in a heap, like a pair of drunken trousers. For spectral warriors, the words of command tend to mean what they say.

The General looked round, and bit into his cigar-butt.

'Whassa matter?' he snapped. 'You never seen an immortal soul busted before?'

Complete silence. When, eventually, the late 8765B's collar-pin hit the ground, it sounded like a small explosion.

'All *right*,' growled the General. 'Move it.'

There was a crash of boots on the tarmac.

With a grunt of satisfaction, the General gave the signal, and the column moved forwards at a terrified quick march towards the waiting trucks. Perhaps it would have comforted the spectral warriors to know that, about a quarter of an hour's drive away, exactly the same person as the hundred-per-cent bastard who was staring at them and willing one of them to have forgotten to blanco his bayonet frog was cowering under a chair and making noises like a petrified kitten.

Maybe not.

There was a hushed silence. You could almost hear the thought, feel the tension. If there had been a barometer nearby, it would have screamed.

Eventually: 'Yeah,' said the Count of the Saxon Shore, 'I'll have the veal as well. So that's three veal, one chicken, one osso bucco, and three bottles of the red.'

The Emperor's sister shook her head. 'Veal's off, sorry,' she said. 'I forgot to mention. Goddamn butcher didn't deliver again today.'

The Electors looked at each other for a long time. It was the County Palatine who eventually put it into words.

'Hey,' he said, 'what's going on around here?'

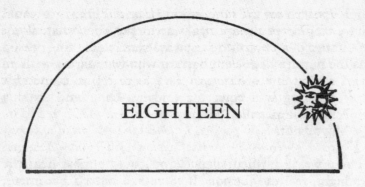

EIGHTEEN

Meanwhile, in the interests of clarity and a comprehensible narrative, take the next exit on the left, over the flyover, and back down the Pastbound lane almost as far as you can go . . .

To a time when there was virtually no Time at all, when the world was young and fresh, and still thinking, *Stuff it, it's years yet before I have to start thinking about pension schemes.*

A vibrant new administration has just moved into spanking new purpose-built offices, with state-of-the-art information technology, a highly trained and motivated young staff and an instruction manual. Which reads like this:

Congratulations! You are now the owner of a new Terra 57636. If properly looked after, it will give you many years of reliable and pleasurable service.

Although the Terra 57636 has been hand crafted using only the finest quality materials, in order to get the very best in performance and reliability from your machine, you should observe the following basic rules:

(1) Ensure that all surfaces are clean and free from excess oil. Do not remove the trees, as this interferes with the supply of oxygen to the intake manifolds.

(2) Try to avoid discharging toxic waste into the oceans. This can upset the ecological balance and lead to excessive wear on the icecaps.

(3) Nuclear weapons should not be used in the Terra 57636. It has not been proofed to withstand the pressures likely to be generated by nuclear explosions. The manufacturers cannot be held responsible in the event of accident or damage resulting from non-observance of this warning, which will also invalidate the guarantee

And so on. Most of the manual is in fact taken up with awful warnings as to what will happen to anybody who infringes the manufacturer's patent or makes unauthorised copies of the software; and a garbled version of this has survived to this day in the form of the Revelation of St John the Divine. The rest of the text was lost many centuries ago.

A minor but ambitious young official has just been appointed deputy head of the Sun Department, a relatively unimportant post, but even high-flyers have to start somewhere. It's his job to ensure that the sun is flown on exactly the right trajectory to ensure that it delivers just the right amount of light and heat to the world busily evolving below. Too little, and Life will be stillborn. Too much, and there's a risk that it'll turn out the wrong way. Strange, warped mutants with malfunctioning components and entirely unsuitable evolutionary matrices will emerge from the bubbling green soup that covers the surface, instead of the superbly constructed designer life-forms that the manufacturers intended.

Look very closely, and in the corner of the hangar you'll see a scruffy individual in the first ever pair of worn-out jeans and the primal Def Leppard sweatshirt, loafing aimlessly around with a broom in one hand and a pair of headphones over his ears. It will be many millenia before the Sony Walkman is invented, but he's getting in some early practice. His chances of promotion are slim.

And on the sixth day, the minor but ambitious young official woke up, put on his shiny black leather flying jacket and his goggles, and strolled confidently down towards the hangar. So far, he told himself, he'd done a pretty good job. The Boss himself had said so, and he ought to know. Pretty good job you're doing there, young 'un, he'd said, and you couldn't put it more clearly than that if you tried.

He climbed into the cockpit, checked the rear-view mirror and the oil gauge, and fastened the safety harness. Pretty good job, young 'un. Well, absolutely. Credit where credit's due, and all that.

'Flaps?' he shouted.

'You what?'

The official sighed. 'I said,' he yelled back, 'flaps.'

'What about them?'

'Are they engaged or aren't they? Come on, man, I haven't got all day.'

'Flaps engaged.'

'Switches?'

'Yeah.'

The young official made a despairing gesture. 'Oh, for crying out loud, are the switches on or off?' he cried. 'Or do I have to come and check them for myself?'

'Switches on.'

'Hoo-bloody-ray. Right then, contact.'

Pause.

'I said,' growled the young official, 'contact. But of course nobody is listening. I am talking to myself. Which is just as well, because it's the only way I'm going to get an intelligent conversation around here. CONTACT!'

'Yeah, right. Sorry.'

There was a thud; then a roar; then the hangar started to shake, as the huge machine's four enormous compression chambers slowly filled with cold, blue fire. The young official pulled his goggles down over his eyes, put the choke halfway in, and called out, 'Chocks away!'

And then he was flying. For a few seconds the world seemed far too small to contain such a wild extravagance of movement; then the airbrakes caught and the giant projectile burst through the thin haze of water-vapour that hung over the sparkling new oceans, levelled out and started to fly straight and level.

A pretty good take-off, young 'un, said the minor but ambitious official to himself. Neat work. Nothing to it, really; all you have to do is hang on to this handle thing and it'll fly itself.

He leaned forward in his seat and peered over the side. Far away, he could glimpse through loopholes in the clouds a shining blue horizon, textured by the breeze into a million regular waves. In there somewhere, at this very moment, the atoms were rubbing together in a miraculously improbable way. Life was just around the corner.

Smiling, the minor but ambitious young official relaxed back into his seat, looked up at the endless blue ceiling above him and began to dream.

All right, *right now* he was doing a job that was little better than Executive Grade 2 status, but that wasn't going to last for ever. It wasn't as if they could just take a trainee, however talented, and plonk him straight down in a fifth-floor office; there were motions to be gone through, knees to be browned. Just as soon as you proved to them that you could do all this noddy stuff with one hand tied behind your back, they'd have you out of it and

sitting behind a desk in no time flat. That would mean
Clerical status; and once you'd got that, you were halfway
there. Anyone with an ounce of go in him could whizz
up the Clerical ladder like a rat up a drain with the bailiffs
on its tail; and then you'd be in Admin. No more dealing
with actual things, no more flying suns or grading
snowflakes or lugging about tectonic plates. In Admin,
they only dealt with the really important, totally nebulous things – five-year plans, forecasts, projections,
economic models, cost-effectiveness ratios, overall strate-
gies. There would be committees, sub-committees,
quasi-autonomous review panels, watchdog commissions,
one-man working parties. You would have absolute
control, and maybe even a chair that swivels.

And then would come the real quantum leap; first to
departmental status, before soaring upwards to the
Empyrean heights of supervisory management; to permanent chairmanship of a committee so vast and so
indefinable that the whole curved universe itself would
be only part of its jurisdiction. As yet, nothing so mind-
bendingly huge existed anywhere in the cosmos, apart
from in the minor but ambitious official's imagination;
but if it ever came to pass, it would have to have a name
that was abstract to the point of stretching the parame-
ters of applied metaphysics.

Finance and something. Finance and Ultimate Purposes.
Something like that.

The minor but ambitious official smiled. He and the
world were young, talented and going places together. He
and the world were like *that*.

Oh.

Oh shit!

Actually, that too was way ahead in the future, but as
we've already seen, the minor but ambitious official is
way ahead of his time.

A long way below, but still rather closer than it ought to be, the surface of the sea boiled. Huge banks of water-vapour drifted up into the sky, bumped jarringly into temperature shifts, liquefied and fell back. Out of the water, jagged points of rock poked nervous and embar-rassed fingertips, like guests who have turned up far too early for the birthday party of somebody they scarcely know. And deep down, in the very dregs of the ocean, something that had no business moving, moved.

It wasn't quite the way it's depicted on the ceiling of the Sistine chapel. There's no inter-digital fireworks, no snap and crackle of white fire. There should have been, of course; and speeches, and a tape to cut, and a special presentation pair of silver shears, and a band. But there wasn't.

This is the way the world begins; not with a zap but a cock-up.

With a frenzied jerk on the joystick, the minor but ambitious official hauled the Sun back up to its proper place in the sky, and sagged forward against the straps of the safety harness. In his mind's eye, he saw two visions:

. . . The first, of the world as it should have been – the calm, dignified procession of perfectly formed organic pioneers rising serenely from the depths of the ocean to colonise the purpose-built land-masses, to evolve in a purposeful way into demi-gods, to begin the long but completely orthodox march towards reunion with their Creator, to the moment when they turn their smug faces to the sun and see only their own reflection . . .

The second, of the world as it was going to be – nasty green slimy things slopping up on to premature beaches, twitching apologies for mandibles in the germ-ridden air; slowly squeezing themselves into all manner of outlandish shapes – ammonites, dinosaurs, mammoths, monkeys, things even more obscenely ludicrous than monkeys;

things that would slip out of control and start smashing the place up, building motorways, exterminating whales, waging wars, wearing fluorescent green beachwear . . .

Very carefully, the minor but ambitious official looked all around him, and then down at the seas below.

Maybe nobody would notice.

Not yet, anyway. And by the time they did, who could possibly tell whose fault it had been? He fixed his eyes on the western horizon, steadied his grip on the joystick, and began to whistle aggressively.

Some time later, he made a faultless landing back at the hangar, cut the motors, and climbed rather unsteadily out of the cockpit. As he walked the long, long way across the hangar to the big double doors, nobody came running up, nobody called his name; there were no thick-set men in raincoats, no soldiers, nothing – just the erk with the broom and his headphones, prodding half-heartedly at the first few molecules of dust as they drifted through the still-pure air. He closed his mind to the problem, and gradually the problem began to disintegrate. Fragment of the imagination, trick of the light, nothing moved at all. Pretty good job, young 'un. Thanks, sir, glad you liked it.

'Bit low there, weren't you?'

The minor but ambitious official spun on his heel and stared. For his part, the erk with the broom made a more than usually half-hearted stab at an atom of grime, and scratched his ear where the headphones chafed the lobe.

'Sorry?'

'I said, bit low there this morning. Could've been an accident, going as low as that. You know, could've set something off before its time.' The erk raised his head and grinned. 'You want to be more careful,' he added.

'I don't know what you mean,' replied the official, apparently through a mouthful of cotton wool. 'I kept at exactly the right height all the way.'

'That's all right, then,' replied the erk, widening his grin. 'Must've been imagining things.'

'Well, don't do it again,' the official snapped. 'And get on with your work. This place is an absolute tip.'

But the grin only became wider, and the official turned away and nearly ran for the doors. As he retreated, he may or may not have heard somebody muttering something like, Calls himself a *high*-flyer, big joke. *Low*-flyer'd be nearer the mark . . . He grabbed the door, hauled it open, and slammed it.

And it came to pass exactly as the minor but ambitious young official had foreseen. He got his promotion, the world got mankind, and nobody said anything. True, there were a few heads shaken at hyper-departmental level, and there was a full internal inquiry. And then nothing.

Nothing, except a face burned deep in the official's mental retina, a grin, the memory of a tiny movement in the depths of the sea. Meanwhile, two careers developed: one dizzily ascending, one sort of slithering along the bottom. Maybe, said the official to himself a hundred times a day, he's forgotten all about it. A brain like that needs all its capacity just to make sure the beer ends up in the mouth and not down the front of the shirt. If he was going to say something, he'd have said it by now. And then the grin would float by like a stray patch of anti-matter, and whisper, *Don't kid yourself. He hasn't forgotten.*

As an interesting footnote to all this, it's worth recording that the evolutionary development of the human waste disposal system was the result of the young official's subconscious desire to have something appropriate to mutter under his breath every time he thought of it.

★　　★　　★

'Oh,' Bjorn said.

'Exactly,' Ganger interrupted. 'That's why, as soon as he was appointed chairman of the Finance and General Purposes committee, the first thing he did was have you spirited away to an idyll and kitted out with a brand-new identity. It was a good try, but doomed to failure from the start.'

'Oh,' Bjorn repeated. He was thinking, Stuff me, what a lot of long words this jerk knows. 'Come to think of it, I remember something like what you just said. But I never thought . . .'

From the floor there was a howl that set all the atoms in the cosmos on edge. Ganger stared.

'You mean you hadn't . . . I mean, it didn't occur to you . . .'

'Nah,' Bjorn replied. 'Course, now you tell me, it all sort of makes sense. Yeah, you've got a point there.' He leaned down and put his lips close to Finance and General Purposes' ear. '*Bastard!*' he shouted.

'Well,' said Ganger quickly, 'anyway, that's beside the point. Now we all know, and that's what really matters, isn't it? In case you're wondering how I found out . . .'

'You read his mind, didn't you?' said Staff quietly.

'So?'

Staff was white as a sheet and trembling. 'That's not *fair*,' he said. 'You shouldn't do things like that.'

Ganger looked as if he'd just been kicked in the nuts by an angel. 'Oh come off it,' he said. 'You've just heard me say that this jerk is responsible for *everything*. He's a goddamn evolution criminal, that's what he is. You do understand that, don't you?'

'Of course I do,' Staff shouted. 'That still doesn't make it right. You can't just go about peering in through people's ears like that.' He turned away. Ganger shook his head in disbelief and turned to Jane.

'You don't think it was wrong, do you?' he said.

Jane thought about it for a moment. On the one hand, she didn't hold with bugging. On the other hand . . . She thought for a moment about Homo sapiens, and many things crossed her mind: toothache, the division of the species into two genders, acne, comfort eating, split ends, clogged pores, catarrh, armpits. You could forgive most things, given time, but you've got to draw the line somewhere. And feet. If this guy was responsible for feet . . .

'He had it coming,' she said; then she, too, leaned forward. 'Why five toes, you scumbag? Go on, answer me. Why five, for God's sake? Four not good enough for you or something?'

Ganger nodded. 'Motion carried, I think,' he said. 'Now then, all we've got to do is . . .'

The room suddenly filled with white light. From the street below, a tannoy invited them to reflect on the fact that the building was surrounded. If they had weapons, it might be a shrewd move at this stage to throw them out of the window.

Jane cleared her throat.

'Excuse me,' she said, 'but who's that, exactly?'

Ganger looked round at her. 'Out there, you mean? The ones with the searchlights and the PA system?'

'That's right.'

'I have an idea it's my colleagues from Security,' Staff interrupted. 'This is just a wild guess, but I think they want to arrest us.'

'I see,' said Jane. 'Why?'

'It's what they're best at, I suppose,' Gange said. 'I mean, why do painters paint? Why do potters make pots? The question we should be addressing is, will they succeed?'

For his part, Bjorn gave them the kind of stare that large, stupid people reserve for their intellectual betters when they're indulging in verbal fireworks instead of getting on with the job. That's great, it said, and you won't mind if I leave you to it and just look around for a gun or something. He started to search the drawers of the desk, and soon he'd found what he'd been looking for. The bad guys always have small, pearl-handled guns in their desk drawers.

'Right,' he said.

He crossed to the window and hurled a chair through it. Then he flattened his back against the wall, extended his arm through the shattered glass, and pulled the trigger.

Down below, a spectral warrior felt something land on top of his head. Gingerly he reached up and felt the crown of his cowl. It was damp.

Meanwhile, Bjorn was staring at the prisoner with contemptuous disbelief.

'A water-pistol,' he croaked. 'What sort of chicken-shit wimp keeps a pearl-handled *water-pistol* in the top drawer of his desk?'

'A pacifist?' Ganger suggested. Staff sighed and pointed at the three tall potted ferns on top of the filing cabinet, just before they disintegrated in a hail of automatic fire from the street below.

'Not so much a pistol,' he mumbled (inevitable, since he was now hiding under the desk, with his head wedged sideways into the carpet) 'as a novelty plant-mister. I seem to remember the lucky dip at the office party a few years back . . .'

'They seem to be shooting at us,' Jane remarked, enunciating the words with bell-like clarity. 'Should they be doing that, I wonder?'

Staff raised his head painfully and glowered at Bjorn. 'I think we seem to have started it,' he growled. 'They're just defending themselves.'

'Fine,' Jane replied. 'I can quite see their point. I mean, a water-pistol at this range, you could get absolutely *soaked*. You could get pneumonia.'

There was a hollow thump down below them somewhere, followed about half a second later by an explosion in the office. The room was suddenly full of charred and shredded paper.

'Somebody would have appeared to have taken out the filing cabinet with a wire-guided missile,' Staff announced. He sounded for all the world like a BBC Radio Royal Wedding's compère commentating on Armageddon. 'I can only assume they have their reasons, because . . .'

There was a faint *whoosh*, and something whirred past Staff's hiding place and vanished into the hole in the far wall where the filing cabinet had once been. It was Bjorn, jumping up, grabbing Jane in one hand and the hostage in the other, and running for it.

Staff realised that he was on his own. It crossed his mind that he shouldn't be.

Something else crossed his mind. On tiptoe.

'It won't do you any good, you know,' he sighed wearily. 'I mean, if I go, you go too, so you're just fooling yourself.'

Maybe, replied a voice somewhere in his memory, but it's all as broad as it's long. Besides, there's some amazingly good places to hide in here.

'Where?'

Well, said the voice, can you remember that time you went on that fact-finding visit to those caves, right down in the heart of that mountain somewhere?

'Vividly.'

Thanks. Yes, this'll do nicely. You can't remember a light, can you? It's as dark as a bag down here.

'No, I can't.'

Or a sandwich, maybe? Come on, you must be able to

remember something to eat. I could be down here for a very long time.

Staff didn't bother to reply. Instead, he crawled out from under the desk, ducked as a lump of ceiling smashed down a few inches away from him, and then picked up his feet and ran.

He made it to the hole in the wall just a fraction of a second before it closed up.

'. . . me *down*!' Jane yelled, and then landed with a bump. 'Ouch,' she commented.

'Sorry,' Bjorn replied. 'I thought you said "put me down", so I did.'

Jane sat up and rubbed her shin vigorously, sending small and entirely unintentional electric signals running the length and breadth of Bjorn's spinal column. 'Where are we, anyway?' she growled.

'Dunno,' Bjorn said. 'Wherever this is, though, I don't reckon we should stay here. Those guys out there weren't just ordinary Security, you know. More like spectral warriors.'

Jane nodded, and then grabbed hold of the hostage by his nose.

'You,' she said. 'What's happening?'

The hostage, still tucked under Bjorn's arm like a quivering football, made a tiny mewing noise of pure terror. Jane sighed.

'Can you do anything to make him talk?' she asked Bjorn. He nodded.

'Mind you,' he added, 'all he'll probably say is "oh shiiiit", and "ouch, you're breaking my arm", and stuff like that, but . . .'

There was a nervous cough from under Bjorn's armpit. *'You're in the vaults of the Central Administrative Section, directly under the closed file store,'* it twittered, *'and if you hurt so much as a hair of my head, then so help me I'll rip your lungs out and make Chinese lanterns out of them.'*

Bjorn stared down. 'You what?' he demanded.

'Don't blame me,' whimpered the tiny voice. *'That's not me talking. I'm absolutely terrified of you. It's him who's making the threats.'*

'Him?'

'Well, me. Other me. Him. Mercy!'

Bjorn frowned. 'You mean there's two of you?'

'Sort of. Well, no. There's just the one of me, but in two halves. One mind, two bodies, each body containing an undivided half-section of the same integral whole.' The voice hesitated. *'I'm the meek, cowardly one.* AND I'M THE COMPLETE BASTARD. *It's all to do with making schizophrenia work for you rather than being a handicap.'*

'All right,' said Jane, 'that'll do. At least we know where we are now.' She paused. 'Where are we?'

Bjorn furrowed his brow. 'We're under the closed file store in the vaults of . . .'

'Quite,' Jane interrupted. 'I meant, where are we in relation to the way out. The sort of answer I'm looking for,' she added helpfully, 'is either "This way" or "Follow me".'

Bjorn nodded. 'Follow me,' he said.

It was turning out to be a bad day.

The sun was refusing to start. A crew of seven muscular mechanics had given it their best shot and all they'd managed to do was flood the engine and bend the starting handle. The bright spark who'd suggested putting a set of jump leads on the battery of the moon was now in hiding, helped considerably by the fact that there was now no light of any description.

As a result of a freak short-out on the mainframe at Weather, it was now slashing *up* with rain over two continents. The same fault was having drastic effects in Perjury, where the thunderbolt cannons had jammed themselves on automatic override and were giving insurance salesmen, Presidential spokesmen and the organisers of awards ceremonies a very hard time indeed. Fortunately, the manifold cam rocker on the Liefinder unit had sheared its locking stud, which meant that each shot landed precisely eighteen inches to the left.

Gremlins in the signal-box at Chronology processing meant that the Western hemisphere had just had sixteen consecutive bank holidays in the space of fifteen minutes.

The random selector needle at Requisitions, the central prayer-answering agency, had stuck solid on *God save the Queen*, with the result that Her Majesty had had a truly unpleasant morning being repeatedly snatched from the jaws of sudden and unexpected death by supernatural forces. A gang of maintenance men were crawling towards the stylus across the main resonator disc with big hammers and extremely mixed feelings; because if they got the bloody thing free and then it went and stuck on *Give us this day our daily bread*, they were definitely not going to be held responsible.

All dreams delivered within the last forty-eight hours had been returned marked *Not Known At This Address*. Some of them were ticking.

And finally, as if that wasn't enough to be going on with, the music of the spheres was suddenly distinctly audible throughout the length and breadth of the cosmos, and had turned out to be *That's Entertainment*, played with one finger on a Yamaha organ.

This is what happens when no-one's in charge.

'CHARGE!'

'Er, chief . . .'

'ARE YOU QUESTIONING A DIRECT ORDER, TROOPER?'

'Not as such, chief, certainly not, no, perish the thought. It's just, me and the lads, we were wondering . . .'

'WHAT?'

'Like, like, sort of, charge *where*, chief, because I mean, charge, yes, behind you every step of the way there, absolutely one-hundred-and-ten per cent commitment on all sides, no sweat, *guaranteed*, only it's just that as orders go, sort of like, ninety-nine-point-nine-*nine* per cent absolutely brilliant, but directionally speaking, I wouldn't say it was vague exactly, really *not* vague at all, vague's quite the wrong word for this situation, more sort of general, in fact, more *flexible* really, yes, that's it, flexible, but maybe just this once, you know, in the circumstances, perhaps if we were to play down the flexibility angle just *somewhat* in the interests of greater, well, er, precision, if you sort of catch my general drift, perhaps, well, it was just a thought, you know, maybe, er.'

'FOLLOW ME!'

'Thanks, chief. Got that. Right on. Right.'

'You're lost, aren't you?'

Bjorn stopped dead in his tracks and frowned. Having a vocabulary marginally smaller than that of the average phrase-book compiler has its drawbacks. What Bjorn wanted to do was to explain that the sort of place where they were now, you were always, by definition, lost; the crucial thing was to be lost in the right way; because then, once all your directional preconceptions had been stripped away and you were floating free, like a magnetic needle in a saucer of water, the chances were that (because, in a truly random environment, objects take the line of least resistance) the barometric pressure of conven-ience would draw you on in the right direction, much more swiftly and surely than if there was a bloody great yellow line drawn on the floor with THIS WAY painted in fluorescent letters every five yards.

What he actually said was 'Yuh.'

'Thought so,' Jane sighed. She sat down on something – it was too dark to see exactly what – slipped off her shoe and massaged the sole of her foot. 'I had this horrible feeling, you know?'

Bjorn braced himself and took one final slash at the cliff-face of language. 'We're, like, meant to be lost, right? 'Cos this isn't a place you can sort of find on purpose. It more sort of finds you.'

To his great surprise, Jane nodded. 'I see what you mean,' she said. 'Like the public lavatories in Italy. Yes, I can relate to that.'

There was a thoughtful silence, broken only by a faint, muffled, rather wet noise as the hostage surreptitiously tried to gnaw through the length of clothes-line by which he was tethered to Bjorn's wrist. Since the hostage had small, uneven teeth and the washing-line was the same hawser-like article Bjorn had helped himself to before leaving the Idyll, they were content to leave him to it until there was a risk of him choking on his own displaced fillings.

'Only,' Jane mused, 'you still haven't said where it is we're supposed to be going. I take it you do actually know? Or is that cheating?'

Bjorn made perhaps the greatest effort of his life. Well, not the very greatest; that had been when he'd passed by a pool of drying cement in the street and not left foot-prints in it. 'Well,' he said, hand-turning the words with exquisite care, 'yuh, I do sort of know where we're going, it's just I don't sort of *know*, you know? It's more like the place knows, and I don't.'

Jane tested the statement carefully and decided that it had the logical equivalent of a bent axle. 'You mean we're lost,' she said.

'Yuh.'

Jane stood up. 'That's fine,' she said. 'Follow me.'

She didn't know how she knew, she just *knew*. So she walked directly into the wall.

'Ouch!' she said, a moment later.

And in her mind, along with a tasteful display of coloured lights and a dull throbbing sound, like the sea, a voice said, 'Nice try, but you were a foot to the left. Try again.'

She tried again. And vanished.

Bjorn stared. There was the wall, and Jane had just walked through it. No dynamite, no careful feeling for the seams, not even a zip fastener or a yard or so of velcro. That was *cool*.

There was a soft clink. The hostage had broken a tooth.

Wearily, as if noticing his presence for the first time and deciding he didn't really hold with it, Bjorn grabbed the hostage in one hand and his knapsack in the other, then he emptied out the sack and stuffed the hostage into it.

The hostage was small, but not that small; there was no way he was going to fit in there, at least not without the sort of pruning and editing usually reserved for a young reporter's first major story. The head would have to go for a start . . .

He fitted. The sack could have been made to measure for him. How this came to be possible nobody knows, although it may have had something to do with the fact that the hostage sensed that if he didn't, he was going to end up reduced to his bare essentials, like a Jerusalem artichoke. Bjorn buckled down the flap, adjusted the weight on his shoulders, and took a long, shrewd look at the wall.

Some people are cool by nature. The rest of us have to try just that little bit harder.

He lowered his head and charged.

*   *   *

Jane sat up.

'I'ink I'oke y'ose,' she said.

A party of nuns shifted their hand luggage from hand to hand and stared at her. A young couple sitting under the departure board giggled. Nobody moved to help her up, or anything like that.

A few seconds later, Bjorn stumbled heavily forwards, fell over her and landed in the lap of a sleeping Japanese businessman, who woke up and stared at him for a long half-second before ostentatiously taking out his handkerchief and wiping blood from his collar. The blood was coming from a nasty but superficial gash on Bjorn's scalp; nothing serious. Bjorn's head, it should be apparent by now, had the density of a collapsed star. In a head-butting contest, he could have taken on the whole of Mount Rushmore and won.

'Bloody hell,' he said. 'For a minute there, I thought we were in an airport.'

There was a pause, just long enough for Jane to satisfy herself that her nose was indeed still at unity with itself.

'You were right,' she said. 'I suppose it had to happen eventually.'

There was a voice, and it wasn't inside anybody's head, and what it said was:

Leydis and Gennelmein, thiz iz the lazzt corl for Bee Dubbyu Ay fly nummer Six Six Sebben to Blyblollolob. Passgers for Bee Dubbyu Ay fly nummer Six Six Sebben to Blyblollolob procee to gate nummer zerch where borin izz in progrez.

– just like flight departure announcers the world over.

(It's worth putting on record the fact that they don't deliberately mislead or misinform; it really gets to them after a while, and a lot of them end up with serious psychological trauma. It's just that they have this awful superstitious hang-up about not saying the names of places or the numbers of departure gates, which makes them subconsciously slur the words, or at best say them through three layers of compacted paper tissue.)

'Jeez,' Bjorn gasped, 'we *are* in an airport. Hey . . .' He froze, then his hand flicked behind his back where he could feel a spreading, soul-chilling dampness making its way slowly down from between his shoulder-blades to the base of his spine. In his experience, only one thing seeped quite so thoroughly, and that was blood. He brought his hand back, placed it under his nose, and sniffed the tips of the fingers.

Actually, *two* things. True, one of them is indeed blood. This was the other one.

'Just out of interest,' Jane remarked, 'why have you got a baby strapped to your back?'

'That's not a baby, that's the hostage,' Bjorn said. Once he'd said it, of course, it occurred to him that you don't say words like *hostage* in airports, even airports that probably only exist in the vague and unfrequented dimensions under the stairs of the human brain. By then, of course, it was too late.

'I see,' Jane said, and nodded. 'He's turned into a baby.' She continued looking at Bjorn – just over his shoulders, to be precise – but her next words were addressed vertically. 'Well,' she said, 'that's fine. Don't mind me; after all, it's your continuum, you do whatever you like.' She shuddered. 'Anyway,' she went on, 'you agreed that we seem to be in an airport?'

'Looks like it,' Bjorn confirmed. He was trying to stuff a very, very disreputable handkerchief up the back of his shirt.

'Well, why not?' Jane replied, smiling brightly. 'Where better than an airport, if we want to go somewhere? I mean, we don't have any passports or tickets or anything like that, let alone any money, and . . .' She stopped herself, and then started again. 'That's not going to be a problem, though, is it?' she said. 'Now then, where was it we wanted to go?'

'Um,' said Bjorn.

'It's very logical,' Jane went on, sorting through her pockets with a sort of manic confidence. 'We wanted to go somewhere. Therefore we are in an airport. I think we can put that down to good old-fashioned cause and effect, somehow.' She paused, and considered briefly. 'In the old days,' she added, 'I think there was a lot of tedious mucking about with genies and lamps and three wishes, but I suppose they rationalised all that. Ah, here we are.'

She held out two passports, and two tickets.

Although she wasn't in the least surprised at the way they'd materialised, she was intrigued to notice that they were return tickets. One was marked THERE, the other BACK.

'Oh come *on*,' she exclaimed testily. 'Either the whole free will thing was a gag or it wasn't. You can't have it both ways.'

A nun looked at her.

'You keep out of it,' she snapped.

Jane and Bjorn Blyblollolob, passgers on Bee Dubbyu Ay fly nummer Squirch Frow Squirch to Somewhere Else, pliz proceed immidyatly to gate nummer miaow, passgers Jane and Bjorn Blyblollolop, fankyow.

Jane winced. Then she looked directly upwards once more.

'Thank you,' she said. 'And about time, too.'

'THIS WAY!'

'Actually, chief, that way's a . . .'

Splash.

★   ★   ★

Staff stopped running and collapsed against a door. It swung open, and he fell through.

It is important to remember that all offices are one office, all corridors are one corridor, and all fire extinguishers, wherever consciously situated, end up directly on a level with the kneecaps of stumbling people. Staff swore.

He was in his own office,

'Now hold on,' he panted to nobody in particular. 'If we're going to play silly beggars with each other, we might as well do it properly.'

The light switched on, apparently of its own accord. There was suddenly a cup of tea on the desk. Staff knew without tasting it that there were two sugars.

He realised that he hadn't had the faintest idea who he was talking to, but whoever it was had listened. It was terrifying.

'Ganger,' he whispered. 'Can you hear me?'

There was silence, internal as well as external. He shook his head frantically, but nothing rattled about in it. He even tried blowing his nose, but no dice.

'Um, can you hear me?' he said. 'How about one . . .' He looked about frantically, and saw the cup of tea. 'One digestive biscuit for yes, two for no.' Two digestive biscuits slid out of the air and into the saucer. They seemed to be grinning.

'I see,' Staff muttered, his teeth set. 'It's going to be one of those days, isn't it?'

(. . . And outside, in the world, a split pin in the gravity induction drive mysteriously floated out and fell on the floor with an unheeded tinkle. It caused a very localised problem; the world was unaffected except for a square mile of Amazonian rain forest, where the trees were suddenly sucked down into the ground.)

Staff walked deliberately round to his chair, sat down and put his feet up in one of the drawers. He reached out for the tea and biscuits. They moved, gently but firmly, six inches to the right.

'I suppose telling me who you are would be out of the question,' he said.

Two digestive biscuits, travelling like the razor-sharp throwing-discs of the Japanese Ninja, scythed through the hair on the top of his head and embedded themselves in the wall. He glowered at them.

'Fair enough,' he said firmly. 'I can wait.'

The universe – or at least the part of it filling Staff's office; the *relevant* part – held its breath. There was a puzzled silence. Staff folded his arms, leaned his head back and gazed at the ceiling.

Time, of course, is tricky stuff, and it would be fatuous to say 'half an hour passed,' or 'an hour ticked by,' under the circumstances. Better to say, 'some time passed,' and leave it at that.

Staff sat still, saying nothing, surrounded by nebulous bafflement. After a while, the ceiling began to flicker, and suddenly was covered with a profoundly weird version of Michelangelo's vision of creation. But Staff just closed his eyes.

Some time passed . . .

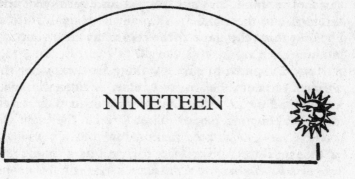

NINETEEN

A brief note on the culture, lifestyle and overall world view of spectral warriors.

Spectral warriors only know one joke. It goes like this:

Q: How many spectral warriors does it take to change a light-bulb?

A: One, and a stepladder. At a pinch, of course, he could stand on a chair.

Like all crack military units, they have marching-songs, the best-loved of which goes:

Underneath the lamp-light, by the barrack gate.

Darling, I remember the way you'd always gone by the time I got there.

Spectral warriors come into being when freeze-dried dragons' teeth are sown on the ground, and cease to exist when an enemy kills them, or (more usually) when they transgress their own Byzantine disciplinary regulations. Being composed entirely of spirit and ether, they do not require food and drink, or at least, they never get any. Very few of them survive long enough to find out whether or not it actually matters.

It would be wrong to say that spectral warriors are

afraid of nothing: they're afraid of an enormous variety of things, and their anxiety is usually thoroughly justified. The only thing they aren't scared of is the enemy, because anything their opponents can do to them is going to be playtime compared to what's waiting for them when they get back to camp. This is, of course, intentional.

Platoon 384657J, Blue Company (known in the service as the Whimpering Eagles) burst through the plate-glass windows at a fast trot, fanned out and assumed the legendary Reverse Tortoise formation, a manoeuvre designed to enable the front-line troops simultaneously to envelop the enemy and get as far away from the commanding officer as possible. Then they took cover, deploying in the specially developed triplex enfilade pattern unique to the unit. Then they stood up and looked sheepish.

The lance-corporal turned to face the crowd of staring holidaymakers, and cleared his throat self-consciously.

'Wrong airport,' he said. 'Sorry.'

The entire section then withdrew, putting into practice the time-honoured embarrassed slouch.

The general drew a deep breath, as if to shout, but the words came out at an unexpectedly gentle muzzle velocity. It was like being cooed at by a man-eating dove.

'Right,' he said. 'This way, I think.'

'We haven't got *time*,' Jane hissed. 'Come on.'

Bjorn looked round, stupefied. He'd never seen so many cans of lager in his entire life. It was, he decided, either a vision of paradise or a challenge. He wanted it to be a challenge.

'Um, yuh,' he said. 'Just let me, uh, choose a six-pack, and I'll be right with you.'

He turned back, and gawped.

It wasn't the first time he'd been in a Duty Free, of

course, but it was the first time he'd ever been in a *perfect* one. The thing which made it different from all the rest was the way it had nothing but beer. Lots of beer. There were cans as far as the eye could see; in fact, if he'd thought about it, he'd have realised that so much specific gravity in one place at one time was a direct contravention of the laws of physics.

'Stone me,' he whispered. 'They've even got Rottweiler Nine-X.' His hand reached out instinctively, like a seedling reaching for the sun – and with about as much chance of making contact, because Jane had caught hold of his ear and was pulling.

'For pity's sake,' she was saying, 'you may be a moron, but I'd have thought even you could recognise an obvious trap when you saw . . .' She stopped dead, her mouth hanging open, and her fingers slowly relaxed their grip.

Odd, Bjorn thought, I didn't notice there was a perfume counter. In fact, there wasn't one when I came in, just sixty thousand cans of Budweiser. He tried to interest Jane in this fact, but he was wasting his time.

'Please yourself, then,' he said. 'I'll just go back and have another look at the . . .'

The beer had gone. It had been replaced by a million bottles of scent. Either the shelf-stackers had access to some fairly advanced technology, or something peculiar was going on.

Behind his back, the hostage started to cry.

'Hey!' Bjorn protested. 'That's not fair. I was just going to . . .' He hesitated, while the world flickered. 'Oh,' he said. 'Right, that's more like it. Thanks.'

For her part, Jane was standing looking at the bottle of Chanel she'd just decided to buy and was trying to figure out why the label now read Jackal Extra Lite, Original Gravity 1034°–1038°.

Bjorn scratched his head. 'You know what,' he said

slowly. 'I bet if you opened one of these cans there wouldn't be any beer in there anyway.'

Jane looked at him absently. 'Sorry?' she said.

'I think,' Bjorn replied, 'that all this is a thing. You know. Illustration. Illusion. Figment of the whatsisname, imagination.'

'I know,' Jane said. 'And it was so *cheap*, too.'

They looked at each other.

'I don't like this,' Jane said. 'I wish we knew where we were.'

Bjorn shrugged. 'Doesn't matter,' he said. 'It's where we're going that matters.'

That sounded terribly impressive, and Jane nodded. 'Well said,' she answered. 'And where's that?'

Bjorn looked around. The Duty Free had vanished, and had been replaced by one of those little stalls that sell impractical pink socks. An electric trolley lumbered past and vanished into a gap between two delaminating dimensions.

'Dunno,' he said.

'Excuse me.'

The security officer looked round, and then looked up. About a foot above his head he could make out two tiny points of red light, like . . . Well, if he was a rabbit standing in the middle of a five-lane freeway, and if articulated lorries had red headlights, that's what they'd have looked like, only less, well, cosy.

'Sorry to bother you,' said a voice from a long way away, 'but could you possibly tell me the name of this delightfully appointed airport?'

The security guard licked his tongue round the inside of his parched mouth, and told him. The lights flickered for a moment as the black column they were attached to nodded. 'Thank you,' it said. 'Very much obliged to you.'

Then it turned, inserted what would have been fingers if it had had hands into the black hole where its mouth would have been had it been fitted with one, and whistled.

The front of the entrance hall blew out in a confetti-storm of shattered glass, and the floor shook with the almost subterranean thumps of exploding stun-grenades. Disconcerting shapes, like clouds of black nothing, swung in on ropes, tried unsuccessfully to stop, and crashed into electronic departure boards with pyrotechnic results. There was a really revolting sort of burning smell – not exactly indescribable, because language is capable of an infinity of subtle modulations, but describing it with any accuracy would be a pretty antisocial thing to do. An abandoned luggage trolley quietly folded its wheels inwards and tried to crawl backwards into the wall.

Last of all, the general strode in. He stepped over the dazed body of the security guard, marched over to one slumped heap of smouldering black cloth, and prodded it with the toe of his jackboot.

'Idiots,' he said.

The remaining black shapes – still plenty of them – gathered reluctantly around him, as he studied the check-in area thoughtfully.

After a long time, the general turned due east, wiped melted soldier off the sole of his boot, and pointed.

'They went thataway,' he said.

Bjorn shuddered. The damp patch was expanding with all the speed of the First Mongol Empire, and was threatening to annex his sleeves.

'Er,' he said, before the embarrassment caught up with him and clogged up his vocal cords. He blushed.

'What?' Jane said, without turning her head. She was trying to follow the arrows that pointed the way to pass-port control, and was wondering whether it was the third or the fourth time they'd passed that photograph booth in the corner there.

'Um,' Bjorn mumbled, 'I think the, er, hostage needs changing. You know, like *now*, maybe. Sort of thing.'

'Changing?' Jane raised an eyebrow. 'You mean back into an adult? I don't think it's as easy as that. I'm coming to the conclusion that this whole thing is somehow linked up with the interpretation of empiric sense-evidence through a number of different logical systems, which means that . . .'

'No,' Bjorn insisted, 'I mean change like in, you know, nappies.'

Jane's face relaxed. 'Oh, I see,' she said. 'Right, you carry on, and I'll see if I can find out where these signs are supposed to be leading.'

Bjorn shook his head vigorously, like a dog drying itself. 'No,' he repeated. 'Like, I don't know how. Where all the bits and ends and pins are meant to go.'

Jane shrugged. 'Me neither,' she replied.

'But . . .' Bjorn managed to say, despite the fact that his lower jaw was doing its best to fall off his face. 'But you're a, um, female. You know about these things.'

'Uh-uh,' Jane replied firmly. 'Sorry, can't help you there, I'm afraid. All I know about babies is that you're not supposed to put them in washing machines. Makes the colours run, presumably.' She turned away pointedly and stared at the signs on the wall, until Bjorn gave up trying to outstare her and slowly unslung the knapsack from his back. His face was the colour of bolognese sauce as he grabbed hold of a pin at random and pulled. To judge by his expression, he was expecting an explosion on the count of five.

'And anyway,' Jane added, 'it's not a baby, it's a hostage, and traditionally it's the man's job to stay home and look after the hostages.' She looked round and then quickly looked away again. Bjorn gritted his teeth and tried to tell himself that what he was holding was in fact a crankshaft case, and what was running down inside his sleeve was in fact gearbox oil. It helped, slightly.

The bang they then heard was the front of the building being demolished.

Jane and Bjorn looked at each other.

'I think I know where it is we're going,' Jane said.

'Yeah?'

'Away,' said Jane firmly. 'Come on.'

In a belated attempt to appear inconspicuous they walked quickly rather than ran towards the nearest exit. A man in uniform tried to stop them, and then recoiled like a salted slug when Bjorn put a wet nappy in his outstretched hand. He made no further attempt to impede their progress.

They were in the baggage hall.

'Wrong way,' Bjorn muttered. 'We should have gone left back there by the . . .'

Jane shook her head. 'This'll do,' she said. 'If there's someone chasing us, we'd better hide until they've gone. If we just mingle in with the crowd here, maybe they won't see us. Anyway, they'll have assumed we've made a run for the planes.'

Trying to look tired and bored, they wandered down towards the carousel, Jane making little cooing noises to the hostage as they went. The hostage started yelling.

'That's fine,' Jane whispered. 'People naturally tend to avoid yelling children in airports, I've always found. It's good cover.'

'Great,' Bjorn snarled. There was about a mile of wet cloth wrapped soggily around his wrist, and a safety-pin had worked its way inside the sleeve of his shirt.

They made their way down through the crowd – and there was something odd about the people comprised in the crowd, but it doesn't do to stare – towards the baggage carousels, where they mingled.

'Here,' Bjorn whispered. 'There's something odd about . . .'

'Yes,' Jane hissed. 'I know. What do you expect me to do about it?'

Bjorn shrugged. Although he wasn't usually given to ruminating on the nature of the universe, he had long ago come up with a reason why female logic is different from male logic. It was complicated, internally coherent and had a lot to do with the fact that women, being on average the shorter sex, spend a lot of their time nearer the ground and are thus likelier to have their brains interfered with by geothermic radiation. He considered explaining it to Jane but decided not to.

'Excuse me,' Jane said, elbowing a bystander out of the way. 'Thank you.'

The funny thing about the other passengers was – well, it was hard to explain it exactly, but . . . no, the hell with it, there's no point lying when the only person you're going to deceive is yourself. Bjorn grasped the mental nettle, and then his dazed mind looked round frantically for a mental dock leaf.

They were transparent.

No, not quite; you could see through them, but only at certain angles. It was as if someone had cut out life-size pictures of people and then pasted them to life-size tailors' dummies made of ice. Or glass. You couldn't get paste to stick to ice, because it would melt or slide off or . . . Bjorn caught his train of thought by the scruff of its neck and whisked it back to the matter in hand. If you looked at these people at certain angles, they weren't there.

Fine, Bjorn thought. So what? I'm no bigot. I can handle black, white, brown or yellow, so I can handle transparent as well. No problem.

Not surprisingly, Jane had been working on the same problem, and the answer she'd come up with wasn't a million miles away from the truth.

(. . . The truth being that the other people in the baggage hall were there all right, but not one hundred per cent. One of the disadvantages of long-distance travel which has never properly been sorted out is the unfortunate truth that whenever a living creature goes an appreciable distance from home and is parted from his possessions, a portion of his soul stays with them until the eventual reunion. And when part of a man's soul is being hauled around on fork-lift trucks on to a conveyer belt after several hours crammed into the hold of an aircraft, it's only to be expected that there will be physical side-effects. Normally, of course, nobody ever notices, because everyone in a baggage hall is in the same situation, except for the porters, who are used to it. Since Jane and Bjorn had no luggage, they were able to see things as they really were, usually through the ribcages of the people standing next to them.)

'These people aren't all here,' she whispered. 'Don't worry about it.'

'I wasn't,' Bjorn replied. And then he stared.

Sailing up towards him was a large cardboard suitcase, a scuffed imitation leather hold-all and a canvas kitbag, none of which he'd seen for well over a thousand years, since the baggage handlers aboard the *Argo* had sent them to the Garden of the Hesperides by mistake.

'Um,' he said. 'Excuse me.' He leaned forward and grabbed the handles, which crumbled into dust in his hands. A thousand years is a long time to go round and round in circles.

'What are you . . . ?' Jane screeched, as Bjorn leaped up on to the carousel and kicked the cases to the floor. He staggered, righted himself, and then collapsed backwards on to the toes of a small, elderly-looking man who was sitting on a very ancient suitcase indeed.

'Sorry, mate,' he mumbled.

'That's all right, Bjorn,' replied the elderly man. 'Could happen to anyone.'

To his great surprise, Bjorn managed to say something. It sounded like 'Ggnnk.'

The General walked up and down the improvised line, inspecting his troops.

'Right,' he said. 'This is the big one. What is it?'

'The big one, chief,' said those few spectral warriors who were directly in his line of sight. The rest of them shuddered. Looking back, they were thinking, it hadn't been so bad being dragons' teeth. Hot, maybe, and smelly from time to time, and perhaps if you were really unlucky you'd get filled, but at least you knew where you were coming from.

'And you're utterly fearless spectral warriors, what are you?'

'Terrified.'

'WHO SAID THAT?'

There was a squeak from the end of the line; then a flash of blue light; then a tiny puff of smoke, and then there was an empty black robe lying on the ground. It was neatly folded, and had its canteen, mess tin and water bottle lying on top of it. Habits get deeply engrained when you're in the Army.

'Now then,' said the General. 'What are you?'

'Utterly fearless spectral warriors, chief,' quavered the line as one shit-scared spectral warrior.

The General paused and looked up and down the line slowly. 'Good,' he said. 'So let's get to it.'

*   *   *

'Long time no see, Bjorn,' the elderly man continued. 'How're you doing, anyway?'

'Yeah,' Bjorn mumbled. 'Hey . . .'

The old man frowned slightly, although it was hard to tell; his face seemed to have set rock hard, like araldite, as if it had been marinaded and case-hardened in boredom. He spoke in a relentless dead monotone, like somebody's cousin showing you holiday snaps. 'Aren't you going to introduce me to your friend?' he said.

Bjorn swallowed hard. 'Jane, this is Ulysses. Ulysses, Jane,' he said. 'Ulysses and me go way back,' he added, trying to avoid Jane's eyes. 'Haven't seen you since . . .'

Jane looked again. The sack-shaped thing the man was wearing, the droopy leather hat, the sandals . . . 'Excuse me,' she said, 'but are you . . .'

Ulysses nodded. 'You heard about me, then?' he said. 'Shocking, isn't it?'

Jane rewound her memory quickly; fairy-stories, a film with Kirk Douglas, something they'd made her read at school. In any case, shocking wasn't the word she'd have chosen herself. 'Oh yes?' she ventured.

'If it goes on much longer,' Ulysses droned on, 'I'm going to complain about it. It shouldn't be allowed, really it shouldn't.'

'Um.'

'I mean,' Ulysses said, scratching his nose with his little finger, 'there I was, Trojan War over, all set to go home, got my return ticket and everything. Only Penelope – that's my wife, Penelope – she said, "You be sure and bring me back some of that purple wool they got over there." Very keen on embroidery, my wife. With her, it's nothing but embroider, embroider, embroider, all the time. Anyway, I remembered to get the wool, and I packed it in my small suitcase, and then when I got off the plane I came down here to collect it . . .'

Jane tried to cover her ears, but found it impossible to do this without moving her hands, and her hands wouldn't move.

'The big suitcase came through all right, but God only knows where the little one's got to. I think they may have lost it, you know.'

'Two thousand years,' Bjorn hissed in her ear. She nodded and smiled brightly.

'Very possibly,' she said. 'Maybe it got sent on some-where else.'

Ulysses nodded. 'Maybe,' he said. 'I think I'll just wait a little bit longer, though, just in case. She won't half play me up if I go home without that wool, you know.'

There was a long silence, during which Jane and Bjorn tried walking backwards, a few millimetres at a time. This silence was broken by a number of sounds.

There was a yell from Ulysses as he caught sight of a small, battered leather suitcase on the belt and threw himself on to it.

There was a similar shout of triumph as a man in a long raincoat pounced on a bundle wrapped in news-paper, which happened to contain the Maltese Falcon.

There was a deafening bang as the stun-grenades thrown by the spectral warriors (or, in one unfortunate case, not thrown by a spectral warrior) exploded.

There was a shrill scream from the hostage, who had woken up and wanted his teddy.

There was a confused whooshing noise as Bjorn hurled Jane, his long-lost baggage and himself on to the conveyer, which whisked them round for a few feet before thrusting them both under the little rubber flaps that separate the world of light and life from the black void where the luggage comes from and, ultimately, goes back to.

And then there was silence.

It didn't last. When the smoke cleared, there was

coughing and swearing and whimpering (from the spectral warriors) and shouting (from the General), while the tannoy announced the arrival of Flight TR8765 from Atlantis, and part of the ceiling collapsed on to the carousel.

When it came round for the second time, most of the debris had little stickers on it.

'Where *are* we?'

'Hey, this is great, you know? All these years I've been wishing I knew where this lot'd got to, and now . . .'

'It's okay,' Jane said. 'I think I know where we are.'

As if in answer, the lights came on.

Or at least the conveyer belt brought them out into the light. They looked up, and saw the baggage handlers.

It wasn't a pretty sight. Take a line through what ordinary baggage handlers are like (which is bad enough) and then imagine what they'd look like in industrial-grade heavy-duty distorting mirrors.

'It's okay,' Jane said, extending her legs and stepping lightly off the carousel. 'It's all okay. Relatively speaking, of course.'

'Is it?' Bjorn looked at her and so failed to notice the overhead derrick. 'Ouch,' he added.

'Stop fooling about and follow me,' Jane replied. She walked rapidly away, leaving Bjorn in the position inherited by all males at airports of running after a female while holding more luggage than he could cope with.

'Look,' he grunted, 'slow down a minute and explain. What's come over you all of a . . . ? And you can shut up, an' all,' he added, as the hostage wailed at him and tried to poke its wee fist through his head.

'It's very simple,' Jane replied. 'Gosh, if I'd realised it before, we could have been out of here an hour ago. Come on. I never knew anyone who dawdled so much.'

She had marched up to the nearest wall, and now stood facing it. She put her hands on her hips, smiled, and said 'Open.'

It ignored her. She might as well have been talking to a brick wall.

'Oh,' she said. 'That's awkward.'

Bjorn arrived. The suitcases and the hostage's carrycot (which had materialised somewhere inside the works of the carousel, and had pink ponies on the sides) were only adhering to him through a misunderstanding of the basics of gravity. He sagged, and his burdens flumped to the ground.

'You see,' Jane went on, 'I'd thought, you know, we wanted to go somewhere, so suddenly there was an airport. We needed tickets, suddenly we had tickets. We needed luggage, we've got luggage. And then all that business with the Duty Free shop; I mean, it was as if someone was reading our minds for what, deep down, we really wanted in a Duty Free shop. So I thought, this is all basically wish fulfilment.' She frowned at the wall. 'Only it doesn't seem to work quite like that. Maybe it's got to be consistent with the illusion, or something.'

Bjorn looked over his shoulder. 'Look,' he said, 'I don't want to hassle you or anything, but there's . . .'

Tentatively, Jane prodded the wall with her fingers. 'If it was wish fulfilment, you see,' she said, 'then it'd be easy to work out where we were, we'd still be somewhere inside our own heads. Or somebody's head. A sort of generalised head; you know, the collective subconscious or the race memory or something. Species memory, probably, only of course, you're not . . . What are you pulling my arm for?'

'Because,' Bjorn replied urgently, 'there's a platoon of spectral warriors coming through the baggage machine and . . .'

He was wrong, at that. The baggage machine was

spitting out empty black cowls, while the strips of black rubber over the gateway between the two halls were rising and falling in a manner suggestive of chewing teeth.

'Yuk,' said Jane. 'Come on, let's get out of here.'

'Pathetic,' the General observed.

There were still quite a few of the spectral warriors; only, like the British at New Orleans, there weren't quite so many as there had been a while ago. Had the General more experience in commanding spectral forces, he'd have known better than to try and bump them across dimensions. As it was, he was angry.

The remaining spectral warriors fell into line quickly. The General paced up and down, snarling.

'This time,' he said, 'no mistakes, right?'

'Right, chief.'

'No getting blown up. No getting sucked away. No forgetting to jump off the escalators and being dragged screaming down into the works. Got that?'

'Got it, chief.'

'Fine. Now then.'

There were two gateways.

One was green, one was red. That was all right. It was what was written over them that worried Jane.

The green one said SHEEP and the red one said GOATS. There was also a huge needle, with the hindquarters of a camel sticking out of its eye. Two men in Italian suits were standing behind it, pushing, while a third was making frantic efforts with a bar of soap.

Jane sat down on Bjorn's suitcase, took off her left shoe and examined a large hole in the sole of her stocking. It shouldn't be like this, she thought. In fact, if she had her way, pretty soon it wouldn't be. But they had to get out of here first.

They became aware of someone standing over them. At first he looked like a spectral warrior, but it was a superficial resemblance only. Same black baggy cowl, absence of face, unpleasant metallic-looking sidearms, but this one had a badge with his name on it.

His name was George.

'Having trouble, miss?' asked George.

Jane looked up. 'As a matter of fact I am,' she said. 'I wonder if you could help me?'

The black hole that was George's face flickered into the anti-matter equivalent of a smile. 'Do my best, miss. That's what we're here for, after all,' he said. 'Now, what seems to be the trouble?'

Jane took a deep breath. 'For starters,' she said, 'where are we, what happened to the dimensional shift, who is it chasing us, and how do we get back to the mainstream dimension without going through those gates over there? I take it you do have to be dead to go through there.'

'Quite right, miss,' George replied. 'Although dead is as dead does, as I always say. Still, that's by the by, isn't it?'

In the far depths of his hood, something twinkled cheerfully. Jane nodded and smiled encouragingly.

'Well,' George went on, 'where you are now, miss, you're in the main entrance hall of judgement control. That's where you have to show your credentials to Immigration, to see if you're going to go first class or economy, smoking or non-smoking. Your baggage will be weighed, and if it's tried in the balance and found wanting then you get charged excess. And like you said just now, miss, being dead is essential. No exceptions, you see. Rules is rules.'

Jane nodded. 'I quite understand,' she said. 'So we're quite a few dimensions away from normality, I take it.'

'Absolutely right, miss,' George replied. 'Well spotted, if I may say so. If I were to hazard a guess, I would say you left the mainstream by falling through an artificially created hole in the dimensional shift. I wouldn't be at all surprised if it happened while you were in a restaurant somewhere. Does that sound right to you?'

By this stage, Bjorn had given up listening. He was going through his kitbag. It was a thousand to one chance that the big jar of Greek olives was still in there, but it was worth a shot.

'I think I was kidnapped out of my own dimension by an official called Finance and General Purposes, to stop me finding out about why he's trying to sabotage the human race,' Jane said. 'Would that account for it, do you think?'

'Oh, I should say so, miss,' George replied. 'Happens more often than most people realise, that sort of thing. We get a lot of that down here.'

Jane nodded. 'And then,' she went on, 'I think he hid me away in the back of his mind – well, in his conscience, actually, which is the nastiest place he could think of. It's where all the horrible things which he knows deep down inside ought to happen to him are stored. I didn't like it much in there, to be honest with you.'

'Don't blame you, miss,' said George. 'Dodgy places, consciences. Then what happened?'

'Well,' Jane said, trying to remember, 'shortly after that . . .'

'Got them!' Bjorn shouted. 'Hey, that's brilliant!'

'Shortly after that I was rescued, and I'm not quite sure where I was then, but I suppose it must have been in one of the Administration office blocks, because if I'd just escaped from inside this person's head, it would stand to reason that I'd end up pretty close to where he was, don't you think? Or am I way off beam?'

'Sound right to me, miss,' said George encouragingly. 'Go on.'

Jane thought for a moment. 'That's where I sort of lost track,' she said. 'You see, my . . . this man here, he sort of pulled some dimensions apart and we just sort of fell through, and here we are in an airport sort of thing.'

'A very neat way of putting it, if I may say so, miss.'

'And at first I thought I must be inside my own head this time, or at least sort of, because everything I wanted to happen sort of happened, only not quite, if you see what I mean. And I thought, Yes, because all through my life people have been telling me that where I've been going wrong is not really knowing what I actually want.'

George nodded, or at least the gash in the side of reality which he represented wobbled a bit. 'Pretty close, miss,' he said. 'You're on the right lines, but not quite there. If I might explain?'

'Please do.'

'Hey, *and* my Proud To Be Weird T-shirt. I've really missed this, you know?'

'Bjorn,' Jane said, 'shut up.'

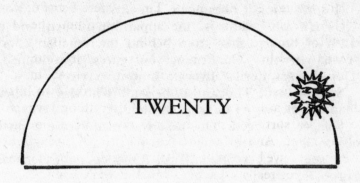

TWENTY

ALL RIGHT, said the wall, YOU WIN.

Staff nodded and opened his eyes. I'm listening, he thought. Can we do this the easy way, because I've had a hard day, and burning bushes or anything like that really wouldn't be a good idea.

. . . And then there was a flash, and a cloud of foul-smelling yellow smoke, and a buzzing sound, like all the flies in all the kitchens of all the transport cafes in the whole world . . .

'Stubborn, aren't you?' said a voice from the chair opposite. 'I expect you're going to insist on visual inter-face as well?'

''Fraid so, yes.'

'More fool you, then.'

. . . And another flash, red this time, and the chair was full of a huge scarlet figure, with horns at one end, cloven hooves at the other, and a sour look somewhere in the middle.

'What a bloody pantomime the whole thing is,' it said. 'The dressing up, I mean. You've no idea how uncom-fortable this get-up is, especially when it's hot. Do you think we could have the window open?'

'I don't think it does open, actually.'

'Don't you believe it,' the apparition replied, and a crash of broken glass from behind the Venetian blind proved its point. 'Confirming your guess,' it continued, 'Dop Ganger, devil's advocate, at your service.'

Staff nodded. 'Thought so,' he said. 'Who was the other chap, by the way? I quite liked him.'

Ganger shrugged. 'Oh, that was me. I have a dual personality, you see.'

'I see,' Staff replied. 'Like Finance and General Purposes, you mean?'

Ganger nodded. 'Exactly,' he replied. 'It's one of the few real executive perks there is. And you don't have to declare it on your tax return. At least, I don't,' he added.

Staff rubbed his chin thoughtfully. 'But of course,' he went on, 'the Ganger I've been running about with – oh I *see*, your *double*; oh, very clever – he's just a tiny part of you, like the tip of the iceberg or something?'

Ganger moved his head slightly in confirmation. 'It's a staff-saving exercise,' he said. 'We're really hot on that in our department. Instead of having lots of different members of staff, you see, we just have the one. But I'm flexible. I spread myself thinly, you know.'

'Lots of different hats, you mean?'

'Some with holes in them, some not,' Ganger replied smoothly. 'We call it going corporate, but that's just a term of convenience.'

'I see,' said Staff. 'So, why you?'

'Someone has to do the audit,' Ganger replied, 'and I suppose we're naturally type-cast for the role of auditors, aren't we?' Staff allowed himself a brief smile. 'We remain separate entities,' Ganger continued, 'even though we work for the same main boss. And if your lot are way off course, we have to give you a helping hand now and then.

Unfortunately – from your point of view, that is – we can't help introducing a little . . .'

'Devilment?'

Ganger scowled. 'That's supposed to be a joke, I suppose,' he said. 'Do you want me to write it down, or do you trust me just to remember it?'

'So we're way off course,' Staff said quietly. 'I thought so. Is it all to do with him? You know, Finance and . . . ?'

'Mainly,' Ganger said carefully. 'But your lot helped. Believe me, they really did. Some of them have a real natural talent for . . .'

'Yes,' Staff interrupted, 'I dare say they do. That's Administration for you.' He stopped briefly and his brow wrinkled. 'Hold on, though,' he said. 'I thought you told me you weren't a . . . or at least the bit of you I knew as Ganger wasn't a . . . that he was sort of co-opted. That's why I was so keen to try and introduce mortals, you see, because you said you'd tried it and it worked.'

'Oh, absolutely,' Ganger replied. 'We do. We subsume the part into the whole, that's all. The only problem we have with that is getting rid of the squishy bits afterwards.'

Staff shuddered slightly. Separate entities, he reminded himself. 'Okay,' he said, 'I'm all clear on that one. And you've done a thorough audit, and you've worked out that where it all went wrong is with Finance making a cock-up with the sun that time. And now you're in a position to nail him, once and for all. Is that it?'

The air was becoming thick with yellow smoke, and there was an offensive smell of brimstone. Ganger nodded.

'We shall make a full report,' he said, 'and we'll make it stick, because we've got a witness. We shall recommend that he be redeployed in our department.' And Ganger licked his lips noisily.

'That's fine,' Staff replied, looking away. 'The only thing is, you seem to have lost your witness.'

'Not quite,' Ganger said (and his voice wasn't a voice any more so much as the buzzing of a million flies). 'In fact, he's right where he should be.'

'Is that so?'

'*Indeed.*' Staff tried not to look as the shape which had been Ganger turned out to be the illusion of a solid body created by a huge swarm of flies in close formation. *Where better? Rather than go to all the trouble and expense of arresting him and arranging for him to be delivered to the Seat of Judgement under armed escort, why not just persuade him to go there himself? You learn little wrinkles like that when you're a . . .*

'And all that mucking about,' Staff said, leaning forward until his head was in the centre of the swarm. 'All that trying the poor girl out in various departments and so forth, that was just to lure him into the trap?'

Certainly not. That would have been pretty inefficient. We think she's ideal for the job, don't you?

'Which job?'

Buzz.

'Don't ask me,' Rosa said. 'Twenty years in catering and suddenly he decides he wants to be a monk. A monk,' she repeated. 'Can you beat it?'

The County Palatine exchanged glances with the Count of the Saxon Shore. 'It's a phase he's passing through,' said the County Palatine. 'And even in monasteries they've gotta eat, you know?'

Rosa stared for a moment. 'You know,' she said, 'I think you guys are as crazy as my crazy brother. I'll get you the check.'

She walked away. The Electors looked at each other.

'Pity,' the Lord High Cardinal said. 'That Rocco, maybe

he makes a lousy Emperor, but give him a pound of mozzarella and a bucket of anchovies and you're in business.'

'And the profiteroles,' groaned the County Palatine. 'Don't forget the profiteroles.'

'I mean,' added the Count of the Saxon Shore, 'Charlemagne, yes. Charles the Fifth, yes. But could they do you tagliatelle verde that's absolutely *al dente* and still leave you change out of twenty bucks? Like hell.'

The Lord High Cardinal nodded sadly. 'Still,' he said, 'there it is.' He glanced down at his watch; and a strange-looking watch it was, at that. Where your watch has hands, it had eyes. 'Hey, we'd better shoot.' He picked up the bill and signed it. 'So long, Rosa,' he called out. 'Our best to Rocco, tell him to say one for us.'

He stood up, emptied the toothpick-glass into his pocket, and led the way.

'I see,' Jane said. 'We were brought here.'

'Yes, miss.'

'Just so as to bring him here?'

'That's right, miss.' George extended a largely non-existent arm and took firm hold of the carrycot. 'And your friend, of course. He's our star witness, you see, miss.'

'I see,' Jane repeated.

George hesitated, and bit the whirling expanse of nothingness that would have been his lip. 'I expect you're a bit upset, miss, what with the way you've been treated and everything. Only to be expected if you are, miss, if I may say so.'

Jane shrugged. 'You'd have thought so,' she said, 'but I'm not really. Or at least I am, but . . . You see, all my life I've really wanted to know what was going on, and why it's all such a *mess*. And now I'm beginning to see. Or at least, I think I am.'

'That's the spirit, miss,' said George. 'Now, can I just see your passports a minute, please?'

Jane nodded, and produced them. After a moment's perusal, George handed them back to her. They were both open.

Jane's passport had her name, and her photograph, and the rather embarrassing bit where it says about any distinguishing marks, the bit she tended to keep her thumb over whenever possible. Bjorn's, however, had a name and a photograph, but . . .

Bjorn took it from her and grinned sheepishly. 'When these lads say under cover,' he explained, 'boy, do they mean *deep* cover.'

He reached up into his face and pulled. Jane gave a little scream, and then opened her eyes. Bjorn was holding a limp rubber mask in his hand and grinning.

Only his name wasn't Bjorn, of course.

'Just one question,' she asked. 'Why Bjorn?'

'Because,' Bjorn replied, and shrugged. 'I happened to see it on the back of a packet of cornflakes, if you must know, and . . .'

'Thank you,' Jane said, bitterly. 'Serves me right for asking, I suppose.'

(Because what Bjorn's passport gave as his name was, in fact, Gabriel; and what Jane really wanted most of all right now was somewhere where she could be sick in reasonable privacy.)

'It wasn't easy for the lad,' George was saying. 'Personality surgery, all that sort of thing. Very proud of him, we are, back in the department.'

Jane turned on him furiously. 'Oh yes?' she said. 'And what department would that be?'

There was a puff of yellow smoke.

★   ★   ★

'Right,' said the General, 'We go in, we zap everything that moves, we rescue the hostage, we come out again. All clear so far?'

The spectral warriors nodded uneasily. That wasn't what was worrying them.

'And afterwards,' continued the General, 'we have a full kit inspection for the survivors. If there are any survivors, that is. Do I make myself clear?'

There was a murmur of assent from the spectral warriors, and then they shuffled into battle formation, ready for the attack. Despite the mechanical precision of their combat drill, there was a certain amount of unseemly pushing and shoving for places in the front rank and other positions of maximum danger. Although spectral warriors naturally tend to think of survival as something that only happens to other people, there was no point in taking unnecessary risks.

'On the command Charge,' the General snarled, 'charge. Understood?'

'Understood, chief.'

'That's fine. Now then, boys. *Cha . . .*'

The word froze on his lips as a door, which hadn't been there a few seconds ago, opened and a figure in uniform came through it.

Spectral warriors are trained in destruction rather than mathematics, but they can count pips, and the newcomer had more pips on his shoulders than you'd expect to find in a fruit-juice factory.

He strolled along the line and stopped, about three yards away from the General, who for his part seemed to have frozen solid.

'Stand easy, men,' murmured the newcomer, and the overhead strip lighting gleamed on the gold lace of his epaulettes and the peak of his cap. The odd thing about his cap was the fact that it had two neat round holes in it just above his ears, for the horns to go through.

With a tremendous effort the General opened his mouth, but nothing came out except a few woodlice and a rather laid-back-looking spider.

'Arrest that man,' said the newcomer. 'Come on, look lively about it.'

Sixty-seven spectral warriors were suddenly very, very happy.

The world stopped.

It didn't come to an end, of course, it simply stopped. The sun jerked to a halt in mid-air and hung there, its engine idling. The earth seized on its axis, but without the juddering crash there should have been, as so much inertia suddenly found itself with nowhere to go. There was a general paralysis of clocks, water stood still in rivers, winds evaporated. Entropy's meter stopped running. Raindrops hung in the air like astronauts in zero gravity.

Except, of course, in New York, where they always have to be different. Anyone looking very closely indeed would have detected some movement there, but only a tiny amount. The majority of the citizens were caught in the general freeze-frame effect; but there was a small party of rather fat men strolling up Thirty-Sixth Street with their hands in their pockets. Three of them were smoking big cigars. They weren't in any obvious hurry.

At the corner of Thirty-Sixth and Broadway, they stopped and waved. A yellow cab without wheels floated noiselessly over the top of the motionless traffic and pulled in to the kerb. Metal steps extended themselves to side-walk level, and the fat men climbed aboard. The cab pulled away, drifting at the speed of, say, a rather slow gondola, and slowly climbed up into the sky until it was lost among the clouds.

By an oversight of the sort which was only to be expected, given the overall level of efficiency of the Administration in general, there was another tiny cell of people left awake and functioning during the general shutdown. They were sitting in an office in Wall Street when it happened; two men and a girl. The girl was the first to speak.

'Darren,' she said quietly, 'I think it's the end of the world. What'll we do?'

The man called Darren thought for a moment. 'You sure about that?' he said.

'Jesus Christ, Darren,' the girl yelled back, 'just come to the window and look for yourself.'

Slowly, Darren put down his telephone, stood up and walked to the window. Years in Wall Street had trained him to analyse situations immediately.

'Yep,' he said, 'it's the end of the world all right.' He sighed; then he strode back to his desk again. 'Okay, guys,' he said. 'Let's get to it.'

'So,' the other man shouted, 'so what do we *do*?'

Darren smiled. 'Sell,' he said.

'Basically,' the Lord High Cardinal summed up, 'we find you guilty as charged of – what was it? Tony, where are my goddamn reading glasses, you know I'm as blind as a bat without . . . of gross negligence, failure to disclose material information, mismanagement, misappropriation of funds and – hey, what's that, I can't read your writing – yuh, being guilty. You have heard the testimony of Mr, uh, Gabriel. Have you anything to say?'

The accused, formerly head of the Finance and General Purposes committee, mumbled inarticulately but said nothing. The six layers of insulating tape over his mouth may have had something to do with it, of course.

'No? You're sure? Well, okay then, I guess that just

leaves the sentence. Any thoughts on the sentence, guys?'

There was a brief exchange of whispers on the podium; then the Lord High Cardinal leaned back in his chair, straightened the white bands at his neck (which looked very like a napkin tucked into his collar if you looked closely) and set his features in a judicial expression.

'Opinion,' he said, drumming his fingers on the desk in front of him, 'is a bit divided here. Tony says rip your lungs out with a plastic fork, Louie says no, that's too good for a scumbag like you, you ought to be shoved down the toilet along with the alligators until you've learned your lesson, and my learned friend the Count of the Saxon Shore . . . Yeah, well, anyway, I disagree.'

There was absolute silence in court. Sixty-seven spectral warriors stood as still as rock-hewn statues, their faces behind their masks bathed in silly grins.

'Personally,' continued the Lord High Cardinal, 'I say, so what, everybody makes mistakes now and then.' He frowned. 'The point is,' he added savagely, 'only losers get found out. Hey, Tony, where's that stupid cap thing? No, not that, dumbo, that's somebody's sock. Right, now then, where were we?'

The other accused wailed, and waved his hands and feet in the air. Nobody took any notice. When it comes to changing the nappies of the guiltiest creature on God's earth, there are no volunteers.

'This court,' said the Lord High Cardinal, 'sentences the two of you as follows. You first. Stand up.'

The erstwhile General was lifted to his feet. He made a mooing noise against the tape, but no-one heard.

'By the special request of the prosecuting advocate,' intoned the Lord High Cardinal, 'and in recognition of your special talents in the field of administration and public relations, you are to be assigned to the staff of the Prosecuting Department.' The Lord High Cardinal winced. 'Hey, you know, that's *inhuman*. Oh well, never mind. As for you – somebody lift the kid up so he can hear, all right? – as for you, since you have temporarily taken up residence in the body of a mortal, this court – say, who thought this one up? It's *wicked* – this court has no jurisdiction over you. You will therefore be deported back to the world to live as a mortal.' The Lord High Cardinal grinned. 'In Kansas City,' he added; then he turned to his closest colleague and winked. 'Okay, Tony?' he said. 'Does that beat the plastic fork idea, or what?'

There was a scuffle, and the two accused were taken away. The Lord High Cardinal settled himself more comfortably in his chair, and took off the black cap.

'Which brings us finally,' he said, 'to the last item on today's agenda.'

How, you may ask, does the Administration work?

It doesn't, of course; but supposing it does . . .

There are the Departments. Each separate department is manned by a permanent staff of officials, and is headed by an officer of Grade II or above. The heads of department form the Finance and General Purposes committee, which passes resolutions for the approval of the College of Electors. It is the job of the Electors to turn the recommendations of the committee into draft orders for ratification by the Main Boss.

The Main Boss. The Man Himself. Numero Uno. The Top Brass. The guy you'd eventually get to see if you absolutely *insisted* on seeing the manager. The Emperor.

All perfectly logical, yes? It would be quite wrong, after all, for the real power to lie in the hands of career civil servants who don't even belong to the same category of life-form as the people being governed. The main boss inevitably has to be a mortal. The trouble has always been finding the right mortal for the job.

Many centuries ago, the Electors hit on the clever idea of not actually telling the Emperor what his job consisted of.

They didn't lie to him, of course, perish the thought. But they were distinctly parsimonious with the truth. To begin with, they did at least tell him that he was the Emperor, without going into all the tedious details of what the job description actually entailed. But even that little snippet of information caused severe problems, so they got into the habit of making sure that when they told him, he wasn't actually listening.

In practical terms, it worked, up to a point. It was intended as a temporary measure only.

In the last hundred years or so, the Emperor has been encouraged to keep a low profile. Rocco VI, as already noted, made pizzas. His immediate predecessor, Wang XIV, ran a small bicycle repair workshop in the back streets of Hong Kong, right opposite the best Cantonese restaurant in the Colony. Neville III (better known to history as Neville the Magnificent) had a paper round outside Macclesfield, and did a little window-cleaning on the side, strictly cash in hand. Joseph XXXIX Ncoba carved little wooden elephants. Gupta IX moonlighted as a petrol pump attendant, and was one of the few Emperors ever to abdicate as a result of an irreconcilable conflict of interests. François XXIII spent his entire reign in a room nine feet by five, firmly convinced that he was a ratchet screwdriver. He was, everyone agrees, one of the better twentieth-century Emperors.

Rocco, Wang, Neville, Joseph, Gupta and François were the successes; the rest weren't quite so hot. The worst was probably Wayne XI, whose five-hour reign was the second shortest in Imperial history. It wasn't the Electors' fault, of course; the first they knew about his disastrous latent tendencies was when he put up the Greenpeace poster in the front window of his tiny flat in downtown Brisbane.

The shortest reign on record was that of Everton I, who was deemed to have abdicated when he missed an easy chance at slip off Courtney Walsh.

The great problem facing the Electors is that only the true Emperor is going to be any good at the job; and the one and only qualification for being Emperor is being the heir apparent, by right of birth. That was why Rocco VI was originally chosen – but further enquiries revealed him to be nothing but a distant cousin of the rightful heir. It was the discovery of the true identity of Charlemagne's closest living relative that set in train the whole sequence of events; because this time, things were going to have to be slightly different. Even temporary measures have to come to an end eventually.

It was obvious who Rocco's successor was going to be; but this time there would have to be a little vocational training beforehand, because the next reign was going to be the crucial one . . .

And you will by now have guessed what Jane looks like – straight nose, strong jaw, the distinctive high cheek-bones familiar from a hundred Imperial portraits. And you won't need telling that her second name, the name that appears on her passport, is Hapsburg.

'Oh,' said Jane. 'Fancy that.'

The world, which had stopped, started again.

Starting implies a beginning. Maybe it's just a cheap-skate verbal trick, but we'll repeat it to let the true significance sink in. The world started again.

Nobody noticed, of course, apart from a few market-makers in New York who suddenly realised that they'd sold everything three minutes before the most colossal upwards swing the markets have ever experienced. By the time the markets stopped rising, staggered helplessly and then quite simply ceased to exist, they'd all pinned letters of resignation to their chairs and gone off to Wisconsin to make new lives for themselves as raffia weavers, and so never knew how right they'd actually been.

Starting implies a beginning. Within ten minutes, things were already very different. The sun moved along its inevitable course. The grass grew. The rain fell. Time ticked, gravity pulled, history coagulated, the tides rose and fell, men and women tripped and blundered their way through the darkened china-shop of human existence. On the wall of Plato's cave, nobody noticed the brand-new notice asking the last person to leave to make sure that the lights were switched off; but that was because, somehow or other, it had been there all the time.

What was different was that it was doing it all by itself. There was nobody running it. It was just . . . happening.

('Hey,' said Ganger, in the back of Jane's mind, 'you can't do this. Stop it at once.'

Why not? I'm the Empress, aren't I? I can do what the hell I like.

Ganger howled, as his fingers started to lose their grip on the projecting shelf of subconscious he was desperately clinging to. 'But it won't *work*,' he shouted. 'There's got to be somebody to run things, or they won't work. They won't run themselves, you know.'

Won't they? We'll soon see about that.

What Ganger meant to say was, 'Maybe they'll work for a while, if you give the sun and the moon and the earth and rain and wind and time and all that sort of thing some kind of semi-sentience, but who's actually going to supervise it and fix it and put it all back on course if it starts to go wrong? Now I suppose you'll say you will, but you're mortal, you won't be around for ever, and so you'll have to train a successor, and that won't be easy, believe you me, oh no.' But since it's impossible to say anything at all if you've suddenly just ceased to be, he only got as far as 'Ma . . .'

What Staff, the Electors and the rest of them said is unrecorded, which is probably just as well. (It's unlikely to have been anything nice.)

And then, with a sigh like the switching off of a hundred million computer screens, the great army of celestial officers, functionaries, administrators, schedule clerks, programmers and timeservers faded away into the air from which they had originally come; and after them their offices, their desks, their files, their hardware, their software, the memory of their existence – until all that was left was one bright, golden paperclip, spinning and sparkling in the upper air, falling or rising weightlessly into the sublime emptiness which is all that remains when Order has finally been tidied away.

And Jane thought, Right then, got that sorted, it should work fine now. I could murder a glass of orange juice.

And in her mind, something said, No, not orange juice, you'll get indigestion, think what happened the last time you had orange juice on an empty stomach, you'll . . . but never got any further, because a moment later it too was sucked away, to its great surprise, and Jane was left alone – definitively alone – with her thoughts.

And finally, the Empress saw everything that she had sorted out, and behold, it was no worse than she'd expected, all things considered. And the evening and morning were the sixth day.

And on the seventh day she ended the work which she had made, and she rested; or at least she tried to rest. But all the milk in the fridge had gone off because of a power cut, and none of the shops were open because it was a Sunday.

The sun rose.

Being nothing more than a dollop of burning gas, it had no way of knowing that it was bang on schedule, right on course and in exactly the right place at precisely the right time.

Because nobody was watching, the slight movement on the face of the waters as the first organism twitched into life went completely unnoticed. No reception committee, no ribbon to cut, no brass band, nothing.

Because nobody was taking notes or filing reports to the appropriate quarters, the flawlessness of the sun's landing and the seamless interface of day and night were completely wasted.

Because it was nobody's responsibility and nobody's fault, the very first living cell was completely alone as it jerked open the window of its consciousness and let out the primordial scream of birth. But it screamed nevertheless. And screamed again. And waited.

There was no reply. There were sounds: the lapping of the waves, the sighing of the wind, the soft grinding of tectonic plates, the distant echoes of the scream itself wrapping themselves doglead-like around the poles and drifting back, but there was nobody to hear them except for one lonely consciousness.

It waited. It screamed again. It listened. Splash, swish, sigh, grunge, hiss. Nothing.

Now, when you're feeling uncertain and apprehensive and you're not a hundred per cent sure you should be here anyway, there's nothing quite so beneficial to morale as a good old sing-song. There was a small, embarrassed cough and then a reedy, squeaky but grimly determined voice began to sing . . .

The sun has got his hat on,
Hip hip hip hip hooray . . .
It was a very small voice, a still, small voice, an infinitesimal voice alone in an infinite sea.
The sun has got his hat on . . .
it repeated firmly. Silence.

A few yards away, something stirred. The movement was so tiny that even if there had been anyone to see, they'd have missed it. But it stirred, and listened, and became alive; and sang:
The sun has got his hat on,
And he's coming out today.

And that was that. There was no going back from here. The continents braced themselves, contorting their rocky coastlines into sheepish grins. They were going to be needed after all.

So, when the next dawn came, not one but many voices – soprano, alto, contralto, tenor, baritone, bass, flat, thin, loud and soft – many millions of voices were raised to greet it, and they sang:
Here comes the sun, little darling,
Here comes the sun,
It's all right . . .

And the evening and the morning were the eighth day.

ODDS AND GODS

Dedications are traditionally used for currying favour.
Accordingly:

To Chris Bell and David Barrett, for the favour
And to Michelle Hodgson and Menzies Khan, for the curry

CHAPTER ONE

On the cloudy heights dwell the gods. They are spirits of light, deathless and ever young. They feast continually in palaces wonderful beyond description, and theirs is a happiness which mortals could never possibly attain.

Indeed. Pull the other one for a veritable feast of campanology. The true facts of the matter are as follows.

In the Sunnyvoyde Residential Home dwell the gods, the whole miserable lot of them. They are cantankerous old buggers, deathless but decidedly no longer young. They witter and bicker continuously in day rooms painted that unique shade of pale green used only in buildings set aside for the long-term storage of the sick and elderly, and they hate it like poison.

All except for Ohinohawoniponama, a vegetation spirit formerly revered by a small tribe of Trobriand Islanders. Since the entire tribe died of influenza a century ago, taking their language with them, nobody can understand a word he says; but it doesn't seem to matter. He smiles a lot, is no trouble at all to anyone, and spends most of his time in the television room watching Australian soap operas.

'Of course he's happy,' commented Marduk, over lunch in the dining room. 'Poor bloody savage, he's never had it so good. Probably thinks he's died and gone to Heaven.'

Marduk had been the warrior god of the ancient Sumerians, which made him one of the oldest gods in Sunnyvoyde. He was, by his own reckoning, six thousand years old, crippled with arthritis, and (in the words of Mrs Henderson, the matron) a bit of an old crosspatch. Which is like defining death as feeling a bit under the weather, or describing the Second World War as a free and frank exchange of views.

'Let me just stop you there, Mardie,' interrupted Lug, shadowy and enigmatic god of the pre-Christian Celts, as he walloped the bottom of an inverted ketchup bottle. '*Died and gone to Heaven.* I mean, we are talking about an immortal god here, and I just wondered if you'd care to clarify . . .'

'You know perfectly well what I mean.'

'Ignore him, Mardie,' said Freya, the Germanic Queen of Heaven, surreptitiously polishing her fork. 'He's just being insufferable.'

'I thought I was being enigmatic and shadowy, Fre.'

'Your tie is in the gravy.'

There had been a, let us say an *understanding*, between Freya and Lug ever since the World had been created out of the bones of Ymir the Sky-Father (or, in Lug's case, scooped out of the churn of the stars into the butter-pat of Time; the Creation is a highly personal thing to all gods and they get very embarrassed if you ask them to talk about it). Obviously, since Freya's people spent most of their time massacring Lug's people and driving them into the sea, nothing could ever come of it; until now, when it was really rather too late.

'I don't know why they let his sort in here,' Marduk carried on. 'Lowers the tone, I say.'

'His sort?' Lug asked, ignoring the kick on his shin from the other side of the table. 'Footnotes, please.'

'Wogs,' Marduk replied. 'In my day, we'd have had his lot up the top of the ziggurat and tied to the altar in three minutes flat. Now, of course, we've got to have them in here with us, which I say is wrong. And they get special food.'

'Live and let live, I say,' mumbled Adonis, Greek god of spring and beauty, through his few remaining teeth and a mouthful of soup. As usual, nobody paid him any attention, and he continued his noisy struggle with the Spring Vegetable.

'Special food, Mardie?' Lug smiled at Marduk over a forkful of lemon sole.

'It's only the Hindu lot,' Freya said. 'And that's just because they're vegetarians.'

'Vegetarians!' In his prime, Marduk had feasted on the hearts and entrails of prisoners of war. Nowadays virtually everything except plain bread and butter gave him wind. 'Stuff and nonsense. What do they want to be vegetarians for? It's just attention-seeking, that's all.'

'I think it's something to do with their religion, Mardie.'

Marduk scowled. 'What the devil do you mean, religion? They're supposed to be *gods*, for crying out loud. Gods can't have religion. Makes you go blind.'

'Would you pass the salt, please?' said Freya briskly.

Gods do not possess eternal youth; they grow old, just like everybody else. Only rather more slowly.

It is also a fallacy that gods are better than anybody else; quite the reverse. Since there's absolutely nobody who dare criticise them, for fear of being blasted with thunder, they are free to behave exactly as they see fit, which is usually very badly.

It therefore follows that Sunnyvoyde is even trickier to run than the average, run-of-the-mill old folks' home. The fact that Mrs Henderson manages it at all is little short of a miracle. That she runs it with a rod of iron only goes to show the quite devastating force of personality she has at her disposal.

For example, when Quetzalcoatl, the Feathered Serpent of the Aztecs, finally and reluctantly agreed to let his godsons book him in, he was implacably determined to have his own bathroom with hot and cold running blood, all his meals served up in jewel-encrusted skulls and his own retinue of seven thousand dog-headed fiends to devour the souls of anybody foolish enough to give him any lip. After five minutes of negotiations with Mrs Henderson, however, his demands were rapidly revised to staying in bed an extra half-hour and being allowed to substitute a fresco of souls in torment for the framed print of happy kittens above his bed. The happy kittens have, by the way, now crept back to their rightful place, and Quetzalcoatl is usually in his seat in the dining room for breakfast by 7.15.

Only one resident of Sunnyvoyde, therefore, is allowed to have his meals in his room. When asked, Mrs Henderson explains that he's not as young as he was and it wouldn't be fair to expect him to make the effort to come down to the dining room three times a day. Which is, indeed, part of the truth.

'Just put it down on the table, Sandra love,' said Osiris, 'and pass me the remote control thing while you're there.'

'Huh.' The nurse feigned irritation. 'And what did your last servant die of?'

'Atheism.'

'Ah.'

'And the one before that was eaten by crocodiles.'

'Right.'

'Sacred crocodiles, naturally.'

'It's apple crumble again today,' said Sandra cheerfully. 'You like apple crumble.'

Osiris sighed. 'Sandra pet,' he said, 'I'm an omniscient god. Lying to me is the proverbial hiding to nothing. I can't abide apple bloody crumble.'

'Then turn it into something else, Mr Clever,' Sandra replied, arranging the napkin tastefully in the shape of a pyramid. 'Go on, say Whoosh! and turn it into chocolate mousse.'

'I'm not allowed chocolate mousse, and well you know it.'

'There you are, then,' said Sandra. 'Go on, you know you like it really.'

'Get out,' Osiris said, 'before I turn *you* into a hedgehog.'

Sandra grinned at him and shut the door. A nice girl, that. Pretty too, if you like them a little bit on the plump side. Ah, thought the erstwhile Egyptian god of plenty, if only I was two thousand years younger.

The reason why Osiris got his meals in his room instead of having to come down and be sociable wasn't because he was more powerful than the other gods, or more sublime, or even particularly older. It was just that he owned the place and could, if he so chose, give Mrs Henderson the sack.

Several millennia of being ritually murdered each sunset by his brother Set, torn into small pieces and reassembled in a hurry and pitch darkness by his slightly-less-than-nimble-fingered wife Lady Isis in time for his daily resurrection at dawn had left the old boy a physical wreck. Several of his component parts were palpably in the wrong place; and even now he still had nightmares about the many times Isis had finished the reassembly job, sewn him back up again and then turned to him and said, 'Ooh, I wonder where this bit was supposed to have gone.'

His mind, however, was as sharp as ever, or so he kept telling himself; and he attributed this to the fact that it had spent so much time out of his body, while the good lady wife had been rewinding the intestines and poring over the wiring chart. Osiris was firmly of the opinion that a mind in a body is like a racehorse pulling a brewer's dray, or a girl with three Ph.D.s becoming a housewife and dissipating her talents on ironing shirts and buying groceries. All that time and mental energy burnt up in operating limbs and keeping the senses ticking over took its toll, and eventually you were left with something barely capable of working the heart and keeping the bladder under some semblance of control.

He contemplated his lunch.

Apple crumble. You knock your pipes out for thousands of years re-enacting the primal struggle of light and darkness, and at the end of it, some chit of a girl tells you that you like apple crumble and expects you to believe it. And hot custard! If he had a shilling for every time he'd told them he couldn't be doing with hot custard . . . well, he'd still be the richest being in the cosmos, only more so. Hot custard!

He paused, slamming the door on his train of thought.

I'm going soft in the head, he said to himself. Here I am, the embodiment of sublime wisdom, having a paddy over a bit of hot custard. This is worrying. I've been here too long.

Instinctively, he stretched his back and tested his legs against the floor. There was no strength left there at all, only pain. Damn.

Osiris had never been a solar deity. If there was one thing that irritated him more than hot custard, it was being confused with a glorified tram-driver who had nothing to do all day but lean on a dead man's handle and try not to bump into too many clouds. His eldest boy, Horus, did that job (hence the name of the family firm, Osiris and Sun) and it suited him perfectly. Horus had, of course, retired long since and lived in the opposite wing of Sunnyvoyde where (as Osiris liked to think) they put the *old* people. They rarely met these days, although whenever they did Osiris never missed the opportunity to get up his offspring's aquiline nose by shouting out, 'Hello there, young 'un,' across a room full of people. Isis too lived a separate life in a small room in the annexe, which she had decorated with an extensive collection of photographs of the British royal family. Good riddance to them both, Osiris felt. If he hadn't had to drag out his life surrounded by idiots, he could really have *been* somebody.

There was a knock at the door; which meant it was Sandra back again. None of the other nurses bothered to knock.

'A visitor for you, Ozzie,' Sandra said.

Osiris blinked. 'Are you sure?' he said. 'I don't have many visitors. I was inoculated against them years ago.'

'Well, you've got one now, isn't that nice? It's your godson.'

'Oh bugger.'

The meek shall inherit the Earth.

Eventually. When everyone else has quite finished with it, and the meek have stopped saying, 'No, please, after you.' Until then, the cocky little bastards shall inherit the Earth; which means that by the time the meek get their hands on it, they'll wish the old fool had left them some money or a clock or something instead.

Hence the institution of the godchildren. Everybody knows that when it comes to affairs of the heart, gods come second only to the characters in a long-running soap opera for spreading it around. At the height of the Heroic Age, the average god scarcely dared set foot outside his own temple for fear of process-servers with paternity suits.

And the mortal children of the gods had children, and so on, and so forth; and eventually the divine spark became sufficiently dilute to allow the ultimate descendents to pack in minotaur-slaying and damsel-rescuing and become chartered accountants instead.

But in each generation there are throwbacks, particularly where the bloodlines of two or more gods happen to coincide; and from this genetic sump Humanity has always tended to draw its statesmen, its generals, its social reformers, its idealists, its princes of commerce and all the other unmitigated pests who have contrived to make a ball of wet rock spinning in an infinite void into the camel's armpit it is today.

These are the godchildren. And, sooner or later, they find out who they are; and, more to the point, what they stand to inherit, if only . . .

'It's not supposed to do that.'

Predictably enough, there was a moment of complete silence.

'Yes, George, we know that,' said Sir Michael Arlington, breaker of awkward silences to Her Majesty's Nuclear Inspectorate. 'That's why we sent for you, all the way from bloody Iowa. Do you feel up to hazarding a guess as to why?'

'You could do really good baked potatoes in it,' said a white-haired scientist at the back of the gathering. 'I mean, a quarter of a nanosecond in there, add a knob of butter and there you go.'

'You could indeed,' replied Sir Michael. 'And when it was ready it'd probably be able to walk out on its own. Any *sensible* suggestions would be very welcome.'

'It's gone wrong.' Professor George Eisenkopf, resident nuclear genius at the University of Chicopee Falls, Iowa, and the State Department's leading authority on civilian atomic power, scratched his nose with the plastic coffee-stirrer he'd been given on the plane. 'It isn't working properly,' he added, in case there were any laymen present.

Sir Michael winced. 'Please, George,' he muttered, 'don't worry too much about blinding us with science. In what way has it gone wrong?'

'I don't know.'

'Great. Is it about to blow up?'

'Too early to say.' Professor Eisenkopf leaned forward and tapped a couple of keys on the computer keyboard in front of him. The screen flickered, flashed a few columns of figures and announced itself ready to play Monster Nintendo.

'Sorry,' mumbled the baked potato enthusiast, nudging past and pressing some other keys. 'Only my wife's nephew came to see the place the other day, and I haven't had time to . . .'

'Don't worry about it.' Professor Eisenkopf studied the data he'd called up, and pursed his lips. 'You're going to find this a bit hard to relate to, guys, but there's something alive in there.'

'In where, George?'

'In the core,' the professor replied. 'As far as I can tell from this box of tricks, sitting on top of the goddamn pile.'

Sir Michael nodded. 'Probably grilling a few sausages,' he said.

'Pardon me?'

'To go with the potatoes.'

* * *

Not all the gods retired. Some of them still soldier on, mainly because they're horribly overworked and never had time to train a successor.

Just such a one was having a well-earned sit-down and a cold beef sandwich in the infernal heart of Bosworth Pike power station. His name was Pan, and if you add -ic to his name, you get his portfolio in the sublime Cabinet.

'Knit *one*,' he said to himself, squinting at the diagram, 'and pearl *two*.'

He was knitting a matinée jacket for Truth (who, as is tolerably well known, is the daughter of Time) and he had an uneasy feeling that he'd gone wrong somewhere. He had a further unpleasant suspicion that the faint brown check which had crept into the pattern about twelve rows back was in fact his beard.

'Nuts,' he said, and let go of the needles. The knitting flopped, suspended from his chin. He reached for the scissors.

The fact remained that his analyst had recommended knitting as tremendous therapy for hypertension and stress, and over the last few millennia he'd tried just about everything else, several times.

Under him, the ground started to glow green. He licked a fingertip, pressed it ever so gently against the side of the pile, and was rewarded with a loud sizzle. Just nicely ready, in fact. He stood up.

Pan is, of course, a nice god; or at least it's wise to believe so, because our beliefs have a profound effect on the divine self-image. This isn't a comfortable thing for the gods themselves – the Egyptian deity Serapis, for example, never tries to eat a piece of toast without cursing the Faithful for believing in the existence of a crocodile-headed god – and it's by no means unknown for a god to wake up one morning to find himself a totally different shape or species simply because of some thoughtlessly imaginative revival meeting held on the previous evening. Mortals believe that Pan, although an incurable practical joker with a sense of humour that would have appalled Josef Goebbels, is fundamentally one of the good guys and incapable of doing anything that would actually result in lasting harm.

He was going to have his work cut out this time, though.

On the other hand, he was a god; and to the gods, all things are possible, at least in theory. Thus it was that when the emergency repair squad broke into the reactor cell three days later, wearing their lead suits and clinging like covetous limpets to their lucky rabbits' feet, their Geiger counters showed up a radiation level several points below the normal ambient reading.

What they did find was a toasting fork, an unopened pat of butter and five stone cold baked potatoes.

There are some people who like lawyers.

For example, Ashtoreth, the antediluvian moon goddess of southern Palestine, was thrilled to bits when her great-great-great-great-great-great-great-great-great-great-great-great-godson Hyman was made a partner in the leading New York firm of Kaplan and Hart, and drove the other occupants of Sunflower Annexe to the brink of violence by talking loudly and incessantly about Her Godson Hymie, The Lawyer.

Other deities with whom lawyers are popular include: Ahriman, the Father of Darkness; Hermes, patron god of thieves; the Scandinavian Loki, god of lies and deceit; and Belenos, in whose honour the Druids burnt men alive in wicker cages. You can't beat a lawyer, according to Belenos, for the generation of plenty of hot air.

Osiris, for his part, had always reckoned that he could take them or leave them alone, with a marked preference for the latter option. Visits from his current godson were therefore as welcome as a rat in a morgue.

And that, he felt, remembering where he was, is no bad analogy. I really shouldn't be in this place. Hellfire, if only the dozy old bat hadn't had the exploded diagram the wrong way up the last night we did the reassembly, I wouldn't be. I'd be out there, bombarding snotty little tykes like Julian with meteorites.

'How do, Julian,' he said, as his godson entered the room. 'Brought me some grapes, then.'

'Yup.'

'Can't stand grapes.'

'No matter.' There was a gonglike sound as the bag of grapes hit the bottom of the tin wastepaper basket. 'Look, I've got to be quick, I'm due in a meeting in forty minutes. How's life treating you, anyway?'

Osiris paused, stroking his chin. 'Life,' he pronounced, 'is a bit like mashed swede. A little bit's nice for a change now and then, but you wouldn't want to live on it.'

'Yup.' Julian stared at him for a few seconds and blinked twice. 'The leg still playing you up, then?'

'Aren't you going to write it down?'

'Write what down?'

'What I just said,' replied Osiris testily. 'That was a Teaching, that was. You're supposed to write down Teachings.'

'Um.'

'And don't give me that boiled cod look, because there's been dafter things than that said out of burning bushes, take it from me. How's Phyllida?'

'Sorry?'

'Your wife.'

'Oh.' Julian glanced at his watch. 'Fine. I'd have heard if she wasn't. Look, I hate to rush off like this but it really is a very important meeting . . .'

'And Ben? And little Julia?'

'They're fine too. Ask after you all the time. Anyway, it's been great seeing you.'

'Your children,' said Osiris icily, 'are in fact called Emma and Clinton. Keeping busy, are you?'

'Yup, thanks. It's been an uphill job, holistically speaking, with the recession bottoming out, but the medium- to long-term overview of our bedrock client base is definitely more positive than negative, and . . .'

'Just remind me,' said Osiris, 'what it is you do.'

Julian sighed. 'I'm a lawyer, Oz,' he replied.

'Oh,' said Osiris. 'Oh well, never mind. You've just got to try not to give up hope, that's all. I heard a good joke about lawyers the other day.'

'I know them all, thanks, Oz. Look, I'll call you. You look after yourself. Don't do anything I wouldn't do, okay?'

'Son,' replied Osiris with conviction, 'I wouldn't do anything you would. Shut the door on your way out.'

Julian looked at him. 'You feeling okay, Oz?' he asked.

Osiris looked up, startled by his tone of voice. 'I believe so,' he replied. 'As well as can be expected for someone whose small intestine now runs slap bang through the middle of his bile duct. Why?'

'Oh, nothing,' Julian replied absently, as he picked at the handle of his briefcase. 'You just seem kind of odd today, that's all.'

'Odd. Right.'

'Not quite, you know, a hundred and ten per cent.'

'Julian, my boy, if I was a hundred and ten per cent, there'd be a seven-and-a-quarter-inch-high replica of me standing beside me on the hearthrug. Go on, now, sling your hook.'

'You haven't been, for example, hearing strange voices or anything?'

'Yes,' Osiris snapped, 'yours. Now piss off.'

'Okay, okay. Same time next week, right?'

'Right.' Osiris sighed. 'Unless, of course, I'm in a meeting. The doorknob is the round brass thing about three feet up from the floor. A half-turn to the right usually does the trick.'

As Julian retreated down the corridor, he played back his mental tape of the interview, ignoring the crackles. Yes, the old fool had sounded strange; but on reflection, no stranger than usual.

Hey!

Julian stopped, standing on one foot; and suddenly grinned.

He'd just had an idea.

CHAPTER TWO

Once, long ago and far away, a bard sang in the mead-hall of King Hrolf Kraki.

There was dead silence from the King's warriors, his carls and servants as the poet traced the intricate pathways of kenning and metaphor, trope and simile, in the still, tense circle of the tawny glow of the hearth. Nobody moved, and the dark yellow mead glistened untasted in the drinkhorns, as the words of the lay sparkled in the air like frozen dewdrops on a spider's web. This moment, this splinter of time, caught like a fly in amber, mounted in a ring of golden firelight.

It was an old song, so old that nobody knew where it had come from or when it had first been sung. It began at the beginning, when Ymir the Sky-Father had first opened his eyes and seen nothing, nothing but the cold and the wind and the loneliness of the first day. On it swept, gathering pace as the singer peopled the shadowy corners with ghosts: Sigurd the Dragon-Slayer; Arvarodd, who once strayed into the land of the Giants; Weyland the craftsman without equal, whose skill brought him only sorrow; Brynhild, who slept for a thousand years on the fire-girt mountain. And now it crawled on to its terrible end, this song without pity, under the control of no singer; the last days, the rising of the Frost-Trolls, the swallowing of the sun and moon by the Wolf, the last battle on the Glittering Plains, the going-down of the gods themselves. As the poet sang, the world seemed to grow tight and brittle, and King Hrolf nervously motioned for more logs to be heaped on the fire.

And then the poet told of the new dawn of the gods; how they rise again from the ashes of the burnt Valhalla and build a new castle that will never be thrown down, a shimmering, sublime fortress of golden stone where Odin and Thor and Tyr the One-Handed and Frey, who is the friend of wretched mortals, will reign for ever, feasting and delighting in the song and restoring vintage traction engines. And there will be no more winters in this . . .

'Doing what?'

The poet shut his eyes. For one blessed moment he thought he'd actually got away with it.

'Um,' he said, 'restoring vintage traction engines. And no more shall hoar-frost fasten on hawthorn . . .'

'Vintage what?'

Sod, fuck and bugger this stupid, lousy song, muttered the poet to himself. Because some bastard always stops me and asks *What's a traction engine?* and I don't sodding well *know*. And neither did my father nor his father before him, and does it really bloody well *matter* anyway?

'Traction engines. I think they're, um, things that gods sort of, well, restore.'

King Hrolf leaned forward, gathering the cowl of the poet's hood in his frying-pan-broad fist. 'Are you,' he growled, 'taking the piss?'

'No, honestly, that's what it says in the song, and . . .'

'The last one of you clowns,' the King went on, knitting

his brows into something like a long, scraggy thorn wind-brake, 'who thought he could come here taking the piss . . .' The King's face melted into a savage grin. 'Thorfinn, tell this ponce what happened to that other ponce, will you?'

Thorfinn, whose eyebrows were slightly less bushy than his lord's but would nevertheless have made ideal starter-homes for discerning partridges, obliged. Usually a man of few words, he seemed to strike a vein of eloquence that would have allowed the poet to jack in minstrelsy and open a nice little newsagent's shop somewhere quiet.

'. . . Right up his jacksy, and then set fire to it. Talk about a pong, we had to have the roof off in the end, and you still get a taste of it when the wind blows in from the fjord. Was that the one you meant, chief?'

'That's the one.'

The poet twitched. 'Honest,' he said, 'it really and truly says traction engines. Do I look like the sort of bloke who could make up a thing like that?'

There was a long, horrible silence; and then King Hrolf smiled.

'Oh,' he said, 'right. *Traction* engines. That's where you get two bits of rope and a winch and you tie one rope to the bloke's ankles and the other round his neck, and you – yes, got you, fine. Just the sort of thing you'd want in Valhalla, for when it's raining out. Sorry, you were saying?'

Twelve hundred years later, it's safe to point out that Hrolf had got it all wrong. By traction engines, the primeval bard had meant big steam-powered locomotives with lots of shiny brass handles and valves and tappets and bright green paint. Or rather, to be precise, one such machine.

She was called *Pride of Midgarth*, and right now she had just emerged from under a layer of old dustbin liners and potato sacks in the big coalshed round the back of Sunnyvoyde. It had taken a millennium of painstaking effort to get her looking the way she did now; which was a right mess.

'I told you,' said Thor, taking a step backwards. 'Wait till the first coat's completely dry before you bung on the second, otherwise it's going to smear. But no, someone had to know best.'

Odin scratched his head. 'The paint must have been no good,' he said. 'I told you, just because it's cheap . . .'

'Nothing wrong with army surplus paint,' Thor replied. 'Provided,' he added irritably, 'it's allowed to dry properly. Provided some great jessie doesn't go slapping a second coat on while the first's still tacky.'

'I think it looks rather nice,' said Frey, absently chewing a peppermint. 'Sort of dappled.'

Thor ignored him. 'It'll have to come off,' he said. 'Strip it right down all over again, then go over it top to bottom with wire wool and Trike, and then back to square one. God, what a waste of bloody time!'

'Not necessarily,' replied Odin mildly. 'We could always—'

'Look, pillock,' Thor interrupted, 'it's my bloody engine, we'll do what I say just for once. Before you ruin it completely.'

Odin shrugged. It was indeed Thor's engine, and always had been. Two thousand years ago it had been the chariot of the thunder, on which the Lord of Tempests rode across the sky on his way to do battle with the Frost-Trolls. One thousand nine hundred and fifty years ago this Wednesday fortnight, however, it had popped a gasket in the upper inlet manifold, flooded the outer compression chamber and seized the main driveshaft bearing solid on the integral cam. After belting it around with his hammer and using a certain amount of intemperate language, Thor had dumped it in an outhouse and bought himself a replacement; a sort of twenty-thousand ton fire-spitting phosphorescent milk float with scythed wheels and a built-in rev inhibitor that limited the maximum speed to six miles an hour. It was pathetically slow but very cheap to insure, and it didn't keep breaking down in the middle of the Glittering Plains, slap bang in the epicentre of enemy territory and miles from the nearest call box.

Thirteen hundred and twenty years ago come Lammas Eve, Odin had idly remarked that they could have fun doing it up again once they retired. It would be a nice little hobby for them, he'd said. They could get it running and hire it out for flower shows and village fetes and gymkhanas.

Nine hundred and ninety-six years ago, the gods of the Great Aesir had clocked off for the last time, received their signed testimonials and gold watches from the Scandinavian nations, and retired to New Valhall, a purpose-built specially-designed complex in the upmarket suburbs of Musspellheim. It was replete with every conceivable feature required by the discerning ex-god – ceaseless feasting, piped eddas, twenty-four-hour-duty Valkyrie service and so on – and the Aesir valiantly put up with it for three very long weeks before sloping off in the early hours of the morning, leaving a note propped up against the Test-Your-Wrath machine and no forwarding address. And taking with them the vintage traction engine.

'Maybe,' Odin suggested, 'we could just rub it down with wet-and-dry and paint over it.'

'Don't be such a pillock,' Thor replied.

Four hundred and seventy-five years ago, Mrs Henderson had put her foot down. She had no objection, she had said, to her residents having little hobbies. Jigsaw puzzles, yes; also ships in bottles, even one-seventy-second scale models of the Temple of the Gods of Death and Destruction in Tlaxopetclan built out of matchsticks, provided always that the person concerned tidied away afterwards and didn't get glue on the carpets. Great big oily traction engines in her newly decorated television suite, no. Either it went, or they did.

So it went; as far as the coalshed, and for four hundred and seventy-five years (ever since Pizarro conquered Peru, and long before Sir James Watt was even thought of) Odin, Thor and Frey had snuck out after lunch on the pretext of taking a walk, and snuck back in several hours later to wash up and leave oily handprints all over the towels in the downstairs cloakroom.

'Quick,' Thor hissed, 'someone's coming.' There was a frantic scrabble and a heaving of potato sacks, just before the door opened. But it was only Freya, come to ask her brother Frey if he wanted to make up four for bridge.

'Not now, sis,' Frey replied. He glanced downwards, subconsciously aware that something seemed to be wrong, and observed that he was standing in one of the tins of green paint. He sighed.

'You're not playing with that thing again, are you?'

'What thing do you mean, sis?'

'You know perfectly well.' Freya tutted. 'Like silly children, the lot of you. I think you'd better get cleaned up and come back inside before Mrs Henderson catches you.'

'But sis . . .'

'Come on.'

Frey sighed. He'd had a sister ever since the earth was without form and void, but even now he sometimes caught himself thinking, Why me? What harm did I ever do anyone? 'All right,' he muttered. 'But I'm not going to play bridge with a lot of old—'

'Yes you are. And you two . . .' She looked round. The

other two gods had somehow managed to disappear. 'Children,' she repeated.

As soon as the shed door had closed, Odin and Thor crawled out from under the sacking and dusted themselves off. They looked at each other.

'Women,' said Thor.

'Quite.'

Legend has it that the massive glass and chromium offices of Haifisch & Dieb, the greatest law firm in the world, have never been totally empty since the firm was established, on the second day of Creation, to cope with the anticipated flood of product liability claims.

On this night, the lights were still bright on the top floor, home (to all intents and purposes) of Julian Magus, the firm's managing partner. He was sitting at his desk, talking through an idea with a colleague from the Probate and Trusts Department.

'Basically,' said the colleague, rubbing his lead-heavy eye-lids, 'your options are somewhat restricted.'

'Go on,' replied Julian.

'Well,' the colleague continued, 'on the inheritance front, expectations-wise, I feel I have to advise that we're into a pretty narrow band in relation to the justifiable aspirations position. Like, prima facie and on the facts as presented to me, before there can be an inheritance, there has, strictly speaking, to be a death.'

'Yes.'

'This is going to be a problem, isn't it?'

'There's no such thing as a problem, Leon,' Julian replied slowly, 'only an opportunity in fancy dress. You'd do well to remember that if you ever want to get on in this profession.'

'Well, yes,' said the colleague, his palate suddenly dry, 'absolutely. I think we're one hundred per cent *ad idem* on that viewpoint. Sounding a slight note of caution, however . . .'

'Yes?'

'I mean,' said the colleague, 'obviously we've got to get the terminology up together before we can progress this. I mean, if we start with the actual definition of death, maybe we could do something there. Like, where in the book of words does it actually say you can't be dead till you stop moving? There's judicial authority to support a view that—'

'No,' said Julian, 'you were right the first time, the death side is a complete washout. Hiding to nothing time. I was thinking,' he went on, leaning back in his chair and steepling his fingers, 'of approaching this from another angle entirely.'

'Laudable,' said the colleague quickly. 'And the precise vector you had in mind?'

'How about,' said Julian, 'a power of attorney?'

The colleague winced. It was bad enough having to be here, on his own, with Julian Magus, the Great White Shark of the legal profession, knowing that a misplaced comma, let alone an inopportune word, could torpedo an entire career that had been thirty years in the carving out. The golden rule is, never disagree with The Man. Any lawyer worth his clove of garlic and silver bullet will tell you that.

'Highly lucid thinking there, Jule,' he therefore said. 'Certainly an avenue we must explore with the last breath in our bodies. But just very briefly turning it upside down and looking at it in the mirror, I've got this little niggle somewhere that says that all the gods gave the godchildren powers of attorney hundreds of years ago. Like, when they retired? I must have lost you somewhere.'

'Powers of attorney, yes,' Julian replied, staring at the corner of the ceiling. 'But not permanent ones. They could be revoked like *that*, any minute. What we want is something a bit more lasting.'

'But.' The colleague could feel the hot breath of Mr Cock-Up on the back of his collar, but somehow he couldn't help himself. 'I mean, I'm clearly being really *dumb* here, but all powers of attorney can be revoked. Can't they?'

Julian smiled. It was a long, slow smile. Generations back in its evolutionary matrix, wolves and bears and sabre-toothed tigers had played their part in its development. That smile alone was worth hundreds of thousands of dollars every year to the firm of Haifisch & Dieb.

'Not if the person giving the power is certified insane, Leon,' he said. 'I'd have expected you to have thought of that one for yourself.'

CHAPTER THREE

'Oh come on. Not again.'

Mr Kortright, supernatural agent, the only man in history ever to tell the goddess Kali that she probably had something there but it needed a lot of working on, shrugged. 'It's the best I can do for you,' he said. 'Good solid work. You should be grateful.'

'But it's so *demoralising*. I'd rather do voice-overs.'

At his end of the telephone connection, Mr Kortright smiled wryly. 'Pan, good buddy, if I could find some way for you to break into voice-overs, I'd be a very happy man. You've just got to face facts, buster. Your stuff – well, these days the kids don't want it, okay? They got video games, they got consciousness-expanding drugs, they got all kinds of stuff they never dreamed of in your day. Jumping out from behind bushes and shouting "Boo!", you're lucky to be working at all.'

'I can do other things,' Pan replied nastily. 'I can turn you into a tree, for starters.'

'Go ahead,' Kortright sighed, 'faites ma jour. As a tree I wouldn't have to try and find something positive to say about Herne the Hunter and his Amazing Performing

Roedeer. And it wouldn't change the fact that passé is passé. Look, you want the job, or do I give it to Huitzilpotchli?'

Pan blinked. 'Who?'

'Little Pre-Columbian guy, square ears. He also does ritual chants and juggles with the skulls of enemies slain in battle.' Mr Kortright cringed involuntarily. 'Usually he drops them. Go on, the choice is yours.'

'All right,' Pan said, 'I'll do it. But it's the last time, all right?'

'That's the spirit, kid. You can't beat an old trouper.'

Pan replaced the receiver, and allowed his shoulders to slump. It hadn't always been like this.

'Taxi!' he shouted.

Back in the old days, before all the rest of them packed it in, he'd really been somebody. Back then, of course, they didn't have all this psychology.

A yellow cab drew up to the kerb, and a bald head appeared through the driver's window. 'Where to, mac?' it said.

Back then, if you wanted to have an emotion, you had to have a god. If you wanted to feel jealous, you were visited by Eris, Lady of Strife. Anybody who fancied a spot of overweening pride had to wait until Hybris, the spirit of Arrogance, worked through her backlog sufficiently to fit you in next Thursday morning. Sexual desire was impossible without the presence of Eros, the blind, flying archer; a deity so overworked that it was a miracle humanity reproduced itself into the third century BC. And if you wanted a spot of blind terror, Pan was your man.

'Wall Street,' Pan replied, opening the passenger door. His hooves clunked on the sill of the door. For all that he kept them discreetly hidden in Helena Rubinstein designer chinos and top of the range Reeboks, Pan had the legs and feet of a goat. Worse; a goat with rheumatism.

'And get a move on, please,' he added. 'It's absolutely essential I get there by ten.'

The cab driver turned round in his seat and scowled at him. 'Hey,' he said, 'I'll get there as fast as I can, don't panic.'

'Sorry. Force of habit.'

Nowadays, they had emotions. Like all manifestations of the Do-It-Yourself tendency, emotions were quicker, cheaper and somehow, to Pan's way of thinking at least, infinitely tawdry. And there was no romance any more, no glamour. You couldn't bribe Paranoia with a sacrifice of firstling lambs, or appease Claustrophobia with a hymn and a prayer. All right, Lyssa and Hecate wouldn't have taken a whole lot of notice either, but at least you'd have had the feeling of getting a personal service, provided by trained professionals. And say what you liked about the gods, they'd had style.

Once.

'Thanks,' Pan said, leaning forward and putting his hand on the doorhandle. 'Anywhere here will do.'

'Okay.' The cabbie drew up, looked at the meter and asked for his fare. Pan stared at him. It wasn't the best he'd ever done, but it was still good enough.

'Hey, mac, no offence. So maybe it's a bit on the high side. Let's just talk it over, and . . .'

Stare.

'The ride's on me, okay?'

Stare.

'Look.' The taxi driver was sweating. 'How'd it be if I gave you fifty bucks and we forgot the whole thing?'

'Done.'

Perks, Pan thought, folding the money into his pocket and cloppity-clopping his way up Wall Street; one of the few fringe benefits. And am I prostituting my Art, putting the wind up tradesmen? Yes. Good.

Wall Street. Again. It was as bad, he felt, as appearing on chat-shows. He pushed open a pair of huge smoked glass doors and trudged in.

His mind wasn't on the job and he overdid the stare he gave the security guard. He felt a bit guilty as he walked on, leaving the poor man cowering under the front desk with a paper bag over his head.

He overdid the elevator, too. As soon as he got out of it, the wretched thing bolted straight up to the thirty-second floor and stayed there. It was gone midnight before the maintenance men were able to talk it down.

It was, he realised, because he was feeling depressed and bad-tempered after talking to Kortright. And the reason it had got to him so badly was that what Kortright had said was true. He was indeed over the hill. Over Everest, even. Maybe it was time he retired, like all the others.

By now he had won through to the dealing room itself, and he stood in the doorway, looking for a suitable victim. His eye lit on a small, round young man with glasses and just enough hair remaining to thatch a toolshed in Lilliput. He walked over and leaned on the computer terminal.

'Hi,' he said.

'Yes?'

'In twenty minutes,' said Pan, staring, 'the dollar is going to fall so far it'll probably burn up on re-entry.'

The market maker gazed at him out of round, glazed eyes. 'Why?' he said.

'It's the British,' Pan replied. 'The War of Independence was fixed. Results of tests show that George Washington was on steroids.' He paused, turned up the stare by about three degrees, and bent it into a grin. 'If I were you, I'd start selling now.'

'Thank you. Thank you very much.'

'Don't mention it.'

By the time he reached the ground floor, walking down fire stairs that seemed to want to edge away from him, the dollar was so far down you couldn't have traced it with a metal detector, and switchboards were jamming and systems going down right across the world as the financial rats scrambled to leave the floating ship. As he pushed through the doors and set hoof to pavement, Pan was acutely conscious of the buzz, the high feeling of having scared the recycled food out of tens of thousands of people who'd never done him any harm in their entire lives. It was a good feeling. It was what being a god is all about.

But, he reflected as he clattered down into the subway, it's still only a cheap commercial job, and I'm lucky to get that. Dammit, it *is* time to retire.

Definitely.

First thing tomorrow.

'The rear crankshaft cotter pin, thirty-six,' Odin repeated, 'is connected to the offside flywheel, seventy-two, by a split pin, nine.' He peered through his bifocals at the diagram.

'Give it here,' demanded Thor impatiently. 'You've probably got it upside down again.'

Odin tightened his grip on the instruction manual, which was twenty centuries old and held together with brittle yellowed Sellotape. 'It's perfectly simple,' he said, for the seventh time. 'We must just have overlooked some perfectly obvious . . .'

'Where does this bit go?'

Odin and Thor looked round, and saw Frey, patron god of all those who stand about with their hands in their pockets while other people do all the work, held up a small oily widget. 'I found it on the floor,' he explained.

'Bloody hell,' Thor exclaimed, 'that's the manifold release pawl. Why the hell didn't you mention it before?'

'You were standing on it.'

'Give it here.'

Twenty minutes with a screwdriver later, Thor straightened his back, wiped his forehead with the dirtiest handkerchief in the universe, and picked up the widget; which sprang salmon-like from his fingers and was at once lost to sight in the deep carpet of wood-shavings, empty crisp packets and bits of paper that covered the floor of the shed.

'I think,' said Frey, 'it landed somewhere over there.'

Odin sighed. 'Now then,' he said, 'let's all stay calm. Everything is always somewhere.'

'Not necessarily,' Thor replied, burrowing his way head-first into a pile of empty sacks. 'What about Excalibur? What about the lost kingdom of Atlantis? What about . . . ?'

'You know what I mean.'

'Only because I'm a bloody good guesser.'

'Excuse me.'

Thor looked up. His hair was full of coal-dust and a dead mouse had entangled itself in his beard. 'Now what?' he demanded.

'This time you're kneeling on it.'

'Am I?' Thor said. 'Ouch!' he added. 'Yes, you're quite right, well spotted. Right then, let the dog see the rabbit. Now, where did I put my screwdriver?'

'The rear crankshaft cotter pin, thirty-six,' said Odin, 'is connected to the offside flywheel, seventy-two . . .'

'I've just done that.'

'You can't have.'

'Why not?'

'Because,' Odin replied, 'here's the split pin in my hand.'

Yes, thought Thor, so it is. If I was to kill you now, there's no way it would be murder. Pesticide maybe, but not murder. 'Fine,' he said. 'Frey, pass me the mole wrench.'

Atheists would have you believe that there are no gods, but this is patently absurd; because if there were no gods, who made the world? Look at the world, consider the quality of design and workmanship. Consider who is supposed to have made it. Convinced? Of course you are. The San Andreas fault wasn't San Andreas' fault at all.

'Now then,' Thor said. He'd skinned his knuckles, banged his head on the rocker arm and caught his nose in the overhead cam. He was also a thunder and lightning god, and thunder gods, like doctors, never really retire. It would be as well for the world's sake if the engine started first time.

'Ready?'

'Ready.'

Thor turned the crank, and there was a loud groaning noise. It could have been the gears waking from nearly two thousand years of sleep; or it could have been the laws of physics saying that there was no way the engine was going to work because all the bits had been put back in the wrong places, and being told by the other forces of nature to put a sock in it. Whatever it was, it was followed by a splutter and a roar and then a peculiar sound like a hippopotamus pulling its foot out of very deep mud . . .

'It's working,' Thor shouted. 'Sod me, it's bloody well working! Will you just look at—'

. . . Followed by a loud bang, and then silence. Small bits of sharp metal dropped down through the air. There was a very peculiar smell.

'I don't think it was meant to do that,' said Frey.

★   ★   ★

'Are you a doctor?'

'No,' replied the postman, 'actually I'm a postman. Did you want to see a doctor?'

'Are you sure you're not a doctor?'

'Yes. Now if I could just get past . . .'

Minerva, former goddess of Wisdom, stood her ground. She was still in her dressing gown, worn inside out, and her slippers were on the wrong feet. 'I told them,' she said, 'I want to see a doctor. I keep telling them, you know, but they don't listen. Will you have a look at my knee?'

'If you like,' said the postman, taking two unobtrusive steps backwards. 'But I am in fact a postman, and—'

'They're still trying to poison me, of course,' Minerva confided. 'You tell them, they'll believe you if you're a doctor.'

The side door opened, and Thor put his head round. Having taken in the scene at a glance, he winked at the postman, tiptoed up behind Minerva and shouted very loudly indeed in her ear.

'Right,' he said, a few moments later, 'shouldn't have any more nonsense out of her for a day or two. Last time she didn't come down for a week. Have you got a parcel for me? Registered?'

'Um,' replied the postman. Of all the places he delivered to, Sunnyvoyde was the one he dreaded most. Since his round also included the Grand Central Abattoir, the explosives factory and the Paradise Hill Home for Stray Killer Dogs, this was probably significant.

'Name of Thor?' he asked.

'That's me.'

'Sign here, please.'

Back in the seclusion of his room, Thor ripped the package open and ploughed his way through the obligatory balls of rolled-up newspaper and grifzote shapes until he found what he was looking for. He examined it.

For once they hadn't sent the wrong bit. He was impressed. Maybe his luck was about to change.

He stuffed the small metal object into the pocket of his cardigan and stumped off to find Odin. On his way he bumped into Frey, who was trying without much success to hide a bunch of bananas down the front of his jacket.

'Has it come?' Frey asked.

Thor nodded, and produced the object. 'Probably not quite to size,' he said, 'but we can soon have a few thou. off it with the file, and then with luck we should be in business. Why are you trying to hide those bananas up your jumper?'

'Sssh,' Frey hissed. 'I'm not supposed to eat bananas, the old bag thinks they give me wind.'

'And do they?'

'Whose side are you on, exactly?'

Half an hour later, the vital component was in place, and the three gods stood nervously beside their pride and joy. Somehow the thought that when the crank turned, this time the engine might fire and run and the beast would be back in action once again was extremely unnerving, and the emotions registering on the gods' unconscious minds must have been akin to those of a doctor who, having managed to eliminate all known illnesses and cure death itself, suddenly remembers that he has a wife, three children and a mortgage to think of.

'Ready?'

'Suppose so.'

Odin rolled up his sleeve, gripped the handle firmly, and turned it. There was a clatter, a dull thump and—

'Gosh,' Frey said, 'it works. Well I never.'

'There's no need to sound quite so surprised,' Odin replied. 'I mean, it was really pretty straightforward when you think about it.'

'Was it?'

'Oh yes.'

'Where did I get the idea that it was horrendously difficult from, then, I wonder.'

They stood for a while, staring. Ten seconds later, it was still working. And ten seconds after that. And ten seconds after that . . .

'Okay,' Thor said briskly. 'Now we've got it going again, what are we actually going to do with it?'

To the gods all things are possible, all things are known. 'Um,' said Odin.

'I mean,' Thor went on after a longish pause, 'there's all sorts of things we *could* do with it.'

'Oh yes.'

'All sorts of things.'

'The possibilities are endless.'

'Only . . .' Thor bit his lip. 'Just now, like on the spur of the moment, I can't quite remember, you know, offhand . . .'

Small, muffled bells rang in Frey's memory. 'Something to do with fun-fairs, I think,' he said. 'And church fêtes and that sort of thing.'

'Really?'

'I think so,' Frey replied. 'Of course, it's been a long time.'

Odin came to a decision. 'Why don't we take it for a ride?' he said. 'You know, a test drive. Just to make sure it actually is working all right. Before we actually do, um, whatever it was we were going to . . .'

'Good idea.'

'Fine.'

In retrospect it was a pity that, in the excitement of the moment, they drove out through the shed door without remembering to open it first; but at least it proved that the old jalopy was still as robust as ever. The gods, however, didn't let it worry them, once they'd brushed the bits of doorframe and hinge out of their eyes. Almost as soon as the engine started to move, a strange exhilaration seemed to sweep over them; a longing, almost, for some long-forgotten sensation that had something to do with speed, the open sky, the wind in one's hair . . .

They were airborne.

'Thor.'

'Yes, Frey?'

'Is it meant to be doing this?'

'Doing what, precisely?'

Odin was poring over the map. In his left hand he had a magnifying glass, and in the right a compass.

'Estimating our windspeed at thirty knots,' he said, in a loud, clear voice, 'that down there must be Budleigh Salterton.'

Frey turned and looked at him, vertigo temporarily pigeon-holed. 'What did you say must be Budleigh Salterton?'

'There,' said Odin, pointing, 'just below us now. I always was pretty clever at this dead reckoning stuff.'

'You mean that there?'

'Yes. Which means that, if we continue this course for another—'

'That's a cloud, Odin.'

'No it's not, don't muck about. We've got a schedule to work to, remember?'

Thor and Frey suddenly remembered Odin's thing about maps. It had slipped their memories until now precisely because, a very long time ago, they had induced Odin on pain of being gutted on his own altar never to so much as look at another map for as long as the world existed. For his part Odin knew for a certainty that he was an excellent map reader, but the landscapes mucked him about by moving around when he wasn't looking. Other things that mucked Odin around included doors, piles of cans in supermarkets and all known electrical appliances.

'If it's not a cloud,' Frey persisted, 'how come it's grey and wispy and you can see the ground straight through it?'

Odin sat still for a moment, staring at the map and chewing the end of a pencil. The pencil in question had once been part of a pen-and-pencil set presented by God the Father to God the Son on the occasion of his passing his Religious Education O-level. 'All right,' he said, 'Budleigh Salterton is somewhere over there.' He waved an arm in a circle round his head. 'So I make it that if we carry on the way we're going, we should be in Papua by nightfall.'

'Since when,' Thor interrupted over the clatter of the turboprops, 'did we want to go to Papua? Come to that, where is it exactly?'

'Now you're the one doing the kidding around.'

'Straight up,' said Thor. 'I had this mate, you see, who was really into hang-gliding. He could read a course off a map sooner than you could say Jack Robinson.'

'Who's Jack Robinson?'

'He's a figure of speech.'

'Oh,' said Frey. 'One of them.'

'It's in the middle of the Indian Ocean,' said Odin, holding the map about an inch from the tip of his nose. 'Principal exports include—'

'Yes, but why do you want to go there?'

Odin looked up. 'I don't,' he said. 'All I said was, if we carry on this line till nightfall, that's where we'll fetch up.'

'Oh I see,' Frey said, 'it wasn't an announcement, it was a warning.'

'Would you mind shutting up for a moment, please,'

Odin said. 'Only I am trying to navigate here, and it's never easy at the best of times.'

'So don't fly at the best of times,' Frey replied. 'In fact, not flying at all would be all right with me. Have either of you two noticed how far we are off the ground?'

'For pity's sake, Frey,' Odin said, not looking up, 'don't be such a baby. Are you chicken or something?'

Frey scowled. 'I am a god, remember. I can be anything I jolly well like. Only I'd prefer to do it down there, if it's all the same to you.'

Thor sighed. 'You know,' he said, gazing out over the kingdoms of the earth, spread out before him like items of kit at an army inspection, 'I used to be really good at this. Flying around and stuff. Only somehow,' he went on, biting his lip, 'somehow I'm not sure I can still—'

'Don't be so feeble,' Odin replied. 'It's not something you forget; it's like riding a bicycle.'

'Sure,' Frey muttered. 'You wobble about for a while and then you hit the ground.'

'That's not what I meant at all.'

'And anyway, when was the last time you ever rode a bicycle?'

'Don't change the—'

'Come to that, have you ever ridden a bicycle at all? Ever?'

'Loads of times.'

'Name one.'

'Look,' Odin said, struggling to pull together the various strands of his thought processes, 'this isn't about riding bicycles, this is about flying. And here we are doing it. And we know *exactly* where we . . .'

For ever afterwards, the locals of that part of Cornwall referred to the rocky outcrop into which the Aesir now flew as Shooting Star Hill. The giant crater formed by the crash became a popular venue for outings and picnics, and attractive colour postcards are available at several local newsagents.

'What,' said Frey, struggling to his knees and spitting out earth, 'happened?'

'Easy mistake to make,' replied a voice, conceivably Odin's, emanating from the upper branches of a fir tree. 'Could have happened to anybody.'

'Will somebody please get this traction engine off me?'

'Low cloud,' Odin went on, 'and a damn great pointy hill; you're bound to have accidents sooner or later. Whoever created this region had absolutely no consideration whatsoever for the safety of air traffic. In fact I've a good mind—'

'But you keep it for special occasions,' interrupted Thor, from under the engine. 'Look, stop fartarsing about, you two, and get me out of here.'

'Yes,' grumbled Frey, grabbing hold of the front fender and heaving, 'but what happened?' To the gods all things are possible, and their strength has nothing to do with muscle and sinew; rather, they draw power from the earth, the sky, the sea. 'Don't just stand there, you prune,' he shouted at Odin, who had made it down from his tree and was scrabbling about for his map, 'grab the other end of this before I drop it on my toe.'

'Coming.'

'Too late.'

'When you've quite finished larking about,' said Thor's voice, from some way down, 'perhaps you'd get on with the job in hand.'

'All right, just give me a minute, will you?'

'The sooner I get out, you see, the sooner I can kick Odin's arse from here to Christmas.'

Between them, Odin and Frey manhandled the hundred-ton machine out of the way, rested it gently on the ground and rescued Thor, who had made a man-shaped hole of the kind usually only seen in Tom and Jerry cartoons.

'Are you saying,' Frey enquired, 'that he managed to fly us straight into the side of this mountain?'

'Actually,' Odin said, 'she's not that badly damaged. Not badly damaged at all. Front wing's a bit the worse for wear, but a few minutes with the lump hammer and you'd never know it was there.'

The reason why gods never fight among themselves is quite simply the futility of the exercise, combined with the prodigious danger to the environment. Two all-powerful, immortal, invulnerable beings going at it hammer and tongs are guaranteed to damage absolutely everything within a fifty-mile radius, with the sole exception of each other.

'Lump hammer, did you say?'

'That's the ticket, Thor. Just pass it over, would you?'

'On its way.'

Five minutes or so later, Frey (who had found the packed lunch and eaten the honey and raisin sandwiches and two of the chocolate mini-rolls) got up, wandered across the now considerably enlarged crater and stirred one of the two recumbent forms with his toe.

'All right, chaps,' he said. 'Now you've got that out of your systems, shall we be cutting along?'

'Good idea.'

'Where to, exactly?'

CHAPTER FOUR

'Yes,' said the thug. 'As a matter of fact, I am a doctor. What's it to you, prune-face?'

'Oh.' Minerva, former Roman goddess of Wisdom, blinked. Vague thought-shapes swirled in her brain, struggling to fight their way through the fog and the mist. 'You don't,' she quavered, 'look much like a doctor to me.'

'Shows how much you know, you daft old bag,' the doctor replied. 'Now sod off, will you, there's a love, because we've got things to do.'

Minerva hesitated. The next line was welling up in her mouth, the words that she always said to everybody; but somehow, for once, they didn't seem appropriate, and she wasn't even sure why she wanted to say them. Nevertheless, she did.

'I shouldn't be here, you know,' she said. 'I shouldn't be here at all.'

The second thug, who was also a doctor, grinned. 'Too bloody right,' he said. 'In a pine box ten feet under's where you should be. Now sling your hook.'

'I'm terribly ill, you know,' Minerva said, or at least her lips shaped the words. Prompted by a massive sense of danger, her mind, what was left of it, was doing something it hadn't done since Machiavelli was an adolescent. It was thinking. Little flashes of electricity were crawling along the overgrown, corroded synapses of her brain. 'By rights,' she went on saying in the meanwhile, 'I should be in a hospital.'

'Let go of my sleeve or you will be.'

Two intrepid electrical discharges met in a jungle of decaying silicone somewhere in Minerva's cortex. It was like Livingstone and Stanley; and the one who might have been Livingstone might have said *Another fine mess you've gotten me into*, because the next words Minerva uttered were comparatively rational but factually incorrect.

'You're not a doctor,' she said.

'Get stuffed.'

The first thug, who really was a doctor, gave her a shove and she sat down heavily on an aged sofa, twisting her knee. Thirty centuries of outraged divinity suddenly woke up and screamed at her to turn this arrogant little mortal into a beetle. She tried it. She missed.

'Come on, Vern,' said the second doctor. 'Let's get it over with and get out of this dump.' He strode forward, not aware that in doing so he'd stepped on Inanna, the great goddess of Uruk, who went *splat!*

In the corridor that led from the day room to Lilac Wing, a nurse blocked their path.

'Excuse me,' she said, 'but who are you and what are you doing?'

'We're doctors.'

'Nobody told me anything about any doctors.'

'So bloody what?'

The nurse, who was the same Sandra who had managed to make Osiris eat hot custard, moved her feet slightly, making it impossible for the two men to brush past her without actually knocking her over. 'May I ask what you're here for?'

The two doctors looked at each other. Because they really were doctors, and had therefore served their time as the lowest form of life in a busy hospital, they still had buried deep in their psyches the basic fear of nurses that all doctors carry with them to the grave. This fear springs from the subconscious belief that the nurse knows a damn sight more about what's going on than they do, and for two pins will show them up in front of the patient.

'We're here to see someone.'

'Oh yes? And who might that be?'

The first doctor glanced at the back of his hand, where he'd written the name in biro. 'It's a Mr O'Syres,' he said. 'We're here to—'

'To give him a medical,' the second doctor interrupted.

'That's right, a medical.' The first doctor started to feel better; this was convincing stuff. He decided to expand it. 'He's thinking of taking out some life insurance,' he went on, 'and so we were asked—'

'You're sure about that?'

'Course we're sure.'

'*Life insurance?*'

'That's right, love, so if you'll just show us the way.'

'Yes, of course,' said Sandra. 'Just follow me.'

She led them to the big broom cupboard and opened the door a crack.

'This is Mr Osiris' room,' she said. 'I won't put the light on because he's asleep at the moment. If you just go in quietly and wait for him to wake up.'

As soon as they were inside, she turned the key and ran for it.

By the time she'd reached Osiris' room, the penny had dropped. Two doctors. What is it that needs two doctors? Easy. She pushed open the door.

'Oh,' she said. 'Sorry.'

She hadn't actually seen Mr Osiris without any clothes on before. True, she'd heard things about him; how he'd undergone a lot of surgery in the past, had all sorts of bits removed and so on. She wouldn't have been worried by scars. Zip fasteners, though, were another matter.

'For pity's sake,' Osiris said, reaching for a towel. 'You could have given me a heart attack.'

'Sorry.'

Osiris looked down at the middle of his chest, and grinned. 'Weren't expecting to see that, were you?'

'No,' Sandra admitted. 'Doesn't it get rusty when you have a bath?'

Osiris shook his head. 'Stainless steel,' he replied. 'I had them put in to make it easier for my wife.'

'Ah.'

'Was there something you wanted?'

Sandra's brain dropped back into gear. 'Get dressed, quick, and I'll help you into your wheelchair,' she said. 'There's two doctors come to certify you.'

'I beg your pardon?'

'Certify you,' Sandra hissed, grabbing a dressing gown and shoving it on to his lap. 'Say you're mad. I've locked them in a broom cupboard.'

Despite the ravages of time, Osiris still retained a fair proportion of the vast mental capacity required of a supreme being. He scowled.

'It's that little bugger Julian,' he growled. 'You wait till I get my hands on him, I'll make him wish—'

'Quickly!'

She helped bundle Osiris into some clothes and got him into the chair. The corridor was empty.

'Typical bloody lawyer's trick,' Osiris was muttering under his breath. 'Have me certified and then take over all my powers with one of those damned attorney things. I knew I should never have signed it.'

'That's awful,' Sandra replied absently. 'If we can just make it to the service elevator, we'll have a clear run out the back to the car park.'

'Mind you,' Osiris went on, 'you've got to hand it to him for brains. Chip off the old block in that respect. Mind out, you nearly had me into the wall there.'

'Stop complaining.'

As they passed the door of the broom cupboard, they could hear the sound of strong fists on woodwork and, alas, intemperate language. It looked to be a pretty solid door, but that wasn't something you could rely on. Never trust something that was once a tree, Osiris reflected. He'd met a lot of trees in his career as a nature god, and had learned a thing or two about them in the process. One: don't sit under them in thunderstorms. Two: never lend them money.

'All clear.'

'Hold on a moment,' Osiris said. 'Where exactly is it we're going?'

Sandra glowered at him impatiently. 'Somewhere you'll be safe, of course,' she said. 'Look, they'll be out of there in no time at all, so do you mind if—'

'*Where?*'

'My mum's, of course.'

'Ah,' said Osiris. 'Right.'

'Is there somebody in there?'

The first thug, who was of course a doctor and there-fore well aware of which of the small bones in his hand he'd broken while banging furiously on the door, stopped hammering and yelled, 'Yes! Let us out!'

There was a pause.

'Are you a doctor?' said the voice.

★　　★　　★

'What do you mean,' said Julian, 'escaped?'

The first thug pressed a coin into the slot, taking advantage of the hiatus in the conversation to choose his words with care. 'He got away,' he said. 'One of the nurses locked us in a cupboard. When we got out . . .' He shuddered. It had taken a long time, and he was still getting nightmare flashbacks from the conversation he'd had with Minerva through the door. 'When we got out, he wasn't in his room. We searched the whole place from top to bottom. He's legged it.'

'Wheeled it,' suggested his colleague, shortly before collapsing against the side of the phone booth with severe abdominal pains. Since he was of course a doctor, he could have told you the technical name for them.

'You buggered it up, you mean?'

'Yes,' admitted the first doctor; then, recalling who he was talking to, added, 'without prejudice, of course.'

'Fine,' said Julian, after a while. 'I do hope for your sakes that you're heavily insured, because I happen to specialise in medical negligence claims.'

'Hey,' said the second thug, grabbing the receiver, 'that's not fair, we were only . . . Why are you laughing?'

'I'm sorry,' Julian replied, 'it's that word you just said, fair. Always has that effect on me. Now listen, you find him and get him committed like immediately, or the two of you'll find yourselves having trouble getting work as snake oil salesmen, let alone doctors, kapisch?'

'Now hang about,' shouted the second doctor, and the pips went.

'Damn,' said his colleague. 'Now what do we do?'

'What the man says would be favourite. Any idea how we go about it?'

'No.'

'And you call yourself a doctor.'

'Shut up.'

*　　*　　*

Situated in its own extensive grounds among acres of
rolling cloudland, Sunnyvoyde commands extensive views
over three galaxies, but is a bit of a cow to get to if you
have to rely on public transport. Add a wheelchair into
the equation, and x suddenly equals extreme difficulty.

'You're sure there's a bus?' Osiris demanded. He was
starting to feel the cold.

'Of course there's a bus. How do you think I get to
work every day?'

'And what is a bus exactly?' Osiris wrinkled his omniscient brow. 'I mean, I've heard of them, of course, but I
don't think I've ever actually seen one. After my time,
really.'

Sandra blew on her hands and jumped up and down
until the sensation of a cloud wobbling under her feet got
too much for her. 'It's a sort of square box,' she replied,
'with a wheel at each corner and seats inside.'

'It's a box you go inside?'

'That's it.'

'Ah. You mean a coffin.'

'No. Coffins don't have wheels.'

'Bet?'

'It's bigger than a coffin.'

'Bigger than a large coffin?'

'You can judge for yourself.'

Exactly on time, the bus drew up and stood for a
moment, its engine running and doors closed, as if it was
catching its breath. 'Have you,' Sandra asked, 'got any
money for the fare?'

'Money?'

'Round flat metal discs with someone's head on one
side and—'

'I mean,' replied Osiris irritably, 'I didn't know you had
to pay to go on these things. Yes, thank you. Would two
gold pieces cover it, do you think?'

'I would imagine so.'

'Hold on, then.'

'What are you doing?'

'It's a bit,' Osiris grunted, 'like I imagine putting contact lenses in must be. Come on, you little – oh blast, I've dropped one.'

'No,' Sandra explained patiently, 'you don't have to put them on your eyes. The man just takes them from your hand and gives you a ticket.'

'What's a ticket?'

'Just leave all the talking to me, all right?'

'Ruddy funny way to go about things, if you ask me.'

Osiris' bad temper soon evaporated when he found that he was only charged half price, and after a few minutes it was obvious he was enjoying himself immensely. The way he kept yelling 'Whee!' and pretending to steer told its own story.

'Will you stop that. People are staring.'

'I'm used to that.'

'Yes,' Sandra whispered back, 'but we want to be inconspicuous, remember. We're escaping. Running away. Or had you forgotten?'

Osiris had the good grace to look embarrassed. 'Sorry,' he said. 'Hasn't really sunk in yet. I've been a lot of things in my time, but Most Wanted wasn't one of them. Usually,' he added, 'quite the reverse.'

'Really?' Sandra searched in her bag for a peppermint. 'I thought you gods were loved and worshipped. You know, revered and stuff.'

'Revered, yes,' Osiris replied. 'Loved, no. All right, people say a lot of nice things to you when you're a god, but it's either because they want something or they're frightened of getting a thunderbolt up the jacksie, not because they think you're fun to be with. Masses of prayers and sacrifices, but nobody ever remembers your birthday.'

'Gosh,' said Sandra through her peppermint. 'I didn't even know gods had birthdays.'

'Proves my point, doesn't it? Should I be sitting here, do you think? Only it does say, *Please give up this seat if an elderly or disabled person needs it.*'

'I think you qualify on both counts.'

'Do I? Well I never. It must be very complicated, being a mortal.'

It was one of those slow buses. From Sunnyvoyde, it meandered at the pace of an elderly glacier with corns past the Islands of the Blessed, across the Elysian fields, round the back of Valhalla – long since sold for development and converted into possibly the most nerve-jangling theme park and paintball game center in the cosmos – along the Nirvana Bypass to the Happy Hunting Grounds Park and Ride, where the bus suddenly filled up with dead Red Indians carrying shopping bags. Shortly after a brief stop at the Jade Emperor's palace, Osiris fell asleep, and only woke up when Sandra tugged at his sleeve. He looked out of the window.

'Come on,' Sandra was saying, 'the next stop is ours. I'll get your wheelchair out of the rack.'

'Hey,' said the god. 'Where *is* this?'

'Wolverhampton.'

'But it's so ruddy *small*.'

'You should have thought of that before. Like on the sixth day, for instance.'

'That wasn't me,' replied Osiris, defensively. 'That was the other bloke. Thing, name begins with a J.'

'Up we get.'

Although he never dared mention it to his priests for fear of causing immortal offence, Osiris had never been a great one for ceremony and fuss; but there are certain ways of going about things that are bred in the bone, and when a god visits Earth, he expects more of a welcoming party than a small child on a bicycle and a stray cat. Osiris sighed.

'And people actually live here?' he said.

'Yes.'

'How do they fit in those titchy little houses?'

'We manage.'

'Which way now?'

'Actually,' Sandra said, opening the gate and pushing the wheelchair through, 'we're here.'

'Surely not.'

'Look. If you're going to be difficult we can turn straight round and go back. Just because you're a god doesn't mean you own the place.'

'Well, actually . . .'

'You know what I mean.'

Sandra opened the front door, parked Osiris' wheelchair in the small front parlour, and went through into the kitchen. From behind the kitchen door, Osiris could hear a buzz of voices. The door opened.

'Mum,' said Sandra, 'meet Mr Osiris; he's a god. Mr Osiris, this is my mother.'

Sandra's mother was a small, potato-shaped woman, who looked as if she'd been repeatedly washed in bleach but not ironed. She stared at the god suspiciously.

'Is he staying for his tea?' she asked. 'Because I was going to do liver.'

'Actually, Mum,' Sandra replied, 'Mr Osiris'll be staying with us for a week or so. You see, he's escaping from his godson, who wants to take over the world by having him certified.'

'He'll have to have our Damian's room, then.'

'That'll be fine.'

Sandra's mother sniffed. 'He's not one of those vegetarians, is he? Only I thought we could have steak and kidney tomorrow. There's vegetable soup if he'd rather, but it's only packet.'

'Steak and kidney will be fine, Mrs . . .' Osiris said. 'I really don't want you to go to any trouble on my—'

'And what about clean towels,' Sandra's mother went on, 'what with him being in a wheelchair and everything, because it's Thursday tomorrow and the man's coming to fix the aerial in the morning.'

'Mum . . .'

'And you haven't forgotten I have my feet done Mondays now instead of Wednesdays, have you?' Sandra's mother sighed. 'Though I suppose he could have the small chair from the lounge and I'll move the nest of tables into the kitchen. For now,' she added. 'Can he use the, you know, on his own?'

'Mr Osiris is a *god*, Mum. I'm sure he'll be no trouble at all. Will you?'

'You'll hardly know I'm here, Mrs . . .' Osiris sucked his lower lip. Either he was missing something or else Julian's doctor friends were well within their rights wanting to have him certified. Two weeks in this place, he added to himself, and I might even give myself up.

'Does he want a scone?'

'Yes.'

'Right.'

Sandra sat down and took her shoes off. 'I'm sure you two'll get on like a house on fire,' she said, looking at the ceiling. 'She likes visitors really.'

Well quite, Osiris muttered to himself. After a day or two she probably puts vases of flowers on them. 'It's very kind of you,' he said aloud, 'doing all this for me. You're sure it's no trouble?'

'No trouble at all.'

'Oh.'

'We are *not* lost.'

Thor glanced up at the sky. 'Anyone else saying that,'

358 • Tom Holt

he said, 'would have grounds to be worried about sudden bolts of lightning.'

'What?'

'Perjury,' Thor explained. 'If it's any help, that down there looks very much like Bury St Edmunds.'

'What do you know about Bury St Edmunds?'

On the chariot flew, whirling like a fast black cloud over the sleeping landscape of (for the record) northern Italy. Where its shadow fell, thin and ghostly in the pale moonlight, dogs whined and sleepers turned in their beds, crossing themselves and dreaming strange dreams.

'A damn sight more than you do, probably,' Thor replied. 'Look, there's the High Street directly below us, and that bright light there must be Sainsbury's.'

'Sainsbury's?'

'Since your time,' Thor replied, not without slight embarrassment. Odin and Frey looked at each other.

'All right,' Thor snarled, 'so I've got this, um, acquaintance in Bury St Edmunds, and from time to time she sends me the odd postcard . . .'

'*She.*'

'She's seventy-five years old, for crying out loud,' Thor snapped.

'Well, you're no spring chicken yourself.'

'Shut up and navigate.'

There had been a time – not so long ago in divine chronology, but for the gods all things are different – when the passing of Thor's chariot made the skies boil and the earth shake; but no longer. There were many reasons – the decay of faith, the decomposition of the ionosphere, the fact that when Odin put the main crankcase assembly back together he somehow managed to connect up the swinging arm direct to the connecting rod without linking it up to the reciprocating toggle – and all probably just as well. Mankind cannot bear too much unreality, and there are rather too many military airfields and guided missile bases on the north-east Italian border to make overflying in an environmentally disruptive UFO a sensible course of action.

'What's she called, then?' asked Frey.

'What's who called?'

'Your bit of stuff in Bury St—'

'She is not,' Thor growled, 'my bit of stuff, okay? Mrs O'Malley is a highly respectable—'

'Carrying on with married women now, are we?'

'. . . widow who happens to have a sincere and scholarly interest in Scandinavian folklore, and who happens to have consulted me on a few points of reference concerning the—'

'What's her first name, then?'

'None of your business.'

'Ethel. I bet you it's Ethel.'

'Look, can we please talk about something else, because I find this whole conversation extremely childish and pretty damn offensive.'

'So it is Ethel.'

'No it's *not*.'

Beneath them, a flash of silver, a few silhouettes against the sky, the glitter of the moon on a broad expanse of still water. The early fishermen of the Venetian lagoon looked up from their nets and wondered what they had just seen; a black cloud flitting across the moon, a cold, sharp breeze ruffling the lagoon into a myriad feathery waves, a distant sound as of far, unearthly voices bickering.

'And *that*,' said Odin triumphantly, 'must be Scarborough.'

CHAPTER FIVE

M rs Henderson frowned.
It hadn't been a good day, so far. She'd completely
lost one resident, another was out loose somewhere on
the transparent pretext of buying socks, she'd had
intruders on the premises claiming to be doctors (which
unsettled some of the more ethnic gods, to whom doctors
were people in leopard skins with short tempers and
impaling sticks) and now one of the nurses had called in
sick. Her intuition told her that Chaos was back in town
looking for a rematch.

About three quarters of the residents of Sunnyvoyde
would have you believe that they had been solely responsible for putting Chaos in her place and giving Order the
confidence to come out of her shell and form meaningful
relationships; but Mrs Henderson knew better. Chaos, as
far as she was concerned, was a Greek word for what
happened when you let people try and run their own
lives, and it wasn't something that she permitted in her
establishment, thank you very much. Had Mrs Henderson
been in charge of the Garden of Eden, stewed apple would
have been on the menu every second Wednesday, and

anyone who didn't eat it all up would have had it put in front of them at every meal until they did.

'Melanie,' she said into the intercom, 'just come in here for a moment, will you?'

It was time, she decided, to stop getting in a fluster and start sorting things out. The doctors had gone, and any further reference to them would be firmly discouraged. Mr Lug would be back eventually, and she would have a few well-chosen words with him when he did, and that would be all right. Sandra, the nurse who had had the misfortune to contract some unspecified illness, would be given the opportunity to select a career more conducive to her obviously delicate health. Mr Osiris, though, was a different matter entirely. Although the precise situation wasn't totally clear, Mr Osiris would appear to have booked out for good; his toothbrush was gone, as were his gold watch (presented to him by the people of Egypt in recognition of four thousand years of loyal service; he was ever so proud of that) and the little jar he kept all his leftover organs in. And Mr Osiris owned the place. She wasn't quite sure what to do about him.

By way of explanation: an unresolved uncertainty in Mrs Henderson's life would be a bit like a Tyrannosaurus in Central Park; out of place, extremely rare and, after a fairly short interval, extinct.

'Yes?'

'Melanie, I want you to put a call through for me. It's a Los Angeles number. Fairly urgent, if you don't mind.'

She wrote the number, and a name, on a yellow sticky and handed it to her secretary, who glanced at it, looked up sharply, caught her employer's eye and left the room quickly.

There, said Mrs Henderson to herself, problem solved.

★   ★   ★

There was no reply to Melanie's call, except for the inevitable answering machine.

Thank you for calling Kurt Lundqvist Associates. There's no-one in right now to take your call, but if you leave your name, your number and details of the supernatural entity you want killed after the tone, we'll get back to you as soon as we can. Bleep.

On the credit side, Osiris was blissfully unaware of the second front that was just opening up against him. On the debit side, he was sitting in front of a big plateful of Sandra's mother's rhubarb crumble.

'Gosh,' he croaked. 'How delicious. And is all that for me?'

It was a prospect, he felt sure, that would have intimidated anyone. To someone whose stomach currently lay sideways alongside his left lung, the result of a fairly basic misunderstanding on the part of Lady Isis of pages 34 to 56 inclusive of the instruction manual, it was enough to cool the blood.

'Tell him,' said Sandra's mother, 'he needn't finish it if he doesn't want it all.'

'Yes, Mum.'

'Mind you, there's starving children in the Third World who'd be really glad of a nice bit of rhubarb crumble.'

It'd certainly make them count their blessings, Osiris reckoned. He picked up his spoon and picked tentatively at the southerly aspect. Care was needed in making the first breach in that impressive structure; one false move and the whole lot might come crashing down on him.

'Yes, Mum.' From behind the cover of the big vase of plastic flowers, Sandra winked at him, setting off an alarming sequence of memories which he thought he'd cauterised years ago. Dear God, yes, the first time he ever went to tea with Isis's parents. Isis's father was the Word and her mother was the Great Void; and they weeded out their daughter's ineligible suitors by means of the diabolical practice of Trial By Massed Vegetables.

With a start, Osiris realised that all these goings-on were causing him to revisit his lost youth; which was a nuisance, to say the least. He hadn't enjoyed his youth one little bit. In fact, far from losing it, he'd left it behind, so to speak, by means of an open window and a rope of knotted sheets.

'Tell him,' said Sandra's mother, 'there's some nice hot custard if he wants it.'

'Oooh yes,' Sandra replied. 'Mr Osiris *loves* hot custard, don't you, Mr Osiris?'

Gods don't make particularly good liars; they don't get the practice, because they don't feel the need. Nobody asks a god why he's late for work this morning, or was it him who broke the window, for fear of getting a response along the lines of, Yes, and you want to make something of it? Several thousand years of married life had, nevertheless, left Osiris with a reasonable grasp of the basics of the craft.

'Yes,' he said. 'How delightful.'

While Sandra's mother was out of the room, doing whatever it is you do to bring about hot custard, Osiris leaned across the table and grabbed Sandra by the wrist.

'No offence,' he hissed, 'but you've got to get me out of here. Much more of this *Does he like cold custard?* stuff, and somebody not a million miles from here is going to go to bed a different shape.'

'Don't be horrid. That's my mum you're talking about.'

Osiris sighed, letting go of Sandra's wrist. 'I know,' he said, 'and I'm being very ungrateful. Old god's privilege, that is. But she treats me like I don't exist. You shouldn't do that to a god, you know. We're insecure enough as it is without people not believing in us all over the place.'

Sandra bit her lip. 'I don't think she can see you very well,' she said.

'Ah.' Osiris nodded. 'I might be able to help you there. What is it, cataracts? Glaucoma?'

Sandra shook her head. 'No,' she said, 'her eyes are fine. I think it's her, um, imagination that's a bit wanting in places. I don't think her disbelief suspends very well. After all, this *is* Wolverhampton. There haven't been any gods in these parts for, oh, I don't know how long. There's certainly never been any gods on the Orchard Mead Housing Estate.'

'That's terrible,' Osiris said, shaken. 'I mean to say, surely everybody is capable of believing in gods. We built you that way, for pity's sake.'

'I'm afraid you're a bit out of touch, Mr Osiris.'

'Strewth.' Osiris leaned back in his chair and thought about it. It wasn't a concept he found easy to get hold of. People could dislike gods, sure enough. Despise them, certainly; hate them, even. But not believe in them at all – that was like people not believing in rain just because they didn't like getting wet.

'I'm sorry.'

'Not your fault.' Osiris sighed. 'You're quite right, I am out of touch. No wonder I've felt all weak since I got here. There's much of it about, is there, this not believing?'

'Lots and lots.'

'What do people believe in, then, if they don't believe in gods?'

'Hard to say.' Sandra rubbed her nose pensively. 'The telly, of course. And family life. And Wolverhampton Wanderers Football Club, which only goes to show what you can do if you really set your mind to it.'

Osiris shook his head slowly. Belief is to gods what atmosphere is to other, rather more temporary life-forms; they live in it, and it shapes them, in the way that millions of tons of water overhead shape the curiously designed fish that live at the very bottom of the sea. This can, of course, have its unfortunate side. When, for example, the Quizquacs of central Peru had finally had enough of their god Tlatelolco's obsession with human sacrifice *à la nouvelle cuisine* (one small human heart, garnished with fine herbs and served with the blood *under* the meat) they exacted a terrible revenge, not by ceasing to believe in him, but by believing in him with a fervour never before encountered even in such a pathologically devout race as the Quizquacs. They also chose to believe in him in his aspect as an excessively timid field vole inhabiting an enclosed kitchen full of hungry cats.

'I've definitely got to get out of here,' Osiris said. 'Look, don't let me put you to any more trouble. Just call me a taxi and I'll go and find a hotel somewhere.'

'A hotel?' Sandra laughed. 'You wouldn't last five minutes.'

'Wouldn't I?'

'No chance.'

'What makes you say that?'

By way of reply, Sandra reached for her handbag and produced a mirror. Osiris took it from her, automatically smoothed his hair, and had a look . . .

'Oh,' he said. 'Oh I see.'

'Exactly. Now perhaps you understand why Mum doesn't choose to be able to see you very well. It's just as well she's got such a limited imagination, or she'd be halfway up the wall yelling for the Social Services by now.'

The face Osiris had seen in the mirror was, beyond question, his own. That was, of course, the problem. The plain fact of the matter is, gods are radiant. They shine; and no amount of face powder and foundation was ever going to have any effect on the dazzling glow that was pouring out of him. You could have got a healthy tan just by briefly catching his eye.

'It hasn't done that for ages,' he said weakly. 'Why's it doing it now?'

'They've got some sort of infra-red thing back at the Home,' Sandra replied. 'Suppresses it, or filters it out, something like that. Out here, of course . . .'

'Gosh.'

'I'm used to it,' Sandra went on, 'and besides, all of us nurses are given these special contact lenses, otherwise we'd spend all day wandering about bumping into things. It's a dead giveaway, I'm afraid.'

Osiris handed back the mirror, noticing as he did so that the plastic frame was just starting to melt. 'Any suggestions?' he muttered.

'Well.' Sandra helped herself to a planklike slice of bread and butter. 'At first I thought of seeing if we could get you a job as a lighthouse keeper . . .'

'Good thinking.'

'Only that would take some time to fix up, and we've got to keep you out of sight until I've had a chance to find out exactly what's going on. Really, your best bet is to stay here and sweat it out.'

'Sandra . . .'

'What choice do you have?'

'Yes, but that mother of yours. I mean, please don't get me wrong, salt of the earth . . .'

'If by that you mean she makes you feel like having a very big drink, yes, I find that myself, too.'

'It wouldn't be so bad,' Osiris said mournfully, 'if only she'd admit I was here. Actually talk to me, things like that.'

Sandra nodded. 'Actually,' she said, 'I reckon it might be possible to get her to do that.'

'Oh yes? How?'

'You could try offering her a very substantial sum of money.'

Even with Sandra's mother talking to him, Osiris found it hard to settle. True, he now had his own room, with a view out over the shunting yards and a small black-and-white portable television capable of receiving two channels; but the waves of disbelief were definitely getting to him, and he didn't like the effect it was having. Twice he'd dropped things because his hands suddenly became translucent and feeble, and he was getting pins and needles all over his body. He scarcely had the strength to wheel himself over to the telly to change programmes.

Never mind. He looked up at the clock, which told him it was almost time for *The Young Doctors*. Soap operas were something of a lifeline to him, on the grounds that if the inhabitants of this peculiar country could watch this sort of thing without serious credibility disorders, they were capable of believing in anything. He switched on the set and settled back in his chair.

Adverts. Was there time to plug in the kettle and make himself a nice cup of . . . ?

He knew that voice.

. . . *Absolutely free when you buy two or more packets of new Zazz with the unique biological fragrance* . . .

Surely not. He must have retired years ago. Only, Osiris reflected, if he had then surely I'd have seen him about the place, and I haven't. And nobody could call him inconspicuous.

But hurry, hurry, hurry, because this special offer must end soon, so don't miss out on this unique chance to save, save, save . . .

It was him, for sure. Osiris could tell by the way that, in spite of everything, he was gripped with this insane desire to buy fabric conditioner. Not because he wanted it, but because he was afraid of missing out on the unique special offer. Very afraid. Panic-stricken, even.

'The old bugger,' Osiris chuckled. 'Well, fancy that.'

'Guess what?'

'I've brought you some tea,' said Sandra, putting the tray down on the bed. 'It's boiled chicken with cabbage and mashed potatoes, with stewed plums and custard to follow.'

Osiris looked away. 'I've just seen someone I know, well, more heard than seen, and you'll never guess—'

'Come on,' Sandra said, 'eat up. Don't want the custard getting—'

'And,' Osiris went on, 'I've made up my mind what I'm going to do next.'

Sandra narrowed her eyes. 'I don't like the sound of this,' she said. 'I thought we'd agreed that you were going to be sensible and stay here until we'd got things straightened out.'

'Ah yes,' Osiris said, 'but that was before I found out my old friend Pan's still on the loose.' He produced a theatrical chuckle. 'Talk about a complete lunatic, the times we've had together, it'll be a holiday just—'

'Pan?'

Osiris took a deep breath. 'He's a god,' he said. 'And he's doing voice-overs on the commercial breaks. Obviously he hasn't retired yet. And we go back a long way, Pan and me. He wouldn't begrudge a bit of house room for an old chum. So, first thing in the morning, I'm going to phone that TV station and leave a message for him.'

'I see,' said Sandra stiffly. 'And you think—'

'Yes.' Osiris scowled. 'Please don't take this the wrong way, but I feel that at my time of life I'd be better off with my own kind. I've made my mind up, and—'

'It'll all end in tears, you mark my words.'

'I'm a god,' Osiris said grimly, 'and I'll do what I damn well please. I invented free will, dammit, so why shouldn't I have some for a change?'

Sandra shrugged, and put the tray on his lap. 'All right,' she said, 'that's fine. Only what makes you so sure this Pan person will want you descending on him out of the blue and getting under his feet?'

'Don't worry about that,' Osiris said, and a grin the size of Oklahoma spread slowly across his face. 'That's not going to be a problem, you mark my words.'

'Eat your nice tea.'

'And that's another thing . . .'

'Or,' Sandra said meaningfully, 'there'll be second helpings of everything.'

'Oh. Right. Yes.'

'Don't worry,' Thor said, wiping his forehead with his sleeve and scrabbling in the toolbox. 'I can fix it. No problem. Just get out of my light and let the dog see the . . .'

To the gods, all things are known. 'I still think it's the main bearing,' Odin said. 'Else why was it making that tapping noise?'

'What tapping noise?'

'I distinctly heard a tapping noise five minutes or so before she seized,' Odin replied. 'I'd have mentioned it only you'd have bitten my head off.'

'I'm hungry,' Frey observed, from under the shade of his golf umbrella. 'We've missed dinner and breakfast and I'm damned if we're going to miss lunch too.'

'Belt up, Frey,' Thor replied, rubbing his beard with his oily left hand. 'Odin, can you remember which way round the cotter pin's supposed to go on this axle?'

Frey stood up and shaded his eyes with his hand. In

front of him, the Alps rose in dizzying white majesty, blinding in the cold, clear sunshine. 'Are you sure that's Matlock over there?' he asked.

'Nowhere else it could be,' Odin replied. 'But look at the map if you don't believe me.'

'I think I'll just go for a stroll.'

'Don't get lost.'

Frey grinned. 'I'm only going as far as the nearest place they sell food,' he said. 'I don't suppose I'll be very long.'

He walked away down the slope, picking his way with care through the rocks. Hm, he thought, gazing out over the surrounding landscape, so that's why they call this the Peak District.

He hadn't gone far when he came across a man and a woman walking slowly up the hill. The man was about sixty, the woman perhaps a year younger; they were plainly but neatly dressed, and the man was leading a laden donkey. Frey smiled; here was a source of inside information.

Now there is a well-established tradition that when the gods walk abroad among men, they do so in some form of disguise; gods manifest themselves as beggars or weary travellers, goddesses as washerwomen or old crones gathering firewood. Men say that this is typical underhand management behaviour, sneaking about and spying, like unmarked police patrol cars on motorways. Gods know that the real reason is to spare gods the embarrassment of not being recognised by their adoring worshippers. Frey shrugged his shoulders and became in a fraction of a second a weary traveller *à la mode*; aertex shirt damp with perspiration, heavy flight bag over one shoulder, suitcase in hand, crumpled sun-hat perched on head. He cleared his throat.

'Excuse me,' he said. The couple turned and looked at him.

'Excuse me,' he repeated, his memory trying to recollect the local cuisine of north Derbyshire, as reported by popular television drama. 'Could you possibly tell me where I might be able to get cod, mushy peas, pickled gherkins and a really tasty chip butty, please? And jam roly-poly and a nice strong cup of tea,' he added.

The man and the woman looked at each other and conferred in a foreign language, which Frey (to the gods all things are known) thought was probably Portuguese.

'Sorry,' said the man haltingly. 'No understan Inglis. Sorry.'

Between gods and men there are differences, and there are similarities; as between, say, the very rich and the very poor. Divine public relations have in the past tended to play down the similarities, understandably enough; but in more recent years this approach has been revised. Hey guys, the gods now say, we aren't really all that different. We're just guys and gals, same as you. If you prick us, they say, do we not bleed? Well, no, actually, they admit, we don't; and anyway that's not a particularly apt example to choose, because anyone trying to prick us is likely to find himself on the bad end of many millions of volts of static electricity. But you know what we mean.

Accordingly, it's not too remarkable that as Frey continued his journey down the hill, and the man and his wife plodded on up the hill, exactly the same phrase should have leapt spontaneously into their minds.

'Bloody tourists,' they all thought.

'Of course,' said Mrs Henderson, 'we're all extremely concerned. Extremely. Taking off like that, a god of his age.' She paused, and Julian's extra-perceptive senses caught a whiff of a point being surreptitiously made. 'I'm very much afraid,' she said, 'that Something might Happen to him.'

'Really? Such as what?'

Mrs Henderson shrugged, as if to say that in a curved universe, anything is by definition possible.

'I'm sure he'll be all right,' she said. 'After all, he is a god and fundamentally quite sensible, for his age. But with this terrible cold weather we've been having . . . And he hasn't taken his blue pills with him.'

'You don't say.' The two looked at each other, and electricity crackled in the air. It was as if the two thieves crucified on either side of Our Lord on that first Good Friday had put their heads together and decided to cut out the middle man. 'His *blue* pills,' said Julian slowly. 'That could be serious.'

'Very.'

'I dread to think what might happen to him without his blue pills.'

'Not that anything will, of course . . .'

'No, of course not.'

'It's just that it's always advisable to consider the *very worst* that might happen. Just in case.'

'Quite so.'

'Which is why,' said Mrs Henderson, taking a deep breath and hoping very much that she hadn't completely misinterpreted the messages emanating from under Julian's eyebrows, 'I've taken the liberty of engaging a, um, private enquiry agent to see if he can, um, find your godfather for us.'

'Splendid. Splendid.'

'A Mr Lundqvist.'

'*Ah.*'

'He came very highly recommended.'

'Top rate man. Exactly what I'd have done, in your position.'

'Oh I *am* glad.'

Julian allowed himself the luxury of a smile. It would

cost a paying client about a year's salary to be smiled at by Julian, but he treated himself to a smile a month at cost. 'If Kurt Lundqvist can't sort this business out,' he said, 'nobody can.'

The same Kurt Lundqvist was, at that precise moment, locked in hand-to-hand combat with a tall gentleman with projecting teeth and a conservative taste in evening dress at the bottom of an open grave somewhere in what used to be called Bohemia.

It should have been a perfectly straightforward job – go in, garlic under nose, whack the hickory smartly through the aorta and home in time to catch the closing prices on Wall Street – but he'd recently taken on a new assistant, and she wasn't yet a hundred per cent *au fait* with the technical jargon of the supernatural contract killing profession.

'Look,' he gasped through clenched teeth as the Count's icy fingers closed around his throat, 'can we cut this a bit short, because I'm due in Haiti for a rogue zombie at six-thirty. I don't like to rush you, but . . .'

A right pillock he'd looked, reaching into his inside pocket and fetching out a five-pound lump hammer and a prime cut of best rump steak. He would have various things to say to Ms Parfimowicz when he got back.

'Nothing personal,' grunted the Count, 'but I'd rather we went through the motions. Aaaaagh!'

'Okay, that's fine,' Lundqvist replied, as his right hand finally connected with the butt of his .40 Glock automatic. 'I'm about through here anyway.'

The bullet wasn't, strictly speaking, silver; but it was a Speer 170-grain jacketed hollow point, backed by six grains of Unique and a Federal 150 primer. By the time the echoes of the shot had died away, the Count didn't seem in any fit state to discuss the finer points of metallurgy. You would have to be abnormally thin-skinned to take 'Gluuuurgh!' as any sort of valid criticism.

Nevertheless, Lundqvist felt peeved. It wasn't the way these things ought to be done. You had to preserve the mystique. Once people cottoned on to the fact that any Tom, Dick or Harry could blow away the Undead with a factory-standard out-of-the-box compact automatic, they wouldn't be quite so eager to pay through the nose for the services of a top flight professional.

A quick glance at his watch told him he was badly behind schedule. A quick scout round produced a three-foot length of broken fence post, and a few strokes of his Spyderco Ultramax lock-knife put enough of a point on it to do the job. He was just dusting himself off and searching the pockets for any small items of value when his bleeper went.

'Lundqvist here.'

'Oh Mr Lundqvist, I'm sorry to disturb you like this, I hope I haven't called at an inconvenient moment.'

'No, it's okay. While I think of it, what I had in mind when I gave you the equipment list this morning was stake S-T-A-K-E, not—'

'Oh gosh, Mr Lundqvist, I'm most terribly sorry, really I am, I never thought—'

'That's fine,' Lundqvist broke in – in order to have the time to wait for a natural break in the flow of Ms Parfimowicz's apologies you had to be a giant redwood at the very least – 'it wasn't a problem as it turned out. Just remember for next time, okay?'

'I will, I promise. I'll just quickly write it down and then I'll be sure to remember. That's stake spelt S-T-A . . .'

'Ms Parfimowicz,' Lundqvist said firmly, 'quiet. Now, what was so goddam important?'

'Oh yes, I'm sorry I got sidetracked, I must stop doing that, it must be so *irritating* for you. A Mrs Henderson called – she's not in the card index but she knew the private number so she must be genuine, don't you think – and she wants you to kill a god.'

There was a brief pause while Lundqvist grabbed for the receiver which he had somehow contrived to drop. 'I don't think I heard you right,' he said. '*Kill a god?*'

'That's what she said, Mr Lundqvist. Of course I could have got it down wrong, I know I'm still having trouble with taking the messages off the machine, but I'm pretty sure—'

'Mrs Henderson, you said?'

'That's right, Mr Lundqvist. Do you want me to spell that back for you?'

'I'll be straight back. Call Haiti, cancel the zombie, make up some excuse. This is more important.'

'Oh.' The voice at the end of the line quavered slightly. 'What excuse can I make, Mr Lundqvist?'

'Tell them . . .' Lundqvist grinned. 'Tell them I had to go to a funeral.'

CHAPTER SIX

Love, according to the songwriters, is the sweetest thing; but tea as made by the great god Pan must come a pretty close second. It's just as well that Pan is immortal, because if he were ever to die, several third world countries whose economies depend in whole or in part on the cultivation of sugar cane are likely to fall on hard times.

'Have another biscuit,' said Pan with his mouth full. Osiris shook his head.

'Too full of cake,' he explained. 'Couldn't eat another thing.'

'To the gods,' Pan replied, helping himself, 'all things are possible.'

'All right, then. I like these little ones with the coconut on top.'

All living things yearn for their own kind; and it had been a long time since Pan had spent any time with a fellow god. As far as Osiris was concerned, he had several thousand years' unhealthy eating to catch up on. So many doughnuts, so little time.

'Well, then.' Pan leaned back in his chair and nibbled

the chocolate off a mini swiss roll. 'So what have you been up to all this time?'

'Nothing.'

'Nothing at all?'

Osiris nodded. 'The first six hundred years after I retired, I just had a bloody good rest. After that, I found I'd got out of the habit of doing things. My own fault, really.'

'Institutionalised.'

Osiris let his eye wander around the room. His reactions were mixed. On the one hand, he thought, the very idea of an immortal god, one of *us*, being afforded so little respect by mortals that he could only afford a bed-sitting room over a chemist's shop in a suburban high street was so infamous that it made his palms itch for a thunderbolt. On the other hand, it was a damn sight bigger than his gloomy little kennel at Sunnyvoyde (and he *owned* the horrible place, remember), and it was quite plain from the most cursory inspection that Pan didn't have little chits of teenage girls in white pinnies barging in whenever they felt like it, moving his possessions about and confiscating his digestive biscuits. True, there was about a thousand years' arrears of washing up in the sink, but the price of liberty is eternal housekeeping. He wrenched his mind back to the subject under discussion.

'I suppose so, yes,' he said wistfully. 'To begin with you think, Hey, this is the life, five meals a day brought to your room by beautiful young girls. Then you realise that for the last thousand years you've noticed the food but not the girls. Then you start to wonder what's happening to you.'

'Yeah.' Pan nodded, but in his mind's eye he could picture his compact, thoroughly modern, utterly squalid kitchen. He had a perfectly good dishwasher, but it was a while since he'd actually seen it, because of all the dirty plates piled up on every available surface. 'Mind you, five meals you haven't had to cook for yourself. It's definitely got something going for it.'

'Not much, though.' Osiris shifted slightly in his wheelchair, which seemed to have shrunk. 'How come you never retired?'

'Couldn't afford to,' Pan replied. 'Purely and simply a question of money.'

'Really?'

'Really. I look back now and I say to myself, If only I'd had the good sense to take out a personal pension plan back in the third century BC, I wouldn't still be having to get out of bed at six-thirty every morning to go to work. Mind you, it's always the way. When you're that age, you think you're going to live forever. Or, more to the point, you think you *aren't* going to live forever, so why bother? Were you, um, planning to stay long?'

Osiris nodded. 'Depends on how long it takes.'

'How long what takes?'

'For me to outlive my godson,' Osiris replied. 'The way I see it, all I've got to do is stay out of the way of him and his precious doctors until they kick the bucket. And in our timescale, that just gives us time for a quick game of poker before I've got to be getting back.'

'Poker?'

'It was only a suggestion. If you'd rather play snakes and ladders or . . .'

Inside his soul, Pan grinned. The ability to cause sudden panic isn't the world's most useful skill; it's not like plumbing or carpet-laying, the sort of thing that'll always keep the wolf strictly confined to the downstairs rooms. But it surely gives you the edge when playing poker.

'You're not proposing,' he said coyly, 'that we play for money, are you?'

'Money?' Osiris looked at him. 'I didn't know you could.'

'I've heard that it's possible.'

'Gosh. I suppose you sort of bet on who's going to win each hand.'

'I suppose so. Want to give it a try?'

'Why not? Do you know how we go about it?'

'I expect we'll pick it up as we go along.'

Three hours later, Pan came to the conclusion that maybe he'd been a trifle injudicious. Given that he was immortal, and assuming that he managed to continue doing these lucrative voice-overs he'd just broken into right up till the scheduled destruction of the Earth, he'd probably be able to pay Osiris back eventually, provided he didn't get charged interest and went easy on the food and electricity:

'You've played this before,' he said.

'I learned recently,' Osiris replied. 'About six months ago. One of the nurses at the Home has a boyfriend who's a lorry driver. Apparently they spend a lot of time in transport cafés playing cards. We usually have a game or two every Friday evening while he's waiting for her shift to end.'

'I see. Do you think your godson's likely to be dead yet?'

Osiris glanced at his watch. 'I doubt it,' he said. 'There's this other game he's taught me if you'd like to try something else. I'm not *quite* sure of the rules, but—'

'No thanks.'

'Oh.' Osiris shrugged. 'Well, in that case we'd better settle up. I'd rather have cash, if it's all the same to you.'

Pan winced. 'To be absolutely frank with you,' he said, 'I'm just the teeniest bit strapped for cash at the moment. Would you mind if I, er, owed it to you. Just for a week or so, you understand . . .'

Osiris smiled pleasantly. 'I can do better than that,' he said. 'You do me a small favour and we'll call it quits. How does that sound?'

There was a deafening crash, and the air was suddenly full of broken glass.

All over the building, alarms should have gone off. Haifisch & Dieb had security systems that projected into several as yet undiscovered dimensions; so sophisticated were they that bells rang and lights flashed on monitor screens if a hostile philosopher started postulating that lawyers might not exist in a perfect universe. But even the most elaborate setup won't work if someone has been round snipping vital wires and stuffing socks in the mechanism at strategic places.

'Hi,' said Julian, not looking up. 'Take a seat, with you directly.'

Kurt Lundqvist let go of the rope on which he'd just abseiled in, and with an easy movement drew an enormous handgun from a huge shoulder holster. He levelled it at Julian's heart, and cleared his throat discreetly.

'Fifty-calibre Desert Eagle,' said Julian, apparently to the seventy-page lease open on his desk. 'What's wrong with the trusty old Glock, then?'

Lundqvist winced slightly. 'My new assistant,' he said. 'Goddamn woman will insist on tidying the place up. It'll turn up eventually.'

'Tsk.' Julian clicked his tongue sympathetically, drew a few squiggles on the page with a red felt-tip, and closed the lease. 'Good of you,' he said inevitably, 'to drop in.'

'I was just passing.'

'Sure. Now then.' Julian leaned back in his chair – it was the sort of chair that was designed to define its occupant, and it told you better than any words could

that you were sitting on the wrong side of the desk –
and steepled his fingers. 'I got a job for you,' he said.

'So I'd heard.'

'I think you're the right man for this job.'

'Thanks.'

'You come recommended.'

'Glad to hear it.'

Julian reached across the desktop and drew a file
towards him. 'Highly recommended.' He opened the file,
flicked through a couple of pages and nodded. 'You've
been around a fair while, I see. Like, it was you who
finally killed Dracula in 1876.'

'Yup.'

'And 1879. And 1902. And 1913.'

'You can't keep a good man down.'

'And 1927. But not since.'

Lundqvist shrugged. 'Actually, you can keep a good
man down, just so long as you use a big enough stake.
In this case, a telegraph pole.'

'Cool.'

'It worked.' He smiled faintly. 'First time, anyhow.
Though I hear they get some really bizarre wrong
numbers in those parts even now. What is it you want
done?'

Julian shrugged and turned a few more pages. 'Hey,'
he said, 'this one you did a year or so back, that really
was a bit out of the ordinary.' He tossed over a polaroid
of a stunted green shape, vaguely humanoid but with a
weird head and strange, long fingers. 'I thought he made
it back to his own planet eventually. There was a film
about it. Lots of kids with bicycles.'

Lundqvist said nothing, but shook his head. Julian
suddenly felt ever so slightly unnerved.

'But he was kinda sweet, wasn't he?' he said.

'So what?'

'How did you find him, exactly? I thought he was well hidden, after the story broke.'

'I tapped his phone.'

'Figures.' Julian closed the file. 'Well, I want you to think of this job as the culmination of your extremely impressive career. Afterwards, of course, you'll have to retire. You'll never be able to work again.' He paused and smiled. 'Mind you, you'll never need to work again. The package I have in mind is extremely favourable.'

'Look.' Lundqvist leaned forward and stared at him across the desk. 'The only packages I know about go tick tick. Cut to the chase, okay?'

'Okay.' Julian folded his arms. 'I've got a god needs taking for a ride.'

'A god. I see. Any particular one?'

'Osiris. You know him?'

'By repute.' Lundqvist's eyes glowed. 'Any reason, or just general resentment about the Fall of Man?'

'My business,' said Julian quietly. He picked up the pen and fiddled with the cap. 'Let's say he's taking up space required for other purposes. And time, too.'

'Yeah?'

'Yeah.'

Lundqvist stood up. 'I ought to blow your fucking head off right now,' he said.

In a curved and infinite universe, everything has to happen eventually, somewhere. Julian stared. For the very first time he was at a loss for words.

'Now listen to me,' Lundqvist hissed. He reached out a hand and gathered a palmful of Julian's tie. 'Two points. One, gods are immortal. This makes them pretty damn difficult to kill. Not,' he added with a hint of pride, 'impossible. But difficult, certainly.'

'Not for you, surely.'

'That's beside the point.' Lundqvist tightened his grip

on the tie. 'The second thing is, I don't kill gods. I'm the good guy, dammit. I'm on their side. I sort out the bad guys, that's what I do. Talking of which, the only thing standing between you and reincarnation under a flat stone is professional ethics.' Lundqvist grinned suddenly. 'And I wouldn't rely on that too much.'

'You'll be sorry.'

Lundqvist's face was white with rage. 'Hey, man,' he growled, 'I'd have thought you'd have known, threatening me is not wise. The last guy who threatened me is now an integral part of the Manhattan skyline.'

'No threat intended. All I meant was, you don't take the job, you don't get paid a very large sum of money. I'd be really sorry if I missed out on a chance like that.'

'Stuff your money,' Lundqvist replied. 'I got principles, okay?'

'Principles?' Julian raised an eyebrow. 'Kurt, for god's sake, you're a multiple murderer. Isn't it just a bit late . . . ?'

Julian found himself hovering in the air about six inches away from his seat, with a square foot of his shirtfront twisted in Lundqvist's hand. 'I got principles,' he repeated. 'You touch a single hair on that god's head and you'll wish you'd never been born. Or rather,' he added, with a disconcerting grin, 'you'll wish you had been born. In vain, it goes without saying. You copy?'

'Save it for the customers, Kurt,' replied Julian, although he could have done with the air he used in doing so for other, more urgent purposes. 'How much? Name your own—'

'Fuck you.'

'Actually, I was thinking that money would be more appropriate. Still . . .'

Julian hit the back of his chair like a squash ball, and his head slumped forwards on to the desk. A splash of blood from the cut on his forehead fell on the lease, fortuitously blotting out an unfavourable rent review clause he'd previously overlooked.

'Am I to take that as a definite maybe?' he asked.

For a moment, Julian was convinced Lundqvist was going to kill him. The gun reappeared from under his arm – God, Julian thought, as he stared down the endless black tunnel of the muzzle, after a hard day's work that thing must smell *awful* – and there was a click as the hammer came back. But there was no bang; because Lundqvist was a professional, a highclass operator, and the golden rule of top specialists is: no free samples. A moment later, there was only a space where Lundqvist had been, and the wind blowing intrusively through the smashed window.

'Shit,' Julian mused aloud. 'Ah well, never mind.' He swivelled his chair round to the computer terminal on his desk, tapped a couple of keys and waited while the machine bleeped at him.

Ready.

Julian frowned. 'Ready what?' he said.

Sorry. Ready, sir.

'That's more like it. Right, do me a scan on the following wordgroup.'

He tapped again. The machine flickered, told him a lot of things he knew already about all rights being protected, and finally produced a column of names. The heading was:

International A–Z Compendium of Atheists

CHAPTER SEVEN

The visitor looked startled.

'Yes,' he replied. 'Of philosophy. What seems to be the problem?'

Lug elbowed the visitor tactfully in the ribs. 'Ignore her,' he whispered. 'She says that to everyone.' He started to tap his head meaningfully, caught Minerva's eye and tried to make it look as if he was scratching his head. The visitor ignored him.

'Will you take a look at my leg?' Minerva said. 'I keep asking to see the doctor but they never listen.'

'We really ought to be getting on, because we've got a lot to—'

'Certainly,' said the visitor. 'I shall be delighted to look at your leg, although it's a pity you didn't ask me six thousand years ago, before it got all wrinkled and yuk. Still, better late than never.'

'Really, you shouldn't encourage her, she can be a real—'

'Yes,' said the visitor, 'that's definitely a leg. I'd know one anywhere. It's the foot at the end I always look for. Mind you, who is to say that I'm not in fact an ostrich dreaming that I'm a doctor of philosophy looking at a leg? A very charming leg, it goes without saying, even now.'

A hand in the small of the back propelled the visitor out of the television room and into a small enclosure used for the storage of cleaning equipment. Lug closed the door.

'Since when have you been a doctor of philosophy?' he demanded.

'Not long,' Pan admitted. 'I saw one of these adverts in a magazine. You send them fifty dollars and they give you a degree. I could have been an emeritus professor, only they don't take credit cards.'

'Right. Look . . .'

'Chicopee Falls.'

Lug blinked. 'I'm sorry?'

'Chicopee Falls, Iowa. University of. If you're interested I can let you have the details.'

'No thank you,' said Lug firmly. It was, he decided, a bit like having a conversation with someone positioned twenty minutes in the future, with frequent interruptions from someone else five minutes ago in the past. 'Look, will you stop changing the subject? You're getting me all muddled up.'

'Sorry,' replied the god of Confusion. 'Force of habit. What can I do for you?'

Lug moved a dustpan and brush and sat down on the electrical floor-polisher. 'I don't know,' he replied. 'You came to see me, remember?'

'So I did.' Pan leaned on a vacuum cleaner and grinned. 'Got a message for you.'

'Oh yes?'

'From Osiris.'

Lug looked at him blankly. 'His room's just down the corridor from mine,' he said. 'Why can't he tell me himself?'

'Because,' Pan replied, idly unwinding the flex and tying knots in it, 'he's done a runner. Gone into hiding. Didn't you notice all the kerfuffle a few days ago, when those two doctors came to declare him insane?'

'Declare *him* insane?' Lug thought about it. 'It's a good point, though,' he added. 'I mean, if she asked them if they were doctors, they wouldn't find it odd at all. Sorry, I'm doing it now. Why were they trying to do that?'

'So that his loathsome godson could take over his powers and get at his money, he reckons.' Pan leaned down and buffed his nails on the polishing mop. 'Apparently, the godson's managed to get him to sign a power of attorney.'

'Sneaky.'

'Very.' Pan yawned. 'Anyhow, I'm here just to tell you so you won't be worried about him. That's about it, really.'

'Why me, though?'

Pan shrugged. 'No idea,' he said. 'But he was absolutely clear about it, you were the one I had to tell, so if you wouldn't mind just signing this receipt, I can be on my way.'

'Oh. Sure. Have you got a pen handy, by the way, because I think I've—'

Just then the door opened, and a small head the colour and shape of an acorn appeared round it.

'You doctor?' it asked. 'Doctor of phirosophy?'

Pan raised an eyebrow. 'Sorry?'

'Minerva say you doctor of phirosophy. Please, you take rook at soul for me? Soul not very good, maybe sick. You maybe give prescliption or something.'

'That's Confucius,' Lug whispered. 'He doesn't speak very good Eng—'

'I'd be delighted,' Pan replied. 'Now then, where does it hurt?'

The rest of Confucius followed his head into the room.

'Not hurt at all,' he replied, bowing from the hips. 'Maybe not exist at all. Plato he say—'

'Ah,' Pan replied. 'I think what you really need is a doctor of theology. Sounds more a theological job to me.'

'So. You know where I find doctor of theology?'

'It just so happens that I'm a doctor of theology. University of Chicopee Falls, Iowa, class of '87. Just go next door and take your id off and I'll be with you in a jiffy.'

As the door closed behind him, Lug frowned. 'Do you have to do that?' he asked. 'It's going to be a complete bloody shambles here for weeks now, you realise.'

'Sorry,' Pan replied. 'But I've got my Hypocritic Oath to think of.'

'You mean Hippocratic.'

'I know what I mean,' replied the Father of Misunderstandings. 'Now then, I've given you the message. Be sure not to tell *anyone*. You got that? Anyone at all.'

Lug blinked. 'If I'm not to tell anybody, why tell me?'

Pan got up, brushed himself off and winked. 'Don't ask me,' he replied, 'I'm only the messenger. Moving in a mysterious way just sort of goes with the territory, don't you find? Thank you for your time.'

Force of habit can be a tremendously powerful influence. Between the broom cupboard and the front door. Pan diagnosed three prolapsed souls, five ingrowing personalities (doctor of psychiatry, University of Chicopee Falls, Iowa; buy two, get one free) and a nasty case of entropy of the mind's eye. He got out of the building about thirty seconds ahead of the security guards and their ten-stone Rottweiler.

He was strolling back towards the bus stop when he realised that someone was following him. A mortal, female, young and, if you were in the habit of confusing quantity with quality, reasonably attractive. She was wearing a white overall thing and had a watch pinned to her front. He stopped until she'd caught up with him.

'Excuse me,' she said. 'Are you Pan?'

'Who wants to know?'

'I do.'

'That's all right, then. Only you can't be too careful these days.'

The girl frowned at him. 'I'm looking for Mr Osiris,' she said. 'Is he staying with you?'

'How did you find out?'

'He heard your voice on a telly commercial just before he left my house without saying where he was going,' replied the girl. 'When the commercial came on in the television room back at the Home, I asked around the residents to see if they knew whose the voice was, and they told me it was you. Then when somebody said Pan had just been in the place causing trouble—'

'Bloody cheek!'

'. . . I rushed out after you and here I am. Will you take me to see him?'

Pan considered for a moment. 'How do I know you're on his side?' he asked.

'If I wasn't, would I be asking you?'

'But you work at Sunnyvoyde, don't you? I don't think he's particularly keen to go back, you see.'

The girl smiled ruefully. 'Not any more I don't,' she said. 'I got sacked for helping him get away.'

'You must be Sandra.'

The girl nodded. 'He needs looking after,' she said. 'Don't get me wrong, I think he's awfully nice, but . . .'

'You think so?' Pan scowled. 'Let me give you a word of advice. If you're holding two pairs, kings and jacks, and he's sitting there with that befuddled look on his face as if he's trying to remember which century he's in, fold immediately. Better still, just play for matchsticks.

Provided,' he added, 'you have the title deeds to a couple of rainforests tucked away somewhere. I can think of a lot of ways of describing your friend, and awfully nice is definitely on the B team reserve list.'

Sandra giggled. 'He's good at card games, isn't he? My boyfriend owes him ninety-seven million pounds, at the last count. And he only learned to play recently.'

'Beginner's luck, huh?'

'He's told you,' Sandra went on, 'what that nasty godson of his is trying to do to him?'

Pan nodded. 'Ingenious little sod,' he said. 'I forget now who it was thought up the idea of mortals in the first place, but they've got a lot to answer for. Present company excepted, of course.'

'You should try doing my job,' Sandra replied, nettled. 'Have you ever tried getting lightning stains off formica?'

'Oh, gods aren't perfect, I know,' Pan said hastily. 'But at least we don't—'

'Or clearing up after they've been playing Sardines? I hate to think what it must've been like when you lot were running things.'

Pan sighed. 'Pretty much like it is now,' he said, 'except your lot had someone definite to blame. Sometimes,' he added, 'I think that was all we were there for. It worked, too. The race that despises together rises together, I always say.'

'Here's the bus, look.'

'Oh good,' said Pan, patron deity of all those who couldn't organise piss-ups in breweries. 'Somehow I always feel at home on public transport.'

'We have to plan our next move,' said Osiris, 'very carefully.'

To the gods all things are possible, all things are known. Ask a god what's the quickest way to the post office and he'll be absolutely sure to know, even if he's never set eyes on the town in question. And Pan was a god (he had certificates to prove it; seventy-five dollars each or ninety-nine dollars fifty if you opt for the deluxe parchment-look display version). But how he came to be in a beat-up yellow van with a plump girl, a monolithic driver with spiky hair and an earring and the Son of Nuth, Opener of Ways, remained a mystery to him for ever.

'You can drop me off at the next traffic lights,' Pan said hopefully. 'Thanks for the lift.'

'Sorry, I need you to help me with a few things,' Osiris replied. 'You don't mind, do you?'

'I'd really have loved to help out, but . . .'

'I'll pay you.'

There was complete silence except for the sound of an old van with a dicky exhaust going over a pothole.

'Actual money?'

'The currency of your choice.'

'How much?'

'How much did you have in mind?'

And Pan thought, Gosh. I could retire. I could pack it all in and buy a little place somewhere and stay in bed till gone eight o'clock in the morning. No more horrible poxy jobs just to pay the rent. No more Panicograms. No more promotional videos for fallout shelter manufacturers. No more jumping out of cakes at rich depressives' birthday parties.

'Count me in,' he said.

'Fine.' Osiris nodded. 'As I was saying, we have to plan our next move very carefully. Use our heads, that sort of thing.'

As he said the word, he looked at his companions. There was Carl, Sandra's boyfriend; six foot nine of mortal muscle, a man only too delighted to use his head if it involved breaking down doors or stunning opponents.

There was Sandra herself; female, it had to be admitted,
but her heart was in the right place, which was more than
he could say for himself. And there was Pan. As for him;
well, there are many legends concerning the genesis of the
gods, but the version that Osiris gave the most credence
to was the one where, on the eighth day, the Creator found
Pan at the bottom of his packet of breakfast cereal. Put
another way, Pan was the sort of god Mankind probably
found it necessary to invent, if only by way of getting its
own back. Still . . .

And there was him. Which made it all sort of all right.
In a way.

'Our objective,' he went on, 'is to stop my godson Julian
getting control of the Universe by having me certified and
taking my place by virtue of a power of attorney. Agreed?'

'Can we stop at the next service station?' Sandra
contributed. 'I knew I shouldn't have had that last cup
of tea before we—'

'In other words,' Osiris said, 'we're up against a lawyer.
A really clever, unscrupulous, dishonest, conniving lawyer.
Now, who do you think we ought to go to for help?'

Silence again.

'Anybody got any ideas?'

Pan shifted in his seat. 'Let's get this straight,' he said.
'You're asking us who we think is likely to prove a match
for this ultimate legal vulture godson of yours, somebody
who can play him at his own game and win?'

'That's right.'

'If you want my initial reaction,' Pan replied, 'might I
ask if the expression "a hiding to nothing" is at all familiar
to you?'

'Excuse me.'

For a moment Osiris was bewildered, and looked round
the van to see who was the amateur ventriloquist. Then
he realised. Carl had said something.

'Go on,' he said.

'How about we get a better lawyer?'

'Don't be so . . .' Osiris stopped himself from finishing the sentence. To the gods all things are known; except, apparently, the bleeding obvious.

'Good idea,' he said feebly. 'Yes, I was wondering who was going to be the first to—'

''Cos a better lawyer, right, he'd be able to run rings round this other lawyer. Stands to reason.'

'Is there a better lawyer?' Sandra interrupted. 'I thought your Julian was the best there is.'

'Rubbish.' Pan blew on the window and started to draw a smily face in the condensation. 'He's just another mortal, right? You get an immortal lawyer, and Julian won't know what hit him. Well, not what hit him first, anyway. I expect the second, third and fourth time he'll be saying, Hello, godpapa.'

'An immortal lawyer,' Osiris mused. 'You know of one, do you?'

Pan laughed. 'Sure,' he replied. 'Of course, he doesn't *call* himself a lawyer, too much self-respect, but to all intents and purposes that's what he is.'

'Oh.' Osiris came from a culture whose written language consisted of hieroglyphic picture writing, and so the thought that crossed his mind at this point was little-sketch-of-a-light-bulb-being-switched-on. 'Oh, *him*. Yes, that's very good. I think we're actually getting somewhere at last.'

'Who are you talking about?' Sandra asked.

Pan grinned. 'He has many names,' he said.

'What, you mean like Sanderson, Linklater, Foot and Edwards? Lawyers are funny like that, aren't they?'

'No,' Pan replied wearily. 'I mean, different people know him by a lot of different names, but in fact he's the same person.'

'The same as who?'

'Himself, of course.'

'He's the same as himself. I see.'

Pan gave Sandra a long look, assessing her as a potential apprentice. There was definitely raw natural talent there.

'He's one bloke,' he said slowly, 'but he's known by different names to different people. Got that?'

'I really would like it if we stopped somewhere soon, because—'

'All *right*.'

The van changed lanes and took the next exit, signposted to the Pinfold Gap Service Area. The occupants got out and Sandra sprinted off, leaving Osiris in his wheelchair between Pan and Carl. A few seconds later, a big Japanese four-wheel-drive with tinted windows purred in and parked just behind the van.

'Where are we?' Osiris asked.

'I dunno,' Pan replied. 'Godforsaken place, wherever it is.' He looked down at the wheelchair. 'In a manner of speaking, that is. I thought you knew where we were going.'

Osiris shrugged. 'Away was the general idea when we started off. Now we know where we're going, it might be a good idea to get the map out and plan a route.'

Pan shook his head. 'I wouldn't worry about it,' he said. 'Where we're going is dead easy to get to, wherever you start from.'

'But you know a short cut, I suppose.'

'Only in my professional capacity,' Pan replied. 'I know short cuts to everywhere for business purposes, goes without saying.'

Osiris nodded. 'We'll take a look at the map,' he said.

The door of the four-wheel-drive opened slowly, and its driver climbed down and came up behind the three of them, walking with practised stealth. He was holding something dark and shiny down by his side.

'Osiris,' said Pan quietly. 'Don't look round, but I've got a feeling . . .'

'Freeze!'

'Thought so.'

Behind them, Kurt Lundqvist levelled his gun. 'You in the chair,' he said, 'roll forward five paces. You other two, turn slowly round.'

Pan swallowed. He was, of course, immortal and invulnerable. He also wanted to stay that way, and a good working definition of immortal is someone who hasn't died *yet*. He raised his hands.

'Has he got a gun?'

'How should I know?' Osiris replied in a loud whisper. 'I haven't got eyes in the back of my head, you know. I did once, mind,' he added. 'That was the day she forgot to put her lenses in.'

'Shut it,' Lundqvist snapped. 'You two, hands on your heads. Quickly.'

They did as they were told.

'Okay.' Lundqvist took a good look at them over the sights of the Desert Eagle. 'Now then. Are you two guys doctors?'

Many years ago, when the world was so young that parts of its rocky skeleton were still soft and flexible, Pan had been to the first of a series of evening classes on Coping With Stress. By the end of the evening he was so tense with frustration and rage that he had to see a physiotherapist, but elements of the recommended procedures still lingered down in the back of the sofa of his mind.

Relax, he told himself. Make a conscious effort to loosen the muscles of the back, neck and chest. Take a long, slow, deep breath. Smile.

'A doctor of what?' he asked.

'Medicine,' Lundqvist replied. 'And keep your goddamn hands where I can see them, okay?'

Hang on, Pan said to himself, I know that voice. He turned his head slightly, just enough to get a splendid view down the barrel of the gun.

'Kurt,' he ventured, 'is that you?'

'Yes,' Lundqvist admitted. 'Now answer the question.'

'Not,' Pan replied, 'of medicine. Look, Kurt, it's me, Pan. Stop waving that bloody thing about, will you, because you're giving me bad vibes, and I can get all of them I want at trade discount.'

'How about him?' Lundqvist said. 'He looks like a doctor to me.'

'Well he isn't,' Pan snarled. 'And what would you know, anyway? The only doctors you come across tend to be arriving as you leave.'

'All right,' Lundqvist said, lowering the hammer and putting the gun reluctantly away. 'You can put your hands down now, but no . . .'

Osiris turned round and scowled, giving Lundqvist the impression that he'd just arrived in the next life only to find he'd spent the last sixty years devoutly worshipping the wrong god. 'Who is this idiot?' Osiris asked.

Pan grinned. 'Meet Kurt Lundqvist,' he said. 'He kills people. Well, people is pushing it a bit, I suppose. Things would be nearer the mark.'

'Does he really,' Osiris said. 'How interesting. We have a name for that where I come from.'

'Yeah?' Lundqvist tried a sneer, but his reserves of bravado were down to barrel-bottom level. 'And where's that, exactly?'

Osiris grinned, and pointed.

'Kurt,' said Pan quickly, 'I'd like you to meet Osiris. He's a god. I think it'd be a really good idea if you two could somehow start again from scratch, because—'

'I was hired to kill you,' Lundqvist said.

'Were you, now? What an interesting life you've led so far. Which,' he added, 'is probably just as well.'

'Yes.' Lundqvist nodded. 'I refused. First time I ever turned down a commission.'

'How extremely sensible of you.'

'And,' Lundqvist continued, scrabbling about for a few vestigial threads of the initiative, 'I came to warn you.'

Osiris raised an eyebrow and looked at Pan, who was staring fixedly at the petrol pumps in an effort to convey the impression that he was somewhere else. 'Warn me of what?' Osiris asked.

'There's two doctors looking for you, to certify you as insane. So, when I saw you with two suspicious-looking characters . . .'

'Wasn't that thoughtful,' Pan said quickly, realising as he did so that he was well up in the running for Asinine Remark of the Aeon, burning off 'peace in our time' and close on the heels of 'when I grow up, I want to be a lawyer'. 'Don't you think that was a thoughtful thing to do?'

'Very,' Osiris said. 'You seem to know this idiot from somewhere.'

'Sure,' Pan said. 'We go way back, Kurt and me. Why don't we all go and have a . . . ?'

There was a chunky, solid sort of a noise, and Lundqvist slowly toppled forward and fell on his nose. Behind where he had been standing was Sandra, holding a brick.

'Oh marvellous,' Pan said. 'Look, grab his legs and let's go and have a coffee. We'll all feel much better with a nice hot drink inside us.'

Mrs Henderson narrowed her eyes, until it was hard to imagine any but the most anorexic of photons scriggling its way through to her retina.

'Won't do it?' she said. 'How very strange. You did offer him money?'

Julian nodded impatiently and would have said something sarcastic had he not foolishly got in the way of Mrs Henderson's eye. She made him feel uncomfortable. Sure, he still knew deep down that he was the only possible candidate for Senior Partner of the World, but something at the back of his mind was telling him that, nevertheless, his hair was uncombed and his socks smelled.

'A great deal of money?'

'A very great deal of money,' said Julian, with feeling. 'More than I earn in a month.'

'How very odd.'

Julian got up and walked to the window. From Mrs Henderson's office, you could see all the kingdoms of the earth on a clear day. 'Not that it matters,' he said. 'There are more ways of killing a cat.'

Although he had his back to Mrs Henderson, he could feel death rays on the back of his collar, and realised that he'd said the wrong thing. Of course, Mrs Henderson kept cats. Probably three of them, with matching names. Meeny, Miny and Mo would be a fair bet. And they'd have their own little baskets and their own little saucers with their names on, and birthdays and favourite chairs with smelly old blankets on them; and anybody crazy enough to kick one of Mrs Henderson's cats was definitely not long for this world, and very likely on dubious ground for the next.

'More ways,' he said, 'of sorting out our problem than the obvious one,' he therefore said. 'How come,' he added, without looking round, 'my godfather owns this place, anyway?'

Mrs Henderson shrugged. 'I needed some capital,' she said, 'he wanted somewhere to retire to. At the time it seemed a perfectly sensible arrangement. And it has been, too, until lately.'

Julian sat down on the window-seat and gazed out over the cloud-meadows, marking them off in his mind's eye into a grid plan of building plots. 'So what happened to change your mind?' he asked.

'Well.' Mrs Henderson paused for a moment, marshalling her thoughts. 'I suppose you could say there's been a lot of latent friction between us for some time. Your godfather has, well, ideas about how this establishment should be run. I have my own ideas. They are the correct ones. I have devoted a lot of time, energy and money to this project, and I have no intention of seeing it come to nothing.'

A twinkle of light appeared in Julian's mind. 'You want to raise the fees,' he said.

'Among other things, yes.'

'And he wasn't happy with that?'

'Correct.'

Wow, Julian thought. For that, she's prepared to murder a god. He turned slowly round and looked at her, dispassionately. Yes, she would have made one hell of a lawyer.

'Of course,' she went on, 'this wilfulness on his part suggests most strongly to me that your poor godfather is, let's say, a wee bit confused in his mind these days, perhaps not quite up to looking after his business affairs. It's for that reason I really would welcome his being examined by a doctor. For his own good, of course. But if he won't co-operate, then really, perhaps the euthanasia approach might well be the kindest thing.'

'For his own good.'

'The welfare of the residents is, naturally, my one and only consideration.' She smiled. 'All the residents, naturally.'

'Naturally.'

When I am master of the universe, Julian memorandised to himself, Mrs Henderson's permanent welfare will be one of my first considerations. It would be a positive pleasure devising something that would be in her best interests, ideally with nine dozen six-inch nails playing a prominent role.

'Anyway,' he said, wrenching his mind back from this agreeable digression. 'If he's disappeared, so much the better. All we need is for him to stay disappeared for the prescribed period of time and we can legally presume that he's dead. That ought to be—'

'But he's a god,' Mrs Henderson interrupted. 'Surely—'

'So?' Julian grinned. 'Everybody is equal in the eyes of the law, remember. And the law says that someone who can't be traced after a certain period of time is legally dead. End of problem.'

'And if he does turn up within the time?'

'Easy. We get him certified. It's what we in the legal profession call Catch-44.'

'I see.' Mrs Henderson rubbed her nose with the knuckle of her left forefinger. 'And meanwhile?'

'Meanwhile,' Julian said, 'I hold his power of attorney.' He sat down opposite her and crossed his legs. 'Exactly what level of fee increase had you in mind?'

'Let me get you some tea,' said Mrs Henderson.

CHAPTER EIGHT

To get from the Pinfold Gap Service Area to the Garden of the Hesperides, you can follow one of two routes: the easy, long way, or the quick, difficult one.

'Turn off here,' Osiris said. 'We haven't got all day.'

The easy, long way is overland to Folkestone, ferry to Ostend, through Germany and Austria to what used to be called Pomerania, then turn right and on down through Armenia to the Caucasus, follow your nose and you're there. When you find yourself falling over backwards trying to see the tops of the mountains, you know you've arrived. There's even a chair-lift to the top, although it's not a hundred per cent reliable; it was installed in 1906 and the only maintenance they've got around to doing is one coat of paint on the railings at the bottom and a dab of grease on the ratchet once every change of General Secretary.

'Are you sure you—?'

''Course I'm sure,' Osiris replied. 'I've got the map, haven't I?'

The other way is overland to Greater Pinfold, leave the van in the car park opposite the church, scramble three quarters of the way up Pinfold Fell to the small cave that very few people know about, and summon a demon, using the handy implements provided. The demon then does the rest. In theory.

'Wouldn't it have been simpler,' Sandra interrupted, 'just to phone his office and make an appointment?'

The two gods and Kurt Lundqvist looked at her.

'Well?' she said.

'No,' Pan replied.

'Why not?'

'For one thing,' Pan said, 'he hasn't got an office. For another, he's not on the phone. For a third, he doesn't keep appointments. Satisfied?'

Sandra frowned. 'Funny sort of a lawyer,' she said. Pan shook his head.

'Not in context,' he replied. 'You wait and see.'

'Oh.' Sandra thought for a moment. 'So what exactly do you have to do if you want to see him, then?'

Osiris and Pan looked at each other. 'It's a long story.' Pan said.

'I expect we've got time.'

There was a rumbling from the driver's seat. It could have been thunder in a tin-panelled canyon, or Sandra's boyfriend talking.

'Signpost,' he said. 'Greater Pinfold, half.'

It took two divine brains a comparatively long time to work out that he meant half a mile. 'That's fine,' Osiris said. 'Once we're in the village, go along the main street and then just keep heading uphill. You can't miss it.'

'Why hasn't he got an office?'

The two gods exchanged glances and then turned to Lundqvist, who was occupying the time in honing the edge on his Sykes-Fairbairn combat knife on the sole of his boot.

'You explain it,' they said.

'Me?'

'Yes.'

'All right, then.'

The gods, Lundqvist explained, created the first man and the first woman.

Their motives for doing so are lost in the mists of comparative religion, and speculation is now probably futile. The most convincing explanation is that at the time they were destruct-testing the maxim 'everybody makes mistakes'.

The first man was called Epimetheus, and the first woman was called Pandora. Contrary to what the scientists would have you believe, neither of them was four feet tall, hairy, stooped and equipped with a jaw like a snowplough; although Epimetheus did have a mole on his nose and Pandora's black hair had a grey wave running across it from the moment she came to life, the result of Athene neglecting to wait till the paint was completely dry.

And there they were, just the two of them; and it occurred to the gods that, apart from comprising a complete set of first editions, they weren't much use for anything.

'They're not *supposed* to be any use for anything,' Athene replied, when this point was drawn to her attention. 'They're just supposed to *be*. They're,' she added, 'the meaning of the universe.'

The other eleven gods looked at her.

'Man,' she said, looking away, 'is the measure of all things.'

'Come again?'

'Man,' said Athene, 'defines the cosmos. Man is the independent life force, entirely separate from the Creator and possessed of free will, who by the very act of observing

causes all things to exist, simply by virtue of being susceptible of objective observation.'

There was a short pause.

'Fair enough,' said Vulcan, god of fire, metal and (in
due course) cordless screwdrivers. 'So what's the other
one for?'

Venus, goddess of love, frowned, wrinkling her lovely
nose. 'Which one do you mean?' she said, and sneezed.
She had just been created herself from the sea-spray
crashing against the rocks of Paphos, and towelling robes
and electric hair-dryers were still several giant conceptual
leaps away in the future.

'The shorter one with the round bits sticking out,'
Vulcan replied. 'By the way, is it meant to look like that,
or did you take it out of the oven too early?'

'Easy,' Athene replied. 'She tells Man what to do.'

There was another silence, marred only by the distant
groaning of tectonic plates and the grating sound of Time
running in.

'I thought you said he's got free will,' said Mars, god
of war.

'Sure.' Athene turned round slowly and gave him a
long, cool stare. 'And he freely decides to do what he's
told. If he knows what's good for him, that is.'

'Ah. Right. Yes, that sounds pretty logical to me,' said
Mars, briefly usurping Athene's prerogative as goddess of
wisdom. 'So, do we cut a tape or break a bottle of wine
or something, or is that it?'

'That's it for now,' Athene said. 'We just let them get
on with it.'

'With what, Thene?'

Athene gave her new sister a glance of disapproval.
'Venus,' she said, 'I think you and I need to have a little
talk.'

To begin with, there were the inevitable minor glitches.

For one thing, Venus completely misunderstood Athene's whispered explanation of her new duties, with the result that Mars spent the first few days of human history dragging the first humans off each other before they gouged each other's eyes out; while Vulcan rather shamefacedly admitted that while installing the digestive system and associated plumbing he'd had the blueprints upside down and read the scale as inches rather than centimetres. It was, however, too late to do anything about that now, and fortuitously the system as installed did actually work, just about.

It wasn't until much later that the real design faults began to show up.

Apollo, god of the sun, was the first to notice; and for a day or so he was inclined to ignore his misgivings. It was too improbable for words. Surely not . . .

But no. He was right. He was going to have to tell the others.

'Cheerful little sods, aren't they?' he therefore observed casually over dinner. 'I mean, to look at them, you wouldn't think they had a care in the world.'

He reached for the salt, and in doing so became aware of eleven pairs of eyes fixed on him.

'Cheerful?' Mars said.

'That's the way it looked to me,' Apollo replied, a slightly defensive tone creeping into his voice. 'Of course I could be wrong. Probably am. But . . .'

'Of course they aren't cheerful,' Athene replied quickly. 'They can't be, they're mortals. Creatures of a day. Out, out, brief candle. Don't say silly things like that, Pol, or you'll upset people.'

Nevertheless, first thing the next day, Athene crept out of Heaven by the back door and hurried down to Earth. Disguising herself as a clothes moth (an inept disguise, since there were as yet no clothes, but she was flustered) she buzzed through the lazy summer air and hovered for a while outside the mouth of the cave where the mortals had taken to cowering during the hours of darkness.

Inside, she could hear giggling.

Not, she had to admit, an auspicious start; but it was probably just a freak occurrence. Any minute now they'd start snivelling and bemoaning their lot, like they were supposed to do. She spread her wings and, since she was missing breakfast, spent a thoughtful quarter of an hour in a mimosa bush.

When she returned, the first thing she noticed was a smell. A delicious smell. So enchanting was it that before she knew what she was doing she'd flown straight into the bole of a tree and knocked herself silly.

It was the smell of cooking; to be precise, mushrooms and fried tomatoes.

The gods, it should be explained, ate their food raw and drank rainwater. After all, when you're immortal the risk of catching some fatal disease from raw food is minimal; and since there's no way a god can die of starvation, meals were in any case little more than a ritual observance designed to while away half an hour of endless, all-the-shops-are-shut-and-it's-raining Eternity.

Nothing but salad for the rest of Time. Small wonder that the gods were all as miserable as sin; small wonder, too, that they regarded this as the proper state of affairs. Happiness wasn't a concept they could easily get their heads around.

Athene uncrumpled her wings, adjusted a bent antenna and took off. Something would have to be done about this.

About a week later, Epimetheus and Pandora were just waking up from a nice lie-in and wondering whether to breakfast on plantain fried in honey or glazed eggplant with cinnamon when there was a knock at the cavemouth. They looked at each other.

'Visitors,' said Epimetheus.

'Oh *goody*,' replied his wife. 'Just think, Ep, our first guests! Isn't this wonderful?'

'Rather,' said our common ancestor, jumping up and running to the cavemouth. 'Gosh, life's fun.'

Outside the cave stood a tall figure in a blue uniform, with a peaked cap. There was, Epimetheus subconsciously noticed, a strange, almost unfinished look about him; almost as if he'd been called into being by someone who had a vague idea of what he should look like, but insufficient detailed knowledge to complete the job. Epimetheus couldn't help feeling that, viewed from the back, he wouldn't be visible.

'Sign here,' said the man.

'Certainly. How do I do that, exactly?'

The man showed him, and Epimetheus followed suit enthusiastically, until the man took the pen and clipboard away from him. Then he handed him a parcel.

It was big, and chunky, and it rattled excitingly when you shook it. It also said *Do Not Open This Parcel* on the label in big red letters, and if Epimetheus hadn't been so completely carried away with the delirious excitement of it all, he might have wondered how the hell he could read the writing, bearing in mind the fact that he was only sixteen days old and writing hadn't been invented yet.

'Hey, what are we supposed to do with this?' he asked the man, except that the man wasn't there any more. He shrugged, grinned with pleasure and took the parcel back into the cave.

Seven minutes later, of course, they'd opened the parcel.

'What is it?' Pandora asked.

Epimetheus shrugged again. 'Hang on,' he said, 'there's writing on the side here.'

'What's writing?'
'This is.'
'How absolutely wonderful.'
The writing said:

*Congratulations! You have been chosen as a lucky winner
in our special grand gala free-to-enter Prize Draw!!*

*Please accept this wonderful alarm clock radio
(batteries not included) as your special introductory gift,
absolutely free!*

*All you have to do to be allowed to keep your wonderful
new free gift is to select six items of your choice from the
enclosed catalogue, crammed with exciting special offers
chosen with you in mind, and let us have your order plus
your cheque within seven working days. So hurry!*

'Gosh,' said Pandora, after a long pause. 'What's a catalogue?'

'This is, I suppose,' Epimetheus replied, lifting a thick
glossy book out of the carton. He flicked a couple of
pages and whistled. 'Hey,' he whispered, 'you wait till you
see what's in here!'

The very next day, the order arrived: an electric blender
(plug not supplied), a video recorder, a washing machine,
a power drill, a microwave oven and an exercise bicycle.
And, tucked in with the packaging, an invoice for three
thousand, six hundred and thirty dollars, ninety-five cents
(including delivery and packaging).

By the afternoon of that day, there was a certain cool-
ness in the atmosphere at the cave. Epimetheus, if asked
to account for it, would have explained by saying that
Pandora had cracked the jug on the blender, jammed the
washing machine and broken the exercise bicycle by over-
vigorous use. Pandora's version would have been that
Epimetheus had made a complete mess of wiring up the

plugs and plumbing in the washing machine, with the result that all the appliances had blown themselves up and the floor of the cave was an inch deep in suds and soapy water. In addition, there had been a degree of asperity in the discussion as to who was going to pay the bill.

It occurred to neither of them to ask where the electricity supply and the mains water had come from; partly because they were innocents living in the first dawn of the Golden Age, but mostly because they were too busy arguing over whose fault it was that Epimetheus had used the electric drill to drill slap bang through the middle of a power cable; after which, anything to do with the electricity supply was pretty well academic.

The next morning they overslept (the alarm clock radio didn't work, because (a) Epimetheus had put the batteries in the wrong way, or (b) because Pandora had set it up all wrong, despite Epimetheus' totally lucid explanation of how to do it). What finally woke them was the sound of the bailiffs breaking in to repossess the blender, the video recorder, the washing machine, the microwave, the power drill and the exercise bicycle.

This led, inevitably, to a free and frank exchange of views on the subject of budget management, impulse buying and some people who were so mean that other people couldn't be expected to live with them one minute longer; which was in turn interrupted by the arrival of the men from the electricity company to disconnect the supply for non-payment of the bill.

By nightfall, the cave was empty. Pandora and Epimetheus had moved to smaller, damper caves at opposite ends of the mountain and were corresponding bitterly by carrier pigeon over who was to get the alarm clock radio.

As the argument raged, and the air vibrated with the clatter of hurrying wings, something moved at the bottom of the original box, out of which the free gift had come. It stirred. It blinked. Feebly, it spread stunted wings and lifted itself into the air.

In their excitement, Pandora and Epimetheus had over-looked the little creature; that slow, patient, long-suffering stowaway in the box of troubles. It didn't mind. It suffered long. Painfully stiff after its long confinement, it fluttered away towards Pandora's cave with its message of hope.

As you will have guessed, the little creature's name was Litigation, friend to all wretched mortals who have suffered wrongs and been oppressed. Next morning, when it perched on the rock outside Epimetheus' hovel and handed him a writ, it had somehow grown slightly larger and maybe even a touch fatter; but it had deep, grey eyes that seemed to say, Trust me.

By the time it arrived back at Pandora's cave, bearing a counter-writ, it was the size of an ostrich and virtually spherical, and its soft velvety paws had been replaced by whacking great talons. By then, of course, it was ever so slightly too late.

Lundqvist didn't put it quite like that, of course; his account was rather more pithy. But that, more or less, was the basic outline.

CHAPTER NINE

'Italy?' Odin asked, smiling. 'What on earth makes you think that?'

Below them, the traction engine ran smoothly, purring across the sky like an enormous flying cat. It had been Thor who'd fixed it eventually, and in doing so proved yet again the validity of his theory of simple mechanics; namely that, just because something's inanimate and incapable of perception doesn't mean to say it can't be scared shitless by being threatened with a whacking big hammer.

'Well, for a start,' Frey replied, 'the place is full of Italians.'

Odin shook his head in gentle scorn. 'It's a well known fact,' he said, 'that there's a substantial emigré Italian population in the north of England. More a Yorkshire phenomenon than Derbyshire, I'd always understood, but obviously you came across an enclave . . .'

'A whole townful?'

'They like to stick together.'

'Escorting a statue of the Madonna through the streets to a Romanesque cathedral?'

'Probably nineteenth-century Gothic.'

'Past a town sign saying *Bienvenuto in Bolzano*?'

'Twin town scheme. Very popular idea these days, twinning. Never had it in our day, of course. Nearest we ever got was, we burn your crops, you throw decaying corpses in our water supply.'

Thor, propped on one elbow on the roof of the cabin, snarled irritably. 'You'd better be right, sunshine,' he said. 'Because if this is Italy, then we're a long way from home, and the further we are, the later it'll be before we get back, and the likelier it is that She'll have noticed we've gone. And you know what that means.'

'Are you suggesting that I'm frightened of Mrs Henderson?'

'Yes.'

'Rubbish.'

Frey shifted uneasily in his seat. 'If it helps at all,' he murmured, 'I'm absolutely terrified of Mrs Henderson.'

'Huh.' Odin sniffed. 'I always reckoned you had a yellow streak in you.'

Frey stiffened. True, he wasn't the most warlike of the Norse gods; he was, after all, a god of peace and fruitfulness, of nature and the quickening earth; or, as his devotees had put it back in the good old days, a wimp. True, in the Last Days, when the Aesir had ridden forth for the last battle with the Frost-Trolls, it had been Frey who'd volunteered to stay inside Valhalla and man the switchboard and co-ordinate supply chains and monitor intelligence reports and all the other things one can find to do indoors in time of war. But these things are relative; and even a wimpish Norse god is on average rather more quick-tempered and volatile than a barful of marines at closing time on pay day. 'What was that,' he enquired, 'you just said?'

'I don't know about you two,' Thor interrupted, 'but I'm scared of her. And so are both of you, if you get right down to it.'

Odin shrugged. 'All right,' he said, 'and so am I, but that's beside the point. We're on our way home, and she'll never even know we've been gone, and that's a promise.'

'Is it?'

'Yes.'

'I was afraid you'd say that.'

'We're exactly on course,' Odin continued icily. 'Another three minutes and we'll be directly over Warrington.'

A look of recollected pain crossed Frey's face. 'It's the way she draws her eyebrows together just before she tells you off that gets me,' he said. 'As soon as you see those eyebrows move you say to yourself, Right, here it comes, but there's like this sort of twenty-second gap, and it's the waiting that gets you down. I'll swear she practises in front of the mirror or something.'

'And the tone of voice,' Thor replied. 'Don't forget the tone of voice. The way she says, "What *do* you think you're doing, exactly?" It makes you feel so . . .'

'I know.'

'Will you two stop going on about Mrs blasted Henderson?'

Thor shook his head, and looked down over the side at the ground below. It was at times like this, when he found himself gazing down from the heights upon the kingdoms of men, spread out beneath him like some enormous chessboard, that he felt an overpowering urge to drop something heavy over the side. He resisted it.

'So what's that lot down there, then?' he asked.

'Which lot where?'

'The major city with all the suburbs and arterial roads and things.'

So high up was the chariot that all a mortal would have seen was a splash of grey, flickering intermittently through the veil of thin cloud. But the gods can see things which

we cannot; not with their eyes but with their minds, which
thrill to the subtlest harmonies of the planet. With their
minds they can see Time, smell light, hear the grinding
of the Earth on its axis, feel the vibrations of the changing
seasons. Thus, from this height, a god would have no
trouble at all making out the Coliseum, the Forum, the
Baths of Caracalla, Trajan's Column, St Peter's Square,
all the crazy cross-hatched jumble of junk and jewels that
make up the Eternal City.

'Easy,' said Odin, throttling back and gently feathering
the airbrake. 'That's Droitwich.'

Ever since the world began, there has been a windswept
hillside under an iron-grey sky where three grey women
sit beneath a bent tree and spin.

What name you give them depends on who you are;
but you can never be wrong, whatever name you choose,
simply because what mortals call them is completely and
utterly unimportant. Whether you refer to them as
Parcae, Norns or Weird Sisters, nothing you can say or
do will affect them in the slightest degree, because they
were here first. More to the point, they will still be here
long after you, and everyone else, have been entirely
forgotten.

They sit, and they spin. Some people will have you
believe that they are asleep, and in their sleep they dream,
and their dreams are thoughts and their thoughts supply
the world with wisdom. Others claim that what they spin
is the web of life; its warp, its weft and the final little
dismissive click of the scissors. The truth, insofar as such
a concept has any validity in this context, is that they sit,
and they spin, and occasionally speak softly to one
another, just as they have always done, and what you may
care to believe is your own affair entirely.

'I spy with my little eye' – they have no names, but let

them be labelled One, Two and Three – 'something beginning with O.'

For a time they were called Graeae, and it was held that between the three of them they had one eye, one ear and one tooth, which they passed from hand to hand. This is almost certainly untrue.

'Outcrop.'

'Correct. Your go.'

'I spy with my, sorry *our* little eye something beginning with . . .'

'Hang on, I've still got the ear,' said Two. 'Here, Elsie, catch.'

'She's dropped it.'

'She couldn't see, because you've got the eye.'

'That's right, it's all my fault, as usual.'

'Where is it?' asked Three, scrabbling in the short, wiry grass with her gnarled fingers.

'Left hand down a bit, steady as you go, getting warmer.'

'She can't hear you.'

'Oh for crying out loud.'

Their sleep is dreaming, their dreaming is contemplation, their contemplation is eternal bitter resentment about who forgot to pack the spare organs. 'Got it,' said Three, 'no thanks to you two.' It is perhaps unfortunate that the only organ they have in triplicate is tongues.

'Ready?'

'Ready.'

'I spy with our little eye something beginning with R.'

'Ravine.'

'Correct. Give Betty the ear, Elsie, and do please try not to drop it.'

'I like that coming from you.'

One of the drawbacks that comes with playing I Spy for at least five hours each day in the same place ever since the beginning of Time is that you reach a point where you know all the answers.

'Mountainside,' said Two.

Three scowled. 'You might wait till I actually ask the question.'

'It's the right answer, isn't it?'

'That's beside the point.'

'Oh for pity's sake,' said One, 'let's play something else.'

'All right.'

What is undoubtedly true is that they are wise. All the wisdom in the Universe has at one time or another made the circuit of that little ring before drifting out into other, more prosaic dimensions. This means that the Three are very powerful, very wise and . . .

'Name me three rivers whose names begin with Y.'

'Yangtze-kiang, Yarra and Yellow.'

. . . Very, very bored.

'Let's play something else instead,' sighed Two. 'What about consequences?'

'No.'

'Why not?'

'Because,' replied Three, 'you cheat.'

The ear flashed from hand to hand, until it became a blur. The eye, meanwhile, lipread.

'I do not.'

'You do.'

'It's impossible to cheat at Consequences.'

'You seem to manage.'

'You two,' growled One. 'Just shut up and spin, all right?'

They sat, and they span, and Time ran round the circle. Time running in an enclosed circuit generates Truth. Truth sparking across the points of Knowledge becomes Wisdom.

'We could,' suggested Two, 'play Twenty Questions.'

'Are you out of your mind? After last time?'

'What?'

'I said, are you out of your mind, after last time.'

'What?'

'She's gone and dropped the ear again.'

'We ought,' opined One, 'to tie a bit of string to it, and then we wouldn't have any of this—'

'What?'

'Oh forget it.'

On the skyline, about seven hundred yards away, a tatty yellow van materialised and crawled painfully over the rocky ground. There was the occasional scrunge as some component or other hit a stone.

'There they are,' said Osiris, pointing. 'You see them, Carl? Just under that funny-shaped tree.'

'I got that, Mr Osiris. I think we just lost the exhaust.'

Pan closed his eyes. 'Look,' he said, 'are you absolutely sure about this, because those three old boilers really get up my nose.'

'Absolutely essential,' Osiris replied. 'Here, Carl, watch out for that—'

'Sorry, Mr Osiris.'

'It doesn't matter.'

Pan winced. 'You sure,' he said, 'we couldn't just look him up in the phone book or something? I mean, we haven't actually tried that, have we?'

'Shut up, Pan, there's a good lad. Right, park here and we'll walk the rest of the way.'

Under the tree, the three sisters stiffened, the web suddenly still in their hands.

'Visitors,' observed Two with disgust.

'Not again,' One sighed. 'That makes three times this century. What does it take to get a little peace and quiet around here?'

'What's she saying?'

'I said—'

'She's dropped it *again*.'

'One of these days,' remarked Two, after a short scrabble, 'it's going to go in the cauldron and get cooked, and then where'll we be, I should like to know.'

Folklore abounds with different versions of how to approach the sisters and implore their assistance. All known versions are completely incompatible with each other, except that all agree that the sisters must be treated with the very greatest respect. Failure to observe this simple precaution will inevitably mean that any request for information will fall on deaf ear (even if the ear hasn't rolled away under a stone or taken refuge in the lid of the sewing box), and there are rumoured to be even worse consequences as well.

'Wotcher,' Osiris called out. 'Hands up which of you's got the ear.'

'Who wants to know, shortarse?'

Osiris cleared his throat. The next bit always made him feel terribly self-conscious.

'Look,' he said, I conjure you by the dread waters of Styx, you who know all that is, all that was and all that will be. Tell me now—'

'I can't hear you,' said One, putting on her irascible crone voice. 'You'll have to speak up.'

Pan leaned forward, grabbed the ear from One's withered hand and held it to his lips like a microphone.

'He said,' he shouted, 'he conjures you, lots of stuff about how clever you are, and he wants to ask you something. Got that?'

The three sisters sat for a while, waiting for the ringing inside their skulls to stop.

'There is no need,' said One frostily, 'to shout.'

'Sorry?'

'I said, there's no need to—'

'Sorry?'

'What did she say?'

Pan grinned. 'SHE SAID THERE'S NO NEED TO SHOUT,' he said, and tossed the ear towards Three, who fumbled the catch. There was a plop as the ear went in the big black pot that stood in the middle of the circle. The sisters shrieked in chorus.

'Butterfingers,' said Pan. 'Now then . . .'

Sandra darted forward, plucked the ear out of the soup, picked a few lentils and split peas out of the funnel-shaped bit and handed it carefully to One.

'Thank you,' she said. 'All right, fire away.'

Somewhere near the French-Belgian border, a giant Mercedes lorry thundered south-westwards through the night. Swiftly it went on its sixteen wheels, and its iron belly safeguarded a consignment of two thousand cases of tinned prunes.

The driver, a Breton, stared with weary eyes into the cone of white light his headlamps projected and whistled a tune to keep himself awake. It had been a long day and he had many miles to go, but the magnitude of his enterprise stirred in him a sense of adventure he hadn't felt since he was a lad. For there was a serious shortage of prunes in France, so the rumours said, and it was mildly flattering to be chosen to be the man who brought the canned fruit from Ghent to Aix.

As he approached the border, he braced himself for a potentially tiresome passage through customs. You didn't need too exceptional an imagination to forecast the re-action of a bored excise official to the information that the cargo aboard the truck consisted of half a million prunes. There would be funny remarks, and witticisms, doubtless at his expense; and at three in the morning after a long drive, he could do without that sort of thing, thank you very much.

So preoccupied was he with these and other similar thoughts that he didn't notice the fact that he seemed to have acquired a shadow, in the form of a big, black, four-wheel drive with tinted windows.

The first he knew about this vehicle, in fact, was when he came round a sharp bend to find the road blocked by a tractor. He slammed on his brakes and slithered to a halt; whereupon three shadowy figures jumped out of the four-wheel drive, ran up to the driver's door and pulled it open. Something metallic sparkled in the pale light of the stars.

'Just climb out slowly,' said a shadowy figure in abysmally accented French, 'and you won't get hurt. Okay?'

The driver nodded quickly. 'Fine,' he said. 'You do know what I'm carrying, don't you?'

'Shut up.'

'Okay.'

(By pure coincidence, another identical lorry owned by the same road freight company was carrying a load of twelve million cigarettes along the same route, only about three quarters of an hour behind. Because of the prune famine, the schedules had been rearranged somewhat.)

Shortly afterwards, the lorry continued its journey, with a different driver, and headed for a different destination; namely a deserted hockey field on the outskirts of Cambrai. On arrival, it was driven into a big shed, and the doors closed behind it. Lights came on, and men hurried to the tailgate to start unloading.

The gate opened.

'Hang on,' said a voice from inside the container body. 'This isn't right, surely.'

The speaker, when fixed in a spotlight, turned out to be a white-haired old gentleman in a wheelchair. He was flanked by a plump girl, a large, stocky man with an expression like bad amateur taxidermy, a tall, thin man in camouflage gear holding a very large handgun and an even taller, thinner character with goat's feet.

Slowly, the hijackers backed away. Even those of them who could stomach the sight of Lundqvist's Desert Eagle felt distinct bad vibes from the expression in the old man's eyes and the curious terminals of Pan's legs. In the version they'd heard, it had been an old lady with an axe in her shopping-basket, but this was clearly an updated rescension of the same basic urban folkmyth.

'Sorry about this,' Pan called out. 'Only, we needed a lift, you see, and there was your lorry, and we thought . . .'

There was a shot. Maybe it was fear, or perhaps just a nervous finger tightening reflexively on a trigger. The bullet hit Pan in the forehead, passed out the back of his head as if through thin air and buried itself in the mountain of boxes behind. Brown juice started to seep through the cardboard.

Then there were more shots – Lundqvist giving area fire with the .50 calibre, which made a noise like a portable indoor volcano and took out most of the lights. The hijackers responded in kind. There were suddenly prunes everywhere.

'Stop it,' said Osiris briskly, 'at once.'

Simultaneously, every firing pin in the building jammed solid, and the lights came back on. This time, however, they were supported by unpleasantly-shaped figures with the heads of jackals; and for all their brilliance they seemed to produce more shadows than light. The hijackers came forward.

'Now then,' Osiris said. 'Someone tell me where we are.'

The gang leader, nudged forward by his colleagues, unravelled six inches of tongue from round his Adam's apple and explained. He also apologised profusely, expressed extreme regret for having inconvenienced such obviously distinguished supernatural persons, and asked if they would very kindly care to turn the prunes back into Marlboro Hundreds, as he had a customer waiting.

'Oh no you don't,' Osiris replied. 'We've got to get to Aix by morning, and you're going to take us there. Otherwise,' he added with a pleasant smile, 'something around here's going to get turned into cigarettes, but it sure ain't going to be the prunes. Kapisch?'

The journey was resumed. This time, however, the chief hijacker travelled inside the container, with the muzzle of Lundqvist's gun nestling in his ear and Carl standing behind him with a tyre iron.

'Going far?' the hijacker asked.

Osiris grinned. 'You could say that,' he replied. 'I don't think you'd want to know where we're headed, really I don't.'

'That's fine,' the hijacker replied quickly. 'Only making conversation.'

'But I'm going to tell you anyway,' Osiris replied maliciously. 'That way, either you'll tell someone else, and they'll lock you up in a loony bin for the rest of your life, or else you'll keep it to yourself and probably go stark staring mad anyway. Serve you right. We're gods.'

'You don't say.'

'And,' Osiris went on, 'we're headed for the Kingdom of Death, if it's still there. Last time I heard, they were trying to turn it into some sort of ghastly drive-in theme park, but I don't suppose they ever got the planning permission. I mean, imagine the problems you'd have with off-street parking.'

'Indeed.' To those whom the gods wish to destroy, they first give pins and needles in the left foot. The hijacker rubbed his leg against the side of the van, but it didn't help much.

'We need to go there,' Osiris went on, 'because the Three Wise Women told us that in order to locate the last hiding place of the Golden Teeth of El Dorado (which, as you know, lie at the world's end and are guarded by an enormous fire-breathing, hundred-headed answering machine) we have to find and read the Runes of Power chalked on the wall in the little boy's room immediately adjacent. That's what they said, anyway,' Osiris concluded. 'It's not April the First today, by any chance?'

'You certainly have an unusual job,' said the hijacker. 'Did you always want to be a god or did you just sort of drift into it?'

'We need the Golden Teeth,' Osiris went on, 'in order to pay our lawyer. That's just something on account, by the way, to cover initial expenses, setting up the file on the computer, routine administrative work, that sort of thing. He's very expensive, even for a lawyer.'

'He must be very good, though.'

'Oh he is. Very.'

CHAPTER TEN

'If this is Droitwich,' muttered Thor, 'they've definitely been fiddling about with it since I was last here.'

'And when was that, then?'

'1036.'

'Well, there you are, then.' Odin stood on the extreme edge of the kerb, wavering. Being omniscient, he knew all about cars; and besides, he'd seen them often enough on the telly. It was just that, en masse, thundering past like some stampeding herd of square steel cattle, they seemed a trifle, well, unnerving. Or would do, if he was a mere mortal. And there is, of course, this wretched convention that when gods walk abroad among mortals, they have to blend in. If it wasn't for that, of course . . .

'Get a move on, will you?' Thor grumbled at his elbow. 'We haven't got all day, you know.'

'Shut up,' Odin replied. 'We can't just go charging through the traffic and have all the cars bouncing off us, it'd be too conspicuous. We've got to wait for those little coloured lights to come on.'

'What, those ones up there on that stick?'

'That's the ones.'

'And that's what mortals do, is it?'

'Yes.'

'It's a funny old world,' Thor said. 'And so we've got to do like they do?'

Odin nodded. 'When in Rome,' he said.

At his other elbow, Frey made a face. 'Odd you should say that,' he said.

It hadn't been Odin's fault. Admittedly, it was the inner valve ring seal gasket that had blown, and it had been Odin who'd fitted it, and because you just couldn't get the parts for these older models nowadays it had been Odin who'd gam-shacked up a substitute out of brown paper and treacle. But the brown paper and treacle gaskets of the immortal gods are by definition more lasting than diamonds, and in Odin's opinion there was no way it should have blown if the inlet manifold had been properly set up in the first place. They were now looking for a car parts store, Odin having a hunch that the gaskets off a 1991 Leyland Roadrunner would probably do the trick at a pinch.

'How do you mean, Frey?'

'I think we are.'

Odin scowled. 'What's he on about now, Thor?' he demanded. 'Because if this is some sort of wind-up you two are making up between you, I'm really not in the mood.'

Thor, who had been conferring with his colleague, shrugged. 'Sorry,' he said. 'Our mistake. Of course this is Droitwich.'

'Thank you.'

'And that . . .' Thor pointed to their left. 'That must have been the Droitwich Coliseum we went past just now, and those must be the Baths of Alderman Wilkinson, and that big square building over there is probably the world famous Temple of the Engineering, Municipal and Allied Trades.'

'And what about that over there?'

'Where?'

Frey pointed towards the forbidding gateway in front of them, with its curiously garbed attendants.

'Oh that,' Thor said. 'I think that's the Catholic church.'

Enormous lorry thundering its way through the Provencal night. Exhausted driver blinking hazily through a fly-splattered windscreen. One step out of line would guarantee that he spent the rest of his life on a lily-pad.

Round a hairpin bend, to find a tractor standing right across the road. Marvellous new fifth-generation air brakes pull the rig up short before the two vehicles combine together in a Jackson Pollock of twisted metal.

If he'd been looking in his rear-view mirror, instead of sprawling over the dashboard with a gearlever up his right sleeve, he'd have seen a dark green four-wheel drive with tinted windows purr up behind the tailgate.

His door is jerked open. He looks down into the muzzle of a big black handgun.

'Okay,' hissed the masked man behind it. 'Do as I say and you won't get—'

The driver blinked twice. 'You what?' he said.

'Do as I say,' replied the hijacker, irritably, in abysmal French, 'and you won't get hurt.' He scowled. 'Trust me,' he added, 'I'm a doctor. Really.'

'I don't believe this.'

'Straight up. That's a nasty cut you've got on your forehead, by the way.'

'Must be where my head hit the wheel.'

'You should get that seen to. Any dizziness, nausea, double vision?'

'I don't think so. I've got this migraine coming, I think.'

'No spots in front of the eyes?'

'No.'

'Take two aspirin,' said the hijacker, 'get a good night's sleep and we'll see how you are in the morning. Meanwhile,' he added, 'get out of the cab before I blow your fucking brains out.'

'Yes, doctor.'

Shortly afterwards, the lorry continued on its journey, with a new driver. If it was supposed to be going to Aix-en-Provence, it was going the wrong way.

'All right,' said the customs official sleepily, 'what've you got in there?'

The driver leant out of the window. 'You're going to laugh when I tell you,' he said.

Out of wind-scoured, sleepless eyes the customs official glowered at him. 'I don't think so,' he said. 'Come on, where's your bill of lading?'

The man in the passenger seat rummaged about in the glove box, and handed down a packet of papers. The customs official sighed.

'Fine,' he said. 'Prunes. Okay, you two out and let's see inside.'

There was a brief flurry of conversation inside the cab.

'Hang on,' said the driver. 'Diplomatic thingummy.'

'I beg your pardon?'

'Immunity,' the driver said. 'Just a tick, here we are, passports. And this lot here's a diplomatic bag, okay?'

'Get real, will you? It's a bloody juggernaut.'

'Ah.' The driver nodded. 'Diplomatic juggernaut, though, innit? You want an international incident, be my guest.'

There was a moment's silence.

'You're absolutely sure,' said the customs official, 'that it's prunes you got in there?'

'Absolutely,' replied the passenger. 'Look at it this way. Would we say it was prunes if it wasn't?'

The customs official thought about it. The argument had a certain specious attraction. Tractor spares, yes. Engine parts, certainly. Any time a customs official sees Engine parts on a manifest, he ducks for cover and calls up the bomb disposal guys on the radio. But prunes . . .

'No armaments, then? Drugs, illicit diamonds, rare species?'

'Not as far as I know, officer.'

'Pirate radio equipment? Dutiable goods such as alcohol, perfume or tobacco? Works of art requiring an export licence?'

'Don't think so. Are you feeling all right, by the way?'

The customs official raised an eyebrow. ''Course,' he said; and then, catching the driver's eye, added, 'Or at least I think . . .'

'You look a bit under the weather to me,' said the driver, putting his head on one side and pursing his lips, 'if you don't mind me saying so.'

'Oddly enough,' said the customs official, 'just lately I've been getting these sharp stabbing pains round about here . . .'

'Been eating regularly?'

'Not very regularly, no . . .' the customs official looked up. 'Why?' he demanded.

'We're doctors,' the passenger explained. 'Any heartburn or related symptoms?'

'Not that I'd noticed.'

'Headache?'

'Can't say I have.'

'Sure?'

'Positive.'

The driver looked up and down the road. At this time of night, they had the place to themselves. There was nobody else to be seen in the customs post. Accordingly, he swung open the door of the lorry, dealing the customs official a sharp blow just above the ear. The customs official, predictably, fell over.

'Laymen,' the driver called out, putting in the clutch and pulling away. 'What do they know? And when you wake up, take two aspirins.'

The Swiss guard hesitated, his mind scrolling back through recent memories. He'd seen something, just subliminally, for a fraction of a second; but there had been an anomaly – an abomination, even. Something had been where there should be nothing. He stood for a moment, like a statue representing Contemplation on some baroque triumphal arch; then he remembered, and sprang into action. Just as he'd thought.

Down by the side of the sentry box, four-fifths hidden in the shadows, was an empty crisp packet. He snatched it up, marched over to the receptacle provided, and binned it. Another blow struck, he congratulated himself, against the forces of entropy.

Prompted by this thought, he reviewed his position in the cosmos, and saw that it was good. Only three months since he'd left his Alpine canton and joined the standing army of the Papal State, and already he was standing guard at the gates of the Vatican. All right, yes, the goods entrance of the Vatican, which was pretty much like goods entrances anywhere, but only if viewed superficially. I had rather be a goods entrance keeper in the house of the Lord than dwell in the tents of the ungodly.

Then the ground started to shake. Instinctively, his hands tightened on the shaft of his halberd; but a glare of white light and the low roar of massive engines reassured him. Just a lorry.

A lorry. At three o'clock in the morning. What could it be, he asked himself. And, in due course, the driver.

'Prunes.'

'Prunes?'

'That's right. Now if you'd just open the damn gates, we can unload this lot and I can go to bed, all right?'

The guard narrowed his eyes. 'Prunes?' he said.

The driver leant out of the window and manoeuvred his head until the tip of his nose was but a few microns from the guard's forehead. 'Look,' he said, 'prunes it is, and if you want to go and get the Big Fella out of his pit and ask him what he wants six million dried plums for, then jolly good luck to you and send me a postcard from Hell. Otherwise, open this flaming gate before we all die of old age.'

'Yes, but *prunes*.'

A few seconds before the driver would otherwise have put his foot down on the throttle and crashed the gate, the passenger leant across, smiled placidly, and said, 'Perhaps I can explain, my son,' he added.

'Gosh,' said the guard, stepping backwards and standing stiffly to attention. 'I didn't see you there, Your Reverence.'

'No matter.' The passenger removed the cardinal's hat and put it on the seat beside him. 'The Holy Father's compliments,' he said, 'and may we please proceed?'

'Of course, Your Reverence. Only . . .'

'Yes?'

'Prunes, Father. It just seems . . .'

'Yes?'

'Just a moment and I'll do the gates for you.'

Monsignor Donatus O'Rourke did up the last buckle on his crimson flak jacket, muttered a final Hail Mary, and drew back the plunger of the syringe, flooding the chamber with holy water. His bell jingled faintly in its shoulder holster.

'Okay, lads,' he growled into his walkie-talkie, 'this is it. Don't screw up, and let's go for it.'

Mgr O'Rourke was no back-street exorcist; he was a pro, from the tips of his asbestos gloves and ring with built-in geiger-counter to the toes of his rubber boots. People called him a mercenary, a theologian of fortune, have bell, will travel; he laughed in their faces. Whenever he did a job, he knew he was doing it for the Big Guy, in the way that he knew was right, even if the redhats round the Curule Chair had declared his methods anathema. The substantial sums of money that found their way to his Swiss account he regarded simply as contributions to the war chest. Fighting the old gods with the new technology wasn't cheap, and he'd long since learnt not to expect any funding from Holy Mother church (or, as he preferred to think of it, the Organisation). As a result, he had to do business with some pretty dubious characters, who he suspected were motivated by concerns not one hundred per cent connected with the struggle against the forces of darkness. So what? As he'd said in his evidence to the Walinski Commission, he knew that what he was doing was right, and if he had to raise his own funds in order to do it, that's the way the eucharist crumbles. Not, of course, that he'd ever even considered selling holy water to the Shi'ites as the yellow press had alleged; but even if he had, his conscience would still be clear.

His men – all hand-picked, the flower of the priesthood – should all be in position by now. He turned to the man crouched beside him, and said, 'Well?'

The man, who was a doctor by profession, nodded. 'What are we waiting for?' he said.

'Okay,' replied Mgr O'Rourke. 'Let's nuke some spooks. Go, men!'

On his command, three priests in black balaclavas abseiled down from the balcony above, landing with pinpoint precision beside the tailgate of the lorry. From their backpacks they unslung heavy black chainsaws. A second or so later, the night was torn by the sound of steel on iron.

'Second wave into position,' Mgr O'Rourke barked into the walkie-talkie. 'This is it, guys. Remember Joppa!'

Twelve priests with reeking censers scuttled out from the shadows and hit the deck, pineal glands pumping, brains clamouring, What on earth does he mean, remember Joppa? As soon as they were in place, the second section scrambled forward, dragging behind them an enormous sled-mounted bell.

'Nice work,' snapped the Monsignor. 'Red Section stand by, and – *candles*.'

On all four sides of the courtyard, enormous spotlights snapped on, drenching the ancient stones with photons. At precisely the same moment, the chainsaws screamed through the last few millimetres of the tailgate, which fell out into the courtyard with a tinny clang. The censers, launched with unerring aim, sailed through the air into the back of the lorry, filling the confined space with thick billows of scented smoke. The bell boomed.

'Doing good, guys,' O'Rourke muttered. 'Now, in there with the book, and . . .'

His lips froze. Damn. Damn. There's always something, isn't there?

'Listen up, guys,' he said, as casually as he could. 'Anybody out there got a spare bible?'

Inside the body of the lorry, the situation wasn't good. By the time Osiris had recovered from the effects of an unexpected lungful of incense and had tumbled to what was going on, it had almost been too late. Absolute chaos, he reflected, absolutely typical. Still, what the hell do you expect from a generation that believes that the Earth revolves around the sun?

He rallied his forces, which had been reduced to a manageable size by a snatch squad of PVC-cassocked priests who had knocked out Kurt Lundqvist with a weighted crucifix and whisked him away. Admittedly, the man had been trying to help; but elbow room inside the lorry had been limited at the best of times, and Lundqvist rolling around firing his gun and lobbing stun grenades had taken up rather more of it than his net usefulness warranted. Someone would no doubt get him back in due course. When the time was right.

'Carl,' he shouted. 'Fetch a tyre iron.'

'This,' Pan coughed, fanning incense out of his eyes, 'is ludicrous. Why don't we just turn them all into woodlice and be done with it?'

Osiris shook his head. 'A bit out of touch, aren't we?' he said. 'No can do, ever since we all signed the Ravenna Convention.'

Pan blinked. 'The what?'

'The Ravenna Convention.' Osiris ducked to avoid a hand-thrown rosary. 'Part of the handover deal when we packed it all in. Basically it says that the Christian mob can push us about all they like and we can do bugger all about it.'

'You're kidding!'

'Wasn't my idea,' Osiris replied. He reached up, caught a censer in mid-flight and threw it back. 'It was the Roman lot, I seem to remember, always quarrelling among themselves, reckoned they needed some sort of peace-keeping force once they retired, to stop them cutting each other's throats in the TV room and shoving laxatives in the Sanatogen.' He gave Pan a meaningful look.

'Nothing to do with me,' Pan replied. 'Never heard of it, in fact. Certainly never signed anything.' His face brightened. 'Which means, surely, I can change them into anything I like and nobody can touch me for it.'

'You,' Osiris replied, 'no. Me, yes. If you so much as transform a hair of their heads, then I'm mythology. But not,' he added grimly, 'before I turn you into a sewer god. Understood?'

'You wouldn't?'

'It's a dirty, rotten job,' Osiris replied, 'but someone's got to do it.'

'Fine.' Pan sighed. 'So what are we going to do now?'

'That's what I need the tyre iron for. Thanks, Carl. Break open those crates, will you?'

'Can I help?' Sandra, who had spent the last ten minutes sleeping peacefully after a direct hit on the side of the head from a hassock, crawled to the wheel-arch and crouched down behind a crate. It was at times like this, she felt, when the battle is raging all around and the menfolk are battling desperately for mere survival, that you wish you'd brought your knitting.

'I expect so,' Osiris replied. 'When did you last eat anything?'

Sandra considered. 'I had a packet of crisps on the ferry,' she replied, 'and a Mars bar and an apple a couple of hours after that. I'm farnished,' she added.

'Fine,' said Osiris, as Carl reduced the nearest packing case to matchwood with a well-aimed blow of the tyre iron. 'Have a prune.'

'Bless me, Father, for I have sinned.'

From behind the curtain there was a faint snap, as the priest lit a Lucky Strike. 'Yeah, sure,' he said wearily. 'Okay, let's hear it. And what trivial misdemeanour is bothering us today?'

'Um.' The penitent hesitated. 'Well, I missed confession yesterday.'

'Big deal.' The priest yawned. 'You didn't have anything

to confess, right? C'mon, you must be able to do better than that.'

'Well . . .' There was a pause, during which the priest drew down a lungful of smoke and coughed savagely. 'I also harboured uncharitable thoughts about Brother Justinian.'

'You harboured uncharitable thoughts against Brother Justinian.'

'Yes.'

'That's it?'

'Well, yes. I suppose so.'

'You guys, you make me want to puke, you know that? Sins? You don't know sins from *nothing*. Where I come from, now, we could teach you wimps a thing or two about sinning.'

'Er . . .'

'Where I come from . . .' the priest paused, hawked mightily and spat, ringing a spittoon somewhere on his side of the curtain like a gigantic gong. 'Where I come from,' he continued, 'we wouldn't give you the snot from our noses for anything less than a double aggravated rape. And you come hassling me with goddamn uncharitable thoughts. Get outa here, will you?'

There was a long, puzzled silence; then the penitent said, 'Shall I say three Hail Marys?'

'Hey.' The priest clicked his tongue. 'I get this feeling,' he said, 'that you're gonna say them no matter what I tell you, so basically yeah, go for it, do your karma. Now get . . . Jesus H. Christ, man, what was *that*?'

As the shock waves of the tremor died away, the priest ripped aside the curtains of the confessional and sprinted away down the cloister towards the presumed source of the noise, scattering popcorn as he went.

About thirty seconds later he turned a corner into the small courtyard by the goods entrance and stopped dead in his tracks, as if he'd just run straight into a transparent breeze-block wall.

'Holy shit!' he whispered. Not entirely without justification.

He saw, in the eerie glow of blue flares and bright white floods, a lorry in the middle of the yard, ringed by monks crouched down behind such cover as they could find. From the back of the van emanated a succession of scintillating and extremely colourful sparks and forks of lightning, which arced and buzzed their way round the yard before earthing themselves back into the van. By way of return fire, the monks were lobbing in smoking censers, lighted candles and handbells. Two rather more worldly figures on an adjoining balcony were blazing away with automatic pistols, although to no perceptible effect. There was a stifling odour of sanctity and sulphur; and, from inside the lorry, audible even above the sundry bangs and crashes, the sound of steadily chomping jaws, punctuated by the occasional rending belch.

'Hey,' breathed the priest, as the penitent scurried up and ducked down beside him, 'this is *real*, you know? Sure, back home you don't go out the vestry door without your can of Mace and your shiv, but this is something else, you know?' He laughed for sheer joy. 'Man,' he breathed, 'this is better than *Ghostbusters*.'

Two monks wheeled in a supermarket trolley laden with the biggest bible the penitent had ever seen, under cover of three Augustinian canons with perspex riot shields. A particularly flamboyant sparkle whizzed through the air, splattered against a shield, and dissolved into a floral tribute of green and orange cinders. Two monks ran up and doused the flames.

'Support group,' crackled a bullhorn, 'deploy the holy water cannon. Come on, guys, move it.'

A platform of monks darted off into the shadows and

returned with one of the Papal fork-lifts from the goods entrance (painted bright yellow and emblazoned with *In hic signo vinces* stencilled on the wings). On the forks was an enormous contraption like an outsize fire extinguisher, out of which led a hundred yards of black rubber hose. Two of the monks contrived to tangle their feet in it and fall over. A pale lilac sparkle soared through the air in a graceful parabola and lit on the roof of the forklift, which promptly vanished from sight in a retina-engraving flurry of colours.

'C'mon, guys, this is sloppy,' snorted the bullhorn. 'Blue section, give cover. Purple section, deploy the book.'

With cries of 'Geronimo!', 'Yee-haaah!' and 'Blessed be the name of St Teresa of Avila, whose day this is', parties of monks wheeled the trolley forward under the cover of huge asbestos screens. All around, handbells clanged, candles flared. It was, the priest remarked to the penitent, like Bloody Septuagesima all over again.

Inside the lorry, the atmosphere was tense; and, of course, thick as cream cheese with incense from the censers. Pan, with a handkerchief over his face and a barricade of smashed crates affording some slight cover, was shooting coloured lightning from his fingertips and doing his best to dodge flying handbells at the same time. Behind him, Osiris, Sandra and Carl huddled round a heap of empty tins and chewed grimly.

'That's it,' Sandra groaned through a full mouth, 'I can't eat another one, I'm sorry. You'll just have to leave me.'

Osiris said nothing – his mouth was stuffed so full his lips could scarcely meet – but instead grabbed a can, slit the top off with his thumbnail and thrust it at her. She winced and took it.

They were eating prunes.

And, of course, spitting out the stones into an upended crate, which by now was three-quarters full. The floor of the lorry was six inches deep in empty tins, and there was syrup everywhere.

'Are you jokers nearly done?' Pan yelled over his shoulder. 'There's no way I can keep this up for much longer.'

'Tinker, tailor, soldier . . .'

'Stay with it,' Osiris mumbled back. 'Just a few more dozen should do it, if only you can . . .'

'. . . Sailor, rich man, poor man . . .'

Osiris turned his head and stared. 'Carl,' he said. 'Just what do you think you're doing?'

'Beggarman,' replied Carl, looking up. 'Eating prunes, like you said. Thief.'

'Yes, fine, but what's all this soldier sailor stuff? Have you gone completely—?'

'It's what you say when you eat prunes.'

'Is it? Why?'

'Dunno.' Carl considered for a moment, his jaws moving. 'Brings you luck, I s'pose.'

'Does it?'

'It's s'posed to, I s'pose.'

Osiris thought about it. 'Oh well,' he said, 'can't do any harm, I guess. Chartered surveyor, inspector of taxes, research physicist . . .' He paused, ejected a mouthful of stones into the crate, and wiped a torrent of juice off his chin. 'Management consultant, systems co-ordinator . . .'

'It's a shame,' Sandra observed, 'there isn't any custard. My mum always does lots of hot custard with prunes.'

'Computer software designer, trainee account executive, there, that'll have to do.' Osiris spat out the last few stones, took a deep breath and drew the crate towards him. 'Right,' he said. 'This is what—'

'Builder, milkman, postman, bookie's runner . . .'

'This is what we have to do.'

*   *   *

The monks had finally succeeded in manhandling the trolley with the book in it right up to the tailgate of the lorry. Not without heavy losses: seven of their number were ambling aimlessly round the courtyard clothed from head to foot in bright blue fire, bumping into corners and singing quietly to themselves. Another dozen lay on their backs on the flagstones, glowing alarmingly and giggling at the moon.

'Okay, you're doing great, guys,' rasped the bullhorn. 'On my command, open the book.'

And then there was a horrible moment as the whole courtyard seemed to fill with a bright green flare, as handfuls of prunestones flew out of the lorry into the air. A split second later they came down, rattling on the flags, bouncing and skittering. And there they lay.

A monk, who was on fatigues for a week for dropping a loaded chalice on the sergeant-major's foot, stared at the stones and whimpered. Bloody tourists, he thought, who exactly do they think is going to have to sweep that lot up?

Crack.

One prunestone, which had chanced to fall into a shallow pool of fizzing blue light, twitched sharply. Out of one side a tiny green shoot nuzzled its way out, groped with a tendril and touched down on the courtyard floor. A second later, it wasn't alone.

'Come *on*,' Osiris muttered under his breath. 'What the hell's keeping you?'

It all happened in a fraction of a second. There was a fusillade of tiny cracks, a scurrying of prunestone shells, a filthy smell . . .

. . . And then there was a forest. All the prunestones were suddenly sprouting. Like the fingers of a martyr to rheumatism their roots clawed a couple of times at the flags, scratched a few times at the surface, and thrust a taproot down through the stones and into the bowels of the earth. The trees grew.

When they were all twenty feet high, Osiris tapped Carl on the shoulder . . .

('Farmer, painter and decorator, handyman. Um . . .')

. . . pulled him to his feet and shouted in his ear. Carl nodded, grabbed Sandra by the hand and hauled her after him out of the lorry into . . .

Indeed. Into the forest.

Forest was, by now, the only apposite word for it. True, it was made up of nothing but plum trees (Victorias) and it didn't actually cover very much ground, but it was quite definitely a forest. What it lacked in the horizontal axis was more than adequately compensated for by the sky-scraping height of the vertical.

'It seems to be working,' Osiris said. His face was green, and he kept swallowing hard. 'That's splendid. Now then, somebody give me a push and we'll get out of here.'

The wood – to be precise, the sacred grove – was still going strong. A snatch squad of monks who had been trying to sneak into the lorry through the front passenger door were suddenly smothered in long, leathery twigs, shaken violently, and hurled backwards into the middle of the yard. No prizes for guessing whose side the timber was on.

'That's the trouble with this business sometimes,' observed one of the two doctors to his companion, as they watched the plum forest below them explode into blossom. 'Sometimes, you just can't see the wood for the . . .'

The rest of the sentence was drowned out by the crash of falling masonry. A handful of prunestones had chanced to fly through an open window, and now there were large holes in the walls, with plum-laden branches sticking out through them. A task force of monks with strimmers and electric hedge-trimmers were fighting a desperate rear-guard action to save the auxiliary paraffin store.

There was a crash, as of a sash being thrown up. Mgr O'Rourke froze in the act of lobbing a chasuble and glanced up, to see an open window and an all too familiar form silhouetted in the frame. It was wearing purple silk pyjamas.

'You there,' boomed a voice from the window, 'keep the noise down. There's people up here trying to sleep.'

'Yes,' muttered Osiris, 'point taken. All I can say is, it seemed like a good idea at the time.'

'Did it?' Pan frowned at him. 'There was a time, then, when you thought it'd be a really spiffing wheeze to hem us in with an impenetrable grove of supernatural plum trees. Fine. Any similar ideas about how we're going to get out of here?'

'Look, I said—'

'And,' Pan continued, making the most of what was for him a unique opportunity to tell someone so instead of being told so by somebody else, 'any further brain-waves about how we're going to slip past all those loony monks and priests and so on once we've managed to get out of here? Or didn't you want to spoil the spontaneous excitement of it all?'

Osiris scowled at him. 'That'll do,' he said. 'There's no need to get all amusing about it. We'll just have to apply our minds a bit, that's all.'

'Maybe,' Sandra suggested, 'they'll get bored and go away.'

'That's what you reckon, is it?' Pan demanded. 'They'll eventually wander off to watch the flying pigs, or something. Well, you never know, do you. Or perhaps the sky will fall on their heads. Perhaps,' he went on, making the most of it while it lasted, 'the gods will come and rescue us. You know, *deus ex machina*, all that sort of caper.'

'Now calm down,' Osiris interrupted sharply. 'We're in enough of a hole already without you indulging in flights of fancy.'

'Flights of fancy what?'

Osiris was about to answer this with a homily on the childishness of low-grade irony when the sky darkened, the earth began to shake, and a loud crack of thunder made his teeth vibrate in his head. He looked up.

'No, we are *not* going to crash,' retorted Odin testily. 'I fixed the locknuts myself, everything is entirely under . . .'

The engine crashed.

There was silence, apart from the death-rattle of the engine as it feebly spun a flywheel or so. A few of the riper plums fell from the tree and splatted on the rear mudguard.

'. . . Control.'

'We seem,' Frey remarked, hauling himself out from under a fallen branch, 'to have landed in some sort of a forest. Odd, that.'

'Quite.'

'A forest in the middle of Droitwich.'

Odin's head popped up from inside the cab. He was covered in oil, and his spectacles lay at a crazy slant across the bridge of his nose. 'Probably a park or a picnic area,' he said. 'Look, shin up that tree there and see if you can spot something like goalposts or a bandstand, something we can navigate by.'

'Must I?' Frey gave him a troubled look. 'Come on, Odin, you know about me and heights, I get vertigo standing on tiptoe. Can't someone else do it?'

'Leave it to me,' Thor grumbled. He knelt down, tucked his socks inside his boots and laid a hand on the nearest treetrunk. 'I'm going up now,' he said. 'I may be gone for some time. If I'm not back in half an hour, bloody well come and find me, okay?'

'Okay. Oh, Thor . . .'

'Yes?'

'Before you go . . .'

'Yes?'

'Have one of these plums, they're not at all bad.'

With a bad grace, Thor started to climb the tree. Odin, meanwhile, was studying the AA book of town centre plans. Frey had found a rather squashed, almost two-dimensional banana and was eating it.

After a less than flawless climb – the tree was designed more for aesthetic and horticultural purposes than ease of ascent – Thor reached the top. He rested for a moment, then shaded his eyes with his hand and looked out. And saw . . .

'Hey, you two!'

'Well?'

'You'll never guess what I can see.'

'What?'

'I said, you'll never guess.'

'I wasn't,' said Frey, through a mouthful of banana, 'proposing to try. Are you going to tell us, or are we going to have to wait for your collected letters and diaries?'

'I think,' said Thor, 'we're actually inside the Vatican.'

Frey glanced up. 'Nah,' he said. 'I read a book about it once, the decor's all wrong. For a start, it's not the right ceiling.'

'Yes, but . . .'

'The ceiling in the Vatican,' Frey continued obliviously, 'is sort of wide and covered in these paintings. I never heard anything about plain navy blue ceilings with tiny white dots.'

'Listen . . .'

'Very famous, the Vatican ceiling,' Frey went on.

'There's this really famous picture of the two electricians wiring something up, only they've obviously not earthed it properly, because where one geezer is handing something to the other one – probably a screwdriver or a pair of tinsnips – there's this big flash and sparks running up and down the guys' arms. I think it's one of those public information posters, something like Increasing Safety in the Home.'

'I meant to say,' said Thor patiently, 'inside the Vatican grounds.'

'What makes you think that?'

'Divine intuition.'

'Oh.' Frey folded the banana skin neatly and threw it over his shoulder. 'Any people about?'

'Odd you should mention that,' Thor replied. 'Yes, there's quite a few milling about down here. You know something? This place is crawling with priests.'

At the bottom of the tree there was a hurried conference.

'Ask them,' Frey called out, 'if we can borrow a set of welding gear.'

One of the few remaining advantages of being a god, Pan said to himself, as he raced along behind Osiris' wheelchair through the darkened streets of Rome, is that you don't have any hang-ups about believing in miracles. For instance, there we all were, trapped, no way out. Next minute, something like an enormous traction engine materialises in the sky, swoops down, smashes a gap in the outer wall, ploughs through the plum trees and lands slap bang on top of the lorry, allowing us to make a smart getaway while the priests and monks are having severe hysterics and crises of faith. Not many mortals could handle something like that, but for a god it's all in a day's work.

'Any idea where we are?'

'No,' Pan replied. 'Years since I was in Rome. Last time I was here, in fact, I remember watching the Christians being thrown to the hamsters.'

'You mean lions.'

'No,' said Pan, 'hamsters. It was a Wednesday matinée. Are they following us, do you know?'

Osiris glanced back over his shoulder. 'I don't think so,' he replied, 'but let's not take any chances. Go easy a minute, let the mortals catch up.'

'Any idea what that big engine thing was?'

'I reckon it must have been a *deus ex machina*.'

'Fancy.' said Pan. 'I always wondered how those things worked. Bloody handy, the way it just turned up like that.'

'Maybe it was fate, or something.'

'I didn't think we were supposed to get any of that,' Pan said, 'being gods.'

'Maybe it wasn't for us. Maybe it was for the mortals. Anyway, who cares? Let's just accept it and be grateful, eh?'

'Sort of a *fate accompli*, you mean?'

Osiris sighed. He was tired, frustrated, disorientated and very, very full of prunes. It was probably just as well that the Lady Isis had at some stage mislaid most of his pancreas, because otherwise he would probably be feeling a bit under the weather by now.

'We lost Lundqvist, then,' he observed.

Pan shrugged. 'You can't make omelettes,' he said. 'I expect he'll be all right. After all, he is a professional assassin, and they're a load of monks and things. Supposed to turn the other cheek and all that. Knowing Kurt Lundqvist, he'll have no difficulty knowing what to do with a turned cheek.'

'You know him from somewhere, I gather.'

Pan nodded. 'A long time ago,' he said. 'I was up around

Thessaly someplace, on a job. He was there doing his thing. Not a very nice person to be around when he's working, unless you know exactly who it is he's there to see to. I was very relieved to find out it wasn't me.'

'It wasn't, then?'

Pan shook his head. 'Nah,' he replied, 'just some local fertility spirit they needed knocking off. You know, one of those matinée idol types who has to die each winter so that the crops may germinate and the corn ripen.'

'And Lundqvist was there to assassinate him?'

Pan nodded. 'At the time he specialised in that sort of thing,' he said. 'I believe he's what they call a cereal killer.'

'If I never see another prune as long as I live,' Osiris remarked, 'that'll be absolutely fine by me. Ah, here they are. Come on, you two, we may be immortal but we haven't got all day.'

Sandra and Carl came round the corner, red-faced and panting; the result, Pan presumed, of violent exertion on a full stomach.

'Are you being followed?' Osiris demanded.

'I don't,' Sandra gasped, took a deep breath, and went on, 'think so. Haven't looked for a while. Haven't heard anything.'

'Prunes getting to you?' asked Pan, sympathetically. Sandra nodded.

'No custard,' she explained.

For some reason the mention of custard made Osiris restless. 'Right then,' he said, 'time we weren't here. Lead on.'

Pan frowned. 'Where?' he asked.

'I don't know, do I?' Osiris replied. 'You're supposed to be a god, use your flaming initiative.'

He had hardly finished speaking when they all heard an ominous sound in the distance: the blowing of whistles, and the faint sussuration of many men singing the

23rd Psalm under their breath while running. 'This way,' said Pan, decisively, and he put his weight behind Osiris' wheelchair and started to push strenuously. The two mortals found themselves struggling to keep up.

As observed previously, the art of leading the way down narrow alleys on the pretext of knowing a neat little short-cut is an essential part of the craft of spreading confusion, and accordingly Pan set a brisk pace through a maze of back-streets. By the time the mortals gave up the struggle and sagged in a shop doorway, announcing that they were incapable of one more step, it was nearly light, and several tradesmen were rolling up their shutters to catch the early customers on their way to work. Into one such shop Pan led the way.

It turned out to be a typical old-fashioned small back-street barber's shop, with four well-worn chairs, a foxed mirror and a small bald man with a brown liver-spotted head and enormous eyebrows standing ready to greet them. On seeing him, Pan did an immediate double-take.

'Buon giorno, signori, signorina,' trilled the barber, indicating his chairs with a fine, practised flourish. 'Per favore, si sedrai qui. Che bella giornata oh my gawd it's you!'

Pan grinned sheepishly. 'Hiya, Miffy,' he said. 'Nice place you've got here.'

The barber drew his substantial eyebrows together like curtains. 'Gitonoutavityabastard,' he snarled. 'How you've got the bloody cheek to come waltzing in here after all you—'

'Excuse me.'

The barber turned on Osiris with an angry gesture, registered the wheelchair and moderated his tone with a visible effort. 'Look here, chum,' he said, 'you tell your mate here to sling his hook, otherwise I'm bleedin' well gonna sling it for him, okay? If he's not out of here by the time I count to . . .'

Osiris raised an eyebrow. 'You two know each other, then?'

The barber laughed savagely. Pan, who had stepped behind the wheelchair at the start of the exchange, nodded.

'We go way back,' he said. 'This is Miffy – sorry, Mithras, God of the Morning. He's a sun god.'

'Was,' said Miffy emphatically. 'Was a sun god. Packed it in fifteen hundred years ago. And keep your bloody voice down, will you?'

In the street outside, Osiris could hear the tramp of sandalled feet, the ominous clinking of censers. 'Look,' he said, 'we're gods. I'm Osiris, in fact, used to do the sun lark, just like you. Egypt and Upper Nubia. We're in a bit of a jam, and we'd really appreciate it if you'd just let us hide out the back there for a while. All right?'

Mithras narrowed his eyes and peered. 'You're Osiris?' he said.

'That's right.'

'Cor,' said the barber, with a faint chuckle, 'stone me! I had you down as this big tall geezer with a broad chest and a sort of Kirk Douglas chin.'

'That was me two thousand years ago,' Osiris replied. 'Rather let myself go a bit since then.'

'I used to know your lad once. Horace.'

'Horus.'

'That's it, Horus. Great lanky ponce with the head of a sparrowhawk or something.'

'That's him.'

The barber considered the position for a minute. 'All right, then,' he said, 'straight through there, you can hide in the stockroom. But as soon as you've got rid of who's chasing you, I'm gonna pull his lungs out!'

'Fair enough,' Osiris said. 'This way?'

* * *

Time was when the dungeons of the Vatican were the most fashionable in Europe, attracting a cosmopolitan elite; and the post of Chief Jailer was regarded as the *ne plus ultra* of the turnkey's profession. Nowadays, most of the cells have been turned into offices for the lesser officials or closed file stores, and the Chief Jailership has been amalgamated with the office of Assistant Downstairs Caretaker and Deputy Inspector of Drains.

The Vatican is, however, a proudly conservative and traditionalist institution; and therefore there is always one proper, old-fashioned, honest-to-goodness dungeon ready and waiting, just in case a really important heretic turns up out of the blue, with its own specialist jailer and genuine fitted rats. True, the Health and Safety insist that the rats be kept in a cage and fed and watered regularly by a fully certified and trained rat care operative, in accordance with the EC Statement of Practice; but it's the thought that counts.

'Definitely over-reacted, if you ask me,' Odin said, for the fifth time. 'Granted we were trespassing, and maybe we did inadvertently damage some masonry and a few trees, but even so.' He scowled with indignation. 'This would never have happened,' he added darkly, 'in Accrington.'

'Whosa woosa itty bitty ratty, then?' said Frey in the corner. 'Who's got the dearest little ratty paw-paws in the whole wide world?'

'You still haven't explained,' said Thor, 'why we can't just beat the shit out of them and push off. I mean, for crying out loud, Odin, we're *gods*.'

'Exactly.'

'What do you mean, *exactly*?' Thor snapped, standing up in the escape tunnel he'd already started digging. It was already shoulder high; they'd only been there twenty minutes and the equipment available to him was a half broken china mug and a toothbrush. 'One of these days, Odin, you're going to wake up and find the bailiffs have repossessed your brain.'

'Exactly because we're gods,' Odin replied. 'This is a Christian jurisdiction; we shouldn't be here. If we cause trouble, it could lead to a serious theological incident.'

'Not if we only pulped them a bit. Just enough so's we could escape, plus a few kicks up the jacksie for luck. I don't suppose anyone'd even notice.'

'Little rattikins want nice piece of coconut ice? Very nice, yum yum? No? Not want nice bit of—?'

'Frey, will you stop talking to that sodding rodent!'

'Oh, yeah?' Frey replied. 'And where else am I going to get an intelligent conversation in here?'

'Serious,' Odin went on, 'theological incident. Which in turn means the Pope or whatever he calls himself writing a stiff letter to the Henderson. Which means . . .'

'All right,' said Thor, 'point taken. If only I hadn't listened to you in the first place.'

'I like that, coming from you. You knew we were in Rome all along. Why the devil didn't you say anything?'

Thor made a rude noise and returned to his digging. Being a god (and to the gods all things are known) he had already worked out that his tunnel, if continued on its existing course for seven hundred and fifty yards, would bring him out slap bang in the middle of the main laundry room. They could dress up in sheets and pretend to be ghosts.

'By the way,' said Frey, in between enquiring of his new friend who exactly had the sweetest little iskery whiskery woos in the whole world ever, 'anybody got any idea who he is?' He jerked his head towards the slumped figure by the door. 'Whoever he is, looks like they gave him a right old seeing-to.'

'Dunno,' said Thor. 'He was in here when we arrived,

I think. You could wake him up if you wanted.'

'All right,' said Frey. He leant across, took a firm hold of the figure's ear, and twisted smartly.

'Ow!' said Kurt Lundqvist, waking up. 'Gug. Where . . . ?'

Frey smiled reassuringly. 'We don't actually know that ourselves,' he said, 'But we think it's the Vatican. I'm Frey, by the way, that's Thor and he's Odin.'

'Kurt Lundqvist. Hey, what am I doing here?'

'How should I know?' Frey replied. 'Actually,' he admitted, 'I should, because in theory I know everything, but there it is. We were supposed to go on refresher courses, but we never bothered.'

Lundqvist looked them over. 'You're gods, aren't you?' he said.

'Give the man a big cigar,' Frey replied. 'Of course, we're retired now. How about you?'

Lundqvist considered. As noted above he was basically a very religious man – you had to be in his line of work. Atheism to a supernatural hit-man would be as unthinkable as freeze-dried rain – but he was painfully aware that from time to time he'd been called upon to commit some fairly sacrilegious acts in the course of his duties, up to and including the destruct-testing of some deities' eternal lives; and for the life of him he couldn't remember whether this particular pantheon had crossed his path before. Best, he decided, to be a little bit discreet.

'I'm a journalist,' he therefore said. 'War correspondent with the Chicopee Falls Evening Intelligencer. Hey, what are you guys doing in here? And why don't you just—?'

'Because,' Thor said, 'that great jessie over there won't let us. Don't thump the guards, he says. Don't smash down the walls, he says. Wait for someone from the High

Commission to come and bail us out. Fat chance.'

'Thor, you know perfectly well there are proper procedures . . .'

'Bearing in mind,' Thor went on, 'that the High Commission was closed down in AD 332 on the orders of Constantine the Great. Yes, I know Nkulunkulu the Great Sky Spirit of Zululand has a chargé d'affaires still, but I gather he consists of a few small clouds and a build-up of latent static electricity, which really isn't going to be much use to us in here.'

'Oh I don't know,' Frey yawned. 'Sounds like he could cause dry rot in the joists or something, and then they'd have to move us out to a hotel. Take time, though.'

Kurt Lundqvist levered himself up on to his hands and knees and looked around. As always with him, ever since he popped out of the womb and immediately grabbed the forceps and dived for strategic cover under the incubator, his first thought was to locate a usable weapon and a defensible position to fall back on. Limited scope in the conditions prevailing, and he had to content himself with seizing Frey's left shoe and crouching in the corner of the cell.

'Let's get this straight, shall we?' he said. 'You guys are gods, right?'

Thor nodded.

'And you want to bust out, but you can't.'

'Yup.'

'Not,' Lundqvist went on, 'because you haven't the capability, but because it'd be a serious breach of protocol, right?'

'Exactly.'

Lundqvist nodded. 'So,' he said, 'if you could secure the services of, say, a highly trained soldier of fortune who could bash in the guards without any nasty theological comebacks, you could do all the rest of the escaping, like, you know, the rope ladders and waiting helicopters bit, standing on your heads.'

'I guess so,' Thor replied.

'Fine.' Lundqvist smiled and felt in his pocket. 'Allow me,' he said, 'to give you my card.'

CHAPTER ELEVEN

'I t's all right,' said Mithras, 'they've gone.'

(From the same team that brought you *How many angels can dance on the head of a pin?* we proudly present the very latest in abstruse theological conundra; namely, what do retired sun gods now running small hairdressing-businesses in the backstreets of Rome keep in their back rooms? Answers on a postcard, please.)

'You might have warned us,' Osiris protested.

'There wasn't time,' Mithras replied, defensively. 'Besides, I forgot it was there. Only came last evening. Bloke with a horse and cart came in for a haircut, and when I'd done he said he'd come out without his wallet, would I be interested in doing a bit of barter? And since I've got the allotment—'

'Yes,' Pan said, 'all right. We get the message.'

Mithras turned on Pan, snarling. 'Besides,' he snapped, 'I only did to you what you did to me all those years back, you bastard.'

'Did I?' Pan frowned in thought. 'Oh, I see,' he said, 'it's a sort of play on words. Yes, very good.'

Osiris raised a hand for silence. 'Excuse me,' he asked

Mithras. 'I'm sure it's none of my business, but what exactly did he do to you?'

'Hah!'

'It was all perfectly innocent,' Pan muttered, as he put the width of a barber's chair between Mithras and himself. 'Just bad luck, that's—'

'There I was,' Mithras said, 'at my retirement party. Super do it was, champers, horse doofers, bits of minced-up fish in pastry cases with thin slices of egg, the works. Three thousand years in the public service, and a nice comfortable retirement and a decent pension to look forward to.' He paused to give Pan a look you could have freeze-dried coffee with, and went on. 'And just when the party's going well and I've had a few jars, up comes this creep here, all innocent like, with his, Excuse me, but have you given any thought to the long-term benefits of a personal pension scheme specially tailored to your individual requirements? Gordon Bennett, did he see me coming, or what?'

'It was a perfectly legitimate investment proposal,' Pan replied, his face covered with synthetic anger, as if he'd just been eating a doughnut filled with wrath. 'You were at perfect liberty to take independent financial advice.'

'Oh yeah,' Mithras sneered. '*Trust me, I'm a god.* Went and stuck the while lot into Mount Olympus 12½ per cent unsecured loan stock, he did, just six weeks before the battle of the Milvian Bridge.'

'Final defeat of the pagans by Constantine the Great,' Osiris asided to Sandra, who hadn't been listening anyway. 'Christianity becomes the state religion and worship of the old gods forbidden.' He nodded a few times. 'I can see your point,' he said to Mithras. 'In the circumstances, I think ripping his lungs out would be perfectly reasonable behaviour.'

Pan smiled fiercely. 'All water under the bridge, now, though,' he said, 'and anyway—'

'Is it hell as like,' Mithras growled. 'I make it you owe me ninety billion gold dinars, plus interest. I'd prefer cash, if you've got it.'

'So you couldn't retire after all?'

'Been working in this dump ever since,' Mithras replied sullenly. 'Only thing that's kept me going was the thought of what I was going to do to chummy here just as soon as I got my hands on him.'

'I think that's very sad,' Sandra said.

'*You* think . . .'

Pan folded his arms. 'It was an honest mistake,' he said firmly. 'And besides, think of all the tax you've saved just by virtue of being grindingly poor.'

A spasm of doubt flitted across Mithras' face. 'Cor,' he said. 'I never looked at it like that before.'

'You see?' Pan replied, simultaneously crushing Sandra's foot beneath his own on the off chance that she might have been about to point out that gods don't pay tax anyway. 'That's the trouble with laymen, of course, they're incapable of adopting the holistic viewpoint. Strictly speaking, of course,' he added, 'I should be entitled to my ten per cent commission on everything you've saved, but as a gesture of goodwill . . .'

'Gosh. Thanks.'

'That's all right.'

'That's really kind of you.'

'Don't mention it.' Pan unfolded his arms and extended a hand to Mithras, who shook it warmly. 'And by way of a thank you, maybe you could help us with this little job we're doing.'

'There's a door,' said Carl slowly, 'in this wall.'

Everyone else in the room turned and looked at him.

'Straight up,' he added. 'Look, you can see for yourselves. Here, under the wallpaper.'

Careful examination did indeed reveal the edges of a door, together with a slight bulge for the lockplate. 'Well, bugger me,' said Mithras. 'I've been here one thousand, six hundred and eighty-three years, and would you believe I never even noticed it there.'

Pan knitted his brows. 'That suggests,' he observed, 'that it's a pretty old door. Does it lead anywhere, do you suppose?'

Mithras nodded. 'Must do,' he said. 'That's what doors are all about, stands to reason.'

'Any idea where?'

To the gods all things are . . . Yes, well, in theory. Let's instead say, To the gods all things are known, but most of them have memories like car boot sale colanders.

Osiris smiled. For some reason he had good vibes about this. Not that that was quite so significant as it seemed; among other things he'd had good vibes about the South Sea Bubble, Neville Chamberlain's 1938 peace initiative, the groundnut scheme and Polly Peck. Nevertheless, he was prepared to ride his hunch. Being a god means never having to say you're sorry.

'Only one way to find out, then,' he said.

Twenty minutes later, it looked very much like he was going to have to get off his hunch and walk. To the casual visitor, one catacomb is very much like another, and they all smell distressingly of distant sewage and bonemeal.

'Don't mind me,' Pan said smugly. 'What with my line of work and everything, the only time I really know where I am is when I'm hopelessly lost.' He looked around ostentatiously and added, 'Home sweet home.'

'Don't worry,' said Osiris, artificially calm. 'Everything always leads somewhere. We'll soon be—'

'Sure. Has it occurred to you that this tunnel might have been undisturbed for two thousand years for a very good reason?'

Suddenly Osiris jammed on the brakes of his chair, licked one finger and held it up. 'It's a draught,' he said. 'I think we're in business.'

'Are there any of those prunes left, I wonder,' said Sandra. 'I'm hungry.'

The draught, it transpired, came from a low, unfinished-looking tunnel running off to their right. There was something about it which didn't inspire confidence.

'Right,' said Mithras, 'that'll do me. You're on your own from now on. I've got a shop to run.'

Osiris glowered at him. 'You mean you're scared. Admit it.'

Mithras shrugged. 'All right, I'm scared. It's spooky.'

'*Spooky?* You're a god, dammit.'

'Retired. And anyway, I'm well off my own turf here. Sun gods aren't meant to fool around in dark tunnels hundreds of feet underground. Well known fact, that.'

Osiris shrugged. 'Please yourself,' he said. 'Right, on we—'

'Hold on a moment, will you?' Pan interrupted. 'You're not seriously suggesting we go down there, are you?'

'Yes.'

'Why?'

Osiris considered; and while he did so, Pan reminded him that their objectives were (a) short term, to escape from the two doctors and all those lunatic monks, and (b) long term, somehow to get their hands on enough loot to pay their incredibly, monumentally expensive lawyer. Neither purpose, he ventured to suggest, would be materially advanced by going down a dark, dodgy and probably entirely futile hole in the ground.

'Okay,' said Osiris. 'Because it's there. How does that grab you?'

'Not much.'

'Ah.' Osiris smiled. 'That's because you lack insight, initiative and the holistic viewpoint. Last one down the tunnel's a cissy.'

He grabbed the wheels of his chair, shoved off and vanished into the darkness. Sandra and Carl immediately followed, Sandra expressing the view that she doubted there was anything to eat down there but she supposed it was worth a try. For want of other company, Pan turned to his sworn enemy and smiled pleasantly.

'Well,' he said, 'it takes all sorts, doesn't it. Now, what's the quickest way back up to the—?'

'About my money,' said Mithras. 'Oh, and by the way, the interest is of course compound, at let's say a flat rate of fifteen per cent, so that makes, let's see, ten to the power of nine hundred and four times sixteen point three seven eight, divide by three hundred and sixty-five and multiply—'

'Ciao,' said Pan quickly, and darted up the tunnel.

What with falling over his feet and not having a torch, not to mention ominous scuttling sounds and the smell of bonemeal, Pan found it slow and hard going. It was pitch dark and he couldn't see a thing; but, bearing in mind the scuttling sounds, that wasn't necessarily a bad thing. Don't panic, he said to himself. Well, no, I wouldn't would I? On the other hand, I could be rationally and reasonably terrified, no trouble at all. Let's give that a try and see what happens.

HALT.

Pan halted. He had no idea where the voice had come from, if in fact it had been a voice at all.

STAY EXACTLY WHERE YOU ARE.

Pan did as he was told, and as the seconds turned into minutes, the white heat of his terror began to cool ever so slightly. There was something about the voice that reminded him very faintly of something else.

DO NOT MOVE OR IT WILL BE THE WORSE FOR YOU.

'Okay. Point taken. What next?'

YOU ARE IN MY WHIRR CLUNK POWER. SURRENDER OR DIE.

'I'll take surrender, please, chief. So what's next on the agenda?'

A full minute passed; a very long time, in context, and an even longer time down a dark, scuttling tunnel. Pan began to clap his hands together slowly.

DO NOT MOVE OR IT WILL BE THE—

Pan clicked his tongue. 'I think we've covered that bit already, thanks. Can we please get on with it?'

SORRY. I SHOULD WHEEENG PINK I SHOULD HAVE SAID ABANDON HOPE ALL YE WHO ENTER HERE.

Slowly, a grin spread across Pan's face. 'You're a recording, aren't you?'

DO NOT MOVE OR IT WILL—

'Who said anything about moving? Look, can't we just fast-forward a bit and get on to the main feature?'

YOU ARE IN MY—

'—Power, surrender or die. Yes, fine.' He tapped his fingers noisily against the wall. 'I know you've got your stuff to do and all that, but it's really not a bundle of fun standing around in a dank tunnel, probably with nightmarish insects and giant rats and snakes and things loafing around the place, so if we could just—'

RATS?

'Bound to be. There's always rats in these claustrophobia sequences. So if we could—'

I *HATE* RATS.

Pan blinked twice. 'Is that so?'

YES.

'Funny,' Pan said. 'I thought you were just a recording.'

Pause.

DO NOT MOVE OR IT WILL BE THE WORSE—

'Oh no you don't. Come on, tell me what all this is in aid of, and then we can all go home.'

DO NOT MOVE OR—

'Squeak.'

Silence. A long, eerie silence, broken only by a faint scuffling sound. This was in fact caused by Pan running his fingernails across the rough-hewn surface of the tunnel wall, but it did sound uncommonly like the scampering of rodent paws.

CUT THAT OUT, WILL YOU?

'Cut what out? Squeak, squeak.'

THAT SCAMPERING NOISE. AND THE SQUEAKING.

'What squeaking?'

ALL RIGHT, ALL RIGHT, YOU WIN. I AM AEACUS, GUARDIAN OF THE PORTALS OF DEATH AND WINDER-BACK OF THE TAPE OF OBLIVION. YOU AND YOUR FRIENDS HAVE TRESPASSED INTO THE KINGDOM OF DEATH, FROM WHOSE BOURN NO TRAVELLER RETURNS, AND—

'Bourn?'

BOURN. SORT OF MILESTONE. FROM WHOSE BOURN NO TRAV—

'From whose milestone no traveller returns?'

Pause. DON'T ASK ME WHAT IT MEANS, I DIDN'T WRITE IT. AND . . . OH NUTS, I'VE LOST THE PLACE NOW, I'LL HAVE TO GO BACK TO DO NOT MOVE OR IT WILL BE THE—

'Gorblimey,' said Pan, 'that was a big 'un. Great big brown hairy brute, tried to climb right up my trouser leg. Go on, shoo!'

EEEEEK!

Pan made some more scuffling noises and then called out, 'It's all right, I've got him. Here you are, have a nice piece of cheese. Sorry, you were saying?'

AND HERE YOU MUST STAY FOREVER UNTIL THE SEAS RUN DRY AND THE SKY CRACKS ARE YOU *SURE* YOU'VE GOT THAT THING UNDER CONTROL?

'Absolutely,' Pan replied. 'No question – whoops, oh no you don't, here boy, nice cheese.'

LOOK, FOR CRYING OUT LOUD—

In the darkness, Pan grinned and made a few extra-spine-shivering squeaking noises. 'Gotcha,' he said eventually. 'Now then. Here I must stay forever, is that right? Oh well, if that's the case I might as well let this rat go . . .'

It should be explained that the voice was not so much a voice as a reverberation at the back of the head, a mote on the mind's eye, tinnitus of the inner ear, a septic memory. Hitherto, at any rate. Now it was beginning to sound – well, panicky.

HERE YOU MUST S-S-S-STAY FOREVER, it said quickly, *UNLESS* YOU HAPPEN TO GO THROUGH THE HIDDEN DOOR IMMEDIATELY TO YOUR RIGHT, TAKING YOUR SODDING RAT WITH YOU, IN WHICH CASE YOU'LL FIND YOURSELF IN THE ATTENDANT'S ROOM OF THE PUBLIC LAVATORY AT ROME AIRPORT. IT WAS NICE MEETING YOU, GOODBYE.

'Hang on,' said Pan, dragging his fingernails across a jagged piece of scree. 'I may be many things but I'm not the sort to walk out on my friends. If they've got to stay here for ever, I guess I have to as well. No, ratty, stop that, come *back*! Who's a naughty little tinker, then?'

ALL *RIGHT*; JUST A MINUTE, I'LL BE STRAIGHT BACK, DON'T MOVE.

'Or it'll be the worse for me?'

SOMETHING LIKE THAT.

'Fortuitous,' Osiris said.

'Yeah, well.' Pan shrugged his wide, thin shoulders – a poor choice of gesture, since Carl was standing on them, trying to reach up into the cistern. 'Fortuitous is what being a god's all about, innit? I mean,' he added, remembering something he'd heard somewhere, 'the way I look at it, we hold the Fates bound fast in iron chains, sort of thing, and with our hands turn Fortune's wheel about. As it were.'

'Do we?'

'I think so. It sort of goes with the territory.'

Osiris shook his head. 'Funny ideas you Mediterranean types have,' he said. 'Where I come from, godding is basically just making sure the crops grow and remembering to switch out the lights before going to bed. Has he found it yet?'

'No,' Carl replied. 'You sure it's here?'

'Must be somewhere,' Osiris replied. 'Everything always is.'

'Oh.'

'You were there when those three old boilers gave us the directions,' Osiris went on, 'you know as well as I do. The Runes of Power are somewhere in the gentleman's convenience immediately adjacent to the Kingdom of Death, which is where we've just been. I still think that was one hell of a coincidence, by the way.'

'The Kingdom of Death has many doors.'

'What say?'

'The Kingdom of Death,' repeated Pan firmly, 'has many doors. Well known fact. And this is a gent's bog immediately adjacent. And,' he went on, 'according to Herschel's Law of Inverse Commodity, the bigger the public building, the fewer the number of khazis. The Kingdom of Death is probably the largest public building there is; ergo, a maximum of one bog, just enough to comply with the planning regulations.'

'Cor,' Osiris said. 'Herschel's Law and everything. Where did you learn all that stuff?'

'I've been around, you know.'

'So it would seem. All right, we'd better try the next one.'

'Excuse me,' said Sandra.

Pan winced and swore. 'Mind where you're putting your feet, you idiot,' he said. 'That was my ear.'

'Sorry.'

'Excuse me,' Sandra reiterated, 'but would these be them here?'

They turned and looked. Sandra was pointing to a small framed notice on the wall just above the electric hot-air hand dryer.

'Oh.'

'Only they do say,' Sandra went on, '*Directions for finding the Golden Teeth of El Dorado*, and I gathered that was what we wanted.'

Osiris frowned. 'They're supposed to be Runes of Power,' he muttered. 'This whole carry-on is getting way above my head.'

'They probably are Runes of Power by local standards,' Pan interrupted. 'Shall we just have a look and see what they say?'

Sandra, meanwhile, had produced a small notebook with flowers and bunnies and things on the cover and written the directions down. The two gods looked at each other and shrugged.

'That's what it says,' Pan ventured after a while.

'Well.' Osiris rubbed his chin, making a noise like clapped-out sandpaper. 'We might as well give it a go, then.'

Perversely, the traction engine started first time.

'Hey,' Thor enquired, dumbfounded, 'how the devil did you do that?'

Lundqvist shrugged. 'I just pulled this handle thing here,' he said. 'Look, let's get the hell out of here, all right?'

'Switch it off and do it again. You can't have done it right.'

'Oh, for crying out loud,' Frey muttered. A Cistercian SWAT team had just discovered the stunned sentry. 'Give it some welly and let's go, quickly. Any more of this nonsense and I shan't be responsible.'

The Vatican authorities plainly hadn't had the faintest idea what one is supposed to do with a captured supernatural traction engine deposited out of the blue in one's back courtyard. Anyone with an ounce of sense would have disconnected the main rotor arm from the forcing toggle and withdrawn the split pin from the auxiliary drive sprocket, thereby immobilising the entire subordinate transmission; but the helpless unworldly monks hadn't even unclipped the Hodgson cable or overridden the HST. In all likelihood, Thor speculated, as the engine roared into life and lifted off vertically into the air, if a lightbulb goes they pray at it till it comes back on again. Idiots.

'Where to now?' Thor shouted over the roar of the flywheel.

'Home,' Odin replied, 'sharpish. There's still an outside chance She won't have noticed we're not there.'

'Pretty thin chance.'

'Never mind. Set a course north-north-west.'

'Right you are.' Frey was at the controls; a classic example of the wrong man in the wrong place at the wrong time. 'Which one's that?'

'The lever on your left,' Odin replied, 'just above your cufflink.'

'What, this one?'

'No, that's the cigar lighter.'

Lundqvist leant back against the smoke-stack, speculating as to who the hell these imbeciles were, and how soon he'd be able to get away from them. So far, he was painfully aware, his role in the quest to frustrate the diabolical schemes of Julian and the godchildren was very similar to that of sugar in petrol. What he needed in order to get his act together was a few hours to gather his thoughts and regroup, at least three self-loading firearms and a nice strong cup of coffee; none of which were likely to come his way as long as he was stuck on this amazing contraption with these three geriatric lunatics.

'Guys,' he said, 'where is it exactly you're headed?'

'Droitwich.'

'Where?'

'Well, just outside Droitwich, to be precise,' Thor replied. 'About three miles west and two miles straight up. The postal address is Sunnyvoyde.'

Lundqvist hazarded a guess. 'The retired gods' home, right?'

'Yeah.'

This, Lundqvist felt, just wasn't good enough. Wherever Osiris was headed, it most certainly wasn't the place he'd escaped from. Instinctively, though knowing in his heart it was in vain, he frisked himself for some sort of weapon. Anything, anything at all – even a Walther Model 9 in 6.35mm loaded, if need be, with 50 grain jacketed hardball – would be better than nothing. Still. Needs must.

'Okay,' he snapped, standing up and (as the engine passed through a patch of slight turbulence) sitting down again, 'this is a hijack. Turn this thing round and fly it to Tripoli.'

'Why?'

Lundqvist shoved his hand in his pocket. 'I have a gun,' he said.

'Is this ponce serious, do you think?'

'Where's Tripoli?'

'I think it's somewhere in Tuscany, isn't it?'

'Why should having a gun make him want to go to Tuscany?'

'I thought it was in Egypt.'

'It's not a very Egyptian sounding name, Tripoli. All the places there are called Tell something.'

'Telford?'

'I think you're thinking of Tivoli, not Tripoli. Though I'm not sure Tivoli's in Tuscany, come to that.'

'We can drop him off at Telford, no trouble at all. We'll be virtually passing the door.'

'All right.' Lundqvist was back on his feet again, and maintained himself thus with a sort of bow-legged crouch. 'Okay, so I haven't got a gun. First time in over four hundred years,' he added miserably. 'But what I have got . . .' He cast his eye around the immediate vicinity, and grabbed awkwardly. 'What I have got is this spanner . . .'

'Actually, that's a four by nine Stilson,' Odin commented. 'You use it for shimming up the interfacing on the cam nuts.'

'. . . This four by nine Stilson, and unless you all do

exactly what I say, you're all dead. You got that?'

There was a pause.

'Yes,' said Frey at last, 'but where exactly is it you want to go?'

'I've found Tivoli,' Odin said, looking up from the atlas. 'It's in completely the wrong direction, of course.'

'You've got the map the wrong way up, you daft old –'

'Doesn't matter, it's still completely the wrong –'

'We could go there anyway,' Frey suggested, 'and then he could maybe get a bus.'

Odin and Thor froze in mid-bicker and stared at their junior colleague. 'Don't talk soft,' Thor said, 'Tivoli's where he wants to go, what would he want to get a bus for?'

Frey shrugged. 'I've always wanted to go on a bus,' he said, 'ever since I can remember. One of those open-topped ones with the windy staircase at the back.'

'All *right*,' Lundqvist shouted. 'Forget it, will you? Forget I ever said Tripoli. Just drop me off anywhere, and that'll be fine.'

'Just drop you anywhere?'

'That'd be just fine.'

Thor shrugged. 'No problem,' he said; and did so. There was a scream, which rapidly dopplered and died away as the speck diminished away out of sight below them.

'I think,' Frey ventured, 'we're passing over the sea.'

'That's lucky,' Thor replied. 'Hope he can swim.'

Julian sat at his desk and toyed with a paperclip. It was a quarter to three in the morning, he had a headache and he hadn't made any money for well over ten minutes. He scowled.

Somehow, he couldn't concentrate. This was a nuisance; absolute, laser-like concentration, together with a total disregard for basic human dignity, is the key to success in the legal profession, and he'd always prided himself on his ability to blot out from his mind everything except the job in hand, the blood currently in the water.

Why hadn't he heard anything from those two buffoons yet?

Dammit, he'd practically done the whole job for them – fixed things up with the Cardinal, arranged for enquiry agents to trace the old bastard to Belgium, hired the heavies, planned the second hijack, everything short of actually going there himself and doing the business with the holy water. Try as he might, he couldn't for the life of him imagine how anything could possibly go wrong. A one-legged panda could have done the job standing on its head.

Yes. Well. Maybe he should have hired a one-legged panda. As it was, he was going to have to make do with what he'd got. He picked his nose thoughtfully for a while, turning over various options in his mind.

So much, he said to himself, for brute force and violence. Too clumsy, he'd always said, too gauche. There must be another way, one more in tune with the professional man's ethos. He chewed a pencil, his mind moving in many planes simultaneously.

Ah.

There is a saying, attributed to ex-President Richard Nixon and much quoted by lawyers, to the effect that once you have them by the balls, their hearts and minds will follow.

Find the weak point, the mental scab, the little encrustation of half-healed guilt, and there insert your questing fingernail. Prod and pick around the compassion of the gods, their love for their creation, their eternal subconscious self-reproach as they consider everything that they have made: *You got them into this mess, it's up to you . . .*

Yes, thought Julian, that ought to do the trick.

He lifted the telephone.

CHAPTER TWELVE

Squelch, squelch, squelch. Pause. Squelch.

This is the sound of Kurt Lundqvist moving semi-noiselessly, like a black shadow on the very edge of sight, up the beach and into the cover of the trees.

Semi-noiselessly, because even if, like Kurt, you spent forty years as Kawaguchiya Integrated Circuits Professor of Stealth at the Central Ninja Academy after several lifetimes of practical experience at the cutting edge of the silent killing profession, it's pretty well impossible to move in absolute silence when your boots are full of water and your socks feel like overweight jellyfish under your toes.

Having gained the relative safety of the trees, he sat down, yanked off his left boot and emptied it. Out came a pint and a half of sea, some green slime and a small golden fish.

For some reason which he could never quite account for, Lundqvist whipped off the other boot, taking care not to spill its contents, scooped up the fish just as it was on the point of coughing its gills up, and dropped it into the boot. With a flick of its shimmering tail it sought safety in the toe. Lundqvist sighed; then, in his stocking feet and with a complete absence of stealth, he plodded back across the oily black mud of the beach to the water's edge and flung the contents of the boot out as far as he could. There was a tiny *plop!* as the fish hit the water. God, said Lundqvist to himself, this is it, I've finally flipped my lid. If the guys down at Kali's Diner ever found out I'd saved a fish from drowning in air, I'd never live it down.

There was a deafening peal of thunder, followed by lightning, fireworks and piped music. Lundqvist found himself face down in the mud. A small crab scuttled up his trouser leg.

'G'Day. I am the Dragon King of the South-East. The fish you saved was my only son. I am forever in your debt. Name your utmost wish, and it is as good as done, no worries.'

Lundqvist looked up. Hovering over the wavetops was a dragon, of the sort familiar from countless thousands of porcelain jars, cups, soup-bowls, painted silk screens, soap-stone carvings and netsuke. Its head, bewhiskered and leonine, was supported by long, sinuous curves of scaly neck and body, which in turn rested on four taloned claws, which gripped the edges of a huge jade surfboard. Around its bejewelled waist, the marvellous beast wore a pair of long fluorescent bathing trunks, and in one talon it gripped a can of beer.

Yes, thought Lundqvist, Dragon King of the South-East. Dragon Kings come from China, and south-east from China is exactly where I'm thinking of.

'Hi,' he said. 'Look, are we talking three wishes here?'

The Dragon King nodded his enormous head. *'Fair dinkum,'* he said, and his voice was like the crashing of surf on a reef of jade. *'If it hadn't been for you playing the white man back there, the little fella'd be history by now, so I reckon I owe you one. Or rather three,'* he added. *'Fair go, after all. Have a beer?'*

Lundqvist nodded, and a foaming can of lager appeared between his fingers. Dragon King of the South-East, he muttered to himself, just my goddam luck. Of all the cardinal points of all the compasses in the world, why do I have to stray into his?

'Okay,' he said, 'Let's start with some warm clothes and dry footwear.'

The air sparkled; and when Lundqvist looked down he saw that he was now wearing the same pattern of big eye-hurting beach shorts as the dragon, together with an oversize sweat-shirt in the same unfortunate colour scheme, an oversize baseball cap, plastic slip-on sandals and white socks. Something told him that it would be a good idea to get the other two wishes over and done with as quickly as possible.

'*Suits you, mate*,' said the Dragon King, thereby placing himself in the running for the Kurt Lundqvist Pillock of the Year Award. '*Now then, what else can I do for you? Fire away.*'

Lundqvist sighed and rubbed his eyes. What he really wanted right now was six hours sleep, a .40 Glock and a mammoth pastrami sandwich, in that order. From long experience, however, he knew better than most that what gift horses generally have in their mouths is big, sharp fangs.

'I'm looking for some guys,' he said. 'Maybe you can tell me where they are.'

'*Shoot through on you, did they, the bludgers?*' replied the Dragon King sympathetically, rubbing a splash of zinc cream on to the scales of its chest. '*Tell me who these blokes are, and they're found.*'

Lundqvist told him.

'*You're serious?*'

'Yes.'

'*Fair crack of the whip?*'

'Whatever that's supposed to mean, yes.'

'Right-oh.' The Dragon King closed his eyes, and suddenly his whole body became almost translucent, like some weird mirage. 'Central America,' he said. 'Mexico. Sort of Mexico. One of those little bitty countries just down and across a bit from Mexico. San something or other. Big mountains. Make any sense to you?'

Lundqvist nodded. That left wish number three, and it was patently obvious what it was going to have to be. He braced himself.

'Now then,' he said. 'Tell me what they're doing there and why.'

The Aztecs (explained the Dragon King) are famous for three things: gold, the incredible savagery of their gods, and chocolate. All three are inextricably linked.

Quite obviously, chocolate was reserved as the special food of the gods. Therefore, the gods ate nothing but chocolate; all day, every day. Toothbrushes, it should be noted, were unknown in pre-Columbian Central America, and fluoride was not a concept with which they were familiar.

The result: toothache. Toothache of the kind only gods can suffer. Not just the paltry, everyday, diamond-tipped pile-drivers and psychotic gnomes in the upper jaw variety that mortal men have to put up with, but the real thing. Hence the bad temper.

And after the toothache had run its hideous course, gods with no teeth. Which in turn meant no solid food. All that the Aztec pantheon could manage to get down were liquids and a little extremely soft meat that could be mumbled into digestibility between agonisingly sensitive gums. And chocolate too, of course, taken in liquid form.

Hence the notorious human sacrifices of the Aztecs, at

the culmination of which the blood and hearts of the victims were laid on the altars as a banquet for the gods. The way the gods saw things, suffering isn't something you hoard, it's something you share.

Except for one god, the Highest, the Most Supreme; Azctlanhuilptlil, God of War and Dental Hygiene, aloof and apart in his unutterable splendour (or, as his colleagues muttered to themselves, bloody selfish). When all the other Aztec deities finally gave up the unequal struggle and retired to Sunnyvoyde and meagre helpings of chicken soup, Azctlanhuilptlil remained behind, able to keep going by virtue of his unique, jealously guarded, most valued possession: a gigantic set of false teeth, wrought (for this is Mexico, land of inexhaustible mineral wealth) of the finest, purest gold.

Finally, when Cortes and his conquistadores burst into Mexico, smashed the centuries-old civilisation of the Aztecs and suppressed the worship of the old gods, Azctlanhuilptlil in turn was overthrown and reduced by a unanimous vote of his extremely resentful erstwhile devotees to mortal status. His eventual fate is shrouded in obscurity, although legend has it that he ended his days, dentureless and utterly miserable, as a quality control officer at Hershey's.

As to what became of his teeth, nobody knew; but a garbled recollection of their memory circulated among the Spaniards, leading many brave fools to their deaths in the fruitless quest for the Man of Gold. The truth of the matter (so the Dragon King asserted) is that the teeth are still there, soaking the centuries away in the bowl of an extinct volcano, guarded by a dragon or something such and preserved imperishably in sixty billion gallons of Steradent.

'Thanks,' said Lundqvist, getting up and brushing mud off his legs. 'I'll be going, then.'

The Dragon King stirred. *'What about the third wish, mate?'*

'That's all right,' Lundqvist replied, 'keep the change.'

Half past twelve. Lunchtime at Sunnyvoyde.

It was a favourite adage of Mrs Henderson that one of the greatest problems with gods is that they have no sense of time. For them, day merges seamlessly with day, year with year, century with century. The result: vagueness, leading to dementia, leading to wet beds and residents tottering about the corridors on zimmers at three in the morning demanding to see a doctor. Accordingly, there was a routine at Sunnyvoyde, and nothing interfered with it. Breakfast at seven sharp; lunch at twelve thirty, on the dot; afternoon tea at four exactly; evening meal at six thirty, come rain or shine; and finally, the Twilight of the Gods at nine fifteen, lights out and not a peep do I expect to hear out of you lot until breakfast.

By and large the system worked. It instilled a sense of order into many a hitherto purposeless and unstructured divine existence. It is, to put it mildly, embarrassing for a supreme being to find himself waking up in the middle of the night asking himself questions like 'Why am I here?' and 'Is there a reason behind it all?' In Sunnyvoyde, the gods knew that they existed for the sole purpose of being present at the ordained mealtimes. Maybe it cut down on the free will side of things; but you can't be a god for very long without realising that free will and the proverbial free lunch have a great deal in common.

'Kedgeree,' grunted Nkulunkulu, Great Sky Spirit of the Zulus. 'Why does it always have to be flaming kedgeree for Friday dinner?'

'Such a bore,' agreed Ilmater, the Finnish Queen of the Air, adding that the custom of always having fish on Fridays must be somebody's idea of a sick joke, in context.

Nkulunkulu nodded, and asked her to pass the salt.

'No salt at table any more, I'm afraid,' Ilmater replied. 'It's bad for us, apparently. Too much potassium or some such, or at least that's what She said. Really, it's enough to drive one frantic, don't you think?'

'No salt?' Yama, the blue-faced Hindu god of Death, scowled horribly. 'We'll bloody well see about that. Here, you. Get the manageress. I demand to see the manageress.'

The nursing auxiliary thus addressed looked through Yama as if he wasn't there and swept past, wheeling her trolley laden with covered aluminium dishes. In theory she was perfectly within her rights in doing so; Sunny-voyde houses no less than forty-six different Kings of Death, which is far in excess of the number permitted under the Health and Safety Regulations. In order to get round this, Mrs Henderson had long ago organised a rota, whereby each one of them had a number of days on as duty King of Death; on their off days, the various Kings were deemed not to exist (but they still had to be punctual for meals).

'Haven't seen Osiris in a long time,' Nkulunkulu remarked, surreptitiously calling a small pillar of salt into being under cover of his table napkin. 'Wonder if the poor old sod has finally pegged out.'

'Pegged out what?'

'You know, pegged out. Handed in his dinner pail. Shuffled off this mortal coil. You know,' he added with rising frustration, 'kicked the bucket.'

Ilmater looked up from her plate. She had been forking through, picking out the pieces of boiled egg and depositing them carefully on her sideplate. 'Sounds like he's been terribly busy doing all those strenuous things,' she said. 'No wonder we haven't seen him for a while.'

'Died, you dozy old bat. I wonder whether Osiris has finally died.'

Yama shook his head. 'I doubt that very much,' he said, ''cos I'd have been notified if he had. We get a circular every evening,' he explained, 'to avoid duplication and conflict of interests.'

There was a flash, as Nkulunkulu's pillar of salt turned itself into a miniature model of Lot's wife, holding in her hands an LCD display reading *I told you, no salt*. 'I don't know,' he said. 'You work your fingers to the bone creating the world, making it nice for them, stocking it up with edible plants and gullible animals, and what do you get at the end of it all? Stone cold kedgeree and no bloody salt to go on it. It's enough to turn you Methodist.'

'Maybe he's on holiday.'

'Who?'

'Osiris.'

'Excuse me, young man, but are you a doctor?'

'Last time I saw him,' said Yama, 'he was talking to that nurse, you know, the chubby one. Haven't seen her in a while either, come to think of it.'

'Pity,' Nkulunkulu replied. 'Had a bit of meat on her, that one did. Not like so many of these nurses you seem to get nowadays.'

'I don't think you're actually supposed to eat them, Nk.'

'I was speaking figuratively.'

'Oh.' Yama shrugged. 'Maybe Osiris got fed up with kedgeree and booked out,' he went on. 'I wouldn't be all that surprised, knowing him. Always did have balls – not in the right place, I'll grant you, but . . .'

Ilmater shook her head. 'I don't think so,' she said. 'I rather believe booking out is against the Rules, otherwise we'd all have done it by . . . Nk, who is this strange old woman and why is she showing me her knee?'

'That's Minerva,' the sky god replied. 'Ignore her and she'll go away. Tell you what, though, I'd like to see precisely where in the Rules it says you can't book out. Worth looking into, that.'

'Maybe he and the nurse eloped,' Yama mused. 'Difficult, of course, with the wheelchair and everything, but to the gods all things are – I don't believe it, rhubarb *again*. Take it away, woman, take it away, I don't want any.'

'Custard?' asked the waitress.

'No.'

The waitress looked over his head at Ilmater. 'Would you ask him if he wants custard?' she asked. 'Only I haven't got all day.'

Ilmater smiled, what she hoped was her patronising reassuring-the-servants smile. 'I don't believe he does, thank you,' she said. 'Sorry, Nk, you were saying?'

'About getting out of here,' Nkulunkulu replied. 'There probably is a way, you know, if only we could find out what it is. I'd be game, for one.'

'Just look, will you, that stupid woman's just poured custard all over my pudding. I really must insist on seeing the manageress.'

After lunch, say the Rules, residents will enjoy the peace and quiet of the common room. Nobody knows what the penalties for not enjoying the peace and quiet of the common room are, but only because nobody has ever had enough foolhardy courage to find out. As Nkulunkulu sat and stared at the television set, however, his mind remained unwontedly clear. Something was buzzing around in it like a fly in a bottle, and he wasn't quite sure what it was. Then he noticed the empty chairs.

Three of them, over by the repulsive picture of a small child with a kitten. Frantic ransacking of his memory turned up three names: Odin, Thor, Frey.

Stone me, muttered Nkulunkulu to himself, four of them AWOL. Four of them not enjoying the peace and quiet.

How many does it take, he wondered, to make up a Precedent?

'It was somewhere around here, I seem to remember,' said Osiris, looking up from the map, 'that they had the final shoot-out.'

Pan, who was trying to stand on one hoof while extracting a stone from his shoe, quivered. 'Who did?' he asked nervously.

'Butch Cassidy,' replied Osiris, 'and the Sundance Kid.'

Gravity is an evil bastard, Pan reflected as he wobbled, staggered and put his bare hoof down hard on a jagged flint. 'that was Bolivia,' he muttered.

'Oh.' Osiris shrugged. 'That's just down the road that way, I think. We might stop and have a look on the way back, if we have time.'

Pan silently vowed that they wouldn't have time, not unless he could have a nice comfy wheelchair too. 'We'll see,' he said. 'This volcano,' he went on. 'Shouldn't we be able to see it from here?'

'Look for yourself.'

Pan took the map. 'Oh hell,' he said, 'it's one of these awful modern ones, I can't read them. If it hasn't got dragons and Jerusalem in the middle I can't make head nor tail of it.' He screwed up his eyes. Not that he needed glasses – to the gods, all things are visible – but another reason why modern maps were so useless was the minuscule nature of the print. 'I'm sure you know what you're doing,' he said, and handed it back.

Nevertheless, he continued to have reservations – not a particularly unusual state of affairs; on any given subject, Pan generally had more reservations than the entire Sioux and Blackfoot nations combined – and the complete lack of distant prospects of volcanoes did little to resolve them.

Nuts, he said to himself, we're lost. Again. And it's not even my fault.

'Where exactly,' he was therefore moved to ask next time they stopped, 'did you get that map from?'

'The airport,' Osiris replied. 'And you know, I have to say I don't think very much of it. That range of mountains over there, for example. Not a sign of it in here. Must be new, I suppose,' he hazarded, narrowing his eyes. 'Still, it's a poor show selling out-of-date maps, if you ask me.'

Pan nodded. 'New mountains, I see.' He took the map, looked at the cover and handed it back. 'That,' he said, 'is a street plan of Mexico City. According to which,' he added, 'that lot over there is the headquarters of the municipal fire service. How'd it be if we went back the way we came and tried to hire a taxi?'

As he spoke, the earth shook. Gods ought to be used to such things, but Pan never quite managed it; he still felt terribly guilty when, in spring, at the time of the quickening of the soil and the reawakening of the life force, he walked across somebody's nice new carpet without thinking and left behind him a trail of newly flowering primroses.

'Look,' Osiris said, and pointed.

Three of the distant mountains appeared to be on fire. Sheets of red flame were rising hundreds of feet into the air, which was now full of soft grey ash and little hot cinders, some of which settled on the back of Pan's neck.

'Headquarters of the municipal fire service,' Osiris repeated. 'Yes, you could say that. Lads, I think we're in business.'

It was, apparently, a good day for pyrotechnic displays of all kinds; because they hadn't gone more than a few hundred yards towards the mountains when the sky was lit up by a dazzling flash, and some huge fiery object

482 • Tom Holt

streaked across it, travelling at some bizarrely high speed, and vanished over the horizon, followed for a relatively long time after by a deafening sonic boom.

'I told you,' Thor screamed, as the controls writhed in Odin's hands. 'Those head coil gaskets, I said, they're only sealed in with beeswax, go up too close to the sun and they'll melt. And what does the stupid prawn go and do?'

'Calm down,' Odin bellowed, as the slipstream ripped off his white silk scarf and sent it fluttering away into the air. 'Panicking won't solve anything. Now, when I say the word, I want you both to lean as far as you can over to your left. Right?'

The engine wobbled, jinked and turned a complete revolution around its central axis, but with no noticeable effect on its speed or trajectory. Frey, however, lost his left glove, ripped from his hand by the wind.

'I think we'll have to try an emergency landing,' Odin shouted. 'I'm just going to look around for a suitable spot.'

'Great.' Thor tried to wriggle down further into his seat. 'We're in enough trouble as it is without you crashing this poxy thing *deliberately*. Why not just sit back and let nature take its course?'

'I . . .'

'*Oh my god!*'

A fraction of a second ago, the mountains hadn't been there; then, all of a sudden, there they were. Later, Thor swore blind that they missed the peak of the tallest and sharpest of them by no more than twelve thousandths of an inch.

'That was interesting, what you just said,' roared Frey, with his eyes shut.

'Was it?'

'You said *Oh my god*. Didn't know you were religious, Thor.'

'Just an expression.'

'Ah.' Frey's knuckles whitened on the grab handle. 'Pity. We could do with some divine assistance right now.'

Odin was still wrestling with the joystick. 'What irresponsible fool put those mountains there?' he growled. 'Some people just don't think, that's their trouble.'

He jerked the joystick again, snapping it off. He stared at it for a moment and then put it carefully away under the seat. Probably get it back together again with a spot of weld, he reflected.

Thor leant out over the side. Up to a point his former view – the back of Odin's neck – had suited him fine, since it blocked out a lot of rather disturbing things, like the ground rushing up to meet them. On the other hand, he was so sick of the sight of his colleague that right now, anything would be preferable.

'Oh shit,' he groaned. 'More mountains.'

'Volcanoes,' Odin corrected. 'Active ones, by the looks of things. That's odd, you know.'

'Odd!'

Odin nodded. 'I think we may have wandered off course a bit,' he shouted. 'I don't recall there being any active volcanoes in Staffordshire.'

All this while, of course, they had been gaining rather than dissipating speed. It should therefore have been some comfort to them to reflect that even if the joystick hadn't snapped and even if the rudder had been working, there still wouldn't have been time to avoid the huge crater they now flew into . . .

But not out of.

'*Si, senor*.' The old peasant nodded and pointed. With a wave, the driver of the leading armoured personnel carrier waved and let in his clutch. The column moved off.

'*Medicos Yanquis*,' the peasant explained to his wife as they glumly contemplated next season's cabbage crop, over which the column had driven.

The peasant's wife scratched her brown nose, and smiled. On the other hand, she said, there was the compensation.

Compensation?

Compensation, she confirmed. When the Yankee drug police burnt down old Miguel's tomato plot last year thinking it was drugs, they paid him twice its value. And when they napalmed Salvador's beans and shot up his turnips with the helicopter gunships, he ended up with a profit of something like three hundred per cent. This year he was seriously considering hanging paper cut-out flowers on his onion sets to make them look like opium poppies, just in case they came back this way.

The peasant shook his head. Not drug people, he explained. Doctors.

Gringo doctors, his wife corrected him.

True . . .

CHAPTER THIRTEEN

The Guardian of the Golden Teeth stirred in his sleep. It had been a long time since anybody had come – even mortals learn eventually, and twenty acres scattered with wind-bleached bones help to concentrate the mind. In actual fact, the bones were a job lot from a bankrupt ossuary, but the Guardian liked them. He felt they added tone.

Under him, the ground trembled, troubling his sleep with dreams of water-beds and passing trains. His subconscious mind reassured him that it was just the volcano playing up, and the dreams returned to their previous even tenor: a green baize cloth, coloured balls, a man in a waistcoat leaning pensively on a wooden shaft. The Guardian hadn't the faintest idea what the dream was supposed to be about, but so what. After the first ten years it was strangely hypnotic.

The fact of the matter was that, many years ago, a group of cunning and unscrupulous Australian television magnates, unwilling to meet the cost of launching a satellite, had found a way of using the Guardian's slumbering brain as a relay station, with the result that his primordial sleep was populated with soap operas, American films and round-the-clock sports coverage, all rattling around in his frontal lobes and frequently seeping through into the parts that processed the dreams. At one time, when the Melbourne Olympics coincided with the birth of Linda's baby and the TV premiere of *Lethal Weapon 9*, the Guardian's dreams were probably the most bizarre mental images ever generated since the death of Hieronymus Bosch.

Mortals. He could smell mortals, not too far away. And, he realised, another smell; a strange one, this, something that he could just faintly remember from a very long time ago. A worrying smell, presaging trouble.

(*'And where's one cue ball going to end up this time? Oh dear, that's exactly where he didn't want it to go. And how's Steve going to get himself out of this one, I wonder?'*)

Not mortals, the other things. Immortals. Gods. There were gods on his mountain. Dammit, when would they learn they weren't welcome here?

'Fine,' Pan said, sitting down on a rock and sinking his chin in his hands. 'Now all we have to do is find some way of moving them. Anyone think to bring a wheelbarrow?'

Below them lay the Teeth. The clear, tranquil, still slightly effervescent pink liquid that filled the crater served to distort the outline of the huge yellow objects that lay – how deep? A few metres? Fifty? A hundred? – below the surface, but in spite of that, and despite the distance from the lip of the crater to the bottom, the sight was little short of staggering.

Interesting to compare the reactions of the members of the party. Osiris had jammed the brake on his wheelchair and was gazing with one of the wildest surmises ever seen in those parts, silent on an extinct volcano in

Nezahuancoyotl. Pan, as stated above, was wretchedly speculating as to who, in accordance with his usual rotten bloody luck, was going to be called upon to do the heavy lifting. Sandra was thinking, Right now, what wouldn't I give for a whacking great big cheese-burger. As far as we can tell, Carl wasn't thinking anything at all.

'Amazing,' Osiris said at last. 'All that wealth, all that ingenuity, all that manpower, and all the silly sods needed to do was invent the toothbrush.' He sighed. The older he got, the more firmly he was convinced that all gods were, basically, pillocks.

'Excuse me,' Pan interrupted, 'but if you've got some subtle scheme for shifting that lot, now would be a very good time to mention it.'

Osiris brought his mind back from its reverie with an almost audible click. 'No problem,' he said. 'We cheat.'

'We can do that, can we?'

''Course we can. We're gods, aren't we? Where's the point in being a god if you can't bend the rules now and again?'

'There's bending rules,' Pan muttered, 'and there's the law of conservation of matter. And before you ask,' he added, 'yes, if they catch you breaking it they do come down on you like a ton of bricks. Even for a first offence I believe the minimum penalty is four thousand years' community service.'

'Relax,' Osiris replied. 'To the gods all things are possible, remember?'

'I was afraid you were going to say that.'

'Don't be so damned negative about everything,' Osiris said irritably. 'That's the trouble with you. At the first little sign of difficulty you start to panic, and—'

'Well I would, wouldn't I?'

Osiris sighed. 'We cheat,' he said decisively. 'And this is how we do it.'

★   ★   ★

Because, after all, the laws of physics are like all other laws everywhere: designed to make life difficult and unpleasant for the small fry like you and me, while the rich and powerful take no notice of them whatsoever.

The basic, back-of-an-envelope logic behind it all was as follows:

(a) Only things that are possible may be done without violating the fundamental laws of the universe.

(b) However, to the gods, all things are possible.

(c) Therefore, *ipso facto*, anything a god chooses to do is by definition possible, and consequently entirely legal.

Fine; but that wasn't getting an extremely heavy set of false teeth shifted from the bottom of a very big crater. In order to achieve that objective, a degree more detail was required. Thus:

(a) It is extremely difficult to move a set of dentures which is huge and made of solid gold.

(b) On the other hand, it's extremely simple to move a set of dentures which is standard size and made of the latest in lightweight hard plastics.

(c) To the gods, who are eternal and enduring, all that is temporary and corruptible is pretty well the same; the atoms and molecules remain, but from time to time they make up an infinite variety of different shapes. To a god, the myriad shapes and forms that the atoms compose themselves into for a while before decay and entropy do their ineluctable stuff seem very like the individual frames that make up a length of cine film; each individual image is so transitory that the divine eye cannot perceive it, but the general theme remains behind once the image, and tens of thousands like it, have faded away into oblivion, and each single image goes towards building up the whole picture.

(d) Therefore, to a god, everything is what he wants it

to be. Including ginormous sets of gold bridgework.

'Here we are,' Osiris said. He put the teeth carefully away in a jiffy bag, and stowed the parcel in his inside pocket. He turned his head towards Pan, and grinned. 'You see what you can achieve by thinking things through,' he added. 'Saves no end of mucking about.'

'Well done,' Pan replied, while his inner thoughts added *Bloody show-off*. 'And now I think we'd better be getting along, because I have this funny feeling that . . .'

In the crater, the lake was beginning to froth.

'You're paranoid, you are.'

'Am I?'

'Believe me.'

'Maybe,' Pan answered. He was looking down into the crater, where the froth was clearing on the meniscus of the lake, which was now starting to boil. 'Have you ever asked yourself what made me paranoid in the first place?'

Osiris followed his line of sight. 'On the other hand,' he said, 'standing round here chattering isn't achieving anything, and we've got a lot to do, so maybe we should . . .'

And then the volcano shook, and from the bottom of the now empty crater a waterspout leapt up, whirling and spinning. As it spun faster it seemed to take on a shape, a form branded on to the divine subconscious and signifying hassle. A few spins later, and it was solid.

'Strewth,' Carl muttered under his breath. 'It's a bloody great big snake.'

Out of the mouths of babes and morons. It was no longer even translucent; it was depressingly material, a monstrous serpent, towering above them, making a giant Redwood look like a dwarf geranium. At the top of the metallic scaled neck perched not one but very many small, diamond-shaped heads, each with its own fangs and flickering forked tongue. For the record, the Guardian had seventy-three heads, each one capable of independent action. Through his still sleeping brain, meanwhile, weird and incomprehensible messages flashed and were gone, leaving behind a sort of glow, like the flash of floundering colour you can still see with your eyes closed after looking at the sun.

Marvellous stuff, Steradent. Not only does it preserve dentures from decay and kill the lurking germs that find their way into the recesses of even the best false teeth; when the need arises, and some deadly peril threatens the teeth placed in its charge, it can (if infused with enough magic to poison a convention of wizards) turn itself into a hundred-foot-tall mythical serpent and devour all known intruders.

'Funny the way it's still bright pink,' Sandra observed. 'I wonder if it still tastes minty.'

One of the advantages of having the god Pan in your party is that you can get all the blind, unreasoning terror you could ever possibly need, the finest quality, trade. As the hydra uncoiled its grotesquely long neck and lunged, hissing (not exactly hissing; more a sort of bubbling fizz) and darting out countless pink tongues, the denture-thieves scattered and fled, leaving Osiris stranded directly in its path.

'Pan, you sodding coward!' they heard him shout. 'What the bloody hell do you think you're . . . ?'

Oh no you don't, Pan reflected as he hurled himself into a narrow crevice between two split rocks and covered his head with his arms. I *know* what I'm doing, and I prefer it this way. I may be immortal, but I'd really rather not spend the rest of eternity inside the digestive organs of a fucking great snake, thank you all the same. And being a god means never having to say . . .

Oh *balls*!

Painfully and with infinite regret, he levered himself back out of safety, banged his head on a jagged rock in doing so, and ran back towards where Osiris had been.

The Guardian shuddered.

He was, of course, still fast asleep; the unofficial tenants of his brain saw to that. If he were to wake up, even for a moment, television reception on three continents would be interrupted and millions of viewers switching on for that day's episode of *The Young Accountants* would find themselves watching a rather slow and extremely esoteric documentary about the thought-processes of a pool of denture cleaner.

Since he couldn't wake up, he dreamed strange dreams. For example, his seventy-third head, through which passed live coverage of the Melbourne Open Golf Championship, was haunted by the image of one of the contestants suddenly grabbing the ball from the ninth green and making off with it. Head 34 (*A Million Menus*, with Yvonne Wilson) buzzed with a mouth-watering recipe for intruder fried in butter with fresh parsley and new potatoes. Head 41 (the popular game show *Name Your Poison*) cut out in the middle of the pushing-innocent-civilians-down-coal-shutes-and-pouring-hot-tar-on-their-heads round and started a new game entirely from scratch, the objective of which was to capture your opponent's knight's pawn and rip his lungs out with a meathook. One thing on which all the heads were decided was that as soon as there was a commercial break, they'd be out of there and hammering on the franchiser's door in search of a refund.

Burglars, whispered the night-watchman in his subconscious. Get on and eat the fuckers. Blearily, he turned his heads from side to side, scanning the surrounding area for someone to devour.

What his seventy-three pairs of eyes saw was a little old man in a wheelchair, shaking a liver-spotted fist at him and shouting angrily in a high, reedy voice. Burglars, the heads cried in unison. Do us a favour. That old codger couldn't burgle the Dogger Bank.

The Guardian was just about to give the whole thing up as a bad job and go back to his nice muddy bed when a flurry of movement caught his eyes. He hesitated, and saw another human figure sprinting awkwardly over the jagged outcrops of rock towards the old guy in the wheelchair and yelling. Two of them; rather more like it.

And a big hand, please, for our two brave contestants, who're going to step forward tonight and play Hiding To Nothing.

The wheelchair lurched forward, and it appeared that the older man was trying to move towards the younger. That, the Guardian reckoned, was thoughtful; one cyanide gas sneeze from Head 72 would do for both of them, and there was plenty of meat on the second one, even if the first was probably a trifle stringy.

The Guardian frowned and, on the basis that if two heads are better than one, seventy-three must be pretty damn smart, he considered the position in some detail, quickly drawing up a number of alternative courses of action, each one nothing more than an alternative means to the common end of making these two clowns wish they'd never been born. By the time the heads had taken a vote and decided to go for straightforward violence and mayhem, the running burglar had grabbed the handles of the wheelchair and set off as quickly as he could towards a large heap of rocks.

The hydra yawned. Oh well, he said to himself, here we go again. Another day, another mangled bag of crushed limbs.

*   *   *

'I don't know, Pan, there are times when I despair of you.'

Pan paused for a moment, panting for breath. This gave Osiris further scope to develop his theme.

'Call yourself a god,' he went on, 'I've seen beermats with more divinity than you. Your trouble is,' he continued, with the air of someone who had long been minded to make the ensuing points, 'you've got no sense of altruism. Can't be a god unless you care. You'd only take away the sins of the world if you could be sure of getting money back on the empties.'

'Osiris,' Pan replied, 'shut up.'

'It's all very well you saying—' Osiris got as far as saying before Pan clamped his hand firmly over his divine colleague's mouth. With the other hand he tried to push the wheelchair.

And it's Second Burglar on the inside, Second Burglar with Old Codger making a last-minute effort, is he going to make it or has he left it too late, Second Burglar coming up hard now on the inside, maybe finding the going a bit too hard for him . . .

The Guardian swooped, his heads swaying on his neck like over-heavy buds on a broken stalk, and lunged at Pan, who made a desperate effort to jump clear without letting go of the wheelchair. If the traffic wardens of physics had been standing by, they'd have given him a ticket for a flagrant breach of gravity. As Heads 63 and 47 snapped vainly at his heels he landed awkwardly, turned his ankle and bolted, jolting Osiris so violently that he almost swallowed his teeth.

'Mmm,' shouted Osiris through Pan's tightly gripping fingers. 'Mm mmm mmm mm mmm *mmmmmmmm* mm *m*!'

'I'll pretend I didn't hear you say that,' Pan gasped in reply. 'Hell's bells, that was close!'

The situation was deteriorating somewhat. He was

tiring rapidly, he could feel the hot breath of Numbers 42–67 inclusive on the back of his neck and he had a sharp pebble in his shoe. It would be nice, he couldn't help thinking, if someone did something to help. Fairly soon would be nicer still.

There was a loud bang.

When a man has been in the contract killing and supernatural pest control business as long as Kurt Lundqvist, he learns to adopt a robust attitude to false modesty.

Just getting here, Lundqvist reflected, was enough to earn him a nomination for the Golden Uzi at this year's Beirut Festival. He'd walked barefoot across scalding hot deserts, climbed snow-capped mountains, living off small birds and insects and drinking the foul juice of cacti. By sheer dead reckoning he'd found his way to the only airport in a thousand square miles, hijacked a plane with nothing more lethal about his person than five days growth of beard and a plausible manner, overpowered five members of a commando unit sent to dispose of him and armed himself for the job he now had to perform from their rather inadequate kit. He was a big man, and the commandos had been highly trained, deadly and ruthless but nonetheless a bit on the petite size when it came to footwear. The largest boots they'd had between them were two sizes too small.

His seventh sense had warned him to expect to find trouble, and so he had approached the volcano circumspectly. Now, as he lifted his head and peeked out, he could see that he had been justified.

Huge pink hydras no longer fazed him. There had been a time, a great many years ago, when a sight like the one now confronting him would have given him pause for thought, and quite possibly permanent psychological damage; but not any more. All that passed through his mind as he ducked down back out of sight was, Pink hydra, shit, how in God's name am I supposed to take out a pink hydra with this garbage?

The plane he had commandeered, it should be noted, was the flagship and one hundred per cent of the operational fleet of Air Easter Island, the recently formed national airline of that state; and although it wasn't actually powered by a rubber band, that was about all you could say for it. The commando squad sent to eliminate him had therefore been the elite forces section of the Easter Island Defence Force, and their equipment, though perfectly adequate for their purposes, was a few points behind NATO standards in terms of propinquity to the state of the art. Surveying what he'd got, Lundqvist reckoned, he'd be prepared to go a bit further than that. The only art this lot was anything like state of was probably Surrealism.

A quick mental inventory revealed:

Item; a Daisy air rifle, circa 1952.

Item; a surface-to-air rocket.

Item; a launcher for the rocket, consisting of a stick and an empty milk bottle.

Item; a Zambian Army Knife, all blades except the cork-screw broken.

Item; a Sony Walkman, 1982 model, and a tape of the Band of the Coldstream Guards playing Souza marches.

Item; a potato gun, with three rounds of Aran Piper.

Item; an RPG-7 anti-tank missile and projector.

The last item hadn't in fact come from the Easter Islanders. He'd found it in the glove compartment of the plane, and the only conclusion he could logically draw was that it had been left behind by some absentminded member of a previous hijack squad. It wasn't what he'd have chosen, but in context it was probably going to have to do.

He shouldered the RPG-7 and glanced through the sight. What met his eye wasn't the most encouraging of scenes. There was the hydra, huge great big thing with lots of heads, and directly underneath it, dodging about like a blindfolded hedgehog in the Los Angeles rush hour, was Pan, pushing Osiris' wheelchair with one hand and making feeble shooing gestures with the other.

Quickly he considered his options. In the circumstances, a head shot (his usual choice) was out of the question. That left the heart or the point of the shoulder; and since it was anybody's guess where the heart was, he opted for the latter. A well-placed hit there ought to break the spine, provided that the projectile had sufficient oomph to achieve the desired result. Probably not, he had to concede, but there's no harm in trying.

He steadied his aim, took up the slack on the trigger, aligned the sights and slowly squeezed off the last pound and a half of the trigger pull. There was a loud bang.

The Guardian froze, and all seventy-three heads turned slowly and in perfect unison towards the source of the noise . . .

. . . Which proved to be a man sitting behind a rock, holding what was undoubtedly an anti-tank missile launcher. There was no rocket in the breach. You could use the laucher as an impromptu vase for flower arranging, if you filled it with water, but that was about it.

By reflex the Guardian raised a paw and swatted at where the missile should have hit him, had it gone off. It hadn't, or rather, it had done exactly what it had originally been designed to do; it had produced a loud noise and pushed out from the muzzle a small, tatty flag, embroidered with the word:

BANG!

Marvellous, Lundqvist muttered under his breath. Millions of these RPGs were scattered about the world, and I have to get the one converted into a joke novelty. He reflected, apropos of nothing much, on his boyhood, playing tag with his father in the orchard out back of the house. His competitive instinct had compelled him to win, and on the occasion he had in mind, his father had been in hospital for three days afterwards.

The hydra, meanwhile, was turning towards him, looking with its seventy-three heads like nothing on earth so much as a very elderly mop of the sort that is made up of lots of batch ends of frayed string. It was coming this way.

'What I need,' Lundqvist said aloud, 'is an act of goddamn God.'

Which is precisely what he got.

The act in question had been performed by Odin; and to be absolutely precise it wasn't an act so much as an omission. It had been understood that when they were putting the traction engine back together again after picking it out of the side of the mountain they'd flown into, it was Odin's turn to clear out the intake valves. If that wasn't done, Thor had reminded him, the whole bloody contraption was liable to blow up.

'Can't be expected to work miracles,' Odin replied. 'All we can do is our best, that's what I always say.'

'Your best?' Thor laughed harshly. 'Are you sure you've got one? Or is it just one of your many worsts?'

Frey stirred. 'Actually,' he murmured, 'you can.'

'I can what?'

'Work miracles. It's dead easy, actually. Turn water into wine, for instance . . .'

The traction engine stalled. For a split second it hung in the air like a large, malformed cloud; then it began to fall to earth.

'Or there's loaves and fishes,' Frey continued, his hands so firmly over his eyes that powerful hydraulic rams would have been needed to dislodge them. 'I read a book about it when I was a kid. All you need is two loaves, five fishes, some sticky-backed plastic and a couple of old washing-up liquid bottles with the ends cut off . . .'

'I'm getting sick of this,' Thor growled. 'After all, it's my bloody engine, I'm a god and I've had it up to here. I'm going to do some magic.'

Odin frowned. 'We're not allowed –' he started to say.

'Bugger that.' Thor spread his arms and knotted his brows, trying to remember how you went about it. It had been quite a while and time tends to blur the sharp edges of the brain. All he could recall offhand was that in his particular method of disrupting the chain of causality, sticky-backed plastic and decapitated squeegee-bottles were conspicuous by their absence.

It was probably, he decided, a bit like mending a broken machine. You shouted at it, and if that didn't work you belted something with a bloody great big hammer.

'Right,' he yelled. 'Airbrakes!'

Nature, that much-abused personification, grinned. You want airbrakes, she whispered, you got them.

And this time it looks like the big fella's going to be in luck, he's bringing his number 42 head into position, and it looks very much like it's the end of a very courageous fight-back by Burglar, a very sporting loser here at the . . .

BANG!

The Guardian blinked, seventy-three times, simultaneously, and then fell over.

'What,' screamed Thor, who had pushed Odin aside and was wrestling ferociously with the joystick, 'the bloody hell was that?'

The traction engine was vibrating horribly; but, in some peculiar way, the impact had steadied it – broken its fall, you might say. Also, the quite stupendous jolt had had the effect on it of being thumped, very hard indeed, with a two-hundred-pound lump hammer.

It was a machine, and as such only understood one thing. Being clobbered with big hammers was something it could relate to. The motor, which had been simpering in a smug, self-satisfied way in preparation for total shut-down, coughed a few times, spluttered, caught and roared into life. They had lift-off.

'I beg your pardon?' Frey yelled back.

'I said, what was that?'

To the gods, all obscure things are clear, all hidden things are plainly visible. A god sees what is really there, disregarding the deception of form, the meretricious tricks of morphology.

'I think,' Frey therefore replied, 'we just hit a lake.'

We apologise for the temporary interference with reception, which is due to technical problems. Normal service will be resumed shortly.

The Guardian stirred, winced, and felt the side of his head. It hurt. Vague flashbacks of memory crept back, like a film of drifting smoke played backwards. A bang, a sharp blow; the silhouette of a tiny figure against the rim of the crater, with some sort of gun in its shoulder. Some bastard had taken a shot at him.

Right. We'll see about that.

On TV screens across half the globe, the test card flickered and vanished, and was replaced by what could loosely be described as drama: a huge giant kicking the innards out of a diminutive figure with a gun wrapped round its neck. *We interrupt our scheduled programme to bring you up-to-the-minute reports from our newsdesk. The attempt on the life of the Guardian of the Teeth earlier today has led to violent clashes between the Guardian and an unidentified burglar . . .*

Slowly, and with a certain amount of subdued fizzing, the Guardian stood up, wobbled for a moment and looked round. Because he was looking for one individual human being in particular, he failed to notice Pan, Osiris and party making a sharp tactical withdrawal in the opposite direction (taking the Teeth with them). Eventually he found what he was looking for. After a moment's thought he stooped down, uprooted a substantial boulder, and hefted it for weight and balance. Then he advanced.

Kurt Lundqvist, meanwhile, had dumped the RPG-7 and most of the rest of his captured arsenal, and was running like hell back towards where he'd left his transport. It went without saying that he did so with panther-like stealth, gliding like a dim ghost across the rocky terrain, or at least would have done if his feet hadn't kept jumping out of the tiny shoes.

He was almost in sight of safety when the light was blotted out in front of him by, he realised, a very large shadow. No need to look round and see what was causing it. Oh *god*, he muttered as he slithered and scrambled his way over the treacherous shale. God, I wish I . . .

'*Good on yer, mate. Told you you'd need the third wish sooner or later, didn't I?*'

'Screaming Jesus,' Lundqvist gasped. Although there was nothing to see, he could feel the Dragon King's presence in the air, smell its beery breath. 'You again.'

'*G'day. Looks like you've landed yourself in a spot of grief here, mate. Want me to sort it out for you?*'

'No,' Lundqvist shouted, 'absolutely not, no way. I have the situation perfectly under—'

A giant foot thundered down a mere thirty yards away,

making the ground shake. The shadow grew slightly darker, if that was possible.

'*Fair go, sport, looks to me like unless you have some help smartish, you're gonna be history. You're sure about this?*'

'Yes, positive. Bugger off.'

'*I'll be saying g'day, then.*'

The air cleared around him, which only left the problem of the Guardian and his enormous rock. The latter was presently hovering about a hundred and twenty feet above Lundqvist's head, as the Guardian took aim and allowed for ground speed and windage.

Getting out of this one, Lundqvist admitted to himself, was going to be one of the most challenging problems of his professional career; and he had about half a second to do it in.

It's a truism to say that Fortune favours the brave; but the thing to remember about truisms is that they got that way by frequently being true.

Lundqvist got out of there with a margin of perhaps a fiftieth of a second; but get out he did. When the rock finally hit the ground, smashing a crater which, if flooded, would have made a wonderful yachting marina, Lundqvist was already a fair distance away, and moving fast. A specialist in gift horse dentistry might have pointed out to him that he was gripped firmly in an enormous, apparently disembodied, hand, which had appeared out of nowhere, scooped him up and carried him off; but Lundqvist was in no mood to find fault. Better, he reflected, a Lundqvist in the hand than a mangled corpse in the bush. Or words to that effect.

'Thanks,' Lundqvist called out. 'I owe you one, whoever the hell you are. Just drop me anywhere here and that'll be fine.'

'Don't tempt me.'

Lundqvist looked down. They were still many hundreds of feet above sea level, but at least they were over dry land. An island, to be precise. What was more, it had a strangely familiar look, although Lundqvist knew for a certainty that he'd never been there before.

'It was very kind of you to rescue me,' he called out. The hand tightened its grip very slightly; just enough to allow Lundqvist's circulation to continue working.

'What makes you think you've been rescued?'

Obviously, Lundqvist assured himself, a joke. After all, whoever this hand belongs to saved me from certain death.

He looked down again, and then up. You had to say this for certain death: at least it was certain. And, Lundqvist added, drawing on wide experience obtained over many years as Death's leading sales rep, it didn't usually involve hovering high up above islands tucked in the palm of giant hands, or at least not when he was administering it. A 200-grain full metal jacket slug from a .40 Glock was more his style, and by and large he had seen nothing in this character's *modus operandi* to make him revise his views. Death Lundqvist-style might be prosaic, but it avoided the vertigo and the travel sickness, and was over rather more quickly.

'Excuse me,' he asked, 'but where the hell are we?'

The air above him quivered as the proprietor of the hand chuckled disconcertingly. 'You don't recognise it?'

'Can't say that I do.'

'Look closer.'

Lundqvist did so; and it didn't take him long to notice the long rows of large, bleak, stylised anthropomorphic statues that stood in rows all over the beach and immediately contiguous area. The land mass below was Easter Island.

Ah.

'Look,' he shouted, as soon as he was able to get his larynx up and running again. 'If it's about the hijack I can explain.'

'I see. That's another useless talent you've got, is it?'

When the hand eventually stopped and the fingers relaxed a trifle, Lundqvist was no more than twelve feet off the ground, and was able to make a perfectly competent emergency landing on his head.

'By the time I've finished with you,' said the voice, 'I'll make you wish you'd never been born.'

The air swam for a moment; and then the rest of the body to which the hand was attached materialised in front of him. Still no clues as to who or what it was, but it made the Guardian look like something found at the bottom of a breakfast cereal packet.

'Welcome,' it said, 'to Easter Island. I am Hotduyrtdx.'

'*Gesundheit.*'

'No,' said Hotduyrtdx, 'that's my name. And this,' it went on, making a sweeping gesture around the whole island, 'is my home. Or it was, at any rate. You see the statues?'

Lundqvist nodded.

'That's your fault.'

'But I've never been here in my life before.'

'Irrelevant. You're sure you don't remember what it is you've done?'

'Positive.'

The voice sighed. 'Then I'll explain,' it said.

A long time ago (said Hotduyrtdx) there was an island.

It had a population, of sorts; but far too many for the island to be self-sufficient in food. When Hotduyrtdx arrived to take up his new post as divine observer and acting pro-consul, the first thing he did was cast about in his mind for a suitable cash crop; something that would show a high, quick return on capital with minimum risk and no tax implications, making the most of locally available raw materials.

Now then, Hotduyrtdx asked himself, what is it that we have the most of? Answer: rocks. Lots of them. A fine crop, in its way, requiring the minimum of watering and potting on; but not, unfortunately, readily marketable. Think of something else.

And so Hotduyrtdx went away and thought hard and because he was a god (to whom all things are possible) and blessed with an elementary knowledge of economic theory, it wasn't long before the solution presented itself. Forget agriculture entirely. Go for broke with light industry. Make something for which there is an insatiable demand, and you're home and dry.

Such as?

Such as toupees for gods. Do you have difficulty in finding cranial accessories in your size, given that in your natural shape you're a hundred foot high and morphologically unstable? Have over-work and the pressures of executive office resulted in hair loss and premature baldness, leading in turn to a decline in worshipper credibility? Worry no longer. Easter Island Head Cosmetics will come to your rescue. Nobody, not even your fellow gods, will ever be able to see the join.

Hence the statues. None of your cheapskate synthetic rugs in a high-class establishment like this; each hairpiece was hand-made from only the very finest materials by dedicated craftsmen bound by the most dreadful oaths not to make sarcastic comments, no matter how illustrious the customer. For reasons that will shortly be made clear, the hairpieces themselves are now all long gone; but the wigstands remain behind, relics of a once massive industrial civilisation. Hundreds of them; tall angular stylised heads carved out of huge blocks of granite and basalt, all of them bald as billiard balls. Most of them, in fact, are still there to this day.

'Hey,' Lundqvist said, backing away, 'I think maybe you're overreacting a bit here. The plane's perfectly safe, I promise you. I even stopped off on the way and filled her up with gas on my AmEx card.'

Hotduyrtdx snarled, and advanced a step further. 'I'm not talking about the aeroplane,' he said. 'In fact, how do you think the plane came to be there, all nice and conveniently waiting for you? Why do you think you were able to overpower the guard and hijack it so easily?' He grinned, revealing a mouthful of teeth like the 'Before' stage of a hard-sell orthodontics advert. 'I think *set up* is the phrase you people use,' he added.

'But what have I done, man?'

A spasm of rage briefly contorted Hotduyrtdx's face (which hadn't exactly been cuddly-looking to start with; imagine a Hieronymus Bosch watercolour left outside in the rain, and you'll get the general idea). 'For one thing,' he growled, 'I am not a man. Thanks to you I'm not a god either, not any more. But I think you've done enough damage already without adding insult to . . .'

Lundqvist tried to back away further, but an ill-mannered tree impeded his progress. 'What did I do?' he repeated. 'And when?'

'July 17th, 1469. Don't pretend you don't remember.'

'I don't have to pretend.'

'Ah well.' Hotduyrtdx shrugged. 'Actually, they say extreme agony sharpens the memory, so don't give up hope just yet.'

He swept out a talon, which Lundqvist only just avoided, and made a sound like tearing calico.

'Hey . . .' Lundqvist was just about to protest further when the librarians of his memory emerged, dusty and with cricks in their necks, from the uttermost filing cabinet of his mind. Easter Island. Yes.

It had been a very long time ago; back in the days when business had been slow and he'd supplemented his income by doing odd jobs for the Theological Survey Department. It had all been a bit of fun – his five-year mission; to explore new worlds, seek out new life forms, that sort of thing – and on the way home they'd stopped off, yes, *here*, dammit, to mend a puncture and take on water and garlic butter for the final leg of the journey. This place had changed a lot since then, of course. He shuddered.

'Remember now?' Hotduyrtdx asked. Lundqvist nodded.

One of the responsibilities of the Survey was to make routine checks on any gods or purported gods they came across, to ensure that they were complying with the various Practice Directions issued by the Department on various matters, most of them to do with the keeping of full accounts in the prescribed form and maintaining a proper level of professional indemnity insurance. It so happened that, on inspection, Lundqvist had found discrepancies and breaches of the rules, and had reported them. That, as far as he had been concerned, was the end of the matter. Certainly he'd heard no more about it at the time.

'They struck you off?' he said.

Hotduyrtdx nodded. 'And you know what for?' he went on. 'You know what it was I'd done that was so terrible I wasn't allowed to be a god any more? Go on, guess.'

'I can't.'

'I hadn't been filling out my green sheets in duplicate, like I was supposed to. Instead I was just filling out the top copy and taking a photocopy for the file. That was it. Heinous stuff, yes?'

Lundqvist cast his mind back. Green sheets – god, yes,

them. He remembered now. Back then, all gods were supposed to fill out these idiotic forms each time they did a miracle. It was something to do with input tax, and the whole scheme was abandoned a short while afterwards.

'They struck you off for that?'

'Conduct unbecoming, they said.' Hotduyrtdx smiled grimly. 'The way they saw it, it was just an administrative error, and to err is human. If it'd been something really heavy, like bringing the dead back to life or wiping out a century's worth of history, I'd have got away with a reprimand, because to forgive is divine. Marvellous system, huh?'

Lundqvist nodded. He couldn't think of very much to say.

'The business had to close down, of course,' Hotduyrtdx continued remorselessly. 'All my customers were gods, see, and so I wasn't allowed to trade with them. As a result the whole population were put out of a job, they drifted back into subsistence agriculture and died out. I've been here ever since. Thanks to you.'

'I never meant . . .'

Hotduyrtdx scowled, and wisps of strange brown vapour drifted from his nostrils. 'I don't imagine you did. Your sort never do. Ever since, I've been holed up here, brewing up moonshine magic out of anything I could lay my hands on, ready for the day when I could get even with you, you scumbag. It's been a long time.'

He advanced another two paces, until his shadow engulfed Lundqvist completely. It was hard not to notice the claws on the end of his feet.

'Would it help,' Lundqvist said tentatively, 'if I told you I was in a position to put a good word in for you with some very high-ranking gods indeed? I mean, like really top-flight . . .'

'No.'

'Okay.' He sighed. 'In that case,' he went on, 'you leave me no alternative.'

Hotduyrtdx blinked. 'What d'you mean, *I* leave *you* no alter . . .'

Lundqvist braced himself for the desperate expenditure of energy that was to come. Good old pineal gland, always been there for me when I needed you most, come through for Daddy just one more time, we all know you've got it in you. 'I just want you to know,' he said solemnly, looking for the right spot, 'that I really hate doing this. If there was any other way at all . . .'

'Doing what, for pity's sake?'

With a violent explosion of muscular effort, possible only because of countless years of specialist training, Lundqvist jumped between Hotduyrtdx's legs, hit the ground, rolled, regained his feet and used them.

'Running away,' he shouted back over his shoulder. 'I'll get you for this, you sucker!'

'Now just a flaming minute . . .'

But Lundqvist wasn't there any more. He had always been a good runner, although in different circumstances (he had always specialised in *after* rather than *away from*) and the thought of the claws and the quite staggering size of the horrible thing somehow made him able to set a pace that would have had Carl Lewis tripping over his feet in about twelve seconds. As tactical withdrawals went, it was pretty slick.

There is only so much percentage, however, in running away from someone when you're on an island; and running, as the man said, is one thing, hiding is quite another. As he ran, Lundqvist's mind kept itself occupied with figuring out how many of Hotduyrtdx's strides it would take to traverse the island from one side to the other. Not many, he decided. Not nearly many enough.

'*Ready yet?*'

'I told you,' Lundqvist panted, 'bugger off. I've got enough problems of my own without you to contend with.'

The Dragon King of the South-East shrugged his shoulders. '*Blimey, mate,*' he said, '*you're a hard bloke to help, no worries. Just say the word and I'll have you out of there in two shakes of a possum's—*'

'Go away! Piss off! Get the hell outa here!' Lundqvist yelled. 'This is your last warning, okay?'

'*Be like that,*' said the Dragon King huffily, and vanished.

Five minutes of flat-out running later, Lundqvist was so demoralised that he was beginning to wonder whether the Dragon King mightn't have been such a bad idea after all when he came to an unscheduled and quite involuntary stop. Some idiot, it seemed, had built a damn great wall right across the road. To make matters worse, they'd painted it invisible.

'Are you hurt?' said a disembodied voice.

Kurt tried to move; but the parts of his brain responsible for motor functions told him to forget it. He groaned.

'Because if you are,' the voice went on, 'we might be able to help. We're doctors, you see.'

At which point, the two doctors stepped out from behind the invisible wall. They were carrying the inevitable black bags, together with assorted firearms, hand grenades, surface-to-air missile launchers and extremely hi-tech edged weapons; in other words, almost exactly the way the young Kurt Lundqvist had imagined Santa Claus looked, except that they didn't have red robes, long white beards and flak jackets.

'Mind you,' said one of the doctors, 'it's partly your own fault for not looking at the signs.'

Lundqvist spat out a tooth. 'Signs?' he croaked.

A doctor nodded. 'Back there,' he replied, pointing. 'Big signs saying, *Caution, invisible wall*. Of course they're invisible too, but . . .'

Numb, Lundqvist lay still while they examined him and, eventually, prescribed two aspirin and a good lie down. 'What the hell do you think you're doing?' he asked.

A doctor looked at him. 'You are Kurt Lundqvist, aren't you?' he asked.

Lundqvist nodded. 'Why?'

'Good.' The doctor took out his stethoscope, blew down one earpiece and listened to Lundqvist's chest. 'Your friends are coming to rescue you,' he said. 'That's why we're setting up these invisible road-blocks. Clever, yes?'

'How did they know I was here?'

'*I told 'em, of course,*' replied the Dragon King of the South-East, materialising in a deck chair in mid-air about four feet over Lundqvist's head. '*The way I saw it, if you're such a galah you won't ask me to help you, it's up to me to use a bit of initiative.*'

Lundqvist groaned and lay back on the ground. 'I shall count to ten,' he said. 'If you're still here . . .'

'*Cheerio for now, then. Remember, you've still got one wish.*'

'I wish you'd disappear up your own arse, you fucking stupid goldfish.'

'*I'll pretend I didn't hear that,*' said the King cheerfully, and vanished.

Kurt propped himself up, painfully on one elbow, and turned to the two doctors, who were planting invisible landmines. 'You heard that,' he said, 'you're witnesses. I made a perfectly valid wish. I asked him to vanish, he vanished. Okay?'

A doctor looked at him. 'Who vanished?' he asked.

'Concussion,' said his colleague.

'Oh yes, of course. Silly me. Here, Mr Lundqvist, you'd better make that three aspirins.'

Why bother? Lundqvist said to himself. He whimpered, got slowly to his hands and knees, and crawled away behind the wall.

Fortuitously, it turned out; because no sooner had he vanished from sight than Hotduyrtdx suddenly hove into view, making the ground shake with his footsteps.

'Oy, you,' yelled a doctor. 'Not this way, there's a mine-field, you could get—'

Bang.

There was a short pause, during which large chunks of uprooted turf plopped back down to earth.

'Excuse me, but are you injured at all?'

Hotduyrtdx snarled; difficult, because his body was now in more pieces than one of those incredibly complex jigsaw puzzles you were given by aunts for Christmas in your formative years, and which went straight up into the loft first thing on Boxing Day morning.

'I got blown up,' he grunted. 'I'd leave me well alone if I were you.'

The two doctors exchanged glances.

'Ah well,' one of them said at last. 'Now at least we know they still work.'

To the gods all things are possible. Well, virtually all.

'Marvellous,' Thor growled. 'Absolutely bloody wonderful. Now what do we do?'

Frey pointed. 'There's a little sticker,' he said, 'look, there on the windshield. That probably tells you the procedure.' He leant forward and read aloud: "This vehicle has been immobilised; do not attempt to move it . . ."'

'Yes, thank you, I can read,' Odin said. 'The question is, how do we get rid of the confounded thing?'

One of the things – the very, very few things – not possible to gods is removing wheel clamps from illegally parked traction engines, using only the rudimentary tools usually carried in the glove box. 'We could pay the fine,' Frey suggested. 'I gather that usually does the trick.'

Thor snarled. Not for nothing had he been the god of thunder for countless centuries; it started to drizzle with rain.

'Over my dead body,' he said. 'Nobody wheelclamps a god and gets away with it.'

'Fine. So you do know how to get it off, then?'

'Yes. I'll, um, remember in a minute.'

Always the way, isn't it? A quick pitstop in the suburbs of Mexico City, to buy gasket sealant and gear-box oil; Odin's cheerful assurance that they could park in the No Parking zone with impunity since they were only going to be three minutes, and there were no traffic wardens in sight of his all-seeing eye. And here they were. Stuck.

Thor pulled himself out from under the chassis, oily-faced but grinning. 'I think I see how to go about it,' he said. 'Odin, I'll need the tin of grease and a cold chisel. Frey, my hammer.'

A quarter of an hour passed noisily, at the end of which time Thor had hit everything he could reach (including, on a regular basis, his own fingers) and the clamp was still there.

'All we have to do is give them some money and they come and do it for us,' Frey insisted. 'Come on, it's easy. Mortals can do it, even.'

'Shut up, I'm thinking. Odin, go and buy a hacksaw.'

Twenty minutes later; the hacksaw blade had eventually snapped, taking a lump out of Thor's thumb as it did so. Otherwise the situation was pretty well unchanged.

'On the other hand,' Frey said, 'we could stay here for ever and ever. You know, find jobs, settle down, get married, that sort of thing.'

'I said shut up.'

'Leave Frey alone, Thor. It's not his fault.'

'Yes, but he's being aggravating, and if he carries on like that I shall knock his block off with my hammer.'

'He's always aggravating. I don't notice it any more.'

'. . . Ready-made start in the scrap iron business . . .'

'You see? How am I supposed to concentrate with him mithering on all the time?'

'You've just dropped the three-eighths spanner down that grating.'

Thor sighed. 'I seem to remember,' he said dismally, 'we had a damn sight fewer problems when we were creating the Earth.'

Odin nodded. 'Me too,' he said. 'On the other hand, it's one thing making something from scratch, but mending it once it's bust is another matter entirely. Besides,' he added wistfully, 'we had the proper tools then.'

'God, yes.' Thor sighed in nostalgic reverie. 'Remember that seven-mill Bergsen cutter with the adjustable three-way head? Went through igneous rock like a knife through butter.'

'And what about the old rotary magma plane?' Odin smiled involuntarily. 'Whatever became of that, by the way? It must still be about the place somewhere.'

Thor shook his head. 'Swopped it with the Celtic mob for a set of river-bed props and a beach grinder. Load of old tat that was, too. Worst deal I ever did.'

'Bet you they let it get all rusty.'

'Never cleaned anything in their lives.'

'Excuse me,' said Frey, 'but are we going to do something about this wheel thing or are we just going to stand here chattering on until they pull the city down and build a new one?'

His two colleagues looked at him.

'Oh, shut up,' they said.

*   *   *

'Whose damnfool idea was this, anyway?' Osiris demanded, scratching his ear and wriggling uncomfortably in his wheelchair. 'It certainly wasn't mine.'

It was a hot day and the hill was steep. Pan therefore had to save up his breath, like a child with a piggy bank, in order to have enough to answer.

'Don't look at me,' he said.

Neither of the mortals said anything, mainly because neither of them had a very clear idea of where they were or what they were meant to be doing. One moment they'd been escaping from an anthropomorphic oral hygiene accessory, the next they were on a Lear jet flying southeast.

'He's your friend,' Osiris retorted. 'I naturally assumed . . .'

Pan shook his head, while his lungs went into overdraft. 'I knew the man once, many years ago, but I wouldn't say we were friends. Generally I try not to associate too closely with people who spend most of their time bloody to the elbow.'

Osiris sighed. 'Well,' he said, 'we're here now, we might as well do the job. Then I suggest we get out of here as quickly as possible. This whole thing is getting unnecessarily complicated, if you ask me.'

'Behind you all the way,' Pan replied, and in his mind added, Yeah, pushing. Same as usual. Why do I get all the rotten jobs?

'Excuse me.'

Osiris looked back over his shoulder. 'Well?' he asked.

'Excuse me,' said Sandra, 'but the gold teeth things. What did you do with them?'

By way of reply Osiris grinned and patted his trouser pocket. Then the grin became a frown, the patting became frantic thumping, and spread to his other pockets like plague in a sixteenth-century seaport.

'You're not going to believe this,' he said.

But Pan believed it all right. In fact, he'd been waiting for it for a long time, and in a sense he was relieved it was over.

'Where,' he asked tonelessly, 'did you have them last?'

All living things are good at something; and Osiris' innate gift was for losing things out of pockets. When he was still an active god, before his retirement, this unfortunate habit was the main thing standing between him and high office within the Federation. (To give just one example: the lost kingdom of Atlantis was a centre of Mediterranean trade and marked on all the maps until one day it was Osiris' turn to lock up and switch off all the lights after the other gods had gone home. Atlantis remained lost for over four thousand years, until it eventually turned up, dusty and covered in bits of grey fluff, down the back of Osiris' sofa.)

'They're here somewhere,' Osiris was saying, in the tone of voice that implies that everything will come right just so long as you have faith. This didn't convince Pan, who knew from long experience that faith does indeed move mountains, but always puts them down again in the wrong place and invariably loses or breaks a couple of foothills in the process. 'Just bear with me a second and I'll . . .'

'You've lost them, haven't you?' he said.

'Of course I haven't lost them. How can anyone lose a set of false teeth the size of Mount Rushmore?'

'To the gods all things are possible.'

'Ah,' Osiris said, 'here they are.'

From his inside jacket pocket he produced a shiny yellow object which, on closer inspection, proved to be the upper set. Of the lower set there was no trace.

'Brilliant,' Pan said. 'Well, there's nothing for it, we'll just have to retrace our steps. It shouldn't be too hard a job,' he added grimly. 'All we have to do is find a country we've passed through or flown over which has suddenly quadrupled its national wealth overnight. Look out for new, expensive-looking warplanes with the cellophane still on the seats, that sort of thing.'

'Excuse me,' said Carl.

'Or maybe we could try the lost property offices,' Pan continued. 'Ask if anyone's handed in any gold icebergs. There are some honest people left in the world, after all, and—'

'Excuse me.'

The two gods turned round, to see Carl balancing the missing dentures on the palm of his hand. Pan swallowed hard, and grabbed.

'I think,' he said, gently but determinedly relieving Osiris of the other set, 'I'll take charge of these little tinkers for the time being. I'd prefer it if any further outbreaks of alarm and despondency were my fault. After all, that's what I'm good at.'

Osiris nodded meekly. 'Best thing to do,' he said, 'would be to get this lot cashed in as quickly as possible.'

'Cashed in?'

'Realised. Turned into money.' He hesitated, musing. 'Mind you,' he added, 'that's easier said than done. I don't think we can just wander into a jeweller's shop and expect to be paid cash.'

'We need a specialist, you mean?'

Osiris nodded. 'And come to think of it,' he said, 'I know just the very chap. More or less down my old neck of the woods. Retired now, of course, but stayed in those parts. Don't think he had much choice.'

'Excuse me.'

'Yes, thank you, Carl, we've found them now,' Pan said irritably. 'Get on with evolving into a sentient life-form or something, there's a good—'

'It's them doctors,' Carl said. 'I thought you'd want to know, that's all.'

'Where?'

'Over there.'

'*Where?*'

'Look,' said Carl, pointing. 'Just there, behind that big grey thing.'

'Oh.'

'You know something,' said one of the doctors to his colleague, as they lowered the lid of the tank into place and tightened up the restraining bolts, 'when this job is over I think I might retire. Pack all this in.'

His colleague wiped sweat from his forehead with the sleeve of his white coat. 'Yeah?' he said.

The doctor nodded. 'Think so,' he replied. 'Retire, open a little clinic somewhere, make people better. You know, sick people.'

His colleague frowned. 'You reckon there's a future in that, do you?'

'Could be. I mean, it's worth a shot, isn't it?'

'Might work, I suppose. Right,' he added, lighting the blowtorch. 'We'll just seal up the interstices with molten lead, and then that's that job done.'

It had been a remarkably efficient operation; basically a larger-scale version of catching rabbits with the aid of a ferret, except that the net had been a three-foot-thick sheet of invisible glass dumped across the road, and the ferret had been the two doctors plus a large group of stage extras hired for the day, equipped with uniforms, collecting tins, leaflets and Gideon Bibles.

'How was I to know,' said Pan, inside the tank, bitterly. 'They looked just like real Jehovah's Witnesses to me.'

'We should have stood our ground, in any case,' Osiris

replied. 'You don't just turn tail and run as soon as you see a lot of God-botherers walking up the path.'

'I do. And so, I seem to remember, did you.'

'True.' Osiris nodded sadly. 'Basic inbuilt reflex action.' He scratched his head sadly. 'And another thing,' he went on. 'They call themselves witnesses, but they can't be. They're all too young, for a start.'

The tank was a masterpiece of applied theology. Specially built in Germany, where they still know a thing or two about craftsmanship, to exquisitely precise specifications, it was proofed to withstand internal pressures which would make the Big Bang seem like a car backfiring, while the lining of pulped copies of standard nineteenth-century Nihilist philosophical texts was capable of damping out supernatural manifestations equivalent to 7.9 miracles. Anyone able to get out of there would have to have been capable not only of parting the Red Sea but folding it up like a newly ironed tea towel.

'Well,' Sandra said, 'you'd better hurry up and get us out of here. I really am starving, you know?'

'I'm doing my best,' Osiris replied. 'Who do you think I am?'

'Well . . .'

'Yes, point taken. Any suggestions?'

Sandra considered. Her mythological knowledge was limited to stray particles of legendary matter that had adhered to the fly-paper of her imagination. 'How about turning yourself into a shower of gold?' she suggested.

Pan and Osiris looked at each other, and simultaneously sighed.

'Listen, love,' said Pan. 'Two thousand years ago, no problem. These days, with the best will in the world, I think that at our age, between us, the best we could manage would be a small wad of Italian lire. It's a case,' he explained, 'of the spirit being willing but the currency being weak.'

Sandra wrinkled her nose. 'I see,' she said. 'All right, what about a burning bush? You could cut your way out, like one of those oxy-acetylene torch things.'

'Nah,' Osiris replied, 'that's not us, that's more your Judaeo-Christian touch. Different cultural heritage entirely.'

'Not solar-based,' Pan agreed. 'Completely different technology. Besides, we'd need goggles. We've just got to face facts, we're stuck in this bloody thing until somebody lets us out.'

'Oh yes?' Sandra enquired. 'Who, for instance?'

'Gawd only knows.'

CHAPTER FOURTEEN

L undqvist woke up.
   He found himself in a dark, gloomy cave, rank
with the smell of stale air and rotting vegetation. His arms
and legs were securely bound with thick electric cable;
he was gagged with what tasted like a very old and lonely
sock, and there was a guard with an Armalite rifle sitting
about five yards away, reading a pornographic magazine.

Ah, he said to himself, back to normal. I was beginning to worry back there.

It had been, he reflected, a pretty bad run so far, by
his standards. He'd divided his time on this project so far
between standing about like a bottle of brown sauce at a
state banquet, getting under people's feet and being in
the way (which was bad enough) and being chased, scared
out of his wits, abducted and made to run away (which
was *awful*). He was confused, unarmed and thoroughly
depressed, and he hadn't killed anything except time for
as long as he could remember. The way he'd been feeling,
if a spider had run up his leg he'd probably have tried to
trap it in a matchbox and put it outside the door.

Now, however, things were looking up.

It was the work of a moment to fray through the cable against the rock behind him; a mere bagatelle to chew the sock in half; a trifling inconvenience to roll over, break free from his bonds and stun the guard with one blow. In fact, if he hadn't slipped on (of all things) a banana skin and nutted himself on a low shelf of rock, he'd have been out of there in less than six minutes, thereby shattering for ever the record set by Clignancourt and O'Reilly at the Grande Convention Mondiale des Assassins et Espions Professionels in 1967. As it was, he merely equalled it.

Once outside, with a rifle in his hands and (presumably) people to rescue against overwhelming odds in the face of certain death, he felt much better. His manner as he worked a steady and decidedly businesslike way through the various heavily armed men he found here and there about the place was positively jovial. He smiled as he dodged the hail of bullets from the Browning .50 calibre machine gun mounted on the back of the half-track beside the big grey rectangular box, and grinned as he kicked open the rear cargo doors and beat the occupants into insensibility with the butt of his rifle. Somwhere nearby, he felt sure, he could hear nightingales singing.

Then he caught sight of the two doctors.

Yum, he thought.

Please, he said to himself, please let them open up with a couple of Uzis, so that I can take cover, return fire, lob in a couple of these beautiful stun-grenades I found lying about over by the jeep and then go in with the cold steel. And please let them be wearing Kevlar body armour. And please let them have reinforcements standing by to try and keep me pinned down while I dynamite the lid off that big box thing.

A few helicopters wouldn't come amiss, either.

And so the day went on. The sun shone, bullets flew, plastic explosive detonated, and for once someone somewhere in the world was, for a while at least, completely well-adjusted and happy with his lot. There were, admittedly, only three helicopters; but one of them had an Oerlikon 20mm cannon, which made up for quite a lot, particularly when it crashed.

And finally, to round off a beautifully mellow afternoon, he found a tub of Semtex, blew the lid off the tank, and threw down a rope.

'*The sun has got his hat on* . . . Come on, you guys, it's time to split,' he yelled. 'Grab the rope and let's get our butts outa here . . . *The sun has got his hat on and he's coming out today* . . . Come on, let's *move*!'

In the gloom inside the tank, Osiris stirred and looked up. Someone had just dropped a rope on his head.

'Good grief,' he exclaimed, 'it's that maniac friend of yours. The one who got us all in this mess in the first place.'

Lundqvist froze. He could feel the confidence and *joie de vivre* ebbing away. God, he hated being around gods. They did something to him.

'Took your bloody time, didn't you?' Pan said, yawning and massaging his leg, which had gone to sleep. 'Next time, a bit less of the prancing about shooting at people and more attention to the job in hand, all right?'

'Yeah, okay,' Lundqvist mumbled. 'Look, could you kinda get it moving, because they outnumber us fifteen to one and—'

'Is that all? I thought you did this sort of thing for a living.'

'I do.' Lundqvist ducked as a bullet skimmed off the side of the tank a mere inch from his head. 'I'm doing pretty damn good, if you must know. Now can we—?'

'The shooting bothering you, is it?' asked Osiris ironically. 'Well, we'll see what we can do, shall we? Just a moment. There.'

The shooting stopped.

'Hey,' Lundqvist demanded, 'what happened?'

Osiris smiled. 'I turned them all into frogs,' he replied. 'Now, will somebody please give me a hand with this rope thing?'

'You turned them all into frogs.'

'That's right.'

'Just like that?'

'Piece of cake.'

Lundqvist bit his lip. 'I see,' he said. 'Fine.'

'I mean,' Osiris went on, 'if I'd had to wait for you to finish fiddling about we'd be here all night.'

'Yeah. Right. Thanks.'

'And another thing,' Osiris added, pushing the rope aside and levitating smoothly out of the tank. 'Next time you need rescuing, get somebody else. Take out insurance or something. We're busy people, you know.'

Lundqvist looked down at his rifle, sighed, and threw it away. Never wanted to see another silly old rifle as long as he lived.

'Sorry,' he said.

In the introductory booklet that accompanies his best-selling video, *Kurt Lundqvist's Paranormal Assassination Techniques Workout*, Lundqvist was later to write that 'in ninety-nine cases out of a hundred, actually doing the job on some vampire or ghoul is the piss-easy part; getting there is where the real hassle comes in'. He wrote, obviously, from bitter experience; and some of his biographers pinpoint the journey from Easter Island to the Sinai desert as the crucial catalyst that led him to formulate this justly famous aphorism.

Hijacking a passing destroyer and hitching a forced lift as far as the Solomon Islands was, comparatively speaking, a walkover; it was the scheduled flight to Tel Aviv,

followed by the train journey, followed by the taxi ride
that nearly brought him to his knees. The combination
of Pan's extreme fear of air travel ('If we'd intended
ourselves to fly we'd have given ourselves wings.') and
Osiris' undisguised contempt for all forms of technology
not directly based on magic and superstition, plus such
minor details as their complete lack of either money or
passports, made for a trip that was memorable in the
same way that death is a unique, once-in-a-lifetime
experience.

'Well,' Pan remarked, as they paid off the taxi and lifted
out their luggage, 'here we are. Changed a bit since I was
last—'

'Follows,' Osiris replied. 'Changed a hell of a lot since
I was last here. It's fallen down, for a start. Now, who's
got the rams' horns?'

There are few more evocative place names in the world
than Jericho, and it's hard to know what to expect. The
modern town, snuggled under the mountains, is just a
town – 'the sort of place,' as Sandra observed, 'where you
could probably get a bath and something to eat'. A few
miles beyond, you come to the remains of the massive
stone walls of the ancient city which, so archaeology tells
us, were shaken down by an earthquake some time around
1200 BC.

'It's around here somewhere,' Osiris said, shielding his
eyes against the glare of the sand. 'Exactly where, though,
escapes me for the moment. I always used to get my bearings from Ameneshke's kebab stall, and I think he went
bust about three thousand—'

'Me too,' Pan replied. 'Dunno why, because the old
sod did a mean camel kebab. Besides,' he added, 'the old
place does seem to have fallen down rather, which I find
has a somewhat disorientating effect.' He prodded a pile
of fallen masonry with one toe. 'Hence the expression

'Jerry-built", I guess,' he said. 'Well, you have a poke
about, I'm just going to see if I can't get forty winks under
this bit of shade here.'

He selected a pile of millennia-old rubble, brushed
away some of the dust, and lay down, his head leaning
against a fragment of pillar. It moved.

The scene changed. The landscape changed. For a start,
Pan was now lying on a broken column forty foot up in
the air.

'Ah,' Osiris said, 'you've found it. Good lad.'

The city of Jericho, as observed above, was destroyed by
an earthquake.

This snippet of misinformation emanates from the
same source as the reassurance that flying saucer sight-
ings are all hoaxes, crop circles are caused by modern
fertilizers or unscheduled helicopter landings, ghosts are
all done with mirrors by unscrupulous mediums and the
crew of the *Marie Celeste* abandoned ship as they did
because of a surprise visit from the excise men.

The city of Jericho is still, of course, there; and the
piles of untidy rubble shown to visiting coach parties are
mere camouflage, surreptitiously inserted by a League of
Nations task force under pretence of excavating the site,
shortly after the First World War.

Despite this universal conspiracy of silence (unmasked
in all its Machiavellian deviousness by the late Danny
Bennett in his seminal but hitherto unpublished masterpiece, *The Holy Grail and the Holy Graft*), getting into
Jericho is in fact child's play. All you have to do is . . .

'When you've quite finished,' Osiris called out, 'you can
come down here and do something useful for once.'

Pan, suffering from quasi-terminal agrophobia on a
narrow chunk of rock which would have done St Simeon

Stylites very nicely as a shooting-stick, racked his brain for an appropriately scintillating jewel of repartee.

'Help!' he said.

Lundqvist eventually got him down with the help of a long piece of rope and a few rocks; and the fun began.

To get into Jericho . . . The phrase is misleading. It's more a case of getting Jericho back.

'Because,' Osiris explained to Sandra, as he gave his ram's horn an experimental puff, 'the old place wasn't so much destroyed – how you're supposed to play one of these things I have absolutely no idea – as put away in a safe place so that it wouldn't get lost.'

Sandra squinted. 'How can you lose a city?' she replied.

Osiris grinned. 'Well, the best way is to put it in a safe place and then forget where. In fact, it's about the only way.'

'Ah.'

At the next attempt the ram's horn did indeed make a noise. It was very faint and extremely vulgar, and it made Osiris realise that there was more to this than met the eye. He wondered whether a saxophone would do instead, at a pinch.

'Now I bet you're wondering,' he went on, jabbing about inside the horn with a piece of wire to see if there was anything inside, 'why anyone should want to lose a city. Yes?'

'Well . . .'

'Easy. It's a sort of prison.'

'Right.'

Osiris frowned. 'Well, when I say prison, more a sort of remand centre. For gods.'

Sandra looked up. 'Gods?' she repeated.

Osiris nodded. 'It's all rather sad, actually,' he said. 'Long time ago now, this area was absolutely crawling with gods. Elamite gods, Hittite gods, Phoenician gods,

Philistine gods, Moabite gods, Edomite gods—'

'I thought Edom was a sort of cheese.'

'—Jebusite gods, Hivite gods, Amorite gods, Canaanite gods . . .' Osiris paused, having run out of fingers, '. . . hundreds of the little tinkers, all squabbling and bickering over who could have what and whose drains went under whose driveway and whose hedge was eighteen inches too far to the left, all that sort of thing. Well, it had to stop.'

Sandra, who had learnt a thing or two about gods during her time at Sunnyvoyde, raised an eyebrow. 'Why?' she asked. 'Sounds perfectly normal behaviour for gods, if you ask me.'

'It was letting the side down,' Osiris replied stiffly. 'Mortals were getting involved. Anyway, all the other gods got together and give them an ultimatum: pack it in, or else.'

'And?'

'Else,' Osiris replied grimly. 'They refused to take a blind bit of notice, and so we had to take steps. We locked 'em up.'

Sandra stared at him. 'Put them in jail, you mean?'

Osiris nodded. 'We had no choice, really. They were making a laughing stock—'

'Your own kind? You locked them away, just like that?'

'If there had been any other way . . .'

'Huh!'

Osiris frowned and fidgeted with his ram's horn, in which he had just discovered a mouse nest. 'Anyway,' he said, 'here's where we put them, in Jericho. Then we sort of vanished it.'

'Sort of vanished it.'

'That's right.' Osiris rubbed his eyes. Put this way, it did seem a bit extreme. At the time, though . . . 'Jericho lies on this huge geological fault, you see,' he continued, 'and we just opened it up, dropped the city in and closed it up again. It was only a temporary measure,' he added, catching Sandra's eye, 'just to give the ringleaders, Ashtoreth and Melkart and Mammon and the rest of them, time to patch up their differences and learn to get along with each other like civilised adults.'

'Really.'

'After which,' Osiris continued, red in the face, 'they'd be sort of paroled . . .'

'Let out on Ba'al,' Pan interrupted, strolling up and rubbing Germoline into the rope burns on his hands. 'Never got around to it, though, did you?'

'The time never seemed exactly right, somehow.'

Pan nodded. 'Exactly,' he said. 'The fact that you lot divided up their territories between you was neither here nor there. And neither, of course, were they.'

'I see,' Sandra said. 'And now you're going to let them out again.'

'Strictly on a trial basis.'

Pan grinned. 'He needs a favour,' he explained.

'Does he?' Sandra looked puzzled. 'From a load of gods who've been locked up in a cave for thousands of years? What on earth—?'

'Money.' Pan shrugged. 'What else?'

'They're going to pay him money?' Sandra hazarded. Pan shook his head.

'Not pay money,' he replied, grinning. 'Launder it.'

Once again, Sandra looked surprised; shocked, even. 'Launder it?' she said. 'But isn't that what criminals do? Thieves, and so on?'

'And gods, too,' Pan replied. 'Perfectly ordinary, reputable, divine behaviour. Hence such well-known phrases as "Honour among gods" and "Gods' kitchen" and "Like a god in the night". So—'

'What Pan is trying to say,' Osiris interrupted, 'is that

this is an opportunity for these hitherto troublesome and disruptive members of the divine community to redeem their previous antisocial behaviour by . . .'

Like most superstitions, the concept of widdershins has its origins in very pertinent fact.

As witness . . .

Two gods, one contract killer, one lorry driver and one state registered nurse, all clutching ram's horns, all clumping very self-consciously round and round (widdershins, of course) a frost-damaged basalt pillar in the middle of the desert.

'When I say blow,' Osiris called out, 'blow your horns.'

Pan scowled. 'Who does he think he is?' he muttered, 'Count Basie?'

'Is something going to happen?'

'Wait and see, Carl my old mate,' Pan replied, lifting his horn to his lips and making a noise rather like prrrp.

Tramp, tramp, tramp they went, seven times round the pillar; and to mark the end of each circuit, a fanfare on the horns. There have been louder fanfares, it's true, and more melodious and impressive ones too. But a crummy fanfare is still a fanfare.

'We must be complete idiots, letting ourselves get talked into—'

'Shut up, Pan. Now then,' Osiris said, quickly checking the tally he'd made on his fingers, 'that's seven, so all we have to do now is shout.'

Pan raised an eyebrow. 'Shout what, pray?' he asked.

'I don't know, do I? Anything so long as it's loud.'

'*Sorry*, for instance?'

'If you must, yes.'

'Thanks,' Pan replied. 'Sort of two birds with one stone, really.'

And so the party halted and, feeling right clowns,

shouted. Nothing happened. The echo died away in the desert.

And then the ground shook, and cracks began to form in the sand, giving one the impression that this was a bit of the Earth's crust the creation of which God subcontracted out to a couple of lads He'd met in a pub somewhere. There was dust, and noise and . . . movement.

And the walls of Jericho came tumbling up.

There are gods of every conceivable sort and description in the universe, all of them created, in some way or another, by Mankind in his own image. Most nations subconsciously customise their pantheon to suit their world view and basic needs, and it's largely true that humanity generally gets the gods it deserves.

Thus the Greeks created their gods in order to give names, faces and addresses to various oversize notions banging away inside their brains. The Hindus shaped their gods in order to ensure that in times of trouble there'd always be Someone standing by to lend a helping hand (or, indeed, hands; in extreme cases arms, in large quantities) whereas the various Middle Eastern ethnic groups responsible for the gaggle of divine beings locked up in Jericho (if the theory is correct) fleshed out their immortal beliefs purely and simply to tie in with some urgent need of the tribe; quite likely the need to believe, with good reason, that however daft they may look, however nastily they behave, they're still a bunch of choirboys compared with the everlasting gods.

This is probably the most useful thing a god can do for his people; but, job satisfaction aside, it doesn't have very much to recommend it. Not if you have to live, for ever and ever, with the consequences.

*   *   *

'And that,' said Osiris, 'is Jericho.'

'Um,' Sandra replied. She wasn't sure that she liked the look of it much. Certainly it wasn't anything like the picture in the *Illustrated Children's Bible* she'd doodled all over in Sunday school; for one thing the version depicted by the artist hadn't had so many searchlights, barbed wire entanglements and machine-gun emplacements. Nor had there been a big signpost with a skull and crossbones on it reading MINEFIELD – DO NOT ENTER right in front of the main gate.

'I gather,' Pan remarked in a conversational tone, 'that they've been digging an escape tunnel for the last three thousand years. Hasn't got very far, though.'

'No?'

Pan shook his head. 'Dimensions inside a geological fault get a bit muddled,' he explained. 'Damn thing kept on coming out slap bang in the middle of the same tunnel a week after they started digging. The diggers from the future were able to tell the diggers from the past not to bother after all. This,' he added with a grin, 'led to all sorts of problems, as you can imagine.'

Sandra preferred not to. 'Sorry if I've missed something,' she said, 'but aren't they going to be a bit – well, fed up after all this time? I mean, when we open the gates and go in and . . .'

Pan shuddered. 'Not bloody likely,' he said. 'No way we're going to let any of them out until . . . Oh for crying out loud, what's the stupid old fool think he's doing now?'

Osiris, pushed by Carl, was speeding towards the main gate, weaving an apparently perfectly remembered course through the minefield. In his hand he held a big bronze key.

'Can't you stop him?' Sandra hissed.

Pan smiled. 'No,' he said. 'What a pity.'

*　　*　　*

Knock. Knock. Knock. Knock.

'Who's there?'

'Osiris.'

'Osiris who?'

'Stop pissing about, you pea-brain, and let me in.'

A panel in the gate shot back and a hideous face was glimpsable for about half a second. Half a second would be approximately four hundred and ninety-six milliseconds too long.

'No, that's not it,' said a voice from the face. 'That doesn't sound right at all.'

'I said open this door, you—'

'I think,' continued the voice, 'you mean Osiris walkin' down the lane, All in the month of May—'

'Sabre-toothed ponce, or I'll make you wish . . .'

'Or maybe it was Osiris eyes are smiling,' continued the voice. 'It was something like that. Not a very good one, anyway.'

Osiris closed his eyes and counted up to ten. This wasn't to help him calm down and keep his temper. Quite the opposite.

'Hang on,' said the voice, 'isn't it, A kiss is just a kiss, Osiris just a sigh, The fundamental thi—?'

'*Right!*'

There was a flash of lightning, a peal of thunder, and a very loud crash; and the door came away from its hinges and fell. A second later, a small, weary voice was audible from somewhere underneath where it had landed.

'Okay,' it said. 'Anybody spot my deliberate mistake?'

'Ah.' The doorfiend, now visible in all his biological improbability through the vacant doorway, scratched his head. 'It was deliberate, was it? Because I thought to myself, when the hinges melted and then the door started to fall *outwards*, I thought—'

'Shut up and get me out of here.'

The doorfiend swiftly obliged, lifting Osiris out of a god-sized hole he'd been hammered into by the sudden descent of several hundred tons of wrought bronze gate.

'What was the name again?' asked the fiend.

Osiris told him.

'Coo!' said the fiend, grinning. 'I wouldn't go letting them in here find out, 'cos that's the same name as the little shit who's responsible for all this, and they might just think you were him.'

'Might they?'

The fiend nodded. 'And that'd be bad news,' he went on, ''cos really the only thing they do to help them pass the time is planning what they're gonna do to him, the real Osiris, I mean, when they get out.'

'Let me guess. Buy him dinner?'

'No.'

'Flowers?'

'Not unless you count sharpened bamboo poles as flowers, no.'

Osiris shrugged. 'Never mind, he said. 'Now then, which way to the Governor's office?'

Knock. Knock. Knock.

'Who's there?'

'It's me, Governor.'

'No, I'm the Governor, who are you?'

Osiris, having made some passing comment about crying out loud, blew open the door (this time not repeating the deliberate mistake; with the result that the door fell heavily on the doorfiend, driving him fence-postlike eight inches into the ground).

'Bloody hell fire. You!'

Osiris smiled pleasantly. 'Ba'al, my old mate,' he said, extending a hand. 'Long time no see and all that. I see they made you a trusty, then.'

534 • Tom Holt

'You?'

'Nice office you've got here. Splendid view of the . . .' Osiris craned his neck. 'Of the exercise yard, well, that's wonderful. You always were fond of sport, I seem to remember.'

'You!'

'It's a funny thing,' Osiris went on, wheeling himself in and taking a cigar from the box on the desk. 'I was just thinking to myself the other day, I wonder how my old friend Ba'al's getting along these days. And that set me thinking, of course, about the old times. You remember the old times? Of course you do.'

'You . . .'

Osiris lit the cigar, inhaled, and coughed. 'And I thought,' he went on, 'it's never right, I thought, my dear old chum Ba'al locked up in there with a load of criminals and undesirables, there must be something I can do, see if we can't get him out on parole or whatever, I mean, what's the use of having power and influence if you can't—?'

'. . . *bastard!*'

'And so,' Osiris said, 'here I am. Got a little deal to put to you which might—'

'*CALL OUT THE GUARD!*'

'—interest you.'

'Right,' said Ba'al, rubbing his hands together. 'Any suggestions?'

The packed dining hall echoed with shouting voices. There were nine hundred and six gods jammed into a space designed to hold three hundred gods in modest discomfort. During their long imprisonment, the gods and goddesses of ancient Palestine hadn't exactly been idle.

'One at a time, now,' Ba'al shouted, waving his arms.

'Best of order, ladies and gentlemen, please. You at the back there, Mammon. I think you were first.'

Osiris, bound hand and foot in the middle of the throng, smiled serenely. This was better than he had dared hope.

'Well,' said the god at the back, 'it's got to be the oil, hasn't it. Thirty years up to his neck in boiling oil, I mean, we did discuss this in committee . . .'

'Tar.'

'I beg your pardon?'

'The chair,' yelled Ba'al forlornly, 'recognises Tanith, Queen of Darkness.'

'It was tar, you silly old fool,' said Tanith irritably. 'We put it to the vote, remember, and it was five hundred and thirteen for tar, three hundred and forty-three for oil, fifty abstaining.'

'It was not, it was oil. I distinctly remember asking where we are going to get that much oil from.'

'Pitch, you daft old cow. When we took the vote, tar hadn't even been invented.'

'Not to mention,' Mammon continued, 'fuel efficiency. To maintain tar at a constant one hundred degrees Celsius—'

'Tar, pitch, does it really matter? The point is—'

'The point is,' shouted Melkart, a short, fat god with hairy ears, 'twelve minutes in oil, the bugger'll be fried to a crisp and that'll be that, whereas with tar—'

'Thank you,' Ba'al bellowed, 'but I think we had this debate before. Will someone just look up the minutes?'

'What minutes?'

'The minutes of the—'

'I think you'll find there aren't any. I remember saying—'

'Are you telling me there aren't any minutes?'

'The chair recognises—'

'And you can shut your face and all, you daft old—'

Ba'al scowled. 'Hoy,' he growled, 'this is a democratic—'

'Since when? We're gods, aren't we?'

'Excuse me.'

Dead silence, instantaneously. It must have been, Ba'al later reflected, the way he said it.

'Thank you.' Osiris cleared his throat. 'I just wanted to say,' he went on, 'that if any of you want to get out of here – ever – then this is probably your last chance.' He paused; still silence. 'And if I were you, I'd hold the oil just for a while.'

'Not oil. Pitch.'

'Whatever.' Osiris frowned in the general direction of the heckler, and then continued. 'First,' he said, 'outside this building I have a crack team of commandos, led by someone whose name is, I feel sure, familiar to many of you . . .'

'*Lundqvist,*' someone whispered, at the back of the hall. '*He must mean Kurt Lundqvist.*' Osiris was impressed.

'Secondly,' he went on, 'the reason I'm here today is purely and simply to offer you imbeciles . . .' He paused, letting the word hang in the air. Good, he reflected, as the silence persisted, I've got 'em. '. . . imbeciles the chance of a free pardon. If you do exactly what you're told, of course. If not . . .'

The silence lingered; mellowed; ripened. And then was broken.

'I still say it was oil. I mean, boiling tar, just think of the smell . . .'

'*Sssssh!*'

It is a terrible thing to be shushed by nine hundred and five gods simultaneously. The nearest precedent is probably the piecemeal tearing of Orpheus by the Thracian Women; except that piecemeal tearing is, comparatively speaking, quick and painless. Torn piece-meal, you don't find yourself still waking up years later at three in the morning, sweating and pink to the ears with embarrassment.

'Hush, please!' Ba'al banged with his gavel for silence and smiled weakly at Osiris, who nodded affably back. 'Sorry about that,' he said politely. 'Please, do go on.'

'The way we do it,' said Ba'al, 'is this.'

Osiris nodded politely. 'Ah,' he said. 'Yes.' To the gods all things are possible, but some of them are still bloody difficult; for example, keeping your eyelids from fore-closing when someone is explaining to you how to operate a complex bond-washing deal on a five-dimensional stock exchange.

'You've heard,' Ba'al's voice was saying, 'of selling forward, like in exchange rate and commodity trans-actions? Well, that's basically what we do here, except we sell back. It's really pretty straightforward . . .'

Creak, creak, creak went the drawbridges of Osiris' eyes, and the strain of keeping up so much weight unsup-ported is pretty extreme, particularly if you're trying to stay awake at the same time. 'Good Lord,' Osiris heard himself say, 'isn't that clever.' He hoped, vaguely, that the context was right.

'. . . Whereupon the brokers *backwards* in time, who are of course selling their stocks of gold *forward* against early settlement in a bull market, buy *retrospectively* so as to get the advantage of the reverse exchange rate differ-ential, which washes out the coupon, resulting in a very useful capital loss for tax purposes. And it's at precisely this point that we step in and buy *forward*, on a *bear* market, thereby . . .'

'Really.' If Macbeth really did murder sleep, Osiris mumbled dreamily to himself, I can quite believe that he was provoked beyond endurance. 'Now that you've explained it,' he hazarded, 'it all seems so very simple.' He smiled.

'It is,' Ba'al replied, nodding. 'And of course the effect is redoubled if you then sell back through a parallel universe, creating a Doppler effect on the commodities markets in this universe while still getting your settlement ex div *over there*.' He paused; and an allegorically minded artist, requiring a model for Smugness, need have looked no further. 'All my own idea,' he said, 'and completely legal and above board. Mind you,' he added in a whisper, 'it can have side-effects, like the San Francisco earthquake of 1906, but you can't make omelettes, can you?'

'Hmm?' Osiris woke up suddenly from a short but vivid dream involving stuffed crocodiles. 'Tricky,' he answered. 'I always find it helps stop them sticking if you whisk up the yolks in an egg-cup first.'

'Quite. Well, I'd better be making a start, hadn't I?'

'Absolutely.'

Ba'al smiled. 'Strictly speaking, of course,' he said, 'I already have. That's the joy of it, so little paperwork.' Then he laughed, indicating that that had been a funny, albeit technical, joke.

'Ha ha,' Osiris therefore said. 'Look, roughly how long will this take, because I have people waiting.'

'Ten minutes.'

'That's fine.'

'Or seventy-three years, of course, depending on temporal refraction. We'll probably get a slightly better rate if we wait for the upturn in the fiscal sinewave.'

'Oh, let's keep it short and sweet,' Osiris replied. 'Just so long as we get there in the end.'

'You're the boss.'

'Am I?'

'Yes.'

'Oh good.'

Ba'al turned to the computer console on the desk in front of him and tapped precisely four keys. 'Cup of tea while we're waiting?'

'That would be nice, thank you.'

'Milk and sugar?'

'Just milk, thanks.'

Ten minutes exactly later, the door opened and a minor demon came in with a silver tray, on which rested a small rectangular slip of paper. Ba'al picked it up, glanced at it and handed it over.

'Bearer bond,' he said. 'Best way, we always find.'

Osiris looked down at the paper. It was heavy paper, apparently composed of five per cent wood-pulp, ninety-five per cent watermarks, and the printing made his eyes hurt. In among all the squiggles, he could make out Gothic lettering, as follows:

BANK OF HELL

SEVENTY-FIVE DOLLARS

Seventy-five dollars?'

Ba'al nodded. 'We caught the market at its absolute crest,' he said contentedly. 'I mean, in financial terms you're holding the ultimate Doomsday device, because there just isn't enough real money in the cosmos to cover it. Just wave it under a bank teller's nose and *kerbang!* there goes the economy of the solar system down the pan.'

'I see.' Osiris scratched his head, making a noise like fingernails on a blackboard. 'The, um, Hell dollar's pretty strong at the moment, then?'

There was a peculiar noise; Ba'al sniggering. 'That's a good one,' he said. 'I must remember that. Anyway, as I was saying, it doesn't actually matter so long as the money never leaves the system. I mean, it can be capitalised and written off over the years, there shouldn't be a problem. Well, very nice doing business with you.'

Osiris gripped the handrails of his chair. 'Likewise,' he said. 'And no, er, hard feelings?'

'Hard feelings?' Ba'al looked at him. 'About what?'

'About you and your friends being locked up here for the last—'

'Oh that.' Ba'al shrugged. 'I should think this makes up for it, don't you? I mean, our commission on this deal's a fiftieth of a per cent, so we aren't grumbling, are we? I think we can say that leaves us quits.'

'Oh good. And now of course,' Osiris added, 'you're free to go.'

'Yes.' Ba'al hesitated. 'I suppose so, quite. Actually,' he went on, looking slightly to one side, 'we've been thinking about that.'

'So I gathered.'

'No, not like that.' Ba'al bit his lip. 'About whether we should in fact leave or alternatively, well, stay.'

'*Stay?*'

'The thought did cross our minds, yes,' Ba'al replied sheepishly. 'Because of being offshore, you see.'

'Offshore?'

'Sort of offshore. Being in a different dimension, you see, it means we can offer our clients a distinct tax advantage.'

'You can?'

'We believe so, yes. On the basis of, if we don't exist, then how can we pay tax?'

Osiris rubbed his chin. 'Well,' he said, 'there's a sort of specious logic there, I suppose. But surely—'

'It was Mammon's idea,' Ba'al continued. 'Ever since he got out of human sacrifice and into financial services there's been no holding him. No, I think we'll stay as we are, thank you all the same.'

'Fair enough.' Osiris folded the paper carefully and put it away in his top pocket. 'I'll be saying goodbye for now, then. Thanks again.'

'Don't mention it,' Ba'al said. 'Any time. Oh, and could you lower the walls again when you leave?'

'It'll be a pleasure,' Osiris replied.

In his office, Julian leant back in his chair and scowled.

Things, he felt, were getting out of hand; and that always annoyed him. In his view, a perfect universe was one where he had everything firmly in hand, preferably with his thumb jammed hard against its windpipe. At present, however, things were far from perfect.

The latest update on the Teletext showed a colossal rise in share prices, fed by rumours of a massive input of some huge but unspecified quantity of wealth from an uncertain source. Added to this he had in front of him the latest report from his medical advisers, which wasn't exactly hopeful. The clowns had lost him. Again. This time, apparently, on Easter Island, which was in itself peculiar. Until now, Julian wasn't aware that there was anything you could lose on Easter Island, no matter how hard you tried.

And what exactly was the old fool up to? That was the question he kept coming back to, and still he couldn't fathom it. Was he just running aimlessly away? In which case he was going about it in a distinctly peculiar manner. True, he had so far succeeded amazingly well; but that could be explained away entirely in terms of the complete and utter brainlessness of his chosen contractors. Osiris was up to something. But what?

What would I do if I was in his position?

Well, said Julian to himself as he absent-mindedly

flicked through the franchise agreement on the desk in front of him, here adding a few noughts, there crossing out a paragraph, if I were in his shoes I'd find myself a bloody good lawyer, ha ha.

A bloody good lawyer . . .

But . . .

Surely not.

Suddenly, with the depressing inevitability of a car approaching at ninety miles an hour when you've just got your heel stuck in a grating as you cross the road, Julian could feel the pieces clicking smartly into place. The running about. The ducking and diving. The sudden pressing need for fabulously vast sums of money. All entirely consistent with going to consult a lawyer.

But who?

Not just a good lawyer, he mused, but the best. And there is only ever one best at a time; not that the post falls vacant very often. Ever since the legal profession began, there had only ever been one best. So far as he was aware – and if the situation had changed he'd have heard, just as the news of the end of the world would have filtered through to him somehow – the best was still the best; reclusive, all but retired from practice, but still occasionally coming out of retirement to kick the spines of young pretenders up through their ears. When it came to putting on the writs, there was only one master.

And if Osiris has gone to see him, Julian reflected, then it's time for a drastic change of approach. Like now.

He picked up the phone.

'Get me those two idiots,' he said.

CHAPTER FIFTEEN

'A nd what,' said Teutates, the warrior god of the ancient Celts, 'the hell is this supposed to be?'

'Rice pudding.'

Bearing in mind their unlimited power and total lack of accountability, gods are generally extremely tolerant. You can burn their temples, rape their priestesses, massacre their suppliants in the sanctuary of their holy altars, with no worse consequences than a slight upward movement of the all-seeing eyebrow. But there are limits. Gods are, after all, only human.

'Go on, eat it up,' continued the waitress. 'You like rice pudding.'

Still waters run deep; the only visible reaction from Teutates was a slight crinkling of his brow. 'You reckon?' he said.

'Look, it's getting cold and I've got all the rest of the dinners to do. You don't want me to have to get Mrs Henderson.'

Like soldiers in riots, war gods are obliged to go through certain set procedures before letting rip. Procedure one: try calm, conciliatory negotiation.

'No,' Teutates snarled, 'you look, you raddled old boiler. Either you take this pigswill away and bring me a bloody great hunk of Stilton and a box of Ritz crackers, or tonight you go home in a matchbox. Kapisch?'

This, by divine standards, is calm, conciliatory negotiation verging on wimpishness. The waitress tutted.

'Don't you use that tone of voice with me,' she replied sniffily, 'or I'll tell Mrs . . .'

Procedure two: fair warning. 'Okay, prune-face, go ahead and try it. I can't turn you into a frog because by the looks of you someone's beaten me to it, but I'm sure I'll think of something else just as appropriate.'

'That does it. Mrs Henderson!'

Procedure three: there is no procedure three.

'Mrs Henderson,' said the waitress, 'Mr Teutates is being very rude to me and he won't eat up his nice keekee-keekeekeekeekee.'

It was, in all fairness, pretty slickly done and Mrs Henderson, who had seen many such phenomena over the years, couldn't quite manage to keep the overtones of grudging admiration out of her voice.

'Thank you, Mr Teutates,' she nevertheless said, 'that'll be quite enough of that, thank you very much. Now, would you please turn Mrs Hill back into her proper shape before you put the other residents off their food.'

Teutates grinned. 'That is her proper shape,' he replied. 'Stands to reason. I've said it a hundred times, Mrs Hill's really a polecat turned into a human and it's high time someone turned her back. Ask anybody.'

'Mr Teutates . . .'

'I'm not blaming you. Must be really difficult getting staff on the wages you pay. Still, like they say, if you pay peanuts you must expect to employ monkeys. That,' he added darkly, 'can also be arranged.'

'That will do.' Mrs Henderson drew her eyebrows

together, creating a formation fully as intimidating as an advancing battalion of the Imperial Guard. 'Now I've warned you about this before, and . . .'

She stopped, struggling to regain her balance. The force of the attack, the sheer malevolence, had taken her by surprise.

'Mr *Teutates*!'

It had been a long time – oh, over forty years – since one of her residents had tried to turn her into something, and never in all her experience in the residential care business had anyone ever tried to metamorphose her into one of *those*. Quite obviously there was something going on here.

Something that had to be sorted out. Just for now, though, best to play it cool.

'Really, Mr Teutates, you know better than that.' She folded her arms and gave Teutates the Number One cold stare. 'Honestly, I'd have thought you'd have more sense, at your age.'

Teutates nodded curtly, admitting that she had a point. Quite understandably given the nature of her position, Mrs Henderson was hexed about with enough protective charms, amulets, written undertakings and runes of power to withstand a direct hit from an atomic bomb. Low voltage transmigration spells bounced off her like tennis balls off a dreadnought.

'I do not,' Teutates said slowly, 'like rice pudding. Understood?'

'Now, then,' said Mrs Henderson, shaken but firm, 'of course you like rice pudding. It's good for you.'

Teutates glowered at her. 'Listen, missus,' he growled. 'In the beginning I created the Heavens and the Earth out of the curds left at the bottom of the churn of Eternity. Singlehanded I subdued the Wolves of Famine, the Three-headed Dragon of Pestilence and the Wild Dogs of Death.

I can count the stars in the sky, the sands on the seashore and the days that are past. Stands to reason I can make up my own mind whether I like rice pudding or not. And I don't. You got that, or shall I write it down for you?'

'Oh.' Mrs Henderson hesitated. There was definitely something here she didn't understand; she could sense it, and it disturbed her. 'Then why didn't you say so before, you silly man?' she rallied bravely.

'I did.'

'Be that as it may,' Mrs Henderson said, 'that's no reason why poor Mrs Hill should have to be a polecat. I must insist that you turn her back at once.'

Teutates considered his options. On the one hand he was a war god, and he hadn't felt this good in nineteen centuries. On the other hand, he had to go on living here, because he had nowhere else to go; and one of the first rules you learn when you're a war god is, Don't take work home with you.

'Do a deal,' he said. 'No more rice pudding ever again and the polecat walks.'

There was a pause.

'Certainly,' said Mrs Henderson, putting a smile on her face with the same ease as one spreads butter still rock-hard from the fridge on to newly baked bread. 'You only had to ask, you know. We always bend over backwards to make life as pleasant as possible for all our residents.'

As she escorted the newly restored Mrs Hill back to the staff room for a nice lie down and a slice or two of raw liver (there's always a brief period of readjustment after a metamorphosis) Mrs Henderson came to a firm conclusion.

Something was badly wrong, and she didn't know what.

Something would have to be done about that.

*　　*　　*

The first really ominous thing that Osiris and his companions came across on what was, they fervently hoped, the last leg of the journey was a big notice nailed to a tree. It said, in big capitals:

YOU DON'T HAVE TO BE DEAD TO ENTER HERE, BUT IT HELPS

and below, in small italics:

PS All hope to be abandoned prior to entry. Please help keep eternity tidy by placing your hope in the receptacles provided.

'That's all right,' Pan commented, 'I haven't got any with me anyway. How about the rest of you?'

Nobody said anything; but nobody made an effort to abandon anything either; and into the valley of death trudged the five.

'Is where we're going hard to get to?' Sandra asked.

'To get to, no problem,' Pan replied. 'To get out of is an entirely different proposition. In theory, Ozzie and I have sort of implied return tickets – well, season tickets, really – but what I always say is, theory is fine in theory. As for you three, *if* I was in your shoes I'd be using them to get out of here fast. This place,' he summarised, 'gives me the creeps.'

'It does?'

'Always has.'

Sandra raised an eyebrow. 'You've been here before, then?'

'A couple of times, yes. Trade delegations, diplomatic junkets, that sort of thing.'

'You got out all right then, didn't you?'

Pan shrugged. 'It was different,' he replied. 'Those times, I was meant to be there. They gave me one of those little plastic badges you pin on your lapel that says who you are. You've no idea how comforting it is having one of them when you're down among the dead men.'

Thus far, the environment had been fairly normal, if not exactly welcoming. From Reykjavik they had caught the scheduled bus north as far as Thingvellir, and thence by a succession of progressively older and more decrepit minibuses up into Vididal. The last conveyance, which had been held together by insulating tape and force of habit, had shaken itself to bits ten miles back, since when they had dragged themselves over rocks and past the messy dribblings of volcanoes, taking it in turns to push the wheelchair, until they had arrived . . .

. . . Well, here; wherever the hell (so to speak) it was. It consisted of a cave in a cliff, which someone had rather half-heartedly tried to disguise as the result of perfectly natural seismic activity. There was a marked smell of sulphur, brimstone and stale vinegar.

Lundqvist shifted his rucksack on his back and suppressed an urge to whimper. His work had taken him to some pretty unpleasant places – the mountain lair of Mazdrhahn, King of Bats, being one example that stuck in his memory, the Los Angeles sewer network another – but while those places had been terrifying, nauseating, spine-melting et cetera, none of them had ever come anywhere close to this in sheer unmitigated dreariness. He also felt virtually nude, armed as he was with little more than a Macmillan .50BMG rifle, a .454 Casull revolver, an Ingrams sub-machine gun custom-chambered for .44 Magnum and a big sack full of hand grenades; which was the basic minimum as far as he was concerned, the sort of things he stuffed in his dressing-gown pockets if he had to get up in the night for a pee (for his motto had always been not so much *Have gun, will travel as Haven't gun, won't*). What he really needed in this context, he felt sure, was a squadron of main battle tanks, tactical air support, two divisions of special forces and, for choice, his mummy.

'This is it, huh?' he asked, trying to keep his voice gruffly baritone and failing.

'Sort of,' Osiris replied, aggravatingly chirpy. 'Tradesmen's entrance, really. This is the laundry chute.'

Lundqvist did a double-take. 'Laundry?'

'Oh yes,' Osiris replied airily. 'Guards' uniforms, bedlinen, tablecloths, winding-sheets, that sort of thing. They used to do it in-house but now they use a lot of outside contractors. That's why,' he added, jerking this thumb at the mysterious laundry basket thing they'd been taking it in turns to lug over the rocks and mountains, 'we need that.'

'I was wondering when you'd explain about that,' Pan said. 'What is it, exactly?'

'It's a laundry basket.'

'And what's in it?'

'Laundry.'

'I see.'

'It's our cover.'

'I thought he said it was laundry.'

'Shut up, Carl.'

'It's a freshly laundered cover,' Pan explained. 'Has to be dry-cleaned to get the bloodstains out.'

'What bloodstains?'

'Ignore him, everyone. Now,' Osiris went on, 'if you open the lid you'll find some uniforms. White coats, that sort of thing. Also, like I said, lots of pillow-cases, table-napkins, socks and the like. When you've got into the uniforms, I want you to put me in the basket and carry me through the doorway. And try and look natural, all right?'

A few minutes later, the procession found itself in total

darkness, which was a blessing in fairly transparent disguise; anything you could see in a tunnel like that would probably keep you awake at nights for several years. The way the floor crunched underfoot was particularly evocative.

'It's all right him saying act natural,' Pan grumbled, 'but it's not as easy as that. I've been trying to do it all my life and I've never quite seemed to get the hang of it . . .'

The floor shook. To those of the party who had never experienced anything of the kind, it was an eerie moment; not violent, certainly not enough to shake you off your feet, but quite remarkably disorientating; rather like being told by your mother that she never really liked you anyway. And then the lights came on.

Not much to see, but what there was of it wasn't precisely reassuring. A huge wooden doorway, without a door; and nothing but shadows and a heavy smell of something unpleasant (but extremely familiar).

'Oh balls,' Pan muttered. 'I'd forgotten all about this bit. I still maintain we should have gone to the seaside again. Even Weymouth would be better than—'

'Hey,' Lundqvist interrupted. 'What goes on here, then?'

Osiris chuckled. 'You don't know?' he said. 'Read what it says over the door.'

Lundqvist did as he said, and saw the words:

BEWARE OF THE DOG

The fact that none of the three mortals turned and fled at this stage only goes to show what a disadvantage it is to try and make out in life without the inestimable benefit of a classical education.

'That's it, is it?' Lundqvist said, and relief slugged it

out with disappointment for control of his voice. 'A dog. Hell, for a minute there you had me wor—'

Enter the Dog.

'Gaskets?'

'Yes.'

'Cotter pins?'

'Yes.'

'Camchains?'

'Yes.'

'Tappet return springs?'

'Yes.'

'Reciprocating mainshaft lubricator baffles?'

'Yes.'

'Mendelssohn cables?'

'Yes.'

'Cigar lighter?'

'*Yes!*'

Thor shrugged. 'Okay, then,' he said. 'Fire her up.'

The engine quivered, chugged, roared, raced and died. Thor and Frey looked at each other.

'I take it,' Thor said pleasantly, 'that you did remember to put some coal in the furnace.'

'Ah.' Odin frowned. 'There's always something, isn't there?'

'Not always, no. Only when you have anything to do with it.'

Odin ignored that, and shovelled some coal into the firebox. A few minutes later the engine quivered, chugged, roared, raced and then went catumple-catumple-catumple quietly under its breath.

'Right,' said Thor, 'and off we go.'

Slowly but with gathering momentum, the enormous engine rolled forward and thundered across the improvised jungle runway. It took it rather longer than anticipated; but the environmentally aware can rest assured that none of the trees flattened as it cut a swathe through the virgin forest was an endangered hardwood, and most of them were run-of-the-mill renewable resource softwoods.

'I'm sorry if this is a silly question,' Frey shouted, pulling bits of twig out of his beard, 'but this time are we sure we know where we're going?'

'Yes.'

'Why?'

'Because,' Thor called back, 'this time I'm navigating. All right?'

'Yes. I feel better now.'

'Thought you'd say that.' Thor glanced down at the map on his knees, consulted the position of the sun and nodded approvingly. 'Now then,' he said, 'those hills over there are quite definitely the Pennines, so that down there must be Leeds, and in another five minutes or so we'll see the M6 directly below us.'

Slowly, ponderously, in its own unique way magnificently, the giant traction engine flew on across the Amazon jungle.

'It's not,' hissed Pan, backing away, 'quite as bad as it seems.'

'No?'

'No. It's still pretty bad, but not that bad.'

'Ah.'

The Dog, also known as Cerberus and the Hound of Hell, rolled its six eyes and bared its three pairs of teeth, but stayed where it was. The massive iron chain fastened to the collar that surrounded the place just below where the three necks diverged probably had some influence on this, but probably not a decisive one. The chain hadn't been forged which could withstand a determined tug from Cerberus.

'Basically,' Pan went on, trying to back behind the laundry basket but finding it hard because all the space was already taken, 'it's just another official. A civil servant, if you like. Only doing its job, and all that.'

'Really.'

'Really. That explains why it says everything in triplicate.' Pan tried to sidle an extra few microns in the direction of relative safety and tripped over his own feet. 'Good boy,' he mumbled.

'Okay,' said Lundqvist, 'you guys just leave this to me.'

With the deftness of long practice he heeled a round into the chamber of the Macmillan. Bloody great big animals with teeth were what he was good at, and the combination of his skill and experience and six hundred and fifty grains of jacketed hollow-pointed bullet flying at three thousand feet a second ought, he reasoned with himself, to give him the slight edge that, in the final analysis, makes all the difference.

He stood up, took aim and fired. The bullet sang in the air for a fraction of a second too small to quantify on even the most modern equipment, and hit the Dog more or less where the heart should have been.

And bounced off.

The second, third and fourth bullets landed within half a minute of angle of the first, were flattened into thin lead and copper discs, and fell to the ground. The fifth went high, ricocheted off the Dog's collar, cannoned backwards and forwards down the passageway, and embedded itself in a large nugget of hard quartz sunk into the wall. The chips of stone thereby caused would, if properly cut, have made the Kohinoor look like the tip of a very cheap industrial glasscutter.

The grenades weren't much more use, either; and all the armour-piercing rocket that constituted Lundqvist's ultimate rainy-day backup managed to achieve was to cut the chain neatly in two. The Dog, deprived of the chain's support, lurched forward a pace or so, and growled.

'Don't be such a lot of babies,' remarked a voice, apparently inside the basket. 'They're far more afraid of you than you are of them.'

'In which case,' Pan replied, 'the poor thing must be absolutely fucking terrified. Doesn't look it, though.'

'Talk to it,' urged the voice. 'Firmly. Let it know who's the boss.'

By now there were flecks of foam on the Dog's jaw; exactly the same amount in precisely the same place on each of its three heads. It had its eye, or four of them at least, on Lundqvist's neck.

'There, boy. Sit.'

The Dog sat. After a breathless second, it wagged its tail, panted and held out one paw.

'I think,' said Carl, 'he wants to shake hands. Don't you, boy?'

'Excuse me.'

'Yeah?'

Pan swallowed and pointed. 'You sure this is working?' he asked.

Carl nodded. 'I'm used to dogs, see,' he explained. 'My sister in Neath, she's got a dog. Bigger'n this one, too.'

Two gods and two mortals stared at him as if he'd just pulled a blackcurrant and kirsch gateau out of his ear. The Dog, meanwhile, had produced three identical rubber bones out of nowhere and was offering them to Carl with the air of an envoy trying to interest Tamburlaine the Great in a spot of tribute.

'Here,' said Carl, 'fetch.'

He stooped down, picked up a stone and hurled it away. From the outer darkness there came an indignant cry. The Dog picked up its feet and scampered away, its tail thrashing like an amphetamine-crazed metronome.

'It's gone,' said Carl. 'We can go on now.'

Pan and Osiris looked at each other.

'So that's why we brought him,' said Pan, his voice heavy with enlightenment. 'I knew there had to be a reason, what with us being gods and all that.'

'Suppose so, yes.'

'We must have foreseen the Dog, or something.'

'Must have done.'

'Aren't we clever.'

'Very.'

Pan nodded. 'Absolutely bloody brilliant,' he said. 'Now, let's get out of here before it comes back.'

It was, they found, the sort of tunnel or corridor that grows on you less and less the further down it you go. It was still as dark as three feet up a drain, but by now their eyes were getting used to it, showing thereby a degree of zeal that was quite uncalled for in the circumstances; and the ill-defined shapes that loomed up at them through the darkness as they passed weren't the sort of thing you like to be in the same frame of reference with, let alone the same narrow, winding, slippery-floored, underground passage.

'Can you smell something?' Osiris asked.

'Kippers.'

'Which of you said that?'

'I did.'

'Yes, thank you, Carl, I'd rest on your laurels for a bit if I were you. Look, can anyone beside me smell a sort of deserty stable smell?'

'I can.'

'And which one of you said—?'

'Me.'

'Thanks. And who's me?'

The lights went on . . .
'Me,' repeated the camel.

'Our demands,' said Teutates, his tone of voice belying his air of confidence, 'are as follows. One, we want . . .'

The wind howled, bringing with it small, hard bullets of rain that bit into the back of his neck. It was also, he couldn't help noticing, a long way to the ground, even for a god like himself. He tried to huddle down a few millimetres further into his dressing-gown.

'I do wish you'd all stop being such sillies and come down from there,' replied the voice of Mrs Henderson, blared metallically through a megaphone. 'You'll catch your deaths of cold in this weather.'

Teutates steeled his heart. About ninety-three per cent of him by volume (ninety-five per cent by weight) wanted to capitulate, scramble back down the ladder and wrap itself round a big bacon sandwich and a steaming mug of hot chocolate. The other seven (or five) per cent of him, however, being the parts of the brain i/c policy formation, held the casting vote.

'We stay,' Teutates shouted back. 'You want us; come and get us.'

'Please yourselves,' Mrs Henderson megaphoned back. 'As I always say to guests when they first arrive, so long as accounts are settled promptly and you don't upset other residents, this is Liberty Hall. I'll see you at dinner, I hope.'

'Our demands,' Teutates yelled, 'are, like I said, straightforward. First, we want a fast car, and a doctor, and two million gold zlotys, and . . .'

(*'Did he say he was a doctor?'*

'I don't think so.'

'I need a doctor for my leg. It's like a sort of cramp, just here, whenever I bend my knee. Are you a doctor, too?')

The great sit-in on the roof of Sunnyvoyde had started off with at least one bang and a wide selection of the very latest crashes, quality bespoke sound effects you can be proud of. Twenty-four hours later, there was just Teutates, Nkulunkulu, the Great Sky God of the Zulus, and a small, unidentified hairy deity of no apparent usefulness and incapable of saying anything other than 'Uk!'. By the look of him he was probably a vegetation spirit from the Maldives, but it was just possible that he was a reporter or something in disguise. Most of the time he slept.

'Our demands,' shouted Teutates hopelessly. As the wind ate his words and the rain finally found a narrow accessway down the back of his collar, he found himself reflecting that rice pudding, in moderate quantities and with due notice, can make a pleasant change and is not unpalatable. 'Are negotiable,' he howled, just in case anyone was listening.

Back inside the comfort of her warm, dry sitting room, Mrs Henderson caught a faint echo of the last two words and smiled. Give them another three hours and then send the odd-job man out with a ladder.

Nevertheless, it was worrying; very worrying. Mercifully, the manifestation the dissident tendency had chosen on this occasion had been wildly inappropriate, given that she had confiscated the keys of the thunder from Thor when he first moved in, and could summon up wind and rain whenever she chose. Next time, they might use their common sense before selecting their course of action.

It was all the fault of *naughty* Mr Osiris, she reflected. They only dared behave like this because he was still on the loose, making them think things and giving them a precedent, and hope. The sooner he was dealt with, the better.

There was a spluttering noise from her desk, and she saw a fax worming its way through the rollers. When it had finally wiggled to a halt, she read it, and smiled again before scribbling an answer and sending it off. The number she dialled was unlisted and known to very few people, probably because the last thing the Judges of the Dead need is piles of junk faxes.

Oh *good*, Mrs Henderson thought.

It was a very odd-looking camel indeed. It was tall, with long spindly legs, and you didn't need to look twice to see that it had all its ribs. In fact it was so thin that it was probably the only known life-form capable of wearing a Calvin Klein original without bursting the zip.

'Hi,' it said.

Osiris drummed his fingers on the arm of his wheel-chair. 'What,' he asked, 'the hell is going on here?'

'Weighbridge,' replied the camel, with its mouth full. 'Sort of weighbridge, anyway. At your service, distinguished patrons.'

Pan, who had been looking around, saw what he'd been looking for, and grinned. 'Clever,' he said. 'Strictly within the rules, helps keep the riff-raff out; yes, I like it. Your own idea?'

The camel shrugged, giving the impression of a conga of coathangers. 'Alas, no,' he said. 'I am merely a loyal, hard-working employee dedicated to the ideal of old-fashioned personal service. Three hundred thousand zlotys to go through.'

Osiris was becoming impatient. 'Somebody explain,' he demanded. 'To go through what, precisely?'

Pan pointed.

At first it looked like an ordinary archway, until you realised that archways aren't usually made of chrome-plated steel. Once your eyes grew accustomed to the bewildering perspectives involved, you realised that it was . . .

'The eye of a needle,' Pan said. 'You pay your money, the camel does his bit, you're in, free and clear. I assume there's a certificate or something to say you got to the other side?'

The camel nodded. 'Duly witnessed and legalised by a notary public,' it said. 'I am, as it happens, a notary public.' It lowered its voice. 'I took the exams and everything.'

'I'll bet you did,' Pan replied. 'Look, thanks for your time but we're all of us poor as church mice, so I guess we'll just carry on the way we were—'

'Ah,' said the camel. 'You mean via the toll road?'

'That's not quite what I meant,' Pan replied cautiously, 'but do please go on. You will note, by the way, that my friend over there is carrying a very big rifle, which I believe has strong Freudian overtones in his case but is nevertheless loaded.'

The camel shuddered slightly, reminding Pan of a xylophone yawning. 'There's no need to get boisterous,' it said, and pointed with a hoof towards a side tunnel. 'Pedestrians are requested to keep to the footpaths at all times,' it added. 'Have a nice day, now.'

About twenty yards in, the side tunnel grew narrow and low, so that everyone except Osiris had to duck their heads. Underfoot the ground was spongy and soft without being damp, and the sides had the same sort of feel to them. It was unnervingly like being inside somebody's intestines.

'Painfully unimaginative use of imagery,' Pan explained, wiping something sticky and yuk out of his eyes. 'If that back there was the jaws of death, this must be its gullet or something.'

'Talking of eating things,' said Sandra.

'I can hear water.'

Pan stopped. True, Osiris was a god, and gods can hear

the turning of the earth, the graunching of the stars on their badly lubricated axles; but even gods can imagine things. Pan was a god too, and all he could hear was the rumbling of Sandra's stomach.

'Sorry,' he said, 'but all I've got left is a couple of cough sweets and an aspirin. They may have a handful of calories between them if you want to try.'

'Thanks,' Sandra replied, 'but I think I'll wait. There must be a diner or a Little Chef or something around here somewhere.'

'Over there, maybe,' said Osiris. 'By the river.'

There was indeed a river.

Tremendous efforts have been made in recent years to clean up the great waterways of the civilised world. Salmon now spawn in the Thames. The Loire sparkles through central Paris like Perrier on endless draught. The Tiber and the Ganges are now so pure that local inhabitants use it neat to top up their car batteries, and a company has been formed to bottle the Hudson and sell it in health food shops. But cast your mind back to the bad old days, when the smell of your average urban waterway was enough to bubble varnish, and a brick thrown from Waterloo Bridge would have bounced off the surface in a way that would have had Barnes Wallis dancing with joy.

'Where's this, then?' Pan asked.

'The Styx.'

'Sure, it's hardly downtown LA, but—'

Osiris spelt it for him. 'All we have to do,' he went on, 'is cross over and we're there. Home and dry. Well,' he amended, 'home. Now, somewhere around here there should be a ferry . . .'

And sure enough, there was a ferry. It was, Pan realised with horror, more or less exactly how he remembered it from his last visit here, back in the days when there wasn't so much of this science nonsense about and you could have a really good blow-out, take in a show and still have change out of the burnt entrails of a ram. The auto-cauterising function of his memory had compiled a nice thick sheath of mental scar tissue over the whole business; it took just one look at the blunt, squat boat that nosed its way up to the bank to pick off that particular scab, leaving a big patch of raw reminiscence bare and unprotected.

'Hang on,' he said. 'We'll need tickets.'

Osiris raised an eyebrow. 'I thought you just paid the ferryman,' he said.

'Shows how much you know.' Pan took out his wallet and extracted a selection of major credit cards, supplied to him by various leading banks who afterwards found themselves trying hard to remember what the very good reason at the time had been. Then he reached across and abstracted Lundqvist's Sykes-Fairbairn knife from its scabbard on his hip.

''Scuse fingers,' he said.

'You're welcome,' Lundqvist replied automatically, and then added, 'Hey, that's my knife you just . . .'

Pan ignored him. Taking great care not to lacerate the ball of his thumb, he was cutting circles approximately three quarters of an inch out of the cards, two from each one.

'Origami?' Sandra asked. Pan shook his head.

'The trick is,' he replied, not taking his eyes off the job in hand, 'when crossing the Styx on that horrible contraption over there, not to get caught without a ticket when you're half way across; because if you are, you get thrown off the boat. Into that,' he particularised, pointing with the knife at the turgid crust of the river. 'No joke,' he added. 'So if you'll all just hold your water a moment.'

Osiris, meanwhile, had given his colleague up for nuts

and commanded Carl to wheel him up the gangplank that the ferryman had laid down.

'Five, please,' he said. 'Two gods and three adults. Return.'

'You what?'

'Return tickets, please. What's so funny about . . . ?'

The ferryman, who seemd to consist entirely of a big black hood and two unnervingly bony hands, stopped sniggering as if he'd just been switched off at the mains. 'Tickets,' he said.

'But I thought we pay you as we board,' Osiris replied, confused. 'Surely—'

'Not enough money in the world,' the ferryman said. 'You wanna know why you can't take it with you?'

'Why?'

'Because I takes it off you first. Show us yer ticket or sling yer hook.'

Before Osiris could remonstrate further, Pan finished sectioning the last card, gave Lundqvist his knife back and hurried up to the river bank. 'Here we are,' he said, handing out the little celluloid discs. 'Tickets.'

'Pan,' Osiris said, 'they're just little round bits cut out of credit cards. What are we supposed to . . . ?'

He tailed off. Pan was now lying on his back, screwing the plastic circles into his eyes like oversize contact lenses. The ferryman leant over him, like the devil's optician making a house call.

'That'll do nicely, sir,' he grunted. 'Hold on just a mo while I write down the number.'

'It all started,' Pan explained, some time later, as they lurched nauseatingly across the river in the little boat, 'with the first big dose of inflation they had back along, just after the first sack of Rome. Apparently, Chummy here . . .' He indicated the ferryman with a jerk of his thumb. 'Chummy here got so sick of being paid in devalued Roman currency that he started to get funny about it. Started off demanding Swiss francs, even though they don't fit properly and the milled edges cut your eyelids; then it was Deutschmarks, then US dollars for a while, and then it was yen, just for a short time. Now it's plastic or nothing. And if your credit rating doesn't match up, then it's just hard luck.'

Osiris shook his head sadly, adding slightly to the already disturbing oscillation of the boat. Ever since – well, ever since he'd left Sunnyvoyde, he'd had this feeling that things were wrong. Not, of course, that they'd ever been right, not ever (as far as he could remember; and he could remember the universe when it had been in the interstellar equivalent of its very first Babygro); but never, surely, as wrong as this. True, the system had been unjust and unfair and stacked against the poor bloody mortal from the outset; but at least it had been efficient, and it had worked. Now, of course, it was all different. Gone were the days of arbitrary authority and the Divine Whim, and as a result it looked as if you needed private health insurance just to be allowed to die.

I leave them to their own devices for just five minutes, and look what they've done to it all.

He turned to the ferryman and tapped him on the shoulder. It was a bit like playing a very short piece by Stravinski on the xylophone.

'Excuse me,' he said, 'but do you own this boat?'

'What, me?'

'Yes, you.'

The cowl wobbled sardonically. 'Get real, chum,' said the ferryman. 'I just work here, all right? You got anything to say, you say it to the bloody management.'

Osiris nodded. 'I will,' he replied, 'you can count on that. Who would that be, incidentally? The management, I mean.'

'Bloke called Julian something owns this boat,' the ferryman replied. 'Least, it's a group of companies, whatever that's supposed to be, but really it's the same thing.'

'One of the godchildren, is he?'

The ferryman shrugged. 'Dunno,' he replied. 'Like I said, I only work here.'

'Thank you so much for all your help.'

'Piss off.'

It was, inevitably, Sandra who noticed it first.

'Hey,' she said, 'over there, look.'

Osiris followed her pointing finger. His eyesight was not quite so good as it might have been, what with the advancing years and the fact that the Lady Isis had, on the last occasion on which she had reassembled him, put the right eyeball in back to front; but you'd have had to be stone blind not to see the big neon sign, glaring out of the inky darkness.

THE LAST SUPPER

Best Diner in Hell

TRY OUR FABULOUS SELECTION OF BAKED MEATS

'All right,' he sighed. 'Maybe just ten minutes for a cup of coffee and a doughnut or something. We can ask the way.'

The diner was empty except for a waitress, two animated skeletons quietly eating Danish pastries in a corner, and a tall, thin man sitting on his own over an empty cup of coffee, apparently talking to himself. On closer inspection he turned out to be dictating into a pocket dictaphone. As Osiris' party passed by he put the machine away sheepishly.

'Just filing my report,' he said. 'Got to try and make the final edition.'

Pan looked at him. 'The final edition of what?' he asked. 'Are you a journalist or something?'

The man nodded. 'Danny Bennett,' he said proudly, 'special correspondent. I'm on an assignment to . . .' He looked around furtively, and whispered, 'to find out the truth. You know, what's really going on around here. At least,' he added uncertainly, 'I assume I am. Otherwise, why the bloody hell am I here?'

Pan stroked his chin, trying to remember how you did tact. 'Maybe,' he said carefully, 'it's because you're dead.'

There was a moment of profound silence; the sort of silence you get at the bottom of very deep wells, or the back of long-unopened airing cupboards. 'Nah,' the man replied at last, 'not me. I've got so much to live for – you know, my career, my public, this really incredibly big scoop I'm working on right now.'

Pan nodded. 'Been here long?' he asked.

The man rubbed his eyes. 'Now it's funny you should ask me that,' he said. 'I don't think so, but it's a weird thing, trying to keep track of time in this place really isn't easy. I may have been here weeks for all I know.'

As nonchalantly as he could, Pan looked away. 'Well,' he said, 'keep up the good work.' He drew a little nearer, and added conspiratorially, 'if you want a hot tip, check out the ferryman back there. It's all completely unconfirmed, of course, and don't quote me, but . . .'

The man nodded. 'Strictly on a sources-close-to basis,' he whispered. 'You have my word as a journalist.'

'What I've heard,' Pan went on, 'is that he's running the biggest illegal immigrant scam in the universe, right under our very noses.'

The man's eyes widened. 'Boat people?'

Pan nodded. 'Thousands of 'em,' he said. 'I mean,' he added, 'you're not going to tell me all the guys out there were born here, are you?'

The man nodded excitedly, his hand reaching for a

566 • Tom Holt

napkin and his three-colour pen. 'It all adds up,' he said. 'God, I wish I could find out who's behind it.'

Pan looked round. 'Who do you think?' he said. 'The Mob.'

'You mean the Mafia?'

'Nah.' Pan shook his head. 'Not that bunch of choirboys. *The* Mob. The Organisation. *Them!*'

Frantically the man grabbed at Pan's sleeve. 'The Masons?' he demanded. 'The Klan? The Bruderbond? M15? The CIA? The International Standing Commission on Food Additives? Come on, for Christ's sake, you've got to tell me. The public have a right to . . .'

Pan looked him in the eye. 'You mean to say,' he hissed, 'you don't know who *They* are?'

'No,' the man said, half hissing and half screaming. 'All my life I've been trying to find out and I don't fucking know!'

'And you call yourself a journalist?'

'Yes. I *am* a bloody journalist. Look, you have a duty to tell me, I'm Press.'

Pan looked round once more, lifted the sugar jar and shook it, and put his hand over the spout. 'I suggest,' he said, 'you look them up in the phone book. Under T.'

'Right.' The man jumped up, scrabbled up his notebooks, pens and scraps of paper, and ran for the door. Pan shook his head sadly.

'I don't mind there being one born every minute,' he said. 'It's one dying every minute that lowers the tone of this place so much. Here, Sandra, mine's a cappuccino, three sugars.'

'Well,' Pan said, 'here we are.'

It was a door. Just a door, painted white, with a round doorknob and a brass plate, set in an entirely conventional doorframe in a perfectly nondescript wall. The two gods looked at each other.

'I think,' Pan went on, 'we'll just wait for you, um, out here. Don't want to intrude, after all.'

'Oh.'

'I mean to say, if you've got private family matters to discuss, last thing you'll want is us lot standing around gawping.'

'That's very . . .' Osiris paused, trying to find the appropriate words. 'Nice of you,' he continued, failing. 'I don't, er, expect I'll be long.'

'You take your time,' Pan replied, turning up the collar of his coat and trying to hide behind it. 'All the time in the world. We'll just hang about here and, well, admire the scenery.'

No god has ever really mastered the knack of lying – not for want of trying, but simply because it's alien to their intrinsic natures, in the same way that water finds it hard to be thirsty. There was no scenery, none whatsoever. Apart from the building they were standing in front of, there was nothing to be seen in any direction.

'Be seeing you, then,' Osiris said.

'Bye.'

With his free hand, Osiris turned the doorknob, opened the door and wheeled himself through. He found himself in a marble-floored hallway, and in front of him were the doors of an impressive looking lift. Over the doorway, in neon letters, was the word:

QUICK

while the ornate oak-banistered staircase in the corner of the hallway was marked:

DEAD

Osiris pressed the call button, and almost instantaneously the lift doors opened. He wheeled himself in and closed the doors, noticing as he did so that they were made of seasoned, exquisitely polished pine, fitted with elegant brass handles. The inside of the lift was lined with red satin.

A moment later the doors opened again, and Osiris found himself facing a broad, impressive-looking desk, with four telephones on top of it and a middle-aged lady with a pleasant smile behind it. He rolled forward and said, 'Excuse me.'

The lady looked up. 'Mr Osiris?' she asked brightly. 'We've been expecting you.'

Osiris nodded. 'Good,' he said. 'Is he ready for me now?'

The woman looked down at a display board with coloured lights on it. 'He won't be a moment,' she said, 'he's just on the telephone. If you'd care to wait.'

'That's fine.'

'And.' The lady smiled. She looked for all the world like the better class of aunt; the sort that doesn't expect thank-you letters and doesn't mind a bit if you forget her birthday. 'The payment, please.'

Osiris blinked. 'In advance, is it?' he said. The lady nodded, and Osiris handed over the bearer bond. It went in a drawer and was gone.

Twenty minutes later, a buzzer went on the nice lady's desk. She looked up and smiled.

'You can go in now, Mr Osiris,' she said.

The god sighed, put down the August 1974 edition of *Practical Fishkeeping* and grasped the handrails of his chair firmly.

'Right,' he said. 'Thanks.'

'My pleasure.'

As the door closed behind him, the nice lady made a

note in the visitors book and scratched her ear with the end of her pencil; then she vanished, and was replaced by a thirty-foot coiled serpent with five heads and fangs like pickaxe blades. She still looked like someone's aunt, because even serpents have families, but not quite so reassuring and friendly.

'Mr Osiris. Please sit down. May I offer you a cup of tea?'

The lawyer turned round in his swivel chair, picked up a handful of something white and fluffy, and dropped it into a big, chrome-plated shredder that stood beside his desk. There was a chomping sound, and the very faint echo of distant screams.

'No thank you,' Osiris replied. 'Can we get straight down to business, please?'

'Of course.' The lawyer was fat, even by the standards of his profession, bald-headed and dressed in a rather shiny blue suit with a faint white pinstripe. It suddenly occurred to Osiris that the fluffy things were souls.

'Quite right,' the lawyer said; nodding. 'When people say that I'm in a soul-destroying line of work, they don't know how right they are. Now then, what seems to be the problem?'

'It's like this,' Osiris replied; and as he went through the facts of the matter, he couldn't help noticing that the lawyer's eyes were very round and green, and not in the least human. Par for the course, he rationalised, and nothing to worry about; but nevertheless. There was, he calculated, more humanity in a nest of soldier ants.

'I see.' The lawyer put the tips of his fingers together, and sniffed. 'We seem to have reached an impasse,' he said. 'And you want my advice as to what you should do next.'

'That's right.' Any minute now, Osiris said to himself,

that tongue'll come darting out, wrap round somebody and dart back in again. 'So what do you . . . ?'

The lawyer leant forwards, giving Osiris a splendid opportunity to confirm his earlier observation that there were no lids to those bright green eyes.

'If I were you,' he said, 'I'd settle.'

There was a moment's silence.

That is a very dull, banal way of putting it; try again. There was a short interval of the sort of silence usually associated with the fraction of a second between the referee dropping the handkerchief and the faster of the two duellists pulling the trigger of his pistol. Or: there was a pause, with sound effects reminiscent of that small, sharp splinter of time that separates the mighty upward swing of the bat and the crunch of broken glass, during which time all the persons present stand rooted to the spot, watching the ball follow its inevitable parabola greenhouse-bound across the sky.

'Oh,' Osiris said. 'You would, would you?'

The lawyer nodded. 'I don't want to be overly down-side-orientated,' he said, 'but I can't help but feel that the term *hiding to nothing* has a definite relevance in the context in which we presently find ourselves. Obviously,' he went on, leaning back slightly and patting the sides of his gut with the palms of his hands, 'you're right up close to the problem, so objectivity might be a little bit on the problematic side, but for me as an outsider looking in, *not* looking at the situation through rage-tinted spectacles, so to speak, I think you really ought to seriously consider the potential negative fallout of defending this action, both finances-wise and in general terms, viewing the position as a whole and from a holistic viewpoint.'

'You mean,' said Osiris slowly, 'you think I'd lose?'

The lawyer spread his hands, as if waiting for mustard-and-cress seed to fall from heaven. 'We have a saying in litigation,' he said, 'along the lines of, Going to law is a bit like picking a fight with a fifteen-stone, six-foot-nine policeman made entirely out of horseshit; even if you win, you may very well end up wishing you'd never got involved in the first place. Your best bet is to try and get the best terms you can and bow out gracefully, and I say that on the basis of five thousand years in the Law. I'm sure that, given time, I could negotiate for you a very worthwhile financial settlement, very worthwhile indeed.'

Osiris scowled. 'I'm not interested in money,' he said.

The lawyer's eyes grew rounder and rounder, making him look even more like a locust than he had done previously. 'I beg your pardon?'

'I said I'm not interested in money,' Osiris replied. 'I'm a god, remember. Money means nothing to me.'

'Really?' The lawyer scratched his ear, perplexed. 'We are talking about the same thing here, aren't we? Crinkly paper stuff with someone's head on one side and—'

'Yes. Money. The hell with it, as far as I'm concerned.'

'No, but really, I think you must be getting confused here, I'm talking about *money*, the stuff that goes in banks, makes the world go . . .' The lawyer fell silent, sat still for a while and then shook his head until his chins danced. 'My word,' he said, 'maybe it is time you ret . . . I'm sorry, I'm digressing. Very well,' he continued, smiling a smile not entirely unlike the grin of a peckish hyaena, 'now you're about to say that this is a matter of principle and you're damned if you're going to let the proposed plaintiff push you around, and all the rest of it. Well, that's all very fine and splendid and I want you to know that I respect principles very much, in a general sense. On a more particular level, looking towards a more balanced position of principle tempered with healthy pragmatism, I'd say forget it. I mean, what on earth do you stand to gain? You've retired anyway. Why not let Julian take some of the load off your shoulders? I mean, you can trust him implicitly, after all, he's a lawyer, for God's sake. No, I really must urge you to consider matters very carefully, taking account of all the circumstances of the case and not allowing your judgement to be clouded by extraneous factors in any shape or form.'

Osiris bit his lower lip thoughtfully. 'You ever met my godson Julian?' he asked.

The lawyer shrugged. 'I am,' he said, with a flicker of pride, 'the spirit of Litigation, I embody the Law. All lawyers are, in a sense, my children. In that respect I've known him, and his kind, ever since the first caveman filed suit against his neighbour for violating his patent on the wheel. A dispute,' he added smugly, 'which is still dragging on in some higher court or other, so I believe.'

'I see.' Osiris nodded. 'Figures. You remind me a bit of Julian, oddly enough.'

'You must be very proud.'

Osiris shifted a little in his seat, which was the archetypal lawyers' office client's-side-of-the-desk chair. Legend has it that the prototype was designed, five millennia ago, for a three-foot dwarf with granite buttocks who had lost both legs in a mining accident. 'Let's just go over this one more time, shall we?' he said. 'You're advising that I should hand over control of the Universe to my godson, who's a lawyer, because trying to resist his attempts to have me declared officially senile would be a lot of hassle and expense. Is that it?'

'Broadly speaking,' replied the lawyer, polishing his spectacles, 'yes. I must, however, qualify that statement by urging you to consider the precise definition of hassle in this context, bearing in mind the complexity of the grey areas of the Law in this particular arena, not to mention the consideration that the Court is likely to take a poor view of your purportedly wasting its time, speaking entirely prima facie and playing devil's advocate here for a moment, in resisting an application that really does make good practical sense from the feasibility and administrative viewpoints and is probably the best outcome for all parties when push comes to shove. I take it we're basically in agreement on that score.'

Osiris stood up. 'That's your advice, is it?' he said quietly.

'In broad brush terms, taking a simplistic overview, yes, to a certain extent it is.'

'Right.' Osiris smiled. 'Then fuck you.'

'I beg your pardon?'

With a certain amount of surprise, Osiris noticed that he was standing up, which wasn't bad going for someone who'd been confined to a wheelchair since Charlemagne was in nappies. 'I said,' he said, 'fuck you. I can spell that if you like.'

The lawyer raised one eyebrow. 'You're provisionally pigeonholing my advice for mature consideration at a later date?' he hazarded.

'I'm telling you where you can stick your advice,' Osiris replied, wiggling his toes. 'If your basic anatomy's a bit rusty, it's the part of your body you seem to talk through. Goodbye.'

'But I'm your *lawyer*,' the lawyer said, and Osiris noticed that he'd gone bright red in the face, giving him the appearance of a giant strawberry. 'You really ought to give very serious consideration—'

The door slammed.

For about fifteen seconds (or, to look at it another way, eighty-six thousand dollars exclusive of taxes) the lawyer sat motionless, staring at the closed door and wondering what on earth was going on. Then he leant forwards and pressed a buzzer on his desk.

'Has Mr Osiris left the building, Miss Fortescue?'

574 • Tom Holt

'Yes, sir.'

'Did he pay in advance?'

'Yes, sir. Bearer bond.'

'Ah.' The lawyer relaxed, and smiled. 'That's all right, then,' he said.

In the corridor Osiris stopped and collected his thoughts. For the first time in centuries he found that he had nearly the complete set, including most of the first day covers.

Marvellous, he said to himself, money well spent. Now I know what to do.

Avoid going to law, because it doesn't do any good.

The Law is my shepherd, wherefore shall I have nothing. He maketh me to lie down in green pastures, shamming dead.

If Julian inherits the earth, that's what God will look like for ever and ever.

I can stand up.

We created the world, they screwed it up. We created atoms, they split them. We gave them a garden, and now all that's left is a few nibbled-off stumps, some patches of oil and the silver trails of lawyers. We gave them everything, and they have made it into nothing. We gave them Justice, and they invented the Law. And on the ninth day, they tried to have us locked up.

Cautiously, trying not to notice himself doing it in case his brain suddenly remembered about the paralysis business, he glanced down at his feet, then his shins, then his knees. Been a long time, he thought. Still, it's like riding a bicycle. Well, hopefully not at all like riding a bicycle, which is all about wobbling precariously along for two or three yards and then falling over. He raised one foot and put it down, and then repeated the experiment with the other foot. And again. And again.

Gee whiz, World, my feet work! Isn't that amazing?

I can use them for standing.

I can use them for walking.

I can use them for running.

I can use them for standing on tiptoe to reach things on high shelves.

I can use them for dancing.

And, (said the god to himself and thereby parenthetically to the cosmos at large) best of all, I can use them for giving Julian a bloody good kick up the backside.

The science of surgery has come a long way since the days when a doctor was a sawbones and the contents of his little black bag looked horribly like a collation of a carpenter's tool-roll and a torturer's equipment chest. The modern surgeon tends to use such precision implements as the fine scalpel, the forceps, the roll of suture, the miniature laser . . .

The 105mm recoilless rifle . . .

'There he is,' hissed the first doctor. He slammed in the high explosive shell and closed the breech. 'Remember, squeeze the trigger, don't pull.'

Even in his semi-trance of private meditation, Osiris heard the click of the breech-block falling into place. He turned and stared . . .

'Ah,' said the first doctor, grinning in the shadows. 'Now then, hold still, this isn't going to hurt one little bit.'

Before Osiris could move or speak, the second doctor squeezed (not pulled) the trigger, and the ground shook with the thump of the artillery piece going off. The muzzle blast knocked the first doctor to the ground.

'Hoy,' said his colleague, scrambling to his feet, 'did I get him?'

The first doctor nodded. 'You could say that,' he replied. 'All the king's horses job, by the look of it.' He removed a finger – not his own – from his ear and discarded it. 'Put another way,' he went on, 'all his insides are now outsides. Let's get out of here, quick. I never did like the sight of blood.'

The second doctor sneered. 'Huh,' he said, 'you're just like him, aren't you?'

'Am I?'

'Absolutely,' replied the second doctor. 'At the first sign of trouble you go all to pieces.'

CHAPTER SIXTEEN

'As a slogan,' said Ahura Mazda, sun god of the ancient Persians, 'it lacks a certain something, don't you feel?'

Baldur, Norse god of fertility, looked up irritably, aerosol in hand. 'You reckon?' he said.

'Well . . .' Ahura Mazda took a step back and scrutinised the wall further. 'You do want me to be honest, don't you?' he said.

'Not neces . . .'

Great oaks from little acorns; very prudently, the Sunnyvoyde Residents Direct Action Committee had decided to try out its blitzkrieg graffiti campaign on the back wall of the coal bunker, down at the far end of the garden, behind the compost heap. That way, if it turned out not to be the stunningly effective medium of protest they confidently anticipated, nobody would ever know.

'I mean,' Ahura Mazda drawled on, 'banality is all right in its way, but if we were going all out for the trite approach, we can still do better than that.'

'Such as?'

'Such as, let me see, um, "Gods united can never be

defeated". Or "Rice pudding? No thanks". Or "Together we can stop the courgettes". Something like that.'

'"Gods of the cosmos unite",' suggested Nkulunkulu, the Great Sky Spirit of the Zulus. '"You have nothing to lose but your . . . your . . ." Hell,' he said, furrowing his brows into a single black hedgerow. 'Nothing to lose but what, for pity's sake?'

'I like it,' Baldur growled. 'I think it has relevance.'

On the wall he had painted:

MISIS HENDRESUNS A SILY OLD BAGE

in wobbly green letters. On the other hand, it was his aerosol.

'I still think,' muttered Vulcan, the Roman god of fire, 'you should have said something about that tapioca last Thursday. It was really horrible, I thought, and lumpy, too. I can't be doing with lumpy tapioca.'

'The tapioca was fine,' retorted Viracocha, the pre-Inca All-Father of Argentina, 'compared to that yuk we had yesterday, whatever it was supposed to be.'

'Pease pudding,' said Vulcan.

'Whatever,' Viracocha snarled. 'It was absolutely yetch, you know?'

'Absolutely,' Ahura Mazda agreed. 'They make a dessert and they call it pease. I still don't think we've quite taken the possibilities of this medium of expression to their absolute limits, do you?'

Ogun, the Nigerian god of war, shook his head. 'I'm going in,' he said, 'before I catch my death of cold. If anyone wants me, I'll be in the television room.'

'Scab,' Baldur hissed, shaking the aerosol aggressively. 'Blackleg.'

Ogun gave him a long stare. 'I'll take that as a statement of fact,' he said frostily. 'So long, losers.'

Baldur sighed. In his face was reflected the transcendent pain and sorrow of all organisers everywhere who come up against total unrelenting apathy. 'Right,' he said, 'fine. From now on you can use your own bloody aerosol. I'm going to my room.'

The other members of the committee lingered a little longer, contemplating the despised graffiti. So nearly there, they thought, but not quite.

What we need, they realised, is a Leader.

'I think there's a spelling mistake in there,' Viracocha observed. 'Aren't there two Gs in Bage?'

'I wonder where Osiris has really got to?' somebody asked.

Ahura Mazda nodded. 'Good question,' he replied. 'Typical of him, that, making himself scarce as soon as he's needed.'

'He'd know what to do.'

'Oh come on.' Ahura Mazda yawned and polished his spectacles. 'We all know what to do. It's how to do it that's got us a bit stumped just at the moment.' He looked round. 'Any suggestions, anyone?'

'Are you a doctor?'

'I suppose we could look it up in a dictionary,' Viracocha suggested.

'Look up what?'

'Bage.'

Ahura Mazda sighed. Then, from the pocket of his raincoat, he produced his own aerosol (cobalt blue gloss, for touching up scratches on 1974 Cortinas). He shook the can, playing a merry if avant-garde tune with the little ball bearing in the neck.

'Try this,' he said, and started to spray.

What he sprayed was:

HELP

Once, in the Great Night that preceded the First Day, a woman had stooped over the mangled corpse of her husband. Red to the elbows with his blood, she had gathered the torn scraps of his body in a basket and stolen them away. Under the dim light of the newly lit stars, she had put them back together, refusing to acknowledge the existence of Death, as if it had been some unstable totalitarian regime in some little dominion far away.

In her hand, cupped against the faint breezes of the first dawn, she had shielded the guttering flame of his life. Because she did not recognise Death, because she had refused to admit the possibility of something ending, her work was successful and the body, stitched together with papyrus thread and linen bandage, eventually twitched and stirred; and the mouth opened and said, '. . . -Handed cow, you've gone and bolted my trapezus slap bang in the middle of my pectoral major. Do you realise that from now on, whenever I want to scratch my ear I'm going to have to wiggle my toes?'

But that was a long time ago; and since then, Death has opened his embassies and consulates in every corner of the cosmos. Undoing Death's work is no longer a matter of putting the bits back together and turning the starting handle. Or so they say.

'Search me,' said Pan, scratching his chin. 'Try turning it round the other way and belting it a few times with the heel of your shoe.'

Sandra looked up at him. Her clothes were soaked in blood, there was blood on her face, in her hair, everywhere. In her hand she held seven inches of warm grey tubing and a bone.

'You're not really helping, you know,' she said.

Pan shrugged. 'I was beginning to wonder,' he said glumly. 'I think I'll go and see if I can get hold of lots of hot water and some clean towels.'

With an effort, Sandra cleared her mind. On the one hand, it surely stood to reason; in the old days, he was always being dismantled and put together again, so there had to be a way of doing it, a simple way that a trained nurse like herself could work out, from first principles if necessary. On the other hand . . .

'Thigh bone,' she muttered under her breath. 'The thigh bone connecka to the hip bone, the hip bone connecka to the—'

Find my head.

She looked up. The voice had sounded just like him, except that there had been no sound and no voice. She pulled herself together and picked a few bits of fluff out of what she believed was the left kidney.

Find my head and I can tell you what to do. Please.

'Osiris?' she asked faintly. 'Osiris, is that you?'

No, it's Maurice Chevalier. Of course it's me. This is my soul speaking.

'Where are you? I mean, where is it?'

You're kneeling on it.

Sandra stood up hurriedly. 'Sorry,' she said. 'Gosh, so that's what they look—'

Find my head. I'll tell you what to do. But hurry. This really isn't the most comfortable way to have a conversation, believe me.

There is something horribly comic, under all imaginable circumstances, about a head with no body attached to it. No matter how desperate the grief, how bewildering the shock, there is always the temptation, lurking in the blackness of the mind, to stick one's fingers up the neck and try to say *Bottle of beer* without moving one's lips.

When you've quite finished.

And, when the First Day dawned, the wicked prince Set looked out from his throne and saw the sun. And he turned to his two brothers and asked them what it might be.

And his brothers turned to each other in amazement (they had perfectly good names but somehow always ended up being called Game and Match) and confessed that they did not know. Something, they suspected, had gone wrong somewhere . . .

And Osiris had risen from the dead, made whole again by the love and faith of his wife, and had thrown Set and his treacherous brothers into the Pit. Thenceforth there had been day and summer, and there was no more Death except for those who did not truly understand . . .

Or so they say. It's one thing to believe in the existence of a video recorder, and another thing entirely to build one from scratch out of a cardboard box full of knobs and bits of old wire.

Except that to the gods, all things are possible . . .

'Yes, but where does this bit go?'

Osiris' head blushed; quite some feat considering that his blood supply was some five yards away. 'Stay at home a lot in the evenings, do you?' he said.

'Yes,' Sandra replied, frowning, 'as a matter of fact I do. Why?'

The head sighed. 'I wouldn't worry about it,' he said. 'I haven't actually used that bit for so long that I'm not absolutely sure myself. Ask Pan, he'll know.'

Kurt Lundqvist, meanwhile, had wandered off, quite unnoticed by his companions, on the pretext of finding the two doctors and pulling their lungs out, but really to go and have a nice sulk in the bushes, if he could find any. All this time, he reflected, he'd been tagging along like some accredited observer, pleased and grateful if anyone asked him to pass a spanner or lift a wheelchair. True, whenever he had had centre stage to himself he hadn't exactly cut the most heroic of figures, but that wasn't his fault, he felt sure. Perhaps he should just leave them a note and slip quietly away.

'Hoy, you!'

He turned.

'Whatsyername! Thingy!'

He was being addressed, he realised, by a disembodied head; and although this wasn't in fact a novel experience for him (compare the Grendel contract of AD 792, for example; or the Medusa hit, right back when he was just starting out in the business) it was nonetheless a sufficiently rare occurrence to leave him standing there with his mouth open making a sort of *Gark!* noise.

'I've got a job for you,' said the head. In his already bewildered state it took Lundqvist several seconds to notice that the head was being supported by a column of ants, none of whom seemed to know particularly how they came to be doing this.

'Pardon me,' he eventually managed to say, 'but shouldn't you be, um, over there. With the rest of you?'

The head sighed. 'They're in conference,' the head replied. 'Trying to work out which order the toes go in, would you believe. I think they've got as far as the little piggy who had roast beef. Anyway, it'll be ages before I'm needed. So I thought I'd take this opportunity to give you your orders.'

Lundqvist took a deep breath. 'Thanks,' he said, 'but I've been thinking it over and I guess I'm not really achieving anything here, and I've got this pretty major practice of my own back home that needs my full attention, so maybe it'd be better if we just call it a day, huh? I won't be sending in an invoice, naturally, because . . .'

And so on. That at least was what he intended to say, but in reality he only got as far as, 'Tha.' Academic, in any case, as to the gods all things are known and no secrets are hidden.

'Easy little job,' the head continued. 'For someone with your qualifications and experience, that is. Spot of fighting, a touch of abseiling in through windows and throwing grenades, silent elimination of sentries, all that sort of carry-on. Right up your street, I reckon.'

Lundqvist nodded eagerly. 'Sure,' he said. 'No problem, glad to be of service. What exactly did you have in—'

'Well.' The head grinned. 'What it boils down to is, I want you to liberate Sunnyvoyde.'

'I beg your . . .'

The head ignored him, and a seldom-used part of his subconscious mind reflected on the humiliation of a six-foot-seven man being talked to by a severed organ positioned the height of an ant's shoulders above the ground. 'Go in there,' he said, 'take out all the guards, get the residents organised, lead them to death or glory. Well, glory anyway. You think you can manage that?'

'I guess so,'

'You're sure you don't want any backup? Helicopters, armoured personnel carriers, dog-headed fiends from the land of the Dead, that sort of thing?'

'No, that's fine,' Lundqvist replied, mentally reviewing his various pre-departure checklists. 'When do I start?'

'Now,' replied the head.

'No time to lose, huh?'

The head nodded, and in doing so squashed flat about forty members of its escort. But that sort of thing is par for the course if you're a tiny individual caught up in the ebbing and flowing of the tide of Destiny; just as you're about to overthrow the forces of Darkness and bring back the old King or whatever, along comes some bastard and treads on you. Still, there it is.

'If I were you,' the head said, 'I'd get on to it right away. Tell them,' it added, 'I sent you, okay?'

'That'll help, will it?'

The head considered. 'I expect so. Still here?'

Lundqvist nodded; and then frowned, as a thought struck him. 'Hang on,' he said. 'Which way is Sunnyvoyde from here?'

The head grinned, and rolled its eyes directly upwards. 'If you lie on your back,' it said, 'just follow your nose.'

Misha Potemkin, assistant distribution manager for the Novosibirsk Tractor Co-Operative, woke to find himself in the toilet of a standard-class carriage of the Trans-Siberia express. This was pretty much what he'd been expecting.

Painfully, he pulled himself to his feet and pulled up his trousers. Too much vodka on an empty stomach at the Jaroslavsk Tractor Industries Fair, combined with not getting all that much sleep over the last four days, had obviously caught up with him. Just his luck, he reflected bitterly, massaging his querulous temples with the palm of his hand, if he'd missed his station. If he had, it'd be another twelve hours before he'd be home again.

Cautiously, he rolled back the door, staggered out into the corridor, and looked out of the window. He observed three things which gave him cause for serious thought.

He saw no train.

He saw no track.

He saw no ground.

With a gurgling noise he collapsed back into the toilet and slammed the door, bolting it behind him. His senses told him that outside the window there was nothing at all. Not even a distant prospect of the ground, such as one might expect to see if the train had derailed on a hairpin bend in the mountains, leaving half the carriage hanging out over a ravine; or clouds, or sky.

A man who has spent twenty-seven years in the nationalised tractor business knows better than that. Obviously he was suffering from hallucinations, the result of cheap

Georgian vodka (probably made from freeze-dried oven chips), and until they'd stopped he was likely to be better off where he was. The last time he'd had the DTs, immediately after the Miss All-Siberian Reaper and Binder awards ceremony the May before last, he'd hallucinated some pretty unsettling things, all of which had been far too large to fit inside a small, confined space like this. They'd be hard put to get just their heads in without banging their noses on the sink.

Half an hour later his head still felt like the contents of a turbocharged cement mixer, but he hadn't had to contend with so much as a single sabre-toothed wolfhound coming through the wall at him holding a bunch of flowers. Probably, he decided, it's better now. Just to make sure, however, he opened the door on the other side of the corridor and looked out.

Still no train.

Still no track.

But at least there was some ground; there was, in fact, a stereotypical Siberian landscape (snow, snow and more snow under an iron-grey sky that looked like a photograph taken with poor quality ASA 400 film). That, he reflected, was a material advance. He closed the window, crossed to the other door and looked out.

No train.

No track.

No ground!

The holding of high-level peace conferences in railway carriages straddling the borders of the conflicting nations is an inoffensive, even picturesque tradition, and its very lack of originality gives it a degree of innate respectability, extremely useful when organising a last-ditch attempt to reach a negotiated settlement between two implacably hostile factions.

It had been Pan's idea, of course, and a very good idea too. Since Osiris had refused to return to Earth, and Julian had declined categorically to visit the extended parallel dimension, at right angles to reality, in which Osiris had pitched his base camp, it was also pretty well the only option. It had, however, taken some setting up. Simply getting the dispensation from the Physics Board of Control had been bad enough.

But there the carriage was, half in and half out of the universe of space and time, and on board were the two teams of delegates: the hand-picked elite of the legal and accountancy professions at one end of the carriage, all briefcases and laptop computers and go-anywhere fax machines, and Pan, Carl, Sandra and an old Olivetti portable at the other. Whether by luck or by judgement, however, the divine delegation had scored one of the most telling victories of the conference before a single word was spoken; they'd got the end of the carriage with the toilet.

'All right,' said one of Julian's team, a jet-propelled intellectual property lawyer from New York, attended by no less than three Principal Minions and seven Nodders First Class, 'we're prepared to back down on the water-cress *if*, and this is a very big if, you guys can see your way to accommodating us on the pastrami. How about it?'

Five hours into the conference and they were still discussing what to have in the sandwiches.

All this had come about because Kurt Lundqvist had stormed Sunnyvoyde. Scroll back and edit; not so much stormed, perhaps, because he'd gained admittance by ringing the front door bell and asking to be let in, on the pretext that he'd come to mend the ballcock. Once inside, however, he had made inflammatory speeches, distributed subversive pamphlets, done all that could be expected of a front-line professional agent provocateur and diagnosed Minerva as having tonsillitis. His appearance had at first had the effect on the residents of a small Friesian calf in a ceramic pipe factory, but eventually . . . Mrs Henderson was now besieged in the linen cupboard, fifty thousand tins of tapioca pudding had been dumped in the swimming pool, and the gods had signed a hurriedly drafted Declaration that dealt in lofty terms with such concepts as life, liberty and the pursuit of Black Forest gateau.

It is one thing, however, to storm the Bastille; quite another to consolidate your position to the extent that you can start issuing your own postage stamps. The godchildren had immediately retaliated by sequestrating all divine assets invested in the World Below; and, since these consisted of about ninety-five per cent of the World Below, this constituted one of the few known cases of effective economic sanctions. The next step could only be war; and, as is well known, you can't have a proper war without a failed peace conference first. It's like having dinner in a really expensive restaurant and skipping the starter.

Pan looked round and conferred briefly with his colleagues.

'Okay,' he said, 'I think we're not as far apart on this as you imagine.' He drew a deep breath. 'We'll hold our hands up on the pastrami if you'll consent to a multilateral regulatory agreement on the mineral water.'

'Policed by UN observers?'

'If necessary, yes.'

The lawyer frowned. 'We must insist.'

'Sure.' Pan nodded gravely. 'It should be plain by now that we have nothing to hide. Can we move on now, please?'

There was a general shuffling of papers. 'We now come,' said the lawyer, 'to item number two on the agenda, and

I'd like to take this opportunity to point out that your party are already in flagrant breach of the pre-conference consensus on this one.' He shook his head, like a wet dog trying to shake off the sins of the world. 'I mean, come on, guys. We specifically agreed that the five coathooks nearest the doors were going to be ours.'

Pan hesitated. True, the first rule of negotiation is, Give the bastards a hard time on absolutely everything. On the other hand, his knee itched and he was getting pins and needles in his left foot. 'Okay,' he said. 'It's no big deal. You can have 'em.'

There was stunned silence on the other side of the table. 'We can?'

'Certainly. Be my guest.'

Frenzied conferring on the other side. 'But,' the lawyer pointed out, 'your coats are already in position.'

'Move 'em.'

'Are we talking a phased withdrawal here, under the auspices of a UN watchdog force, or—'

'Sling 'em on the floor,' Pan replied, smiling. 'They're only a couple of old anoraks and a parka.'

It was, one of the godchildrens' delegation admitted later, profoundly unnerving, the way Pan just sat there for the next thirty-seven minutes, giving way on every single piece of trivia they could contrive to throw at him. You got the impression, he went on, that either the guy was an absolute pro or a complete novice. When negotiating at this level, it's hard to say which is more deadly.

'We now come on,' said the lawyer, sweating, 'to item seventy-six. Who's going to rule the universe? Well, I think we can probably just flash past this one—'

'No, we can't,' Pan said. The lawyer looked the god straight in the eyes and turned quickly away. Pan didn't just have a poker face; his was the sort of expression that would convince you that he held at least four aces even before the seal had been broken on the deck of cards.

'All right,' the lawyer said, stifling a yawn. 'We propose that it should be us. You got a problem with that?'

'Sort of.'

'Nothing we can't handle, I'm sure. What's the bottom line here?'

Pan grinned. 'It's because you're useless,' he said. 'Totally and utterly incompetent. If the very best of you was given the job of organising the Budweiser annual Christmas staff party, sooner or later someone'd have to go to the off-licence. I rest my case.'

'You call that a case?' the lawyer sneered. 'Man, that'd be hard pressed to be a handbag. Where's your evidence?'

Pan laughed, raucously and on his own, for at least seventy seconds (which is a very long time), before wiping his eyes with his sleeve. 'If you want evidence,' he said, 'look around. There's nothing in the universe that isn't evidence.'

'Except woodlice.'

Pan stopped dead in his tracks and stared at the small, plump lawyer who had just spoken. 'Beg pardon?' he said.

'Woodlice,' replied the small lawyer. 'If (as if not admitted) we've cocked anything up, we sure haven't cocked up wood-lice. They're doing really well under this administration. Productivity up and everything. You just go and ask one if you don't believe me.'

'And stalagmites,' added a senior accountant. 'Under this administration, stalagmites have risen by an average of sixteen point four seven two per cent. I call that a pretty conclusive argument, don't you?'

'Look . . .' said Pan.

'And,' interrupted a bald, almost circular lawyer who had hitherto been asleep, 'rotary washing lines. What did your people ever do to help facilitate open air laundry dehydration?'

'Look . . .'

'Or time,' said an even more senior accountant, pointing at Pan with a forefinger like a bratwurst. 'No fewer than five centuries actually completed ahead of schedule. That's the sort of results you just can't argue with.'

'Look . . .'

'Mountains, now,' chirruped a thin, brittle-looking actuary from the back row. 'This administration can truthfully say that it hasn't lost a single major peak since it took office. In fact, I'd venture to say that there are more quality mountains now than at any time in the last—'

'*LOOK.*'

Thank you (said Pan).

Be still and know that we are your gods. In the beginning we created the heavens and the earth, and we were without form and void.

Don't get me wrong. That was cool. It was like slopping round in your old clothes on a Sunday morning, not having to shave or put your teeth in. That's basically the way a god ought to be. And then you came along.

I remember saying to Osiris at the time, Look, Oz, just create them in your own image, it'll be a whole lot less hassle in the long run. But no, he said, that's not good enough, I want them to have all the advantages we never had. I want them to have souls, and know right from wrong. I want them to have good and evil, otherwise what purpose will there be in their poxy little lives? I want them to be *better* than us.

So we gave you morals. We gave you sensibilities. We gave you ethics – and it wasn't easy, believe you me. You ask the average god to explain the difference between right and wrong, he'll look puzzled and ask if wrong's a dialect word for 'left'. But we wanted you to have the best of everything, and we managed, somehow.

And that meant (Pan said) that instead of just hanging loose in the void having a good time, we had to look after you. We shaped your destinies, judged your dead, zapped your perjurors, grew your crops, all that stuff. It wasn't what we wanted to do, but we did it.

And what thanks did we get? Prayers? Sacrifices? Temples with nice cosy armchairs where a god can put his feet up with the paper and have forty thousand winks? Not a bit of it. We had to put up with your suffering, your complaining, your why-me-whatever-did-I-do whingeing, your goddamned holier-than-thou attitudes. You made us doubt ourselves in everything we did. Every time we rained, we had to ask ourselves, Do the crops need rain this time of year, are they having droughts or floods down there? We couldn't so much as sneeze without running the risk of flattening one of your rotten little cities. We tried our best, and yes, I think we did a bloody good job; but every time we made just one little mistake, you were on us like a ton of bricks, with your sickeningly smug ours-not-to-reason-whying and your agnosticism and your general air of putting up with us out of the kindness of your hearts. And you know what? We respected you for it. We admired you. You made us feel really small.

And (Pan said) in the end we thought, Why bother? They're much better than we are, they've got justice and morality and all that sort of thing, and all we do is the flies-to-wanton-boys stuff. Let's hand it all over to them and call it a day. So we did. Dammit, we *believed* in you.

And look what happened. Ye have made of my Father's house a suite of offices. You've given the world over to the charge of lawyers and accountants and politicians – men whose only function in life is to make the truth appear lies and lies appear the truth. No more gratuitous violence, you said, no more inexplicable disasters, no more meaningless suffering, no more war, no more hunger, no more hatred, no more oppression.

Yes. Well.

Which is why (Pan said, and his voice shook the carriage and the surrounding hills) we're calling a halt. We never claimed to be better than you, but at least when we destroy a city or flatten a harvest we don't mean anything by it. No god ever killed anything for a principle or ruined the lives of millions for ten per cent of the gross. We may be clumsy, but evil is something you thought up all by yourselves, along with martyrdom, litigation and financial services.

And that is all I have to say on the matter.

'Fine,' said the lawyer, 'so it'll have to be war. Unless,' he added innocuously, 'you'd rather we did it the civilised way and took it to law. Just a suggestion.'

Pan thought for a moment, and grinned. 'Law?' he said. 'You mean have a trial and may the best man win?'

'Sure.' The lawyer managed to keep a straight face, because it's something you learn over the years, but his heart was rubbing its hands. We've got them, the dozy old buggers, it was saying.

'Done with you,' said Pan. 'We elect for trial by combat. We find that it's cheaper, quicker, fairer and a damn sight less traumatic for the participants. Agreed?'

The lawyer hesitated. 'All right,' he said, 'but it'll have to be by mortal rules, and with champions. You've got to admit, we'd be on a hiding to nothing fighting to the death with one of you lot.'

'Fair enough.'

'And,' said the lawyer quickly, 'we have first choice of champions, okay?'

'I suppose so, yes.'

'In that case,' said the lawyer, 'we nominate Kurt Lundqvist.'

CHAPTER SEVENTEEN

'You sure about this?' asked Pan, for the forty-third time. 'I mean, you don't have to if you don't want to.'

'He's sure,' Sandra replied.

The heat from the floodlights was enough to fry eggs in sweat, and the air was the consistency of lard. Everyone who was anybody, everybody who had been anybody, and seventy-five per cent of everyone who was going to be somebody at some indeterminate point in the future, were here, shuffling in their seats, whispering excitedly, eating popcorn. In his private box in the epicentre of the dress circle, Lin Kortright, supernatural agent, focused his opera glasses, every fibre of his being intent on spotting the fresh, raw theological talent that would set the twenty-seventh century alight. On the western side of the arena, broadly speaking, sat the mortal contingent, the godchildren, their aides, assistants and support staff, demurely charcoal-suited and poised like hawks to pounce on any technical infringement of the rules. On the eastern benches sprawled the gods, a pan-dimensional charabanc trip to Weymouth, opening paper bags, pouring from thermoses, arranging rugs, crossing legs against importunate bladders, complaining incessantly and (in the front three rows at least) setting up the chant of, 'Come on, you Reds.'

Pan shook his head. 'I want you to know,' he said, 'that I have grave reservations about this whole thing.'

Carl looked up and peered at Pan through his visor. 'Grave reservations?' he repeated.

'That's right.'

'Oh. I didn't realise you had to book. I thought you just turned up in a box and they—'

'It's going to be all right,' Sandra said firmly, looking up from buckling on a shinguard. 'Don't fluster him.'

'I see. It's going to be all right, is it?'

'Yes.'

'You know this for a fact, do you?'

Sandra nodded. 'Osiris told me so himself.'

Pan's face exhibited a smile the consistency of office canteen coffee. 'Right,' he said, 'Osiris said so, point taken. Sandra, I don't want to be a wet blanket here, but I've known him rather longer than you have, and—'

'He's a god, isn't he?'

Pan blinked. Right now, he realised, her faith was strong enough to send Mont Blanc whizzing into orbit like a marble from a catapult. 'True,' he said. 'So'm I. So are all those incontinent old duffers you can see over there. For crying out loud, Sandra, you used to have to put them to bed and remind them what day of the week it was, surely you don't imagine . . .'

Sandra shook her head. 'They're not gods,' she said, 'they're just very old people. Mr Osiris is a *real* god, you can tell.'

'Oh?' Pan scowled. 'How?'

'Because,' Sandra replied with utter conviction (and it may be worth mentioning at this juncture that her grand-mother was the great-great-great-great-great-great-great-

great-great-great-great-great-great-great-great-great-great-great-grand-daughter of Joan of Arc's second cousin), 'he's the only person I know who can put a hot cup of tea down on a french-polished table and not leave a white ring. Only a true god could do that.'

'Um . . .'

'Only a true god would be that considerate. If it was someone else's table, I mean.'

Pan shook his head and wandered away. In his considered opinion, they'd been hopelessly outflanked at the very last moment, and it was time to pack it in and call it a day. It had been a good try, they'd had some fun (although offhand it was hard to call to mind a specific instance of this) but one had to be brutally realistic. The other side had Kurt Lundqvist – despite his recent mediocre form indisputably the deadliest two-legged fighting machine in the history of combat – whereas the only mortal the gods had been able to call on to fight their corner was Sandra's boyfriend Carl, he of the big ears and vacant expression large enough to store furniture in.

Carl. He'd been along from the start, Pan reflected as he marched along looking for a bookie who'd accept any odds at all on a Lundqvist victory, ever since they'd broken out and set off on this fatuous exercise; but try as he might, he couldn't actually call to mind anything the boy had done, except stand about and help with the heavy suitcases. There were some positive things about him, sure enough. He was toilet trained, he didn't seem particularly fussy about what he ate and his shoes were always dazzlingly brightly polished. More relevantly, he stood about six feet in his socks and had shoulders like an American footballer. His brain, however, seemed to be another matter entirely; like the vestigial vein of gold-bearing quartz directly underneath Bloomingdales or the

Ascension Island tourist industry, it was an understandably under-exploited resource. Face facts, the lad was only slightly more sentient than a traffic light.

We're going to lose, Pan muttered to himself. What a pity. And where the devil has Osiris got to?

Ready?
'Yes, boss.'
You know what to do?
'Yes, boss.'
Remember, when I said leave all the thinking to me, I really did mean all the thinking, all right?
'Yes, boss.'
Got everything? The baseball bat? The bag of sand?
'Yes, boss.'
Clean underpants?
'Yes, boss.'
Splendid.

Lundqvist looked up, and whimpered.

Outside, in the arena, he was going to win; he knew it as a depressing certainty, as hopeless and ineluctable as Monday. At his side was the .40 Glock, his trademark, with which he could shoot the ash off a cigarette at a hundred yards. Strapped to his ankle, the Sykes-Fairbarin fighting knife. In his left hand, the slide-action Remington twelve-gauge. And this, he reflected bitterly, was the absolute minimum he'd been able to select when offered choice of weapons without laying himself open to a charge of throwing the match.

The other side had chosen a baseball bat and a bag of sand. Probably thought it was funny.

It goes with the territory. He could just about refuse to fight gods, on conscientious grounds, but there was no way he could turn down a contract to fight a fellow human being. It was part of the price he had to pay for being a professional, and being the best. If he hadn't been the best, he could have chickened out on grounds of cowardice – perfectly legitimate for any other member of the profession except himself to do that. And if he hadn't been a professional – but he had been, for more years (thanks to the exemption from the rules of chronology that came with his Federal licence) than anybody could remember. If he wasn't a professional, one hundred per cent impartial and doing it purely and simply for the money, then there were one hell of a lot of dead people out there who had grounds for some extremely trenchant criticism. The defence of only-obeying-orders only holds good so long as the orders are actually obeyed.

LAYDEES AN GENNULMENN YOUR ATTEN-SHUN PLEEEZ . . .

It was a very special arena – unique, the first and last of its kind. They'd had to search long and hard to find a site that was a temporal anomaly and a moral vacuum and also had adequate parking for seventy million cars. The beer tent alone had required licences from no less than sixty-four different authorities, many of them the same authority at different points in time. The floodlights were all dying stars, and the PA system had been in the Beginning, and had been with God and (according to some versions of the story) was God. Certainly it hadn't come cheap.

FOR THE HEAVYWEIGHT CHAMPIONSHIP OF THE UNIVERSE . . .

And it'll all be my fault, Lundqvist said to himself. The bastards, they've gone and made me into a lawyer, a *lawyer*, for gods' sake. I may have done some pretty filthy things in my time, but I never thought it'd come to this. I wish I'd never been born.

IN THE *BLUE* CORNER REPRESENTING HEAVEN . . .

Too late now to make a bad day's work good. Eventually there comes a time when all that matters, or at least all you think about, is doing the job and doing it well, and it doesn't matter whether or not it's a lousy rotten job that someone has to do. At the end abide integrity, skill at arms and the money, these three, and the greatest of these is the money. Everything else is vanity, vanity of vanities.

AND IN THE *RED* CORNER REPRESENTING MARKET FORCES . . .

A very great deal of money, it went without saying.

'Well?' demanded Bragi, the blind Norse god of poetry. 'Have they started yet?'

There are those who'd have you believe that the post of Norse god of poetry must be, at best, a sinecure and, in all likelihood, a leg-pull (like the First Lord of the Swiss Admiralty or the Australian cultural attaché). Very few such sceptics have ever said anything of the sort to Bragi's face, however, and those foolish enough to have done so tend to be easily identified by their false teeth and crooked smiles. It's amazing how much damage a lead-weighted white stick can do at close quarters.

'I don't know,' replied Ahriman, the Parsee Prince of Darkness. 'That dozy cow in front of me's got her hat on, so I can't see a damn thing.'

'I heard that. And it's not a hat, it's the top of my head.'

'Sorry, Medusa, didn't realise it was you. Look, *have* they started yet?'

The serpent-haired Queen of Terror shook her head. 'Our chap's out there already but their bloke hasn't shown yet. With luck he'll be out of time and we can claim victory by def . . . No, here he is, dammit. Booo!'

Medusa scowled. If looks could kill – if looks could still kill despite cataracts and glaucoma . . .

'What's he got?' Bragi demanded.

'Um.' Medusa squinted. 'Guns and things, I think. To be honest with you, I'm not very well up on these modern gadgets.'

'If it's Kurt Lundqvist,' Ahriman interrupted knowledgeably, 'it'll be the .40 Glock and the Remington 870. He's done all his best jobs with them.'

Bragi raised a redundant eyebrow. 'What's a Glock?' he asked.

'It's a sort of gun. Actually it's a state-of-the-art compact polymer-framed double-action semi-automatic handgun with—'

'*Glock?*'

'That's right, Glock.'

'Oh for crying out loud,' exclaimed Bragi. 'You sure it's not a Colt or something? There's masses of rhymes for Colt.'

Ahriman pushed aside a dreadlock of vipers and peered through his binoculars. 'No,' he said, 'definitely the Glock. Adopted by law enforcement agencies worldwide, this revolutionary design—'

'Block,' muttered Bragi, 'clock, dock, hock, jock, knock. What are they doing now, by the way?'

'Shaking hands, I think. That or arm-wrestling.'

'Lock, mock, nock, rock, sock . . .'

'And now,' said Ahriman, 'the referee's talking to them. Saying he wants a good clean fight, I expect, though personally I never saw a clean fight in all my life. Dust on your trouser knees at the very least.'

'Is there such a word as yock?'

'I have a feeling,' said Medusa sadly, 'that this is going to be a very short fight. Anyone like a sugared almond?'

'Not for me, thanks. Here, did you know some of your green mambas've got split ends?'

'That's their tongues, idiot.'

'There's absolutely nothing at all that rhymes with Remington,' Bragi complained bitterly, 'except possibly Leamington, and really that should be Leamington Spa, so you'd have to have Spa as an enjambement on the next line. Why can't the bastard use a spear like everybody else?'

'Hey up,' Ahriman interrupted. 'They're going back to their corners. I don't think I want to watch this.'

'Frock, crock, broch, pill*ock* . . .'

The whistle went.

Nothing personal; Lundqvist jacked a round into the chamber of the Remington and fired. There was the usual universe-filling boom . . .

He blinked. At a target fifteen yards away, with a short-barrelled shotgun loaded with #00 Buck, it's virtually impossible to miss unless you're inadvertently standing with your back to your opponent. For a moment his brain was in freefall; and then he picked up a voice on the short wave of his subconscious. Or rather, not a voice. A smirk.

Osiris, you bastard, you're helping him.

Certainly not. It just so happens that all of the little bullet things went wide. No violation of the laws of physics there, I promise you. After all, the shotgun is scarcely an instrument of precision.

You're cheating.

Absolutely not. It was just one of those unforseeable fluke events, like a whole bag of coins falling on the floor tails upwards. What we in the trade call an Act of God.

We'll see about that, Lundqvist growled. He slammed back the action, chambered another round and fired.

Would it be Brownian motion I'm thinking of, or is it

Thingummy's principle of uncertainty? I'm rather a latecomer at physics, because in my day the sky was held up on the back of the goddess Nuth. Now you may think you know a thing or two about lumbago . . .

Before his conscious mind could override, Carl was on to him. Sand exploded in his face while the baseball bat sent the shotgun spinning across the arena into the crowd . . .

('Stock, shock, cock, *who* threw that? Just wait till I get my hands on whoever . . .')

Oh good, said Lundqvist's subconscious mind, mortal danger; now we know where we are. Before Carl could bring the bat down, Lundqvist dropped his shoulder, side-stepped, hit the ground and rolled. By the time Carl knew where he'd got to he was on his feet, the knife in his right hand. Carl struck out hard, and if he'd connected there can be no doubt that Lundqvist's head would have ended up in the press box. As it was, the bat whistled through empty air and a fraction of a second later, Carl was on the sand, vaguely wondering in those parts of his mind still open for business exactly why his legs had suddenly folded up like a Taiwanese shooting stick, and what had happened to the lungful of air he'd invested in only moments previously.

Lundqvist straightened his back and drew his pistol. It was extremely likely that he'd broken a bone in his foot, and there were small bits of glass from his watch sticking in his ear. Apart from that, he was back on top . . .

All right. You win.

When you're around gods, time tends to have all the value and relevance of a fifty-lire note. In the short space of time between the front pad of Lundqvist's forefinger tightening on the trigger of the Glock and the hammer falling, the following subliminal dialogue took place:

Do I?

Seems like it. Go on, pull the damn trigger, get it over with.
But I don't want to.
You don't?
Apparently not.
Tough. Should have thought of that before you became the greatest assassin the world has ever seen, shouldn't you?
But hey, I'm on your side, you fucker. You want me to do this?
I want you to do what's right. That's what we created you people for, for gods' sake. If you can't do a perfectly simple thing like solving an insoluble moral dilemma . . .

The hammer quivered as the sear began to roll out of its notch. In the members' enclosure, Julian was smiling. And something deep inside Lundqvist's head grabbed the mike, and shouted.

'Dragon King of the South-East,' it shouted, 'get your great scaly ass over here.'
G'day.
'Third wish, right?'
Fair go, sport. What's it to be?
'I need,' said Lundqvist, 'an act of God. Can you manage that?'
No worries. Strikes me you don't need one the way you're set, but—
'Do something.'
Like what, mate? I'm not a flamin' mind reader, you know.
'Jam the gun. Take all the powder out of the cartridge. I don't know. Just do it, okay?'
Like a rat up a drain, mate. Here's luck.
The hammer fell.
Nothing happened.

'What's happening?'
'I can't see,' Ahriman snapped. 'Look, either keep your bloody pets under control or get a haircut, all right?'

'I'm sorry. I washed my snakes last night and now I can't do a thing with them.'

'He's just standing there,' Ahriman said. 'The gun didn't go off and he's just standing there like he's waiting for ivy to grow up him or something. He's not even trying to clear the gun, although with the unique toggle action of the Glock, clearing a first position stoppage is an extremely simple—'

'Why?' Bragi howled. 'This is ludicrous. Blow yer whistle, you great fairy!'

'Now he's looking up,' Ahriman went on. 'Blowed if I know what it is he's seen. Hang about, though, there's something . . . Looks like some kind of bird. No, it's too big, it's more like a . . . Well, if I didn't know better I'd say it was a . . .'

'Doesn't look like Old Trafford to me,' Thor objected.

'I can't help it if you can't read a map.'

'And even if it is,' Thor continued, 'somehow I don't think they'd be overjoyed if we go and park this damn great thing right in the middle of the playing area.'

'Ah,' said Odin. 'Actually, it's not as if we've got a great deal of choice in the matter.'

'I see.'

Odin braced himself in his seat and gripped the joystick firmly in his right hand. 'Hold on tight,' he said. 'I should be able to bring her in smoothly if only I could just . . .'

If I were you, I'd get out of there quick.

'Yes, boss.'

I mean really quick.

'Yes, boss. Boss?'

Well?

'How far should I go, boss?'

Oh, I think about five yards should do the trick.

* * *

'Oh,' said Bragi. 'Does that mean we've won?'

Ahriman opened his eyes. He could see Carl, slowly getting up off the ground. He could see the traction engine, or at least the part of it which wasn't embedded in the earth. He could see Thor bashing Odin over the head with a length of mangled driveshaft, while Frey made a show of dusting off his elbows. He could see Julian, standing up and walking swiftly towards the fire exit. He couldn't see Lundqvist; but, since the sight of blood always made him feel faint, that was probably just as well.

'I think so,' he said. 'Just because it was a pure fluke doesn't mean to say it doesn't count.'

'Pure fluke?'

'Act of God, you might say. Right, madam, just so much as another hiss and I'll take you down the salon myself and see to it they give you a perm you'll never forget, do I make myself clear?'

The immortal soul of Kurt Lundqvist stood up, brushed bits of body off its trouser knees, and looked down. Being an immortal soul, it had no lunch to bring up, which was probably just as well.

'Hey,' it yelled at the cosmos, 'I was using that!'

No reply.

In the back of its residual consciousness, it could remember something it had once read in a Gideon Bible about how the trumpet shall sound and the dead shall be raised incorruptible, and it thought, Just my stinking luck. Come Judgement Day, and I'll be the only one going round Eternity with a flat head, one foot at right angles to the other and carrying my left arm. Thank you very, very much.

Unless, it speculated, they patch you up first.

Yes, well, that might be something of a mixed blessing,

bearing in mind the standards of celestial reconstruction work he'd seen recently. If Osiris was anything to go by (and he was a goddam *god*, remember, so presumably he merited the Grade A custom deluxe service) divine reconstitution would leave him looking like something brought home from school by a nine-year-old just starting pottery classes.

It ain't so reliable, what they say in the Bible, it ain't necessarily so. Or at least, the soul fervently hoped it wasn't. It reckoned it had done its bit for these people, one way or another, and the thought of dwelling in the House of the Lord for ever as the human equivalent of a Skoda was not pleasant.

The gods as creators; the whole cosmos a Friday afternoon job if ever there was one. The imperishable part of Kurt Lundqvist shook its head and walked away.

The first thing we'll do, we'll kill all the lawyers.

No, Osiris reflected, that's looking through the wrong end of the telescope. If we're going to do this thing, we may as well do it properly.

He rose slowly out of Carl's body and resumed his own. It was like stepping out of the water back into the air.

'All right, people,' he said, 'gather round.'

The gods went into a huddle.

Nobody knows what actually happened to Julian Magus and the godchildren, although there are a number of extremely imaginative myths, most of which fail to convince simply because they were concocted by people who don't actually know what brimstone is.

The truth is that Julian had made plans for this, as for all other contingencies; and, like ninety-nine point seven per cent of all Julian's plans, this one worked flawlessly.

Within ninety seconds of Lundqvist's death he was clambering into a waiting helicopter clutching two suitcases full of uncut diamonds, while the in-flight plastic surgeon sterilised his instruments.

'Alpha Centauri,' he snapped to the pilot, 'and step on it.'

There are places where even the gods won't follow you; and, once you've come to terms with the fact that the beaches are blue and the ocean is yellow, and the combined power of all three suns isn't enough to convert the first taramasalata pink on the shoulders and back into true California golden brown, the good life can be successfully synthesised as well there as anywhere else. Beware, however, of ninety-nine point seven per cent success. After Julian had been in Alpha City for just under three years he was waylaid by a smooth-talking financial services consultant who persuaded him to invest his entire capital in Amalgamated Heliconium 37½% Unsecured Loan Stock, and is now earning his living as a washer-up at Z[i4kh98/98fß***sgwy's Bayside Diner at the unfashionable end of Neutron Cove.

For the record, he's never been happier; which only goes to show that where gods are concerned there's no justice, but there is, occasionally, mercy.

It began to rain.

'Be reasonable,' Pan yelled, as the water started to seep through the seams of his oilskins. 'What the hell are we going to need tarantula spiders for anyway?'

'Two of them,' Osiris replied, from the shelter of the covered wheelhouse. 'Sharpish. And remember to get a male and a female.'

The level was rising fast. Pan growled, gripped the handles of his supermarket trolley, and squelched away.

When a god wants an ark in a hurry, he doesn't muck

about waking people up in the middle of the night and giving detailed specifications in cubits; he simply ordains, and there it is, riding at anchor, ready for the statutory whack round the gunwales with seventy centilitres of Moet. It was big, comfortable and well-equipped, which was a good thing in the circumstances; because this time, nobody was going to be left behind.

Sandra looked in to report on her inventory of the ship's stores. 'We've got,' she said, 'five hundred billion rounds of egg and watercress, seventy billion small cardboard cartons of orange juice, ninety billion Mars bars, forty-six billion packets of peanuts and twenty-seven billion cubic tons of freeze-dried Red Mountain coffee. Do you think that'll be enough?'

Another good thing about being a god is that people do what they're told. No sooner had the first big raindrop splatted itself like a summer bluebottle against a windscreen than the human race, all of them fast asleep, began to form orderly queues at the designated embarkation points, whence they were collected in winged minibuses. The only small gnat in the ointment was the distinctly unethical behaviour of Mercury, god of thieves, who managed to get the fast food concession for the embarkation points by asking Osiris for it when he was busy with something else. Sad to say, not one human being got on to the ark without first buying a frankfurter in a roll, smeared with blood-red sauce.

'Sugar?'

'I knew I'd forgotten something.'

'Never mind.' To the gods all things are possible. 'Let there be sugar. It doesn't actually matter,' Osiris went on, 'because all this is all illusion anyway, but there's no point in upsetting people unnecessarily. How about biscuits?'

'The whole of C Deck is full of biscuits,' Sandra replied. 'If it's an illusion, why bother?'

Osiris looked up from his charts. They were plain, unmarked blue, apart from a tiny dot representing the peak of Mount Ararat. 'It's like building an office block,' he said. 'You put up hoardings until the work is finished, so that people only see it when it's complete. It looks better that way.'

'Ah.'

Osiris shrugged, so that his yachting cap flopped down over his left eye. 'Besides,' he added, 'the other gods won't believe in it unless we do it this way. You've got to remember that your average god is about as conservative as you can get, or otherwise how come they spent thousands of years making the crops grow on manual?'

The other gods spent the entire voyage on A deck, lounging beside the pool and throwing empty cans and bottles into the water. The New Mythology states that just before the waters subsided on the third day, all these bottles drifted together and formed the continent of Australia. One of the good things about the New Mythology is that it's usually more convincing than the truth.

On B deck mankind spent the voyage bickering, going to work and fighting a few small wars over the possession of the deck quoits area. There was no point, Osiris argued, saving the human race just to have it die of culture shock thirty-six hours into the voyage.

In the engine room, black-faced, sweaty and up to their elbows in grease, Odin, Thor and Frey argued the whole time about whose job it was to lube the main drive shaft bearing. On the blueprint of the ship, Osiris had crossed out the words *Engine Room* and written in *Valhalla*.

On the third day, the waters subsided.

The dove circled.

It was confused. It had only nipped out to gorge itself

on oil seed rape, crap all over a few parked cars and sit on a telegraph wire. All the sudden blue wet stuff was distinctly unfamiliar.

Doves have pretty near three-hundred-and-sixty-degree vision, so their eyes have, properly speaking, no corners out of which to spot tiny specks of darkness in vast blue horizons.

After a few wary approaches to make sure the target area didn't in fact conceal two men in camouflage clothing with shotguns and a flask of coffee, the dove put its wings back, glided down, turned into the wind and pitched on the branch of the olive tree that was, as far as it could tell, the only bit of perch space left in the whole world. It sat for a while, smugly congratulating itself, and then stretched out its neck and nibbled a leaf.

Yuk. Salty.

Don't like it here.

With the leaf still in its beak, it spread its wings and flew away.

When the waters had all subsided, B deck awoke to find that, apart from a certain degree of residual dampness, the world was exactly as it had been; which was nice.

Except that it was clean. It had been a last-minute inspiration on Osiris' part to dump sixteen billion tons of concentrated non-biological washing-up liquid over the side on the evening of day one, and an equivalent amount of fabric conditioner twenty-four hours later. By the time the oceans had receded back into their proper confines, you could have eaten your dinner off the pavement in Trafalgar Square without the unpleasant necessity of being a pigeon.

Behold, said the god to himself, I don't make a new heaven and a new earth, because that would be wasteful and extremely traumatic for the inhabitants. I make the old heaven and the old earth, only rather less grubby.

Not that that'll last; but one does one's best, just as a mother always washes and irons regardless of a world full of mud, oil and chocolate. And this time, the god resolved, a little dirt and grime won't matter very much.

This time, we will run things, but there'll be a difference. We won't let them know we're doing it.

There were some gods, however, who had no wish to go back; and that wasn't a problem, because there were always too many of them, even from the very beginning.

Understandable. It goes without saying that running the world is the ultimate in rotten jobs. It's a god's life, running the world.

For those gods who wanted out, behold he created a new Sunnyvoyde, far above the clouds in the temperate uplands of the Glittering Plains. The post of matron he gave to Sandra, who understood about gods (who are only people with an immunity to death, when all is said and done), shortly before sealing it off from the world below for ever. No reports ever filter down any more, except in very garbled form; but observers at the University of Chicopee Falls Department of Integrated Theology report that there is a seventy-nine-point-six per cent chance that rice pudding was reintroduced within six months of start of business, at the request of the residents.

Where am I?

The cloud wobbled slightly under him, and he grabbed at it. It was nothing but cloud. It righted itself and floated.

'And what the fuck,' Lundqvist demanded, 'have you bastards done to my feet?'

Perfumed winds moved the cloud along, and there was a faint suggestion of the music of stringed instruments.

Below, the world lay still and fresh, the sleep of the newborn.

'What is this?' Lundqvist wailed. 'Leprosy?'

'They're your scales, mate,' replied the Dragon King of the South-East, steering his cloud alongside. *'Have a beer?'*

Lundqvist shook his head. 'What scales?' he said. 'Why have I got claws on the ends of my legs? And what are . . . ?'

He rose six inches or so into the air, panicked and flopped back on to the cloud.

'Wings,' replied the Dragon King. *'You use them for flying and gliding mainly, though if you lie sort of on your side they make a really ace surfboard.'*

'Wings?'

'What you need, my old mate,' said the Dragon King, *'is a mirror.'*

Let there be a mirror. Lundqvist looked in it, blinked, closed his eyes and groaned.

'I dunno,' sighed the Dragon King, *'bloody whingeing mortals. It's really good being a dragon, you'll see.'*

'How soon till it wears off?'

'It doesn't.'

'Shit.'

'I think,' asserted the Dragon King, *'this is your reward for, like, saving the universe and allowing the powers of darkness to be defeated. You ought to be pleased, you ungrateful bastard.'*

'Pleased.'

'Suit yourself, pal.' The Dragon King frowned and spurred on his cloud. Lundqvist panicked.

'Hold on,' he shouted.

'G'day again.'

Lundqvist allowed his eyes to open again. 'Just exactly what does this dragon thing involve?' he asked. 'I mean, what are dragons, for Chrissakes?'

The Dragon King preened himself and opened another

can. *'Dragons,'* he said, as if reciting a slowly learned lesson, *'are the spirits of the blessed, endowed with the wings and the fish-arse cozzie and sent forth to supervise the smooth running of their alloted sector. I cover Australia,'* he added.

'No kidding.'

'Among my duties,' the Dragon King continued, *'are the dispensation of rain, particularly on cricket fields where the Aussies are losing, the regulation of the seasons and the protection of cattle against airborne diseases. Sort of like the Flying Doctor.'*

'How about zapping perjurors?' Lundqvist enquired.

'Nope.'

'Incinerating bearers of false witness? Carbonising blasphemers and worshippers of false gods?'

'Not our job, sport. The lighter fuel up the hooter is purely ceremonial.'

Lundqvist frowned, a difficult thing to do when your forehead is covered with thousands of interlapping molybdenum gold scales. 'That's all you do, is it? Water the garden and worm the dog?'

'You could put it like—'

'The hell with that, man. I'm a trained killer, not a gardener. You know, fingers not so much green as red to the elbow. If they think I'm going to piss about *growing* things for the rest of . . .

The Dragon King looked at him down a runway of glistening snout. *'Steady on, cobber,'* he said mildly. *'You've finished with all that stuff now; you've attained Enlightenment.'*

'I have?'

'Yeah, no worries.'

'Oh *shit!*'

For the first hour, Lundqvist sulked.

Then it occurred to him that since he was a dragon,

he had a right to breathe fire even if only for purely peaceful ends. He tried it. Good fun.

And if he was a dragon, he ought to be able to swoop dizzyingly out of a clear blue sky. Once you'd got used to the reverse G-forces trying to scoop your brain out through your ears, it was easy.

Add a nicely balanced lashable tail, claws which (he noticed) were two feet long and sharp as surgical instruments, teeth like cavalry sabres and little round red eyes that could pick out a fieldmouse at a mile and a half and, all told, it was a pretty neat package. Something you could grow to love, given time. An F-111 would have been preferable, but never mind.

And down there, even among the brassicas and legumes and Merinos and Charolais, there were still the good guys and the bad guys. Greenfly to exterminate. Coltsfoot and deadly nightshade to bring in, dead or alive. Colorado beetles to track down and destroy. Tapeworms to hunt through the labyrinthine entrails of the lowing kine. Seen in the right light, from a sufficiently raked and refracted angle, there is true heroism in pesticide.

Pesticide. Getting rid of pests. The first thing we'll do, we'll kill all the lawyers.

No? Pity. Never mind; because while there's mildew and blackspot and blackfly and ants, let's face the music and dance.

In the warm radiance of the newly polished sun, the Dragon Without Portfolio opened his wings, hiccuped green fire and headed downwards.